William Henry Simcox, George Augustus Simcox, Demosthenes,
Aeschines

The Orations of Demosthenes and Aeschines on the Crown

William Henry Simcox, George Augustus Simcox, Demosthenes, Aeschines

The Orations of Demosthenes and Aeschines on the Crown

ISBN/EAN: 9783337272425

Printed in Europe, USA, Canada, Australia, Japan

Cover: Foto ©Andreas Hilbeck / pixelio.de

More available books at **www.hansebooks.com**

Clarendon Press Series.

DEMOSTHENES

AND

AESCHINES

ON THE CROWN.

SIMCOX.

London

MACMILLAN AND CO.

PUBLISHERS TO THE UNIVERSITY OF

Oxford

THE ORATIONS OF

DEMOSTHENES AND AES

ON THE CROWN

With Introductory Essays and Notes

BY

GEORGE AUGUSTUS SIMCOX,

FELLOW OF QUEEN'S COLLEGE

AND

WILLIAM HENRY SIMCOX,

FORMERLY FELLOW OF QUEEN'S COLLEGE, OXFORD

Oxford

AT THE CLARENDON PRESS

1872

FELICES PROAVORUM ATAVOS: happy the editors who lived before text-books. There were giants in the earth in those days: there could be no question for them what should be the aim of an edition of a classic. A Casaubon or a Lipsius had only to tell all that he knew; the bearing of some particular piece of erudition on a given passage of Athenaeus or Tacitus might be doubtful, but the editor was the only man who possessed it, and the scores or hundreds of scholars who composed the Republic of Letters were always eager to feed on the crumbs that fell from the rich man's table. Even when the vast stores of learning of the sixteenth and seventeenth centuries had begun to be drafted off into separate collections, and their results were beginning to pass into common property, there was still much to be done which only great commentators could do. It is interesting, for instance, to observe how much even in recent commentaries is superseded by a great lexicon—which is only another way of saying how many commentaries were needed to make the great lexicon possible; or, to come closer to our special subject, how much of Dissen and Winiewski has passed into Thirlwall. The study of classical antiquity has hardly ceased to advance, but classical editions are no longer the principal organ of its progress. Tact rather than knowledge, judgment rather than insight, tend increasingly to become the distinctive qualities of the ideal editor. Of the questions which the Orations on the Crown have hitherto suggested, the greater part have upon the whole been adequately answered : only long and wide experience in tuition can supply an answer to the further questions, what an editor ought to expect from the reader, and what he may leave to be supplied by the teacher ; when to quote and when to refer, what to repeat and what to assume. Even with this training it is easy to say too little or too much; and, as other helps multiply, it becomes safer every day to err, if at all, in the direction of saying too little, to avoid repetition as much as possible, and simply to add one's own gleanings to the rich store gathered by the labourers of earlier days.

Viewed in this way, the task of a modern editor comes more and more to resemble that of an ancient scholiast, whose readers were satisfied with an explanation of the text, as they had not to familiarise themselves with Greek grammar, while their needs or desires were satisfied by the most cursory reminder on all subjects connected with history and geography. The scholiast and his readers had of course one advantage, if it is to be called so, over their modern successors—the language of their authors was their own mother tongue. To realise completely the meaning of Demosthenes, it was sufficient to comprehend the relation of the Greek of the fifth century of our era, to the Greek of nine hundred years earlier; we have to compare the ways in which two languages, differing almost as widely as kindred languages can differ, vary not the expression only, but the substance of a thought. And this suggests another difference. Almost every reader of a foreign language translates involuntarily sometimes: many readers translate often: it can hardly be doubted that an editor ought if possible to translate always. This discipline carries home, as nothing else will, a sense of the ambiguity of even such a perfect language as Attic Greek. There are all manner of possible shades of meaning and connection between which any translator has to decide; and the grounds upon which he has to decide are so shadowy, that he may well hesitate to obtrude his decision upon the reader, and where he feels compelled to state an opinion, will have little confidence in its commending itself to any judgment but his own. Such questions, though their importance is for the most part secondary, are likely to give careful readers increasing trouble for some time to come. Their difficulty, perhaps, may be held to excuse some hesitation in the language of an editor (and *a fortiori* in the language of *two* editors). The habit of seeking light increasingly in a microscopical inspection of the text, has an undeniable tendency—which we fear may be visible in our own work—to foster a temper of over-refinement.

It is hardly necessary to say more of what we have tried to do in the exegetical notes, for which, with insignificant exceptions, we are jointly responsible. The different chapters of the introductions are signed by their respective authors. It seemed best, as far as possible, to leave all questions of chronology to specialists. If anything like a consent existed, it would be of course desirable to put the results of enquiry before the tiro; but, when such cardinal dates as the birth of Demosthenes and the battle of Tamynae are still uncertain, to attempt to deal with the subject as a whole would have placed us between the alternatives of fatiguing the student with an exposition of conflicting evidence, which we felt incompetent to sum up, or of inviting him to burden his memory with a column of provisional dates. Leaving chronological difficulties on one side, it seemed possible to bring out some points bearing on the character and policy of the rival orators, which have hardly found an adequate place in the tradition of antiquity, or attracted the full attention at least of English historians. Of course a volume would have been too little to treat adequately of the practical politics of the age of Demosthenes, which have been studied much too exclusively from 'the world-historical stand-point.' It is so easy for posterity, for whom Philip and Demosthenes are the only important and significant figures of their time, to write as if their contemporaries had seen nothing else. When we remember how little we know of men like Eubulus and Demades and Lycurgus—some of whom stood higher with their contemporaries than Aeschines at any time, or Demosthenes during the greater part of his career—we see how fragmentary our knowledge of the period still is, and how imperfect it is likely to remain. Meanwhile, any one who has had occasion to read the Attic Orators carefully, will probably form a few impressions about the conditions and aims of public life in the fourth century B.C., which may serve (at least for hurried readers) to supplement the more solid information to be found in standard historians like Grote, or standard constitutional writers like Boeckh and Schoemann.

This may be the place to apologise for an inelegance in the notes upon Aeschines. The list of various readings was originally intended to appear in a shorter form, at the end of the little history of the text: it was placed in its present position at the suggestion of the Delegates of the Press. Unfortunately the commentary, where the readings which affect the sense were sometimes noticed, had been sent off separately, so that more than once the critical and exegetical notes overlap; while a more serious inconvenience accidentally arose from this change of plan, several readings, including most of those of Schultz and the MSS. collated by him, not being, for a considerable part of the speech, given in the same place with those taken from Bekker. These are of course too important to be omitted, so are inserted in a separate list.

Among previous editions, we have made most use of Bremi, Franke, and Schultz, for Aeschines; of Dindorf (one of the most valuable of variorum editions) and Dissen for Demosthenes. It would be presumption on our part to praise either, especially Dissen, whose anatomy of the rhetorical arrangement of the whole speech, and of every individual paragraph, is worthy to rank with his own analysis of Pindar: while he left little to be added in the way of historical illustration. Besides the histories of Grote and Thirlwall, which of course are indispensable, we found Mitford suggestive: with all his imperfect knowledge and grotesque unfairness, he brings out not a little which has fallen into the shade since his time; one reason is that he wrote from the historians rather than from the orators. Of the German writers upon the Orators, we have found most benefit in Westermann, in spite of his over ingenuity, and Droysen, who has written the history of the period covered by the Documents quoted in the Speech on the Crown, to prove that the documents in our present text do not fit. Boehnecke is rather a diffuse and perplexing writer; and it is perhaps hardly doing him injustice to take his results from continuous histories, which are largely constructed out of his materials.

While feeling the full extent of our obligations to these and to others, we have avoided crowding our pages with references. The class of readers whom all editors must expect, who simply want to make out their author with as little trouble as possible, arc apt to find references simply an encumbrance. The class of readers whom all editors would desire, do not confine themselves to a single edition: when they read an author, they read the best books that bear upon him. To this class we have always thought that references, except to recondite sources of information, must seem an interruption and an impertinence. This consideration applies with especial force to subjects connected with grammar. Those who require to have a phrase or a construction explained, are surely better guided to a clear perception of its force by translation or paraphrase, or by the suggestion of an equivalent English idiom, than by being pointed to its place in a classification which, though elaborate, is not final, and instructed to distinguish it by a name selected from a terminology more complete than significant.

In conclusion, we have to express our thanks to the Master of Balliol for many valuable suggestions upon the way of approaching the questions which came before us in the course of our work; and to the Delegates of the University Press, from whom we received great courtesy and kindness, together with many useful criticisms in detail from the Dean of Christ Church and the Rev. G. W. Kitchin. We owe much also to the great kindness of the Rev. E. L. Hicks, of Corpus Christi College, who, amidst the pressure of his various engagements, has found time to read our proof sheets—a labour always thankless, though we trust not fruitless.

G. A. SIMCOX.
W. H. SIMCOX.

May, 1872.

CONTENTS.

LIFE OF AESCHINES.

It seems from Aeschines' own statements that he can scarcely have, been of genuine Attic descent: he nowhere mentions his paternal grandfather, and his claim (De F. L. p. 47, § 153) that his father belonged to a φρατρία, which had the same family rites as the Eteobutadae, can only be intended to mislead. We know that slaves partook in the family rites of their masters, and it is probable that freedmen would also. At the same time it is obvious that he was connected in some way with an Attic family, and therefore the charge that he was the slave of the Corin- ᾽ thian Elpias (Dem. de Cor. § 164) falls to the ground. The date of his birth can be fixed within a year, by the statement of his son (l. c.) that he was ninety-four at the time Aeschines delivered (or published) his speech De Falsa Legatione. This would throw his birth to 437 or 436 B.C., so ᾽ that he would be quite a young man at the time of the disastrous expedition to Syracuse. After that calamity, many slaves and denizens were admitted to the Attic franchise, and the father of Aeschines may well have been among them. This would fall in with Aeschines' account of his father's recollections of politics between the defeat of the expedition to Syracuse and the establishment of the Thirty, and would give room for the rest of the narrative of his athletic distinctions, of his service in Asia, and of his co-operation in the restoration of the Commons. At this time he must have been already a citizen, for Lysias, who rendered far greater services, was kept through a constitutional scruple in the condition of an ἰσοτελής. It is admitted that he lived in a very shabby condition, first as the assistant and then as the successor of Elpias, teaching letters and the elements of literature. He believed in his profession, to judge by his son's somewhat obtrusive enthusiasm for παιδεία, which in his mouth includes, or rather is equivalent to, what we mean by culture and civilisation. He married a person whose name was Glaucothea, when Aeschines and his brothers had given the family a respectable position: till then her work-a-day name was Glaucis. Demosthenes, who asserts that till then everybody called the father Tromes, which is at any rate a possible name, says the mother was called Empusa (ἀπὸ τοῦ πάντα ποιεῖν καὶ πάσχειν, D. de Cor. § 166), which can only be a nickname. It is stated, and not denied, that she made a trade of initiating the lower orders into mysteries, apparently connected with the worship of Sabazius. Phryne and other women of her profession organised mysteries of their own (Baiter and Sauppe, Attic Orators, p. 362), and it is possible that the mother of Aeschines was accused of belonging to the profession of Phryne, because she organised mysteries. At any rate we should re- member that in his Speech on the Crown, where we find the most picturesque imputations on these points, Demosthenes is retailing gossip at least forty, if not fifty years old. It is to be remembered also, that during the period between the restoration of the democracy and the restoration of the Long Walls, Athens and most of the Athenians were extremely poor; and that until the battle of Naxus, B.C. 378, the pro- cess of recovery was extremely slow, so that it is hard to say how far such gossip, even if true, would affect the relative respectability of its subject.

Aeschines was born B.C. 389–88, for he was in his forty-fifth year when he prosecuted Timarchus (Ae. in Tim. p. 7, c. 49). Demosthenes (De Cor. § 322 sqq.) tells a long story of how he helped as a boy in his father's school, and in his mother's incantations. He himself seems to imply that Demosthenes had called him a schoolmaster, and that he was not ashamed of it (Ae. in Ct. § 217). If this interpretation of τὰς ἐν τοῖς γυμνασίοις μετὰ τῶν νεωτέρων μου διατριβὰς be right (but vid. ad loc.), it gives an explanation of the ostensible occupation of Aeschines, who was never an active politician. At any rate the phrase points to a charge which Demosthenes did not think it worth while to press when preparing his speech for publication.

When he was enrolled as an Athenian citizen, he served for two years· among the περίπολοι, which we might almost translate 'coastguard,' which Demosthenes omits to mention, as Aeschines omits all mention of his connection with the stage. His duties as a 'coastguard' can hardly have been very arduous, and it is at least conceivable that he combined them with occasional exhibitions at country festivals. He left the stage after an unlucky fall (αἰσχρῶς πεσεῖν. Demochares ap. Vit. Aesch. anon., might be synonymous with ἐκπίπτειν, but κατέπεσεν in Apollonius' life hardly can) in the character of Oenomaus. Before this he had been under-clerk to some petty officials (D. de Cor. § 325, p. 314), a discreditable office, as its chief value to the holder was the small perquisites he could earn by conniving at small frauds, being a rascal for two or three drachmas, as Demosthenes puts it (De F. L. p. 403, § 222). He may have left the stage when elected clerk to the Assembly; according to Demosthenes, he took his election with becoming gratitude (D. de F. L. § 360, p. 442). The anonymous life says he was clerk first to Aristophon and then to Eubulus, which would mean that these orators having the official control of public business, the Assembly naturally confirmed their choice of subordinates. This falls in with Demosthenes' statement that Aeschines supported Aristophon's accusation of Eubulus (D. de F. L. p. 434, § 333), while in a later speech (De Cor. § 207, p. 280) he charges him with flattering both, and with the fact that Eubulus treated him as having a claim to protection when prosecuted by Demosthenes.

The author of the life says that in this capacity he became familiar with laws and decrees, and so was led to enter upon politics. Certainly his frequent references (In Ct. §§ 75, 104, etc.) to the value of public records, may be set down to the pride of the ex-official, as his references to παιδεία may be set down to the pride of the ex-schoolmaster. The writer of the twelfth of the letters which have come down to us under the name of Aeschines, makes him say that he entered political life at the age of thirty-three, i. e. B.C. 356-55. There is nothing else to fix either the date or the motive of his change, except that it may have been before the battle of Tamynae in 349, where he distinguished himself, and was sent home with the despatch which announced the victory, and must have been before his embassy in 347 to the Arcadian Assembly in Megalopolis. Embassies to important states on important occasions, generally were assigned to men of weight and position; but embassies which would take a good deal of time, and were sent on a mere chance of doing good, were reckoned as early as the time of Aristophanes (Ach. vv. 65-9c) among the minor prizes of professional politics. The ostensible object of this particular embassy was to enlist Megalopolis in a league against Philip. Thirlwall (vol. v. p. 429, c. 44) very probably supposes that Eubulus, who always (De Cor. § 207) advocated the Theban alliance, hoped by this means to detach Thebes from Philip, since Megalopolis always leant on Thebes. If this could have been accomplished, it would have been easy to settle the Sacred War by supporting the party opposed to the δυναστεία of Philomelus and his successors, Thebes would have been strong enough to support her partisans in Peloponnese, Philip would have had no opportunity for intervention south of Thermopylae, and it would have been preposterous to attempt to divert the theoric fund to military purposes. Aeschines came back (D. de F. L. §§ 9–11, p. 343) full of the fine speech he had made, of the evidence he had obtained of Philip's intrigues in Peloponnese, and of the miseries of the Olynthian captives. He proposed (Dem. l. c.) that ambassadors should be sent all over Greece to enlist allies against the common enemy; and, unfortunately for his reputation and that of Athens, the proposal was adopted. Meanwhile Philip was throwing out the hints of friendly intentions by which he secured the peace of Philocrates. When the first embassy was sent, Aeschines was chosen among nine others, partly no doubt as a not undeserving public servant, partly as an honest and hearty opponent of Philip. He was the youngest except Demosthenes, who messed with him, and said he was warned by him against 'that brute' Philocrates (Ae. de F. L. § 21, p. 360), which is likely enough, as Philocrates was the only one of the party definitely pledged to peace, and Demosthenes and Aeschines had both made themselves conspicuous as opponents of Philip, while Aeschines might suspect Demosthenes of flagging in the good cause, since he had supported Philocrates when prosecuted. On their arrival there was a formal audience, where all the envoys were to make set speeches. The only thing they had to do at this stage was to give as good an impression as they could, and make the case of Athens look as well as possible. They spoke in order of age : the two youngest were the only famous speakers. Aeschines dilated to his great satisfaction on all the claims Athens had to the gratitude and good offices of Macedon and Philip, and glossed over all recent acts which might be thought unfriendly. To our notions, such a manifesto would have been more in place at the beginning than at the end of a war; but Philip had expressed a desire not only for peace, but for friendship with Athens, and professed to be anxious to serve her, so that an harangue of this kind might serve to strengthen his good intentions if sincere, if not, to shame him into sincerity. Aeschines says he left the special point of Amphipolis to Demosthenes, and that Demosthenes broke down, and begged his colleagues to screen him by saying he had spoken to it. Philip made an elaborate reply to the ambassadors, in which he paid special attention to the arguments of Aeschines (Ae. de F. L. § 41, p. 33). All the ambassadors were very much struck by Philip's intelligence and by his fascinating manners; and this was the only tangible result of the mission, except that it was arranged that Philip should send ambassadors with full powers to Athens, and should abstain from all attacks upon the Chersonese until the Athenians had considered the terms to which they were authorised to agree. Perhaps it had been arranged that Philocrates should propose a peace in accordance with those terms.

Two assemblies were held to consider the question. Aeschines says (De F. L. p. 36, §§ 67, 68) that it was intended that the first should be for debate, and the second for voting only. As there were no means of enforcing this understanding, we may believe Aeschines when he speaks as if Demosthenes had disregarded it, and Demosthenes when he speaks as if Aeschines had disregarded it, without quite disbelieving that it existed. According to Demosthenes (De F. L. §§ 15–17, p. 345), at the first assembly Aeschines spoke shortly and reasonably on the necessity of peace, in the second he spoke violently on the necessity of Athens securing her own interests, and rejected all appeals to the brighter days of Athenian history. Aeschines (l. c.) professes that both these sets of topics formed part of a single speech, and maintains, with more plausibility, that his opponent caricatured his tone, he had only warned the people against the indiscriminate imitation of the worst precedents of the past; for instance, the fatal obstinacy of Cleophon, to which he was fond of appealing in later speeches. In fact, after the virtual conclusion of an armistice, practical politicians had no choice; it was morally certain that the renewal of the war meant the loss of the Chersonese, which the Athenians valued more than their honour. It was out of the question to delay the peace till the last roving embassy had returned, or to risk it for the sake of Cersobleptes or the Phocians.

We now come to the most important epoch in Aeschines' life, the period of his second embassy, upon which he honestly endeavoured to serve Athens, but gradually drifted, through Philip's ascendancy and his own selfish vanity, into a position which made him worse than useless to his country. Aeschines believed sincerely in Philip's professions of goodwill. He, like the majority of his colleagues, concurred with the general appointed to escort them in ignoring their instructions dictated by Demosthenes, which bound them to go and look for Philip in Thrace, in hopes of being able to stop his conquests. They had some reasons for disregarding them: Cersobleptes had not been admitted to swear to the peace as an ally of Athens; before they started they heard Philip had already taken Holy Mount, where Cersobleptes kept his treasure. On the other hand, a good many small posts, some important, were still held against Philip, partly by the troops of Chares: it was not impossible that by energetic action some of these might have been retained as outposts of the Chersonese.

We are to remember that for Aeschines the great business of the embassy was to secure the benefits of the alliance; for Demosthenes, to put an end to the war with the minimum of loss. The first object would have been seriously compromised by a long journey to press a doubtful

b

theory of secondary interest. When Philip came back he found the
ambassadors at Pella, and set to work to fool them to the top of their
bent. He contracted Xenia with them, he pressed magnificent presents
upon them : perhaps this was the time that Aeschines received his estate
in Olynthus, and Philocrates one of twice the value (D. de F. L. p. 386,
§ 158). It would be interesting to know whether Philip measured his
gifts by his estimate of the importance of the receivers, or by his estimate
of their services to him. Meanwhile Aeschines improved his intimacy
at court, and lost no opportunity of urging Philip to settle the affairs of
Phocis in such a way as to secure Athens and humble Thebes. Philip
listened, professed goodwill more largely than ever : perhaps hinted
at confidential promises. The situation helped him; if he was sincere,
it was essential that he should keep his intentions secret. Still, he was
so intimate and so encouraging, that the gossip of the court came to
echo the private boasts, perhaps not too private, of Aeschines and his
colleagues. They aided Philip to deceive them; practically, they quite
admitted that Athens was to co-operate with Philip, that Philip might
co-operate with Athens, and they were quite as earnest in persuading
Philip to put them in a position to manage Athens, as in persuading him
to help Athens under their management. Aeschines was vain enough to
hope to manage Athens by his interest with Philip, and Philip by his
interest with Athens : meanwhile he was proud of the honour of Philip's
friendship, and this vanity fed both the others. Like a good many
people, he was given to professing that democracy was admirable if well
and strictly administered; and in his mind the profession covered a
belief that as democracies were always ill and laxly administered, affairs
had better be in the hands of a limited and responsible number. During
the few weeks that his promises were believed, he let his secret convictions appear (D. de F. L. § 361, p. 442). He gave himself the airs of
a cultivated gentleman, and people could always annoy him by talking of
the 'ex-town-clerk' (D. de F. L. p. 42, § 361). He complains that he
was falsely accused of revolutionary designs, and the suspicion clung to
him, as we see by his pedantic parade of democratic loyalty in the speech
against Ctesiphon (§§ 166–168 sqq., etc.) When Phalaecus had secured
his own safety by sacrificing Phocis, Aeschines was sent with some of
his former colleagues to remind Philip of the promises they said they had
received. Instead of going or swearing off, he sent his brother and a
doctor to swear that he was too ill to move. The result was, that he was
free to stay at Athens to do what could be done towards soothing public
opinion at first, and could claim a sort of title to address Philip in the
name of Athens, when the people were likely to be thankful for small
concessions. When the Phocian townships had capitulated, and the

irritation of Athens had taken the form of the affectation of unwise alarm (D. de Cor. § 45 sqq.), Aeschines actually set off and exerted himself heartily and with ostensible effect, both to obtain assurances of Philip's goodwill, and to combat the fanaticism of the little tribes of Oeta who urged the extermination of the Phocians. Indeed he actually induced the Phocians to send representatives to support him on his trial, by a profession of their public gratitude for his valuable services. That trial only came into court, if it came, three years after the embassy on which the alleged offence was committed. Timarchus, an energetic underling of the war party, gave notice of a prosecution: it is not clear whether Demosthenes was to have been his συνήγορος, or whether he simply took up the prosecution *de novo* when Timarchus was disfranchised. That Aeschines should have been able to disfranchise Timarchus is a proof that, even after the Phocian expedition, those who wished to be on good terms with Philip were still the strongest party at Athens. There is some doubt as to the motive of the prosecution. Aeschines of course represents it as a simple measure of defence against a sycophant, Demosthenes (De F. L. § 527. p. 433) represents that the real provocation was that Timarchus had πέρυσι proposed a decree to prohibit the exportation of arms to Philip. The interpretation of πέρυσι depends partly on the date we assign to Demosthenes' De Fals. Leg., and this date depends again on the interpretation of πέρυσι. The ordinary date for the speech, and the ordinary meaning of πέρυσι, would place the date of the decree after the peace of Philocrates. If so, it would be perhaps the earliest measure of the policy of distrust and irritation which destroyed any possible advantages that might have been hoped from the Macedonian alliance. Whatever the motive for the prosecution, Timarchus was disqualified for public life. Aeschines convicted him of an offence against good feeling (the offence against morality was scarcely denied) by an appeal to common fame, and to the suspicious absence of the witnesses who were called to testify in ambiguous language to the worst charges. The commonest cases (Dem. adv. Naus. p. 981 § 7, In Mid. § 114, p. 543) could be left pending for years; and, after this interruption of the trial, it is not surprising it remained in suspense till 343 B.C., when it seems to have been revived as a simple engine to aggravate the public discontent with the peace.

Philocrates was already in exile: he had displayed his wealth too cynically, and avowed too frankly that it was the reward of his services to Philip in carrying the treaty (D. de F. L. § 27, p. 417). Aeschines had a plausible theory to allege in defence of his acts, and the eagerness of Demosthenes to carry the treaty, perplexed him in the management of the prosecution. After all, the only argument of Aeschines' corruption was that when his promises proved fallacious, instead of admitting that he had been duped by Philip, he chose to throw the blame upon Athens, who had failed to secure the advantages of the treaty by prompt and loyal co-operation. He was acquitted (Idomeneus ap. Plut. Vit. Dem. c. 15) by thirty votes, and this acquittal was so far from honourable, that he never ventures to allude to the trial. Demosthenes (De Cor. § 181, p. 275) expresses a fear that the jury may repeat the mistake made after the Phocian war, and regard Aeschines as too insignificant to be guilty of serious mischief, which is an unmistakable allusion to his former acquittal. But the reticence of both the rival orators led even in antiquity (Plut. ubi sup.) to a suspicion that the pleadings on both sides were never delivered or meant to be delivered, and this has been repeated so often by modern writers, that it has almost become a certainty, though it is more than doubtful whether pamphlets in the form of unspoken speeches would have been as effective in the days of Demosthenes as in those of Cicero. After this trial the activity of Aeschines reduced itself mainly to a more or less questionable correspondence (D. de Cor. § 168, p. 271) with Philip until Demosthenes' reform of the trierarchical law, when he was retained with a fee of two talents (D. de Cor. § 368, p. 321) to argue that the law would reduce the number of ships for which trierarchs were then available, and that therefore the existing law should be maintained under which the ἡγεμόνες τῶν συμμοριῶν managed to evade the whole expense. Dinarchus (I. § 42) speaks of the frequent changes made by Demosthenes in the terms of his law; Demosthenes (l. c.) speaks of Aeschines having mangled it;—so that the opposition probably told, though not to an extent to interfere with the efficiency of the measure.

In his office as Pylagoras, Aeschines exercised an absolutely decisive influence in Greek history, or rather was the occasion of an absolutely decisive event. According to his own account of the matter, which is sufficiently credible, the Amphissian Locrians had it in contemplation to propose a fine of fifty talents to be levied on Athens for an alleged irregular dedication of some Theban spoils in the new temple at Delphi. The charge was brought out of compliment to Thebes, on whose protection the Amphissians relied to screen their own encroachments. If pressed, the charge might have been indefinitely troublesome; it was exceedingly probable that if backed by Thebes it would be backed by Philip, and then Athens would have been involved in the peril of an Amphictyonic war. If, as Demosthenes (De Cor. § 192) implies, a citation to Athens was an indispensable preliminary to any action, it was probably judicious to wait, for it was clear that no citation had arrived.

It would have certainly been safe, perhaps not very undignified, to plead, if the citation came, and, if necessary, pay. Aeschines preferred the chance of playing a brilliant part; he called attention with immense theatrical effect to the sin of the Amphissians, at least the leaders of the Theban party then in possession of affairs, in trespassing on the consecrated territory of Cirrha. Considering the extreme insignificance of the Amphissians, it was possible for the Amphictyons to deal with them without calling for the full force of any powerful member of the league. It was certainly no service to Philip to set Thebes and the Amphictyons at variance: to be the acknowledged protector of both was what he had gained by his Phocian expedition. If Athens had sent her delegates to the extraordinary meeting which was very properly summoned, as otherwise the Amphissians would have had time to prepare for resistance, it is hardly likely they would have resisted at all. If either Aeschines or Demosthenes had had complete control of Athenian policy from the first nomination of pylagori, Philip's opportunity would not have come : it came because Aeschines committed the Amphictyons to a conflict with Amphissa, and because Demosthenes made it impossible for them to bring it to an end without the help of Philip. If Aeschines was sent to Delphi as a party measure, the only party object was to find him a place and keep things pleasant. It is curious that the result of his manœuvre to exalt Athens by punishing a dependent of Thebes was to throw Thebes into the arms of Athens. Without the unwilling, unconscious cooperation of Aeschines, the Theban alliance could not have been effected by Demosthenes. As Demosthenes (De Cor. § 242, etc.) boasts that his rival was entirely passive during the interval between the occupation of Elatea and the battle of Chaeroneia, it may be doubted whether even the indictment against Ctesiphon was seriously intended to be pressed : it served its original purpose if it kept Demosthenes from receiving the crown.

Neither the battle of Chaeroneia nor the revolt and reduction of Thebes did anything to place Aeschines in a position of political influence or ascendancy. After the peace of Philocrates, we hear from his rival of his estate in Olynthus; after the destruction of Thebes, we hear again of his estate in Boeotia (D. de Cor. § 54) ; but the real managers of the Macedonian interest in Athens were Demades for the assembly and Phocion for the administration. Aeschines was at once a vain man and an indolent man: he only cared to exert himself when he could make a figure, which accounts for his being rewarded and not employed. In 330 B.C., when the Lacedaemonians had been decisively defeated in Peloponnese, when their king had been killed in battle, and their surviving leaders sent up to Asia to be disposed of at the good pleasure of

Alexander, who it was now known had overcome all the organised power of the Persian empire, Aeschines thought that at last he might hope to inflict an irreparable mortification on his rival, who had rashly counted on the success of Persia to deliver Greece. As Demosthenes said (Ae. in Ct. § 217), he wished to shew off to Alexander, at a moment when, if ever, opinion had definitely accepted Alexander as the champion and the arbiter of Greece. Between 338 and 330 B.C., no such moment occurs; and it is unnecessary to suppose with Westermann, that because Aeschines undoubtedly recast much of his speech after the trial, he also brought its historical allusions up to the date of publication, and that this date was later than the trial. The other members of the Macedonian party had no motive for supporting him: if he succeeded he would only divide the favours which Demades was anxious to monopolise; besides, Demades and Demosthenes were personally on good terms, as it was convenient for political opponents to be. Accordingly, Demosthenes was supported by the whole strength of his party (Ae. in Ct. § 258), while Aeschines, for want of advocates, was reduced to appeal (l. c.) to the memory of great citizens of better days. The result was what might have been expected when the forces were so unequal. It is clear, indeed, that an illegality had been committed: it is certain that Demosthenes' accounts could not have been examined without prejudice, if the vote of thanks for his generosity had passed: it may be doubted whether the proclamation in the theatre was lawful or no. But it is clear that both the certain and the possible illegality had been condoned in exactly similar circumstances, and if the spirit of legality had been strong enough to enforce the letter of the law in political trials, it would have been strong enough to give the cases Demosthenes appeals to the force of binding precedents. Besides, the perverse ingenuity which staked the decision between the two great orators on the trial of an insignificant partisan, throws an air of coldness and unreality over an able and elaborate pleading. The latter half of the speech is a very clever and plausible statement of what there was to say against Demosthenes, but the cleverness only embarrasses the argument. It is probable the ancient critics were right who thought that if Aeschines had been content to treat Ctesiphon as the real as well as the ostensible criminal, he might have convicted him as well as Timarchus; and even this, if it had not recommended him to Alexander, would have mortified Demosthenes.

After his crushing defeat, Aeschines may be said to disappear from history. All we know is, that after the trial, how long after is not clear, he left Athens and went to Rhodes and to Ephesus, in the hope that Alexander would restore him. This expectation was disappointed by

Alexander's death, and Aeschines settled at Rhodes. He died in exile at the age of 75. There was a consistent tradition that the Rhodian school of eloquence dated from his visit. The anecdotes of his exile have come down to us in a form that cannot be tested. As Westermann points out, the most famous of all, which relates that Demosthenes supplied him with money to escape from Athens, is at variance with all that we know from other sources of Aeschines' pecuniary position, and probably originated in the rhetorical exercises on the lives of orators, which under the form of μεταποιήσεις Δημοσθενικῶν χωρίων began as early as Demetrius Phalereus. Perhaps we may believe, on the authority of the letters composed in imitation of those which circulated as early as the time of Dionysius of Halicarnassus, under the name of Demosthenes, that on his arrival at Rhodes he was indebted to the hospitality of Cleocrates, a descendant of the Damagetus celebrated by Pindar, though the information is thrown into the grotesque form of letters to Ctesiphon, who it is implied had taunted him with his misfortunes, and then given him an introduction, which proved useless, to somebody else. Perhaps after all the most characteristic anecdote of his exile is that the Rhodians asked him to teach rhetoric, and that he replied that he did not know it himself. Whether the story is true or no, it fits in very well with the fastidious indolence and contempt for his surroundings which there seems reason to attribute to him.

To judge by his bust and by the taunts of his rival, Aeschines was exceedingly handsome: he was also physically robust, and had a magnificent voice, but it seems (D. de F. L. p. 442, § 361) that in spite of his pompous bearing he was short. He tells us himself that at forty-five, when he prosecuted Timarchus, he had got quite grey, and looked more than his age (In Tim. p. 7, § 49). He admits (Ibid. p. 19, § 135 sq.) that he had made himself unpleasantly ridiculous by his importunate attentions to handsome boys; but he had the support of public opinion in regarding these episodes as blots on his discretion rather than on his respectability. In other ways he seems to have satisfied the ordinary requirements of opinion better than his rival; he was married, he had legitimate children, he shared the common opinions and prejudices and habits, and the Athenians could no longer affect to despise a man for the shifty and precarious way in which he got his living. Then he had managed to pass through life without making personal enemies, or being involved in disreputable personal quarrels. He himself believed devoutly in respectability as the sum of all ordinary routine observances, and naturally his keen sense of personal respectability was compatible with a very low sense of national honour. Like Demosthenes, he was in a way a religious man: he believed in the Gods as a part of the historical traditions of Greek culture; it was the mission of the countrymen of Solon to vindicate the honour of the shrine of Delphi. Perhaps we may infer from the pretentious peroration of the speech against Ctesiphon, that sophistical deified abstractions of the order which Euripides had brought into fashion, had a stronger hold upon his personal conscience.

G. A. S.

LIFE OF DEMOSTHENES.

DEMOSTHENES was the son of a wealthy manufacturer of the same name, who had a cutlery which employed thirty slaves, and an upholstery which employed twenty. Theopompus, who did not admire the son, says (Plut. Vit. D, § 4) that the father was τῶν καλῶν κἀγαθῶν ἀνδρῶν. He was certainly rich, and probably took rank as a gentleman; but it seems there were those who contrasted his position with that of the old landed aristocracy. There is an unmistakable sneer in the concession of Aeschines, 'to tell the truth he was a freeman,' and Demades is said by Tzetzes, who had access to some good traditions (Chil. 6. 129–135), to have taunted Demosthenes with assuming the airs of a Critias, when he was only a cutler's son after all. Demosthenes the elder married Cleobule, the daughter of Gylon, and this marriage involved his family in a cloud which enemies could always exaggerate with effect. Demosthenes (Contra Aphobum 2, §§ 2, 3, p. 836) admits that Gylon was at one time a debtor to the state, but contends that the debt was paid before his death: Aeschines asserts that he had betrayed Nymphaeum, a post in the Black Sea which paid the Athenians a yearly tribute of a talent, and in his absence had been condemned to death. The two stories do not hang well together, and if we had to choose between them, we ought certainly to prefer Demosthenes' statement, if only because it was thirty years nearer the facts. It would account for both stories, if we suppose that at the time of the loss of Nymphaeum Gylon was already a state debtor, and that the fact of the debt may have been a principal proof of his treason. In that case he may have had reason to think that the sentence of death and confiscation would be allowed to remain a dead letter after the original debt was paid. It is certain that he remained in the Black Sea, and settled at Bosporus, where the dynasty gave him the township of Cepi. There he married a Scythian lady. It appears that so far as language went the Scythians were already Hellenised, for Aeschines (In Ctes. § 172) gives a barbarian who speaks Greek as the definition of a Scythian. It is quite certain that this marriage was irregular. It is not clear that it was incurably null. In all probability it took place before the archonship of Euclides after the anarchy, and it appears (Demosthenes contra Eubulidem, § 34, p. 1307) the children of Athenian citizens by foreign mothers born before that date were admitted to the franchise, while the strict law was henceforward to be enforced by the ordinary means. If so, the question whether Gylon's daughters could lawfully marry Athenian citizens, would lie *inter apices juris.* Cleobule brought her husband fifty minae, according to Demosthenes. Demosthenes was born B. C. 385-84. This would make him just over sixty years old at the time of his banishment, which Hyperides expressly states was the case (Frag. 17, ed. Sauppe), and would coincide with the indications Demosthenes gives of his own age. He represents himself as just eighteen in 367-66, and thirty-two at the time of the affair of Midias, which it seems possible to place in 353-52, though it is possible to argue from it in defence of the opinion of those who bring down the birth of Demosthenes with Dionysius to 381-80. Two years after Demosthenes, a sister was born, who married Laches, and became the mother of Demochares. When Demosthenes was seven years and some months old, his father died, leaving a capital of fourteen or fifteen talents. The disposition he made of his property seems to shew that he felt it to be insecure: at least he seems to have tried to bribe three of his most influential relations to protect what was left, by giving them a hold over nearly a third of the property. Aphobus, his sister's son, was to marry Cleobule with a dower of eighty minae, and the use of the house and furniture till Demosthenes came of age; Demophon, his brother's son, was to have two talents and marry the sister as soon as she was old enough; and Therippides was to have the use of seventy minae till Demosthenes should be of age. They realised their legacies at once, did not trouble themselves about either marriage, though Aphobus declined to support the widow until she had put her gold ornaments into his possession. When Demosthenes came of age, they handed over thirty minae and fourteen slaves and an empty house. It is clear that the property had been maladministered in some way. It is a curious question what became of it; how much was downright embezzled, how much simply wasted. We have five orations of Demosthenes upon the whole business (counting the πρὸς Ἄφοβον ψευδομαρτυρίας) which might be expected to resolve the difficulty, but we cannot form even an approximate idea from them of what the guardians' case was like, or even of Demosthenes' own theory of the embezzlement, though we have to remember that he designedly withholds two-thirds of his case. In fact, it is hard to imagine that they could have had a case at all; yet it is clear that there was enough to be said on their side to get up a prejudice against Demosthenes, which could be appealed to with effect many years after. The property was much of it of a very precarious character; for instance, the slaves in the upholstery were pledged by one Moeriades, as security for forty minae (In Aphobum 1, §§ 31-33, pp. 1021, 1022), and it seems (though Aphobus allowed him to borrow five minae more on the same security, which moderate sum was duly repaid) that Moeriades was a very untrustworthy debtor, and as the security disappeared without the debt having been paid, it is quite possible that the guardians were right in stating that the creditors had established a better title to the security. The only arguments urged by Demosthenes in reply to this theory are that the guardians ought to have defended an action to maintain their lien on the slaves, and that his father was not a fool, which is backed up by some makeshift evidence of the solvency of Moeriades. Then two of the guardians had claims of one kind or another against the estate (In Aphobum 1, § 56, p. 828), and it seems were paid what they chose to ask, without even giving receipts for a specified amount. Again, Demosthenes gives an estimate of the materials in hand in both manufactories, which there were no means of checking at the time of the trial; for he makes no profession of producing accounts or vouchers, he only produces the evidence of those who had had ten or twelve years ago the means of knowing what the case was then. It is probable that we have only Milyas'[1] opinion of what was left, and Demosthenes' opinion of what became of it; though Demosthenes makes out clearly that Aphobus ought to have accounted for the stock-in-trade, and did not. Also bottomry, in which more than a talent was placed, was a very hazardous investment, and there were sums of money amounting to a talent and forty or fifty minae lying at call at different bankers, which were more likely if drawn out to be paid away than to be invested. Also we know that Demosthenes all his life was a man of expensive tastes, so that it is hardly necessary to discredit entirely a plea put forward by Aphobus, that there had been considerable advances before the pupilage came to an end. This would be supported by the ambiguous taunt of Aeschines (In Ctes. § 73, p. 78), that Demosthenes had squandered his heritage in a ridiculous way.

---

[1] The confidential freedman of the elder Demosthenes.

Moreover, it is very possible that there actually was a concealed treasure, especially if we believe that Gylon's representatives were liable to have their property attacked for his debts. This liability was put forward as the reason why the guardians did not find some one to farm the whole property, get in the debts, invest the assets, and carry on the business. Demosthenes produces evidence that this had been done in other cases, and had answered admirably, though he does not say whether quite such a complicated or hazardous business had been successfully farmed. He states, further, that the plea of Gylon's debt to the state was put in at the last moment, too late to allow him to bring forward evidence that the debt had been paid, as he asserts it had. At first sight it seems a strong presumption against their sincerity in putting forward this plea, that they had returned Demosthenes as possessing fifteen talents, and liable to contribute on an assessment of three. But as the particulars of his estate were not given in the return, they may have easily made themselves believe that it was safest for their ward to avert, even at a sacrifice, the suspicion of concealed resources, which might have led to enquiry where and what they were. Again, Demosthenes says that as the thirty slaves in the cutlery brought in thirty minae a year, when half of them were sold he reckons that the rest should have brought in fifteen, whereas the return was only eleven minae according to his guardians. It is not very surprising that the profits of a business resumed on a reduced scale, after being almost at a standstill for two years, should exhibit a falling off of something like twenty-seven per cent. If it were certain that the will was suppressed before Demosthenes began to be troublesome, this would be a clear proof of deliberate malversation; as it is, it would almost account for the facts, to suppose that the property was shamefully, indolently, timidly mismanaged, by men who from first to last thought only of their own ease, profit, convenience, and security, and systematically postponed their ward, who perhaps exaggerated his destitute condition, since Aphobus offered before the trial either to prove that he was worth ten talents, or to make him so (In Aph. 1, § 57, p. 829). We have also to remember that Milyas enjoyed opportunities of peculation not so very inferior (on a small scale) to those of the guardians, while Demosthenes had a much better chance of recovering from them than from him.

Demosthenes was a delicate child, and had an impediment in his speech; between the two he got the nickname of Βάταλος, or Βάτταλος. Demosthenes acknowledged the former (D. de Cor. § 281, Ae. in Tim. § 186) as given by his nurse, perhaps in consequence of his stammering, which implies that the other at any rate was a calumny: it conveyed some kind of obscene imputation. He neglected the ordinary physical education of respectable Greeks; out he received the common intellectual training.

He says (De Cor. § 320, p. 312) that he went to the schools that became his rank, and complains (In Aph. 1, § 53, p. 828) that his guardians left his teachers unpaid. This falls in with the rather untrustworthy story that he asked Isocrates to teach him a fifth of his art for two minae, as he could not pay ten to learn all. As Isocrates taught his Athenian pupils gratis (Vitt. X Oratorum, p. 838), the story cannot be true as it stands, though it would be likely to be told of a man whose first form of extravagance had been a taste for expensive lessons. There are other stories which it is less easy to test, of his passion for Thucydides, and his having studied under Plato, and having been electrified by a speech of Callistratus, in which he invited the Athenians to recover Oropus. The first of these derives some confirmation from the harshnesses of Demosthenes' style, of which we have sufficient evidence, though the traces have disappeared from his published speeches. The second rests on less authority, and is intrinsically improbable: when Demosthenes was old enough to learn from him, Plato's influence was almost entirely limited to the circle of professed philosophers. The third may easily be true, but it is curious that Demosthenes, who all his life was a strong partisan of Thebes, should have been electrified as a boy by an anti-Theban orator; and the story was of a kind to pass easily into a legend, and perhaps it is only the legend that has reached us. The only point that we can take as proved in his education, is that he studied under Isaeus, whose influence the ancients traced in his earliest speeches: and on such a point ancient criticism may be trusted implicitly. We do not know, however, whether he consulted him until he had a personal motive in the conduct of his guardians. Demosthenes was enrolled at the age of eighteen. Aeschines implies that there were, or might have been, difficulties raised, since he claims that Philodemus, his own father-in-law (De F. L. § 159, p. 48), smoothed them away. Just before this Aphobus had definitively violated the conditions of his legacy by marrying the sister of Onetor, and Demosthenes, as soon as he was of age, lost no time in urging his grievances. For two years the business remained in the stage of negotiation and arbitration; at last the arbitrators decided against Aphobus, apparently (In Aph. 1, § 57, p. 829) on the ground that the capital had been frittered away in expenses that ought to have been met out of revenue. Demosthenes assessed damages of ten talents against each of his guardians, and apparently had provided himself with evidence that money which would have amounted to that sum under his father's management, had passed through each of their hands, and that they were answerable for the whole of it. We have his opening speech in the action against Aphobus, and his reply, in which we trace something of the line of the defence, which made little impression on the court, for Demosthenes obtained a verdict for the full amount of his claim.

The trial had nearly been frustrated by a curious incident so convenient to the guardians, as to make Demosthenes' charge that they prepared it plausible. Thrasylochus came with his brother Midias to insist (with a good deal of insolence, related at length in the speech against Midias, and not mentioned at all in the speech against Aphobus) that Demosthenes should either relieve him of the expense of a trierarchy, or exchange properties. If the exchange had been accepted, Thrasylochus would have had a right to compound all the actions, which he might have done on very easy terms and yet have been a gainer, as his estate, by Demosthenes' own shewing, was only worth about seven talents. Demosthenes calls no evidence in support of his theory, that the exchange was maliciously and vexatiously proposed. It is even possible that he accepted it freely from a desire to have two strings to his bow, and not risk everything on the success of his action. He accepted, subject to a decision of a court on the comparative value of the two properties, pending which he insisted on retaining possession. The day of the other trial was fixed, and Demosthenes, having refused Thrasylochus possession, was liable for the cost of the trierarchy. Consequently he had to pledge the assets which he acknowledged having received from the guardians, for a sum which enabled him to pay the expenses of the trierarchy, after which he brought an action for slander against Midias, who was condemned in damages of ten minae, which he did not pay (Mid. p. 543, § 114), and spun out for eight years the suit in which Demosthenes tried to recover.

Aphobus, like the other guardians, was a man of wealth and influential position; but he obviously took the verdict against him as a serious danger. He put all his property out of reach (Adv. Aph. §§ 5, 6, p. 845): he paid caution money as a denizen at Megara: after which precautions he came into court again with what was practically a motion for a new trial. His last word (In Aph. 1, § 60, p. 830) both before the arbitration and before the court had been, that after all there was a private treasure of four talents committed to the care of Cleobule, and that Milyas could be made to say where it was. Demosthenes had met this allegation upon the trial by the evidence of three witnesses that Milyas had been emancipated, and could not be made to speak under the only conditions under which his evidence would have been trusted. Aphobus replied by prosecuting Phanus, one of the three, for perjury. If he had gained his verdict, he would not have been legally entitled to a new trial. Perhaps he could have recovered from Phanus; certainly the conviction of Phanus would have discredited the former verdict enough to create a serious prejudice against Demosthenes in any future attempts to enforce it. Moreover, he and his colleagues had wisely reserved the best part of their case till Demosthenes was unprepared to meet it: at this point of the proceedings they brought forward a mass of evidence in support of their own story of the guardianship, doubtless as a presumption that as Demosthenes was pledged to a vexatious prosecution, he had suborned perjury to carry it through[1].

Apparently the prosecution failed, and Aphobus was thrown back on the system of passive defence which he had prepared. Among other precautions, he had sent his wife back to Onetor, and so became his debtor for the amount of her dowry. As security for this he placed his house and landed property, the only asset which could neither be moved nor hidden, in the hands of her brother, and sent Demosthenes to get his remedy from him. The second speech against Onetor implies that since the first Demosthenes had obtained possession of the house (Adv. On. 2. § 18, p. 877), and there we have to leave the story. It appears that the suits against the other guardians never came into court: Demosthenes, some ten years after, says that he could not recover οὐδὲ πολλοστὸν μέρος. One ancient biographer says that he let some of his guardians off for money and others for goodwill, which must be understood of all the people against whom he brought suits in connection with this family quarrel, for three guardians could not be divided into 'some' and others. This seems the place for an action brought against his cousin Demomeles for wilful wounding, and compromised, according to Aeschines (Ae. de F. L. § 99, p. 40, In Ctes. § 213, p. 84), for a pecuniary consideration. Lastly, Zosimus (p. 147, Reiske) gives the matter a sentimental turn, and pretends that Demosthenes, after shewing his skill by getting verdicts for thirty talents, the full amount claimed, shewed his sense of justice by taking only the fourteen talents which were due. It is clear from the way in which Demosthenes speaks of his public and private liberalities, both in the Midias (§§ 196–200) and in the De Corona (§ 332), that he had always money within reach. Probably he converted the fourteen slaves left in the cutlery into ready money, and with what he got from his guardians and their allies, he had a capital of several talents, on which he could live from hand to mouth. He was reproached in antiquity with lending money upon bottomry, which was too insecure

---

[1] The speech πρὸς Ἀφοβον has been discredited on three grounds: firstly, the preparations for evading the decision of Attic courts mentioned there and in the speeches against Onetor, could not precede a fresh appeal to Attic jurisdiction; secondly, the special appeal was useless, since it could not set aside the verdict in the former trial; thirdly, Demosthenes tells the old story to a new audience in the old words. All three difficulties may be met, as they are raised, *a priori*.

an investment, and led to too many disputes to be quite respectable, though of course it enabled a small capitalist to turn his money often. Aeschines, a much better authority (In Ctes. § 173), implies that his main dependence was upon his rhetorical skill, which he exercised both in composing speeches for sale, and instructing those of his clients with whom he had become personally intimate. Beyond this general outline, the years between the trial of the guardians and his entrance into public life, are the most obscure in the life of Demosthenes.

Perhaps this is the time of life to which we should especially refer the sneer of Theopompus which puzzled Plutarch (Vit. Dem. § 13), that Demosthenes could never keep to the same things or the same men. The constancy of his opposition to Philip and Alexander gives at this distance an appearance of unity to his conduct and character, which escaped the appreciation of a splenetic, impartial, and intelligent contemporary. It seems to have been, especially in its latter part, a time of effusive and hardly creditable intimacies, importunate, probably interested, and yet not insincere. By the report of his enemies (Ae. de F. L. § 177, In Tim. §§ 170-176), Demosthenes was the oracle of a fluctuating circle of heady, rich young men, each of whom expected to become the first man in Athens, thanks to his own position and abilities, and above all, to the training of his gifted friend, who meanwhile made the connection serve his own convenience. The earliest and the most lasting, the most business-like, and perhaps the most questionable of these intimacies was with Apollodorus, the son of Pasion, a wealthy banker and naturalised Athenian, who was in a state of constant collision with Phormion, his father's confidential freedman and successor in business, who, like his master, had been naturalised. Apollodorus, forgetting that Pasion had been a slave himself, was angry that Phormion should be better off than himself, and passed a long series of years in disputes with him, which gradually culminated in lawsuits. Apollodorus employed Demosthenes in five cases unconnected with his quarrel with Phormion, which are placed on more or less satisfactory evidence at various dates between 361-60 and 351-50 B.C. As Demosthenes made his first mark as a speaker in 359-58 (Euseb. Chron. p. 345, ed. Mai), Apollodorus, who was some ten years older, must have been his earliest and most consistent patron; but in 351-50 there must have been something of a quarrel, for Demosthenes composed a speech to be delivered, apparently by himself, in behalf of Phormion, in which Apollodorus is very severely handled. Phormion got his verdict, probably thanks to this speech, which begins with a graphic description of the pitiful way in which the poor man had fumbled his own case. Apollodorus, like Aphobus, replied by prosecuting a witness for perjury: the speech he delivered was supplied by

Demosthenes. The transaction was regarded in antiquity as highly questionable; and it would certainly be strange for a barrister now to call a witness on one trial, and accept a brief to prosecute him for perjury on another. It is hardly clear whether this was the whole of the story as Plutarch knew it; he speaks as if Demosthenes had written a speech for Phormion to deliver, which certainly cannot be the ὑπέρ Φορμίωνος that we have.

So far he may be thought to support the far worse charge of Aeschines, put plainly in the περὶ παραπρεσβείας, § 171, and in a more abstract form in the In Ctesiphontem, § 173, that Demosthenes allowed one side a sight of the speech he was engaged to compose for the other. It is clear that in the speech to which Demosthenes, in behalf of Phormion, composed a reply, Apollodorus had dwelt much on the fact of Phormion having been his father's slave, and as the reply professes to give a full account of their quarrels, and mentions no trial in which Apollodorus could be said to prosecute Phormion περὶ σώματος, it is on the whole most probable that Aeschines was exaggerating; that he presumed that Apollodorus claimed Phormion as a slave, because he taunted him with having been one. At the same time it is hardly probable that if Demosthenes did no more than Plutarch says, it would have damaged him, as Aeschines says his conduct did. Aeschines professes that Demosthenes got a reputation for bad faith: by the time of Plutarch this had dwindled to an imputation of bad taste. On such evidence we could not convict any man, especially a great man, and not an unscrupulous man of deliberate treachery; and there are many ways in which we can imagine the charge to have arisen, without imputing this: e. g. Demosthenes may have shewn Apollodorus the speech after the trial, to prove that it was less offensive than he thought; and the charge was one which might easily become obscure when the people who spread it were dead.

We know of two other intimates of Demosthenes, Ctesippus, the son of Chabrias, with whom he was closely connected in 355-54, and whose mother he was expected to marry (Plut. Vit. Dem. c. 15); Aristarchus, the son of Moschus, a violent young man, who killed Nicodemus, apparently for reflecting in the public assembly on his relations with Demosthenes, 'by knocking out his eyes,' Aeschines says, 'and slitting the tongue that dared to speak out to you.' Demosthenes was accused of having instigated the crime: he himself professed to believe in the innocence of Aristarchus, who fled to avoid a trial. Aeschines talks of three talents which Aristarchus had lodged with Demosthenes to provide for his necessities in exile, and which the latter had embezzled (De F. L. § 177). We may perhaps believe that money of Aristarchus' passed through Demosthenes' hands; perhaps also that he had or made reasons for detaining some or all of it.

This seems the place to say something of Demosthenes' personal habits and private character. All his life he seems to have been accused by his enemies of two faults, which seem at first sight to exclude each other: one being an austere morosity, the other profuse, effeminate luxury. We hear of his being ridiculed as a water drinker (D. de F. L. § 51), and of his speeches smelling of the lamp (Plut. Vit. § 8): Hyperides (Frag. 17, p. 19, Sauppe) makes it an aggravation of his crime in embezzling the treasure of Harpalus, that he had rebuked the harmless indulgences of the young men who were bringing him to justice. It is chiefly from Aeschines that we hear of the other side,—of the thin clothes, like a fine lady's, in which he wrote his speeches against his friends (In Tim. § 131, p. 18), of the excesses which made it credible that he had to find a friend to make him a father (Ae. de F. L. § 158, p. 118), of the extravagance which was sure to exhaust the treasures of Persia at last (In Ctes. § 173, p. 78). The second charge is supported to some extent by the number of anecdotes which Athenaeus has collected, of his expensive favourites of both sexes; and perhaps by another story, that when brought to trial in the matter of Harpalus, he had no children to exhibit to move the pity of the court, except those of his Samian concubine, and was ashamed to produce the mother. About the worst charges Demosthenes' enthusiastic admirers were silent throughout antiquity, probably from prudence, not from contempt. It is happily impossible to examine them in detail; they must be passed by with the admission, 'where there is smoke there is fire,' not dismissed with the contemptuous phrase, 'throw mud enough and some is sure to stick.' As we never hear from Aeschines the remotest hint of excesses of the table, it is probable that Demosthenes' temperament was like that of Mahomet and the early Caliphs, abstemious in one direction and voluptuous in another. It is harder to decide why he was so particular to have his clothes spun fine, except on the ground of delicate health; perhaps, too, his timid, jealous, suspicious temper, may be taken as the outcome of a sensitive, irritable organisation, to which the mere physical fret of ordinary flannel might be intolerable. This also would account in some measure for the charge of extravagance: to a timid, nervous man, the act of spending money gives for the moment a pleasant sense of power; and a nature not naturally joyous, needs to be assured that a pleasure is pleasant by its cost. Besides, a man who spends at rare intervals, finds it easiest when he does spend to be lavish; and lastly, it should be remembered that Demosthenes was habitually munificent both in public and private.

We have many details, but no dates, for his severe and thorough self-education as an orator. We know how on his first appearance he broke down; and how he was encouraged and guided by the actor Satyrus; how he declaimed, while marching up hill and by the sea shore, with pebbles in his mouth; how he shaved one side of his head, and shut himself up to meditate. We have more questionable information, that even his first unfortunate attempt was pronounced by old men[1] to be in the spirit of Pericles, and that at last when his lisp was conquered, he was able to appear in the public assembly with the following grotesque piece of exultation, ἥκω φέρων ἐς ὑμᾶς τὸ ῥῶ καταῤῥερητορευμένον. His perseverance in overcoming difficulties is the point on which our authorities have insisted most; and this has given greatest prominence to the shortcomings of his oratory, which were connected with physical defects, because most resolution was required to conquer these. But it seems that besides being ill-delivered, his first speeches were harsh and obscure, and that the sentences were too long not merely for his voice, but for human ears. Another fault, of which Aeschines has preserved specimens ranging from 346 to 330 B.C., was indulgence in violent and unpleasant metaphors. This has not been noticed by ancient critics, so that it is probable Demosthenes himself removed any traces of it from his finished compositions. After all, however, he never attained to perfect clearness and ease, except in the beautiful speech against Leptines; his eloquence rushes, and does not flow; his great speeches are a little monotonous in their intensity; they are overweighted with arguments and earnestness, everything is enforced and 'inculcated;' we look in vain for the repose of secure and confident exposition, of unembarrassed narrative. The ancients were conscious of the want of relief in his astonishing eloquence (Plut. Vit. Dem. § 11), and cultivated contemporaries took unfavourable notice of another consequence of his absorbed and pathetic seriousness. They contrasted his artificial manner, his forced passion, his deliberate pathos, which electrified the groundlings, with the reserve and self-possession of older speakers, 'who discoursed with the multitude in a stately, magnificent way,' and who, if their speeches as compositions were comparatively cold and empty, never merged their own dignity and personality in a torrent of factitious enthusiasm (Plut. Vit. § 11).

On the whole, it seems we ought to place the greater part of this laborious training comparatively late in Demosthenes' life, just before the first speeches on public affairs that have come down to us, the earliest of which is dated 355-54, even if we are to assume that it was over then. Probably the lawsuit with his guardians left him no leisure while it lasted;

---

[1] How old? Aeschines thought it a great thing to have a father who remembered Cleophon.

after the compromise, there would still be four or five years before we can suppose that he had much practice as a speech writer, and these would be occupied in part with rhetorical studies: it appears there were already books on rhetoric, from which it seems, from the ancient guesses that have come down to us, he learnt more than from living teachers. But when he had learned to write a speech he still had to become an orator. He had still as much to learn as a chancery lawyer, who comes to face public meetings, and has to gain the ear of the House of Commons, and in his case the change was peculiarly difficult. Aeschines (In Ctes. § 173, p. 78) asserts that he took to politics because he had no choice after his unprofessional conduct towards Phormion and Apollodorus; the insinuation is without visible or probable foundation,—we have public speeches before the case came on, and private speeches after it was decided. Demosthenes himself (In Zenothemin, ad fin.) gives us a much more valuable clue to the relation between the two sides of his career: he makes his client and relation, Demon, swear to the court that he, Demosthenes, has refused him all support at the trial; because as a politician he finds it impossible to take part in private causes, since this would prejudice those against whom he appeared, against his public measures. Demon refers to his kinsman as a speaker of established reputation, but beyond this we cannot fix the date. Demosthenes' first considerable move was the speech against the law of Leptines, which was delivered 355–54. It was to a considerable extent the choice of a party: the declaration both of the principles on which he would act, and of the persons with whom he would act. Leptines had proposed to resume all exemptions from liturgies, except those granted to the descendants of the tyrannicides, on the common-sense grounds that a good many were enjoyed by very unworthy persons, and that several very rich men were exempted from burthens which there were few rich men left to bear. The proposal was so popular, that the first attempt to combat it was allowed to fall through in consequence of the death of one of the speakers selected by the holders of exemptions to defend their cause. And though the opposition was revived, it was too late to involve the mover in penal consequences. In fact, the opponents felt themselves compelled to bring forward a counter proposal of their own, professing to remedy the undeniable scandals which they admitted to be the strong point of Leptines' case. One of the most curious and amusing parts of Demosthenes' speech, is that (§§ 151–153, pp. 498, 499) where he insists on the means Leptines had for obliging him to go on with this alternative proposal, or at all events for carrying it through himself, when his own was definitively got rid of. The people who were in enjoyment of this grotesque privilege were principally rich denizens or aliens with a business connection with Athens, and naturalised citizens. All had made large presents to the Athenian people of money or money's worth : the naturalised citizens had made many such presents, and been rewarded first with exemption from the denizens' special burdens, then with citizenship, then with exemption from the festival taxes. The son of Chabrias, indeed, enjoyed the exemption as a reward for his father's military services, but his father had raised armies on his own credit, and had enriched the treasury. In point of fact, to maintain the permanence of such exemptions on principle, as essential conditions of Athenian honour and greatness, really implied that Athens was to pursue an ambitious policy in reliance on casual resources, that she was to depend upon large 'benevolences,' and encourage them by shewing that such benevolences were a secure investment; that her foreign policy was to be directed with the concourse of a crowd of cosmopolitan adventurers and potentates, rather than by the free determination of the ancient race of Erechtheus. Perhaps it may be thought, that as we never hear of Demosthenes' paternal grandfather, and do hear of his Scythian grandmother, Demosthenes himself had little old Athenian blood in him, and belonged himself to the cosmopolitan set. On this occasion Demosthenes was successful : Leptines' project was got out of the way, and Demosthenes' counter project fell through, as it was probably meant to fall.

The orator tells us himself that there were many lines of political life at Athens, and that, as might be expected from his speech against Leptines, he had chosen foreign politics for his own. Within three years he had delivered five, if not six, important speeches, of which one only was on a subject of vital interest. In fact, all are the production of a young man in whom legitimate personal ambition quite kept pace with his high abilities and lofty patriotism; it is quite as much his object to bring himself favourably before the public, as to procure the adoption of the definite measures he recommends, as in fact a young man could scarcely expect the public to give immediate practical effect to his plans. The first two of this group of speeches may be placed in 354. One of them was delivered in consequence of a foolish panic, that the danger of Persian invasion was not at an end with the abrupt termination of the Social war, and that the best way of meeting it was to appeal to Panhellenic patriotism, and attack the great king at home by an united effort. Demosthenes points out, that by all experience it would be much easier for Persia, if provoked, to direct a coalition of all Greece against Athens, than for Athens to organise such a coalition against Persia. But the principal object of the speech is to shew that Athens has much to do in order to be ready for war, to which end he has prepared a schedule calculated to set the direct contributions on a better footing.

The other has not come down to us. It was directed against the expedition to Euboea, which resulted in the battle of Tamynae; and as Demosthenes' opposition cannot be set down to a pacific temper, it is safe to take it as the first proof of the partiality for Thebes with which he was often afterwards reproached, with the more plausibility, because during Demosthenes' political life a good understanding with Thebes could only be maintained at the price of bearing a good deal from the Thebans. The speech in favour of Megalopolis explains the reasons of his unpopular determination; he regarded it is an axiom, that no power ought to be allowed to preponderate in Greece, because such a power could be appealed to to thwart the enterprises of Athens, while if matters on the mainland of Greece were balanced and divided, Athens would have free scope to pursue her career of maritime adventures. It required great boldness to deliver, such a speech so soon after the disastrous termination of the Social war, which must have made all schemes of maritime dominion look unpromising, especially as the Athenians had a chance of solid advantage by a hearty co-operation with Sparta. Thebes was exhausted by the struggle with Phocis, and if the Athenians had thrown their weight into the opposite scale, they might certainly have recovered Oropus, at the price of assisting Sparta to regain a modified and precarious ascendancy in the Peloponnese. Between anti-Spartan feeling and anti-Theban feeling, between the counsels of prudence and the stimulus of resentment and ambition, the Athenians did nothing, and most probably did not even decree anything. The Phocian war just then languishing, the Thebans managed to send a contingent into Peloponnese: Oropus was not recovered, and Megalopolis was relieved. The fourth speech of the group shews more clearly than any of the rest, the kind of results Demosthenes thought Athens ought to aim at, the kind of action for which he wished her to keep herself free. The Rhodians appear to have been the prime movers of the coalition which brought on the Social war, while they themselves were set in motion by Mausolus, the hereditary prince of Caria. When the war had terminated to the advantage of the allies, the great Rhodian families who had been in correspondence with the Carian dynasty, thought the time had come to repay themselves and their patrons. Accordingly a Carian garrison was admitted, and the commons were put down. Demosthenes thought that it was possible to take a generous revenge upon the Rhodians, by granting the request of some envoys more or less accredited by a party which desired a counter revolution, delivering the commons from the yoke of their own nobility and the Carian dynasty, and of course restoring the island to its old connection with Athens, which, if strictly interpreted, was hardly very onerous to one party or profitable to the other. In all four orations, there is as yet no trace of any paramount practical object which the speaker had before him. Athens is to guide herself by maxims and traditions, for want of a scheme of comprehensive policy. She is to avoid the risk of a hostile coalition, to put the war taxes on a sound footing, to watch against the growth of any power capable of dominating Greece, to place herself at the head of the democratic interest in maritime Greece, and, if opportunity offer, in continental Greece also; in this way she will be able to maintain and increase her prestige, and to secure the largest share of the small advantages of current politics, which are concisely summarised under the head of influence. It must be admitted that in the absence of results, this policy embodies much generous sentiment and one sound maxim.

At the time when the speeches in favour of the commons of Rhodes and the first speech against Philip were delivered, it would have been unreasonable to require either the orator or his audience to decide which speech contained the prophecy of his career. Both might have reasonably imagined that the decline of democracy was as grave a danger to Athens as the progress of Macedon to Hellenism; in fact, Philip as yet had only appeared as the benefactor of his two nearest Greek neighbours: he had enlarged the territory of Olynthus, he had delivered the great houses of Thessaly from the pressure of the dynasty of Pherae, he had driven back the hordes of mercenaries collected by the Delphic treasure. True he had established his supremacy in towns that had belonged to the Athenian confederacy, and established himself in the important position of Amphipolis; but he had definitely asserted the ascendancy of his own power, which, if not Greek, was in intimate relation with Greek states, over the unmistakable barbarism of the Thracian and Illyrian hordes. Greece had seen Athens lose Rhodes and the Bosporus with great equanimity, as a result of the Social war: Athens herself had recovered the loss. Those who believed that Greece and Athens would lose little if the war with Philip ended in the loss of the precarious footing Athens still maintained on what was called 'the Thracian frontier,' might be pardoned for their shortsightedness, especially as Demosthenes contributed something to fulfil his prophecies by his vigorous and judicious efforts to falsify them. The speech has three main points, the causes of Philip's undeniable ascendancy in the long war, the remedies for this ascendancy by improved administration at Athens, and above all by a reform in the moral tone of the citizens. This last is the key-note to all the speeches prior to the Peace of Philocrates; the Athenians must take the management of their own affairs into their own hands; they must break through the routine established

by the public men who persuaded the commons that the regular supply
of their doles depended upon it; if they took the wages of the state, they
must hold themselves ready for the service of the state in time of war ;
the attempt to secure the good management of affairs by the criminal
accountability of the generals was futile or worse; if the generals were
properly supported, they would succeed, or, if they failed, then it would
be time to punish them.   These doctrines were maintained by Demosthenes throughout his career, with one important omission and one
important addition.   After the capture of Olynthus, he no longer ·
seriously exerted himself to urge his countrymen to serve in person,
and long before that catastrophe, he began to attribute everything that
went wrong to the ubiquitous agency of Philip's gold.   The latest in
date of the series is also questionable in point of authenticity, and in
fact has generally been rejected on the ground that it is a cento made up
from the Second Olynthiac.   Indeed, if we maintain its genuineness, we
must also maintain that after the speech had served its turn, Demosthenes
went back to it as a quarry for the materials of the Second Olynthiac.   In
itself the oration is perfectly coherent and exceedingly clever, and fits
very well into history, though we can only fix its real or supposed date
approximately.   It must be later than the revolution in Rhodes, 352 B.C.,
and before the law of Eubulus, which made it a capital offence to apply
the theoric fund to military purposes.   We know that at one time it was
the habit of Demosthenes to compose speeches for a debate he had just
heard; we do not know how long this habit continued, or if it was left
off gradually.   These questions are all so uncertain, that perhaps the point
may almost be decided by observing that one of the parallel passages is
completed with a happy trait in the speech περὶ συντάξεως (§ 23, p. 172),
which is omitted in the Second Olynthiac.   The object of the speech is
to prove that the Athenians lost much in dignity, and even in profit, by
allowing themselves to be managed by cliques of politicians, and com-
pounding for a few small and certain advantages, instead of the great
results that might be expected from vigorous and self-sacrificing action.
The speech, if Demosthenes wrote it, and if it was ever delivered, produced little effect; it is chiefly remarkable as a manifesto against the
system of Eubulus, upon the whole the most influential and the most
respectable statesman of the generation which was passing away, a sort
of minor Pericles in his conservative policy and his consistent and successful endeavours to bring home to all classes a sense of their material
interest in democratic institutions, though without the palest reflection
of his magnificence of conception or of his imposing personality.

   At the time of the expedition to Euboea, which is identified by Demosthenes (Adv. Mid. §§ 205–207, p. 567) with that which led to the battle

of Tamynae, placed by Westermann 354–53, three years earlier than the
ordinary date, on the ground of the testimony of Hyperides, Demosthenes volunteered to serve as Choregus, as otherwise his tribe would
have been unrepresented in the competition at the Dionysia, as it had
been the year before. Of course this exempted him from service in the
expedition, and it is possible, without any imputation on his courage,
that this consideration stimulated his munificence, just as Midias, though
commandant of the cavalry, chose to fit out a trireme at his own expense,
and serve aboard of her. Besides his dislike to the disagreeables of
campaigning, Demosthenes had an additional motive in his dislike to all
interference in Euboea, as tending to embroil Athens with Thebes. He
made his preparations with perhaps something of his usual extravagance,
ordering a magnificent ceremonial dress for himself, with a gold crown :
perhaps this revived the spleen of Midias, who had an old quarrel with
Demosthenes, going back to the time of the lawsuit with the guardians.
It is possible, too, that he was connected with Nicodemus, who, according
to Aeschines (De F. L. p. 292), prosecuted Demosthenes as a deserter,
and had to be bought off; who also spoke freely against Demosthenes on
some ground, and was murdered about this time by an intimate of Demosthenes. However, he had some motive for annoying Demosthenes, and
he had the power of doing so with impunity. He was rich and well-
born, he was closely connected with other rich and influential men ; he
had no ambition, a strong and rational contempt for his countrymen, a
certain shrewdness and a certain courage, and his only use for all these
resources was to set himself above the law; he desired nothing of his
countrymen, except that they should be afraid of him. The night before
the Dionysia he succeeded in spoiling the orator's finery, and, according
to Demosthenes, he succeeded by terrorism in depriving him of the
prize; it is certain that after the decision he assaulted Demosthenes
with such violence, that twenty years after the event Aeschines could
taunt him with having the marks still about him. He was some twenty
years younger than his assailant, and could therefore plausibly claim
credit for his forbearance in not killing him upon the spot, though probably Midias was the more powerful man of the two. Immediately after
the performance, an assembly was held in the theatre to decide upon all
the complaints which had arisen during the festival, and Demosthenes
brought his case before it and obtained an enthusiastic decision, that,
beside the common assault, Midias had been guilty of a public offence,
by an attack on a public officer during a public festival. As Demosthenes set forth in his speech, there were ample precedents for taking
the severest view of such conduct; but there were precedents also of
respectable citizens who had allowed powerful men to insult them at

their own price, though perhaps not under such aggravated circumstances. In fact, the question at issue was the value of Demosthenes' personal dignity, and this explains the tenacity with which he maintained the prosecution, in spite of threats and bribes and accusations got up against himself by men of straw, who were never meant to press them. At last the question was put before him in this form: that even, if he gained his verdict for the public offence, the influence of Midias would be certain to secure the adoption of the reduced penalty which was due to a common assault, and that he only had the choice whether the half talent (some hundred and twenty guineas) which Midias would pay in any case, should be paid to him or to the state. Whatever happened, Demosthenes was certain to be ridiculous, for the prosecution would be a fiasco if Midias was allowed to fix the penalty. Perhaps a fiasco would have been forgotten sooner than a compromise; at any rate, Demosthenes was never forgiven for taking the only satisfaction he was likely to get. The inflexible civic virtue of his speech, which was not delivered, has enabled the spiteful taunts of contemporaries to find an echo in posterity.

Demosthenes was compensated to some extent for this personal mortification, by an event which gave him an opening to attain something nearer political influence than he had hitherto enjoyed. Much of the mismanagement of the war with Philip had been due to a sceptical indifference at Athens. The Athenians did not see how they were to act with energy north of the Aegean without allies on the spot, as they indeed never had acted before. At last Olynthus declared against Philip, and solicited an alliance with Athens, and there was a chance that the Athenians would attend seriously to the subject which Demosthenes was anxious to make his own. We have three speeches on behalf of Olynthus, which it is generally assumed were delivered at three assemblies, to which another supposition is frequently added, that each assembly had to consider the demands of an Olynthian embassy, and each voted an expedition. The order of the three speeches is an insoluble question, for none of the three speeches dates itself absolutely or relatively; the external evidence reduces itself to balancing the authority of Dionysius, perhaps of Philochorus, against that of antiquity in general; the internal evidence reduces itself to a comparison which of three urgent speeches can be considered the most urgent; any one of the three speeches might have been delivered at any point in the war, and though there are degrees of appropriateness, they are far from being indisputably plain. Confining ourselves to the internal evidence, it is pretty safe to say that the third oration seems later than the other two. There is a keener tone of apprehension for the safety of Olynthus, with broader hints at the necessity of making the festival fund available for military purposes, and there are specific reflections on the inadequacy of past efforts, and this last consideration is almost decisive. The first and second stand upon a different footing: if they came to us without an indication of their author, and the age in which he lived, it would certainly be simplest to take them as alternative speeches composed for the same occasion. The situation is the same in both: the Athenians have long desired such aid as Olynthus can give, let them make the best use of it now that Olynthus presents herself unsolicited, let the most be made of the opportunity. But in the first speech this thought is enforced chiefly by dwelling on alarmist topics; in the second the motive is hope, not fear. Philip is disparaged with singular audacity as a mushroom potentate, whose power is only a parasite of the neglect of Athens, while the Athenians themselves are taunted with their degeneracy, and with the paltriness of the improvements on which they were inclined to hug themselves. That Demosthenes should have written two speeches and only delivered one (if, indeed, he delivered either), would not after all be more extraordinary than that Cicero, when he had a much more prominent and assured position, should have written seven speeches against Verres and only delivered two. It would prove at most that he did not consider his oratorical education over; for we must remember that, besides being a patriot, Demosthenes was an artist, and might choose to treat the subject of Olynthus twice over, as Pope did with the Dunciad and Tasso with Jerusalem. Again, we do not know the real relation of Demosthenes' published speeches on public affairs to those which he actually delivered. It was not his rule to compose an harangue and learn it by heart and then deliver it. Of course it is possible that the public speeches which have come down to us were precisely the exceptions to this rule: it is possible also that they represent the final ideal and shape of the speeches which in their delivery had pleased him best. If so, it is not unlikely that he may have perceived that each class of motives introduced into a single speech on behalf of Olynthus, would have been more effective separately than both had been together. Perhaps this conjecture on the order of the Olynthiacs may take its place with others. Nothing can be cleverer than the way in which Demosthenes urges (Ol. 3, § 14, p. 31) that those who have had the popularity of starving the war and nursing the festival fund, ought to bear the unpopularity of repealing the securities they had taken during times of less pressure, for the exclusive enjoyment of the surplus. And we are not undervaluing the seriousness of the first two speeches, at any rate, when we praise their ingenuity: the speaker wishes to induce his countrymen to fight Philip heartily, and he is uncertain whether the way to attain this is by overrating the danger to be feared from him, or by underrating the solidity of his power. It is

obvious that he wishes to establish an influence as well as to carry a
measure, for if he desired the measure exclusively for its own sake, he
would have been content to advocate it on its own proper grounds, and
convince others as he had been convinced himself. In pursuit of the
influence due to his political talents and earnest patriotism, Demosthenes
was destined to make an even greater display of versatility than that implied in the contrast between the Second Olynthiac and the First Philippic.

After some successes, which the orator warned his countrymen
not to overrate, the head of the Philippising party at Olynthus came
into power; probably he was expected to procure tolerable terms for
the city, but he failed to do anything, whether through Philip's severity
or his own incapacity or treachery. First he surrendered the cavalry
(perhaps his own partisans) and then the city, which altogether lost its
political existence, while many of the inhabitants were reduced to slavery.
Curiously enough, Philip, after this success, unprecedented both in its
extent and the severity with which it had been used, made overtures
through various channels for a cordial accommodation with Athens.
Demosthenes, after having made himself as prominent as he could
in opposition to Philip, determined to make himself more prominent
in advocacy of an intimate understanding with Philip. It is quite true
that, as he argued (De Cor. § 291, p. 305, De F. L. § 260, p. 415) when
he passed again into opposition, after the peace of Philocrates had disappointed both himself and public opinion, that his action had no serious
influence upon the result, and that his influence did no harm. But even
if the position of Demosthenes had been simply that of the fly on the
wheel, it is curious that he should have elected to perch upon that particular cart. In fact, when Philocrates was impeached for a cautious
attempt to reciprocate Philip's cautious advances, Demosthenes went
as much out of his way to defend him as Horace Greeley went when he
offered himself as a bailsman to liberate Jefferson Davis; and in the case
of Horace Greeley the generosity was its own object, in the case of
Demosthenes it was the first step of a series. The truth is, that the
power of Philip was such a new anomalous fact in Greek experience,
that it was impossible for any statesman to take in its full bearings.
Even after the victories of Alexander, there was no one who realised
their effect upon Greece; those who had looked to Persia to deliver
Greece, misconceived the situation almost as much as those who thought
that Greece at last had conquered Persia. In 347 B.C. the situation was
still more perplexing than in 330 B.C. Demosthenes has left us no
explanation of his acts, which he endeavours to reduce to insignificance,
and his denials of the specific statements of Aeschines are too perfunc-
tory to be very important. Aeschines' account is very amusing, and on the

whole consistent and not incredible, though it is doubtless heightened and somewhat distorted by his natural anxiety to make out that Demosthenes would have sold himself to Macedonia if he could. According to him, Demosthenes annoyed all his colleagues on the first journey to Macedonia, by his overweening confidence in a great diplomatic triumph: he was going to stop Philip's mouth with a sound cartrope, without a single flaw or splice in it (Ae. de F. L. § 22, p. 31). It is true, that as Hegesander had expressed his fear that Philip would have the best of the discussion of the merits (as he had certainly the material ascendancy), Demosthenes may have only meant that he might promise a verbal victory for what it was worth. In the presence of Philip, Demosthenes was cowed. Still according to Aeschines, he broke down ignominiously, and when he tried to recover himself, he only blundered into spasms of fulsome flattery (Ae. de F. L. § 37, pp. 32, 33). Henceforward Aeschines represents Demosthenes as actuated simply by an anxiety to propitiate Philip, and by jealousy of his colleagues, for whom he was perpetually laying traps. The first display of this feeling was against Aeschines, whom he reviled for imperilling the peace by the energetic tone of his speech, as if, said Demosthenes, we should ever man the fifty triremes which we voted to keep ready. The fifty triremes were specially intended to defend Thermopylae, as suggested by Demosthenes himself (Ib. § 40, p. 33), and it was certainly natural for him to give vent to his spleen when he saw that others relied upon carrying out his policy, when he perceived that it had irrevocably broken down by the fault of others. Besides, the attitude of rebuke came easily to him; the fault to be rebuked was a secondary consideration. He had rebuked the assembly for desiring war with Persia, before he had rebuked them for their slackness in the war with Philip. After this ebullition, according to Aeschines, Demosthenes next endeavoured to screen his break down by getting his colleagues to report that he had supported the claim for the restoration of Amphipolis, as previously arranged. After this the envoys began to express their admiration of Philip personally, and Demosthenes dared them to repeat their compliments at Athens (Ib. § 46, p. 33). Considering that Philip had as yet no party, and that most of the citizens revenged themselves in the only way they could, by despising him, it is probable that the challenge was only meant as a taunt, though Aeschines says it was meant as a trap. At all events it seems to have acted as one; the ambassadors gravely proceeded to arrange who was to dilate upon each of Philip's accomplishments. When they came to carry out this programme, Demosthenes, who had probably forgotten the whole affair, was disgusted with their behaviour, as, to say the least, unbusinesslike; accordingly he turned all their compliments into ridicule, and wound up by giving a specimen of the style in which necessary and unpleasant business ought to be despatched (Ib. § 53, p. 34). Still he persevered in his attentions to Macedonia, which were the more significant because they were unnecessary: he moved that an assembly should be held to consider the proposals of the ambassadors, even before the ambassadors arrived, and that the ambassadors themselves should be treated with special and elaborate distinction in the theatre; he even arranged that during their stay they should be his guests. It is obvious that if he was not anxious to begin a new career as a Macedonian agent, he wished to leave no trace of his old career as an opponent of Macedon.

What happened at the two assemblies in which these proposals were under consideration, and in connection with the ratification of the treaty by Athens and her allies, is one of the most perplexing questions in the whole history. We have practically to choose between the authority of Aeschines and that of Demosthenes. The only two indisputable facts are, that Demosthenes went out of his way to defend Philocrates and to court the Macedonian ambassadors; these facts have a meaning in the story of Aeschines, they present themselves as isolated anomalies in the story of Demosthenes. In fact, when the speeches on the embassy were composed, Demosthenes had a strong interest in misrepresenting his former attitude, and it seems he did so. It seems probable that Demosthenes was quite as impatient as Aeschines of the delays that would have resulted from any attempt to act in conjunction with the whole body of Greek states. When the peace had become unpopular, those concerned in it naturally bandied the blame about among one another, and fastened upon things to which they had not dreamed of objecting at the time, as the origin of all the mischief. So far as we can see, the only incidental consequence of the peace which Demosthenes seriously endeavoured to prevent at the time, and which he was seriously displeased to see accomplished in spite of him, was the extension of Philip's Thracian frontier in the direction of the Chersonese. So far as we can make out, the original draught of the treaty as moved by Philocrates, stipulated for peace and alliance between Athens and her allies on the one part, except the Halians and Phocians, and Philip and his allies on the other. No doubt this exclusion was copied from the instructions of Philip's ambassadors, and so was put more plainly and offensively than need required. The self-respect of the Athenians revolted against admitting in the same breath that the Phocians were their allies, and excluding them from the treaty; but it still had to be determined whether the Phocians, though not excluded by name, were to be admitted in fact. This was in the first instance a question for the administration, and it was quietly decided against the Phocians. It is true that they had a treaty which they had not violated; but the alliance had been made with the nation, not with the dynasty, and the dynasty had recently affronted Athens by declining to profit by it. Demosthenes does not claim to have protested; as a partisan of Thebes he had no reason for doing so. Cersobleptes stood in rather a different position; he and his predecessors had been the great obstacles to the tranquil enjoyment by Athens of their establishments in the Chersonese, and anything like a stable alliance with the Thracian kings was out of the question; but at the moment an alliance existed on parchment, and had not been recently violated upon either side. On the other hand, Philip's ambassadors had orders not to include Cersobleptes in the treaty, and an alliance with Cersobleptes would certainly be an obstacle to an intimate alliance with Philip, such as many at Athens were anxious to conclude, including Demosthenes, if we may trust Aeschines. Besides, it is to be remembered that the question was whether Athens should make peace on behalf of the Phocians and Thracians, which neither the Phocians nor Thracians had authorised her to do. While the terms of peace were under discussion, there was no mention of Cersobleptes; but, after the peace had passed the vote, one Critobulus of Lampsacus presented himself, and claimed to be sworn as representing Cersobleptes, who was very hard pressed, and in need of help from any quarter. Demosthenes was chairman for the day, and resented the intrusion in characteristic language (Ae. de F. L. § 90, p. 39). He said Critobulus was sponging for a share of the peace like a parasite at a sacrifice, and that another assembly was fixed for the consideration of such claims, and his must wait till then. However, he was forced to put a motion for swearing him to the vote, and so it was probably carried he should be sworn. He came for this purpose into the generals' office, but it is evident that he was not sworn, for Demosthenes accused Aeschines (Ae. ubi sup. § 92) of turning him out; and no doubt Aeschines, like Demosthenes, wished to exclude him. So, according to the writer of Philip's letter (ap. Dem. p. 160), did the Athenian generals; and no wonder, for we do not hear one word of his credentials. It seems the matter was staved off to the next assembly, as Demosthenes originally proposed, and that there Philocrates carried a motion, which virtually excluded Cersobleptes, that those states should be sworn as Athenian allies which had representatives then in session at Athens (Ae. in Ct. § 74). This assembly seems to have been held on the twenty-fourth or twenty-fifth of Elaphebolion. On that very day Philip had taken Holy Mount and the treasure of Cersobleptes. Chares at once sent the news to Athens, and on the third of Munychion, Demosthenes carried a motion in the senate, that the ambassadors should set off at once to find Philip in Thrace, with the avowed intention of stopping his conquests. The

ambassadors had to go as far as Oreus, where there was an Athenian
commander, who had orders to convoy them; but there they halted,
with the full consent of Proxenus. Demosthenes was helpless; he could
do nothing but fret and suspect the worst, especially of Philocrates and
Aeschines, who got on so much better than he with Philip. Perhaps it
was he who inserted the clause in the instructions to the ambassadors,
forbidding private interviews with Philip. After a time they went on to
Pella, and waited there till Philip came back, during all which time the
suspicions of Demosthenes were naturally aggravated, for the reason of
the delay in Philip's return was obviously due to the fresh conquests he
was making in Thrace, and his colleagues had doubtless assured him
that with the capture of Holy Mount all was over, and Philip might
be expected back from one day to another. At last Philip came, and
Aeschines dilated upon the duty of the ambassadors, enforcing a clause
which he had doubtless had inserted in the instructions, that the ambassadors were to do all the good they could. Demosthenes was not in a
temper to take uncongenial advice; he declared he would know nothing
about Philip's expedition to Phocis; the only thing the ambassadors had
to do was to receive the oaths of Philip and his confederates, and get
home without compromising the city by a series of ambitious intrigues.
It was agreed that each ambassador should speak for himself, which is a
sign that neither Aeschines nor Demosthenes was sufficiently trusted by
his colleagues to induce them to silence the other, and to quiet Demosthenes, if possible, it was agreed he should speak first. By this time
Demosthenes had worked himself into a belief that the other ambassadors
were in a conspiracy to betray himself and his country to Philip. Accordingly, while he shewed extravagant deference, or what Aeschines
chose to consider such, to Philip, he contrasted his own language about
Philip at Athens with that of his colleagues, very much to their disadvantage. Aeschines spoke next, and the Macedonians, who had not
witnessed all the bickerings of the last six or seven weeks, naturally
thought his speech more appropriate to the occasion, as well as more
dignified. While the embassy remained at Pella, Demosthenes' position
grew more and more uncomfortable; his colleagues were in confidential
intercourse with Philip, to which he was not admitted; they boasted, on
grounds which he could not control, of having obtained advantages in
which he did not believe; they would not allow him to send home
despatches embodying his alarm; they persuaded Philip to prevent him
from returning alone. Then Philip persuaded them to an open violation
of their instructions. Demosthenes had intended that they should go
first to the Hellespont, and swear Philip and his allies in that quarter,
and then swear his other allies on their way home; but when they were

at Pella, and had been waiting there for weeks, the inconvenience of setting off to the Hellespont was so obvious, that they might be pardoned for receiving the oaths of Philip's allies at Pella, or on the road from thence to Athens. During all this time Demosthenes had been unavoidably in a ludicrous position, and on his return he felt its effects. His colleagues for the moment enjoyed an enormous popularity, on the strength of the good news they brought, and probably believed: Demosthenes professed that he had no knowledge that their promises were true, and that he disbelieved them (De Pace, § 10, p. 59); and he was laughed at for his pains. It does not appear that even now he appealed to the Athenians to defend the Phocians against Philip, though he denied that Philip was coming to defend Phocis against Thebes; he contented himself with urging the Athenians not to send a force of their own to support Philip in his ambiguous expedition, as such a force would only be hostages for their assent to its objects when declared. It was only when Philip had declared himself in favour of Thebes that Demosthenes saw his way to avenge himself on his colleagues for their ill-earned popularity. It was quite certain that if Athens had been disposed to defend the Phocians, she had lost her chance of doing so, thanks to Aeschines and his colleagues; moreover, the alarm created by Philip's measures in Phocis had made the peace for a moment very unpopular, and Demosthenes was, by his own shewing (De F. L. § 228, p. 415), a timid politician who never ventured to intrude on an unwilling audience. From this, it was not a difficult step to the desire to clear himself at the expense of his colleagues. He even persuaded himself that he would never have gone on the second embassy at all, but for his engagement to aid some Athenian prisoners to ransom themselves, which he made on his first visit to Macedonia (D. de F. L. § 190). Meanwhile Demosthenes began for the first time to be taken up by a powerful political combination. The war party proclaimed that every one else had sold themselves, that he was the only man the city could trust (Ae. in Ctes. § 81, p. 65). Still he for some time maintained an attitude of reserve; after the ruin of Phocis, after the decree to put Attica in a state of siege, he delivered an oration in favour of recognising Philip's claims to Amphictyonic rights, which rested on the decision of an assembly whose legitimacy at Athens was considered questionable (De Pace, § 14, p. 60), and which Demosthenes did not care to endorse. His arguments rested upon the old thesis, that Athens could not afford to give occasion for an attack from a Greek coalition. Supposing it were possible to renew the war with Philip alone, under favourable conditions, Demosthenes was ready to do so, though the peace with which he had done his best to connect his name was not yet a year old; but he was still far from the

d

temper, that if free Hellenism was to perish, it became Athens to perish
as its champion. Meanwhile Athens still retained so much elasticity,
that the peace of Philocrates had something of the same effect as the
peace of Nicias; her resources, though no longer adequate to war, were
more than sufficient for a peace establishment (D. de F. L. § 101); the
surplus began to accumulate and the revenue to rise, and public spirit
rose with it. There was no Alcibiades to divert the reviving ambition of
the city to oblique and distant enterprises: it was inevitable that the
peace should be discussed, and except as a *pis-aller* it would not bear
discussion. When it was concluded, a sense of exhaustion had been
general at Athens; but the city was still too prosperous for such a
sense to continue long; and Philip, when he manœuvred for the
peace, had not trusted exclusively to the lassitude of Athens; he had
held out promises which, though vague, were not ambiguous, and had
not done anything that could even be called a commencement of execution. The consequence was, that the politicians of the war party began
to be active and aggressive, while the politicians of the peace party had
nothing to do, and did it. As early as 344 B.C., Philip sent a letter,
backed by embassies from his Peloponnesian allies, to remonstrate against
the hostile attitude into which Athens was gradually drifting; not that the
majority of the people were yet prepared for war, but they were too sore
to repress the anti-Macedonian party, which began to speak much and
act a little in their name. In reply to this remonstrance, Demosthenes
delivered the oration now known as the Second Philippic. He had
a difficult case; for though the Athenians had undoubtedly been misled,
there were no colourable grounds for maintaining that Philip had broken
the treaty; in fact, if he had not given them a right to. judge his conduct
by his professions, it might have seemed positively friendly when judged
by the situation. Demosthenes meets the difficulty by insisting that
every act of Philip tending to extend his influence in Greece was an act
of hostility to Athens, by harping on the fact that he had continued his
conquests in Thrace after the treaty had been ratified at Athens, and
saying that Philip ought to address his complaints not to Athens, but to
his own partisans, whose representations, authorised or unauthorised, had
exposed him to comments which singularly resembled insults. It seems
that Demosthenes spoke often in this tone during the negotiations,
which grew angrier and angrier while the peace was still observed. He
did not propose to abrogate the treaty, but he inflamed the popular discontent with it, and he had already persuaded himself, and exerted
himself to persuade his countrymen, that it was Philip's intention to
take and destroy Athens, as he had taken and destroyed Olynthus.
Still he was timid, and he was not popular; he was probably right in

thinking that he could speak most effectively if he spoke irresponsibly. About a year before the Second Philippic was delivered, Timarchus had undertaken to prosecute Aeschines, and thus exposed himself to a counter prosecution. In this Demosthenes was the leading counsel for the defence, and, by the report of Aeschines, seems to have arranged his case with great ingenuity. Timarchus himself was to speak to the evidence, some general, probably Chares, was to speak to the veniality of the charge, and Demosthenes was to speak to the motives of the prosecutor.

In 343, Demosthenes took up the prosecution against Aeschines himself, in the worst and vulgarest and most tedious of his authentic speeches. It reads less like a speech than like a series of captious and petulant notes upon some statement of Aeschines' case; and even the one strong point, that Aeschines had been a most mischievous tool of Philip's Phocian policy, must have lost much of its effect at the time when men still remembered that Demosthenes himself had done nothing to oppose that policy. Still the growth of angry feeling had been so great, that Aeschines, who, on the strength of his influence as having secured good relations between Athens and Macedon, had been able to procure the conviction of an opponent almost without evidence, was now within thirty votes of being convicted, on evidence scarcely stronger, by an opponent who did not come into court with clean hands. The principal occupation of Demosthenes at this time was a series of embassies, whose object and order it is difficult to ascertain. We hear of him in Leucas, in Ambracia, in Thessaly, in Messene, at Argos, and at Megalopolis, where he set a dyke against the torrent of Python's eloquence. According to his own account (De Cor. § 304) he was uniformly successful, and this is certainly probable, for to most of his audiences the Macedonian alliance was still one of the speculative questions of politics ; in each state there was a small knot of ambitious men who thought to promote their own importance by giving Philip an influence in their native cities, and securing themselves a position as his agents. The advantages of such a course, even where they could introduce a Macedonian ambassador to enforce them, must always have appeared rather problematical, and the sincerity and energy of Demosthenes, even apart from his eloquence, were quite sufficient to rouse Greek jealousy against a foreign king. As the intervention of Philip, armed or unarmed, was generally in support of extra-constitutional powers, it was easy for Demosthenes to represent this vigilant opposition to a power still in alliance with Athens as simply the exposure of unmistakable injustice, which it was impossible for Philip himself to resent. And the same defence applied in the judgment of the orator to his perpetual recurrence to the old grievance about the posts occupied by Philip in Thrace, after the ratification of the treaty by Athens, the recognition of Cardia on the isthmus of Chersonese as an independent ally of Macedon, and especially the occupation of Halonnesus. Upon the first point the Athenians had certainly no case whatever as against Philip; their ambassadors had received the oath of the representative of Cardia, and though Demosthenes' complaints on other grounds had been loud, he tells us nothing of his protests about this. About Halonnesus the case was little better : the sovereignty of the island had never been in debate between Philip and Athens during the war, so that the terms of the peace based on the principle of *uti possidetis* were a virtual recognition of the title of Athens. Unfortunately the Athenian title had not been effectively asserted, and the island was actually in possession of a pirate chief, who insulted the coasts of Macedon. The Athenians were of course the parties to whom Philip should have applied for redress, though we do not know how long they had tolerated the usurpation of the pirate, nor whether they had a more definite title to the island than the general one derived from their command of the sea, nor whether they had a reason for attaching more value to the island than they had hitherto done in practice. However, Philip took the law into his own hands, and the war party made the most of their grievance. Philip's ambassadors were authorised to cede the island, but the war party insisted he should restore it. The distinction was invented by Demosthenes. Philip then offered to submit the question of the original title to arbitration, which looks as if the Athenians had been as careless of their claim to Halonnesus as of their claim to Amphipolis. If the arbitrators decided in Philip's favour, the island was to be ceded; if not, it was to be restored: but the offer was declined. Demosthenes seems to have given two reasons for the refusal—one political, the other diplomatical. The political reason was, no impartial arbitrator could be found (probably because every possible arbitrator had been or would be bribed by Philip); the diplomatical reason was, that Athens could not treat her maritime supremacy or its incidents as matter for arbitration. The same embassy was charged with a commission to invite modifications of the treaty if the Athenians were dissatisfied with it; of course any proposals made were intended to be subject to discussion. The war party put forward three. Each party was to enjoy its rightful possessions (instead of what each actually held at the date of the treaty: i. e. Philip was to cede Amphipolis). The treaty was to be general, and include all Greece, and both Athens and Philip were to have the right of interfering to protect any Greek state attacked by anysoever contrary to the provision. (This clause would give Athens a valid claim to intervene between Philip and his discontented allies.) Lastly, the Thracian posts were to be evacuated. All the proposals seem to have been accepted by the Macedonian envoys, at least *ad referendum;* and an embassy was sent from Athens, with Hegesippus, the boldest, perhaps still the most influential of the war party, at its head, who had carried the proposal to ask for Amphipolis. Of course the first proposal was rejected at once, and the ambassadors who had entertained it were disavowed. The whole proceedings of the embassy were very stormy, and the ambassadors were put in a sort of moral quarantine; which is not surprising if Hegesippus told Philip to hang himself, when he asked what more he could do to please the Athenians, after reciting the concessions, as he considered them, which he had made or was ready to make. The second of the proposals suited Philip's ambition to be the recognised leader and head of Greece in one way, if it suited the jealousy of Athens in another, and therefore was agreed to at once. The third demand Philip was willing to refer to arbitration, which perhaps was as much as could be expected after he had been distinctly and repeatedly charged with violation of a solemn treaty. The negotiation went off on the first point, and the embassy returned to Athens with a new text for Demosthenes' perpetual sermon, that Philip was really carrying on the war against Athens under the forms of peace. This theory had soon to be put upon hard service. Diopithes was stationed in the Chersonese, and the war party had pushed their theory of the treaty so far that he found himself engaged in a war with the Cardians, who had been permitted to swear alliance with Athens. Nor does this appear to have been regarded by Philip or his partisans as amounting to a breach of the treaty. On the other hand, Philip assumed that he violated the treaty even less by defending sworn allies than Athens by attacking them. Diopithes on his part determined to make reprisals, and overran the new Macedonian possessions and the Thracian coast while Philip himself was engaged in the interior. Such violation of the immediate territory of a nominally friendly power was regarded as a clear *casus belli* in the time of the Peloponnesian war. But then the Athenians had been engaged in actual warfare against the Lacedaemonians before they committed this technical and unpardonable breach of peace, and therefore the Lacedaemonians had no motive for deferring the formal renewal of the war. Philip wished still to maintain the treaty, at any rate as a form, which hampered Athens more than it embarrassed him. He sent a formal remonstrance to Athens, and apparently demanded that Diopithes should be put on his trial, which would have involved the break up of the armament raised and kept together by his influence, and so have exposed the Chersonese. Demosthenes was equal to the occasion: he fell back on his old principle that the people ought to deal with their enemies before calling their own servants to account. If Diopithes had done wrong, he said, it might be well to recall him and punish him afterwards, but not to do so at a time when, besides the material advantage to Philip, it would discourage all their commanders everywhere, and deprive Diopithes himself of his power of levying black mail on the Asiatic coast. Moreover, he denied that Diopithes was to blame at all: Cardia itself was Athenian territory, being included within the legitimate boundary of the Chersonese, and Philip was even technically the aggressor, since his aid to the revolted subjects of Athens was really an invasion of Athenian soil. The speech is singularly clever and spirited, though it is surprising that Demosthenes still thought it worth while to address a nation in which it was necessary to support such a cause by such measures and such arguments. Diopithes was neither punished nor recalled, and Philip determined to take reprisals by sea. What he did is not precisely clear; he stopped some ships upon some definite occasion, and in the oration On the Crown Demosthenes expressly asserts that it was this act which led, though not on his motion, to the formal renewal of the war.

If we could trust the compiler or compilers of the papers purporting to be the documents quoted by Demosthenes, it would be possible to give a complete history of the transaction up to Philip's last attempt to settle the matter peaceably by giving up the squadron, after complaining of the secret instructions the commander had received unofficially at Athens; but if this account was accurate, it would be difficult to understand how Demosthenes could have treated the seizure of the ships as the one unpardonable, decisive outrage. Moreover, as Philip's fleet had to pass the Hellespont towards Byzantium, he sent his land force through the Chersonese to protect it from the dangers of annoyance or surprise. Though the precaution was not needless, it was an unquestionable violation of Athenian sovereignty; and to make the matter worse, the troops were permitted to do damage by the way, so that the march could be styled by the speakers of the war party a raid upon Chersonese. The independence and power of Byzantium were incompatible with Philip's designs against Persia, which we may safely admit on the authority of the Third Philippic, for as soon as he was engaged in the interior of Asia Minor his communications would be at the mercy of Athens and Byzantium. Accordingly he seems to have demanded the co-operation of the Byzantines in his measures against Athens, though he still abstained from a formal declaration of hostilities. The Byzantines resolved to maintain their liberty, and accepted the Athenian alliance, which Demosthenes was empowered to press upon them. An expedition was sent to support them under Phocion, and Philip was compelled to raise the siege of Byzantium and Perinthus, and finally to conclude a separate peace with the Byzantines and their insular allies, which it seems was not at variance with their alliance with Athens, for the Byzantines at any rate were sincerely grateful, and voted all kinds of honours to the Athenian people, for which Demosthenes not unjustly takes credit. If the decree of the Byzantines inserted in the text is genuine, as seems not improbable, their gratitude expressed itself in privileges more substantial than honours. Athenians were to be capable of acquiring landed property in Byzantium, though this right had been expressly renounced at the time when the Athenian confederacy had been reorganised in 378. They were to be capable of intermarrying with Byzantines, and the Olynthians are represented by Xenophon as trusting to the effect of intermarriages and this reciprocal right of acquiring landed property to reconcile the rest of the Chalcidic cities to the position of Olynthian Perioeci. If the event of the battle of Chaeroneia had been different, Athens might have begun a new career of prosperous energy, and then Byzantium would have gravitated surely and contentedly into the condition of a dependent ally, and Demosthenes would have had the merit of paving the way by honourable action to an important acquisition. It is clear that Athens continued the war alone : though it no longer had a definite object on either side, it was impossible for either Philip or Athens to propose a peace without confessing that they had been in the wrong. Diodorus indeed, who knows nothing of the peace of Philocrates, introduces a peace between Philip and Athens at this period ; but he is decisively contradicted by Demosthenes, who speaks of the inconvenience Philip experienced from the war, badly as it was conducted, up to the occupation of Elatea.

Meanwhile affairs in southern Greece had gone even worse for Philip than in the Hellespont. Callias, who had got the control of Chalcis, the principal city of Euboea, had pursued his own aggrandisement with little regard to loyalty towards either Thebes or Philip, both of whom had found it convenient to employ him, and both of whom he had courted. Very possibly he broke with Philip when the latter set up independent dynasts in Oreus and Eretria, instead of helping Callias to conquer them for him. At any rate, his appeal to Athens seems to have coincided pretty closely with the Athenian determination to expel the Macedonian garrisons from the island. Though the establishment of those garrisons might be represented as a natural corollary of Philip's legitimate ascendancy in the Pagasaean gulf, it was not the less a menace to Athens, and the garrisons did not take pains to be inoffensive. Consequently, when Callias sent to demand an alliance and to be released from the Athenian confederacy, his petition was favourably received, and an expedition was

sent to Euboea, which expelled the garrisons and made Athens popular.
Callias and Demosthenes pursued their advantage; the former visited all
Peloponnese, Demosthenes went on missions to Acarnania and Megara.
They seem to have returned at about the same time, and both professed to have received pledges, partly public and partly confidential,
frcm the states they had visited. On the strength of these pledges they
led the assembly to expect a general coalition against Philip, with
specified contingents, and a congress to be ready on a specified day in
Anthesterion. As a part of this programme, Callias proposed, and
Demosthenes supported him, that Eretria and Oreus should be released,
like Chalcis, from the general Athenian confederacy, and that a special
league should be formed in Euboea under the presidency of Chalcis,
which should be bound to follow the foreign policy of Athens. The
proposal was reasonable enough ; for the fact that Oreus and Eretria
were still enrolled in the Athenian league, still represented in its
common council, and still paid contributions to its common fund, had
not prevented them from being turned into outposts of Macedonian
aggression. But the fact that definite sums of money under Athenian
control were to be withdrawn, furnished the Macedonian party with a
good text for declamation, especially as the congress and the contingents came to nothing. Probably the pledges which Demosthenes
and Callias had received came from groups of influential men who
might have been able to redeem them if any very vigorous action on the
part of Philip or the Athenians had inspired increased alarm or confidence ; as it was, the states visited waited for Athens, and Athens
waited for the other states ; as Demosthenes said, a little earlier or a little
later, they expected that Chalcis and Megara were going to save Greece.
When the Athenians recognised that they had drifted into war they
recognised the right of the speaker who had advised it to direct their
policy. Probably for the first time in his life, Demosthenes became a
man whom it was worth the while of foreign states to propitiate by
presents. An Athenian embassy was necessary to complete the arrangements for the new Euboean league, to reassure those who were sincerely
attached to Athens, and to silence those who shrank from Chalcis,
though both at Oreus and Eretria Callias had partisans who were glad
to pay for help to get rid of their opponents. According to Aeschines,
Demosthenes had a talent from Chalcis, Eretria, and Oreus for his
services. Chalcis and Eretria paid at once, but the Oreites were poor,
and tried to get off with a statue. The orator was implacable, and
pending payment the city had to pawn its revenue to pay the interest.
Aeschines produces the public documents of Oreus in support of this
piquant anecdote, which contains nothing that, on Demosthenes' own

shewing, the public opinion of his contemporaries condemned, though his reported conduct contrasts painfully with his high professions.

He made a better and more characteristic use of his newly acquired influence by carrying a reform of the trierarchic law, which, at the cost of a slight reduction in the whole number of ships that the trierarchical body could be called upon to equip, made the fitting out of such fleets as were actually voted far more easy, prompt, and certain, while the incidence of the burden was more equally adjusted in proportion to the means of the contributors. The law excited much opposition from the rich, who had contrived to evade their liabilities almost entirely. Under the law of Periander, in ordinary times as many as sixteen members out of a symmoria of sixty contributed equally to the expense of a single trireme, and very commonly the richest of them found a contractor to take the whole expense for the sum which he had received from his partners. Of course the practical effect of the law was that the obligation of trierarchy, instead of a heavy burden, to be met or escaped at comparatively rare intervals, became a moderate charge recurring comparatively often. Demosthenes himself had proposed, three years after the law passed, to improve it by providing that each group of sixty should divide itself into five groups of twelve, each of which was to contain six of the richest and six of the poorest of the members of the symmoria; that each group of twelve so formed should be assessed for as many triremes as the occasion required. It was no doubt intended that within these groups the expense should be shared by private arrangement between the members in some rough proportion to their respective means, but though the law proposed suggested this equitable arrangement more plainly than the law of Periander, it supplied no means for enforcing it. Apparently the law which Demosthenes now carried altogether abandoned the principle of the law of Periander. He took the whole body of property liable to be assessed for trierarchy, and divided it into quotas of ten talents; those properties which fell short of that amount were grouped until they reached it. Each quota of ten talents was liable for one trireme, and if an individual possessed twenty talents he was liable for two, if thirty for three, if more for three and a service boat. It seems probable that the very large intervals at which the liability increased were intended as a concession to the rich opponents of the bill; for Demosthenes never denies having made the concessions which he was frequently accused of selling.

When Philip availed himself of the invitation of the Amphictyons to carry out a project which had been attributed to him ever since his Phocian expedition, and fortified Elatea, Demosthenes was exalted from an influential statesman into the virtual dictator of Athens, almost of independent Greece. The step seemed the justification of all that he had been preaching for many years to deaf ears, of Philip's purpose to destroy Athens and enslave Greece; and the suddenness of Philip's apparition, the want of visible connection between his action and its apparent object, produced a panic in which all ordinary party distinctions effaced themselves, and which the avowed partisans of Macedonia did not venture to combat. Demosthenes was the only man who could come forward with a theory of the situation, and on this unique and supreme occasion he had all the courage of his convictions. He undertook the responsibility of everything, and overruled all opposition. His first step was to secure Thebes from falling into Philip's hands. Though the fortification of Elatea was clearly intended to bridle Thebes (which, indeed, considering the countenance Thebes had given to the sacrilegious Amphissians, was only the duty of all loyal Amphictyons), the habit of acting with Philip and of being guided by his confidants was still powerful; it coincided with the hatred of Athens, which nothing since the battle of Mantinea had weakened, while the ambitious and ineffectual diplomacy of Aeschines had even contributed to strengthen it. The worst the Thebans had to fear was that they might become dependents of Philip, as the Arcadians had been the dependents of Sparta, and they may well have thought this risk less than that of being conquered by Philip. Though Demosthenes represented the Thebans to the Athenians as in greater danger than themselves, it is obvious that he did not really expect the Thebans to think so, for he makes a merit very legitimately of having overcome their reluctance to accept the very liberal alliance which he had persuaded the Athenians to authorise him to offer, on the express ground that it was very mean to seem to take advantage of the extremity to which the Thebans were reduced. If Aeschines is to be believed, even before Demosthenes had drawn up the terms of the alliance, the Athenian troops were in motion towards Thebes, or had even entered Theban territory. Considering that the attack might be expected from the side of Boeotia in any case, it is not improbable that the Athenians advanced to meet it, even before they knew if they would have to meet it alone. The terms of the alliance were such as to give Demosthenes enormous personal power; all measures were to be concerted with the Boeotarchs, so that the movements of the confederacy were directed from Thebes, and Demosthenes installed himself there as resident ambassador, so that he practically directed them. At the same time his indefatigable activity extended to the rest of Greece: the Achaeans and Corinth, Leucas and Corcyra, and Megara were induced to join the coalition; a mercenary force of fifteen thousand foot and two thousand horse were taken into pay. It seems from Demosthenes' own admissions that the conditions which attracted these allies were onerous to Athens; but the precedent of Salamis, to which Demosthenes appeals to prove that such sacrifices were glorious, proves also that they repaid themselves in the long run. We do not know in detail how Demosthenes wielded the coalition which he organised. It appears that he was jealous of interference, even from generals upon military matters; in fact, in the unhappy condition of affairs, there was no one whom he could trust with any portion of his power. Upon the whole he appears to have been an able war minister; two battles were fought which at Athens were considered victories (D. de Cor. § 274, p. 300); (and the military customs of Greece prevented the honours of the field from being often doubtful); anxious despatches were intercepted from Philip to his Peloponnesian allies (Ib. § 280, p. 302), and he began to profess a desire for peace (Ae. in Ctes. § 148, p. 74). To set against these proofs of ability and success we have vague imputations of peculation and arrogance (Ib. § 146), and two definite and serious charges. The first charge is that Demosthenes hired a body of ten thousand mercenaries to the Amphissians (l. c.), which was overwhelmed separately, as he might have foreseen. The criticism appears to be sound, but we do not know how far what was questionable on grounds of strategy was excused by diplomatic or financial reasons, or even by the military necessities of an unwieldy and heterogeneous armament. It would be certainly absurd to suppose with Aeschines, that Demosthenes knowingly imperilled the success of his combinations for a paltry bribe. The second charge is, that when Philip was ready to treat, the violence of Demosthenes made an honourable accommodation impossible, and forced on a disastrous battle. The story of Aeschines (Ib. §§ 149–157, p. 75), which Demosthenes passes by without notice, is that Philip was going to send embassies (apparently to each of the allies) to propose peace, and that it was known that the Boeotarchs were ready to treat; that Demosthenes hereupon swore in the Athenian assembly that he would arrest the first man who mentioned peace, that notwithstanding this the Thebans began to send the Athenian troops back that the terms might be discussed in a full assembly; that lastly Demosthenes shamed them out of their pacific intentions by threatening to propose that the Athenians should request a passage through Boeotia to fight Philip single handed. Even if the confederacy had been sufficiently united to treat as a single body, Demosthenes would probably have been for war; he would have preferred the chance of annihilating Philip to the certainty of prolonging the *status quo*. Whether he was right or wrong in rejecting or ignoring the chances of treating conjointly, he was certainly right in refusing to allow any of the allies to treat separately, which would have

been fatal even if Philip had been a loyal adversary; and after the
Thebans had shown a disposition to withdraw from the war, it was
clearly necessary to decide the war at once.

The decisive battle ended in a rout, in which Demosthenes behaved as
badly as the rest of the troops who were not killed or taken; there were
stories that he had behaved worse. It seems admitted, that physically
he was a coward; and it is difficult to see where he should have looked
for moral strength to run away in the least disgraceful manner possible.
On his return to Athens he had himself appointed to a roving commission
to collect funds in the Aegean, and of course his enemies asserted that
his motive was rather to be out of danger than to be of use. It appears,
for reasons to be more fully examined hereafter, that before he set off on
his mission, he had contributed very liberally to an extempore repair of
the fortifications, and that it was this for which Ctesiphon proposed that
he should receive a crown, at a time when he was still accountable as
overseer of fortifications, to which office he had been appointed after the
peace, when it was desired to put them in a permanent and thorough
state of repair. Public feeling still sustained Demosthenes; he delivered
the funeral oration over the dead of Chaeroneia, and the relatives met at
his house for the funeral feast. The speech has not come down to us,
probably because it was unworthy of the speaker and the occasion, and
the result has been that we have an ancient attempt to supply its place,
which the ancients rightly pronounced to be contemptible. Yet there
appears to have been some strong and not unnatural feeling against him;
he found it convenient to have his recommendations moved *pro formâ*
by Nausicles. On the other hand, we hear of his venturing to support
the prosecution of Lysicles, who had been in command at Chaeroneia.
That decisive battle had for the time the same effect upon Demosthenes
which had been produced by the capture of Olynthus: he accepted its
results to their full extent, and advised the Athenians to elect him con-
servator of the peace (Ae. in Ctes. § 159). The death of Philip, of which
Demosthenes probably had early intelligence from Charidemus (Ae. in
Ctes. §§ 77, 160. pp. 64, 76), changed the whole tone of the orator's
feelings. When the news came he was in mourning for his only daughter,
but he immediately put on holiday garments and offered sacrifices of
thanksgiving, and set up an altar to worship Pausanias as a hero. It
seems that he professed that the news had been revealed to him in a
vision by night, and one need scarcely suspect him of insincerity; when
the wonderful news came he dreamt of it, and then only he ventured to
believe it. While the contest was still pending, he had counted upon
the possibility of Philip's death, and the probability that his system would
die with him. When the possibility was realised, he had no choice but

to wait hopefully for the probability to realise itself. Until Alexander shewed some sign of sinking under the difficulties, which we are tempted to underrate as much as Demosthenes underrated his abilities, it was hopeless to persuade the Greeks to move, and perhaps the Athenians were the hardest to move of all. Northern Greece, at any rate, was effectually garrisoned ; and so when Alexander came down to Corinth, he received the submission of a congress, and was empowered to act as captain-general of the Greek nation against the great king. But as soon as Alexander had crossed the Haemus, and rumours of his death could be circulated, the elements of discontent began to stir. The Theban exiles, who had been protected at Athens, and were in intimate relation with the chiefs of the war party, recovered the whole of the city except the citadel ; the Arcadians put themselves in motion, with what object was not certain, and the uncertainty was an unexpected danger to Macedonia. Lycurgus and Demosthenes supplied the Theban leaders with assistance underhand, and vainly endeavoured to commit the state to a renewal of the war. Aeschines and Dinarchus (In Ctes. §§ 239–241, In Dem. §§ 21, 22) tell a story that Demosthenes contrived to lay hold of seventy talents out of three hundred which the king of Persia had sent to Athens, and which the Athenians had declined to accept. This story does not fit in with another story told by Aeschines, that a little before Alexander crossed into Asia, the king sent down an insolent letter, refusing by anticipation all requests for subsidies, and that when 'entangled by the dangers which surround him now,' he sent to offer a subsidy of his own accord. This would imply that the first Persian money which came into Greece came after the battle of Granicus, or even after the battle of Issus, and therefore too late to save Thebes ; yet both Dinarchus and Aeschines complain that Demosthenes would not expend fourteen talents out of seventy to induce the Arcadians to pronounce against Alexander, and to bribe the garrison to surrender the Cadmea (Ae. et Din. ut sup.) And what makes the matter more curious still, Demochares, in the decree which he moved to his uncle's honour after his death, recites that he bribed the Arcadian leaders to go home without assisting Macedon. It may safely be supposed that if Demosthenes did receive money from Persia, the king understood that he would apply it in great part to his private purposes ; and perhaps we may venture to believe what is intrinsically probable, and was uncontradicted matter of common fame, that he did receive money ; but the subject was one which gave great scope to envy and exaggeration, and if a calumny could not be met by a point-blank denial, it could not be met at all. Aeschines might perhaps be made consistent with himself, if we suppose that the seventy talents came into Demosthenes' hands before the battle of Chaeroneia, and Dinarchus might have made a mistake, being a younger man and writing later; but the evidence is not of a kind to establish even a venial charge. Whatever Demosthenes left undone, he did enough to compromise himself and Athens; the Thessalians actually voted an expedition against the city (Ae. in Ctes. § 71); Alexander demanded, and the terms of the alliance gave some colour to the demand, that Demosthenes, Lycurgus, and eight other leading politicians, should be tried before the congress of allies for high treason against Greece. Though the demand might be plausible, it was impossible for an independent state, such as Athens still claimed to be, to grant it. The military men demanded seem to have left the city; Demades and Phocion appealed to Alexander not to insist upon the extradition; Demosthenes himself, if Aeschines is to be trusted, smuggled a favourite of his own into Alexander's intimacy (In Ctes. § 161), and received through this dishonourable channel a contemptuous assurance of security. During the early vicissitudes of the war, we are told that he measured its probabilities by his wishes, and abandoned himself to the temper which he had rebuked in his countrymen before the peace of Philocrates (Ib. §§ 164–167). He refused to act, because the Macedonian party were too strong, and were training and pruning the city to grow as they pleased; but if he did not act--and it is difficult to see how he could have acted--he boasted the more of the Persian cavalry that would ride over Alexander's whole army, of the terror which he fancied he read in the faces of Aeschines and of his friends, of his own share in the revolt of Thessaly, and of the coalition in Peloponnese; in a word, he lived in the state of unhealthy and undignified exaltation in which the Southern sympathisers in England lived during the last twelve months of the Confederate war. When all was over, both in Greece and Asia, he fell back upon the thought which he had already expressed in the Third Philippic, that a power too strong for men was busy in the world; that a miserable and evil fortune had lighted upon all mankind, and upon Athens among the rest. With these feelings he met the prosecution of Ctesiphon, when Aeschines decided to bring it on at last. After all, the occasion was hardly a worthy one for a great man to sum up a great life upon, and leave his political testament to mankind. Much of the greatest speech of antiquity is devoted to a wrangle with Aeschines, which presents the display of an endless wealth of scorn and sarcasm; but scorn and sarcasm must descend, sooner or later, to the level of their object. Even in the elevation of the speech there is something almost theatrical: we feel that Demosthenes and Athens are posing together for a grand historical tableau. All the unreadiness, all the half-heartedness of Athens, has dropt out of sight; all Demosthenes' own vacillations, all the questionable and unauthorised manœuvres by which he got together an imposing but unstable coalition, are forgotten too in the glorious picture of Athens falling, sword in hand, as the champion of free Hellenism, and Demosthenes as the minister and expression of her heroism and devotion. Of course it was inevitable: he had a right to his crown; he could not have relinquished it even had he wished; he was compelled to defend it, but as we read the defence we see how pitiful it was that his greatest effort should have been made on account of a personal honour that was only honourable if uncontested, and how far we have travelled from the single-minded sincerity, the impersonal fervour of the Olynthiacs and the First and Third Philippic.

For the next six years we know nothing of Demosthenes, except casual anecdotes which point to a life of morose, unsocial luxury, and personal relations overclouded by jealousy and mistrust. In 324, Harpalus, who had been appointed by Alexander to the rich Satrapy of Babylonia, and had courted popularity by magnificent presents to the Athenian people, and by putting magnificent jobs into the hands of any Macedonian partisan whose loyalty was not above corruption, fled from his Satrapy with a treasure of five thousand talents, and presented himself at Sunium with a formidable squadron. This inspired the idea that he meant to seize Athens, and establish himself there as despot, a result which would have been equally unsatisfactory to every party at Athens. Accordingly he was made to understand that if he advanced further he would be treated as an enemy; whereupon he decided to come with a single ship, and a treasure which he afterwards stated at seven hundred and twenty talents, and appealed to the Athenians to join him in declaring war upon Alexander. Hyperides was not alone in wishing to take the risk: Demades had to remind the people that the money he had provided for holiday making was available, if they chose to divert it, for war. Demosthenes also took the same side, the side of common prudence and of common honesty, and it was not surprising that the people took it also. Meanwhile, as might have been expected, a demand arrived for the surrender of Harpalus. To this no one was disposed to agree; there was a wide difference between not co-operating with Alexander's rebels, and surrendering them to Alexander. On the other hand, the impression in Alexander's camp was, that since Harpalus had gone to Athens, Athens must have set the treaty at defiance, and probably commenced hostilities. It seems that, as a precautionary measure, orders were sent to lay an embargo on the corn fleet. To protect, or even to dismiss Harpalus, was too hazardous. His servants were given up, and he himself and his treasure were detained till Alexander's pleasure should be further known. In giving up the servants, the Athenians shewed that they had no romantic sense of what was due to Harpalus, who had put himself freely into their power; we may infer that, in keeping the treasure they were not without hopes of keeping it for good. One can hardly suppose that Demosthenes, who proposed the motion, acted without *arrière pensée;* without committing Athens to a war at once, he might have been willing to keep open the possibility of using Harpalus and his treasure, and the larger treasure which he left with his troops in Crete, if a favourable opportunity came. As Harpalus was arrested to keep him out of the hands of Alexander, it was not likely that he would be kept prisoner till Alexander could send for him. Demosthenes, who proposed his arrest, was not improbably privy to the arrangements for his escape. After his escape, it was discovered that only three hundred and fifty talents had reached the treasury out of the seven hundred and twenty which Demosthenes had stated, on the authority of Harpalus, had come from Crete. Demosthenes, it seems, had known of the deficiency at the time that the remains of the treasure were transferred to the Acropolis, and kept his knowledge to himself. The discovery created much alarm when it came to be known; since Harpalus had escaped, there was no excuse for keeping his money, and as it was reasonably assumed that most of the deficiency had gone in bribes to secure the speech, or even the silence of influential politicians, the people naturally thought that the politicians who had had the money should be compelled to refund. The only evidence as to who these politicians were, that would have been received with any confidence, was inaccessible: the servants of Harpalus who could have been tortured were in Asia. Everybody who had been in communication with Harpalus, everybody who could be represented as having acted in his interests, or not having acted against him, was suspected; there was a general wish to punish somebody, while nobody was ready with definite accusation against anybody in particular. Perhaps it was the best that could be done to refer the matter, as Demosthenes proposed, to the Areopagus, that is to say, to chance and time. The Areopagus was a court of so many old men of strict respectability, who were bound together by no ties of party or of rank, nor yet by any political knowledge or experience, but simply by a strong corporate tradition. They were respected, not because they had any means whatever of going right, but simply because they were exempt from almost all the motives which practically made an Athenian court go wrong. They decided not only by the evidence that came before them in court, but upon the personal knowledge of individuals among them (Ae. in Tim. § 92); that is, upon hearsay, which such individuals chose to trust. After listening for six months to anything anybody chose to tell them, they finally drew up a list of persons, among whom Demosthenes was included, who were debited with different sums of the treasure of Harpalus. These persons had the option of taking their trial for a capital offence, or of paying the sum the Areopagus set down to them. If they elected to defend themselves, they did so at the disadvantage that the one body in Athens which all still respected was the prosecutor. Demosthenes was the first who was brought to trial (Dem. Ep. 1, § 15); the partisans of Alexander and the partisans of Harpalus were between them most probably a majority of the court, and with a hostile majority the authority of the Areopagus would outweigh the eloquence and services of Demosthenes. As for evidence, we do not know whether any prosecutor out of the ten or eleven spoke to it. Dinarchus confines himself to the easy topics, that treason is a great crime, Demosthenes a bad citizen, the Areopagus a venerable court. Hyperides, in his fragments, makes very much the same points, but he also suggests that the line of defence went too much to a mere verdict of 'not proven,' and that Demosthenes' friends had thought of putting forward the dangerous plea, that as treasurer he had made advances out of his own private property, and repaid himself from the money of Harpalus. He was condemned to a fine of fifty talents, and thrown into prison, as he could not or would not pay ; after a few days he escaped to Troezen, where he had leisure to reflect on the machinery by which he had had more than one suspected spy of Macedon put out of the way. The few anecdotes of his exile only indicate a keen and natural sense of popular ingratitude, which was the more reasonable if, as the compiler of the letters which circulated in his name believed, he was the only one condemned of those who ventured to stand a trial.

When Alexander was really dead, and the Aetolians and Athenians had renewed the struggle for independence, Demosthenes exerted himself with success in support of the Athenian embassies sent to recruit for the league in Peloponnese. He was recalled with immense enthusiasm, and the assembly voted him fifty talents for a sacrifice, as the only constitutional way in which they could cancel the fine. He lived honourably and usefully while the war lasted, giving diplomatic help to Hyperides, who had the chief conduct of civil affairs. When it was over, he fled with Hyperides and two other citizens of the same party to Aegina; they were sentenced to death by the assembly, which enjoyed the restricted franchise under the constitution of Phocion. They took refuge in separate sanctuaries at Aegina, whither Antipater soon sent to arrest them. Archias, formerly an actor, was employed to remove Demosthenes from sanctuary if possible without violence. He made promises of good treatment, to which Demosthenes is said to have replied, that he had never been impressed by the acting of Archias. There are different accounts of the way in which he poisoned himself;

e

they all agree that he took care to leave the sacred precinct alive. Demochares, his nephew, took advantage of the discrepancy to believe that he was taken away from the evil to come by the immediate favour of the gods.

There is a good deal of appropriateness in Plutarch's parallel with Cicero. Besides the superficial resemblances, of which he has accumulated enough to be striking, the fundamental tragedy of the situation was the same for both: they saw how to save their country, and with all their matchless eloquence they had no hold on the working political forces of the time. Of the two, Cicero was the more fortunate; he had not to survive the false success of the Philippics so long as Demosthenes survived the false success of the league which was crushed at Chaeroneia. The irreproachable regularity of Cicero's private life may be contrasted with the numerous infirmities of Demosthenes; but the inexhaustible self-complacency of the Roman is heartless compared to the feverish, almost petulant indignation of the Greek, which sprang from a consuming intensity of purpose able to raise a life stained by much weakness, perhaps by some baseness, to the loftiest heights of greatness and heroism.

G. A. S.

PRACTICAL POLITICS OF THE AGE OF DEMOSTHENES.

§ 1. *Authorities—Demosthenes, Theopompus, Isocrates.*

OF the many records of antiquity which have been lost upon their way to us, few are better worth regretting than the copious history of Theopompus. This would have shewn us the age of Philip as it appeared to an acute and disinterested contemporary; and the orations of Demosthenes cannot supply the loss of such a history. A period cannot be understood by the help of the most admirable protests against all that happened in it. If the writings of Mr. Carlyle were our principal authority for what has passed in England during the last forty years, it is conceivable that the inquirer might be guided to the central springs which controlled events; but it is certain that the superficial aspects of the scene, as well as the physiognomy of the actors, would be strangely distorted by the lurid light of first principles. Demosthenes is a less abnormal writer than Mr. Carlyle, and he supplies abundant fragmentary indications which enable us in some measure to check and supplement the first impression produced by the main current of his exhortations. He is as good an authority as a partisan, or rather a practical man, can be; but, after all, he is not as good an authority as Tacitus, and the history of the early Roman empire has always been one-sided, because it has always been written by authors who trusted or distrusted Tacitus. Both the character and the intellect of Demosthenes were far above the level of Isocrates and Xenophon, yet it may be doubted whether he measured such important elements of the situation as the action of Thebes or the power of mercenaries, as intelligently as they. The apathy of Athens, which he spent his life in combating, was itself the symptom of a disease whose causes he left it to Isocrates

e 2

to study; that disease was nothing less than the moral and material anarchy and atrophy of Greece.

§ 2. *Epaminondas, the precursor of Philip and successor of Lysander.*

The pregnant words with which Xenophon closes his ungenerous description of the battle of Mantinea deserve a fuller commentary than they have yet received. There is a sense in which the crowning victory of the great Theban did really augment and perpetuate the confusion of Greece. Like Gustavus Adolphus, Epaminondas is personally one of the most spotless figures of history; like Gustavus, he made himself a name as the champion of a cause which served to ennoble the aggrandisement of his country. Both died in the moment of victory; both left a body of clients behind them, who were forced to look out for new protectors; the clients of both had to accept the protection of a foreign power, whose intervention completed the disorganisation of Germany and Greece. Except in Austria, Gustavus was forgiven even by contemporaries, both for the mischief which he did and for the greater mischief which he prepared. Epaminondas was less fortunate. The pretensions of Sparta and Athens to dispute or divide the supremacy of Greece were condoned by public opinion, in consideration of their services to the common cause at and after the Persian invasion; but ever since the beginning of the Peloponnesian war there had been a sincere and growing aversion to such claims in the abstract, and when Thebes put them forward after the unprecedented triumph of Leuctra, she could appeal to no services and she could be reproached with treasons. If this antipathy had stood alone, it might have given way to events; but the conservative veneration for Sparta was far from exhausted, and had been recently reinforced by Agesilaus' settlement of Peloponnese. That settlement was very arbitrary; but it was not too oppressive to be permanent, and it professed not insincerely to base itself on recognised principles of public right. Epaminondas broke up this settlement by an appeal to the ambition of a few and the greed of many—materials with which it was impossible to erect a permanent structure. Such a policy was unjustifiable, for the Peloponnesians were increasingly reluctant to be used for aggressive purposes; it was unreasonable, for it could not benefit Thebes in the same proportion as it injured Sparta; it encumbered the Thebans with allies who had often to be helped and could not often be led. Athens might perhaps have consented to recognise Thebes as the military head of Greece north of the Isthmus, if her own naval position had been uncontested. It was impossible for her to acquiesce in the pretension of Thebes to concentrate all the land forces north and south of the Isthmus under her own direction. And Epaminondas actually endeavoured to inspire his countrymen with the futile and preposterous ambition of depriving Athens of the dominion of the sea, and transferring the Propylaea from the Acropolis to their own Cadmea. When the Propylaea were built, the wealth of Athens rested partly upon tribute and partly upon trade, and the Corinthians might plausibly imagine that by building more ships and paying more sailors they might deprive her of at least one source of wealth; but in the days of Epaminondas the wealth of Athens rested upon her trade, which could not be transferred to Boeotia, which possessed no harbour that could compete with the Piraeus. The result was, that the Thebans in attempting to gain everything failed to secure anything. The tactical discoveries of Epaminondas enabled them to break the power of Pherae, which was not yet consolidated, and the power of Sparta, which had begun to decline; but as neither Pherae nor Sparta were crushed, both were in a position to resume their aggressions as soon as the great Theban general was taken away.

Epaminondas left nothing behind him except a system of tactics which Philip improved, and a body of dependant allies who had to find a new protector, and found one in Philip, to whom Messene and Megalopolis had begun to turn almost before their precarious independence was twenty years old. This result was due not merely to the weakness of those communities, but to the manner in which they had been set up. Brasidas was the last commander who carried on his diplomatic business with the constituted authorities of the states within reach of his arms. Lysander set the fashion, which was too convenient not to be followed, of dealing directly with influential knots of managers, who undertook by some means or other to carry the authorities with them. In this way the commander secured a body of personal adherents spread over great part of Greece, while the state which sent him was able to act more rapidly and over a larger area. The agents of these *extempore* combinations gained most of all; the fact that they had brought their states into connection with a great power, gave them a Pan-Hellenic rank which they could have reached in no other way, and which they were entitled to retain as long as the connection lasted. The hereditary relation of proxenia was hardly compatible with loyalty as we understand it, for the proxenus was certainly expected to side with the state he represented up to the latest moment that he decently could. The conduct of Fox during the Revolutionary War has been considered more than factious; it would have been considered legitimate in Greece, had he happened to be the proxenus of France. While this dignity continued to be hereditary in the families of more or less intelligent grandees like Callias, whose

pomposity on the Spartan embassy is so amusingly exhibited by Xenophon, its operation, though embarrassing, was not corrupting. But by the
time of Demosthenes the office was a matter of speculative traffic.
Hyperides (Frag. 19, ap. Baiter and Sauppe, p. 352) estimated that
Demades and Demosthenes had made some sixty talents apiece by
decrees (often, no doubt, mere complimentary grants of citizenship) and
proxenias. It is not clear whether the money was made by exercising
the office or selling it; but the first hypothesis derives support from
inscriptions, and the ultimate inference from both is the same, for if
a man spends money on an office, he almost always intends to make
money by it. Probably the *proxenus* of more than one Greek state was
quite as much and as reasonably suspected at Athens as the *xenus*
of Philip, who performed the same kind of services for a better pay-
master. In both cases the agents' functions were the same, to keep
Athens as far as possible in good humour with the foreign power represented, and supply that power with such information as would be useful
in the management of its relations with Athens. The *proxenus* of Chalcis
would have as much to do in giving Chalcis good advice, as in advocat-
ing its interests at Athens ; the *xenus* of Philip was aware that his principal was hardly in a position to need or take advice. The attempts of
Aeschines to have a policy, and to carry it out by the help of Philip,
were even more preposterous, though not much more, than the attempts
of Euphron or Lycomedes to have a policy of his own, and carry it out
by the help of Epaminondas. Philip only extended to the whole of
Greece the system which Lysander had spread over the islands and the
Asiatic coast, and Epaminondas had used on a still more extensive scale
in Peloponnese, not only remodelling old communities, but founding new.
The system disguised itself as it diffused itself, and lost in loyalty more
than it gained in decorum. Lysander's dependants pledged themselves
to obedience with their eyes open, and received in return a positive, distinct assurance, that the whole power of Sparta, so far as he could
influence it, should be exerted to maintain their hold upon their own
cities, where they might gratify their passions or reduce their theories to
practice. Epaminondas presented himself as a liberator; he was obliged
to treat his confederates upon an ostensible footing of equality, but when
they attempted to stand alone, Lycomedes was abandoned to his difficulties, and the handful of disappointed zealots who slaughtered Euphron
were dismissed with applause from Thebes. Philip's dependants had a
still better excuse than those of Epaminondas for being insincere with
themselves if they pleased, for they were ostensibly in many cases not
even confederates, but personal friends; for Philip as a politician with
large schemes, including many distant objects, found it convenient to

keep up an intelligence ripening into an interest in many states, whose immediate co-operation was not required. When such friends were no longer wanted, they were abandoned to the contempt of Philip's courtiers, who were well inclined to insult those, who had once divided the favours of their master, with the convenient name of traitor.

§ 3. *The arrest of the material development of Greece.*

The mendicant ambitions of which Philip had come to be the earthly providence were not a new disease in Greece. To say nothing of the half legendary Alcmaeon, who was reported to have founded the fortunes of his house upon the alms of Croesus, Pausanias and Themistocles had pleased themselves with the thought of ruling over their countrymen as viceroys of the Great King, whom they had defeated. This monstrous egotism, to which everything, even self-respect, is sacrificed, was the natural vice of the first men of a society where the desire for personal distinction was one of the highest of known motives; but, while the society was healthy and vigorous as a whole, the diseased members could be cut off, the peccant humours could be expelled. The new evil of Demosthenes' day was that 'the crop of men who were traitors and takers of bribes and reprobates,' were tolerated and envied and admired (D. de F. L. p. 426, § 300). They had despaired of their country, but they had not despaired of themselves; if they could not carry their fellow-citizens with them up to a higher level of power and prosperity, at least they had emancipated themselves. Their pursuit of an individual deliverance was, after all, the worldly parallel to the spiritual renunciation of philosophers. They were really akin to the sage, as we see him in the *Republic* standing under a wall to let the storm go by, or in the *Phaedo* holding fast to some plank of sound doctrine as he drifts over the waves of this troublesome world; as well as to the wise man of Epicurus hiding in a garden from the useless agitations of the world, and the equally unsocial wise man of Zeno helping to carry on the routine of the world from a sense of duty, while conscious all the time that 'he shall deliver neither sons nor daughters: he shall deliver his own soul only by his righteousness.' Greek society had lost the powers of keeping either the nobler or the baser forms of individualism within bounds, because it had ceased to develope. The population of Greece proper was certainly no greater in the middle of the fourth century before Christ, than it had been at the beginning of the fifth; in Laconia it was certainly less. In other parts of Greece it is probable that there would have been an increase, but for wars and emigration, up to the beginning of the Peloponnesian war; and both wars and emigration, upon the whole, enriched the mother country more than the natural increase of population would have done. But the only way in which Greek society, or indeed ancient society, could continue to advance, was by diffusing itself: it was not sufficiently articulate to increase indefinitely, and to perfect its organisation within a limited area. With the close of the era of colonisation, Greece began to relapse into the predatory state from which it was just emerging when the Works and Days were composed. Even in Aristophanes we see the plague is begun; the passion for confiscation is becoming a force in the politics of the richest city of Greece. After the Peloponnesian war, the aggregate wealth of the community ceased to grow, as population had ceased to grow already. Individual wealth was coming to depend upon accumulation rather than on enterprise; so that Isocrates could say that Megara, the poorest state of Greece, possessed the greatest and the finest houses, obviously because the oligarchy practised the oligarchical virtues of thrift and regularity. Where these existed, the rich continued to get richer while the poor got fewer instead of poorer: elsewhere foreign and domestic politics degenerated into a less and less unconscious, and more and more wasteful struggle for the fragments of a stationary total (see Isocrates de Pace and Panegyricus passim). The sterile rivalries of the greater states had no intelligible motive, except their habitual pretensions and the interested ambition of the commanders, who wished to have their share of the plunder of the Aegean, and these rivalries maintained an equally sterile agitation in all the minor states, where the rich desired a still more exclusive and arbitrary hold upon affairs, while the poor desired to expel or massacre the rich, as a preliminary to dividing their possessions. Neither side could attain even so much tranquillity as is implied in the recognition that things are come to a dead-lock, for so long as the great states were at war, or not at peace, they were on the look-out for partisans who might count upon having a heartier welcome, in proportion as they were more deeply committed. Meanwhile, in the intervals of tempest, continental Greece and Peloponnese were continually drained of all the men of spirit who had failed in one revolution, or were too impatient to wait for the next. These ever-growing swarms of 'men without cities,' were in ever-increasing proportion the instruments with which the great powers of Greece fought out their rivalries. When they were not employed at home, they transferred their activity to the Asiatic coast, and took part in the internal quarrels of the Persian empire. Isocrates saw clearly that a radical remedy was necessary, if the disease was not to eat out the life of Greek society. Athens and Sparta alike must give up their pretensions to the dominion of the sea, which was only a fine name for the power of levying blackmail on the islands. If the great states resolved to be quiet, the rest would be quiet by force, and while

they abstained from external disputes, internal disputes also would remain in abeyance ; the number of the dangerous class of men with
appetites and ambitions, without ties or status, would at any rate cease to
multiply. But these would be only palliatives : only the conquest of Persia would effect a cure. Isocrates' conception of the results of that conquest was falsified by the event. He thought that the principal benefit
would accrue to what remained of a settled, orderly population in Greece.
He expected that all the immense realised movable wealth of Asia would
be poured into Greece, and that then, when nobody was poor, the danger
of the poor plundering the rich would cease. He looked also to the
dangerous classes being cleared off into the new settlements, which would
become possible when the incubus of Persian domination was removed
from the Levant ; but this would be rather a subordinate benefit. He
certainly never imagined that Alexandria and Pergamus and Antioch
would become the moral and material centres of Greek life, while Sparta
and Athens would be deserted and insignificant. Of course if the enterprise had been undertaken, as at first he desired, by free Greece, his
anticipations might have been realised ; but when he directed his eloquence upon Philip instead of upon Athens, he should have realised that
a new power would find itself new seats.

§ 4. *The condition of Athens.*

Of the three great evils which afflicted Greece, Athens was still free
from one, perhaps the worst of all : it was still possible for Athenians to
live at home. There was a continual danger that envy, prompted by
hunger, would become a political power ; there was an increasing number of men who had despaired of the greatness of their country, and had
made up their mind to rise upon her ruins ; but Athens did not contribute to the cloud of mercenaries who hovered between Europe and Asia.
Even the diseases which Athens had, she had in a milder form. Demades,
the greediest and most cynical of the correspondents of Macedon,
affirmed at the time of the arrest of Harpalus, that he took money and
meant to take it, but the country should be none the worse. The reserve
was doubtless a fiction ; but the fiction was intended to deceive himself,
as Tzetzes makes him say he had no wish to see Athens turned into
a cemetery like Thebes: a cemetery could be no sphere for his ambition.
The best reception at the court of Alexander would not have compensated him for the suppression of the assembly which he liked to lead.
Athens still imposed upon even the least loyal of Athenians: those whom
Demosthenes denounced as traitors had not yet ventured to hope that
they might become tyrants. It was as much as they ventured to do, to

give themselves airs of superiority to the institutions which they always professed their desire to maintain.

Demades called the festival pay 'the cement of the constitution,' and this was certainly its most important function. It was really the most elegant form of the universal μισθοφορία, the pleasantest item τοῦ δημοσίου λήμματος, which was the tribute exacted by king Demos from his subjects. Of course Demosthenes was right in comparing such beggarly doles to the diet that physicians gave their patients, which was just enough to keep them alive, and much too little to make them strong and hearty (Ol. 3, p. 37, § 39). He was thinking of the grand old days of Pericles, when the poor had frequent opportunities of leaving their precarious life in Athens for the plenty and independence of Thurii or Amphipolis, when splendid careers were in the reach of individual energy, to say nothing of the ennobling and exhilarating sense of belonging to a great community, which made life a pleasure and a pride to the poorest. When he looked at what Pericles had done for the city, he could not resist the temptation of minimising all the conveniences and elegances which had made Eubulus popular, as ' roads, and fountains, and white-wash, and stuff;' though such improvements were just in place in a city where monumental buildings were erected already, and where public officers were beginning to make such profits that their private houses were finer than the public offices. No doubt in the time of Lysias, in the early days of the restored Democracy, the prosecutor generally wound up his peroration by assuring the jury, that to confiscate the property of the defendant was the only way to provide for their fees, while the defendant quoted instances of confiscations which had proved worthless, concluded that he had better be left to take care of his own money, and appealed to his past conduct as evidence that he would continue to spend it handsomely on public objects.

Even after the reforms of Eubulus had placed the finances on a footing which reduced the force of such temptations to a minimum, after the peace of 346 had begun to recruit the resources of Athens, Demosthenes could still say (De Chersoneso, p. 106, § 68), that to hint at hostilities to Philip, and to expatiate in an irresponsible way on his bad faith and the treachery of his correspondents, required more courage than to ' go ahead,' like some politicians, with endless denunciations and confiscations. The speech against Androtion abounds with instances of the immense annoyance which the fiscal system produced in its working among men of moderate means, and the oppressive contrivances, so convenient that they could be represented as indispensable, which were employed, with very imperfect success, to collect very moderate sums. But after every allowance for the way in which the state machinery jarred, and for the signs which it gave of a possible disruption, it worked much more smoothly and safely at Athens than anywhere else in Greece, more smoothly and safely than it had worked at any time during the Peloponnesian war. Then there had been class hatreds upon one side, and the cruel ambition of unscrupulous cliques upon the other; and though one clique was always ready and eager to sacrifice another to the jealousy of the commons, when there was anything to gain by the sacrifice, yet, as their objects were substantially similar, there was a strong fellow-feeling between them whenever their interests were not in collision. The oligarchs of the generation of Alcibiades were too selfish to act as a party, but they felt as a class. There were political questions at issue, which might have found solid parties in a society where there was space for parties to become homogeneous. Though the ultimate sovereignty of the popular majority was irrevocably established, it had still to be settled how far the popular majority was bound by constitutional forms of its own enactment; it had to be settled where that majority was to look for leaders, which involved the further question, how much liberty of action was to be allowed to the high officers of the executive, who were still in large measure men of hereditary rank and position, long after the lead in the assembly had passed into the hands of low-born agitators, who caught and exaggerated the suspicions and passions of their class? Again, there was the question whether the pay and the doles which the citizens received, on all manner of occasions out of public funds, were to be regarded as the accident or the essence of the constitution; whether, in fact, the majority of Athenian citizens were to support themselves or be supported by the state, at the expense of the rich or of the allies, when there were allies who paid tribute to Athens, or could be brought to carry appeals there. In the time of Demosthenes all these questions had been settled but one, and that was not a party question. The strict regularity of procedure in the assembly and elsewhere was hardly the interest of the oligarchs; though they were a minority, the organisation of the clubs gave them facilities for snatching divisions which seemed of more importance than the chances, which were far from common, of defeating objectionable proposals by a deliberate and dilatory use of constitutional forms. Even politicians as moderate as Nicias could propose without scruple, upon a great occasion, that the president of the assembly should take the grave responsibility of putting a question already lawfully decided, to a second vote. The dispute continued open, for there were always some politicians who desired a reputation for energy, and others who desired a reputation for legality; but the division did not coincide with the degree of their real or professed attachment to democratic principles. Aristophon was famous for the number of impeachments he had braved, but as for his principles, he was as good a democrat as Eubulus, who went on quietly and methodically, and he had no pretensions to be a better democrat. The other outstanding questions had been settled as Cleon would have settled them, and yet the effective power of the assembly had diminished. There were several reasons for this. The misdirected ambition of Thebes had acted as a damper on such enthusiasm and energy as the assembly retained. The feeling of the people could not be roused in favour of a war to extend the blessings of democracy, when extending the area of democracy meant extending the predominance of Thebes. There had always been a sentimental feeling at Athens in favour of the autonomy of the Boeotian towns, and the Thebans had outraged this honourable sentiment, even before they had alarmed the prudence of their natural supporters. The consequence was, that, though the Theban side remained the democratic side, the democratic side ceased to be popular. If the reaction had attempted to throw Athens decisively into the arms of Sparta, its success would have been short-lived; but the party of reaction was too indolent to be imprudent. They desired to direct the attitude of the city in conformity with their own sympathies, and they were glad to have occasional opportunities of displaying their personal gallantry at the head of a small body of picked troops; but they were too thrifty to desire any prolonged or energetic intervention, which would have had to be carried on at their expense. The average aristocrat of the period had no political programme whatever, except to enjoy his independence; he had no longer any shreds of privilege to defend; he was too self-indulgent to wish to reform the license which would have offended Pericles; he was too experienced to dream of making the popular majority the instrument of his personal ambition. The organisation of society under which he lived gave him no advantages which he could or would appreciate. On the other hand, the community had very little power over his class, while they had considerable power over the community. The Athenians were still in the barbarous stage of finance, when all extraordinary expenses had to be met by special taxation imposed for the occasion, unless by singular good fortune there happened to be a treasure in hand. This was not all, there was a risk that an occasional tax which fell upon a limited number of reluctant contributors, might encounter so much passive opposition as to render its yield uncertain. For instance, on one collection there were arrears of fourteen talents, and Androtion made quite a reputation by getting in between seven and eight, though he had persuaded the assembly to intrust him with extraordinary powers, and though he had used them with extraordinary vigour and not with unimpeachable integrity. To obviate this so far as possible, it was usual that when a direct property-tax was levied, the whole amount should be advanced by the richest men in the symmorias, who recouped themselves at leisure. This already conferred a modified power of the purse, for it was unwise to offend men whose ill-humour would be inconvenient. Again, when it was resolved in the assembly to send so many gallies to sea, there was danger that everyone with influence to stand a trial, without too much risk, would begin to shift off the burden upon somebody else[1], or even simply refuse to pay, and trust to a protest of inability. Consequently, the really rich men who took the whole expense and collected it from their 'partners' (as it had become the fashion to call those who shared the outlay), really performed a valuable public service, even if they found a contractor to take charge of the vessel, and pay her out and home for a less sum than they expected to collect from their partners, or employed the vessel for purposes of private trade whenever it suited them to sail themselves. Of course if they sent the vessel with a contractor whose only chance of a profit was cheese-paring, it was likely to be ill-found, and if they employed it for their own business, the punctuality of the squadron was likely to be impaired; but, except on some peculiarly alarming emergency, it was difficult to get an Attic squadron to sea at all, and without such help it would have been impossible. These were the merits which enabled a Midias to set himself at ease above the law, and to enjoy the consideration which private magnificence will always command. He had no wish for power, he despised his countrymen too much to desire to lead them: it suited him better to vindicate his selfishness by taunting them with their imbecillity and shiftlessness.

The fact that men of hereditary position had despaired of political influence (and they always despair as soon as they find that the majority prefers leaders like itself), was of course sufficient to brand politics as a discreditable trade, though, as in America, individual politicians might achieve an honourable reputation. But the name which the aristocrats fastened upon those who had driven them from the arena stuck to the class of public men who remained at the helm. To eschew politics, to be a plain, private man, was an essential of respectability; to have much to do with the law-courts, or even with the assembly, was to be a sycophant; it was easy for a man who would hawk at small game, to make himself sufficiently annoying to become a personage, while a person who wished

---

[1] The two speeches composed for Apollodorus, when he appealed to the courts to secure the crown due to the trierarch who equipped his ship best and quickest, and to enforce repayment of the expenses he had incurred by serving beyond his term, shew that men of established position often eased themselves by trusting to the ambitious vanity and ostentatious gratitude of *nouveaux riches.*

to be useful, even if he spoke well, found it easier to get credit for his speeches than for his intentions.

As it was discreditable to be a politician, the public interest in politics hardly ever went beyond excitement, and generally stopped at curiosity. This favoured the tendency to laxity of administration which was inherent in the Athenian constitution. The assembly was omnipotent; and in the assembly, to borrow the forcible words put into the mouth of Ae-schines, 'One man went and another came, and there was nobody to look after the common good' (D. de F. L. p. 383, § 149). The only check upon its license was the rule that no business should be brought forward in the assembly which had not passed the council; but this was an illusory security, when every speaker could conclude his speech with the draught of a decree to be moved if encouraged by the audience, and while measures of decisive importance could be originated in the council, and smuggled through the assembly as matter of form. The constitution of Athens had arisen at a period of expansion and enthusiasm; it had taken its final shape under the influence of a statesman whose high character and experience enabled him to govern upon his own principles in the name of the assembly. After the death of Pericles, constitutional statesmen confined their endeavours to protecting his institutions, so that Athens was left with a constitution which in ordinary times did not and could not work as it was intended, for want of motive power. The public opinion of Athens was active and intelligent, but helpless for want of organised institutions to give it effect.

The assembly had not even so much organisation as party divisions would have given it. Politicians were divided into cliques, which had an interest in avoiding collisions (Dein. in Dem. p. 102, §§ 103 sqq., In Arist. p. 106, § 15), for their objects seldom required the whole force of the state, and therefore opposition to one another was only a waste of power. Demosthenes happened to have a personal quarrel with Aeschines, and they fought it out in the courts; but he was on good terms with Demades, and saw with great equanimity the extraordinary honours with which the people rewarded his buoyant and convenient sub-serviency. It is true that he had special reasons for his forbearance, as Demades had exerted himself to save him after the second capture of Thebes, besides supporting him when interrupted in the assembly, a service which Demosthenes could not or would not repay in kind. Of course when they had opposite measures to advocate they denounced each other with suitable energy; but they never did this unnecessarily: all through the speech on the Crown Demades is only mentioned once, and then with a compliment. There was little temptation for politicians to do otherwise. Office was a rare incident of public life, and so an orator was rarely excited by the hope of driving a rival from office. The only motive for attacking an opponent was the chance of driving him from public life altogether by a successful prosecution, and from this they were deterred in general by the curious presumption of Athenian law, that a prosecution should be held to be frivolous. This worked in two ways: sometimes a prosecution was left to be undertaken by under-lings of a party whom it could afford to sacrifice, while the leaders, if convenient, supported the ostensible prosecutor, who alone ran any risk; sometimes a prosecution was kept hanging over a man till it was con-venient to press it, like Aeschines' indictment against Ctesiphon, and this was probably the case with Demades, who during the Lamian war found himself disfranchised under no less than seven distinct indictments for having proposed illegal enactments. No doubt the indictments had been accumulating all through the reign of Alexander, and had been duly laid by cautious patriots, who hoped for better times. But these were exceptions: the days of Cleon were long past, when popular leaders had to give effect to popular passions and prejudices by syste-matic terrorism; the cliques who managed the assembly without exciting it, found it easier to wait till circumstances sent the floating majority their way, so that they could carry out their more or less interested pro-jects by its help.

Though the assembly was hardly earnest, it was by no means calm; on the contrary, precautions had to be taken to prevent speakers from bullying the chair. With this object, at some period between 345 and 338 B.C., the tribe from which the chairman for the day was taken, was organised into a body-guard to protect his authority. For order was exposed to two distinct dangers: the first and slightest was simple tur-bulence, the second was the interested violence of orators who wished to extort the connivance of the chair in pushing through some irregular measure, with the aid of a body of partisans who had been warned to stay till the business was over. Supposing that the chairman was really neutral, his tribe might be relied upon to defeat such manœuvres, and elaborate precautions had been taken from the first restoration of the democracy, to secure both his neutrality and his authority. The only possible object of giving the prytanis of the day nine colleagues, selected from the senators of each tribe except his own, must have been to pro-vide the chairman with colleagues to support or control him as occasion might require. If vice-chairmen were all that was wanted, it would be simpler to allow the other prytanes of the same tribe to act when the prytanis whose turn it was was accidentally hindered from presiding. But the prytanis whose accession could be calculated might be secured beforehand, and in times of popular excitement every prytanis could not be expected to display the firmness of a Socrates : it was expected that the nine assessors would obviate both dangers. But the arrangement presupposed a seriousness, a strictness, and a regularity which were not to be found at Athens. The πρόεδροι, as inscriptions shew, more or less gradually superseded the prytanes altogether in the management of the assembly, and the change must have been consummated when the πρόεδρος of the day was provided with a body-guard, composed of all the members of his tribe who were in attendance at the assembly (cp. Rev. E. L. Hicks, in The Journal of Philology, vol. iii. no. 5). The precaution was far from effectual, for the senate was full of politicians who made sure of the seats which might be convenient to their policy. As there were many citizens who never troubled themselves to be drawn for senators at all, those who never missed a chance, found it easy to get one of themselves in, and if this failed there was always a last resource ; there was no arrangement to enable the official to identify those who had drawn the senatorial tickets, consequently a politician could always buy one from a private man, who only valued it for the year's pay, which was not too high for a politician to make an advance upon. Nor was all over when the senate was filled, or packed, as politicians chose to suppose, for it was one of the symptoms of the unhealthy state of politics, that, as in the eighteenth century in England, the gravest charges were bandied about without being tested. One side treated them as too notorious to be proved, the other as too frivolous to be refuted. There was as much danger, or more, of the proedri being appointed corruptly out of a known and limited number, than of the senators being appointed corruptly out of a larger and unlimited number. And if a private man got appointed senator and proedrus without the suspicion of management, he had no experience, and so might be easily managed or frightened by those who had.

The discredit attached to politicians had other consequences, besides the suspicion which it threw upon public measures. It made it practically impossible to set the law in motion without a personal motive, and so discredited the law, because the presumption in the mind of the indifferent majority was, that whoever had been subjected to a legal penalty was an unfortunate man whose enemies had been too much for him, and so was almost entitled to be treated for the future with exceptional forbearance. Public prosecutors instituted by lawful authority did not exist; those who made it their business to supply this defect of the constitution were branded as sycophants, and though the people were not disinclined to use one nuisance to abate another, defendants who had broken the law had a great advantage in being able to reflect upon the prosecution, with the certainty that they would not have the court against

them. This prejudice told in favour of the class who considered insolence and licence aristocratic, because those whom they insulted could
get no remedy except at law, and discredited themselves by seeking it
there. When a comparatively strict politician found an opportunity to
carry a vote that the demes should purge themselves, the sufferer raised
a cry that he was the victim of a local clique, and came before the court
with a lame story half made out (Dem. adv. Eubulidem). Of course he
relied on the fact that others whose story was no better had been left un-
molested; and this might easily happen, considering that there was no
proper proof of citizenship required when a young man was first enrolled.
If he was properly introduced, the guildmen asked no awkward questions,
and when he was once free of the guild no questions were asked at all.
Amateur prosecutors made it their business to shew that they had an
honest family reason for coming forward, and liked to begin their
speeches with the respectable aphorism, that the public profited by
private quarrels. A man whose father was disfranchised as a state
debtor, and who expected to be disfranchised himself when his father
died, came forward to prosecute his father's prosecutor while he could, as
a matter of family duty, and filled up half his speech (cp. In Theoc.
passim) with an eulogium on his own motives, and an elegy on his
wrongs, as if sympathy with his revenge was likely to have more weight
with the court than the proof of such irregularities as were doubtless
condoned every day.

The only direction in which political theorists looked for a check on
the prevailing laxity, was itself suggestive of the exhaustion of Greece.
Isocrates could only suggest that the Areopagus should be invited to
resume the censorial authority which he believed it to have received from
Solon. If this could be effected, he believed the citizens would all have
adequate and ostensible means of livelihood. This would act in two
ways: by enforcing wholesome habits of industry, and by relieving the
citizens from their enfeebling dependance on the public doles, so that
sycophants could not demoralise the assembly or the courts by appeals
to their cupidity. Another very important effect of the censorship would
be that the character of politicians would be uniformly respectable, and
then public affairs would be conducted steadily and honourably and
safely, for Isocrates believed that the city had little to gain by ambitious
enterprises.

Though Isocrates was hardly a practical or a representative politician,
the feeling that things had gone too far was not uncommon; and, though
a censorship was out of harmony with both the vices and the virtues of a
society so advanced as that of Athens, the reaction of opinion was sufficient to make the Areopagus a formidable weapon in the hands of

f

politicians. The Areopagus was the one public body in Athens whose action could be calculated, owing to the personal incorruptibility of its members, and their rigid adherence to a traditional procedure.   Consequently it was often used as a committee of public safety.   It still retained an extensive jurisdiction in matters of impiety, which was easily stretched to comprehend treason.   The attempt to govern Athens by the Areopagus was like the attempt to govern Greece by the Amphictyonic council; and in both cases the august traditional authority was merely an instrument and a screen.   As the Thebans could not convoke a congress of allies to overawe recalcitrants, they tried to avail themselves of the congress at Delphi; as the orators could not trust a jury to rid them of an underling of the opposite party, they set the Areopagus in motion.   If that court could bring the case under their prescriptive jurisdiction, the peculiar rigidity of their procedure destroyed all chance of escape; if the case was only sent before the court for enquiry by a popular vote, though the finding of the court was hardly ever reversed upon the facts, it was not too difficult to set it aside upon the merits.   Whether the Areopagus acted as a court of instruction, or as a criminal court of first or second instance, the same inflexibility which made their decisions respected, prevented them from acting upon any system, so as to produce a permanent effect upon public affairs.   The real evil remained: a fluctuating assembly had, and could have, no policy.   If it had been possible to utilise the prejudice in favour of the Areopagus, the outgoing generals, like the outgoing archons, should have been passed into it, and it should have been invested with the powers, not of the Roman censors, but of the Roman senate.

The real permanent antagonistic forces in politics were the necessity of paying the dividends of the Athenian people, and the necessity of allowing the Athenian generals to find means for paying the armies, which the irritable pride of public opinion made it necessary to engage. The majority saw clearly, that while their dividends were paid they had more reason to value their political privileges than the people of any other Greek state, and they had the sense to observe that some regular system was necessary in order to provide them.   Accordingly they were content to abdicate the control of affairs in favour of any administrator who could inspire them with confidence of regular payment.   If the shareholders of the East India Company, instead of being deprived of their power by the state, had allowed it to be usurped by fluctuating cliques of directors, and had continued to amuse themselves by passing from time to time strong resolutions concerning Indian affairs, which they had no means of influencing, and no effective desire to influence, the result would hardly give an exaggerated picture of the pitiful and grotesque condition of the people which was called by circumstances to contest with Philip the supremacy of Greece.

Demosthenes, with the suspicion always haunting him (Phil. 3, p. 124, § 95) that 'some higher power was driving matters on,' still regarded the desire of ambitious men to aggrandise themselves amid the decline of their country, and the desire of the ordinary citizen to receive public money without performing what Demosthenes regarded as public service, in the light of symptoms of unmitigated but unaccountable depravity. There were two good reasons why the average Athenian was less ready to serve in person than in the age of Pericles. Wars, or rather campaigns, were longer, so that he could not afford to be from home so long; and the art of war had made such progress, that amateur soldiers could no longer compete upon equal terms with professional; nor, it may be added, were civic generals on an equal footing with professional officers. And while the ordinary members of Greek society found their ties multiplied as society grew older, the rudimentary character of Greek civilisation multiplied the number of men who had no ties at all. At the end of the Peloponnesian war, the number of soldiers unemployed must have been at its height, yet Cyrus found it difficult to enlist ten or twelve thousand mercenaries. Sixty years later, after the class had been exhausted by the long and bloody Sacred war, ten thousand mercenaries were a minor contingent in the campaign which ended at Chaeroneia. In general, matters are hopeless when enlightened and public-spirited men are reduced to advocate moral reform, because it is useless to change the mechanism of institutions, and therefore Demosthenes is not to be blamed for the ludicrous inadequacy of the suggestion, that the Athenians should serve in person in sufficient numbers to give them some control over the mercenaries they sent out; or, at least, when they sent out a general, they should provide him with funds to pay the mercenaries he was to engage, because then he would not be obliged to go after his army when they went to look for pay. Perhaps, too, it may be thought that he shews a sense of the situation, when he complains of the significant change of nomenclature (De Syntaxi, § 24, p. 172) by which the victories of the restored democracy were attributed to the general, whereas those of the old democracy had been attributed to the nation. Even here he does not emphasise the cause of the change: Iphicrates and Chabrias and Timotheus levied their own armies and maintained their own fleets. This made them in great measure independent potentates, and naturally disinclined them to residence in Athens; so that it is unjust to ascribe their long absences either to their own arrogance of temper or to democratic jealousy, especially as the sons of Chabrias and Timotheus found it quite possible to air their arrogance and extravagance at Athens, without propitiating democratic jealousy by any imitation of their fathers' services. In fact, it is hardly an exaggeration to say that the revived Athenian empire was made by condottieri, and used by condottieri, and destroyed by condottieri at last, and that the only benefit which the Athenians at large derived from it while it lasted, was the remittances which commanders sent home from time to time for distribution. It is doubtful whether those who stayed at home gained more by the relief of settling numbers of their countrymen in Samos and the Chersonese, than they lost by the expense of maintaining the settlers in possession of their allotments. As for the 'contributions,' Isocrates gave them their true name of 'black mail.' The moderation and uprightness of Timotheus made such a good impression upon most of the minor maritime states, that they thought it would be good economy to compound for freedom from indefinite exactions, by a moderate subscription to maintain the preponderance of Athens in Greek waters. As while the understanding lasted Athens was always at war, it was out of the question that the contributions should afford even a modest surplus for accumulation or expenditure at Athens. This, much more than the fear of Persia, determined the Athenians to acquiesce in the abrupt termination of the Social war. Its origin was the belief of the most powerful of the allies, that it was possible to make a better bargain with Persia than they had made with Timotheus, and, even if that bargain had been observed, they would still have desired to change it. The exactions to which the Athenian commanders were driven, not much against their will, when the tedious campaign against Philip had exhausted the patience of Athenian tax-payers, only precipitated the decision to which Rhodes and Chios were already inclined by their correspondence with the mainland, and Byzantium by the temptation to profit by its situation to tax the corn trade on its own account. The three years of the war had caused an expenditure of fifteen hundred talents for worse than nothing, for whole battalions of Deiares and Polyphontes (Ae. de F. L. p. 37, § 74), who only existed in the braggadocio of the generals. It was quite clear that the allies cost more than they were worth, and if Persia was to be their pay-master, there was no time to be lost in letting them go. This explains also the law of Eubulus, which has furnished the text for so many declamations. Chares and his supporters had wasted fifteen hundred talents (Ol. 3, § 32, p. 36) among them, and there was nothing to shew for it; Eubulus did not see his way to reform the administration of the war office, but he was determined that the 'ring' which profited by the existing system should not reap the fruits of his own provident and honest management. There is no need to suppose that Eubulus himself was at all attached to Macedonia; when the charge was made against

him, he swore, as he wished his children to thrive, that he would be glad
to see Philip undone, but he believed that if Chares were ever so well
supplied, Athens would be impoverished and the festival pay stopped,
and Philip would not be put down. The only advantage would be, that
Chares would find it easier to make remittances to his friends at Athens,
and that those friends would find a better market for their influence with
Chares among those who were liable to be oppressed by him, but he
took no interest in all the ardent patriots who, as Aeschines said, could
not live without work in peace time. Through all, the Athenians shewed
the peculiar equanimity (πραότης) which had been remarked upon by Plato,
and of which the orators complain as often as it told in favour of their opponents. They acquitted Chares as often as he was brought to trial (Dem.
de F. L. p. 447, § 381), on the ground that he really wished them well, and
would have done more if he had been properly supported. They refused
to find means to support him, because they felt that, after all, he was an
adventurer pursuing his own advantage in their name, and, as far as
possible, at their expense. For the rest, apart from the unfortunate circumstances of the parting, Athens lost little by the withdrawal of Rhodes
and Chios from the confederation, and even the loss of Byzantium was
chiefly mischievous so far as it tended to raise the price of corn. Attic
commanders were always able to levy contributions on the Asiatic seaboard and islands, in accurate proportion to the strength and requirements of their squadrons, so that if their armaments had been composed
of Athenian citizens, they would not have wanted the means of subsist-
ence while carrying out Athenian objects. As it was, the armaments
pursued their own interest, as they would have done if the Athenian treasury had received meagre contributions from Chios and Rhodes. It is
obvious from Thucydides, that no scale of contributions, in the palmiest
days of Athenian power, was adequate to maintain a fleet and army upon
active service. When the treasure of the Acropolis was once exhausted,
the tribute had to be supplemented by plunder in ever-increasing propor-
tions. As the Asiatic Greeks were certain to be plundered in any case,
they preferred, on the whole, paying tribute to Persia instead of to
Athens, because Persia was more disposed of the two to take the tribute
as a substitute for all other claims, and to abstain from any attempt to
exercise effective control while it was paid. The net result of the whole
matter was, that the Asiatic Greeks were plundered by everybody and
governed by nobody.

§ 5. *Persia.*

The position of Persia was still much better than it appears to us,
who are wise after the event; the original organisation of the empire

by Darius Hystaspes must have been singularly able, for the Great King continued to accumulate treasure to the last, which is probably more than could be said of any other oriental empire which was more than two centuries old. This power seems to have rested upon the tributes of the rich valljes of the Tigris and Euphrates, whose real prosperity did not seriously begin to decline till they became the battle-field between Eastern and Western civilisation. Even then the wars of the Seleucidae and the Romans against the Arsacidae and the Sassanidae, were hardly long enough to make a desert for Kurds and Bedouins. The Carduchi remained in their mountains, and were content to exact tolls of those who traversed their passes; but, though they still followed the Great King in his wars, even he had to disguise this tribute under the name of largesse. Almost the only other symptom of decline which was yet perceptible, was that the huge mud palaces and temples, splendidly faced in stone and colours, which former dynasties had erected at the centre of their power, were not restored or maintained by a migratory court, which gloried in being accompanied by a formidable camp (Is. Paneg. p. 70 fin., § 168). While Persia retained this source of power, it was safer for the individual mercenary to enlist in the service of the Great King than in that of his rebels, and the court had a clear conviction of the importance of getting rid of the mercenary chiefs as soon as possible, which would have preserved them for several generations from the fate of the Khalifate. The financial superiority of Persia during the latter years of the Peloponnesian war had made more impression upon the imagination of Greek politicians than her military inferiority, as demonstrated by the retreat of the Ten Thousand, and the far less striking successes of Agesilaus.

These causes led to the peace of Antalcidas, and the position then assumed by the Great King tended to perpetuate and enlarge itself. The recovery of Egypt shewed that the spirit of the government was not extinct, and those who depreciated the Great King found that they had to insist on the topic that he was not as rich as was thought, and that the celebrated gold plane-tree was not big enough for a bird to build in.

§ 6. *Macedonian Interests and Policy.*

The Athenian public in the early days of the contest still regarded the Great King as more formidable than Philip: their chief feeling about the latter was resentment at the trouble he gave, and they remembered too much what we forget, that he was king of Macedonia. In fact, it may be said that all his spontaneous measures up to 346 B.C., were directed to securing his ascendancy north of the Aegean; and, moreover, when there was a question of sacrificing his interests on the seaboard to his interests in the interior, even north of the Balkan, or *vice versâ*, it was his invariable custom to sacrifice the former. The wars with the Illyrians, the Thracians, the Scythians, seemed to be his business; the wars with the Greek powers of the coast seemed to be almost a luxury. There was only one exception: he was certainly determined to allow no foreign influence except his own in Thessaly, and he had overthrown Onomarchus when he invaded that country, though he made no attempt to counteract the momentary energy of Athens, which, without losing a moment, sent a squadron to occupy the straits in force. Even this, however, was quite within the limits of a purely Macedonian policy; the troubles of the Macedonian monarchy were not forgotten, nor the profit which the Thessalians had made of its weakness. In the years immediately preceding the peace of Philocrates, he had shewn an intention of cultivating an interest in Greece. Every influential Greek who visited his court brought back a fortune, some even brought back a body of mercenaries, or at least the means of engaging one. Of course to a power which was at war with Athens, and exercised a protectorate in Thessaly, an influence in Greece was more than convenient, but there were as yet no signs that he even desired to convert this influence into a supremacy. The Great King before him, the different dynasties which divided the inheritance of Alexander after him, maintained an influence of the same kind, for longer or shorter periods, without ever dreaming of a supremacy, which politicians like Demosthenes would have regarded as the only adequate return for their costly largesses. When Philip came back to Pella after his Thracian conquests, it cannot be doubted that he had at last determined, if he had ever hesitated, to establish himself as paramount in Greece, at any rate north of the Isthmus. The resolution had sufficient motives in his existing relations to Thessaly and Thebes. When the war with Athens was at an end, it was impossible, if Philip was to retain his connection with Thessaly and with Thebes, the ally of Thessaly in the Holy War, that he should allow the Phocian dynasty to retain positions which menaced both. His intervention once begun, of course all the powers which remained in Greece appealed to him to direct it in their interest, and these appeals assumed that he would hardly shock opinion by his most ambitious schemes. It is probable that he expected from the first to do what he actually did: his substantial ascendancy was abundantly secured by the opportunity of garrisoning the posts which commanded the pass of Pylae, and by the thorough disorganisation of Phocis, the population of which had actually to look to him for protection. Without breaking faith with Thebes and Thessaly, it would have been difficult to secure more. At the same time, it is likely enough that Philip would have liked to carry out the programme which he allowed his intimates to dangle before the eyes of Aeschines. Garrisons round Pylae were good, but garrisons at Orchomenus and Thespiae would have been better. Supposing Phalaecus had shewn more fight, supposing the Athenians had sent a strong contingent under Phocion, it is not unlikely that an unscrupulous potentate would have seized the opportunity of keeping his old allies in dependence by means of his new. Demosthenes, when he was not thinking of the conduct of Aeschines, but of the actual situation (De Pace, §§ 20-22), pointed out to the assembly that, without admitting that Philip had been coerced by Thebes, as the people who had been elated by the promises of Aeschines liked to believe, it was apparent that he had done more for Thebes than it was for his own interest to do, and that probably his motive had been to avoid a useless rupture. There are more examples than one in the history of the first Napoleon, where he seems to have sincerely hesitated which of two or more competitors for his favour he should finally elect to disappoint, when each was equally in his power, and it was convenient to keep each in good humour to the latest moment.

For a drunken savage, whose wife seriously believed that a superhuman being in the shape of a serpent had made her the mother of a superhuman child, which is really one very important aspect of Philip's place in the history of civilisation, he was decidedly good natured and well intentioned. He really disliked the utter waste of the war with Athens, which produced nothing but useless vexation to both parties. This is the explanation of all his effusive overtures after the capture of Olynthus. He had got everything he wanted by the war ; all the establishments of Athens which could serve to annoy or hamper him, were now in his own hands ; he was sorry for the Athenians, and wished them well out of it. If the principal motive of the repeated messages of goodwill had been to deceive Athens for his own interest, he would not have grudged them an embassy after the assembly had graciously voted him permission to send one. The peace was more their affair than his, and he waited for them to move in it, and meanwhile went on with his own business in Thrace. He was perfectly willing to guarantee the Athenian possessions in Chersonese, in order, no doubt, to bind the city to be of good behaviour for the future; and it seems that he was really anxious to conclude not only a peace, but an alliance, since he held out hopes of some definite advantage too great to be revealed until he had been admitted as the ally of Athens. Whether the Athenians were meant to look to the possession of Euboea or the restoration of Oropus, the boon was not of a nature to give Philip an effective hold upon them after he had once performed his promise. All that he would have gained would have been popularity at Athens, until the next dispute about something which excited the assembly more than theories of gratitude. The promise was meant to be performed if it should prove convenient, and at worst it would have done good service, Philip thought, if it was believed till the alliance was secured. Like Demosthenes, he felt that a peace without an alliance would be an unsatisfactory truce, and he made the mistake of thinking that the Athenians, like the Thessalians, would abide by an arrangement substantially advantageous to both parties, though they might have been led to enter it by false pretences. He was probably seriously misled by his own dupes, who made him believe that a knot of well-satisfied partisans could manage the assembly and keep the people quiet. No management was needed to prevent the assembly from doing anything against Philip, and no management was sufficient to keep it from grumbling against him, and even voting against him. In fact, the want of self-control which made the Athenians incapable of energetic action, made them equally incapable of reticence and forbearance ; and if their irritability had needed a stimulus, it was to be found in the scornful sermons of Hegesippus, and in the vindictive constancy of Demosthenes. Every dispute was envenomed by a reference to the promises upon which Philip had procured the peace, and Philip's partisans, who were the only persons who were responsible for anything beyond vague professions of goodwill, and proffers of some advantage too great to be prematurely disclosed, were exposed to suspicion as traitors, and their recommendations of peace were discredited, though up to Philip's attack upon Byzantium, those recommendations were supported by every consideration of prudence and good faith. Philip was appropriately punished for his excessive *finesse*, for the alliance obtained under false pretences was certainly the cause of the termination of the peace.

§ 7. *Macedon and the Policy of Athens.*

There were practically three serious views of what ought to be the attitude of Athens in the face of this new power, each distinct from the general popular feeling of helpless irritation. There was the traditional view that Athens, for the sake of her own interests in the Thracian border, ought to be on good terms with the chief native potentate, whichever that might be. This assumed, of course, that all native potentates were inherently weaker than Athens, or, at least, that their position was less stable and more precarious, for the power of Sitalces in its time had been at least as imposing, though less highly organised, than that of Philip, up to 346 B.C. When the full extent of Philip's ascendancy had declared itself, this view tended increasingly to pass into more or less conscious, and more or less interested servility, though its antiquity gave it a sort of respectability ; so that, even after the Phocian expedition,

Philip's partisans could still appeal to the prejudices of a large class against all complainants 'who did not give Philip a chance of being useful to the city,' even if he would. Another view, held by Phocion and many other respectable men, was less unreal, and, after all, less unmanly. Its advocates probably thought, though they did not say, that Athens was going down hill; at any rate they were clear that it was useless to fight Philip on his own coast, and that any precarious footing which Athens might retain there was certain to cost far more than it was worth. It was better to let Pydna and Potidaea and Amphipolis, and even the Chersonese go, and let the citizens die in Athens and be buried at home. Phocion conducted more than one expedition in central Greece with energy and success; there is no evidence that he disapproved in any degree of *their* objects, which could be obtained once for all without disproportionate exertion, whereas Philip, being on the spot and having more at stake, was certain to succeed in the long run. Nor have we any reason to think that he looked forward to Athens accepting the condition of a dependant ally of Philip, because he looked down upon the Athenians with a half-humourous, half-kindly cynicism: he thought Athens might still manage to be prosperous, and respected if not influential, and powerful enough to protect her reasonable engagements and her serious interests. Perhaps the worst objection to his views was that they were adapted to the position and the history of Argos. Even after Chaeroneia he maintained his independence and sobriety of judgment. He actually ventured to warn the people, who were carried away by enthusiasm for the generosity of the conqueror, of the risk they ran in committing themselves to the resolutions of the congress of Corinth, and when their declaration had excited a revulsion of feeling, he contented himself with pointing out that Athens had acquitted herself honourably as a dependant ally of Sparta, and had afterwards regained her freedom of action. There was something unreal in this optimism, but it proceeded not from insincerity, but from a purely positive way of looking at things, and a resolute dislike to all sounding generalisations. Up to the time of Philip's Phocian expedition, there was much to be said for Phocion's policy (which Demosthenes was ready to adopt for a moment at the time of the second embassy), that is, if it had been deliberately and consistently adopted by the assembly. As it was, the self-indulgence of the people and the laxity of the administration made it possible for Phocion to destroy all possible advantage which Athens might have derived from the energy of Demosthenes, while the irritable vanity of the people, inflamed by numerous orators, made it possible for Demosthenes to destroy all the advantage which was to be expected from the prudence of Phocion. Nor was this all; the gaping majority, who never could make up their minds to any coherent course of action whatever, and consistently shut their eyes to everything else, while they tried to live while they could in a fool's paradise of speculation on Philip's bad luck or goodwill, ultimately thwarted the reasonable politicians upon each side by their votes, and by their wishes and habits everlastingly paralysed both.

The third view of the situation was simply, that the dignity of Athens and the safety of Greece demanded an uncompromising opposition to the ambition of Philip. It was advocated not only by Demosthenes, but by many other speakers who shared his dislike to Philip, without his eloquence or his conscientious zeal for a provident organisation of the force of Athens. If either his system or Phocion's could have been fairly tried, it is difficult to ascertain whether the less noble would not have proved the more prudent. The question depends upon the intentions of Philip, or perhaps rather upon his tastes. Sooner or later, of course, if he had lived, public opinion would have forced him to undertake the crusade against Persia, which was the sole remaining hope of all unprejudiced Greeks ; and, if he had done so before the independence of central Greece was seriously compromised, it may be doubted whether Persian money would have been able to rouse a very effective opposition. Demosthenes refused to believe that Philip could trouble himself about the evil things of Thrace, except as á means to secure the good things of Athens ; it would have been a legitimate extension of the same argument, to infer that he could not have busied himself with the silver of Athens and neglected the gold of Babylon. But such reasoning gave Philip credit for being more single-minded and clear-sighted than he really was. There are great men, like Louis XI and Napoleon, to whom it is almost positively painful to release themselves from the joyous entanglement of their own past activity, and Philip was one of these. It suited him far better to have a number of questions of all magnitudes always open, each of which gave him endless opportunities for enjoying the pleasures of what the Greeks called πλεονεξία, than to concentrate himself upon a single object, and make sacrifices in order to pursue it without interruption. This view of Philip's character, so far as it is well founded, is of course a justification of the policy of Demosthenes : it was no use for Athens to leave him alone, unless he himself was determined to get clear of Greece. If he had lived to conquer Darius, he would have been incessantly posting to and from Ecbatana to the sea, and as often as he came to the sea he would have found a number of Greek deputies waiting for him, all of whom would have gone home with despatches very much more to their own satisfaction than to that of their fellow-citizens. Alexander, towards the close of his reign, violated the treaty he had himself imposed upon Greece, by an order for a general restoration of exiles; Philip would have spread the same amount of high-handed injustice over all the years during which Alexander was buried, so far as Greece was concerned, in the recesses of upper Asia. Demosthenes may have deceived himself—he probably did—when he maintained that Philip was an enemy of the city and of the ground it stood upon, for, when the time to gratify such enmity came, Philip exhibited a forbearance too complete not to be generous, though it was doubtless also politic. But though he wished to bring Athens to his own side with as little injury to her as possible, he would not have allowed her to remain apart in dignified isolation from foreign politics; for this was impossible, unless he had been prepared to isolate himself from the politics of Greece.

The dignity of Athens, however, was not such a safe guide as it had once been to the interests of Greece. The majority of the smaller states wished for repose, and for nothing else. If their citizens were to have a career, they must leave their country, for the absorption of the political unit in any larger organisation was still as distasteful as ever, if not more so, to Greek patriotism. It was easier for a city to reconcile itself to a condition of partial dependence, even when it involved very onerous conditions, than to merge its individuality in that of another state, even upon the most favourable terms. For instance, in 393 B.C. the Corinthians were at war with Sparta and in alliance with Argos, but as soon as the question came before them of becoming free citizens of Argos, or going back to their old unequal alliance with Sparta, they chose at any cost to have a city of their own. The best thing that could happen to small states in such a temper, was to be delivered from the necessity of having a foreign policy, and this was exactly what a foreign protectorate could offer them. Independence, in the sense in which it was understood at Athens, was as unattainable to them as empire, and after Lysander and Alcibiades, no Greek state could exercise a protectorate that rested upon the old foundation of mutual respect and confidence. The speech, anciently attributed to Hyperides, on the obligations of the treaty with Alexander, is a very interesting monument of all that Macedonia had found it worth while to promise, even after Chaeroneia. The treaty guaranteed to every state its internal sovereignty and its existing constitution (p. 214, §§ 11, 17), and established a federal authority, which was to prevent any city from allowing exiles to make it a base of operations (p. 216, § 19) against any other, and to prohibit all other revolutionary manœuvres. There is a good deal of uncertainty about the date of the speech; some refer it to the time when the war party was endeavouring to work up the assembly to support the revolt of Thebes; others to the last year of Alexander's reign, when he had issued a general decree for the restoration of exiles. Of course the practical value of the treaty depends upon the date of the speech, for we only know its stipulations from the proofs which its author adduces of their wholesale violation : if it was colourably observed for ten years, it perhaps had justified its existence. Whenever Alexander decided to override the treaty, he did so without any political motive, in the plenitude of despotic caprice. The treaty, as it stood, guaranteed him sufficiently against the danger of any general coalition, and provided for such contingents as he had chosen to demand for his great expedition, but he did not condescend to understand that it was beneath him to punish communities for the ineffectual ill-will of parties.

G. A. S.

THE DOCUMENTS QUOTED IN THE
ORATION ON THE CROWN.

ALL the direct evidence, both documents and depositions, which was to be produced upon a trial at Athens, had to be given in at the preliminary investigation called *Anacrisis*, and were then sealed up in the *Echinus*. The parties of course retained copies for their own use, or for that of the orators who were to compose their speeches. Upon the trial the *Echinus* was opened, and each party got back the writings they had put in. There was a good deal of difference, both in the form in which such writings were put in, and in the way in which they were used. Aeschines liked everything to be as clear and business-like as possible. He wrote the depositions himself (In Tim. § 67) to which his witnesses were called to swear; he put in just those parts of the laws upon which he relied; he even altered the wording, when a textual extract would have been unintelligible without the context (D. de Cor. § 151). Then he handed piece after piece from the bundle, doubtless arranged with professional neatness, to be used just where it would clench a point of his orderly and deliberate argument. Demosthenes' conception of the perfect orator was much more theatrical. He liked to have as much by-play as possible between the speaker and the clerk and other officers (Lept. § 92, In Arist. § 96). Even if such little scenes led to nothing, they kept the attention of the court alive, and they gave an air of fussy earnestness to the speech, which would commend itself, especially to a writer whose composition was to be recited by a stranger. All the documents were put in *in extenso*, and the speaker had to tell the clerk when to stop (In Arist. § 23), and point out where the quotation was to begin (De F. L. § 45[1], In Arist. § 191); if he left the clerk to find his own place, he was

---

[1] λέγ' ἐξ ἐτέρας ἐπιστολῆς ἐπιδείξας, where ἐπιδείξας is a gloss, to describe the action of the speaker.

at leisure to relax from the main argument, and make a point which took little time in a conversational manner. The great majority of the speeches which have come down to us under the name of Demosthenes, are without any attempt to represent the documents cited, which is exactly what we might have expected, for ancient publishers were not familiar with the convenient distinction of text and notes, under which they might have been introduced *in extenso;* and it cannot be supposed that Demosthenes inserted in the final copy of the speech, the exact passages which he had recited in court.

There was hardly a motive for doing so, considering the kind of publicity at which even such a literary orator as Isocrates aimed. A Greek speech was intended to be heard first in public, and then in private ἐν τῇ τῶν μειρακίων διατριβῇ (Ae. in Tim. § 170); Greek society was not rich enough for copies to be rapidly multiplied by slave labour, and circulated from hand to hand, like the Second Philippic of Cicero. The orator of course introduced the *pièces justificatives* in such recitations; but we have no notice of their preparing their speeches for posthumous publication. Their speeches were left for the most part in the condition of remains: the *Midias*, it is generally agreed, was thrown aside unfinished as soon as Demosthenes had compromised the case. We do not even know that the composer of speeches for sale always kept a copy of his speech; it seems improbable that he did, for otherwise there would have been little uncertainty as to the proper contents of the *Corpus Demosthenicum.* Only one question could have arisen about a given speech: was it or was it not included in the collection of autograph MSS.? which, on such an hypothesis, must have passed from Demosthenes to Demochares, and from Demochares to Laches, if they had not found their way already into a public library. In fact, we find that in the first century of our era a large number of speeches were in circulation under the name of Demosthenes, and that critics were just winding up an attempt to ascertain which of them were genuine. It is obvious that long after the flourishing period of Greek oratory closed, the possessors of old speeches, and even old school exercises, kept bringing fresh matter into the market under the most distinguished name available. The canon of Demosthenes was not closed till he had been dead long enough for the public to regard him as the presumptive author of every good old speech, as they regarded Solon as the author of every good old law. If Demosthenes' speeches, as Dionysius had them, came together in this irresponsible way, it would be easy to account for the attempts made to raise several speeches to a higher standard of completeness than the rest. Whenever the owner of the speech was the person for whom it was written, there was a chance that he could supply the *pièces justificatives* with tolerable completeness, for one trial led to another too often for such documents to be hastily destroyed. For instance, if the speech against Stephanus were published by the family of Apollodorus, they would be able to complete it from his papers, so far as they remained in good order, while the effects of time and carelessness would go far to account for the inaccuracies now visible, especially if the practice of putting in depositions without the names of the witnesses who swore to them, indicated by the documents in the speech against Macartatus, was commonly adopted. The editor, whoever he was, of the speech against Aristocrates, thought it worth while to insert, as read by the clerk, the quotations from the documents read, which the speaker recited after the clerk. If the Midias was left incomplete, it was natural that in preparing it for publication, the editor should have looked through Demosthenes' study for any papers that bore upon it, and not impossible that he should have supplemented their contents by more or less infelicitous conjecture.

None of these hypotheses cover the case of the documents in the great Oration on the Crown, which was carefully finished, and remained in Demosthenes' hands. We have, therefore, to inquire in the first place, were they inserted by Demosthenes himself? in the second place, what degree of credit is due to the compiler who inserted them? for it does not follow that, because he made the most astonishing mistakes, he was wholly without trustworthy materials, and the intention to use them honestly. The first question may be answered without prejudice to the second. Of course any evidence which proves that the documents inserted in our text are not a faithful representation of the documents read in court, proves *a fortiori* that they were not inserted by Demosthenes; but this would be proved equally well if a document were inserted in a place which did not suit it, though the document itself might be shewn, by the strongest internal and external evidence, to be a genuine document of the Demosthenic age (§§ 145, 146). Demosthenes says Nausicles has often been crowned in office for his free gifts to the public; so were Diotimus and, again, Charidemus, when they gave the shields; so has Neoptolemus here. Take the decrees passed in their favour, and read them. We ought, if Demosthenes had inserted the documents, to have had several decrees in honour of Nausicles, one in favour of Diotimus, another in favour of Charidemus, and one or more in honour of Neoptolemus. For we cannot suppose that, as Neoptolemus was in court, the decrees in his honour were omitted, since Demosthenes says τὰ τούτοις γεγενημένα, not τὰ ἐκείνοις. Instead, we have one decree in honour of Nausicles, and one in honour of both Diotimus and Charidemus, who are represented as uniting, though in command of separate arms at separate places, to supply a loss of apparently 800 shields captured by the Macedonians at the river battle. Again (§ 208), the speaker appeals to certain decrees and official replies, to shew the mutual dislike between Thebes and Athens, maintained by Philip and his agents. Instead, we have two decrees in which the Athenians resolve to deprecate the advance of Philip, grounding their alarm, in the latest and most abject, on Philip's success in inflaming the enmity of Thebes; and two dispatches of Philip, one in reply to the second Athenian embassy, taunting them with their unsuccessful attempt to alienate Thebes, and one in reply to a Theban dispatch, congratulating Thebes on having resisted the seductions of Athens. The documents, as we have them, fall as flat as flat can be, and if this were not enough to prove that Demosthenes cited others, he goes on to say (§ 217) that Philip had brought the cities to this pass, and was elated with these decrees before he moved to Elatea with his army. The decrees suppose Philip to have arrived there already, and a classical writer would not have represented him as elated by his own dispatches (§ 200). Demosthenes, after giving his account of the beginning of the Amphissian war, and citing the decrees of the Amphictyons, calls for the times at which these things happened, obviously (§ 197) including the whole series of transactions as well as the decrees. Consequently, if he had inserted the documents, we should have had a long list of dates. We actually have a single date, in the year of a pseudeponymous archon (§§.133, 134). Demosthenes calls for the lists of trierarchs under the old and the new laws. Of course the clerk did not read them through, but he began each list, and did not read what we do—a statement of the liabilities of trierarchs.

Supposing that some other person attempted to do what Demosthenes had not done, we have now to inquire what means he had for supplying the documents which he inserted up to § 239, inclusive. It is clear that he had not, at least in their entirety, either the documents put into the *Echinus*, or the duplicates which Demosthenes must have had in his possession while he prepared his speech. These, it is true, are the only sources from which he could have taken at first-hand documents like the deposition at § 171, or the list of dates § 200, for we cannot suppose that either was preserved textually in any department of the public archives. On the other hand, a person with the documents before him could not have made the mistakes which the compiler made in fitting them into their places, and the single date given instead of a whole list at § 200, is a proof that it, and all other evidence of the same kind, must be derived from second-hand authorities or from sheer invention. This, of course, is a presumption that other evidence, of which authentic originals might have been discovered by systematic search, may have been taken

g

from second-hand authorities, which were abundant, rather than from public archives, or from any systematic collection based upon them. The greater part of the documents quoted consist of Athenian decrees and laws, which of course were preserved in the *Metroon*. It is probable that the decrees of the Amphictyons were preserved at Delphi, and that despatches of foreign states and Athenian ambassadors were preserved at Athens. It was therefore possible for a diligent person, at any time between Demosthenes and Plutarch, to supply from the most authentic sources all the documents cited in the speech, except the depositions of private persons, the dates cited at § 200, and perhaps the indictment (§§ 66–68) and the lists of trierarchs; for though Demosthenes implies that the list of trierarchs, under a law which had been ten years obsolete, was still in existence when he spoke, it does not follow that old lists were preserved for ever.

We may, however, be certain that the decrees in our MSS. were not taken direct from the Athenian archives; for, in the first place, they are dated, with one doubtful exception, by pseudeponymous archons, and, with that exception, the archons not only were not contemporary with the events assigned to their year, but never existed at all. If we suppose with Boeckh (Transactions of the Berlin Academy for 1827, p. 153), that in the Athenian archives the clerk of each prytany indorsed and put up separately the decrees passed in his term of office, so that after the arrangements for distinguishing the decrees of different years had got into confusion, those passed in different prytanies could still be distinguished, it is still out of the question that anybody working in the *Metroon* could have taken the clerk for the archon, as this would have led the inquirer to multiply the years under examination by ten, and to divide their legislative activity in the same proportion. If we suppose a compiler to have worked, not from the parchments in the *Metroon*, but from inscriptions, such a mistake would be still more inconceivable. In the second place, the form of the decrees is often so unprecedented and incomprehensible, that it cannot have been copied from the original. For instance, we have, § 90, ἐπὶ ἄρχοντος Νεοκλέους, which is the usual form, in § 93 we have ἐπὶ Νεοκλέους ἄρχοντος, § 147 ἄρχων Δημόνικος Φλυεύς. If we attribute these vagaries to the defective arrangements of the *Metroon*, we should still be unable to account for such forms as πρυτάνεων λεγόντων βουλῆς γνώμῃ § 148, βουλῆς καὶ στρατηγῶν γνώμῃ § 209, πολεμάρχου γνώμῃ § 211, or for the inconceivable confusion of § 91, where anacolutha are piled upon each other in a manner to beggar Thucydides, to say nothing of suspicious expressions like ναύαρχος § 90, μεμψιμοιρεῖ § 91, ἐνδεχομένως § 212, &c.

Boeckh has proposed a very tempting hypothesis to meet the difficulty of the pseudeponymous archons, which is generally assumed as the starting-point of such attempts as are made to maintain that the documents are in any sense genuine. He supposes that our documents are taken from a collection of decrees which followed the arrangement, as he conceives it, of the Attic archives. Such a collection might have been used by persons whose industry and education were not enough to enable them to consult archives for themselves, and it may be conceded that they might make many and curious mistakes in using it, especially if they tried to make *précis* instead of copying at length; in fact, if we suppose a person of the calibre of Pollux (who, 10. 126, makes Alcibiades archon on the strength of an inscription still preserved, proving that he was treasurer to the goddess) set to make extracts from such a collection, he *might* have imported all the superficial irregularities quoted against their genuineness. We know that several collections of decrees were made in antiquity; the fullest was the work of Craterus, the brother of Antigonus Gonatas, which is repeatedly cited by Harpocration, but we have no evidence but that his work, like those of his predecessors, was based exclusively upon inscriptions. That it was largely based on inscriptions we know, and therefore it is doubtful if the compiler had a motive for following the arrangement of the archives. It may be doubted whether the collector was very scrupulous, for he admitted the record of the peace Cimon was held to have concluded with Persia, though it had already been rejected by Theopompus, on the ground mentioned by Harpocration, s.v. Ἀττικοῖς γράμμασιν, that in carving the inscription the full Ionic alphabet was employed, which was not introduced till after the anarchy. Moreover, Craterus did not confine himself to copies of decrees, but gave such a full description, e.g. of the painting of the Battle of Marathon, that it was possible to argue from his silence, as Harpocration does, s.v. ὅτι διαμαρτάνει. On the whole, therefore, it is far from established that the work of Craterus on decrees was of the nature which Boeckh's hypothesis requires, while no later collection of such a nature was known to antiquity, and the earlier collections, being exclusively based on inscriptions, cannot have misled the editor or copyist who inserted the documents as we read them in the text. But even assuming that such a collection existed, as is required by the hypothesis, the contents of the documents themselves are of a kind to strengthen the presumption created by the presence of depositions and other documents, which from their nature cannot have been taken from authentic records.

The first document cited (§§ 36, 37) is one of the most suspicious. In its general outlines it suits the peace of Philocrates, for which it is quoted, but that decree was passed in Munychion, not on the last day of Hecatombaeon, by the senate alone, not by the senate and people; it named ten ambassadors, not five, and of the five named, the majority are not included in the ten whose names are given in the second argument prefixed to Demosthenes' speech on the embassy. If the document is genuine, it must be referred to a peace concluded in the summer of 339 B.C., after the relief of Byzantium; but the orators know nothing of this peace, though each could have accused the other most effectively of breaking it. In fact Demosthenes (De Cor. §§ 185, 186) clearly implies that, after the deliverance of Euboea and Byzantium, the Athenians continued to worry Philip by fruitless and purposeless hostilities, of which he could only get quit by stirring up an Amphictyonic war, which would open the road to Athens. There can be little doubt that Athens was only included in the pacification between Philip and Byzantium through the carelessness of Diodorus, who knows nothing of the peace of Philocrates. But even if such a peace had been concluded, this decree cannot refer to it, for how could five Macedonian partisans have been chosen, on the motion of Demosthenes, to set off in a hurry to ratify a treaty whose effect at the moment would have been to interrupt the successful operations of Phocion? Wherever the compiler got the decree, and he did not get it from Craterus, his authority, if he had one, was thinking of the peace of Philocrates. The next decree cited (§§ 46, 47) might be genuine (though incomplete, for nothing is said of the fortification of Piraeus, or the sacrifice to Hercules, mentioned Dem. de F. L. § 97), but for its date. The decree of Callisthenes was passed (Ib. § 67) on the 27th of Scirrophorion, 346 B.C.: one decree is dated on the 20th of Maemacterion, and so, if genuine, must be five months later; but Demosthenes says nothing of a second σκευαγωγία, in his repeated allusions (Ib. §§ 98, 99, 374) to the discomfort which followed the peace of Philocrates. Besides, when Philip was in Phocis, did he go home without executing the Amphictyonic decrees, and come back five months after to execute them, or did he stay in Phocis without executing them? Again, Philip presided at the Pythia in Boedromion 345, so he must already have been recognised as an Amphictyon, as Demosthenes recommended in his speech De Pace, which therefore falls not later than Boedromion; then war, to say nothing of invasion, is only a contingent danger. What had happened to excite such a panic two months later? not to mention that in 345 there were only twenty-nine days in Maemacterion, so that the twentieth ought to have been ἐνατῇ, not δεκάτη ἀπιόντος. The letter of Philip (§§ 49, 50) assumes a division between the Phocian towns which capitulated and those which were stormed, which is excluded by the statement of Demosthenes (De F. L. § 68), that not a single town was either stormed or besieged; and it hardly brings out sharply enough the point for which it is quoted (§ 51). It is in the regular style of all

the other state papers which have come down to us under the name
of Philip. It might have been taken from a history. The next document cited is the indictment of Aeschines (§§ 66–68). It will be
convenient to examine this with the decree of Ctesiphon (§§ 151, 152).
The indictment purports to have been laid in Elaphebolion of the year of
Chaerondas, and the decree to have been proposed five months earlier,
in Pyanepsion. As Demosthenes was appointed (Ae. in Ctes. § 27) in
the beginning of Scirrophorion in the year of Chaerondas, it is difficult
to see how he can have begun to be responsible when the indictment
was laid. Boeckh supposes that we ought to read πρὸ instead of ἐπὶ in
the passage of Aeschines, so that Demosthenes should have been
appointed at the end of Ol. 110. 2, instead of at the end of Ol. 110. 3;
Droysen, founding upon the fragments of a decree edited by Franz (p. 79,
Bulletino dell' Instituto di Correspondenza Archeologica for 1835), supposes that, besides the tumultuary repairs mentioned by Lycurgus (Adv.
Leoc. § 44, ed. Tus.), which must have taken place before the peace,
when Demosthenes was collecting stores and money for the siege which
seemed imminent (Ae. § 159), there was a systematic restoration, which
was not completed until Lycurgus' first term of office was over, since the
contractors are directed to account to his son Habron, under whose
name he conducted the administration. If the tumultuary repairs were
such temporary makeshifts, it is obvious that Demosthenes' claim to
a vote of thanks must have rested on his contribution to the permanent
ones, and hence there is no need to alter the text of Aeschines; but
it follows that the Chaerondas of the indictment is a mistake, like the
Euthycles of the decree. The fact that in the indictment we have the
name of a real archon out of place, is of course a presumption against
the hypothesis that the compiler always had the name of the clerk for the
prytany before him. The decree cannot be complete or accurate, for it
omits all mention of Demosthenes clearing the ditches, which began the
real decree (Ae. § 236), and regards the theorica as contributed by the
tribes, instead of distributed through them to the citizens, to say nothing
of the omission of all the honorary verbiage which the indictment purports to cite from the decree. The indictment recites that it is laid
before the archon: it was actually laid before the Thesmothetae.

Next we have two decrees (§§ 90, 91, and 93) referring to the affairs
of the ships seized by Philip's admiral; besides the clumsiness of the
first, Droysen objects, as elsewhere, to the names otherwise unknown;
(the second is the only authority for the existence of two Aristophons
among the contemporaries of Demosthenes, but it is hard to suppose
with Droysen, that the celebrated Azenian was the Aristophon who
carried a decree about νόθοι in the year of Euclides.) The letter of Philip

(§§ 95–97) might belong fairly enough to the negotiations described by Frontinus (Strat. 1. 4. 13), which might lead one to think that Philip offered to restore the ships, and held out hopes of settling the dispute with Byzantium by the mediation of Athens; for collections of anecdotes are seldom accurate, the object is to tell a pointed story with an useful lesson, without caring how it fits into the historical context. One cannot be sure that Philip did not offer to restore the ships, because Demosthenes (§ 89) treats their capture as the decisive act which broke the peace; he would be justified in doing so, if thenceforward hostilities continued without being disavowed, and in § 177 the capture of the ships is put on the same footing as the violation of the Chersonese. It is, however, quite certain that the letter we read is not the one Demosthenes put in, which must be the one quoted by Philochorus (Dion. ad Amm. 2), which was intended to provoke, and did provoke, something like a declaration of war. The next decree (§§ 104, 105) must be at least misdated; it purports to have been passed in the year of Chaerondas, five months after the battle of Chaeroneia, to reward Demosthenes for his services in the deliverance of Euboea, three years before the battle.

∴ We come now to a document which is almost certainly genuine, a decree of the Byzantines in honour of Athens (§§ 112, 113). Even this, however, is not exactly what Demosthenes cited in court. Though there is some uncertainty as to the reading, it is quite clear that Byzantium and Perinthus separately voted a crown to Athens, and that these votes were therefore recited in court. After this, it seems the Byzantines passed a further decree *ad perpetuam rei memoriam* full of details, all of which are credible and significant, which, thanks perhaps to Craterus, has come down to us. It is probable that our decree was taken directly or indirectly from an inscription at Byzantium, and that substantially the same decree was passed at Perinthus, since the Perinthians are described as allies, and therefore must have had an assembly of their own (unless, indeed, the senate had received a communication from Perinthus, authorising Byzantium to confer the same privileges in both states). The allusion to the restoration of the hereditary constitution, etc. may imply that during the alliance with Philip his *xenoi* set themselves above it, or may only mean that the Athenians left Byzantium as they found it: ἔγκτησις must have been a common term all over the Aegean, since the reorganisation of the Athenian confederacy in 378 B.C., in which Athens expressly renounced the right, so we need not be surprised to find it here Doricised, instead of its Doric equivalent ἔμπασις. The next decree of the Chersonesites (§ 114) is unobjectionable, though we cannot say of it as of the Byzantine decree, that it contains facts which could not have been invented. The sixty talents must be explained with Boeckh (Staats-uns halteng des Athenes, vol. i. pp. 28, 29, ed. 1817), as three hundred and sixty drachmae by weight, and the mention of four cantons as having a common council which did not include others, e. g. Crithote, is not a very serious objection, as most of the Chersonese was occupied by Attic out-settlers, who could not thank Athens for the restoration of 'their fatherlands.'

In §§ 132–134 we have documents connected with Demosthenes' reform of the trierarchy. The first purports to be the decree for which Demosthenes was prosecuted; instead it is an account of the unsuccessful prosecution of a law which he proposed, and not a hint of its contents is given. Then we ought to have a list of the trierarchs under the old law; we have not even the law, but a statement of one possible result of its provisions. Lastly, instead of a list of the trierarchs under Demosthenes' law, we have a summary of its provisions. The origin of the confusion is obvious. The compiler had got before him, in the margin or else-where, an historical note on the trierarchical reform of Demosthenes, and he cut it up to make it do duty for three documents. Here, again, we have a proof, if possible more conclusive than that supplied by the first decree, that the compiler did not use transcripts from the Attic archives. After this, it is almost superfluous to point out the inaccura-cies of the two next decrees, such as the pleonasms γνώμη βουλῆς καὶ δήμου, ὅτι δοκεῖ τῇ βουλῇ καὶ τῷ δήμῳ, τοῦ ἐπὶ τῆς διοικήσεως κεχειροτονημένου, and the difficulty of understanding how, if Nausicles took office after the Dionysia, at the beginning of March (which he must have done to be in office at the next), he, or any one else, could be hindered διὰ τοὺς χειμῶνας in trans-porting the necessary pay. The compiler need not have invented the fact about Nausicles' munificence, which might be plausibly placed at the end of the Social war; and the proclamation in the theatre may have been an addition of his own, by way of gilding gold. But after all, the words οὐκ εἰσέπραξε τὸν δῆμον might suggest, that for once Nausicles' admirers waited till his accounts were passed, and that the poor com-piler's authority got hold of just that one decree. We have seen already that the next decree cannot be the *decrees* which Demosthenes cited, and therefore cannot have come directly or indirectly from the archives. If it is an invention, it is strange that the compiler should have made the Athenian army lose 800 shields in the battle of the river, which through-out the speech is claimed as a victory.

It is clear from Aeschines (In Ctes. §§ 41–47), that the Dionysiac law contained much which does not appear in our text (§ 155); it is clear from Demosthenes (§ 156), that the law was read *in extenso*. The extract we read contains nothing which might not have been learnt

from the context; but, if it had been directly taken from it, the clause
ἐὰν . . στεφανοῖ could hardly have been substituted for the verbal citation
in the text, πλὴν . . ψηφίσηται.

The principal objection to the evidence of the Areopagites in § 171 is,
that we cannot imagine how the compiler got it; and it is strange that a
special σύνδικος, in addition to the Pylagori, should be sent to plead
before the Amphictyons of Delphi, while the Amphictyons of Delos, as
appears by inscriptions of the hundredth and hundred and first Olym-
piads, were Athenian officers, and therefore it is hard to see why an
Athenian orator should be sent from Athens to plead before them.   It is
unnecessary to suppose, after our experience of the compiler, that αὗται
αἱ μαρτυρίαι (§ 175) includes the evidence of the Areopagites.   It is
simply a clumsy equivalent for ἡ μαρτυρία τουτῶν.   The witnesses ought to
be cited by the Demes, instead of by the names of their fathers; but
this, too, is a trifle.   It is a more serious difficulty, that we hardly know
what the generals can have to do with Demosthenes' prosecution of
Aeschines, whether he proceeded by *Graphe* or *Isangelia;* perhaps it
may be thought that he wished to avoid the risk and the responsibility of
proceeding upon his own authority; but even then it is curious that,
instead of swearing to the fact, the witnesses should only swear to having
sworn to it; and though it is conceivable that their first deposition might
have found its way to the archives of the senate, and have been endorsed
by the clerk of the prytany, we have seen that the compiler did not
habitually use the archives, and therefore the note with which the deposition concludes is a gratuitous riddle.

The decrees of the Amphictyons (§§ 197–199) are clearly unhistorical,
for they implicitly exclude all mention of the extraordinary meeting
attended by all the Amphictyons except Athens and Thebes, of the
attempt at an Amphictyonic execution on the part of the states which
attended, as well as of its temporary success (Ae. §§ 128, 129).   We
should really gain nothing by supposing that the first decree was passed
at the spring Pylaea of 340–39, and the second at the spring Pylaea of
339–38, except to reduce the time between the occupation of Elatea and
the battle of Chaeroneia to about fifty days, which is insufficient for the
events, even if the name of the 'winter battle' did not suggest a strong
presumption in favour of a winter campaign, and to make us ask how
both could have been passed ἐπὶ ἱερέως Κλειναγόρου.   The impression that
the decrees give, taken by themselves, is, that the writer believed that at
the spring Pylaea, at the instigation of Aeschines, the Amphictyons
decided to beat the bounds of the Cirrhaean plain, and that, being interrupted by force, they at once decided to call in Philip.   On the whole,
there is no reason to attempt to read the history into these decrees,

which give a story complete in itself. If there were any reason for thinking them authentic, it might be possible to explain σύνεδροις, by supposing that there were members of the synod whose representatives were not called ἱερομνήμονες. It is just possible that the sixteenth of Anthesterion (§ 200) might be a correct date for the election of Aeschines as Pylagorus, if we assume that he was appointed for the spring Pylaea, though the course of the Attic year from summer to summer, and Philip's Scythian expedition, which seems to come immediately after the relief of Byzantium, in the summer of 340 B.C., would seem to indicate that he entered office in time for the autumn *Pylaea*.

Philip's letter to his allies in Peloponnesus, is dated at least eleven months before the battle of Chaeroneia, and therefore is not in harmony with the chronology of the Amphictyonic or Attic decrees which precede and follow it. The date seems a little early, if we suppose it to be after the occupation of Elatea, which has been inferred from the words of Demosthenes (§ 201), ὡς οὐχ ὑπήκουον οἱ Θηβαῖοι; but the occupation of Elatea was itself a proof of distrust of Thebes, and it may have been justified by the refusal of Thebes to act upon a summons despatched from Pella or Pherae. The original letter must of course have specified a day by which the contingents were to join him, for it would be absurd to require a contingent to be ready for forty days' service, if the service might begin any day in the month; but if we suppose that the documents appeared in the margin before they appeared in the text, it may be supposed that details of this kind disappeared in the process of transference. As we cannot suppose that the Macedonian calendar had attained any degree of scientific precision in Philip's day, we cannot argue with any confidence, from the fact that *Lous* in the corrected cycle did not correspond with *Boedromion;* we cannot even be sure that the coincidence between the Attic and Macedonian months in the year of Alexander's death is a guide to their coincidence in the year before the battle of Chaeroneia, still less can we found anything on the indications of the scientific Macedonian calendar which came into common use under Alexander's successors.

The next group of documents (§§ 209, 210) is one of the most suspicious. Both the decrees assume that a peace, which can be no other than the peace of Philocrates, was still in existence, and that Philip had violated it by occupying Elatea and by alienating Thebes from Athens. This is not absolutely at variance with what we learn from Philochorus (Ap. Dion. ad Amm. 11), that the Athenians had already, two years or more ago, determined, upon the motion of Demosthenes, to man their ships and take down the column on which the treaty with Philip was inscribed, and to make all other preparations for carrying on active hostilities. This measure was only one degree stronger than that which they had adopted during the peace of Nicias, on the motion of Alcibiades, when the Spartans had moved a body of troops by sea. Then they had left the column on which the treaty was engraved standing, and had only appended a statement that the Spartans had not observed it, after which formality they invaded Laconia without scruple. At the same time the Spartans considered that the treaty still existed, though each side might accuse the other of violating it, and therefore they held themselves bound to preface the expedition of Gylippus and the occupation of Decelea, with a formal declaration of hostilities. International morality had not improved in the interval; besides, the Spartans had certainly kept the peace of Nicias better than Philip kept the peace of Philocrates, and the Athenians had reason to keep the peace of Nicias, while the influence of Demosthenes and other anti-Macedonian speakers, if less commanding than that of Alcibiades, was much more steadily exerted. The form of the decree, as given by Philochorus, almost excludes the belief that the assembly voted unmistakably and irrevocably to go to war; neither in the speech on the Chersonesus, nor in the Third Philippic, does Demosthenes himself demand such a vote, he only insists that as, without their choice, they are engaged in hostilities, the only thing to be done is to prosecute them with vigour. It is obvious that, if a declaration of war was not voted, the object of such a curious piece of reserve must have been to claim the benefits of the treaty, and reproach Philip with its violation whenever Attica was in actual danger, as was certainly the case after the occupation of Elatea. But according to Philip's letter, he appointed a *rendezvous* in Phocis for Boedromion, according to the decree. Six months after, the senate and generals discover, for the first time, that 'he has occupied some cities in the neighbourhood, and is sacking others' (of course the decree means, 'is ravaging their territory'). Elatea is clearly intended by the cities which he has occupied, though it is difficult to see how either Elatea or even Chaeroneia, which was three days' march from Athens, could be called πόλις τῶν ἀστυγειτόνων. Hereupon, they propose to request Philip to grant *the* suspension of hostilities until Thargelion (was a suspension of hostilities stipulated by the peace of Philocrates?), in order that the people may have time to deliberate. Then we have the names of three ambassadors chosen from the senate; the name of the deme of one of them is misspelt, which, in combination with the date, makes the correctness of the decree quite inconceivable. There is hardly a motive for defending its substance, though it might be defended if it stood alone. But the next decree, without any reference to its predecessors, asks again for the suspension of hostilities for the same reason. It is dated five clear weeks later, so that if Heropythus were the clerk of the prytany, the first decree must have been passed on his first day of office, and the second on the last,—a curious coincidence; but, without troubling ourselves about Heropythus, we may observe that the Athenians had had time to deliberate, and that it was strange if they were so panic-struck as the decree suggests, that they waited till the very last day of the armistice to ask its renewal from an enemy at least three days distant. Again, Thebes was certainly an ally of Philip, who was at war with Athens; what does the decree mean by saying he adds yet this (above all his other wickedness), ' to set Thebes at variance with Athens?' The words καὶ γὰρ νῦν οὐ κέκρικε βοηθεῖν ἐν οὐδενὶ τῶν μετρίων prove that the writer of the decree supposed Athens to have been at peace with Philip, at least in continental Greece, up to the passing of the decree. Consequently it is no use to try to find a place for these decrees after Philip had escaped by the stratagem recorded by Polyaenus (Strat. 4. 28) from Parapotamia, and forced his way into the country of Amphissa and destroyed the body of mercenaries detached to defend it, after which he seems to have offered to treat separately with Thebes, and apparently with Athens. Even if they did not assume that Athens was technically and practically at peace, they would be incompatible with what Aeschines, who must have quoted the first decree if it had been passed then, says (§§ 141-151) of the uninterrupted domination of Demosthenes up to the battle of Chaeroneia, and with Demosthenes' own account of the sustained and unanimous enthusiasm of the people. The chronology of the Amphictyonic documents and of these decrees, is perfectly coherent as it stands. On the sixteenth of Anthesterion, Aeschines is elected Pylagorus; without loss of time he procures the election of Philip as general of the Amphictyons. Towards the end of Elaphebolion the Athenians begin to be alarmed, and ask an armistice. At the end of Munychion they ask to have it renewed. In Scirrophorion hostilities begin, and everything was over we know in Metageitnion. It is hardly worth while to wonder why the ambassadors chosen from the senate are distinguished by the names of their fathers, while the herald is designated in the proper form by his deme, or why we are told that he was chosen from the people. If Philip's reply, which fits either decree equally well or ill, fitted the history, we might pass over Θετταλοὺς καὶ Θηβαίους, ἔτι δὲ καὶ Βοιωτούς. Among the anti-Macedonian party at Athens, there would be many who, not satisfied with weaning Thebes from Philip, would have preferred to rouse Boeotia against Thebes. But the writer attributes the abject decree or decrees to which he replies, to the failure of an attempt made (clearly after the capture of Elatea) to alienate Boeotia and Thessaly: for such a failure there is no room in the history. The astounding demand with which the letter closes, that the Athenians shall disfranchise their bad advisers and send them along to Philip, is a clumsy copy of the demand for the extradition of the anti-Macedonian orators after Alexander's capture of Thebes. We cannot say that the reply to the Thebans may not contain the substance of a despatch in which Philip congratulated them on having repulsed some advances of the Athenians, of which we know nothing, except that they were made, if at all, before he occupied Elatea.

It is, of course, conceivable that Demosthenes should have thought it desirable to reply to this menacing act by a formal declaration of war, and such a declaration, if it was to be made at all, after being withheld so long, might reasonably take the form of a rhetorical indictment of Philip, such as we read §§ 232–239. Though rambling, the document is not wholly unemphatic or ineffective, and its discursiveness might be defended on the ground that in a hurried decree, intended to remove a prevailing panic, every available topic had to be introduced. We seem to have the decree very much as its author, whoever he was, left it. It is very tolerably correct in point of form, for διὸ δέδοκται, instead of δέδοχθαι, is a natural result of its being very rhetorical and very long. These considerations make the date assigned unusually important, for one cannot suppose that it was added by the compiler on the strength of an opinion derived from one source, while the substance of the decree might be derived from a better, or simply because he wished to give his work a factitious appearance of completeness. The date given is the sixteenth of Scirrophorion, fifty days before the battle, and more than six weeks after the last decree as given by the compiler. Thus the date suits neither Philip's letter to the Peloponnesians nor the Athenian decrees, as we read them, nor the chronology which is suggested by independent authorities. And the date is not the only difficulty. Who is *the* general and *the* admiral and *the* commandant of cavalry, and why is a squadron sent to Pylae when Philip is at Elatea? It would be possible to get over the date and the fleet sent to Pylae, by supposing that the decree really refers to the time of Philip's advance on Attica at the time of the deliverance of Euboea, which was disconcerted by the energetic action of Athens, and apparently of Callias, her new ally in the Pagasaean gulf. But then we should come into collision with Demosthenes' emphatic boast (§ 304), that he never returned unsuccessful from a single encounter with the ambassadors of Philip, though this would hardly be a fatal objection to the authenticity of a document which appeared in better company.

The result of the whole examination is, that out of all the documents inserted in the speech, only one is unmistakably genuine, while another is unobjectionable. We have now to try to ascertain how the rest arose. We may dismiss the hypothesis that somebody sat down to give a fictitious value to his copy of the speech, by inserting the documents out of his own head, without any materials at all. In the first place he had at least two documents before him, the Byzantine decree and the trisected note on the trierarchic law. Again, though a forger might not have taken the trouble to learn the proper form of Attic decrees, he would have tried to save himself trouble by always using the same, so that the endless variations which we find is a proof of, at least, the qualified good faith of the compiler, as well as of his defective information. Again, though a forger might have been too lazy to invent all the documents which the text required, those which he did invent would be obtrusively appropriate to the context. The person who inserted the halting documents which we read, especially §§ 209–216, was not nearly clever enough to think of making his insertions more credible by their remote yet visible appropriateness. Besides, to make the correspondence about the vessels seized by Philip's admiral close with Philip's offer of restitution, is so plainly inappropriate, that we can imagine nobody inserting it except in good faith. Lastly, the decree of Callisthenes, those in honour of Nausicles and Charidemus, and the decree of Eubulus, and Philip's letter in reply, contain facts and details which are intrinsically credible and look historical, and are certainly not derived from the text.

If all the decrees were like that which is given as carried by Demosthenes in the tumultuary assembly, held when the news came that Philip had occupied Elatea, there would be much plausibility in Droysen's theory, that the decrees at any rate are old school exercises, and in this way we should be able to adopt the only satisfactory explanation of the pseudeponymous archons : we should be able to suppose that they were invented *pro formâ*, which is more than we can believe of a forger, for why did he not look in Philochorus? But we cannot imagine a sophist setting his pupils to compose such shambling stuff as most of the decrees, or neglecting to tear it up if they did compose it; besides, if they did set their pupils to exercises of this kind (which cannot be inferred from Demetrius Phalereus' μεταποιήσεις Δημοσθενικῶν χωρίων, the only authority Droysen cites), the only conceivable benefit of such an exercise would be that the pupil learnt how to draft decrees correctly and showily against he came to take part in the parish politics, which still continued to excite the routine ambition of Greek statesmen. But the majority of the decrees are neither showy nor correct.

It may be doubted whether it is worth while to put forward any theory on an obscure and unimportant question, but the following hypothesis, so far as it goes, explains the facts. Somebody, who had a general inaccurate acquaintance with the history of the period, lectured upon the Oration, and illustrated it as well as he could, and gave a sort of descriptive

sketch of the substance of any documents that he knew of from
hearsay or from reading, or perhaps a copy of an inscription which
he had seen in his native town.   One of his pupils took notes of these
illustrations on the margin of his copy of the speech.   Afterwards this
pupil, or a person who inherited his manuscript, transferred the notes,
with due formality, to the text.   We certainly have one note of this kind
(§§ 132–134).   It is hard to believe that we have not another (§§ 66–68),
ἀπήνεγκε . . γραφὴν and ὡς ἄρα, which are suspicious in a *soi-disant* official
paper, are perfectly in place in an account of one; and the parenthesis
ἔστι . . τεταγμένος is rather too explanatory to be official.   In § 90 we
have the explanatory ὡς ἄρα again, and the anacolutha of the next section
are just what we might expect in notes of an oral lecture, and the peri-
phrastic blundering with which each decree opens, never twice alike, is
just what we should expect from a man who wished to convey that
generals and prytanes and senators had a good deal to do with public
business, without himself well knowing what that was.   If the lecturer we
are supposing was no better than even the better kind of scholiast, he
was quite capable of stopping to tell his pupils something about the
Dionysiac law, which they might have learnt as well or better from the
text.   This theory would explain what wants explaining most—the substance of the decrees.   One might possibly suppose that the archons are
really the authorities from whom the lecturer got his information in each
case; we know that Hermippus found some notes of an unknown author
and founded an important statement upon them, which gives us a glimpse
of a wide circle of obscure activity.   It is certain that the person who
trisected the note on the trierarchical reform, was not too scrupulous to
dress up his text with names that were wanting in his original.   He may
of course have looked through the collection of Craterus, if it was arranged as Boeckh supposes, and got the names of the prytany clerks for
his pains; but, upon the whole, it is perhaps as likely that he trusted to
invention, except for two or three decrees which he thought fell in the
year of Chaeroneia, and so dated by Chaerondas.   This leaves the long
decree of Demosthenes unaccounted for, as well as the two depositions.
The long decree might fairly be explained on Droysen's theory, and it
may fairly be a question whether the two decrees passed ἐπὶ 'Ηροπύθου are
not really two forms, not of the same rhetorical exercise, but of the same
subject for one.   The contrast in both, between the preamble and the
enactment, is ridiculous in a decree, but would be quite in place if the
preamble was simply a summary of the situation for the benefit of the
pupil, who was to draw up a speech in the character of a dignified
member of the peace party, and conclude with the practical provisions of
the decree.   With regard to the depositions, we have to choose between

the theory of their being jotted down at a very early period from adequate knowledge, by some person who could have explained the puzzling
note about Nicias, and that of their being invented. Perhaps Philip's
letters are too numerous and too inaccurate to be taken even from careless histories, and the last compiler may have borrowed them from a
work by the author of the letters of Phalaris.

The documents, as we have them, were used by Plutarch and by the
author whose notes on the lives of the Ten Orators have come down to
us under his name; they were not used by Dionysius, but we cannot
infer that they did not yet exist, for Dionysius always follows the recension represented by the Augsburg MSS., which never admitted more
than the first six of the documents, and probably in his time had not
admitted any.

G. A. S.

PRESENT STATE OF THE TEXT OF THE
TWO ORATIONS ON THE CROWN.

UPON most questions of ancient criticism the evidence is either conflicting or inadequate. In the latter case, the student has the consolation
of reflecting that an author who was neglected in antiquity is not likely
to have been wilfully tampered with; but, where ancient criticism has
been busy with the author, it is impossible to escape from the suspicion
that our MSS. represent, in the last resort, the text of men whose
opinions of what ought to have been, coloured their testimony to what
was. When we remember that whole passages have been retrenched
from the text of Demosthenes on purely aesthetic grounds, this suspicion
rises to certainty. In one sense it is a more hopeless enterprise to
restore the text of an orator than to restore the text of any other writer
except one. No one thinks it possible so to edit Homer, as to reproduce
the verses recited by the author or authors in their original form : it
would be enough for any man, if he could restore the text as Herodotus
or Plato read it, or even if he could replace the problem of its reconstruction in the state in which it lay before Aristarchus. And in the
same way, it is at least a question whether we are to propose to ourselves
the verbal reproduction of the 'Battle of the Orators,' as it was heard in
the law-court, or at least as it was fought over again ἐν τῇ τῶν μειρακίων
διατριβῇ at Rhodes or at Athens, in presence of the original combatants ;
or whether we can go further than the days when an unreal rhetoric had
become a science, and when the orators whose rhetoric had real objects
were sunk into text-books.

For thus much is certain—many of the various readings of our present
text of the orators can be proved to be as old as the Christian era. A
scholar like Cicero or Pliny, a critic like Dionysius of Halicarnassus had

means for ascertaining the best text of Demosthenes or Aeschines which we have not ; but it does not follow that they always used to the full the means at their disposal, and, even if they did, they still had a critical task to execute, one differing from that before us in extent rather than in kind. This will appear, if we reason backwards from the inherited evidence as to the text of our authors now in existence, and compare this with the descriptions or notices of the case as it stood between the first and fifth centuries, which are preserved to us by authorities of that period.

And here we must of course defer the question, whether citations in these writers themselves are to be taken as certainly accurate, when made deliberately ; for this is, in effect, the very point to be determined. Keeping for the present to extant MSS., there are in each of the Orations[1] three more or less well-marked groups or families, traceable, as we shall find, in the last resort, to as many tolerably ancient recensions of the text. The value, however, both absolute and comparative, of the present representatives of the three classes, is very different in the case of the two speeches. Of Aeschines there are few MSS.—apparently only one as yet known or collated, f or F^2 at Paris—as old as the tenth century ; two or three, including it appears one good one, of the thirteenth ; the majority, of all classes, being as late as the fifteenth. The first and, in the judgment of most editors, the best group includes four or five of Bekker's MSS. (*abgmn*), p, the 'Helmstadiensis,' which Reiske admired enthusiastically, z, at Moscow, collated by Hess, and three first used by Schultz, the 'Vatican, Laurentian, and Florentine,' as he calls them : the first he considers ought to displace a in the rank of highest single authority to the text of this recension. (There are one or two other less important MSS. of this family.)

The superiority of a, acknowledged apparently by Bekker, and certainly by Baiter and Sauppe, seems to lie rather in the superiority of its archetype than in any superior intelligence of its scribe. Errors that can plainly be traced to inattention to sense or misapprehension of the sense, and sentences utterly nonsensical or ungrammatical, are rather commoner in it than in the other members of the family. (Not to mention merely clerical errors so obvious as not to require notice, see the critical notes at p. 51, l. 15, p. 52, l. 6, p. 92, l. 3, where, however, he had the excuse of dealing with a passage already corrupt or confused, p. 93, l. 13, p. 103, l. 15, p. 117, l. 10.) Of the rest, g appears to be the best of those at Paris, which are the only ones we have been able to consult personally ; and these having

---

[1] Most of these MSS. include other orations of the same authors ; but it is not necessary to go into details on this subject. Many contain other rhetorical works as well.

[2] The former is the sign used by Bekker and most editors who used his collation ; the latter that adopted by Cobet and Schultz.

all been collated by Bekker, there was no very important work to be done. Nevertheless, it still seems worth while for anyone who has opportunity to re-collate one or two of his MSS., as, out of the vast number that he used, it is nearly certain that in each taken singly a few errors will be discovered, chiefly omissions, or (as at §§ 107, 167, 182, of this speech) identical reports of similar but not identical readings. Slight as our own labour in this matter was, we hope it has not been wholly unfruitful: in § 167, Θετταλίαν seems a reading at least worth recording; and in § 182, κἀκείνῳ γε we believe to be right, as it accounts for the meaningless κἀκεῖνό γε of the kindred MSS.

Of the next group, the chief member is F or *f*, already mentioned; *cdh* also, among Bekker's MSS., belong to it, and *q*, Taylor's and Reiske's 'Meadianus.' The Aldine edition also appears to have been prepared from MSS. of this family: and other members have been added to it by Schultz's collations. These MSS. form for the most part a well-defined group closely akin to one another: *d* is almost identical with *f* throughout, *c* in this oration at least, and *hq*, according to Schultz, in the Timarchus, the text of which seems to be in a more satisfactory state than that of the two more interesting Orations. In it, however, there is a wider divergence than in them between this group and the first.

To the third class belong only three or four of Bekker's MSS.; *ek* throughout, *l* in the whole and *h* in part of this Oration. In the Timarchus, *l* agrees with the first group and *h*, as already noticed, with the second. The latter bears, in fact, an intermediate character between the two. According to Schultz, it belongs unmistakably to the second class in the Timarchus, but passes gradually into the third in the course of the other two Orations. Using Bekker's collation, we should rather have said that it agreed with the second class generally, though not universally, in the Embassy, and almost universally in about the first 112 chapters of the Ctesiphon, while during the remainder of the latter speech, it varies as little from *ekl* as these do from each other. We looked at it at Paris, and inclined to the opinion that its peculiarities are the result of a careful and not wholly unintelligent collation of two or more MSS., representing both families. We found that in the earlier part, while the text is generally in harmony with *f* (almost always, except where the reading of *ekl* has some real attraction), the readings of the other group are either inserted as corrections in the text (words or letters that are to be omitted being underlined) or noticed in the margin, in a differently coloured ink to the original, and in a different but contemporary hand. These corrections are rarely noticed by Bekker, but we thought their presence or absence worth recording, as they probably represent the text of a MS. not now known, of the third family; so we have given all that we found in the part of the speech collated by us. Unfortunately, we had only time to go through the first 105 chapters, so that we just missed seeing whether a change of handwriting accompanies the change of affinity; but I believe not, as Bekker notices such a change where it does occur in *e*, and we looked at a few doubtful passages further on, without being struck by it. The scribe of this MS. was a little overfond of displaying school-boyish learning, and in quotations (see §§ 135, 186) he or his archetype copied direct from the received text of the author quoted, instead of giving the text as Aeschines used it, or was recorded to have used it. But, on the whole, our opinion of this MS. individually was rather raised by our personal examination; and as the general question of the comparative value of the classes between which it fluctuates is disputed by the best authorities, any information on the subject may be worth giving. Bekker seems to have regarded *ekl* as the best authorities for at least the earlier part of this Oration, and Cobet considers *hekls* (*s* being a cognate MS., only as yet collated for the speech on the Embassy) the best of any, not noticing, as Schultz complains, the varying affinity of the first named. Most editors in between have pronounced this group the worst of the three, *f* being worthy of respectful consideration, though not perhaps as good as *a* and its congeners.—One circumstance remarked on by Schultz seems to point to an early connection between the two latter recensions: in § 20 of this speech, the corrupt passage is omitted by *fdq hekl* and two of his new MSS. of the second family. Schultz adds to these three families of MSS. a fourth, which appears to be a sort of refuge for the destitute, whose readings are either corrections of grammarians, or, if traditional, are drawn from such various sources as to defy classification. He refers to it *p* and *c* (but not *h*) among the MSS. above named, and the former has indeed almost as much resemblance to the third class as to the first : in the other case, we failed to see that the facts support the arrangement. And the triple division seems on the whole simpler.

None of these MSS., however, bears a high individual character, or can be regarded as more than one instrument among others for getting indirectly the text of an old recension. With Demosthenes the case is different. The question for the critic is not on what principle we are to choose between the variants of a few bad MSS., or what scope the fact of their variation leaves for conjectural emendation, so much as what amount of authority is to be given to the best of a few good ones. As with Aeschines, we have three recensions to choose between; but each of them has much older and worthier representatives.

The first group of MSS., if it may be called so, consists only of one member, the famous Codex S, or Σ^1, a tenth-century MS. at Paris, which

---

[1] The former symbol was used in the Oxford edition of Bekker's Attic Orators ; in the

is admitted on all hands to be the best extant. It was used to some extent, very carelessly it is said, by Auger in 1790; but was never collated throughout, nor its importance recognised, before Bekker, who employed it largely in preparing the text of his edition of the Attic Orators. Since then, it has been collated again by Dübner for Dindorf's edition of Demosthenes, and, according to the latter's preface (in the third Leipzig edition), it has been consulted by others since, without anything of value being added to his own observations. In view of these authorities as to the readings of the MS., we did not think it necessary to attempt a formal collation ourselves; but, as the precise degree of authority to be given to it is the chief open question about the text of Demosthenes, we visited Paris in August, 1870, with the hope of being better able to form a personal opinion about it, and, rather to our surprise, we observed some ten readings (§§ 26, 64, 88, 314, 321, 324, 342, 383, 385, 386) either unnoticed or not quite accurately reported, by Dübner or Dindorf, as well as by Bekker. Possibly some of these may have been mentioned by the revisers ridiculed by Dindorf; but three or four seem not unimportant, and it appears worth while to indicate them all. But our visit to the Imperial Library (as it then was) was ill-timed: for obvious reasons, we left Paris on the 2nd of September, before we had examined a few points where the reading of the MSS. wants elucidation. (See on §§ 79, 172.)

Our inspection of Σ did not tend to raise our opinion of it, which, from its recorded readings, we had been disposed to place as low as any good authority would place it. Purely phonetic blunders (the confusion of αι and ε is the commonest) are very frequent; but, as this is so in all MSS., it is never held to detract greatly from the value of any one. Only when we come to the question of the omissions of words, which most editors regard as accidental, but Baiter and Sauppe, apparently, as the most valuable part of the whole, these seem to assume a different character, when it is seen that the duties of the scribe were less carefully discharged than those of the editor. And, while it is beyond dispute that Σ either is itself the product of a careful edition, or is a transcript of an archetype that was so, we get indications that the editor indulged in conjectures for which he had no authority whatever, so that his work, as we have it, is not to be received as altogether a faithful reproduction of the best tradition as to the text. This opinion was pronounced by Mr. Shilleto in the preface to his edition of the De Falsa Legatione; and we thought it the

preface to Reimer's reprint of it at Berlin in 1823, it is stated that the notation there used, with Greek instead of Roman capitals, was preferred by Bekker himself. At any rate, it has been generally adopted by continental editors, and we have followed it, as perhaps less confusing to the eye.

likeliest way of accounting for certain variations from the common text, which several editors have inclined to accept. Especially in § 41, the insertion of *εἰ* is more easily accounted for, as a tempting way to get out of an involved sentence and a construction not understood, than its omission in all other MSS. can be, supposing it to be genuine.

No one, indeed, is likely to blame us for not having followed this MS. as blindly as the Zurich editors[1]. It is scarcely credible that they conceived their 'tender passion,' as Mr. Shilleto calls it, under the same unfavourable conditions as Don Quixote or Juvenal's Catullus, though in every case they reproduce, and in many adopt in their text, the errors of Bekker's collation[2]. But they were certainly 'to her faults a little blind,' as well as 'to her virtues more than kind;' they have failed to notice, or to attribute importance to, plain marks of carelessness or hesitation, and have ignored the existence, pointed out by Dindorf, of marks of correction and transposition of words, by the original writer, which shew that he did not intentionally deviate from the common text.

Further, it seems doubtful whether they are right in confining their exclusive honour to the text as it came from the 'first hand.' The original editor was, in all likelihood, a more learned and careful grammarian than even the first corrector; but these corrections, not being as frequent as the variations of Σ from the general text, seem to imply a collation in the eleventh century with another MS. of the same family, and this is an aid not to be despised. It is true, indeed, that Baiter and Sauppe suggest in their preface that the Ϙ (διορθωταί) subscribed to most of the Orations does not apply to Σ itself, but to its archetype, and there seems no doubt that the sign is often thus servilely reproduced; but Dindorf notices that the sign is discontinued simultaneously with the notes of the 'second hand,' and this may fairly be held to prove that it refers to his collation. On this hypothesis, where the peculiar readings of 'pr. Σ' are corrected by his successor into conformity with the vulgate, we may surmise that his reading, if not an accidental slip, still does not represent an authentic tradition of the best MSS., but (whether right or wrong) a conjecture or crotchet of the editor.

Of the second family, the best MSS. are F in the library of St. Mark at Venice, first collated by Bekker, and B at Munich, where it was used by Reiske. These have been compared by Dindorf, and pronounced to be

---

[1] We quote them, in remarks on the text, as 'B. and S.' The common notation 'Edd. Turic.' is rather confusing, while to cite the work as Sauppe's is unjust to his *collaborateur*. We only do so in the case of notes bearing his signature.

[2] Dindorf delicately alludes to them in his preface: 'Non defuerunt qui aliquammultas, quae Codici Parisino S per errorem tributae erant, lectiones falsa auctoritatis specie decepti pro veris amplecterentur, excusabili quidem errore, sed errore tamen.'

practically identical, and in consequence B, the later in date of the two (it is of the thirteenth century, the other of the eleventh), is rarely cited in recent editions, except for its notes or marginal readings, which seem to establish that it is not a mere apograph of the other. This being so, the close agreement of the two is an evidence of the care with which both were transcribed, and so of their substantial fidelity to the older text which they represent. We thus have fair means of ascertaining the genuine text (if it can be called so) of a second recension or edition of Demosthenes; not so old nor so accurate as that for which Σ is our sole entire authority, but perhaps more accurately reported to us, since we have several other MSS. (Φ *opqtuv* among Bekker's) by which to check or correct the casual blunders of F, B, or their common archetype. Before Bekker called attention to the superior claims of Σ, the common text of Demosthenes, from Aldus to Reiske, seems to have been based upon this group critically or uncritically used. The Aldine editions were printed from three not very good MSS. belonging to it, and it is probable that it had been the vulgate text of the Byzantine period generally. This accounts for its being far less of a united group, with readings uniform except by accident, than e.g. the third family of Codices of Demosthenes, or either of the three families of Aeschines. Not only do the MSS. above named vary a good deal among themselves, but there is a separate group (ΥΩΠ: the last does not contain this Oration) which are reckoned to belong to this family, but approach more closely to the readings of Σ than does its general type. Dindorf, in his last edition, reckons one of these MSS. (Υ, in the great Paris library: one knows not how to speak of it more accurately, when the title changes with every revolution) as one of the 'principes secundae classis,' co-ordinate with F and B.

Of the third family, the best and oldest member is A, again of the eleventh century, the 'Augustanus primus' of Reiske, who admired it highly, now at Munich like B. It was collated, very ill by all accounts, for Jerome Wolf, and next by the Reiskes,—for Ernestine's share in her husband's work ought not to be ignored, though prejudiced people may be inclined to suggest that the inaccuracies complained of by later editors in his collations are characteristic of ladies' Greek. Dindorf collated it again, distinguishing, for the first time, he says, the original text from corrections or cited variants, and his collation is here followed. The other (Bekkerian) members of the class are *krs*, all at Paris; of these, *s* is said by Dindorf to have most distinctive character, having some readings in common with Σ, while *kr* are of little more use than if they were apographs of A. Such may be generally the case throughout the whole works of Demosthenes; but, so far as there is any difference traceable among the readings reported from them in this speech, it is usually A *ks* that agree, while *r* not infrequently varies toward the common type, that represented by FΥ and their companions. We have not thought it worth while to notice the minor variations of these copies, for they all are so closely related that their use is as testimonies, rarely discordant, to a common archetypal recension: and where it is plain what the reading of this was, we quote the MSS. representing it as ' A et socii.' This recension seems to have been a careful and scholarly one, sometimes a little over scholarly, falling (in a far less degree) into the habits of over-refinement noted in the third group of the Aeschinean MSS. One mannerism curiously common to both, is the tendency to substitute perfects for aorists in the verb γίγνομαι, γεγενῆσθαι for γενέσθαι, etc. A more important point is their tendency to omit the inserted documents, for which see the Excursus on that subject ad fin.

With *adminicula* as plentiful and of as high quality as these, the text of Demosthenes may be considered as in a tolerably satisfactory state; that is, there are hardly any passages that we are obliged to give up as hopelessly corrupt. We always have the choice between possible readings, and generally have no inducement to choose between them, otherwise than according to the preponderance of MS. authority. But when does MS. authority preponderate? If Σ has a reading peculiar to itself, the other known MSS. all agreeing against it, which is to be preferred? The answer to this question will vary with the character of the reading. Hardly anyone will defend the fanatical devotion with which Baiter and Sauppe follow their favourite MS., heroically regardless of grammatical harshness and of inferiority in style, and quite indifferent to the unanimous opposition of both the independent families of MSS. But where either reading is tolerable, both perhaps equally attractive, or the choice between them absolutely indifferent, as happens with the larger number of various readings in most authors—where, in fact, MS. authority is the sole consideration to determine between them—then the practical question arises, is the authority of Σ to prevail over all the others?

It seems to have been the general tendency of English editors to hold that it does not, of German that it does; and our judgment, for what it is worth, follows that of our countrymen. In a case where considerations of taste, style, or Greek idiom furnished no argument either way, our principle has been somewhat as follows. Where Σ was supported by a tolerably unanimous consent of *either* of the other groups of MSS., we have followed their consent without much hesitation, even when such believers in Σ as Bekker and Dindorf[1] failed to afford us their authority.

---

[1] Dindorf's opinion of the *absolute* merit of this MS. does not seem to have varied much since his earliest edition; but in the later ones he professes to have used it more and more as the paramount authority, as compared with our other copies.

Where Σ stood alone against both the other groups, we considered that they were superior, so far as authority went, the chance being considerable that the variation of Σ was either a blunder or a conjecture, and the presumption being in favour of the majority of witnesses, though liable, in any individual passage, to be set aside upon consideration of the merits of the case.

But, in fact, it is scarcely possible to settle this question by mere discussion of the comparative merits of extant MSS. Those who rate Σ most highly, do so less on the ground that it is a very ‘good’ MS., than in accordance with a theory as to the history of the text—that at some time, long anterior to the date of any extant copy, the text of the Orators underwent considerable corruption, but that side by side with the corrupt text, a tradition of a pure critical one was preserved, which has reached us only through this one channel. We have, therefore, to examine the detached notices we can find as to the state of the text in ancient times : if these appear to support the hypothesis of one correct recension co-existing with other corrupt ones, there is no doubt much to be said for the view that Σ is the representative of the one, and our other MSS. of the others. Much cannot be built upon the fact of the notes of the number of lines in which each speech was written in some original copy : these numbers are found in Σ and several others, so that they prove nothing as to Σ representing a purer tradition than they ; while, according to Dindorf, instead of proving that the common text is interpolated, they agree with the *proportionate* lengths of the speeches, as we have them, so closely that one can calculate what ratio a page of the original MS. bore to a page of Reiske. We therefore are thrown back upon the testimony of classical and Byzantine writers, as to the state of the text in their time; and, having ascertained this, we must use it, as far as possible, to explain the phenomena of the text in ours.

But of course there are differences as to the degree of weight to be given to the testimony of ancient authors. In the first place, we must distinguish between the passing quotation of a writer of general literature, and the deliberate citation of a passage by a grammarian : in the former, a familiar and uncritical text may be followed unthinkingly, while the latter is likely to give the form of words which he knew or believed to be right. Thus, though we get quotations enough from Demosthenes in Roman authors from Cicero downwards, these are of no great importance compared with professed rhetoricians or grammarians, even of much later date. And of these, the most important, for light thrown upon the text of our Orators, are Dionysius of Halicarnassus, Hermogenes of Tarsus—a precocious youth of the age of the Antonines, who, between his seventeenth and twenty-fifth year, earned the reputation of the first rhetorician of his day, when his overtasked brain gave way, and he became insane for the remainder of his life—and Harpocration, a lexicographer of uncertain age, but whose date is held to be fixed as low as the end of the fourth century, by certain references to Athenaeus.

But, even with these writers, we must draw a further distinction. We should suppose that a rhetorician, critic, or grammarian, when he made verbal citations from the author he was discussing, would take care not to speak without book: we can scarcely conceive that he should venture to write on an author, without having the text of that author before him. But it is hard for us to form any notion, except by analogy, of all that the accepted models of oratory were to a Greek rhetorician. Among us it is practically forgotten, that there is such a thing as an art, if not a science, of oratory: eloquence, if it ever exists among us, either springs up by nature or is cultivated quite empirically. But men of culture in our time are familiar with the conception of a science of poetical criticism; and the science of theology is also commonly understood to involve the critical knowledge and use of a certain literary text. Now, what aesthetic philosophers do with poets, and theologians or preachers with the Bible, we may not be surprised to find Greek rhetoricians doing with Greek orators; and the citations made by either of these classes of men are untrustworthy, because their familiarity with the works they use enables them to quote from memory in writing, just as they would in conversation. No one would alter a reading of the Vatican MS. of the Septuagint, merely because the text was quoted with some variation by St. Paul or St. Chrysostom; or—to come at once to our own time, and to the rare case of a modern author whose text is confessedly corrupt—who would substitute 'lips' for 'limbs' in the stanza from Shelley's 'Prometheus Unbound,' quoted in 'Modern Painters,' Part III. sec. 2, c. 3, § 7? Yet this is quoted deliberately as an example of the imaginative way of regarding the human *lip*, the author having confused in his memory this stanza with the next, which is really about lips, but having felt confidence enough in his recollection of the passage to write it as he remembered it, without the trouble of verification. And Mr. Ruskin is more of a poet than Dionysius was of an orator, and so may be credited with more sympathy for his author, and at least equal apprehension of his meaning.

Now, as to Dionysius at least, the evidence is very strong that his quotations from Demosthenes are made in this manner. The passage paraphrased from Plato's Symposium (Dion. Ars Rhet. p. 340), shews he did not mind giving the form of quotation to what he must have known to be paraphrase: with an author like Demosthenes, whom he knew by heart, the temptation to paraphrase would be less, the readiness to write from memory greater. When he quotes (De Comp. Verb. p. 47) the climax from § 130, οὐκ εἶπον μὲν ταῦτα κ.τ.λ., it is no wonder that he should remember accurately so short a passage, and of such marked character ; but he forgets the exact context in which it occurs, and so introduces it with a καί, which he clearly means as part of his quotation, but which it is as clearly impossible for us to suppose to have formed part of any possible text. Again, he twice in the same work (Ars Rhet. pp. 286, 350) quotes a passage from § 229, with one or two slight variations of the text, which serve to shew that he did not look at his book, but knew his lesson very well; but in one of these places he goes on further than he remembered the words, and gives the sense, as in the Plato, by a complete paraphrase. Again, in the 'De Admir. vi dic. in Dem.' p. 1126, where he quotes Aesch. in Ctes. § 166, it is plain from the καί inserted by him, that he does not intend to quote verbatim ; but it is probably unconsciously that he blends into one the two clauses, ἀνατετμήκασί τινες τὰ κλήματα τοῦ δήμου and ὑποτέτμηται τὰ νεῦρα τῶν πραγμάτων, in much the same way as Ruskin, in the passage cited, did to the two consecutive stanzas of Shelley.

Yet, though we cannot accept Dionysius' quotations as verbally accurate, and can least of all build anything on his omissions, it does not follow that he throws no light on the state of the text. In the first place, a paraphrase may illustrate the sense of a passage better than a transcription; in § 166, just cited, though we attach no importance to his omissions, we may to his punctuation, for he doubtless carried the sense of the passage correctly in his head, and is therefore a good authority for connecting ἐπὶ τὰ στενά with what follows, rather than with φορμορραφούμεθα. And more than this, though we cannot stake anything on the accuracy of his memory, it yet may be possible to decide what text it was that he had learnt by heart, in general outline, though not in detail. In this same passage he reads ἐκεῖνοι, not κείνων or ἐκείνων ; the fact that he retains instead of eliding the initial vowel, may be considered accidental, but his use of the nominative cannot. In this matter he agrees with one well-marked group (the third, A and its companions) of the extant MSS. ; and it is held to be established, that Dionysius does represent a text belonging to this family. With this agrees the fact, that he appears to know nothing of the inserted documents, the omission of which is still a characteristic of these MSS.

Now, we may fairly assume that a diligent and tolerably learned writer would not use a text that found no favour with scholars; but, from the other authorities named, we find that the recension which found most favour was one that can hardly be identified with this: their testimony goes rather in support of the distinctive peculiarities of Σ. The copies of

Demosthenes, and of Aeschines at least among the other orators, which
were thought most highly of by early critics, were those of one Atticus,
usually cited under the title of 'Αττικιανά. Who Atticus was does not
appear: he is mentioned by Lucian as a βιβλιογράφος, which would suggest that he bore a character half literary, half commercial—that he was
the Stephanus or Aldus of an age of manuscript. In one or two
instances[1], the 'Αττικιανά are expressly cited as differing from the common
text; and, in one case at least, the same difference exists between Σ and
the common text of extant MSS. The inference seems inevitable, that
the recension of which Σ is now the solitary specimen reaches back to
the date of Atticus' collection; and, indeed, from the internal evidence
of its excellence, we should be disposed to think it likely to be at least as
old as the Augsburg or Dionysian text.

But it does not follow that we are at once to identify the 'Αττικιανά with
the ancestors of Σ, in the sense in which we may, subject to some restrictions, identify Dionysius' copy or copies with those of A. It is not
clear that the 'Αττικιανά amounted to what we call an edition; perhaps
they were scarcely even a 'family of MSS.,' i.e. a group traceable,
mediately or immediately, to a common archetype. The first, indeed,
was a thing hardly possible in antiquity, for the different apographs of a
single MS. would of course present casual divergences greater than can
exist between different impressions from the same type. Too much,
therefore, must not be built upon the fact, that one extant MS. (B) bears
the note at the end of one Oration[2], that it was collated with *two* of
Atticus' MSS. For, at the unknown[3] period when the archetype of B
was written (and the note of course refers to the archetype, mediate or
immediate, not to B itself), it may have seemed worth while to a careful
editor to use two copies of Atticus' text, merely to eliminate casual slips
of the pen. But in another way, this note does tend to shew that the
Attician texts did not exhibit a uniform recension. We here have a
claim on the part of B to represent *an* Attician text; now we can
scarcely suppose that B and its congeners are the representatives of *the*
Attician text, to the exclusion of the far superior Σ, and if not, we must
suppose that both Σ and B, and very likely A as well, had allies, and perhaps ancestors, among the 'Αττικιανά themselves—that Atticus collected
and reproduced the MSS., of whatever family, that seemed to carry the
highest authority among those then known and accessible. Any Attician
text would represent *a* recension thought valuable by a careful critic, but

---

[1] See Dindorf's Preface, ad init.

[2] Unluckily the doubtful one, πρὸς τὴν ἐπιστολήν.

[3] F is not quoted as having the same subscription here, and therefore can hardly be the
actual archetype of B, closely as, by all accounts, the two are connected.

not all the same recension: in all probability, the three recensions that have come to us had each their representatives, and possibly some more than these. Of course variations have been multiplied and complicated, in the course of successive transcriptions by men of successively diminishing classical learning; and cross-divisions would arise, in the classification of MSS., by the transcription of an original which was itself the result of a collation, and in which the readings of one or the other complexion would figure now in the text, now in the margin. But, on the whole, it seems likely that the case is not much worse now than it has been ever since, perhaps, the death of Demochares. If we had all the MSS. collated by Atticus, or all the MSS. sent forth by him, we should have more materials for getting the best text of each of our three recensions; we should, perhaps, have a fourth or fifth that might be deserving of equal respect with any; we should be free from the errors or rash conjectures of Σ, from the merely casual errors that are common to A and its congeners, perhaps from those that are common to F, Υ, and theirs, but we should not have a single uncontroverted text of the speeches of Demosthenes and Aeschines, which everyone acknowledged as what they wrote or what they said. And now, though the task of criticism is harder, it is not hopeless. Mere blunders can be detected with comparative ease, by collation of the eccentricities of one scribe with those of another; and genuine doubtful readings are not much more numerous than they were.

It will follow from this consideration, that we cannot accept as final the authority of any single ancient writer, even though his quotations have the strongest internal evidence of being carefully and deliberately made. It is not likely that Harpocration often wrote without looking out his references, and if Hermogenes did, perhaps his enormous memory could afford to do so without risk of detection. But, though we may accept them, as we cannot accept all writers, as giving us accurately[1] the text that they used, in the belief that it was the best, still their own judgment is not infallible. They had more external means of judging right than we; but still, that which they testify to is a matter of opinion, not of fact, and we need not be afraid to revise their judgment if we see cause. The testimony of either of these writers (and even, in a far less degree, of a later grammarian or lexicographer, such as Suidas or Photius) is usually of higher authority than that of even the best of extant MSS. singly, but hardly of more authority than the *consensus* of a family of MSS. Where the differences between the families of extant

---

[1] Assuming, of course, that their own text is beyond question, which is not always the case: it often is adapted to the vulgate of the author quoted.

copies point, not to the accidents of transcription, but to the divergences of archetypes, modern scholarship has to decide by its own lights. It is an assistance to know what ancient scholars preferred, but we still have to exercise our own judgment to determine what theirs is worth.

This reasoning applies to the text of Demosthenes the more directly of our two Orators, but we may fairly conclude that the case of Aeschines is parallel—that with him also we have the choice of three recensions, not necessarily of equal degrees of authenticity, but between which there is nothing to choose on the score of mere antiquity. What a modern editor has to do is to choose between these recensions on their merits; he may thus hope to obtain a probability—certainty is out of the question—as to the words written by the original authors. It remains to enquire how far this has yet been done. If substantial unanimity had been already attained, it would be possible to give a history of the formation of the text without discussing it, and this is what we should naturally have preferred; but learners who wish to study an ancient writer intelligently, have a right to know something of the principles on which his text is fixed, as well as those on which it is interpreted.

Where questions are still open, and the highest authorities differ, it is impossible always to agree with one; and the practice of following previous editors in the text, while every now and then controverting them in the notes, is exceedingly provoking to the reader, and seems to argue rather indolence than modesty in the writer. But the scope for originality is not large in the treatment of the text of the Orators: though diversities of opinion still exist, their range has been steadily diminishing since the appearance of Bekker's edition. We have used, as a sort of basis for our text, the Teubner editions of the two Orators—Franke's for Aeschines, and Dindorf's for Demosthenes; and, whatever may be thought of our judgment where we differ from either of these, in the majority of cases in which we follow them, there can be no doubt at all of their superiority to older editions. A short history of these will serve best to define our position.

The text of the Orators, as of most Greek authors, has passed through three stages, forming a sort of parody on Comte's three periods of human thought. There is the age of superstitious adherence to a vulgate—that of scarcely less superstitious, but in practice more salutary, allegiance to MSS. considered as ultimate facts—and that of the application of common-sense rules of evidence to the testimony available from any source, MSS., quotations, inscriptions, internal evidence, literary analogy, or anything, regard being paid in all cases to the probable sources of error to which each class of evidence is liable. The second of these stages may be held to begin, in the case of Demosthenes, with the publication of

Reiske's Attic Orators, though heralded and anticipated by the collations of Jerome Wolf and Morell; the third, to date from the appearance of Bekker's.

Reiske, in his long and rather rambling Preface, traces the history of the text up to his time: neither the details of this, nor his judgments on work long superseded, are worth recapitulating. It is enough to say that the principal names of the period are Aldus, Jerome Wolf, and Taylor. Aldus, in the different recensions of the text in his two successive editions, and his table (confusedly executed as it was) of various readings among his three MSS., furnished more indications to his successors of the nature of the work before them, than an *editio princeps* always does. Wolf, though clumsy and arrogant in his manner of approaching the task, had yet a clearer notion of what was to be done, and sounder principles as to the way of doing it, than the editors or reprinters of the next two centuries; for during nearly that time the history of the Orators is virtually a blank. It is not till Taylor that anything to be called critical treatment was applied to them : he may be considered as leading up to and introducing the great work of Reiske, but hardly constitutes by himself an epoch in the growth of the final text.

Reiske's work has the faults which are inevitable where a man has to form his conceptions, both of his object and of his method, for himself, unaided and for the first time; but it certainly is a great work, not only in the sense of being a monument of vast labour, but of labour well bestowed. It simplified the task of later editors largely, to have his text for a basis to work upon instead of that of Aldus; and, though finality was out of the question when an author was edited without the highest single authority on his text being consulted, it was a great step to have an edition made on right principles, with however imperfect materials. The MSS. A for one, and p for the other of our two Orators, are not absolutely of the highest class, nor are they even the best MSS. in existence of these authors; but they are not bad ones, and an edition made by an intelligent use of them is sure to supply a possible text, one worth consideration, and differing in kind from the haphazard work, with late and indifferent MSS., that was the usual manner in which a fifteenth century vulgate took its origin. It may be said that the Reiskes, by their collations, laid the foundation for the final text of the Orators, and, pursuing the metaphor, that Bekker built at least the framework of the structure, however much he left for his successors to add to his work.

For between Reiske and Bekker there was nothing of importance done, so far as the text was concerned; but as regards the interpretation and intelligent treatment of Demosthenes generally, and not merely the single oration, the Prolegomena to Wolf's Leptines may be considered to

mark a decided advance. Auger is not considered to have done anything worth mention, except that he was, apparently, the first person to
call attention to Σ. Bekker's complete collation of this put the whole
question of Demosthenes' text on a new footing; while his extensive
collection of other MSS. of both Orators, would have served as ample
materials for constituting a sound text, even if he had not used his own
critical powers on the work of constructing one.

In fact, as regards Aeschines, Bekker is held to have approached less
nearly than usual to the final critical text. He habitually followed the
class of MSS. which we have ranked third, and which by most later
editors[1] have been held inferior in authority to the other two. But in
Demosthenes, at any rate, there is, since the publication of his Attic
Orators, an incontrovertible basis of fact, and any points that remain
doubtful are points of detail. The only exception to the unanimity of
following editors is Buttmann; who, writing (in his Preface to the Midias)
nearly contemporaneously with the publication of Bekker's work, and
having a private view of his memoranda, came to the conclusion that,
though Σ was the best as well as the oldest individual MS. of Demosthenes, it represented a corrupt recension, as compared with A and its
congeners. But the main stream of criticism went on in the channel
into which Bekker had directed it. The works of Vömel and of Baiter
and Sauppe were founded upon it, and continued it. The latter is,
without doubt, in some respects a great and well-executed work, but too
hasty and undiscriminating in its use of authorities to rank with the very
highest class of criticism. Of the excess of their devotion to Cod. Σ in
Demosthenes enough has been said; but as to Aeschines, they may be
held to fill up a place that was wanting, for it had been generally agreed,
when their work appeared, that Bekker had followed a wrong tack in his
treatment of this author. An edition, of which the basis should be *a* and
its congeners, instead of the group *ekl*, was worth compiling and publish-
ing; but here it seems that the Editors went too much on general principles, and judged individual passages too little on their merits, so that
Franke's edition of the text[2] appears to represent a decided advance
upon theirs, contrasting with it as a production of common sense with
the ingenious crotchets of a doctrinaire.

As already mentioned, we used Franke's text as in some measure the
basis of our own; and, though typographical convenience had something

---

[1] The first distribution of MSS. of Aeschines into three classes, as above enumerated, is
Franke's, in his ' Quaestiones Aeschineae.' He refers to it as already generally recognised :
Schultz's classification, so far as it differs from this, is explained above.

[2] His ' Quaestiones Aeschineae' appeared before Baiter and Sauppe's work, and were used
by them to a considerable extent.

to do with this, we are disposed to prefer his text to any yet published or recommended, in spite of the fact that he, in his latest edition, is inclined (according to his statements in the preface) to adopt many of the corrections that have been proposed since the publication of his Aeschines in its present form in 1859. Schultz gives, in the Preface to his Aeschines, by far the neatest and completest account of the actual state of the manuscript evidence to Aeschines' text that has yet appeared; and has also, as above noticed, added considerably to the material resources of this kind by his own collations. But he appears as well as Franke in his last edition, to give too much weight to the inclination, which no critic of Aeschines can easily avoid, to ómit phrases rashly on internal evidence. The case seems to stand thus: either Aeschines' style had certain faults— notably a peculiar kind of verbosity and false lucidity, rather in harmony than otherwise with the character of the man, which leads to vain repetitions and pointless descriptions—of which we have no business to suppress individual examples; or else it is impossible for us to say what Aeschines' style was, except by a faculty of instinctive and intuitive divination. Now it seems to us that the limits of the safe exercise of this can hardly be placed very wide. A learned man may be followed implicitly by those less learned within the sphere of learning; but it is doubtful whether any amount of learning can make instinct a safe guide where reason fails. At any rate, such instinct can only be acquired where the sympathy between author and critic is very perfect; and one may venture to doubt whether such sympathy is attainable between a modern scholar and an ancient orator. Shakespeare has been carefully and intelligently studied in Germany, but no one but an Englishman could have made Falstaff 'babble of green fields,' which is perhaps the palmary instance of external evidence being overborne by the felicity of an emendation.

On this account, we have found less use than might be expected from the most recent German criticism on the text of Aeschines. It would require great learning and great experience in the critical use of MSS., before anyone was entitled to break a lance with Cobet on a question of technical textual criticism ; but it is, in truth, less rash and less arrogant to differ on first principles, not only from him, but from other critics by no means absolutely of the same school. Whether Bekker's and Cobet's estimate of the MSS. *ekl*, or Franke's and Schultz's be the more just, is a matter in which, though 'doctors disagree' at present, final judgment must be deferred till something like agreement is reached; but, when Schultz and Cobet agree in striking out words merely because they overload a sentence, the question is only in a subordinate degree one of learning, but rather of taste and common sense. It is a poor and obsolete joke to say that learned Germans are wanting in the latter faculties; but in a matter that comes within their cognisance, it is open to anyone to differ from the learned Germans. Supposing (as seems to be the tendency among competent critics) it is decided that Cobet overrates the MSS. named, it seems as though the fact could be thus accounted for. The modern critic and the ancient editor of this recension had proposed to themselves a common object, viz. to make Aeschines write more uniform and (in their judgment) more elegant Greek than, from the evidence before us, it appears that he did. Now, the right object for an editor of Aeschines to aim at, is to discover what Aeschines wrote, not what he ought to have written : and it is not self-evident that he did write what he ought. In spite of the general acceptance of the commonplaces about the perfection of Attic art, all Attic writers are not equally artistic. Even Sophocles was 'for one hour less noble than himself,' when he wrote the Herodotean tags in Antig. 905–912, O. C. 337–341 ; and a reader of Lycurgus or Dinarchus, will recognise that it was quite as possible for a practical orator to be dull, as for a rhetorician like Isocrates. Accordingly, we have gone on the assumption that, though no MS. of Aeschines is known of superlative excellence, yet an inductive and conservative text, founded on the MSS. that are known, is likelier to represent what he actually wrote, than any modern reconstruction, based on the reconstructor's sense of the fitness of things.

As to Demosthenes, Dindorf appears to us to have carried on the work of Bekker, in the same direction as the great master, but a little more boldly. His edition, published at Oxford almost contemporaneously with Baiter and Sauppe's at Zurich, besides embodying a new and more accurate collation of the chief MSS. of all families, seems to be prepared with more judgment as to the value, both absolute and comparative, of their testimony, and to have its canons of criticism more definitely perceived, and more consistently applied, than any of his predecessors. The few modifications which he has introduced into his text in the successive Leipzig reprints, are for the most part obvious improvements; while it seemed that there was room for carrying his principles a little further than he has done, and doing for his text something of the same kind as he has done for Bekker's.

So much for the chief critical editions of either or both of our Orators complete. The critical *remarks* on the text have, in effect, been discussed above, Cobet's *Variae Lectiones* and *Novae Lectiones* being the most important works of this class. Of separate editions of these single Orations, the most important are those of Bremi and Dissen. As treatises on the speech itself, the latter especially is of the very highest value ; but neither of them attempts much in the way of textual criticism,

i

beyond a revision and slight modification of Bekker's text. Bremi is hardly very successful in what he does attempt; Dissen's judgment, where it differs from that of other editors, bears the kind of authority that is due to the view of a powerful interpreter on a matter of internal evidence.

W. H. S.

SUPPLEMENTARY NOTES OF VARIOUS READINGS

IN AESCHINES IN CTESIPHONTEM, §§ 1–164.

p. 3, l. 8. ἐξῆν] Ita z Flor.

p. 7, l. 3. κρείττονες] κρείττους z Flor. b Schultz.

„ l. 18. ἕτερον (omisso τινα) Laur. Flor. Barb.

p. 13, l. 1. Διαλογισμὸς τῶν ἡμερῶν] Om. pr. Vat. *agmnp bl* : ψήφισμα habet *e*.

„ l. 10. ἀποδεκτῶν, καὶ νεωρίων ἀρχὴν καὶ σκευοθήκην ᾠκοδόμουν Schultz.

„ l. 14. λόγους] λόγον recipit Schultz.

p. 15. l. 6. καταλείπεται] καταλείπονται (mox omissis illis τούτους .. εἶναι) Schultz.

p. 17, l. 15. ἀπαγορεύοντα Schultz.

p. 19, l. 4. περὶ habet Vat.

p. 20, l. 2. τῆς ἀπελευθερίας] Om. Schultz.

„ l. 6. Ut nos *ekl* Flor.

„ l. 12. μείζοσι] μείζοσι τιμαῖς *ekl*, μείζονος τιμῆς *p*.

p. 22, l. 11. στέφανον] Om. Schultz.

„ l. 16. ὑμετέρων] ἡμετέρων Vat. Flor. Laur. Barb. *f*.

p. 23, l. 4. προσγέγραπαι] Ita *p* Flor. *ek*.

p. 25, l. 17. πρῶτον ἁπάντων *anp* Vat.

p. 26, l. 3. καιρὸν] Om. Schultz.

„ l. 15. ἐγώ τε ἀποκρίνομαι Vat. *dq*, ἔγωγε ἀποκρινοῦμαι Schultz.

p. 27, l. 19. μετασχεῖν .. συνεδρίου] Om. Schultz.

p. 28, l. 10. ἡμῶν] Ita z Flor. Steph.

p. 29, l. 12. ἕνα] Ita *agmn* Vat. Laur. Flor. *ekl*.

p. 30, l. 2. δὲ] Om. *agmn* Laur. Barb. *fcb*.

p. 31, l. 4. Φιλοκράτη καὶ Δημοσθένη Barb., ut *cd*.

„ l. 6. περιμενεῖτε Schultz.

p. 32, l. 5. ποιεῖσθαι] Superscr. Vat., ut *dekl*.

„ l. 6. ὅτ' ἦν προάγων Vat. Flor. Laur., ut *agmkl*.

p. 33, l. 1. τὰ] Om. Vat., solitus ille quidem articulos omittere.

„ l. 6. ἐν δὲ τῇ] ἐν τῇ post Frankium Schultz.

p. 34, l. 3. ἡμῖν Flor.

„ l. 9. εἰληφὼς] ὑπειληφὼς Vat. *p* Laur. *ekl*.

„ l. 13. προκαταλαμβάνων] προκαταλαβὼν Barb. *ekl* Schultz.

p. 35, l. 11. μηνὸς] Om. Flor. : habet Schultz.

i 2

p. 36, l. 1. λέγω] Om. Schultz.

„ l. 4. ἐν ᾧ γέγραπται] Om. Schultz.

„ l. 11. πρόεεροι Barb. *fcdek.*

p. 38, l. 7. ὑμᾶς] ἡμᾶς *agm* Vat. Laur.

„ l. 10. κατὰ τὴν πρεσβείαν] Om. Vat. *pc.*

p. 39, l. 1. τόθ'] τοῦθ' *anp* Vat. Laur. Flor.

„ l. 17. οἱ τῇ .. ἡσυχίᾳ] Ut editi Vat. Laur.: τῇ om. Flor.

p. 40, l. 2. Γάνον καὶ Γανιάδα Schultz.

„ l. 12. ἐπιστρατεύσαντας] πρεσβεύσαντας z Flor. *ekl.*

p. 41, l. 4. θαυμαστῆς] Sic Vat. *p* Flor. *zekl.*

„ l. 11. ἐπιλαθόμενοι] Sic *agmnp* Vat. Laur. Flor.

„ l. 14. πεζῇ Schultz.

„ l. 17. τοῖς παρακαταθεμένοις] Sic *ekl:* ceteri αὐτοῖς παρακαταθέμενοι : vid. annot.
αὐτοῖς τοῖς παρακαταθεμένοις Schultz.

p. 42, l. 6. ἐνεκωμίαζεν Flor.

„ l. 19. αὐτοῦ z Flor.: αὐτοῦ Vat. Laur. Barb.

p. 43, l. 10. ὑπέβαλλεν Vat. Laur.

„ l. 12. τε] Om. *anz* Laur. Flor. *fcdq* et pr. *gm.*

p. 44, l. 8. ἐγκαταληφθέντι Laur. Flor. Barb.

p. 45, l. 1. προγράψας *agmn* Vat. Laur. Barb. *fdb:* εὐφημίας ἕνεκα πρ. om. z Flor.
Statim καὶ add. Flor.

„ l. 2. προεδρίας Laur. Barb.

„ l. 11. οἱ καιροὶ *pz* Vat. Laur. Flor. Barb.

„ l. 12. τοῦτο *pz* Vat. Laur. Flor.

p. 47, l. 13. αὐτὰ Pr. Vat.

p. 49, l. 5. καὶ αὐτοὶ *p* Reisk. Schultz.

„ l. 6. ὑμῖν] Ita *apc:* ceteri plerique ἡμῖν.

„ l. 9. περὶ ἅπαντ' ὧν] πάλιν ἅπας ὧν eleganter conicit Schultz.

„ l. 10. καὶ] Om. *q* Laur. Barb.

„ l. 13. ἀπὸ τοῦ κλέμματος Vat. *p* Laur. *cekl.*

p. 51, l. 7. τοὺς] Om. *zekl* Flor.

„ l. 15. οἱ πρόγονοι οἱ ἡμέτεροι *fcdq* Barb. Flor.

p. 52, l. 7. ἐργάζεσθαι] Ita *ekl,* ἐργάσασθαι *agmnp* Vat. Laur. Barb *fbȝ,* ἐργάσεσθαι
Schultz.

p. 53, l. 16. αὐτοῖς *m fcd b* Barb.

p. 54, l. 14. ἦν] Om. *gmnz* Flor.

p. 55, l. 13. Λέκκιον Schultz.

„ l. 16. Et passim, 'Αμφικτύονες *ac.*

p. 56, l. 3. ἡμετέρας *gpqt,* Schultziani omnes, et ipse Schultz.

„ l. 5. ἐξαρέσασθαι Corr. Vat.

„ l. 11. εἰς τὸ συνέδριον] Om. Schultz, jubente Frankio.

„ l. 14. γε] Om. *gmnp* Vat.

p. 57, l. 1. ὠνομάζετο Schultziani omnes.

„ l. 3. ἐξείργετ' ἂν z Flor. *bekl* Schultz.

„ l. 5. λέγων] Om. Vat. Laur. *pbek.*

p. 58, l. 5. τῶν 'Αθηναίων Schultz.

„ l. 14. ταῖς] τοὺς *agmz.*

„ l. 17. ἐν τῇ ἀρᾷ γέγραπται] Οm. Schultz. θύσειαν *fȝ* Barb.

„ l. 18. μήτε *fcd* Ba·b.

p. 59, l. 7. ἀνηγόρευε] ἀνηγόρευσε Schultz., ex conjectura Franki.

p. 59, l. 14. ἄπωθεν] Ita a Laur. Flor.: ceteri ἄποθεν.

p. 60, l. 14. τῷ δήμῳ] Om. Schultz.

p. 61, l. 9. δὲ] Om. Vat. Flor. Laur. Schultz.

p. 62, l. 4. μήτε soli habent z Flor. bekl.

p. 63, l. 4. Ἀμφισσεῖς Schultziani.

„ l. 10. γε] Om., ut videtur, Schultziani omnes.

p. 64, l. 10. ὑπερωρίσθαι] ὑπερωρίζεσθαι cdq Barb.

p. 65, l. 3. Θῆβαι] Om. ap Vat. Laur. Barb. fcd.

p. 66, l. 10. πῆμα μέγα δῶκε p Vat.

„ l. 13. νέας ἐν habet a, νῆας ἐν eg.

„ l. 15. ὑμῖν] ἡμῖν Vat.

p. 67, l. 2. πάλαι] Om. z Flor.

„ l. 5. ἡμῖν] ὑμῖν pzt et Schultziani omnes.

pp. 67–68. Inter scholia Vaticanus habet οὗτος στρατηγὸς .. ῥήτωρ καὶ οὗτος .. δημαγωγὸς διάσημος .. ῥήτωρ καὶ οὗτος, quamvis δημάγωγος ante Ἀριστοφῶν (ut
videtur) etiam in textu habeat.

p. 68, l. 1. ῥήτωρ ante Πύρρανδρος soli habent fcdq.   Πύρρανδρος geminato ρ habent
Vat. Laur.

„ l. 2. ἐδυνήθη] Ita acqe et Schultziani : ceteri ἠδυνήθη.

„ l. 13. μόνην] μόνον Vat. p Schultz.

„ l. 17. τῷ δ' ἔργῳ] τὸ δ' ἔργον Vat.

p. 69, l. 3. προσποιησάμενος] προσποιούμενος Vat. p Laur. Schultz.

„ l. 7. πᾶσαν Vat. Flor. pz.

„ l. 8. ἀφιστῆται] ἀφίστηται Vat. Laur. Flor. z.

„ l. 13. ἐπεπόνθεσαν Schultz.

p. 70, l. 7. τὰ] Om. Vat. Laur. Flor. z, τὰ αὐτοῦ Barb., τ' αὐτοῦ f.

„ l. 16. ὅπου Vat. Laur. agmnp bel, ὅποτ' fcdq Barb.

p. 71, l. 4. τοῦ] Om. agmn Laur. Flor. et pr. Vat.

„ l. 13. προγεγενημένης] Sic agmnz Flor. Laur. pr. Vat.

„ l. 15. μὴ καὶ] καὶ μὴ amnp z Vat. Laur. Flor.

p. 72, l. 1. ἤδη] Om. Schultz.

„ l. 6. μικρῷ] Ita Schultziani.

„ l. 7. τὴν] Om. pt et Schultziani.

p. 73, l. 5. κήρυγμά τι τοῦτο Flor. z.

p. 74, l. 13. σπουδαῖα τῶν πραγμάτων πάντων Schultz.

p. 76, l. 4. ἀρετῆς ἕνεκα] Om. ap Vat. Laur.

p. 77, l. 11. ἀνατετραφότα gpz Vat. Laur. Barb. Flor. fqdek.
Ad l. 16, post τὴν Schultz. addit ἀπὸ τῆς πόλεως .. ἀπέδρα γάρ.

p. 78, l. 8. καὶ habent z Flor.

„ l. 9. δ'] Om. z Laur.

„ l. 12. ταῦτα habent z Vat. Laur. Flor.

p. 79, l. 9. πάραλοι] Sic amn z p Vat. Laur. Flor. corr. g.

„ l. 12. ἑτέρων] ἑταιρῶν agmnz Laur. Flor.

„ l. 13. γενόμενος] Om. Schultz.

„ l. 17. Δημοσθένης habent q Barb.

p. 80, l. 9. αὐτῷ afcdq Schultz.

ΑΙΣΧΙΝΟΥ

ΚΑΤΑ ΚΤΗΣΙΦΩΝΤΟΣ

ΛΟΓΟΣ.

ΑΙΣΧΙΝΟΥ

ΚΑΤΑ ΚΤΗΣΙΦΩΝΤΟΣ

ΛΟΓΟΣ.

ΥΠΟΘΕΣΙΣ.

Κτησιφῶν ἔγραψε ψήφισμα στεφανῶσαι Δημοσθένην Δημοσθένους Παιανιέα χρυσῷ στεφάνῳ καὶ ἀναγορεῦσαι τὸν στέφανον ἐν τῷ θεάτρῳ Διονυσίοις τραγῳδῶν, ὅτι διατελεῖ τὰ ἄριστα καὶ λέγων καὶ πράττων τῷ δήμῳ τῶν Ἀθηναίων. τοῦτο τὸ ψήφισμα ἐγράψατο Αἰσχίνης παρανόμων, καὶ εἰσάγει κεφάλαια γενικὰ τρία, ἓν μὲν, ὅτι ὑπεύθυνον ὄντα τὸν Δημοσθένην ἐστεφάνωσε τοῦ νόμου κελεύοντος μὴ ἐξεῖναι ὑπεύθυνον ἄρχοντα στεφανοῦν, περὶ οὐσίας, δεύτερον δὲ, ὅτι ἐν τῷ θεάτρῳ ἀνεκήρυξε τὸν στέφανον ἀπαγορεύοντος τοῦ νόμου μηδένα στεφανοῦν ἐν τῷ θεάτρῳ, περὶ ποιότητος, τρίτον καὶ τελευταῖον, ὅτι καὶ τὰ ψευδῆ ἔγραψεν ἐν τῷ ψηφίσματι· οὐκ εἶναι γὰρ καλὸν καὶ ἀγαθὸν τὸν Δημοσθένην, οὐδὲ ἄξιον τοῦ στεφάνου. καὶ τοῦτο εἰς τὸ παράνομον ἀνακτέον, ἐπειδὴ καὶ νόμος ἔστιν ὁ κωλύων τὰ ψευδῆ γράφειν ἐν τοῖς ψηφίσμασιν· ἔστι δὲ περὶ ποιότητος. ὑποφορὰς δὲ λαμβάνει τρεῖς, πρὸς μὲν τὸ πρῶτον· δισσῶς ἐροῦντος Δημοσθένους, ὅτι οὐκ ἦν ἄρχων οὐδὲ ἔστιν ἀρχὴ ἡ τῶν τειχῶν οἰκοδομή, ἀλλὰ διακονία τις καὶ ἐπιμέλεια· εἰ δὲ καὶ ἀρχὴ, τῷ γε ἐπιδεδωκέναι ἐκ τῶν ἰδίων καὶ μηδὲν εἰληφέναι ἐκ τῆς πόλεως οὐκ ἦν ὑπεύθυνος· περὶ ποιότητος ἀμφότερα. πρὸς δὲ τοῦτο ὁ Αἰσχίνης εἰσάγει στοχαστικὸν κεφάλαιον, οὐ μέντοι κατασκευάζει· εἰ δὲ μὴ παρ᾽ ἑαυτοῦ ἐπέδωκεν, ἀλλ᾽ εἶχε παρὰ τῆς βουλῆς εἰς τοῦτο δέκα τάλαντα, περὶ οὐσίας. πρὸς δὲ τὸ δεύτερον κεφάλαιον παρεχομένου Δημοσθένους νόμον ἕτερον, κελεύοντα ἀνακηρύττειν ἐν τῷ θεάτρῳ, ἂν ψηφίσηται ὁ δῆμος, Αἰσχίνης οὐ περὶ τῶν πολιτικῶν αὐτὸν εἶναί φησιν, ἀλλὰ περὶ τῶν ξενικῶν στεφάνων, περὶ οὐσίας. πρὸς δὲ τὸ τρίτον πολλὰ κατὰ μέρος. οἴεται δὲ τὸν Δημοσθένην εἰς τέσσαρας καιροὺς διῃρηκέναι τὴν ἀπολογίαν, τὰ πράγματα καθ᾽ ἕκαστα εἰς τούτους μερίσαντα. πρῶτον μὲν οὖν φησιν εἶναι καιρὸν τὸν τοῦ πολέμου τοῦ πρώτου τοῦ πρὸς Φίλιππον περὶ Ἀμφιπόλεως γενομένου, δεύτερον δὲ τὸν τῆς εἰρήνης, τρίτον δὲ τὸν τοῦ πολέμου τοῦ δευτέρου καὶ τῆς περὶ Χαιρώνειαν ἥττης, τέταρτον δὲ τὸν παρόντα καιρὸν τὸν περὶ τῶν πρὸς Ἀλέξανδρον πολιτευμάτων. ἐν μὲν οὖν τῷ πρώτῳ αἴτιον αὐτόν φησι γεγονέναι τῆς εἰρήνης, αἰσχρᾶς οὔσης καὶ ἀδόξου, καὶ τοῦ μὴ μετὰ κοινοῦ τῶν Ἑλλήνων συνεδρίου τὴν πόλιν αὐτὴν πεποιῆσθαι· ἐν δὲ τῷ δευτέρῳ, ὅτι τὸν πόλεμον τὸν πρὸς Φίλιππον αὐτὸς παρεσκεύασεν· ἐν δὲ τῷ τρίτῳ, ὅτι τοῦ ἱεροῦ

πολέμου καὶ τῶν περὶ Φωκέας συμβάντων αἴτιος ἐγένετο, καὶ τῆς ἥττης τῆς ἐν
Χαιρωνείᾳ, πείσας μετὰ Θηβαίων ἀραμένους τὸν πόλεμον πρὸς Φίλιππον παρα-
τάξασθαι· ἐν δὲ τῷ τελευταίῳ, ὅτι κατὰ τὸν πρὸς Ἀλέξανδρον οὐκ ἐπολιτεύσατο.
μετὰ ταῦτα καὶ τοῦ βίου παντὸς τοῦ Δημοσθένους κατηγορεῖ, καὶ δὴ καὶ Κτησιφῶντος ἐν ὀλίγοις, ἐν οἷς ἀξιοῖ αὐτὸν ὑπὲρ ἑαυτοῦ τὸν Κτησιφῶντα ἀπολογεῖσθαι.
τὰ μὲν οὖν κεφάλαια ταῦτ' ἐστίν. ἐνίκα δὲ τὸν ἀγῶνα Δημοσθένης.

Μέμφονται μέντοι τινὲς τὸν Αἰσχίνην, ὅτι οὐκ ἐνδιέτριψεν ἐν τῷ παρανόμῳ,
ἀλλὰ καὶ τῆς πολιτείας κατηγορεῖ τοῦ Δημοσθένους, καλῶς πεπολιτευμένου τοῦ
ἀνδρός. αὐτὸς δὲ τοὐναντίον τούτῳ μάλιστα ἰσχυρίζεται, λέγων οὕτως· " ἔστι δ'
ὑπόλοιπον μέρος τῆς κατηγορίας, ἐφ' ᾧ μάλιστα σπουδάζω· τοῦτο δ' ἐστὶν ἡ
πρόφασις, δι' ἣν αὐτὸν ἀξιοῖ στεφανοῦσθαι." μήποτε δὲ ἄριστα τοῦτο ἔπραξεν·
ἐπειδὴ γὰρ εἶχε δόξαν μεγάλην παρὰ πᾶσι καὶ ὑπόληψιν ὁ Δημοσθένης ὡς λαμ-
πρότατα πεπολιτευμένος, εἰκότως ᾠήθη ψυχροὺς καὶ οὐδενὸς ἀξίους φανήσεσθαι
τοὺς περὶ τῶν παρανόμων λόγους, εἰ μὴ δόξαν αὐτοῖς ἐμποιήσει τὴν ἐναντίαν,
ὡς ἄρα ὁ Δημοσθένης κακόνους ἐστὶ τῷ δήμῳ καὶ αἰσχρῶς καὶ ἐπιμέμπτως πεπο-
λίτευται. διὰ τοῦτο ἐσπούδασε περὶ τοῦτο μάλιστα, καὶ ἐν τούτῳ τῷ μέρει τῆς
κατηγορίας τὸ πλεῖστον ἐνδιέτριψε. μέμψαιτο δ' ἄν τις τὸ προοίμιον ὡς τραγικὸν
καὶ περιττὸν καὶ ἐπιλόγῳ μᾶλλον ἐοικός.

Ἡ στάσις τοῦ λόγου ἐστὶ πραγματικὴ ἔγγραφος, ὥσπερ καὶ ἡ τοῦ ὑπὲρ τοῦ
στεφάνου. τὰ δὲ κεφάλαια δηλονότι τῆς πραγματικῆς περιέχει ἅπερ καὶ ἐκεῖ,
οἷον τὸ νόμιμον τεμνόμενον εἰς τρεῖς νόμους, τὸ δὲ δίκαιον εἰς τέσσαρας καιρούς.
ὅρα δὲ, πῶς ἐπιλογικῶς ἤρξατο ἀπὸ συνηγόρων ἐκβολῆς, ὥσπερ καὶ Δημοσθένης.

Τινὲς εἶπον, ὅτι οὐκ ἔχει κατασκευὴν τὸ προοίμιον· οὔκουν οὐδὲ συμπέρασμα δεῖ
ζητεῖν. ἀλλ' οὐκ ἔστιν ἀκατάσκευον· ἔστι γὰρ αὐτοῦ κατασκευὴ " ὑπὲρ τοῦ τὰ μέτρια
καὶ τὰ συνήθη μὴ γίνεσθαι ἐν τῇ πόλει." εἰ γὰρ ἡ αἰτία τῆς προτάσεώς ἐστιν
ἡ κατασκευὴ, διὰ δὲ τὸ τὰ μέτρια μὴ γίνεσθαι ἐν τῇ πόλει αἱ δεήσεις, κατασκευὴ ἂν
εἴη. ἔχει δὲ καὶ συμπέρασμα, " ἐγὼ δὲ πεπιστευκὼς ἥκω " ἕως τοῦ " μεῖζον τῶν
νόμων καὶ τῶν δικαίων."

Τὴν μὲν παρασκευὴν ὁρᾶτε, ὦ Ἀθηναῖοι, καὶ τὴν παράταξιν, 1
ὅση γεγένηται, καὶ τὰς κατὰ τὴν ἀγορὰν δεήσεις, αἷς κέχρηνταί

---

1. ὦ Ἀθηναῖοι] Volgo usque ad Bekk. ὦ ἄνδρες Ἀθ., ut habent codd. ek et plerumque l.

---

§ 1. *The strong conspiracy to set aside the laws does not deter me from a duty*

1. παρασκευήν .. παράταξιν are means and end : the one the preparation to make a show of feeling in favour of Demosthenes, the other the array of supporters thus brought together.

ὦ Ἀθηναῖοι. So all MSS., except the least valuable group, almost everywhere throughout the works of Aeschines, instead of the more usual ὦ ἄνδρες Ἀθ. It seems best to follow the MSS., both in the rule and in such occasional exceptions as § 68 init. It appears to have been a matter in which different orators made different mannerisms : e. g. Lycurgus almost always says simply ὦ ἄνδρες, which seems to have been rude, or at least curt. Cp. Soph. Ant. 162.

2. κατὰ τὴν ἀγορὰν δεήσεις. Appeals to prominent public men, and by them to individual citizens ; among them, perhaps, to some of the dicasts themselves.

τινες ὑπὲρ τοῦ τὰ μέτρια καὶ τὰ συνήθη μὴ γίγνεσθαι ἐν τῇ
πόλει· ἐγὼ δὲ πεπιστευκὼς ἥκω πρῶτον μὲν τοῖς θεοῖς, δεύτερον δὲ τοῖς νόμοις καὶ ὑμῖν, ἡγούμενος οὐδεμίαν παρασκευὴν
2 ἰσχύειν παρ' ὑμῖν μεῖζον τῶν νόμων καὶ τῶν δικαίων. ἐβουλόμην μὲν οὖν, ὦ 'Αθηναῖοι, καὶ τὴν βουλὴν τοὺς πεντακοσίους 5
καὶ τὰς ἐκκλησίας ὑπὸ τῶν ἐφεστηκότων ὀρθῶς διοικεῖσθαι, καὶ
τοὺς νόμους, οὓς ἐνομοθέτησεν ὁ Σόλων περὶ τῆς τῶν ῥητόρων
εὐκοσμίας, ἰσχύειν, ἵνα ἐξῆν πρῶτον μὲν τῷ πρεσβυτάτῳ τῶν
πολιτῶν, ὥσπερ οἱ νόμοι κελεύουσι, σωφρόνως ἐπὶ τὸ βῆμα
παρελθόντι ἄνευ θορύβου καὶ ταραχῆς ἐξ ἐμπειρίας τὰ βέλτιστα 10
τῇ πόλει συμβουλεύειν, δεύτερον δ' ἤδη καὶ τῶν ἄλλων πολιτῶν
τὸν βουλόμενον καθ' ἡλικίαν χωρὶς καὶ ἐν μέρει περὶ ἑκάστου
γνώμην ἀποφαίνεσθαι· οὕτω γὰρ ἄν μοι δοκεῖ ἥ τε πόλις
3 ἄριστα διοικεῖσθαι αἵ τε κρίσεις ἐλάχισται γίγνεσθαι. ἐπειδὴ
δὲ πάντα τὰ πρότερον ὡμολογημένα καλῶς ἔχειν νυνὶ καταλέ- 15
λυται, καὶ γράφουσί τε τινὲς ῥᾳδίως παρανόμους γνώμας καὶ
ταῦτα ἕτεροί τινες τὰ ψηφίσματα ἐπιψηφίζουσιν οὐκ ἐκ τοῦ
δικαιοτάτου τρόπου λαχόντες προεδρεύειν, ἀλλ' ἐκ παρασκευῆς
καθεζόμενοι, ἂν δέ τις τῶν ἄλλων βουλευτῶν ὄντως λάχῃ κληρού-
μενος προεδρεύειν καὶ τὰς ὑμετέρας χειροτονίας ὀρθῶς ἀναγορεύῃ, 20

2. δεύτερον δὲ] ἔπειτα δεύτερον ekl.   4. ἰσχύειν .. μεῖζον] μεῖζον ἰσχ. παρ' ὑμῖν
ekl Bekk.   5. ὦ 'Αθηναῖοι] Hic et passim vid. ad 1.   8. ἵνα ἐξῆν] Sic codex
Mosquensis z: ἔξει a, ἔξον ἤ d. Volgo legebatur ἐξῇ: vid. not. Mirum est, quod ἐξείη
Turicensibus et Bakio praeplacuerit : si librorum ratio est habenda, fortasse scribendum fuit
ἐξῆ, eodem quo ἐξῆν sensu.   13. δοκεῖ] Sic nfcd (f in lit.) : δοκοῖ z : ceteri δοκῇ.
14. ἐλάχισται] ἐλάχιστα ed. 'Fortasse legendum τάχιστα' Bekk.   16. τε] Om. Bekk. :
habent agmn.

1. τινες. It is a rather characteristic
mannerism of Aeschines to use the indefinite pronoun in an invidious sense. We
have several cases further on, §§ 3, 5, 58
etc. In § 166 a similar use is attributed to
Demosthenes. Conscious that public feeling
was against him, Aeschines is always hinting
that it was not the genuine public, but the
wire-pullers of public opinion, that had passed
judgment upon him. Cp. Ae. de F. L. § 156,
p. 47.

§ 2. *Which I wish were unnecessary, as in
an orderly State it would be.*

4. ἐβουλόμην. The imperfect indic. used
of the unattainable, just as in relative sentences with ἵνα or ὅπως (e. g. ἵνα ἐξῆν in the
next clause, si vera l.) The use of historical
tenses with ἄν is the same in principle. We
may explain the thought that leads to this
constr. by saying, that in Greek one says,
'it was my wish' till I knew it was vain;

in Latin or English, 'I should' or 'I could
wish' if it were not vain.

5. τὴν βουλὴν τοὺς πεντακοσίους. The
technical title added epexegetically to limit
τὴν βουλήν (and especially to distinguish it
from ἡ βουλὴ ἡ ἐξ 'Αρείου πάγου). So, again,
§ 20 fin. etc.

6. τῶν ἐφεστηκότων. A more general
term for the presiding Prytanis, whose technical title was ἐπιστάτης.

8. ἵνα ἐξῆν. Conjectured by Bekker,
and met by Bremi with the remark, 'Quod a
MSS. oblatum recepissem.' It is now found
in one good MS., so we have adopted it.
Volg. ἐξῇ.

§§ 3–5. *But the practice of impeachment
is the only check on the licence of politicians;*

17. οὐκ ἐκ τοῦ δικαιοτάτου τρόπου
κ.τ.λ. See the Essay 'Practical Politics'
etc.

τοῦτον οἱ τὴν πολιτείαν κοινὴν οὐκέτι, ἀλλ' ἰδίαν αὐτῶν ἡγούμενοι ἀπειλοῦσιν εἰσαγγέλλειν, καταδουλούμενοι τοὺς ἰδιώτας καὶ
δυναστείας ἑαυτοῖς περιποιοῦντες, καὶ τὰς κρίσεις τὰς μὲν ἐκ 4
τῶν νόμων καταλελύκασι, τὰς δ' ἐκ τῶν ψηφισμάτων μετ' ὀργῆς
5 κρίνουσιν, σεσίγηται μὲν τὸ κάλλιστον καὶ σωφρονέστατον κήρυγμα τῶν ἐν τῇ πόλει "τίς ἀγορεύειν βούλεται τῶν ὑπὲρ
πεντήκοντα ἔτη γεγονότων καὶ πάλιν ἐν μέρει τῶν ἄλλων Ἀθηναίων," τῆς δὲ τῶν ῥητόρων ἀκοσμίας οὐκέτι κρατεῖν δύνανται
οὔθ' οἱ νόμοι οὔθ' οἱ πρυτάνεις οὔθ' οἱ πρόεδροι οὔθ' ἡ προε-
10 δρεύουσα φυλή, τὸ δέκατον μέρος τῆς πόλεως. τούτων δ' ἐχόντων 5
οὕτως, καὶ τῶν καιρῶν ὄντων τῇ πόλει τοιούτων, ὁποίους τινὰς
αὐτοὺς ὑμεῖς ὑπολαμβάνετε εἶναι, ἓν ὑπολείπεται μέρος τῆς πολιτείας, εἴ τι κἀγὼ τυγχάνω γιγνώσκων, αἱ τῶν παρανόμων γραφαί.
εἰ δὲ καὶ ταύτας καταλύσετε ἢ τοῖς καταλύουσιν ἐπιτρέψετε,
15 προλέγω ὑμῖν, ὅτι λήσετε κατὰ μικρὸν τῆς πολιτείας τισὶ παραχωρήσαντες. εὖ γὰρ ἴστε, ὦ Ἀθηναῖοι, ὅτι τρεῖς εἰσὶ πολιτεῖαι 6
παρὰ πᾶσιν ἀνθρώποις, τυραννὶς καὶ ὀλιγαρχία καὶ δημοκρατία,
διοικοῦνται δ' αἱ μὲν τυραννίδες καὶ ὀλιγαρχίαι τοῖς τρόποις
τῶν ἐφεστηκότων, αἱ δὲ πόλεις αἱ δημοκρατούμεναι τοῖς νόμοις
20 τοῖς κειμένοις. μηδεὶς οὖν ὑμῶν τοῦτ' ἀγνοείτω, ἀλλὰ σαφῶς
ἕκαστος ἐπιστάσθω, ὅτι, ὅταν εἰσίῃ εἰς δικαστήριον γραφὴν
παρανόμων δικάσων, ἐν ταύτῃ τῇ ἡμέρᾳ μέλλει τὴν ψῆφον
φέρειν περὶ τῆς ἑαυτοῦ παρρησίας. διόπερ καὶ ὁ νομοθέτης

---

1. κοινὴν οὐκέτι] Poenitet Frankium, se ita cum B. et S. pro volgato οὐκέτι κοινὴν ex
agnup scripsisse. Sed amat Aeschines verba in hunc modum minus usitato ordine disponere.
ἡγούμενοι] ἡγ. εἶναι cdf pr. b Bekk.   2. εἰσαγγέλλειν] εἰσαγγελεῖν Reisk., proban-
tibus Bakio et Hamakero. Habet sane unus cod. εἰσαγγελεῖν in margine, alter εἰσαγγέλειν
in textu.   3. καὶ] Om. z.

2. ἰδιώτας. Opposed not to officials, but
to professional speakers. So inf. § 215.
3. δυναστείας. Always of unconstitutional power, like the Latin potentia. In
Thuc. 3. 62. 4 it is used as the name of
a form of government, stigmatized as the
nearest approach to despotism: so Plat. Rep.
8. p. 544 C seems to imply that it is
something between that and oligarchy. The
fundamental distinction between δυναστεία
and τυραννὶς is, that the τύραννος was
almost always an individual, the δυναστεία
almost always in the hands of a group: and
further, that in δυναστεία private influence
overrides still existing laws and constitutional forms, in the latter law and constitution have been altogether suppressed.
τὰς ἐκ τῶν νόμων. Constitutional
remedies provided in permanence, especially
the γραφὴ παρανόμων itself, called in the

next words the one remaining safeguard of
the democracy.
9. ἡ πρόεδρ. . φυλή. Not merely the
tribe, whose representative in the Five Hundred furnished the πρόεδρος for the time
being, but the tribe appointed to act as
described, Ae. in Tim. § 33, p. 59. See Exc.
on ' Practical Politics.'
13. εἴ τι κἀγώ. 'If I also have a right
to an opinion' as well as Demosthenes.
15. λήσετε . . παραχωρήσαντες. ' You
will find that, gradually and unconsciously,
you have surrendered your government to a
faction.' τισί as noted in § 1. παραχωρήσαντες used in D. de Cor. § 19; also ibid.
§ 83, nearly as here.
§ 6. Which leads to despotism,
19. αἱ δὲ πόλεις . . κειμένοις. For the
sentiment, cp. below, § 23 fin.
23. περὶ τῆς ἑαυτοῦ παρρησίας. The

τοῦτο πρῶτον ἔταξεν ἐν τῷ τῶν δικαστῶν ὅρκῳ, " ψηφιοῦμαι
κατὰ τοὺς νόμους," ἐκεῖνό γε εὖ εἰδὼς, ὅτι, ὅταν διατηρηθῶσιν
7 οἱ νόμοι τῇ πόλει, σώζεται καὶ ἡ δημοκρατία. ἃ χρὴ διαμνη-
μονεύοντας ὑμᾶς μισεῖν τοὺς τὰ παράνομα γράφοντας, καὶ μηδὲν
μικρὸν ἡγεῖσθαι εἶναι τῶν τοιούτων ἀδικημάτων, ἀλλ' ἕκαστον 5
ὑπερμέγεθες, καὶ τοῦθ' ὑμῶν τὸ δίκαιον μηδένα ἀνθρώπων ἐξαιρεῖσθαι, μήτε τὰς τῶν στρατηγῶν συνηγορίας, οἳ ἐπὶ πολὺν ἤδη
χρόνον συνεργοῦντές τισι τῶν ῥητόρων λυμαίνονται τὴν πολιτείαν, μήτε τὰς τῶν ξένων δεήσεις, οὓς ἀναβιβαζόμενοί τινες
ἐκφεύγουσιν ἐκ τῶν δικαστηρίων, παράνομον πολιτείαν πολιτευό- 10
μενοι· ἀλλ' ὥσπερ ἂν ὑμῶν ἕκαστος αἰσχυνθείη τὴν τάξιν λιπεῖν,
ἣν ἂν ταχθῇ ἐν τῷ πολέμῳ, οὕτω καὶ νῦν αἰσχύνθητε ἐκλιπεῖν
τὴν τάξιν, ἣν τέταχθε ὑπὸ τῶν νόμων φύλακες τῆς δημοκρατίας
8 τήνδε τὴν ἡμέραν. κἀκεῖνο δὲ χρὴ διαμνημονεύειν, ὅτι νῦν ἅπαντες
οἱ πολῖται παρακαταθέμενοι τὴν πόλιν ὑμῖν καὶ τὴν πολιτείαν 15
διαπιστεύσαντες οἱ μὲν πάρεισι καὶ ἐπακούουσι τῆσδε τῆς κρίσεως,
οἱ δὲ ἄπεισιν ἐπὶ τῶν ἰδίων ἔργων· οὓς αἰσχυνόμενοι καὶ τῶν
ὅρκων, οὓς ὠμόσατε, μεμνημένοι καὶ τῶν νόμων, ἐὰν ἐξελέγξωμεν
Κτησιφῶντα καὶ παράνομα γράψαντα καὶ ψευδῆ καὶ ἀσύμφορα
τῇ πόλει, λύετε, ὦ Ἀθηναῖοι, τὰς παρανόμους γνώμας, βεβαι- 20
οῦτε τῇ πόλει τὴν δημοκρατίαν, κολάζετε τοὺς ὑπεναντίως τῷ
νόμῳ καὶ τῇ πόλει καὶ τῷ συμφέροντι τῷ ὑμετέρῳ πολιτευομένους. κἂν ταύτην ἔχοντες τὴν διάνοιαν ἀκούσητε τῶν μελλόντων

---

5. μικρὸν ἡγεῖσθαι] Cum atqn μικρὸν omittant, credibilius videtur id ex hoc verborum
ordine factum esse, ubi μηδὲν μικρὸν alterum alteri similia succedunt, quam si μηδὲν
ἡγεῖσθαι μικρὸν scriptum fuisset, ut habent gpekl Bekk. B. et S.   14. τήνδε] εἰς τήνδε
nprbek.   21. τῷ νόμῳ] 'Praestat τοῖς νόμοις' Frank.: quod habent pc †b†ekl.   22. καὶ
τῇ πόλει] Om. ekl. 'Bakius delenda esse vidit' Frank.   23. ἀκούσητε] b ekl et corr. α
et Bekk. ἀκούητε.

---

abolition of the γραφὴ παρανόμων had, in
fact, been the first step in the usurpation of
the Four Hundred.

§ 7. *And is ever to be unmasked and
resisted*

4. μηδὲν μικρὸν ἡγεῖσθαι. Do not treat
Ctesiphon's motion as a merely technical
irregularity: it implies a desire on the part
of Demosthenes and his partisans to be
above the law.

6. μηδένα ἀνθρώπων. Askew inserted
ἐᾶν between these words, to avoid the
change of subject between ἡγεῖσθαι and
ἐξαιρεῖσθαι.

7. συνηγορίας. Properly of speaking in
support of the prosecution, but here no
doubt of the defence, as Ae. de F. L.
195 etc.

11. τὴν τάξιν .. ἣν ἄν. Though ταχθῇ

might perfectly well be followed by a
cognate accusative, that construction would
be a little harsh here; probably the case of
ἣν is really determined by that of its antecedent.

§ 8. *For the sake of the trust you have
received from Athens.*

14. κἀκεῖνο .. ἐὰν ἐξελέγξωμεν κ. τ. λ.
'Another thing you have to remember too :
all the citizens put the city into your hands
to-day—entrusted the constitution to you—
before they came here to listen to the trial,
or went away to their private affairs : do
not betray their trust, do not forget the
laws, the oaths you have sworn : but if' etc.
The secondary predicates παρακαταθέμενοι
and διαπιστεύσαντες are, as usual, the most
important and emphatic part of the proposition.

ῥηθήσεσθαι λόγων, εὖ οἶδ' ὅτι δίκαια καὶ εὔορκα καὶ συμφέροντα
ὑμῖν αὐτοῖς ψηφιεῖσθε καὶ πάσῃ τῇ πόλει.

Περὶ μὲν οὖν τῆς ὅλης κατηγορίας μετρίως μοι ἐλπίζω προει- 9
ρῆσθαι· περὶ δὲ αὐτῶν τῶν νόμων, οἳ κεῖνται περὶ τῶν ὑπευθύνων,
5 παρ' οὓς τὸ ψήφισμα τοῦτο τυγχάνει γεγραφὼς Κτησιφῶν,
διὰ βραχέων εἰπεῖν βούλομαι. ἐν γὰρ τοῖς ἔμπροσθεν χρόνοις
ἄρχοντές τινες τὰς μεγίστας ἀρχὰς καὶ τὰς προσόδους διοι-
κοῦντες, καὶ δωροδοκοῦντες περὶ ἕκαστα τούτων, προσλαμβάνοντες
τούς τε ἐκ τοῦ βουλευτηρίου ῥήτορας καὶ τοὺς ἐκ τοῦ δήμου
10 πόρρωθεν προκατελάμβανον τὰς εὐθύνας ἐπαίνοις καὶ κηρύγμασιν,
ὥστ' ἐν ταῖς εὐθύναις τῶν ἀρχόντων εἰς τὴν μεγίστην μὲν ἀπορίαν
ἀφικνεῖσθαι τοὺς κατηγόρους, πολὺ δὲ ἔτι μᾶλλον τοὺς δικαστάς.
πολλοὶ γὰρ πάνυ τῶν ὑπευθύνων ἐπ' αὐτοφώρῳ κλέπται τῶν 10
δημοσίων χρημάτων ὄντες ἐξελεγχόμενοι διεφύγγανον ἐκ τῶν
15 δικαστηρίων, εἰκότως· ᾐσχύνοντο γὰρ οἶμαι οἱ δικασταί, εἰ φανήσεται ὁ αὐτὸς ἀνὴρ ἐν τῇ αὐτῇ πόλει, τυχὸν δὲ καὶ ἐν τῷ αὐτῷ
ἐνιαυτῷ, πρῴην μέν ποτε ἀναγορευόμενος ἐν τοῖς ἀγῶσιν ὅτι
στεφανοῦται ἀρετῆς ἕνεκα καὶ δικαιοσύνης ὑπὸ τοῦ δήμου χρυσῷ
στεφάνῳ, ὁ δὲ αὐτὸς ἀνὴρ μικρὸν ἐπισχὼν ἔξεισιν ἐκ τοῦ δικα-
20 στηρίου κλοπῆς ἕνεκα τὰς εὐθύνας ὠφληκώς· ὥστε ἠναγκάζοντο
τὴν ψῆφον φέρειν οἱ δικασταὶ οὐ περὶ τοῦ παρόντος ἀδικήματος,
ἀλλ' ὑπὲρ τῆς αἰσχύνης τοῦ δήμου. κατιδών δέ τις ταῦτα νομο- 11

---

1. δίκαια] καὶ δίκαια cf b ekl. 7. μεγίστας ἀρχὰς] Post haec addunt ἐν τῇ πόλει
ekl: ἀρχὰς ἐν τῇ πόλει μεγίστας b, qui mox καὶ τὰς ante προσόδους omittit; μεγ. ἐν τῇ
πόλει ἀρχὰς γρ h. 11. ἀρχόντων] ἀρχῶν ekl Bekk. Et quamvis certum sit, auctorem
hujus familiae codicem nimis per conjecturas suis de Graecitate notionibus Aeschinem
accommodasse, hic atque alias videtur fieri posse, ut hi idioma servaverint, a ceteris in
usitatiorem dicendi formam immutatam.

§ 9. After this prelude, I expound the laws contravened. They were necessary to make accountability serious:
3. μετρίως. 'Pretty well,' a word of modest self-satisfaction. Cp. Ar. Nub. fin.
5. τυγχάνει γεγραφώς. 'The particular laws infringed by Ctesiphon in his motion,' those which, as a matter of fact, he has come into collision with out of the whole number.
8. περὶ ἕκαστα τούτων. 'At every turn'—: they sold both their political and administrative influence. τούτων refers to all the occasions of corruption that either class of office supplied, not to the classes themselves, which would require ἑκάτερα.
10. ἐπαίνοις καὶ κηρύγμασιν: i.e. votes of thanks passed in the assembly, and proclamation of these votes in the theatre.
12. πολὺ δὲ ἔτι μᾶλλον. A judge's responsibility would be greater than an

advocate's: and besides, a numerous Athenian jury would probably include some who had taken part in the vote of thanks.
§ 10. Which otherwise would have been annulled, by the account being anticipated.
17. ἀναγορευόμενος. The technical word: cp. ἀνάρρησις below, §§ 32, 190, D. de Cor. § 71, ἀναρρηθῆναι below, § 45: so ἀνειπεῖν, ἀνερῶ are used as aorist and future.
20. τὰς εὐθύνας ὠφληκώς. This would involve ordinarily a fine, as well as restitution of the money embezzled.
21. οὐ περὶ.. τοῦ δήμου. 'Not on the question of the crime before them, but to save the credit of the people,' i. e. not to consider merely the guilt, however clear, of the outgoing magistrate, but the popular decree already passed in his favour, which his condemnation would stultify.
§§ 11, 12. Hence a law was made against

θέτης τίθησι νόμον καὶ μάλα καλῶς ἔχοντα, τὸν διαρρήδην
ἀπαγορεύοντα τοὺς ὑπευθύνους μὴ στεφανοῦν. καὶ ταῦτα οὕτως
εὖ προκατειληφότος τοῦ νομοθέτου εὕρηνται κρείττονες λόγοι
τῶν νόμων, οὓς εἰ μή τις ὑμῖν ἐρεῖ, λήσετε ἐξαπατηθέντες. τούτων γάρ τινες τῶν τοὺς ὑπευθύνους στεφανούντων παρὰ τοὺς 5
νόμους οἱ μὲν φύσει μέτριοί εἰσιν, εἰ δή τις ἐστὶ μέτριος ἐπὶ
τῶν τὰ παράνομα γραφόντων· ἀλλ' οὖν προβάλλονταί γε τι
πρὸ τῆς αἰσχύνης. προσεγγράφουσι γὰρ πρὸς τὰ ψηφίσματα
στεφανοῦν τὸν ὑπεύθυνον, ἐπειδὰν λόγον καὶ εὐθύνας τῆς ἀρχῆς
12 δῷ. καὶ ἡ μὲν πόλις τὸ ἴσον ἀδίκημα ἀδικεῖται· προκαταλαμβά- 10
νονται γὰρ ἐπαίνοις καὶ στεφάνοις αἱ εὔθυναι· ὁ δὲ τὸ ψήφισμα
γράφων ἐνδείκνυται τοῖς ἀκούουσιν, ὅτι γεγράφει μὲν παράνομα,
αἰσχύνεται δὲ ἐφ' οἷς ἡμάρτηκε. Κτησιφῶν δὲ, ὦ Ἀθηναῖοι,
ὑπερπηδήσας τὸν νόμον τὸ περὶ τῶν ὑπευθύνων κείμενον καὶ τὴν
πρόφασιν, ἣν ἐγὼ ἀρτίως προεῖπον ὑμῖν, ἀνελὼν, πρὶν λόγον, 15
πρὶν εὐθύνας δοῦναι, γέγραφε μεταξὺ Δημοσθένην ἄρχοντα στεφανοῦν.

13 Λέξουσι δὲ, ὦ Ἀθηναῖοι, καὶ ἕτερον λόγον ὑπεναντίον τῷ

---

3. κρείττονες] 'Recte κρείττους ex *b* Bekkerus' Frank. Nos, ubi viri docti dubitant,
decrevimus non codicum fidem, saltem unanimorum, pro Atticistarum legibus deserere.
6. ἐστὶ μέτριος ἐπὶ τῶν] Sic omnes praeter *pekl: ἐστὶ* om. *e, ἐπὶ* om. *pekl* Bekk. et
recentiorum plerique. Sed vid. annot.   8. προσεγγράφουσι] προσγράφουσι
mavolt Frankius, et hic et § 204; quod quidem illic duo codd. habent, hic non video cur
mutandum.   12. γεγράφει] Sic *amnf*: γέγραφε pr. *g, ek,* ceteri ἐγεγράφει. Vid.
annot.   18. ἕτερον] Volg. ἕτερόν τινα. τινα om. *afd* † pr. *b* †.

---

crowning any officer while accountable.
Some attempt to evade this law, but Ctesiphon defies it :
4. τούτων γάρ .... στεφανούντων. A
double designation : 'some of these—one
class of the people who propose crowns for
accountable officers in spite of the laws.'
The whole formal structure of the paragraph
is irregular : Κτησιφῶν δὲ, in the next §,
answers to οἱ μὲν, which itself is an unsymmetrical repetition of τινές.
6. ἐπί. Bekker omits this word on the
authority of his favourite group of MSS., and
Franke in the belief that Aeschines wrote
μέτριός ἐστι τῶν (as Taylor had suggested):
that ἐστὶ was carelessly written before
μέτριος, and then the ἐστὶ after μέτριος,
being superfluous, corrupted into ἐπί. But
though ἐπὶ might have been thus introduced,
it seems too easy to omit to have been
likely to have kept its place by accident :
the best MSS. agree in retaining it. And
ἐπὶ in the sense of 'among' seems justified

by Soph. Ant. 789 (where ἀμερίων ἐπ'
ἀνθρώπων is coupled with the simple genitive ἀθανάτων), and Pind. Ol. 7. 133.
12. ἐνδείκνυται. 'Leaves his hearers
room to perceive' is the force of the preposition, which may be illustrated from that
of ἐνδιδόναι.
γεγράφει. The pluperfect seems appropriate, for his present repentance is to
be strongly contrasted with his past crime :
and the unaugmented form seems most
easily to account for the double variant.
14. ὑπερπηδήσας marks his audacity,
ἀνελὼν his infatuation.
16. μεταξὺ might be joined with ἄρχοντα (as e. g. μεταξὺ θύων, Ar. Ran.
1242), but the rhetorical force of the order
proves that it stands alone ; 'proposed in the
interval (of accountability), to crown Demosthenes in office.'
§ 13. Though he also has his evasion—
that Demosthenes was not 'in office' within
the meaning of the law.

ἀρτίως εἰρημένῳ, ὡς ἄρα, ὅσα τις αἱρετὸς ὢν πράττει κατὰ
ψήφισμα, οὐκ ἔστι ταῦτα ἀρχή, ἀλλ' ἐπιμέλειά τις καὶ διακονία·
ἀρχὰς δὲ φήσουσιν ἐκείνας εἶναι, ἃς οἱ θεσμοθέται ἀποκληροῦσιν
ἐν τῷ Θησείῳ, κἀκείνας, ἃς ὁ δῆμος εἴωθε χειροτονεῖν ἐν ἀρχαι-
5 ρεσίαις, στρατηγοὺς καὶ ἱππάρχους καὶ τὰς μετὰ τούτων ἀρχάς,
τὰς δ' ἄλλας ταύτας πραγματείας προστεταγμένας κατὰ ψήφισμα. ἐγὼ δὲ πρὸς τοὺς λόγους τοὺς τούτων νόμον ὑμέτερον 14
παρέξομαι, ὃν ὑμεῖς ἐνομοθετήσατε λύσειν ἡγούμενοι τὰς τοιαύτας
προφάσεις, ἐν ᾧ διαρρήδην γέγραπται, "τὰς χειροτονητάς" φησιν
10 "ἀρχὰς" ἁπάσας ἑνὶ περιλαβὼν ὀνόματι ὁ νομοθέτης, καὶ προσ-
ειπὼν ἀρχὰς ἁπάσας εἶναι ἃς ὁ δῆμος χειροτονεῖ, "καὶ τοὺς
ἐπιστάτας" φησὶ "τῶν δημοσίων ἔργων·" ἔστι δὲ ὁ Δημοσθένης
τειχοποιός, ἐπιστάτης τοῦ μεγίστου τῶν ἔργων· "καὶ πάντας,
ὅσοι διαχειρίζουσί τι τῶν τῆς πόλεως πλέον ἢ τριάκονθ' ἡμέρας,
15 καὶ ὅσοι λαμβάνουσιν ἡγεμονίας δικαστηρίων·" οἱ δὲ τῶν ἔργων
ἐπιστάται πάντες ἡγεμονίᾳ χρῶνται δικαστηρίου· τί τούτους 15
κελεύει ποιεῖν; οὐ διακονεῖν, ἀλλ' ἄρχειν δοκιμασθέντας ἐν τῷ

---

6. τὰς δ' ἄλλας ταύτας] Sic *g ekl* et *γρb* : τὰς δ' ἄλλας ταῦτα *amn*, ceteri τὰ δ' ἄλλα πάντα.   10. προσειπών .. εἶναι] προειπὼν *ndq* Reisk : οἶμαι pro εἶναι conj. Steph. : Frankio locus corruptus videtur, et alterutra opus esse emendatione.

---

1. ἄρα. Of an absurd or paradoxical assertion, 'for it comes to that,' practically equivalent to the ironical δή, 'you are to know.'

αἱρετὸς ὤν. Opposed to ἃς οἱ θεσμ. ἀποκληροῦσιν and κατὰ ψήφισμα to ἃς ὁ δῆμος εἴωθε χειροτ. ἐν ἀρχαιρεσίαις: κατὰ ψήφισμα being the vital words. Perhaps, as Aeschines uses the plural λέγουσι, Ctesiphon may have advanced this argument: it does not occur, at any rate, in Demosthenes' published speech.

§ 14. *But the law has anticipated this trick, and after enumerating offices like his,*

7. νόμον ὑμέτερον. 'A law of yours.' Opposed word for word to τοὺς τούτων λόγους, 'a law outweighs words: you outweigh Demosthenes and Ctesiphon.' The latter point is enforced by the repetition of the pronoun, ὃν ὑμεῖς ἐνομοθ.

10. προσειπών .. εἶναι is a curious construction: Reiske with one MS. read προειπών: Bekker restored προσ., B. and S. return to προ., and Franke inclines to it, adding that it may be εἶναι that is corrupt. Stephanus and Naber conjectured οἶμαι. προειπών seems unlikely to be the sense intended: if the wording of the law had been so plain as to be thus described, Aeschines would doubtless have quoted it verbatim: and though οἶμαι is not unlike Aeschines'

manner, perhaps the received text is not so impossible as to. be worth altering in uncertainty.

15. ἡγεμονίας δικαστηρίων. These officials had a summary jurisdiction, enforced by fines (cf. ἐπιβολὰς ἐπέβαλλε, § 27), and directed the preliminary proceedings in more serious cases, before the case came to a dicasterion—something like the French *Juge d'instruction.*

§ 15. *Expressly calls them all 'magistracies,' making no distinction such as he tries to draw.*

It does not follow that, because the law of δοκιμασία expressly included the case of Demosthenes' office, therefore the law that Aeschines appealed to included it virtually; nor can we have confidence enough in the consistency of Athenian legal terminology to build, as Aeschines does, on a merely incidental expression. Without a class of skilled professional lawyers, it is not strange if an office was called an ἀρχή (still less if its holder was said ἄρχειν), when it was more strictly ἐπιμέλειά τις καὶ διακονία. Perhaps in this argument, as in the general plan of his case, Aeschines weakens his cause by attempting to prove too much : Demosthenes' other office would fall under the law, if that of τειχοποιὸς did not.

δικαστηρίῳ, ἐπειδὴ καὶ αἱ κληρωταὶ ἀρχαὶ οὐκ ἀδοκίμαστοι, ἀλλὰ
δοκιμασθεῖσαι ἄρχουσι, καὶ λόγον καὶ εὐθύνας ἐγγράφειν πρὸς
τὸν γραμματέα καὶ τοὺς λογιστὰς, καθάπερ καὶ τὰς ἄλλας
ἀρχὰς, κελεύει. ὅτι δὲ ἀληθῆ λέγω, τοὺς νόμους αὐτοὺς ὑμῖν
ἀναγνώσεται. 5

ΝΟΜΟΙ.

16 "Οταν τοίνυν, ὦ 'Αθηναῖοι, ὁ μὲν νομοθέτης ἀρχὰς ὀνομάζῃ,
οὗτοι δὲ προσαγορεύωσι πραγματείας καὶ ἐπιμελείας, ὑμέτερον
ἔργον ἐστὶν ἀπομνημονεύειν καὶ ἀντιτάττειν τὸν νόμον πρὸς τὴν
τούτων ἀναίδειαν, καὶ ὑποβάλλειν αὐτοῖς, ὅτι οὐ προσδέχεσθε 10
κακοῦργον σοφιστὴν οἰόμενον ῥήμασι τοὺς νόμους ἀναιρήσειν,
ἀλλ' ὅσῳ ἄν τις ἄμεινον λέγῃ παράνομα γεγραφὼς, τοσούτῳ
μείζονος ὀργῆς τεύξεται. χρὴ γὰρ, ὦ 'Αθηναῖοι, τὸ αὐτὸ φθέγγεσθαι τὸν ῥήτορα καὶ τὸν νόμον· ὅταν δὲ ἑτέραν μὲν φωνὴν ἀφιῇ
ὁ νόμος, ἑτέραν δὲ ὁ ῥήτωρ, τῷ τοῦ νόμου δικαίῳ χρὴ διδόναι τὴν 15
ψῆφον, οὐ τῇ τοῦ λέγοντος ἀναισχυντίᾳ.
17 Πρὸς δὲ δὴ τὸν ἄφυκτον λόγον, ὅν φησι Δημοσθένης, βραχέα
βούλομαι προειπεῖν. λέξει γὰρ οὗτος " τειχοποιός εἰμι· ὁμολογῶ·
ἀλλ' ἐπιδέδωκα τῇ πόλει μνᾶς ἑκατὸν καὶ τὸ ἔργον μεῖζον ἐξείρ-
γασμαι. τίνος οὖν εἰμι ὑπεύθυνος; εἰ μή τις ἐστιν εὐνοίας 20
εὔθυνα." πρὸς δὴ ταύτην τὴν πρόφασιν ἀκούσατέ μου λέγοντος
καὶ δίκαια καὶ συμφέροντα. ἐν γὰρ ταύτῃ τῇ πόλει οὕτως ἀρχαίᾳ
οὔσῃ καὶ τηλικαύτῃ τὸ μέγεθος οὐδείς ἐστιν ἀνυπεύθυνος τῶν καὶ

---

4. κελεύει] 'Vide ne rectius absit' Frank.　　αὐτοὺς ὑμῖν] Transp. Bekker cum ekl.
7. ὁ μὲν νομοθέτης .. οὗτοι δὲ] Sic agmn : ceteri ἃς ὁ νομοθ... ὀνομ., οὗτοι προσαγ.
18. προειπεῖν] προσειπεῖν agmfcd. Cum hic de vera lectione nemo dubitaverit, probabi-
lius videbitur, ad § 13, codd. plerosque errasse.　　19. ἐξείργασμαι] Sic a, ut videtur,
et corr. b; ceteri scripti -σται.　　22. συμφέροντα] ὑμῖν συμφέροντα cekl : δίκαια ὑμῖν
καὶ συμφέροντα habent gmn : ut nos afdb.

---

5. ἀναγνώσεται. Sc. ὁ γραμματεύς : cp.
below, § 124 fin. This is a quasi-impersonal
construction, like ἐσάλπισε, 'the trumpet
sounded,' literally '(the proper person, i. e.
ὁ σαλπικτὴς) sounded the trumpet,' and is
not uncommon in the orators.

§ 16. And you will be guided by the
laws, not by rhetoric.

10. ὑποβάλλειν combines 'reply' and
'give them to understand.'

οὐ προσδέχεσθε. We should say
'you will not tolerate' or 'you never tolerate
a pestilent sophist,' generalising the fact,
which the Greek idiom states absolutely,
as actual and individual.

§ 17. Nor does the law admit Demosthenes' alleged limitations of responsibility,
any more than his denials of it.

17. ὅν φησι Δημοσθένης. 'As Demosthenes says it is;' φησὶ like φάσκει, used
especially of a false assertion.

19. μεῖζον. 'Greater' than I found it,
or than I was bound to maintain it.

22. ἀρχαίᾳ .. τηλικαύτῃ. These epithets are not mere laudations, but intended
to create an impression that the principle of
universal responsibility must be just and
profitable, since it was sanctioned by the
immemorial practice and the immense prosperity of Athens. Further, it heightens the
force of Aeschines' universal and even paradoxical assertion, 'In all the generations of
the past, in all the multitudes of the present
day, there is not one public servant irresponsible.'

ὁπωσοῦν πρὸς τὰ κοινὰ προσεληλυθότων. διδάξω δ' ὑμᾶς πρῶτον 18
ἐπὶ τῶν παραδόξων, οἷον τοὺς ἱερεῖς καὶ τὰς ἱερείας ὑπευθύνους
εἶναι κελεύει ὁ νόμος, καὶ συλλήβδην ἅπαντας καὶ χωρὶς ἑκάστους
κατὰ σῶμα, τοὺς τὰ γέρα μόνα λαμβάνοντας καὶ τὰς εὐχὰς ὑπὲρ
5 ὑμῶν πρὸς τοὺς θεοὺς εὐχομένους, καὶ οὐ μόνον ἰδίᾳ, ἀλλὰ καὶ
κοινῇ τὰ γένη, Εὐμολπίδας καὶ Κήρυκας καὶ τοὺς ἄλλους ἅπαντας.
πάλιν τοὺς τριηράρχους ὑπευθύνους εἶναι κελεύει ὁ νόμος οὐ τὰ 19
κοινὰ διαχειρίσαντας οὐδ' ἀπὸ τῶν ὑμετέρων προσόδων πολλὰ
μὲν ὑφαιρουμένους, βραχέα δὲ κατατιθέντας, ἐπιδιδόναι δὲ φά-
10 σκοντας, ἀποδιδόντας δὲ ὑμῖν τὰ ὑμέτερα, ἀλλ' ὁμολογουμένως
τὰς πατρῴας οὐσίας εἰς τὴν πρὸς ὑμᾶς ἀνηλωκότας .φιλοτιμίαν.
οὐ τοίνυν μόνοι οἱ τριήραρχοι, ἀλλὰ καὶ τὰ μέγιστα τῶν ἐν τῇ
πόλει συνεδρίων ὑπὸ τὴν τῶν δικαστηρίων ἔρχεται ψῆφον.
πρῶτον μὲν γὰρ τὴν βουλὴν τὴν ἐν Ἀρείῳ πάγῳ ἐγγράφειν 20
15 πρὸς τοὺς λογιστὰς ὁ νόμος κελεύει λόγον καὶ εὐθύνας διδόναι,
καὶ τὸν ἐκεῖ σκυθρωπὸν καὶ τῶν μεγίστων κύριον ἄγει ὑπὸ τὴν
ὑμετέραν ψῆφον. οὐκ ἄρα στεφανωθήσεται ἡ βουλὴ ἡ ἐξ Ἀρείου
πάγου; οὐδὲ γὰρ πάτριον αὐτοῖς ἐστίν. οὐκ ἄρα φιλοτιμοῦνται;

4. μόνα] Sic ng et corr. m: ceteri et Bekk. μόνον. 6. τὰ γένη] κατὰ γένη b et
γρ. m. 14. τὴν βουλὴν τὴν ἐν Ἀρείῳ πάγῳ] τὴν β. ἐν Ἀρ. π. df, †βουλὴν ἐν Ἀρ. π.
pr. b†. 16. καὶ τὸν .. σκυθρωπὸν .. κύριον ἄγει] Om. fdbckl. Habent agmnc†γρb†
καὶ τῶν .. σκυθρωπῶν .. κύριον ἄγειν. Ut nos, marg. Bern., Lambinus, B. et S. τὴν ..
σκυθρωπῶν .. κυρίαν ἄγει Reisk. Bekk.

§ 18. *All public servants are responsible—
priests who handle no public money,*

2. ἐπὶ τῶν παραδόξων. 'In cases where
you would least expect it'—not an in-
frequent use of ἐπὶ, but forming a transition
to that noted above in § 11.

3. καὶ συλλήβδην κ. τ. λ. The whole
body is responsible for each individual : each
individual again is responsible for his own
person. And not merely the fluctuating
masses of individuals are responsible, but
the great permanent priestly families.

6. τὰ γένη. In apposition to ἱερεῖς, i. e.
is added to designate *part* of the class.
The reading κατὰ γ. is not much easier,
and has nothing else to recommend it.

§ 19. *Trierarchs who spend private money,
and that* bona fide, *unlike Demosthenes,*

The responsibility of the trierarchs was
for the condition in which they delivered
their ships. As the hull was provided by
the state, and a certain sum (though far
short of the actual cost) advanced towards
the equipment, Aeschines' argument seems
unfair : Demosthenes' position as τειχοποιὸς
was, at most, a parallel case. But perhaps
the contrast is less with this than with the
theoric fund : 'the trierarchs, though they

never administered the public property,
though *they* are not in the habit' (observe
the change of tense) 'of laying down a
little for your service, while filching largely
from your revenues, and then pretending
that these trifles are a free gift from their
property, not a restitution of yours,' are
made responsible : while *you* administered
the whole finances of Athens, as treasurer
of the theoric fund : as τειχοποιὸς, your
alleged gifts *were* only colourable.

§ 20. *Areopagites, sacred as is their
office and high as are their principles,
Senators, and all.*

16. Whether τὸν .. κύριον or τὴν .. κυρίαν is to be read seems nearly a matter of
indifference. Neither, probably, is what
Aeschines wrote : the latter (making the
Council responsible collectively) perhaps
suits the context better, the other is nearer
to the MS. reading τῶν .. σκυθρωπῶν ..
κύριον ἄγειν. But the latter seems rather
to point to καὶ [ἕκαστον] τῶν .. σκυθρωπῶν .. κυρίων or something similar. All
that can be said is, that the passage is
corrupt, and its sense clear.

18. οὐδὲ γὰρ πάτριον αὐτοῖς ἐστίν.
Cp. Λε. in Tim. § 83. p. 11, for this phrase—

πάνυ γε, ἀλλ' οὐκ ἀγαπῶσιν, ἐάν τις παρ' αὐτοῖς μὴ ἀδικῇ, ἀλλ'
ἐάν τις ἐξαμαρτάνῃ, κολάζουσιν· οἱ δὲ ὑμέτεροι ῥήτορες τρυφῶσι.
πάλιν τὴν βουλὴν τοὺς πεντακοσίους ὑπεύθυνον πεποίηκεν ὁ νομο-
21 θέτης. καὶ οὕτως ἰσχυρῶς ἀπιστεῖ τοῖς ὑπευθύνοις, ὥστ' εὐθέως
ἀρχόμενος τῶν νόμων λέγει, "ἀρχὴν ὑπεύθυνον" φησὶ "μὴ ἀπο- 5
δημεῖν." ὦ Ἡράκλεις, ὑπολάβοι ἄν τις, ὅτι ἦρξα, μὴ ἀποδημήσω;
ἵνα γε μὴ προλαβὼν χρήματα τῆς πόλεως ἢ πράξεις δρασμῷ
χρήσῃ. πάλιν ὑπεύθυνον οὐκ ἐᾷ τὴν οὐσίαν καθιεροῦν οὐδὲ ἀνάθημα
ἀναθεῖναι οὐδ' ἐκποίητον γενέσθαι οὐδὲ διαθέσθαι τὰ ἑαυτοῦ οὐδ'
ἄλλα πολλά· ἑνὶ δὲ λόγῳ ἐνεχυράζει τὰς οὐσίας ὁ νομοθέτης τὰς 10
22 τῶν ὑπευθύνων, ἕως ἂν λόγον ἀποδῶσι τῇ πόλει. ναὶ, ἀλλ' ἔστι
τις ἄνθρωπος, ὃς οὔτ' εἴληφεν οὐδὲν τῶν δημοσίων οὔτ' ἀνήλωκε,
προσῆλθε δὲ πρός τι τῶν κοινῶν. καὶ τοῦτον ἀποφέρειν κελεύει
λόγον πρὸς τοὺς λογιστάς. καὶ πῶς ὅ γε μηδὲν λαβὼν μηδ'
ἀναλώσας ἀποίσει λόγον τῇ πόλει; αὐτὸς ὑποβάλλει καὶ διδάσκει 15
ὁ νόμος ἃ χρὴ γράφειν· κελεύει γὰρ αὐτὸ τοῦτο ἐγγράφειν, ὅτι
"οὔτ' ἔλαβον οὐδὲν τῶν τῆς πόλεως οὔτ' ἀνήλωσα." ἀνεύθυνον δὲ
καὶ ἀνεξέταστον καὶ ἀζήτητον οὐδέν ἐστι τῶν ἐν τῇ πόλει. ὅτι
δὲ ἀληθῆ λέγω, αὐτῶν ἀκούσατε τῶν νόμων.

ΝΟΜΟΙ. 20

23 Ὅταν τοίνυν μάλιστα θρασύνηται Δημοσθένης λέγων, ὡς διὰ

4. ἀπιστεῖ τοῖς ὑπευθύνοις] ἀπαιτεῖ τοὺς ὑπευθύνους gmne, ἀπιστεῖ τοὺς -νους c.

part of the traditional dignity of that
court.

1. ἀλλ' οὐκ ἀγαπῶσιν .. κολάζουσιν.
'They have an ambition; but it is to suppress, not merely crimes,' such as those of
Demosthenes and Ctesiphon ' but venial irregularities,' such as Ctesiphon's might have
been, if Demosthenes were not a traitor.

2. οἱ δὲ ὑμέτεροι ῥήτορες. 'The orators
who come before you,' in contrast with παρ'
αὐτοῖς just above.

§ 21. *Accountable magistrates are subject to all sorts of restrictions, to prevent
their evading their obligations;*

6. μὴ ἀποδημήσω; μὴ repeated from
the μὴ ἀποδημεῖν to which the supposed
speaker is replying.

7. ἵνα γε μὴ κ.τ.λ. 'No, you may
not, in order that you mayn't get public
money or public business into your hands,
and then, having secured your own advantage first, run away' before the public
loss and scandal come to light.

9. ἐκποίητον γενέσθαι .. διαθέσθαι τὰ
ἑαυτοῦ. The spirit of these regulations
clearly is, that as no god, so no man should
be allowed to acquire control over the

property, or establish a claim on it, which
ought to be entirely exposed to reprisals
from the state. It may be suspected, that
the law dated from a very primitive state
of society—adoption being forbidden, because the state could only enforce its claim
through the original household and guild,
testation, because it then amounted almost
to a transfer of property. Bremi suggests,
that the reason for forbidding adoption may
be, that the official might lose his citizenship
on εὐθύνη — in which case the adoptive
father would be left without the heir he
had thought to secure.

§ 22. *And that in all cases, whether they
have handled public property or no.*

11. Ναὶ, ἀλλ'. So below, §§ 28, 168,
D. de Cor. § 313, etc. One hardly knows
whether to translate the word 'yes' or
'nay' in such cases, its use being to point
a climax, a stronger case for the supposed
objector than what has gone before. Cp.
Shilleto's excursus on the word, in his
Demosth. de Fals. Leg.

§ 23. *If then Demosthenes appeals to his
gifts, the law bids you require him to prove
that they were his own to give.*

τὴν ἐπίδοσιν οὐκ ἔστιν ὑπεύθυνος, ἐκεῖνο αὐτῷ ὑποβάλλετε· " οὐκ
οὖν ἐχρῆν σε, ὦ Δημόσθενες, ἐᾶσαι τὸν τῶν λογιστῶν κήρυκα
κηρῦξαι τὸ πάτριον καὶ ἔννομον κήρυγμα τοῦτο, 'τίς βούλεται
κατηγορεῖν ;' ἔασον ἀμφισβητῆσαί σοι τὸν βουλόμενον τῶν
5 πολιτῶν, ὡς οὐκ ἐπέδωκας, ἀλλ' ἀπὸ πολλῶν ὧν ἔχεις εἰς τὴν
τῶν τειχῶν οἰκοδομίαν μικρὰ κατέθηκας, δέκα τάλαντα εἰς ταῦτα
ἐκ τῆς πόλεως εἰληφώς. μὴ ἅρπαζε τὴν φιλοτιμίαν, μηδὲ ἐξαιροῦ
τῶν δικαστῶν τὰς ψήφους ἐκ τῶν χειρῶν, μηδ' ἔμπροσθεν τῶν
νόμων, ἀλλ' ὕστερος πολιτεύου. ταῦτα γὰρ ὀρθοῖ τὴν δημο-
10 κρατίαν."

Πρὸς μὲν οὖν τὰς κενὰς προφάσεις, ἃς οὗτοι προφασιοῦνται, 24
μέχρι τοῦδε εἰρήσθω μοι· ὅτι δὲ ὄντως ἦν ὑπεύθυνος ὁ Δημοσθένης, ὅθ' οὗτος εἰσήνεγκε τὸ ψήφισμα, ἄρχων μὲν τὴν ἐπὶ τῷ
θεωρικῷ ἀρχήν, ἄρχων δὲ τὴν τῶν τειχοποιῶν, οὐδετέρας δέ πω
15 τῶν ἀρχῶν τούτων λόγον ὑμῖν οὐδ' εὐθύνας δεδωκώς, ταῦτ' ἤδη
πειράσομαι ὑμᾶς διδάσκειν ἐκ τῶν δημοσίων γραμμάτων. καί μοι
ἀνάγνωθι, ἐπὶ τίνος ἄρχοντος καὶ ποίου μηνὸς καὶ ἐν τίνι ἡμέρᾳ
καὶ ἐν ποίᾳ ἐκκλησίᾳ ἐχειροτονήθη Δημοσθένης τὴν ἀρχὴν τὴν ἐπὶ
τῷ θεωρικῷ.

---

3. τοῦτο, 'τίς] τούτου τίς amn et corr. k.   11. κενὰς] Sic Stephanus : libri κοινάς.
14. οὐδετέρας δέ πω] οὐδετέρας πω fd + cor. b † οὐδετέρας δὲ ekl, † οὐδετέρας πως b.†
18. ἐπὶ τῷ θεωρικῷ] Sic cd Bekk. et post eum omnes : ceteri τῶν -κῶν. Addebatur ὅτι
μεσοῦντα τὴν ἀρχὴν ἔγραψεν αὐτὸν στεφανοῦν. ἀναγίνωσκε. Haec om. ekl : k in margine
inseruit, ὁ διαλογισμὸς τῶν ἡμερῶν ὅτι .. στεφανοῦν, ἀναγινώσκεται. Et ἀναγινώσκεται
sibi volunt fcdh, dum ἀναγινώσκετε habent : nempe id glossema ex titulo in textum irrepsit.
Ipsum titulum om. agmn bl.

---

3. πάτριον καὶ ἔννομον. These words
suggest the reason why Demosthenes should
have submitted to it, and why Aeschines
should object to its suppression.

4. ἔασον .. εἰληφώς. A specification of
the fraud more vaguely insinuated in
§ 19.

7. τὴν φιλοτιμίαν. 'Your public spirit,'
i. e. your character or reputation for that
quality. Cp. below, § 45, ψευδῆ φιλοτιμίαν
κτᾶται.

8. μηδ' ἔμπροσθεν κ. τ. λ. 'And let
your public action follow the laws, not
outrun them.' It was a perfectly legitimate
πολίτευμα to spend money in the public
service, and then expect a crown for it:
but before doing this, Demosthenes should
have satisfied the laws which prescribed
εὐθῦναι as a condition antecedent to a
crown. For the sentiment of the next
clause, cp. on § 6.

§ 24. So much for their arguments. The
fact, that Demosthenes was accountable,
admits of no argument.

11. οὗτοι. Demosthenes and Ctesiphon.
οὗτος in a judicial speech is constantly 'the
man before you,' so, usually as here, the
opponent of the speaker. However, in
D. de Cor. §§ 15, 103 etc., he calls
Ctesiphon τουτονί : but quite as commonly
τόνδε or τονδί, 'the man by my side,'
§§ 144, 344. In Latin, the distinction between hic, 'the man by my side,' and iste,
'the man before you,' or sometimes (addressing the opponent's advocate) 'your
client' is more regular : the distinction
between the two demonstratives being more
fixed, and their relation to the first and
second persons more symmetrical in Latin
than in Greek. In the next sentence, οὗτος
is Ctesiphon as opposed to Demosthenes,
being the man actually before the court,
while Demosthenes, he says, has no need
and no business to appear there.

14. οὐδετέρας .. δεδωκώς. Cp. D. de
Cor. 149 : he says that he did pass his
εὐθῦναι at the proper time, unchallenged by
Aeschines or any one else.

ΔΙΑΛΟΓΙΣΜΟΣ ΤΩΝ ΗΜΕΡΩΝ.

Οὐκοῦν εἰ μηδὲν ἔτι περαιτέρω τούτου δείξαιμι, δικαίως ἂν
ἁλίσκοιτο Κτησιφῶν· αἱρεῖ γὰρ αὐτὸν οὐχ ἡ κατηγορία ἡ ἐμή,
ἀλλὰ τὰ δημόσια γράμματα.

25 Πρῶτον μὲν τοίνυν, ὦ 'Αθηναῖοι, ἀντιγραφεὺς ἦν χειροτονητὸς 5
τῇ πόλει, ὃς καθ' ἑκάστην πρυτανείαν ἀπελογίζετο τὰς προσόδους
τῷ δήμῳ· διὰ δὲ τὴν πρὸς Εὔβουλον γενομένην πίστιν ὑμῖν οἱ ἐπὶ
τὸ θεωρικὸν κεχειροτονημένοι ἦρχον μὲν, πρὶν ἢ τὸν 'Ηγήμονος
νόμον γενέσθαι, τὴν τοῦ ἀντιγραφέως ἀρχήν, ἦρχον δὲ τὴν τῶν
ἀποδεκτῶν, καὶ νεώριον καὶ σκευοθήκην ᾠκοδόμουν, ἦσαν δὲ καὶ 10
26 ὁδοποιοὶ καὶ σχεδὸν τὴν ὅλην διοίκησιν εἶχον τῆς πόλεως. καὶ οὐ
κατηγορῶν αὐτῶν οὐδ' ἐπιτιμῶν λέγω, ἀλλ' ἐκεῖνο ὑμῖν ἐνδείξασθαι
βούλομαι, ὅτι ὁ μὲν νομοθέτης, ἐάν τις μιᾶς ἀρχῆς τῆς ἐλαχίστης
ὑπεύθυνος ᾖ, τοῦτον οὐκ ἐᾷ, πρὶν ἂν λόγους καὶ εὐθύνας δῷ,
στεφανοῦν, ὁ δὲ Κτησιφῶν Δημοσθένην τὸν συλλήβδην ἁπάσας 15
τὰς 'Αθήνησιν ἀρχὰς ἄρχοντα οὐκ ὤκνησε γράψαι στεφανῶσαι.

27 'Ως τοίνυν καὶ τὴν τῶν τειχοποιῶν ἀρχὴν ἦρχεν, ὅθ' οὗτος τὸ

---

10. ἀποδεκτῶν, καὶ νεώριον καὶ σκευοθήκην] Sic post Dobree. Frankius. ἀποδεκτῶν καὶ
νεωρίων ἀρχήν, καὶ σκ. libri et Bekk. : νεωρῶν pro -ρίων substituit Stephanus, ἀρχὴν delebat
Markl. 14. λόγους] Mala uniformitatis cupidine λόγον substituit Frank.

§§ 25, 26. *Since the time of Eubulus, the treasurer of the Theoric fund has held a combination of offices formerly distinct: Demosthenes therefore was accountable for all.*

8. ἦρχον‥ ἀρχήν, ἦρχον. As in the preceding section, Aeschines uses the word on the applicability of which he is insisting, over and over, so as by repeated begging the question to persuade the hearers to regard the point as self-evident. Here, as often, his rhetorical artifices bear too much trace of self-conscious labour.

10. ἀποδεκτῶν, καὶ νεώριον καὶ σκευοθήκην. The MSS. reading, ἀποδ. καὶ νεωρίων ἀρχήν, καὶ σκ., is hardly credible, though retained by Bekker and Bremi. Stephanus substituted νεωρῶν, which makes sense; Markland omitted ἀρχήν, which makes the style tolerable; Franke, following Dobree, reads as in the text, which when once suggested is almost self-evidently right. Though Aeschines is fond enough of the word ἀρχή, he would not have sacrificed the whole cadence of the passage to secure one more repetition of it.

11. καὶ οὐ κατηγορῶν κ. τ. λ. I do not say that these numerous offices were no* in general well discharged : only, that as so many were included in that of administrator of the festival fund, so many are there for

which Demosthenes was accountable, and so many legal barriers between him and the crown. Demosthenes' reply (de Cor. §§ 142 sqq.) is substantially, ' For my voluntary expenditure as τειχοποιὸς I was not accountable : for my official receipts I was' (in which the theoric fund would be included). ' But my crown was for the former only : and the court were perfectly free to pass my accounts for the latter (which they did) or not, whatever the people might have voted on the other point.' That is to say, the spirit of the law was not violated ; which is as much as to say, the letter was : as indeed Aeschines had proved triumphantly.

§ 27. *And his own motion for appointing commissioners for the walls proves that he intended them to be accountable magistrates :*

17. 'Ως τοίνυν κ. τ. λ. Having proved that Demosthenes held, within the meaning of the law, an ἀρχὴ ὑπεύθ. in regard to the theoric fund, he proceeds to the more doubtful point, that his office as τειχοποιὸς fell within it also. The proof is sought in the wording of Demosthenes' own decree under which he obtained the office—with the proposing of which Ctesiphon seems to have been connected. Not having the text of the decree, we cannot judge of the argument.

ψήφισμα ἔγραψε, καὶ τὰ δημόσια χρήματα διεχείριζε καὶ ἐπιβολὰς ἐπέβαλλε, καθάπερ οἱ ἄλλοι ἄρχοντες, καὶ δικαστηρίων
ἡγεμονίας ἐλάμβανε, τούτων ὑμῖν αὐτὸν Δημοσθένην καὶ Κτησιφῶντα μάρτυρας παρέξομαι. ἐπὶ γὰρ Χαιρώνδου ἄρχοντος θαρ-
5 γηλιῶνος μηνὸς δευτέρα φθίνοντος ἐκκλησίας οὔσης ἔγραψε
ψήφισμα Δημοσθένης ἀγορὰν ποιῆσαι τῶν φυλῶν σκιροφοριῶνος
δευτέρα ἱσταμένου καὶ τρίτη, καὶ ἐπέταξεν ἐν τῷ ψηφίσματι
ἑκάστης τῶν φυλῶν ἑλέσθαι τοὺς ἐπιμελησομένους τῶν ἔργων
ἐπὶ τὰ τείχη καὶ ταμίας, καὶ μάλα ὀρθῶς, ἵν᾽ ἡ πόλις ἔχῃ
10 ὑπεύθυνα σώματα, παρ᾽ ὧν ἔμελλε τῶν ἀνηλωμένων λόγον ἀπο-
λήψεσθαι. καί μοι λέγε τὰ ψηφίσματα.

ΨΗΦΙΣΜΑΤΑ.

Ναὶ, ἀλλ᾽ ἀντιδιαπλέκει πρὸς τοῦτο εὐθέως λέγων, ὡς οὔτ᾽ 28
ἔλαχε τειχοποιὸς οὔτ᾽ ἐχειροτονήθη ὑπὸ τοῦ δήμου. καὶ περὶ
15 τούτου Δημοσθένης μὲν καὶ Κτησιφῶν πολὺν ποιήσονται λόγον·
ὁ δέ γε νόμος βραχὺς καὶ σαφὴς καὶ ταχὺ λύων τὰς τούτων
τέχνας. μικρὰ δὲ ὑμῖν ὑπὲρ αὐτῶν πρῶτον προειπεῖν βούλομαι.
ἔστι γάρ, ὦ Ἀθηναῖοι, τῶν περὶ τὰς ἀρχὰς εἴδη τρία, ὧν ἓν μὲν 29
καὶ φανερώτατον οἱ κληρωτοὶ καὶ οἱ χειροτονητοὶ ἄρχοντες,

---

3. **Δημοσθένην]** -νη *acb* Bekk., qui sic passim. Variat librorum usus, sed plerumque
-νην habent, idque cum B. et S. et Frankio retinemus.   **καὶ Κτησιφῶντα μάρτυρας]**
μάρτυρα καὶ Κτ. *ekl*, μάρτυρα Hamaker, probante Frankio.   8. **ἐπιμελησομένους]** Sic
apckl: ceteri ἐπιμελησομένους quod nunc mavolt Frankius.   9. **ἔχῃ]** ἔχοι *k* Bekk.
13. **εὐθέως]** εὐθὺς *kl* Bekk.: idemque et hic et ad § 21 mavolt Frankius. Ibi habent *ekl*,
sed non recepit Bekk.   **λέγων]** Om. *ekl* Bekk.   16. **βραχὺς .. λύων]** βραχῆ καὶ
σαφῆ καὶ .. λύοντα *ekl*, † βραχὺν (non βραχῆ ut testatur Bekk)† καὶ σαφῆ καὶ ταχὺ
κωλύοντα *b*.   19. **φανερώτατον]** πᾶσι φαν. *fcdb ekl* Bekk.

---

4. **ἐπὶ γὰρ Χαιρώνδου.** See excursus on
documents for the chronological difficulties.
6. **ἀγοράν.** The old word for an assembly of the people, but in speaking of the
whole people superseded by the later ἐκκλησία.
9. **καὶ μάλα ὀρθῶς.** It was right to
appoint special commissioners, holding office
by decree of the people, that the people
might know whom to hold responsible : but
their responsibility was destroyed by Ctesiphon's motion.
§§ 28-30. *The law being too general to
admit of his quibbles about the mode of his
appointment.*
13. **ἀντιδιαπλέκει.** Literally, 'meets this
with a new twist :' for such metaphors from
wrestling, cp. below, § 206 etc.
15. **πολὺν ποιήσονται λόγον.** Cp. above
on § 13.
16. **βραχὺς καὶ σαφὴς καὶ ταχὺ λύων.**

So all the best MSS. : the inferior group has
βραχὺν (or βραχῆ) καὶ σαφῆ καὶ ταχὺ
λύοντα (or κωλύοντα). This makes the
antithesis much more vigorous, and one
could wish that there were authority for
adopting it : 'they will produce a great deal
of irrelevant argument : the law will answer
them with a short and decisive one.' But
perhaps such an abrupt prosopopoeia is, in
its very vigour, unlike Aeschines.
§ 29. Demosthenes complains (de Cor.
§ 156) that Aeschines had garbled the laws
he quoted : perhaps the charge would apply
here, as he seems to wish to reduce three
legal categories to two.   The argument
seems to rest, as before, merely on the use
of the word ἄρχειν, applied to the third
class of offices : or perhaps also it may be
implied, that as they carried with them the
requirement of δοκιμασία, so they did of
εὐθῦναι.

δεύτερον δὲ ὅσοι τι διαχειρίζουσι τῶν τῆς πόλεως ὑπὲρ τριάκοντα
ἡμέρας καὶ οἱ τῶν δημοσίων ἔργων ἐπιστάται, τρίτον δ᾽ ἐν τῷ
νόμῳ γέγραπται, καὶ εἴ τινες ἄλλοι αἱρετοὶ ἡγεμονίας δικαστη-
30 ρίων λαμβάνουσι, καὶ τούτους ἄρχειν δοκιμασθέντας. ἐπειδὰν δ᾽
ἀφέλῃ τις τοὺς ὑπὸ τοῦ δήμου κεχειροτονημένους καὶ τοὺς κληρω- 5
τοὺς ἄρχοντας, καταλείπεται, οὓς αἱ φυλαὶ καὶ αἱ τριττύες καὶ οἱ
δῆμοι ἐξ ἑαυτῶν αἱροῦνται τὰ δημόσια χρήματα διαχειρίζειν,
τούτους αἱρετοὺς ἄρχοντας εἶναι. τοῦτο δὲ γίγνεται, ὅταν, ὥσπερ
νῦν, ἐπιταχθῇ τι ταῖς φυλαῖς, ἢ τάφρους ἐξεργάζεσθαι ἢ τριήρεις
ναυπηγεῖσθαι. ὅτι δὲ ἀληθῆ λέγω, ἐξ αὐτῶν τῶν νόμων μαθή- 10
σεσθε.

ΝΟΜΟΙ.

31 Ἀναμνήσθητε δὴ τοὺς προειρημένους λόγους, ὅτι ὁ μὲν νομοθέτης τοὺς ἐκ τῶν φυλῶν ἄρχειν κελεύει δοκιμασθέντας ἐν τῷ
δικαστηρίῳ, ἡ δὲ Πανδιονὶς φυλὴ ἄρχοντα καὶ τειχοποιὸν ἀπέδειξε 15
Δημοσθένην, ὃς ἐκ τῆς διοικήσεως εἰς ταῦτα ἔχει μικροῦ δεῖν δέκα
τάλαντα, ἕτερος δ᾽ ἀπαγορεύει νόμος ἀρχὴν ὑπεύθυνον μὴ στεφανοῦν, ὑμεῖς δὲ ὀμωμόκατε κατὰ τοὺς νόμους ψηφιεῖσθαι, ὁ δὲ
ῥήτωρ γέγραφε τὸν ὑπεύθυνον στεφανοῦν μὴ προσθεὶς "ἐπειδὰν

5. ἀφέλῃ] ἀφέληται *agmn*: et ad § 45.   6. καταλείπεται] Sic, ut videtur, *n*: *agm*
καταλίπωνται, *l* καταλείπονται, *p* καταλείπωνται, *fcdbgek* καταλείπονται habent.   'Recte C.
Scheibius,' inquit Frank., 'καταλίπονται [sic]' sed deletis verbis τούτους αἱρετοὺς ἄρχοντας
εἶναι, scribi jubet.'   19. μὴ] οὐ *ekl* Bekk. Frank.

4. There are first the magistrates
elected by, or selected by lot from, the
whole nation whom everybody admits to be
magistrates : the *two* other classes recognised
as magistrates by the law must be different
classes of men elected by local bodies.
   8. τοῦτο δὲ κ.τ.λ. For it could not be
pretended that a *merely* local office, appointed by the local body at its own discretion, was an imperial magistracy, and
carried the obligations and disabilities of
one: it was when the local body was only
employed as a machinery for the purposes
of the nation at large, that Aeschines' view
was at least tenable.
   ὥσπερ νῦν. 'As in the present case,'
not of course 'as at the present time ;' for
Demosthenes' office, and the occasion for it,
had now long expired.
   § 31. *Put the two groups of laws together* : 'Nominees of tribes shall enter on
office :' *Demosthenes is an official nominated
by a tribe.* '*An official may not be crowned
before his accounts :' with what right can
Ctesiphon propose that Demosthenes shall* ?
   15. ἄρχοντα καὶ τειχοποιόν. The καὶ
is almost epexegetical, 'nominated him to

an office, viz. that of ....' The order
would perhaps more commonly be τειχοποιὸν καὶ ἄρχοντα, 'commissioner of fortifications, and (as such) a magistrate,' which
illustrates the process of thought by which
the simple copulative gets this force.
   16. ἔχει. The present might be used
merely to contrast his holding the money,
a permanent condition, with the altogether
past individual incident of his nomination (ἀπέδειξε): but Aeschines no doubt
means to insinuate, that Demosthenes
had embezzled the money, and had got it
still.
   18. ὁ δὲ ῥήτωρ. Ctesiphon was not a
professed public speaker (below, § 215): but
(as the better Scholiast remarks) Aeschines
calls him so with a purpose, meaning :—' If
you are speaker enough to make a proposal
in the Assembly, you ought to be able to
defend it in court.' Cp. below, § 243.
   19. μὴ προσθείς. So the better MSS.
μὴ marks the absence of this precaution as
a *condition* of thorough flagrant illegality.
οὐ προσθεὶς would be simply 'and he did
not add,' μὴ προσθεὶς = 'while yet he did
not add.'

16   ΑΙΣΧΙΝΟΥ   §§ 32-34·

δῷ λόγον καὶ εὐθύνας," ἐγὼ δὲ ἐξελέγχω τὸ παράνομον μάρτυρας
ἅμα τοὺς νόμους καὶ τὰ ψηφίσματα καὶ τοὺς ἀντιδίκους παρεχόμενος. πῶς οὖν ἄν τις περιφανέστερον ἐπιδείξειεν ἄνθρωπον
παρανομώτατα γεγραφότα;
5 Ὡς τοίνυν καὶ τὴν ἀνάρρησιν τοῦ στεφάνου παρανόμως ἐν τῷ 32
ψηφίσματι κελεύει γίγνεσθαι, καὶ τοῦθ᾽ ὑμᾶς διδάξω. ὁ γὰρ
νόμος διαρρήδην κελεύει, ἐὰν μέν τινα στεφανοῖ ἡ βουλὴ, ἐν τῷ
βουλευτηρίῳ ἀνακηρύττεσθαι, ἐὰν δὲ ὁ δῆμος, ἐν τῇ ἐκκλησίᾳ,
ἄλλοθι δὲ μηδαμοῦ. καί μοι λέγε τὸν νόμον.

10   ΝΟΜΟΣ.

Οὗτος ὁ νόμος, ὦ Ἀθηναῖοι, καὶ μάλα καλῶς ἔχει. οὐ γὰρ, 33
οἶμαι, ᾤετο δεῖν ὁ νομοθέτης τὸν ῥήτορα σεμνύνεσθαι πρὸς τοὺς
ἔξωθεν, ἀλλ᾽ ἀγαπᾶν ἐν αὐτῇ τῇ πόλει τιμώμενον ὑπὸ τοῦ δήμου
καὶ μὴ ἐργολαβεῖν ἐν τοῖς κηρύγμασιν. ὁ μὲν οὖν νομοθέτης
15 οὕτως· ὁ δὲ Κτησιφῶν πῶς; ἀναγίγνωσκε τὸ ψήφισμα.

                      ΨΗΦΙΣΜΑ.

Ἀκούετε, ὦ Ἀθηναῖοι, ὅτι ὁ μὲν νομοθέτης κελεύει ἐν τῷ δήμῳ 34
ἐν Πυκνὶ τῇ ἐκκλησίᾳ ἀνακηρύττειν τὸν ὑπὸ τοῦ δήμου στεφα-

1. ἐξελέγχω] Sic Steph. Bekk. et alii: ἐλέγξω l, ἐλέγξω gn, ceteri ἐξελέγξω.   4. παρα-
νομώτατα] Sic agmnc : ceteri et Bekk. παράνομα.

2. τοὺς ἀντιδίκους refers to § 27,
Δημοσθένην καὶ Κτησιφῶντα μάρτυρας
παρέξομαι : perhaps also to § 13 init., where
he points out that their own arguments
destroy one another.
  § 32. The manner of proclamation is as
illegal as the thing to be proclaimed.
  9. ἄλλοθι δὲ μηδαμοῦ. From §§ 34, 48,
it appears that this is a verbatim quotation
from the law : in the law given at D. de Cor.
§ 155 of course these words do not appear.
The law which Demosthenes cited was, indeed, a different one from that alleged by
Aeschines here (see below, § 36), but the
text of the law there given seems to be
framed on Demosthenes' speech alone, and
not even to harmonise perfectly with that.
See D. de Cor. § 155.
  § 33. For the law wisely regards services
to Athens as fitly recompensed by Athenian
fame :
  12. τὸν ῥήτορα. Note how Aeschines
damages his argument, at its strongest
points, by giving way to his temper. He
ought to have confined himself here to a
dispassionate exposition of the actual general
provisions and objects of the law : but
instead, he quotes it as though the legislator
were his συνήγορος, and all his words had

been framed with a view to the special case.
In all probability, the law dates from a
time when the most frequent recipients of
crowns would not be ῥήτορες, but either
generals, or citizens to be thanked for
ἐπιδόσεις : it would be a rare coincidence
for the latter to be, like Demosthenes,
statesmen as well. And with a soldier or
private citizen, the danger alleged by
Aeschines would not be likely to arise : the
one would be already known by foreigners,
the other could hardly hope to become so.
  14. ἐργολαβεῖν ἐν τοῖς κηρύγμασιν.
'Make these proclamations a matter of
trade,' 'speculate in proclamations.' The
insinuation is, that to have a vote of thanks
proclaimed before a large number of foreigners was an advertisement of political influence, which it might be worth the while
of foreign states or their citizens to pur-
chase.
  § 34. But Demosthenes is not satisfied,
unless we exhibit his undeserved honours to
our visitors from all Greece.
  18. τῇ ἐκκλησίᾳ must be a dative of
time, being explained by ἐκκλησιαζόντων
Ἀθηναίων below, rather than in epexegetical
apposition with Πυκνί, like τὴν βουλὴν τοὺς
πεντακοσίους, above § 2.

νούμενον, ἄλλοθι δὲ μηδαμοῦ, Κτησιφῶν δὲ ἐν τῷ θεάτρῳ,
οὐ τοὺς νόμους μόνον ὑπερβὰς, ἀλλὰ καὶ τὸν τόπον μετενεγκὼν,
οὐδὲ ἐκκλησιαζόντων Ἀθηναίων, ἀλλὰ τραγῳδῶν ἀγωνιζομένων
καινῶν, οὐδ᾽ ἐναντίον τοῦ δήμου, ἀλλ᾽ ἐναντίον τῶν Ἑλλήνων, ἵν᾽
35 ἡμῖν συνειδῶσιν, οἷον ἄνδρα τιμῶμεν. οὕτω τοίνυν περιφανῶς 5
παράνομα γεγραφὼς, παραταχθεὶς μετὰ Δημοσθένους ἐποίσει
τέχνας τοῖς νόμοις· ἃς ἐγὼ δηλώσω καὶ προερῶ ὑμῖν, ἵνα μὴ
λάθητε ἐξαπατηθέντες. οὗτοι γὰρ, ὡς μὲν οὐκ ἀπαγορεύουσιν οἱ
νόμοι τὸν ὑπὸ τοῦ δήμου στεφανούμενον μὴ κηρύττειν ἔξω τῆς
ἐκκλησίας, οὐχ ἕξουσι λέγειν, οἴσουσι δὲ εἰς τὴν ἀπολογίαν τὸν 10
Διονυσιακὸν νόμον, καὶ χρήσονται τοῦ νόμου μέρει τινὶ κλέπ-
36 τοντες τὴν ἀκρόασιν ὑμῶν, καὶ παρέξονται νόμον οὐδὲν προσήκοντα τῇ γραφῇ τῇδε, καὶ λέξουσιν, ὡς εἰσὶ τῇ πόλει δύο νόμοι
κείμενοι περὶ τῶν κηρυγμάτων, εἷς μὲν, ὃν νῦν ἐγὼ παρέχομαι,
διαρρήδην ἀπαγορεύων τὸν ὑπὸ τοῦ δήμου στεφανούμενον μὴ 15
κηρύττεσθαι ἔξω τῆς ἐκκλησίας, ἕτερον δ᾽ εἶναι νόμον φήσουσιν
ἐναντίον τούτῳ, τὸν δεδωκότα ἐξουσίαν ποιεῖσθαι τὴν ἀνάρρησιν τοῦ στεφάνου τραγῳδοῖς ἐν τῷ θεάτρῳ, ἐὰν ψηφίσηται ὁ

13. τῇ γραφῇ τῇδε] 'Cum edd. Turice. ex agmnp suscepi. Vellem volgatum τῇδε τῇ γραφῇ retinuissem' Frank. 15. ἀπαγορεύων] ἀπαγορεύοντα fcdb Bekk. Cum ceteris mutant Brem. B. et S. Frank.

2. οὐ τοὺς νόμους μόνον ὑπερβάς. The substantial violation of the laws was in proposing the crown at all: changing the place might be called a technical error, though that was bad enough. Still the antithesis is unsymmetrical,—a common fault with Aeschines.

4. τῶν Ἑλλήνων opposed to τοῦ δήμου, much as τὰ Ἑλληνικὰ to τὰ κατὰ τὴν πόλιν πολιτεύματα, D. de Cor. § 139.

§ 35. This point, indeed, they will defend by a quibble,

6. παραταχθεὶς μετὰ Δημοσθένους. This seems to point to the conclusion, already conjecturally mentioned, that Ctesiphon undertook the more technical parts of the defence. Yet § 202 inf. seems to prevent this, unless the two passages refer to different recensions of the speech. The argument is, indeed, mentioned in Demosthenes' speech (§§ 155-56), but briefly and contemptuously, much as if Aeschines had been (or the speaker affected to think he had been) sufficiently refuted already.

7. ἵνα μὴ λάθητε. Contrary to the usual force of this Greek construction, the verb seems to be here more emphatic than the participle. One might translate, 'that if you are deceived, it may not be for want of warning.'

11. κλέπτοντες τὴν ἀκρόασιν ὑμῶν. The trick played is probably the using part of the law—quoting one clause out of its context, which, if taken by itself, might bear the sense required to justify Ctesiphon. If it were certain that Aeschines was referring to the passage in Demosthenes' speech just cited (de Cor. § 156), the expression here would describe very well the way he begs the question by a burst of eloquence (τί οὖν, ὦ ταλαίπωρε, συκοφαντεῖς; κ.τ λ.), and so evades the necessity of replying to Aeschines' careful explanation of the law.

§§ 36, 37. Which it is an insult to the city to allege, not refuting the applicability of this law, but asserting that another contradicts it.

15. ἀπαγορεύων. We follow the MS. authority like most recent editors; but ἀπαγορεύων is the more obvious reading, and -οντα perhaps the more accurate. The force is, 'which I allege to prove my point,' not 'which they describe as telling in my favour.'

18. τραγῳδοῖς like τῇ ἐκκλησίᾳ as explained above, § 34. A similar phrase occurs in the text of the indictment given at D. de Cor. § 67, and of Ctesiphon's motion at § 152, τραγῳδοῖς καινοῖς—explained. in Reiske's Indices, ed. Mitchell, ἐπὶ τραγῳδοῖς

δῆμος· κατὰ δὴ τοῦτον τὸν νόμον φήσουσι γεγραφέναι τὸν
Κτησιφῶντα. ἐγὼ δὲ πρὸς τὰς τούτων τέχνας παρέξομαι 37
συνηγόρους τοὺς νόμους τοὺς ὑμετέρους, ὅπερ διατελῶ σπουδάζων παρὰ πᾶσαν τὴν κατηγορίαν. εἰ γὰρ τοῦτό ἐστιν ἀλη-
5 θὲς καὶ τοιοῦτον ἔθος παραδέδυκεν ὑμῶν εἰς τὴν πολιτείαν, ὥστ᾽
ἀκύρους νόμους ἐν τοῖς κυρίοις ἀναγεγράφθαι καὶ δύο περὶ μιᾶς
πράξεως ὑπεναντίους ἀλλήλοις, τί ἂν ἔτι ταύτην εἴποι τις
εἶναι τὴν πολιτείαν, ἐν ᾗ ταὐτὰ προστάττουσιν οἱ νόμοι ποιεῖν
καὶ μὴ ποιεῖν; ἀλλ᾽ οὐκ ἔχει ταῦθ᾽ οὕτως· μήθ᾽ ὑμεῖς ποτε εἰς 38
10 τοσαύτην ἀταξίαν τῶν νόμων προβαίητε, οὔτε ἠμέληται περὶ
τῶν τοιούτων τῷ νομοθέτῃ τῷ τὴν δημοκρατίαν καταστήσαντι,
ἀλλὰ διαρρήδην προστέτακται τοῖς θεσμοθέταις καθ᾽ ἕκαστον
ἐνιαυτὸν διορθοῦν ἐν τῷ δήμῳ τοὺς νόμους, ἀκριβῶς ἐξετάσαντας
καὶ σκεψαμένους, εἴ τις ἀναγέγραπται νόμος ἐναντίος ἑτέρῳ
15 νόμῳ ἢ ἄκυρος ἐν τοῖς κυρίοις, ἢ εἴ που εἰσὶ νόμοι πλείους ἑνὸς
ἀναγεγραμμένοι περὶ ἑκάστης πράξεως. κἄν τι τοιοῦτον εὑρί- 39
σκωσιν, ἀναγεγραφότας ἐν σανίσιν ἐκτιθέναι κελεύει πρόσθεν

9. μήθ᾽] μὴ agmnekl.

καινοῖς εἰσιοῦσιν εἰς τὴν σκηνήν. In D. de
Cor. § 68, the strange phrase occurs τραγῳδῶν τῇ καινῇ, which looks almost as though
the compiler found the dative used, and did
not understand it.
ἐὰν ψηφίσηται. Cp. ad D. de Cor.
§ 155.
3. ὅπερ διατελῶ σπουδάζων. The object for which Aeschines claims to be zealous is only to prove that he has the law
with him, not simply to enforce the law :
still this sincere eagerness to rest his case on
legal rather than political grounds, is in
harmony with his narrow conceptions and
respectable character.
6. καὶ δύο περὶ μιᾶς πράξεως. καὶ
marks a climax : it is bad enough to have
obsolete laws mixed up with those still valid,
but worse to have two laws mutually invali-
dating each other.
§§ 38-40. *Such folly is not only unworthy
of the city, but impossible in it. The constitution provides an express remedy for any
such danger.*
9. μήθ᾽ ὑμεῖς .. οὔτε ἠμέληται. It is
physically possible but morally impossible
for the nation to disgrace itself : for the
legislator (whose work is complete and
satisfactory, and an object of almost religious reverence) it is not even physically
possible that he should have stultified himself so completely. Such is the motive for

using the two different negatives : occasion-
ally they are coupled together where the
antithesis is less emphatic and serious, e. g.
Soph. Ant. 676, οὔτ᾽ ἂν δυναίμην μή τ᾽
ἐπισταίμην λέγειν. It is hardly necessary
to suppose that Aeschines was consciously
imitating a poetical construction, though as
an actor he must have been familiar with
Sophocles.
11. τῷ νομοθέτῃ τῷ τὴν δημοκρατίαν
καταστήσαντι. Does Aeschines mean to
assert that this particular law dated from
Clisthenes? Solon can hardly be meant.
Every organic law was popularly referred to
him, the more readily that the history of
Athens had really been a development of
his code and constitution. Aeschines' views
on Athenian history were decidedly inaccurate (see de F. L. p. 51, §§ 183-7), though
the mention of νομοθέτης τις (inf. § 44)
as reforming a recent abuse, shows that
he knew everything did not date from
Solon.
17. πρόσθεν τῶν ἐπωνύμων. Before
the statues of the heroes, the Eponymi of
the ten Tribes, which stood in the Ceramicus. This is an argument for the law
being really as old as Clisthenes (whether
Aeschines means expressly to ascribe it to
him or not) : it would be a special object
with him to secure a religious sanction to
his innovations on the old order.

τῶν ἐπωνύμων, τοὺς δὲ πρυτάνεις ποιεῖν ἐκκλησίαν ἐπιγράψαντας νομοθέτας, τὸν δ' ἐπιστάτην τῶν προέδρων διαχειροτονίαν
διδόναι τῷ δήμῳ, καὶ τοὺς μὲν ἀναιρεῖν τῶν νόμων, τοὺς δὲ
καταλείπειν, ὅπως ἂν εἷς ᾖ νόμος καὶ μὴ πλείους ἑκάστης πράξεως. καί μοι λέγε τοὺς νόμους.　　　　　　　　　　　　　　5

ΝΟΜΟΙ.

40　Εἰ τοίνυν, ὦ Ἀθηναῖοι, ἀληθὴς ἦν ὁ παρὰ τούτων λόγος
καὶ ἦσαν δύο κείμενοι νόμοι περὶ τῶν κηρυγμάτων, ἐξ ἀνάγκης,
οἶμαι, τῶν μὲν θεσμοθετῶν ἐξευρόντων, τῶν δὲ πρυτάνεων ἀπο-
δόντων τοῖς νομοθέταις ἀνῄρητ' ἂν ὁ ἕτερος τῶν νόμων, ἤτοι 10
ὁ τὴν ἐξουσίαν δεδωκὼς ἀνειπεῖν ἢ ὁ ἀπαγορεύων· ὁπότε δὲ
μηδὲν τούτων γεγένηται, φανερῶς δή που ἐξελέγχονται οὐ μόνον ψευδῆ λέγοντες, ἀλλὰ καὶ παντελῶς ἀδύνατα γενέσθαι.
41 ὅθεν δὲ δὴ τὸ ψεῦδος τοῦτο ἐπιφέρουσιν, ἐγὼ διδάξω ὑμᾶς
προειπὼν, ὧν ἕνεκα οἱ νόμοι ἐτέθησαν οἱ περὶ τῶν ἐν τῷ θεά- 15
τρῳ κηρυγμάτων. γιγνομένων γὰρ τῶν ἐν ἄστει τραγῳδῶν
ἀνεκήρυττόν τινες, οὐ πείσαντες τὸν δῆμον, οἱ μὲν ὅτι στεφανοῦνται ὑπὸ τῶν φυλετῶν, ἕτεροι δ' ὑπὸ τῶν δημοτῶν· ἄλλοι

---

2. νομοθέτας] Editores plerique νομοθέταις, Dobreeum secuti.　4. ἑκάστης πράξεως]
Legebatur περὶ ἑκάστης πράξεως. Praepositionem cum agmnſcdbq delevimus.　9. οἶμαι]
οἴομαι agmncdh Bekk.　　ἀποδόντων] ἀποδιδόντων agmn.　12. γεγένηται] γένηται
agmn.　18. ἕτεροι δ' ὑπὸ] ὅ τι ὑπὸ volt Cobetus.

1. ἐπιγράψαντας νομοθέτας. So the MSS. and Bekker.　Dobree first suggested νομοθέταις, 'writing (on the notice of assembly) "For the Nomothetae."' Such is doubtless the sense: that would most likely be the actual word written. But the accusative, the word written being treated as the object of the verb rather than an explanation of it, may be defended: it is exactly like κἀμοὶ, λέγω γὰρ κἀμὲ, in Soph. Ant. 32 (contrast ibid. 5. 567).

4. ἑκάστης πράξεως. The simple genitive is like τὸν τῶν ὑπευθύνων νόμον in § 206: we have therefore adopted the MS. reading. Legebatur περὶ ἑκάστης.

8. ἐξ ἀνάγκης, οἶμαι. The fact that there existed an elaborate machinery for preserving consistency in the laws, does not prove that it always worked faultlessly. There seems some likelihood that the system was too elaborate, and that the appointment of nomothetae was such a burdensome delay in the constitutional repeal of a law, that it was often preferred to allow it tacitly to become obsolete, or even to risk a prosecution by legislating without them. But

probably a stricter rule of legal interpretation than ever existed at Athens would hold that Aeschines was right in his main position—that if two laws on one interpretation contradict each other (while neither is specially repealed), another interpretation which reconciled them must be preferred to it.

10. ἤτοι introduces the preferable alternative, the more likely, in Aeschines' opinion, to be adopted; because, if his view of the case was right, it was what the law did actually enforce, and therefore in any case must have aimed at enforcing. For the use of ἤτοι .. ἤ, cp. Thuc. 2. 40, ἤτοι κρίνομέν γε ὀρθῶς ἢ ἐνθυμούμεθα, where ἤτοι introduces the more certain alternative. So perhaps in Aesch. Ag. 849, ἤτοι κέαντες ἢ τεμόντες—burning is the milder remedy, to be tried first, if adequate.

§ 41. The law alleged by them relates to local, private,

16. γιγνομένων .. τραγῳδῶν. The performers put for the performance, as sup. § 36, inf. § 45, etc.: cp. gladiatoribus in Cic. Phil. 1. 15. 36.

δέ τινες ὑποκηρυξάμενοι τοὺς αὑτῶν οἰκέτας ἀφίεσαν ἀπελευθέρους, μάρτυρας τῆς ἀπελευθερίας τοὺς Ἕλληνας ποιούμενοι. ὃ δ᾽ ἦν ἐπιφθονώτατον, προξενίας τινὲς εὑρημένοι ἐν ταῖς ἔξω 42 πόλεσι διεπράττοντο ἀναγορεύεσθαι, ὅτι στεφανοῖ αὐτοὺς ὁ 5 δῆμος, εἰ οὕτω τύχοι, ὁ τῶν Ῥοδίων ἢ Χίων ἢ καὶ ἄλλης τινὸς πόλεως ἀρετῆς ἕνεκα καὶ ἀνδραγαθίας. καὶ ταῦτ᾽ ἔπραττον οὐχ ὥσπερ οἱ ὑπὸ τῆς βουλῆς τῆς ὑμετέρας στεφανούμενοι ἢ ὑπὸ τοῦ δήμου, πείσαντες ὑμᾶς καὶ μετὰ ψηφίσματος, πολλὴν χάριν καταθέμενοι, ἀλλ᾽ αὐτοὶ προελόμενοι ἄνευ δόγματος 10 ὑμετέρου. ἐκ δὲ τούτου τοῦ τρόπου συνέβαινε τοὺς μὲν θεατὰς 43 καὶ τοὺς χορηγοὺς καὶ τοὺς ἀγωνιστὰς ἐνοχλεῖσθαι, τοὺς δὲ ἀνακηρυττομένους ἐν τῷ θεάτρῳ μείζοσι τιμᾶσθαι τῶν ὑπὸ τοῦ δήμου στεφανουμένων. τοῖς μὲν γὰρ ἀπεδέδεικτο τόπος ἡ ἐκκλησία, ἐν ᾗ χρῆν στεφανοῦσθαι, καὶ ἀπείρητο ἄλλοθι μηδαμοῦ 15 κηρύττεσθαι· οἱ δὲ ἀνηγορεύοντο ἐνώπιον ἁπάντων τῶν Ἑλλήνων· κἀκεῖνοι μὲν μετὰ ψηφίσματος, πείσαντες ὑμᾶς, οὗτοι δ᾽ ἄνευ ψηφίσματος. συνιδὼν δή τις ταῦτα νομοθέτης τίθησι 44

2. τῆς ἀπελευθερίας] Post Ἕλληνας ponunt ekl, omitti jubet Cobet.　6. ἀρετῆς ἕνεκα] ἕνεκα ἀρετῆς omnes praeter ekl.　Verborum ordo minus usitatus Frankio et ceteris, credo, editoribus displicuit : nobis haud multum abest quin placeat.　7. οἱ] Soli habent ekl : et omitti, quamvis haud facile, aliquo tamen modo potest.　12. μείζοσι] pekl add τιμαῖς : itaque Bekk. Frank.　13. ἀπεδέδεικτο] l et Bekk. ἀποδέδεικτο.

1. ὑποκηρυξάμενοι. 'Sub praecone' Reiske. The force of the preposition may be illustrated by ὕπαυλος, ' to the sound of the flute.'
§ 42. And especially foreign honours;
4. διεπράττοντο. Perhaps bargained with the states for the crown, to get them undeserved credit at home ; perhaps, having obtained the crown bona fide, gained the privilege of proclamation by bargaining with the theatre manager or the herald. διεπράττοντο must clearly be of something discreditable.
5. ὁ τῶν Ῥοδίων ἢ Χίων. These are the likeliest, as being neutral states, and as islanders possible, though not actual, allies of Athens. For an Athenian to be their friend might make him important at home, as possibly a useful diplomatist. For a man to receive a crown (say) from Thebes might raise a suspicion of treason : from Seriphus would be nugatory and ridiculous. Possibly also there may be an invidious allusion to Demosthenes' speech ὑπὲρ τῆς Ῥοδίων ἐλευθερίας.
8. πολλὴν χάριν καταθέμινοι. ' Having established large claims on your gratitude;' inserted to mark the magnitude of

the favour conferred by the people, which it required so much to earn. The phrase χάριν καταθέσθαι is too common, in this sense, to make it likely that it can here mean only ' making you the people they had to thank,' as inf. § 47, ἵνα μείζω χάριν εἰδῇ τῶν στεφανούντων ὑμῖν.
§ 43. Whose unauthorised proclamation in the theatre was both a nuisance and a bad example.
12. μείζοσι. The reading of all the best MSS. Volg. add. τιμαῖς, which might easily have either got in or slipped out, as a διττογραφία real or supposed. The omission seems preferable, rather as being the less obvious reading than in deference to the authority of the known MSS. of Aeschines. The correction μειζόνως has hardly anything to recommend it. The reason why the honour is greater is twofold : the proclamation is made to a wider circle, and it rests (or appears to rest) only on the individual's merit, not the people's favour.
14. ἄλλοθι μηδαμοῦ. Vid. sup. ad § 32.
§ 44. And is forbidden by the law which Demosthenes quotes, without affecting the one I quote.

νόμον οὐδὲν ἐπικοινωνοῦντα τῷ περὶ τῶν ὑπὸ τοῦ δήμου στεφανουμένων νόμῳ, οὔτε λύσας ἐκεῖνον· οὐδὲ γὰρ ἡ ἐκκλησία
ἠνωχλεῖτο, ἀλλὰ τὸ θέατρον· οὔτ᾽ ἐναντίον τοῖς πρότερον κειμένοις νόμοις τιθείς· οὐ γὰρ ἔξεστιν· ἀλλὰ περὶ τῶν ἄνευ ψηφίσματος ὑμετέρου στεφανουμένων ὑπὸ τῶν φυλετῶν καὶ δημοτῶν 5
καὶ περὶ τῶν τοὺς οἰκέτας ἀπελευθερούντων καὶ περὶ τῶν
ξενικῶν στεφάνων, καὶ διαρρήδην ἀπαγορεύει μήτ᾽ οἰκέτην ἀπ-
ελευθεροῦν ἐν τῷ θεάτρῳ μήθ᾽ ὑπὸ τῶν φυλετῶν ἢ δημοτῶν
ἀναγορεύεσθαι στεφανούμενον, μηδ᾽ ὑπ᾽ ἄλλου, φησὶ, μηδενὸς,
45 ἢ ἄτιμον εἶναι τὸν κήρυκα. ὅταν οὖν ἀποδείξῃ τοῖς μὲν ὑπὸ 10
τῆς βουλῆς στεφανουμένοις εἰς τὸ βουλευτήριον ἀναρρηθῆναι,
τοῖς δ᾽ ὑπὸ τοῦ δήμου στεφανουμένοις εἰς τὴν ἐκκλησίαν, τοῖς
δ᾽ ὑπὸ τῶν δημοτῶν στεφανουμένοις καὶ φυλετῶν ἀπείπῃ μὴ
κηρύττεσθαι τοῖς τραγῳδοῖς, ἵνα μηδεὶς ἐρανίζων στεφάνους καὶ
κηρύγματα ψευδῆ φιλοτιμίαν κτᾶται, προσαπείπῃ δ᾽ ἐν τῷ 15
νόμῳ μηδ᾽ ὑπὸ ἄλλου μηδενὸς ἀνακηρύττεσθαι, ἀπούσης βουλῆς
καὶ δήμου καὶ φυλετῶν καὶ δημοτῶν,—ὅταν δέ τις ταῦτα
ἀφέλῃ, τί τὸ καταλειπόμενόν ἐστι πλὴν οἱ ξενικοὶ στέφα-
46 νοι; ὅτι δ᾽ ἀληθῆ λέγω, μέγα σημεῖον ὑμῖν τούτου ἐξ αὐτῶν

1. περὶ] om aebl : cf. ad § 39.   3. ἠνωχλεῖτο] Sic agmnfcb, ceteri scripti ἐνωχλεῖτο :
Steph. et B. et S. ἠνοχλεῖτο.   9. μηδ᾽] Sic post Sauppium Frank. : libri μήθ᾽.   17. ὅταν
δέ τις] Sic amn cd ekl : ceteri δή.   18. ἀφέλῃ] Sic ekl : ceteri ἀφέληται. Cp. § 30, et
vid. annot. in § 46.

2. οὔτε λύσας ἐκεῖνον .. οὐ γὰρ ἔξεστιν.
'It neither repeals the other, for its object is
different, nor contravenes it by a side-wind,
for that is illegal.'

9. μηδ᾽ ὑπ᾽ ἄλλου. φησὶ, μηδενός. Of
course this would verbally include the Athenian people, but it would not prove in the
least that the other law, relating to crowns
given by them, was to be altered. This law
limited the proclamation of crowns that
might legally (as things then were) be proclaimed in the theatre, and did not license
those that might not.

10. τὸν κήρυκα. It therefore probably
rested with him what proclamations were
made.

§ 45. National crowns have their place
fixed by one law; local and foreign by the
other;

ἀποδείξῃ. The subject must be either
ὁ νόμος or ὁ νομοθέτης : perhaps the latter
is likelier, as Aeschines has been insisting
that the laws (that appointing the Senate-
house or the Assembly as the place of proclamation, and that allowing, under certain
conditions, of the Theatre) are different in

scope, origin. and occasion. He admits,
indeed (apparently), that they differ in date,
and so presumably in authorship : but to this
he is not concerned to attend. In fact the
Greek idiom, making it superfluous to name
the subject, makes it also superfluous to conceive it distinctly.

11. εἰς τὸ βουλευτήριον. The proclamation is spoken at once in and to the
Senate-house; addressed, as it were, into the
midst of the assembled senators

14. ἵνα μηδεὶς .. κτᾶται. 'That no one
may get a false reputation for public spirit
by collecting crowns.' The notion of ἔρανος is simply a contribution; it may be
started by the contributors or by another;
or, again, for their own benefit or for another's.

16. ἀπούσης ...δημοτῶν. 'Since senate,
people, tribesmen, wardsmen are excluded,'
the two latter by this law, the two former,
as Aeschines contends, by the o.her.

§ 46. Subject: to the condition (not only of
a popular vote, but) of consecration of the
crown itself: a condition it would be scan-
dalous to annex to one's own gift,

τῶν νόμων ἐπιδείξω. αὐτὸν γὰρ τὸν χρυσοῦν στέφανον, ὃς ἂν
ἐν τῷ θεάτρῳ τῷ ἐν ἄστει ἀναρρηθῇ, ἱερὸν εἶναι τῆς Ἀθηνᾶς
κελεύει ὁ νόμος, ἀφελόμενος τὸν στεφανούμενον. καίτοι τίς
ἂν ὑμῶν τολμήσειε τοσαύτην ἀνελευθερίαν καταγνῶναι τοῦ δήμου
5 τῶν Ἀθηναίων ; μὴ γὰρ ὅτι πόλις, ἀλλ᾽ οὐδ᾽ ἂν ἰδιώτης οὐδὲ
εἷς οὕτως ἀγεννὴς γένοιτο, ὥστε ὃν αὐτὸς ἔδωκε στέφανον ἅμα
ἀνακηρύττειν καὶ ἀφαιρεῖσθαι καὶ καθιεροῦν. ἀλλ᾽, οἶμαι, διὰ
τὸ ξενικὸν εἶναι τὸν στέφανον καὶ ἡ καθιέρωσις γίγνεται, ἵνα
μηδεὶς ἀλλοτρίαν εὔνοιαν περὶ πλείονος ποιούμενος τῆς πατρί-
10 δος χείρων γένηται τὴν ψυχήν. ἀλλ᾽ οὐκ ἐκεῖνον τὸν ἐν τῇ 47
ἐκκλησίᾳ στέφανον ἀναρρηθέντα οὐδεὶς καθιεροῖ, ἀλλ᾽ ἔξεστι
κεκτῆσθαι, ἵνα μὴ μόνον αὐτός, ἀλλὰ καὶ οἱ ἐξ ἐκείνου, ἔχοντες
ἐν τῇ οἰκίᾳ τὸ ὑπόμνημα, μηδέποτε κακοὶ τὴν ψυχὴν εἰς τὸν
δῆμον γίγνωνται. καὶ διὰ τοῦτο προσέθηκεν ὁ νομοθέτης μὴ
15 κηρύττεσθαι τὸν ἀλλότριον στέφανον ἐν τῷ θεάτρῳ, ἐὰν μὴ
ψηφίσηται ὁ δῆμος, ἵν᾽ ἡ πόλις ἡ βουλομένη τινὰ τῶν ὑμετέρων στεφανοῦν πρέσβεις πέμψασα δεηθῇ τοῦ δήμου, ἵνα κηρυττόμενος μείζω χάριν εἰδῇ τῶν στεφανούντων ὑμῖν, ὅτι

2. τῷ θεάτρῳ τῷ ἐν ἄστει] τῷ θεάτρῳ ἐν ἄστει fcd, †τῷ θεάτρῳ ἄστει b†.   3. κελεύει
ὁ νόμος] ὁ νόμος κελεύει ek Bekk.   5. τῶν Ἀθηναίων] τοῦ Ἀθηναίων ek Bekk. Vid.
annot. ad loc.   11. στέφανον ἀναρρηθέντα] Sic agnun: ceteri transp.   16. τινὰ τῶν
ὑμετέρων] τῶν πολιτῶν τινὰ τῶν ὑμετέρων volt Hamaker, haud sine aliqua ratione. Gaudeo
certe, semel viro docto verba addenda, non tollenda visa esse. *

3. ἀφελόμενος. The middle is used, because the law not only takes the crown
away, but disposes of it. Just above we have
ἀφέλη in the active: there one is simply to
subtract the classes named, and has nothing
more to do with them.
5. τῶν Ἀθηναίων. Bekk. et Brem. τοῦ
Ἀθηναίων: et sic passim. The construction is perhaps more Attic, but it seems
superfluous to assume that it was universal,
in the face of MSS.
μὴ γὰρ ὅτι κ.τ.λ. 'For not to say a
city, there is not a single private man who
would be so mean as, at the same moment,
to proclaim, take away, and consecrate the
crown 'of his own giving,' the strongest of
the Aeschines' arguments on this point, considering how little Athenian law could bear to
be treated as faultlessly systematic. πόλις
is a word of honour, in itself including
moral dignity: cp. ad D. de Cor. § 29.
οὐδὲ εἷς is really an afterthought, ' there is
not only no city, but no individual, not one,
who ...'
9. τῆς πατρίδος. 'Than that of his
country,' τῆς, in all probability, not agreeing

with but governing πατρίδος. It would
have been τῆς τῆς πατρίδος, except on
euphonic grounds.
§ 47. And not annexed to gifts really
national : while both conditions are fitting
with foreign ones.
13. μηδέποτε .. γίγνωνται. For the
sentiment, of men's feelings towards the
nation depending on the nation's treatment
of their ancestors, cp. inf. § 169.
17. ἵνα κηρυττόμενος .. ὑμῖν. 'That
he may, through his proclamation, feel more
gratitude to you for permitting it, than to
those who give the crown.' τῶν στεφανούντων = ἢ τοῖς στεφανοῦσιν : the construction
of the genitive after a comparative is not
common, when the noun in the other construction would be in a case other than
nominative or accusative. A gloss was
added, ἢ τοῖς στεφανοῦσιν, which in the
MSS. appears in the text after ὑμῖν. Though
grammatically this clause is expressed as
being the only object of the law, it is probable that Aeschines contemplates the homage
of foreign states (ἵν᾽ ἡ πόλις .. δεηθῇ τοῦ
δήμου) as part of the benefit.

κηρῦξαι ἐπετρέψατε.   ὅτι δ᾽ ἀληθῆ λέγω, τῶν νόμων αὐτῶν
ἀκούσατε.

ΝΟΜΟΙ.

48 Ἐπειδὰν τοίνυν ἐξαπατῶντες ὑμᾶς λέγωσιν, ὡς προσγέγραπται ἐν τῷ νόμῳ ἐξεῖναι στεφανοῦν, ἐὰν ψηφίσηται ὁ δῆμος, 5
ἀπομνημονεύετε αὐτοῖς ὑποβάλλειν· ναὶ, εἴ γε σέ τις ἄλλη
πόλις στεφανοῖ· εἰ δὲ ὁ δῆμος ὁ Ἀθηναίων, ἀποδέδεικταί σοι
τόπος, ὅπου δεῖ τοῦτο γενέσθαι, ἀπείρηταί σοι ἔξω τῆς ἐκκλησίας μὴ κηρύττεσθαι.   τὸ γὰρ "ἄλλοθι δὲ μηδαμοῦ" ὅ τι
ἔστιν, ὅλην τὴν ἡμέραν λέγε· οὐ γὰρ ἀποδείξεις, ὡς ἔννομα 10
γέγραφας.

49 Ἔστι δὲ ὑπόλοιπόν μοι μέρος τῆς κατηγορίας, ἐφ᾽ ᾧ μάλιστα σπουδάζω· τοῦτο δέ ἐστιν ἡ πρόφασις, δι᾽ ἣν αὐτὸν ἀξιοῖ
στεφανοῦσθαι.   λέγει γὰρ οὕτως ἐν τῷ ψηφίσματι· "καὶ τὸν
κήρυκα ἀναγορεύειν ἐν τῷ θεάτρῳ πρὸς τοὺς Ἕλληνας, ὅτι στε- 15
φανοῖ αὐτὸν ὁ δῆμος ὁ τῶν Ἀθηναίων ἀρετῆς ἕνεκα καὶ ἀνδραγαθίας," καὶ τὸ μέγιστον· "ὅτι διατελεῖ λέγων καὶ πράττων
50 τὰ ἄριστα τῷ δήμῳ."   ἁπλοῦς δὴ παντάπασιν ὁ μετὰ ταῦτα
ἡμῖν λόγος γίγνεται, καὶ ὑμῖν ἀκούσασι κρῖναι εὐμαθής· δεῖ
γὰρ δή που τὸν μὲν κατηγοροῦντα ἐμὲ τοῦθ᾽ ὑμῖν ἐπιδεικνύναι, 20
ὡς εἰσὶν οἱ κατὰ Δημοσθένους ἔπαινοι ψευδεῖς καὶ ὡς οὔτ᾽
ἤρξατο λέγειν τὰ βέλτιστα οὔτε νῦν διατελεῖ πράττων τὰ
συμφέροντα τῷ δήμῳ.   κἂν τοῦτ᾽ ἐπιδείξω, δικαίως δή που
τὴν γραφὴν ἁλώσεται Κτησιφῶν· ἅπαντες γὰρ ἀπαγορεύουσιν

---

4. προσγέγραπται] Sic ek: ceteri προγέγραπται.   Vid. ad loc.   6. ὑποβάλλειν]
ὑποβαλεῖν fcdh.

§ 48. *You are now in a position to see
through their frivolous excuses.*
4. προσγέγραπται. 'Demosthenes and
Ctesiphon will pretend there is a supplementary clause to the law, the truth being
that there is a distinct law about a distinct
matter.' Most MSS. have προγέγραπται,
but it is hardly appropriate to the sense, and
would imply that the law was more explicit
than they could even pretend.
9. τὸ γὰρ .. ἔννομα γέγραφας. For the
very object of the γραφὴ παρανόμων was to
prevent a casual vote of an excited assembly
overriding the permanent law, as, on Demosthenes' view of the effect of the Dionysiac
law, it allowed to be done in the case of
public honours.
§ 49. *I proceed to my main point—that
Ctesiphon's form of proclamation is false in
fact.*
12. ἐφ᾽ ᾧ μάλιστα σπουδάζω. This

hardly contradicts § 37 sup., where Aeschines
lays such stress on the legal aspects of the
case. By the terms of the indictment this
party question was a branch of the legal one.
13. πρόφασις. Depreciatory as usual,
though it is not meant so much that Ctesiphon's real motive was not the alleged one,
as that the allegation itself was false.
§ 50. *He is* not *a salutary counsellor,* not
*a good citizen: for Ctesiphon to call him so
is falsifying our public records.*
21. οἱ κατὰ Δημοσθένους ἔπαινοι. κατὰ
thus used in a good sense is rare, but cp. D.
de Cor. § 271.
οὔτ᾽   ἤρξατο   λέγειν .. πράττων.
Neither the policy he *recommended*, while
no more than one speaker among many,
nor that he has *executed*, since your misplaced confidence in him.
24. ἅπαντες. Here Aeschines judiciously
appeals to 'every law there is:' to quote

24 ΑΙΣΧΙΝΟΥ §§ 51, 52.

οἱ νόμοι μηδένα ψευδῆ γράμματα ἐγγράφειν ἐν τοῖς δημοσίοις ψηφίσμασι. τῷ δ' ἀπολογουμένῳ τοὐναντίον τούτου δεικτέον ἐστίν. ὑμεῖς δ' ἡμῖν ἔσεσθε τῶν λόγων κριταί. ἔχει δ'
οὕτως.

5 Ἐγὼ τὸν μὲν βίον τὸν Δημοσθένους ἐξετάζειν μακροτέρου 51
λόγου ἔργον ἡγοῦμαι εἶναι. τί γὰρ δεῖ νῦν ταῦτα λέγειν, ἢ
τὰ περὶ τὴν τοῦ τραύματος γραφὴν αὐτῷ συμβεβηκότα, ὅτ'
ἐγράψατο εἰς Ἄρειον πάγον Δημομέλην τὸν Παιανιέα ἀνεψιὸν
ὄντα ἑαυτῷ, καὶ τὴν τῆς κεφαλῆς ἐπιτομήν. ἢ τὰ περὶ τὴν
10 Κηφισοδότου στρατηγίαν καὶ τὸν τῶν νεῶν ἔκπλουν τὸν εἰς
Ἑλλήσποντον, ὅτε εἰς ὢν τῶν τριηράρχων Δημοσθένης καὶ 52
περιάγων τὸν στρατηγὸν ἐπὶ τῆς νεὼς καὶ συσσιτῶν καὶ συνθύων καὶ συσπένδων, καὶ τούτων ἀξιωθεὶς διὰ τὸ πατρικὸς αὐτῷ
φίλος εἶναι, οὐκ ὤκνησεν ἀπ' εἰσαγγελίας αὐτοῦ κρινομένου περὶ
15 θανάτου κατήγορος γενέσθαι· καὶ ταῦτα ἤδη τὰ περὶ Μειδίαν
καὶ τοὺς κονδύλους, οὓς ἔλαβεν ἐν τῇ ὀρχήστρᾳ χορηγὸς ὤν,
καὶ ὡς ἀπέδοτο τριάκοντα μνῶν ἅμα τήν τε εἰς αὐτὸν ὕβριν

1. γράμματα ἐγγράφειν] γράμματα γράφειν e, γράφειν l. Illud restitui volt Bakius,
deleri γράμματα Frankius. Equidem Bakio paene assentior. 6. εἶναι] Om. z. 8. Παι-
ανιέα] Itane an Παιανέα hoc verbum scribendum sit, jam ab Harpocrationis diebus quaestio
fuit. Hic Παιανιέα habent libri, idque nos invito Frankio pro contracto παιανιᾶ restituimus.
15. καὶ] ἢ Mead. Reisk. Sed variat consulto Aeschines formam loquendi: vid. annot. ad
loc.

chapter and verse as he did before would have shown that the legislator meant to forbid the falsification of decrees when passed, not the passing of decrees with a false preamble.

§§ 51, 52. *Judge his character by the stories of his private crimes and frauds:*

9. κεφαλῆς ἐπιτομήν. Cp. inf. § 213 (where this story is alluded to, while that of Midias is expressly mentioned), Ae. de F. L. § 99, p. 40.

10. Κηφισοδότου. See Dem. c. Aristocr. p. 670 sq., §§ 180 sqq. He was fined five talents, narrowly escaping a capital sentence: ibid. § 199.

12. περιάγων .. ἐπὶ τῆς νεώς. According to the Scholiast, it was a compliment from the general, to sail with the captain whose ship was in best condition; if so, τούτων ἀξιωθεὶς κ.τ.λ. has a special point: 'he betrayed an old friend, who had strained a point to do him honour.' For without these words, the compliment received from the general might tend to prove Demosthenes a faithful public servant.

συσσιτῶν καὶ συνθύων καὶ συσπένδων. All these would constitute ties which it was impious to violate. We get a similar charge against Demosthenes, inf. § 225.

where we find mentioned·and rejected the plea we should naturally expect, that he had cared more for public duty than for private. Probably general opinion was on Aeschines' side, at least before the rise of Stoicism; it might almost be said that modern opinion is so too, if we compare the case of Essex and Bacon.

15. καὶ ταῦτα ἤδη. He affects surprise, that he has no sooner quitted one disgraceful episode than he finds he has come to another. One might represent ἤδη by 'presently.' Reiske reads ἢ for καὶ with one MS., which is possible, but needless.

16. τοὺς κονδύλους .. χορηγὸς ὤν. The mere affront was a disgrace, besides the disgrace of compromising it.

17. ἀπέδοτο τριάκοντα μνῶν. Grote suggests that the compromise in this case may have been a creditable and legal one, no more than acquiescence in Midias' ὑποτίμησις of a fine of thirty minae, in place of the capital penalty proposed at first by Demosthenes. If the facts had been so, it is conceivable that Aeschines would have represented them as he does; but we have really no grounds for the conjecture, except the supposed impeccability of a high-minded politician.

καὶ τὴν τοῦ δήμου καταχειροτονίαν, ἣν ἐν Διονύσου κατεχειρο-
53 τόνησε Μειδίου. ταῦτα μὲν οὖν μοι δοκῶ καὶ τἆλλα τὰ τούτοις ὅμοια ὑπερβήσεσθαι, οὐ προδιδοὺς ὑμᾶς οὐδὲ τὸν ἀγῶνα
καταχαριζόμενος, ἀλλ᾽ ἐκεῖνο φοβούμενος, μή μοι παρ᾽ ὑμῶν
ἀπαντήσῃ τὸ δοκεῖν μὲν ἀληθῆ λέγειν, ἀρχαῖα δὲ καὶ λίαν ὁμο- 5
λογούμενα. καίτοι, ὦ Κτησιφῶν, ὅτῳ τὰ μέγιστα τῶν αἰσχρῶν οὕτως ἐστὶ πιστὰ καὶ γνώριμα τοῖς ἀκούουσιν, ὥστε τὸν
κατήγορον μὴ δοκεῖν ψευδῆ λέγειν, ἀλλὰ παλαιὰ καὶ λίαν
προωμολογημένα, πότερα αὐτὸν δεῖ χρυσῷ στεφάνῳ στεφανωθῆναι ἢ ψέγεσθαι; καὶ σὲ τὸν ψευδῆ καὶ παράνομα τολμῶντα 10
γράφειν πότερα χρὴ καταφρονεῖν τῶν δικαστηρίων ἢ δίκην τῇ
πόλει διδόναι;
54 Περὶ δὲ τῶν δημοσίων ἀδικημάτων πειράσομαι σαφέστερον
εἰπεῖν. καὶ γὰρ πυνθάνομαι μέλλειν Δημοσθένην, ἐπειδὰν αὑτοῖς ὁ λόγος ἀποδοθῇ, καταριθμεῖσθαι πρὸς ὑμᾶς, ὡς ἄρα τῇ 15
πόλει τέτταρες ἤδη γεγένηνται καιροί, ἐν οἷς αὐτὸς πεπολίτευ-
ται. ὧν ἕνα μὲν καὶ πρῶτον, ὡς ἔγωγε ἀκούω, καταλογίζεται
ἐκεῖνον τὸν χρόνον, ἐν ᾧ πρὸς Φίλιππον ὑπὲρ Ἀμφιπόλεως

5. δοκεῖν μὲν ἀληθῆ] Ita libri : facile est ἀληθῆ μὲν cum Cobeto corrigere. Quod sententia quidem postulat ; sed non Aeschinem tantum, verum etiam scribas, saltem antiquiores,
crediderim cognovisse quantum logicus verborum ordo posset immutari. 7. ὥστε] Sic ek :
ceteri ὡς, quod vix aut hic aut in § 96 restitui potest. 9. προωμολογημένα] προσωμολο-
γημένα fcdb, idque mavolt Cobet. Facilior sane volgati interpretatio. 12. διδόναι] δοῦναι
ekl Bekk. 17. πρῶτον] πάντων πρῶτον ekl Bekk., πρῶτον ἁπάντων an p Tauchn.

§ 53. Stories which there is no need for
me to tell, and which by their familiarity
condemn Ctesiphon.
3. οὐ προδιδοὺς .... καταχαριζόμενος.
'Not that I mean to betray you, or condone
the trial,' as Demosthenes did that of Midias. It is not necessary in Greek, as in
English, to emphasise the antithesis between
the two persons. καταχαριζόμενος = 'to
give up as a personal favour.'
4. παρ᾽ ὑμῶν ἀπαντήσῃ. A rather
strangely strong expression ; 'lest I should
be encountered by you with the feeling,
that .. ' is exactly the sense. Cp. Ae. in
Tim. p. 23, § 164, for a similar phrase,
where, however, the subject is κραυγὴ, not
an abstract thought.
10. ἢ ψέγεσθαι. 'Languet. Sensui
sufficeret ἀπολέσθαι.' B. and S. But the
anti-climax is intentional : Aeschines is not
prosecuting Demosthenes, but only trying to
cancel a vote of thanks in his favour. Supposing such irony intended, there was no
danger of the point being missed when the
speech was heard, not read,—a thing always
to be remembered in judging of the likelihood of rhetorical point.

§ 54. But is a traitor as well as a scoundrel, and that throughout his political career :
the partner of Philocrates.
13. σαφέστερον. 'More explicitly,'
not (like his private life) in mere passing
hints.
14. πυνθάνομαι μέλλειν Δημοσθένην
κ.τ.λ. There is no passage such as this in
Demosthenes' actual speech. He follows
(with many digressions) a roughly chronological order, in enumerating his public services, but nowhere divides his life into
periods ; and, had he done so, it is hardly
likely that a passage so closely connected
with the whole argument could have been
dropped in preparing the speech for publication. It is likely enough that Aeschines had
really heard rumours, not always accurate,
about the line of defence Demosthenes intended to take, so that we need not (indeed
we cannot, without supposing the whole
speech rewritten) imagine that this passage
was added after the date of trial. Details
and illustrations, like §§ 190, 226, etc., stand
on a different footing.
αὐτοῖς. Note that he assumes Demosthenes will speak. Contrast inf. § 200 sqq.

ἐπολεμοῦμεν· τοῦτον δ' ἀφορίζεται τῇ γενομένῃ εἰρήνῃ καὶ
συμμαχίᾳ, ἣν Φιλοκράτης ὁ Ἀγνούσιος ἔγραψε καὶ αὐτὸς
οὗτος μετ' ἐκείνου, ὡς ἐγὼ δείξω. δεύτερον δὲ καιρόν φησι 55
γενέσθαι ὃν ἤγομεν χρόνον τὴν εἰρήνην, δηλονότι μέχρι τῆς
5 ἡμέρας ἐκείνης, ἐν ᾗ καταλύσας τὴν ὑπάρχουσαν εἰρήνην τῇ
πόλει ὁ αὐτὸς οὗτος ῥήτωρ ἔγραψε τὸν πόλεμον· τρίτον δὲ
ὃν ἐπολεμοῦμεν χρόνον μέχρι τῆς ἀτυχίας τῆς ἐν Χαιρωνείᾳ,
τέταρτον δὲ τὸν νῦν παρόντα καιρόν. ταῦτα δὲ καταριθμη-
σάμενος, ὡς ἀκούω, μέλλει με παρακαλεῖν καὶ ἐπερωτᾶν, ὁποίου
10 τούτων τῶν τεττάρων αὐτοῦ καιρῶν κατηγορῶ καὶ πότε αὐτὸν
οὐ τὰ βέλτιστά φημι τῷ δήμῳ πεπολιτεῦσθαι· κἂν μὴ θέλω
ἀποκρίνασθαι, ἀλλ' ἐγκαλύπτωμαι καὶ ἀποδιδράσκω, ἐκκαλύ-
ψειν μέ φησι προσελθὼν καὶ ἄξειν ἐπὶ τὸ βῆμα καὶ ἀναγκά-
σειν ἀποκρίνασθαι. ἵν' οὖν μήθ' οὗτος ἰσχυρίζηται ὑμεῖς τε 56
15 προειδῆτε ἐγώ τε ἀποκρίνωμαι, ἐναντίον σοι τῶν δικαστῶν,
Δημόσθενες, καὶ τῶν ἄλλων πολιτῶν, ὅσοι δὴ ἔξωθεν περιεστᾶσι, καὶ τῶν Ἑλλήνων, ὅσοις ἐπιμελὲς γέγονεν ἐπακούειν
τῆσδε τῆς κρίσεως· ὁρῶ δὲ οὐκ ὀλίγους παρόντας, ἀλλ' ὅσους

1. ἀφορίζεται] ἀφορίζεται τὸν χρόνον Bekk., cum omnibus praeter *ekl*, nisi quod τὸν om.
mar. *n*.   3. καιρόν] Om. *gm* B. et S. Frank.   8. ταῦτα δὲ] †ταῦτα δὴ corr. *b* †.
9. παρακαλεῖν] καλεῖν *fcdb*: παρακαλεῖν habet *k* in γρ.   15. ἐγώ τε ἀποκρίνωμαι] Sic
libri plerique optimi.   Cum ἐγώ τε ἀποκρίνομαι habeant *dg*, B. et S. scribunt ἐγὼ ἀποκρίνομαι
(dum Sauppius ἔγωγε conjicit) ; Bakius ex codicis *p* lectione (ἐγώ τε ἀποκρινοῦμαι) ἐγὼ τί
ἀποκρινοῦμαι ; legit.   Tria verba volt deleta Hamakerus, duo Frankius, ita ut ἐγὼ ἐναντίον
σοι .. ἀποκρίνομαι jungerentur.   Sed vide annot. ad loc.   16. δὴ] δὲ *afcd*, δὲ τε̄ *gmb*, τε *n*,
om. *ekl*.

3. οὗτος μετ' ἐκείνου. For the conflicting evidence of these speeches and those on
the Παραπρεσβεία, see the Life of Demosthenes.

§ 55. The author of our last ruinous war,
our failures in it, and our present impotence:
for he is equally guilty for all,

5. τὴν ὑπάρχουσαν εἰρήνην. 'The
peace we had, such as it was ; ' for in spite
of the treachery of Demosthenes and Philocrates, and all we lost by them in making
peace, it was worth having.

9. παρακαλεῖν. 'Call upon me, invite
me,' to help out his case, referring, apparently, to such an invitation as inf. § 165,
D. de Cor. § 9. Feeling that the word was
a strange one to use of an enemy, several
MSS. have substituted the simple καλεῖν.

12. ἐγκαλύπτωμαι καὶ ἀποδιδράσκω.
To be taken quite literally, 'cover myself
up, and hurry away.' In spite of what has
been said on the last section, these words look
like an actual quotation from Demosthenes'
speech as delivered, or at least as prepared.

§ 56. Since he wishes to know; as I will
prove to you and the strangers in court:

14. ἵν' οὖν μήθ' οὗτος κ.τ.λ. 'So, in
order that he may lose his chance of a strong
point, and you (the court) may be fore-
warned, and I have my answer ready for
you, Demosthenes, before the judges I
answer,' etc. The words seem to support
the view, that Aeschines really had spoilt by
anticipation a point that Demosthenes had
intended to make, and caused the omission
of a vigorous passage in his speech. The
force of ἀποκρίνομαι after ἀποκρίνωμαι is,
'You expect an answer : here is one, which
will serve the two other objects also.'

16. ὅσοι δὴ ἔξωθεν περιεστᾶσι. Compare the remarks on the παράταξις of partisans at the opening of the speech ; also § 8.
ὅσοι δὴ is no doubt the right reading, though
one group of MSS. omits δὴ, and most of
the others substitute δὲ or τε. If δὲ or τε
were read, it would have to be joined with
τῶν Ἑλλήνων ; and then the second ὅσοις
would be unbearably awkward.

οὐδεὶς πώποτε μέμνηται πρὸς ἀγῶνα δημόσιον πυραγενομένοις·
ἀποκρίνομαι, ὅτι ἀπάντων τῶν τεττάρων καιρῶν κατηγορῶ σου,
57 οὓς σὺ διαιρεῖς, κἂν οἵ τε θεοὶ θέλωσι καὶ οἱ δικασταὶ ἐξ ἴσου
ἡμῶν ἀκούσωσι κἀγὼ δύνωμαι ἀπομνημονεῦσαι ἅ σοι σύνοιδα,
πάνυ προσδοκῶ ἐπιδείξειν τοῖς δικασταῖς τῆς μὲν σωτηρίας τῇ 5
πόλει τοὺς θεοὺς αἰτίους γεγενημένους καὶ τοὺς φιλανθρώπως
καὶ μετρίως τοῖς τῆς πόλεως πράγμασι χρησαμένους, τῶν δὲ
ἀτυχημάτων ἀπάντων Δημοσθένην αἴτιον γεγενημένον. καὶ
χρήσομαι τῇ τοῦ λόγου τάξει ταύτῃ, ἣν τοῦτον πυνθάνομαι
ποιεῖσθαι μέλλειν, λέξω δὲ πρῶτον περὶ τοῦ πρώτου καιροῦ 10
καὶ δεύτερον περὶ τοῦ δευτέρου καὶ τρίτον περὶ τοῦ ἐφεξῆς καὶ
τέταρτον περὶ τῶν νῦν καθεστηκότων πραγμάτων. καὶ δὴ
ἐπανάγω ἐμαυτὸν ἐπὶ τὴν εἰρήνην, ἣν σὺ καὶ Φιλοκράτης ἐγρά-
ψατε.

58 Ὑμῖν γὰρ ἐξεγένετ' ἂν, ὦ Ἀθηναῖοι, τὴν προτέραν ἐκείνην 15
εἰρήνην ποιήσασθαι μετὰ κοινοῦ συνεδρίου τῶν Ἑλλήνων, εἴ
τινες ὑμᾶς εἴασαν περιμεῖναι τὰς πρεσβείας, ἃς ἦτε ἐκπεπομφότες κατ' ἐκεῖνον τὸν καιρὸν εἰς τὴν Ἑλλάδα, παρακαλοῦντες
ἐπὶ Φίλιππον, μετασχεῖν Ἑλληνικοῦ συνεδρίου, καὶ προϊόντος

2. ἀποκρίνομαι] ἀποκρινοῦμαι agmnk corr. ἀποκρίνωμαι el.   3. διαιρεῖς] Sic
agmnp: ceteri et Bekk. διαιρῇ.   4. σοι] Om. agmn.   5. ἐπιδείξειν] Sic aekl et γρ.
gm: gmn et superscr. b ἐπιγράψειν, ceteri ἀποδείξειν.   8. αἴτιον γεγενημένον] Transp.
ekl: 'sed cum Taylore abesse malim' Bait.   10. ποιεῖσθαι μέλλειν] Transp. ekl
Bekk.   17. περιμεῖναι] περιμείναντας Reisk.: et Frank., dum περιμεῖναι legit, mox
μετασχεῖν Ἑλληνικοῦ συνεδρίου volit omissa.

§ 57. And that it is no thanks to him that
he has not done more harm than he has.

3. κἂν οἵ τε θεοὶ .. ἅ σοι σύνοιδα. He
continues to address Demosthenes, to make
the final taunt more pointed ; and so is able
to throw the condition of the impartiality
of the court into the third person, which is
less disrespectful to them.

4. ἅ σοι σύνοιδα. 'What I know against
you.' In Latin or English an equivalent
preposition would imply the guilty knowledge of an accomplice.

6. καὶ τοὺς φιλανθρώπως .. χρησαμένους. Especially, of course, Philip himself,
on account of the terms he granted after
Chaeronea ; but the plural may be designed
to include Alexander also, who did not press
against Athens the charge of complicity in
the Theban revolt.

8. ἀπάντων. Demosthenes was the single cause of the misfortunes of Athens, while
there were two causes of her safety. In a
similar spirit he calls the misfortunes of
Athens πράγματα when he speaks of Philip's
use of them, ἀτυχήματα when of Demosthenes' responsibility for them.

13. ἐπὶ τὴν εἰρήνην. During the Olynthiac war, Aeschines had opposed Philip ;
he therefore could not blame Demosthenes
for the war, nor for its ill success, since his
advocacy of strong measures was unsuccessful.

§ 58. But for Demosthenes and Philocrates, you would have had an honourable
peace with Philip, concluded in concert with
all Greece.

17. περιμεῖναι. Reiske's conjecture περιμείναντας makes the style of the passage
neater. A more probable improvement is
Franke's, to omit μετασχεῖν Ἑλληνικοῦ
συνεδρίου, which looks like a gloss, and is
an awkward repetition of εἰρήνην ποιήσασθαι μετὰ κοινοῦ συνεδρίου τῶν Ἑλλήνων.
ἃς ἦτε ἐκπεπομφότες. The peri-
phrastic form of the pluperfect is not
adopted merely for rhythm. It suggests—
men who had sent embassies all over Greece
in a pan-Hellenic cause had done a dignified thing. The Athenians were in enjoyment of this dignity.

19. προϊόντος τοῦ χρόνου. A congress
under Athenian presidency would be a great

τοῦ χρόνου παρ' ἑκόντων τῶν Ἑλλήνων ἀπολαβεῖν τὴν ἡγεμο-
νίαν· καὶ τούτων ἀπεστερήθητε διὰ Δημοσθένην καὶ Φιλοκράτην
καὶ τὰς τούτων δωροδοκίας, ἃς ἐδωροδόκησαν συστάντες ἐπὶ τὸ
δημόσιον τὸ ὑμέτερον. εἰ δέ τισιν ὑμῶν ἐξαίφνης ἀκούσασιν **59**
5 ἀπιστότερος προσπέπτωκεν ὁ τοιοῦτος λόγος, ἐκείνως τὴν ὑπόλοιπον ποιήσασθε ἀκρόασιν, ὥσπερ ὅταν περὶ χρημάτων ἀνηλωμένων διὰ πολλοῦ χρόνου καθεζώμεθα ἐπὶ τοὺς λογισμούς.
ἐρχόμεθα δή που ψευδεῖς οἴκοθεν ἐνίοτε δόξας ἔχοντες κατὰ
τῶν λογισμῶν· ἀλλ' ὅμως ἐπειδὰν ὁ λογισμὸς συγκεφαλαιωθῇ,
10 οὐδεὶς ἡμῶν ἐστιν οὕτω δύσκολος· τὴν φύσιν, ὅστις οὐκ ἀπέρ-
χεται τοῦθ' ὁμολογήσας καὶ ἐπινεύσας ἀληθὲς εἶναι, ὅ τι ἂν
αὐτὸς ὁ λογισμὸς αἱρῇ. οὕτω καὶ νῦν τὴν ἀκρόασιν ποιήσασθε. **60**
εἴ τινες ὑμῶν ἐκ τῶν ἔμπροσθεν χρόνων ἥκουσιν οἴκοθεν τοιαύτην ἔχοντες τὴν δόξαν, ὡς ἄρα ὁ Δημοσθένης οὐδὲν πώποτε
15 εἴρηκεν ὑπὲρ Φιλίππου συστὰς μετὰ Φιλοκράτους,—ὅστις οὕτω
διάκειται, μήτ' ἀπογνώτω μηδὲν μήτε καταγνώτω, πρὶν ἂν

1. ἀπολαβεῖν] †ἐξεγένετο ἀπολαβεῖν corr. b †. 5. ἀπιστότερος] ἄπιστος ekl. 10. ἡμῶν] Sic z et Steph. : ceteri et B. et S. ὑμῶν. ὑμῶν post ἐστὶν ponunt ekl. 11. καὶ ἐπινεύσας] Om. ekl. ὅ τι ἂν] ὁ δ' ἂν f, †ὁ δ' ἂν pr. b †. 16. πρὶν ἂν ἀκούσῃ] Sic post Reisig. B. et S. et Frankius: πρὶν ἀκούσει agmn, πρὶν ἀκ ύσοι kl, ceteri (et superscr. in n) Bekk. πρὶν ἀκούσῃ.

step in the direction of a permanent Athenian leadership.

2. δ.ὰ Δημοσθένην καὶ Φιλοκράτην .. δωροδοκίας. It is insinuated that both had the same motive for pursuing the same policy. Philocrates had been convicted of corruption: Demosthenes was not above suspicion, though Aeschines confesses that it would surprise his audience to hear that he took bribes from *Philip*.

§ 59. *You do not regard Demosthenes as a Philippiser: but facts, like figures, are stronger than opinion.*

5. ἐκείνως. 'In that way (different from your actual spirit in this case) in which you form your judgment, when' etc. The analogy suggested in the passage is, ' If you have left a sum at your banker's, and drawn out various portions at various times, you may think that there is still a balance left; but if he says there is none, you are satisfied if the figures prove it. So you may think that Demosthenes has been a consistent enemy to Philip; but if I prove each one of the points where he did Philip treasonable service, you will regard him as owing a penalty to the state, rather than as having any claim of obligation upon it.' There seems not the slightest ground for supposing an allusion to the εὐθῦναι of Lycurgus after

his five years' office, as Westermann supposes from the turn of expression in Demosthenes' reply (de Cor. § 290). He there speaks as though Aeschines' argument had been, ' You think there is some balance of benefit to you from Demosthenes' actions; I, by enumerating the various items of his treasons, will prove there is none.' ' No,' says Demosthenes, ' in accounts the final result is all that matters; in politics you take account of the items, and thank the man who has won you profit, even though it be cancelled by loss elsewhere.' But it seems easier to suppose that he made an attack on Aeschines that was hardly fair, when he, or at least the court, had forgotten the exact context of the illustration, than to suppose that Aeschines really intended the illustration to apply to Demosthenes' whole career, and not only the first period.

11. ὅ τι ἂν .. αἱρῇ. 'Whatever result the calculation itself may establish,' the *unforced* result of the calculation. αἱρεῖν is common enough in the sense of 'to convict,' and with λόγος as subject, in that of ' prove.'

§ 60. *I will prove—or rather not I, but the facts—that of those two traitors Demosthenes was the more guilty:*

16 μήτ' ἀπογνώτω κ.τ.λ. ' Let him

ἀκούσῃ· οὐ γὰρ δίκαιον. ἀλλ' ἐὰν ἐμοῦ διὰ βραχέων ἀκούσητε
ὑπομιμνήσκοντος τοὺς καιροὺς καὶ τὸ ψήφισμα παρεχομένου,
ὃ μετὰ Φιλοκράτους ἔγραψε Δημοσθένης, ἐὰν αὐτὸς ὁ τῆς ἀληθείας λογισμὸς ἐγκαταλαμβάνῃ τὸν Δημοσθένην πλείω μὲν γεγραφότα ψηφίσματα Φιλοκράτους περὶ τῆς ἐξ ἀρχῆς εἰρήνης 5
61 καὶ συμμαχίας, καθ' ὑπερβολὴν δὲ αἰσχύνης κεκολακευκότα Φίλιππον καὶ τοὺς παρ' ἐκείνου πρέσβεις, αἴτιον δὲ γεγονότα τῷ
δήμῳ τοῦ μὴ μετὰ κοινοῦ συνεδρίου τῶν Ἑλλήνων ποιήσασθαι
τὴν εἰρήνην, ἔκδοτον δὲ Φιλίππῳ πεποιηκότα Κερσοβλέπτην
τὸν Θρᾴκης βασιλέα, ἄνδρα φίλον καὶ σύμμαχον τῇ πόλει,— 10
ἐὰν ταῦθ' ὑμῖν σαφῶς ἐπιδείξω, δεήσομαι ὑμῶν μετρίαν δέησιν·
ἐπινεύσατέ μοι πρὸς θεῶν τὸν ἕνα τῶν τεττάρων καιρῶν μὴ
καλῶς αὐτὸν πεπολιτεῦσθαι. λέξω δὲ ὅθεν μάλιστα παρακο-
λουθήσετε.
62 Ἔγραψε Φιλοκράτης ἐξεῖναι Φιλίππῳ δεῦρο κήρυκας καὶ 15
πρέσβεις πέμπειν περὶ εἰρήνης [καὶ συμμαχίας]· τοῦτο τὸ

3. Φιλοκράτους] μετὰ Φιλοκράτους gfcdb.   7. Post πρέσβεις addebatur οὐκ ἀναμείναντα: quod habent quidem libri, sed loco incerto, varia forma, ita ut glossema videretur etiam
si sensui conveniret. Vid. annot. ad loc.   8. τῶν Ἑλλήνων] Om. agmn : deleri volt
Scheib.   12. ἕνα] Sic agmnnekl : volg. πρῶτον.   15. κήρυκας] κήρυκα ekl et edd.
plerique : κήρυκας habet Tauchn.   16. καὶ συμμαχίας] Om. ekl B. et S. Frank.

decide nothing either way, aye or no,' or
rather, 'no or aye,' the order being determined rather by euphony than idiom. But
one may note, that dissent would acquit
Demosthenes, assent condemn him : Aeschines therefore prohibits first the alternative
which he fears is likeliest, and which would
be false as well as premature.

4. ἐγκαταλαμβάνῃ. 'Surprise,' 'detect.'
The ἐν gives a further reference, which cannot be rendered without undue emphasis, to
the position in which he finds himself when
surprised.

πλείω. Though Philocrates moved
all the more important decrees, those on
points of etiquette moved by Demosthenes
may have been more numerous. The reading μετὰ Φιλοκράτους has nothing to recommend it, either in sense or authority.

§ 61. And if I prove this, confess that
Demosthenes is condemned for the first
period.

7. After πρέσβεις, the MSS. add οὐκ
ἀναμείναντα, which words must be due to a
confusion with the charge already made, of
not waiting for the return of the Athenian
ambassadors—not from Philip, but from the
Greek states. Some MSS. omit παρ' ἐκείνου
to suit the sense ; but the charge is the same
as that repeated in more detail in § 76.

12. ἐπινεύσατε. He perhaps remembers
that he had used the same word in the
simile, § 59; so he repeats it here of the
thing to be illustrated.

τὸν ἕνα. So most and best MSS. :
Volg. πρῶτον. ἕνα, besides having better
authority, makes the request more moderate.
Aeschines says only, 'If I prove this, confess
that I have proved one quarter of my case,'
instead of 'consider that I have proved the
most paradoxical of my assertions.'

13. λέξω δὲ κ.τ.λ. 'I will begin my
narrative at a point from which it is easy to
follow.'

§ 62. He defended Philocrates on his trial,
and got into the Senate to support him :

15. κήρυκας. So most and best MSS. :
Volg. κήρυκα. It is true that probably only
one herald would be sent with the embassy ;
but Philocrates wished to provide for all con-
tingencies, and there might be two embassies
required, either successively or to different
states ; and the plural is thus used, as more
general. Some MSS. repeat it, inf. § 63 fin.

16. καὶ συμμαχίας. B. and S. and Franke
omit these words, less on MS. authority than
because historically inaccurate. But it is
not impossible that Philocrates proposed more
than was actually done immediately, or even
that Aeschines may have anticipated a little.

ψήφισμα ἐγράφη παρανόμων. ἧκον οἱ τῆς κρίσεως χρόνοι· κατηγόρει μὲν Λυκῖνος ὁ γραψάμενος, ἀπελογεῖτο [δὲ] Φιλοκράτης, συναπελογεῖτο δὲ καὶ Δημοσθένης· ἀπέφυγε Φιλοκράτης.
μετὰ ταῦτα ἐπῄει χρόνος Θεμιστοκλῆς ἄρχων· ἐνταῦθ' εἰσέρ-
5 χεται βουλευτὴς εἰς τὸ βουλευτήριον Δημοσθένης, οὔτε λαχὼν
οὔτ' ἐπιλαχών, ἀλλ' ἐκ παρασκευῆς πριάμενος, ἵν' εἰς ὑποδοχὴν
ἅπαντα καὶ λέγοι καὶ πράττοι Φιλοκράτει, ὡς αὐτὸ ἔδειξε τὸ
ἔργον. νικᾷ γὰρ ἕτερον ψήφισμα Φιλοκράτης, ἐν ᾧ κελεύει 63
ἑλέσθαι δέκα πρέσβεις, οἵτινες ἀφικόμενοι πρὸς Φίλιππον ἀξιώ-
10 σουσιν αὐτὸν δεῦρο πρέσβεις αὐτοκράτορας πέμπειν ὑπὲρ τῆς
εἰρήνης. τούτων εἷς ἦν Δημοσθένης. κἀκεῖθεν ἐπανήκων ἐπαι-
νέτης ἦν τῆς εἰρήνης, καὶ ταὐτὰ τοῖς ἄλλοις πρέσβεσιν ἀπήγγελλε, καὶ μόνος τῶν ἄλλων βουλευτῶν ἔγραψε σπείσασθαι
τῷ κήρυκι τῷ ἀπὸ τοῦ Φιλίππου καὶ τοῖς πρέσβεσιν, ἀκόλουθα
15 γράφων Φιλοκράτει· ὁ μέν γε τὴν ἐξουσίαν ἔδωκε τοῦ δεῦρο
κήρυκα καὶ πρέσβεις πέμπεσθαι, ὁ δὲ τῇ πρεσβείᾳ σπένδεται.

2. δὲ] Om. agmnfcb.   4. χρόνος] Volg. usque ad Bekk. ὁ χρόνος.   Articulum om.
afed ekl. ἐπῄει χρόνος delet Hamakerus, et omisso quidem articulo, substantivom certe
friget.   Fortasse χρόνος glossema sive, ut ita dicam, titulus est, ut in D. de Cor. § 200.
12. ταὐτὰ] †τὰ αὐτὰ corr. b †.   ἀπήγγελλε] ἀπήγγειλε Bekk., †quod a pr. m. habet
b † cum nde habeant ἀπήγγελε.   13. τῶν ἄλλων] Om. fd pr. b ekl, † ἐκ τῶν ἄλλων
corr. b †.   14. ἀπὸ] Sic g et post H. Wolf. Bekker et alii : ceteri libri ὑπὸ, Tauchn
παρά.   15. ἔδωκε] Sic ekl Bekk. etc. : δέδωκε Steph. cum ceteris codd.   16. κήρυκα]
κήρυκας fcd pr. b : κήρυκα † corr. b † et ceteri.   σπένδεται] σπένδεσθαι ekl.

1. ἧκον οἱ τῆς κρίσεως .. Δημοσθένης.
'The day of judgment was come : Lycinus,
who drew the indictment, was to make his
accusation : Philocrates was to make his
defence : his defence was supported by Demosthenes.'   Such we must suppose to be
the force of the imperfects, if Aeschines is
to be credited with perfect accuracy, for
Philocrates (Ae. de F. L. § 14, p. 30) was
ill, and did not appear in person.

4. Θεμιστοκλῆς ἄρχων.   'The archonship of Themistocles,' in apposition with
χρόνος.   Similarly in Latin, as in the opening sentence of Tacitus' Histories.

5. οὔτε λαχὼν .. πριάμενος.   'He was
neither drawn in the first lot nor to fi'l up a
vacancy, but made sure of the office and
bought it ;' presumably of some citizen who
had really drawn a senator's ticket, and was
willing to sell it.   According to Harpocr.,
ἐπιλαχὼν does not mean 'drawn to fill up
an actual vacancy,' but 'drawn on a supplementary list,' provided to fill up vacancies if
they occurred.   ἐκ παρασκευῆς refers to the
actual intrigue rather than to the motive,
but it has the same effect on the sense as
our expression 'on purpose.'

§ 63.   And did support him, both there and
on the embassy.

8. νικᾷ.   'Carries another resolution,'
like γνώμην νικήσαντος in Hdt. 1. 61. The
common use of νικᾶν Ὀλύμπια is similar in
principle : it is a cognate accusative of the
matter in which the victory is gained.

11. τούτων εἷς ἦν Δημοσθένης.   It is
extraordinary that Aeschines makes this an
insinuation of complicity with Philocrates,
considering that he himself was another.
Just afterwards, indeed (καὶ ταὐτὰ τοῖς ἄλλοις πρέσβεσιν ἀπήγγελλε), he alludes to
Demosthenes' not very honest prosecution
of him ; but he has sacrificed the chance of
making another point out of his own acquittal, by implying that the ambassadors
were corrupt.

13. σπείσασθαι τῷ κήρυκι, i. e. to grant
him a safe-conduct.

14. τῷ ἀπὸ τοῦ Φιλίππου.   So Wolf, and
the reading has since been found in the MS.
q, and adopted by Bekker and later editors.
All other known MSS. have ὑπὸ, which
can only be justified by supposing ἀποστα-
λέντι or something similar to have dropped
out.

64 τὰ δὲ μετὰ ταῦτα ἤδη μοι σφόδρα προσέχετε τὸν νοῦν. ἐπράτ·
τετο γὰρ οὐ πρὸς τοὺς ἄλλους πρέσβεις τοὺς πολλὰ συκοφαντηθέντας ὕστερον ἐκ μεταβολῆς ὑπὸ Δημοσθένους, ἀλλὰ πρὸς
Φιλοκράτην καὶ Δημοσθένην, εἰκότως, τοὺς ἅμα μὲν πρεσβεύ-
οντας, ἅμα δὲ τὰ ψηφίσματα γράφοντας, πρῶτον μὲν ὅπως 5
μὴ περιμείνητε τοὺς πρέσβεις, οὓς ἦτε ἐκπεπομφότες παρακαλοῦντες ἐπὶ Φίλιππον, ἵνα μὴ μετὰ τῶν ἄλλων Ἑλλήνων,
65 ἀλλ᾿ ἰδίᾳ ποιήσησθε τὴν εἰρήνην· δεύτερον δ᾿ ὅπως μὴ μόνον
τὴν εἰρήνην, ἀλλὰ καὶ συμμαχίαν εἶναι ψηφιεῖσθε πρὸς Φίλιππον, ἵν᾿, εἴ τινες προσέχοιεν τῷ πλήθει τῷ ὑμετέρῳ, εἰς τὴν 10
ἐσχάτην ἐμπέσοιεν ἀθυμίαν ὁρῶντες ὑμᾶς αὐτοὺς μὲν παρακα-
λοῦντας ἐπὶ τὸν πόλεμον, οἴκοι δὲ μὴ μόνον εἰρήνην, ἀλλὰ καὶ
συμμαχίαν ἐψηφισμένους ποιεῖσθαι· τρίτον δὲ ὅπως Κερσο-
βλέπτης ὁ Θρᾴκης βασιλεὺς μὴ ἔσται ἔνορκος, μηδὲ μετέσται
τῆς συμμαχίας καὶ τῆς εἰρήνης αὐτῷ. παρηγγέλλετο δ᾿ ἐπ᾿ 15
66 αὐτὸν ἤδη στρατεία. καὶ ταῦθ᾿ ὁ μὲν ἐξωνούμενος οὐκ ἠδίκει, πρὸ
γὰρ τῶν ὅρκων καὶ τῶν συνθηκῶν ἀνεμέσητον ἦν αὐτῷ πράττειν τὰ συμφέροντα, οἱ δ᾿ ἀποδόμενοι καὶ κατακοινωνήσαντες

---

1. μοὶ σφόδρα προσέχετε τὸν νοῦν] σφόδρα μοι τὸν νοῦν προσέχετε ekl Bekk.
2. τοὺς πολλά] Volg. ante Bekk. τὰ πολλά. 4. Φιλοκράτην καὶ Δημοσθένην]-τη et
-νη habent cd, -νη etiam f: non tamen volgatum hic mutat Bekk., ut in plerisque locis.
5. πρῶτον] 'Hinc altera manus e' Bekk. 6. περιμείνητε] περιμινεῖτε Steph. et marg.
Bern.: περιμείναιτε conj. Saupp. 14. μηδὲ] Sic Bekk. et recentiores: libri μήτε, quod
sunt qui defendant. 15. ἐπ᾿ αὐτὸν ἤδη] ἤδη ἐπ᾿ αὐτὸν ekl Bekk. 16. στρατεία]
στρατία fcd pr. b: †·εία corr. b †. 18. κατακοινωνήσαντες] κατακοινώσαντες k
Reisk. Tauchn.

§ 64. These two being the only ambassadors guilty, as the only ones open to temptation.
3. ἐκ μεταβολῆς. 'When he turned
round' upon Philip. Aeschines sees that
he must take fresh care to distinguish his
own case from that of Demosthenes, if he is
to avoid being damaged by the insinuations
of the last section.
4. εἰκότως κ.τ.λ. This parenthesis gives
the reason why Philip should have selected
these instruments, and also why the speaker
assumes that they were Philip's instruments.
5. ὅπως μὴ περιμείνητε τοὺς πρέσβεις.
See D. de Cor. §. 29.
§ 65. They committed you to an alliance
with Philip, and betrayed Cersobleptes.
8. μὴ μόνον τὴν εἰρήνην, ἀλλὰ καὶ συμμαχίαν. 'Not only the peace' already proposed, 'but also an alliance.'
10. ἵν᾿, εἴ τινες .. ὑμετέρῳ. 'That, if
any should turn your eyes to the people of
your city,' 'respond to the appeal of you, the
Athenian people.' The appeal originally

issued to Greece was the act of the nation:
the disregard and stultification of it, the act
of the conspirators alone.
13. τρίτον δέ. Demosthenes also represents Cersobleptes' exclusion as an act of
intrigue never sanctioned by the nation, and
treats Philip's conquests from him as acts of
absolute treachery: D. de F. L. p. 397, §
200; p. 398, § 202.
15. παρηγγέλλετο .... στρατεία. The
Halians were also excluded, on the ground
that their conquest was inevitable.
§ 66. Acts of legitimate war on Philip's
part, of detestable treason on theirs.
16. καὶ ταῦθ᾿ ὁ μὲν .. ἦσαν ἄξιοι. 'And
Philip did no wrong in paying for this; as he
had sworn no oath and made no covenant
with us, he could not be blamed for seeking
his own profit. But they deserved all your
anger for their share in the bargain—for
sacrificing every bulwark of the state to
their partnership' with Philip and each
other. For the common Greek construction of ὠνεῖσθαι and ἀποδύσθαι of treason,
vid. ad D. de Cor. § 28.

τὰ τῆς πόλεως ἰσχυρὰ μεγάλης ὀργῆς ἦσαν ἄξιοι. ὁ γὰρ
μισαλέξανδρος νυνὶ φάσκων εἶναι καὶ τότε μισοφίλιππος Δημοσθένης, ὁ τὴν ξενίαν ἐμοὶ προφέρων τὴν Ἀλεξάνδρου,
γράφει ψήφισμα, τοὺς καιροὺς τῆς πόλεως ὑφαιρούμενος, ἐκκλη- 67
5 σίαν ποιεῖν τοὺς πρυτάνεις τῇ ὀγδόῃ ἱσταμένου τοῦ ἐλαφηβολιῶνος μηνός, ὅτ' ἦν τῷ Ἀσκληπιῷ ἡ θυσία καὶ ὁ προαγών,
ἐν τῇ ἱερᾷ ἡμέρᾳ, ὃ πρότερον οὐδεὶς μέμνηται γενόμενον, τίνα
πρόφασιν ποιησάμενος; ἵνα, φησίν, ἐὰν ἤδη παρῶσιν οἱ τοῦ
Φιλίππου πρέσβεις, βουλεύσηται ὁ δῆμος ὡς τάχιστα περὶ
10 τῶν πρὸς Φίλιππον, τοῖς οὔπω παροῦσι πρέσβεσι προκαταλαμβάνων τὴν ἐκκλησίαν καὶ τοὺς χρόνους ὑμῶν ὑποτεμνόμενος
καὶ τὸ πρᾶγμα κατασπεύδων, ἵνα μὴ μετὰ τῶν ἄλλων Ἑλλήνων ἐπανελθόντων τῶν ὑμετέρων πρέσβεων, ἀλλὰ μόνοι ποιήσησθε τὴν εἰρήνην. μετὰ δὲ ταῦτα, ὦ ἄνδρες Ἀθηναῖοι, ἧκον 68
15 οἱ τοῦ Φιλίππου πρέσβεις· οἱ δὲ ὑμέτεροι ἀπεδήμουν παρακαλοῦντες τοὺς Ἕλληνας ἐπὶ Φίλιππον. ἐνταῦθ' ἕτερον ψήφισμα νικᾷ Δημοσθένης, ἐν ᾧ γράφει μὴ μόνον ὑπὲρ τῆς εἰρήνης,
ἀλλὰ καὶ συμμαχίας ὑμᾶς βουλεύσασθαι, μὴ περιμείναντας τοὺς

---

5. ποιεῖν] ποιεῖσθαι debl et edd. nonnulli.   6. ὁ προαγών] Sic afcd pr. b: ὅτ' ἦν
προάγων gm::kl: e, ut videtur, ὅτ' ἦν προαγὼν, quod habet Tauchn. τότε ἦν προαγὼν corr.
b †.   7. δ] ἦ f, ἦ c, utrumque profecto pro ᾗ positum : om. a.   8. τοῦ] Om. ekl
Bekk.   9. ὡς] Om. fcd † pr. b †.   11. ὑμῶν] ἡμῶν ekl.   13. ὑμετέρων] Sic k :
ceteri ἡμετέρων.   15. τοῦ] Om. eki. Bekk.   ὑμέτεροι] Sic Ald.: codd. omnes ἡμέτεροι.
17. Δημοσθένης] † ὁ Δημοσθένης pr. b †.   18. ὑμᾶς] Om. ekl, ceteri ἡμᾶς: ὑμᾶς habet Ald.

3. ὁ τὴν ξενίαν .. Ἀλεξάνδρου. Taken
up by D. de Cor. §. 64, p. 350.

§ 67. *Before Philip's ambassadors arrived, Demosthenes had arranged to isolate
you, by hurrying on an assembly on a holy
day.*

6. ὁ προαγών. The meaning is clear,
'the prelude' to the Dionysia. It is commonly accented as in the text, but a few
MSS. have προάγων ; 'fortasse rectius,'
Franke. The derivation may be either 'the
day introducing,' and so 'preceding' the festival, or 'the preliminary contest:' and the
accent will depend upon the etymology.

8. ἐάν. The form of conditional sentence
appropriate to utter uncertainty. Demosthenes would probably have said εἰ πάρεισιν.

10. οὔπω παροῦσι. If they had been
there, the assembly on a holy day might
have been proposed to save time ; but he
must have had a corrupt motive for risking
profanity on a chance.

προκαταλαμβάνων τὴν ἐκκλησίαν.
'Forestalling the assembly for them.' The
article is used because the decree first provided an assembly in advance, and then fixed

the business of *that* assembly in Philip's
interest. For the notice of business given
to the Assembly, cp. sup. § 39, ἐπιγράψαντας
νομοθέτας.

§ 68. *They came : your own ambassadors
were absent. Demosthenes carried a decree
to treat for alliance as well as peace, in the
absence of your own allies.*

15. παρακαλοῦντες .. ἐπὶ Φίλιππον.
Aeschines thus exposes himself to the retort
of Demosthenes (§ 29), that the action he
attributed to Athens was dishonourable.
Technically it was ; substantially Demosthenes' reply was true, though Athens would
have been in a more dignified position if she
could have waited for the return of the last
ambassador from a mission certain to be
fruitless. Aeschines overstates his case, to
heighten the contrast between Demosthenes'
policy and the nation's.

17. τῆς εἰρήνης .. συμμαχίας. As sup.
§ 64.

18. ὑμᾶς βουλεύσασθαι. One may remark here once for all on the uncertainty of
reading between ὑμεῖς and ἡμεῖς, wherever
the sense does not determine it ; as is often

πρέσβεις τοὺς ὑμετέρους, ἀλλ᾽ εὐθὺς μετὰ [τὰ] Διονύσια τὰ
ἐν ἄστει, τῇ ὀγδόῃ καὶ ἐνάτῃ ἐπὶ δέκα. ὅτι δ᾽ ἀληθῆ λέγω,
ἀκούσατε τῶν ψηφισμάτων.

ΨΗΦΙΣΜΑΤΑ.

69 Ἐπειδὴ τοίνυν, ὦ Ἀθηναῖοι, παρεληλύθει τὰ Διονύσια, ἐγί- 5
νοντο δὲ αἱ ἐκκλησίαι, ἐν δὲ τῇ προτέρᾳ τῶν ἐκκλησιῶν ἀνεγνώσθη δόγμα κοινὸν τῶν συμμάχων, οὗ τὰ κεφάλαια διὰ βραχέων ἐγὼ προερῶ. πρῶτον μὲν γὰρ ἔγραψαν ὑπὲρ εἰρήνης
ὑμᾶς μόνον βουλεύσασθαι, τὸ δὲ τῆς συμμαχίας ὄνομα ὑπερέ-
βησαν, οὐκ ἐπιλελησμένοι, ἀλλὰ καὶ τὴν εἰρήνην ἀναγκαιοτέ- 10
ραν ἢ καλλίω ὑπολαμβάνοντες εἶναι· ἔπειτα ἀπήντησαν ὀρθῶς
70 ἰασόμενοι τὸ Δημοσθένους δωροδόκημα, καὶ προσέγραψαν ἐν
τῷ δόγματι ἐξεῖναι τῷ βουλομένῳ τῶν Ἑλλήνων ἐν τρισὶ
μησὶν εἰς τὴν αὐτὴν στήλην ἀναγεγράφθαι μετ᾽ Ἀθηναίων καὶ
μετέχειν τῶν ὅρκων καὶ τῶν συνθηκῶν, δύο μέγιστα προκατα- 15
λαμβάνοντες, πρῶτον μὲν τὸν χρόνον τὸν τῆς τριμήνου ταῖς
τῶν Ἑλλήνων πρεσβείαις ἱκανὸν γενέσθαι παρασκευάζοντες,

1. ὑμετέρους] ἡμετέρους ekl. Vid. annot. ad loc.: quinquies, si semel, mutandum.
[τὰ] Διονύσια] Articulum om. gmne: volg. ante Bekk. μετὰ τὰ ἐν ἄστει Διονύσια.
5. ὦ Ἀθηναῖοι] Om. ekl, post Διονύσια ponunt gmn.   ἐγίνοντο] ἐγένοντο p Reisk.
Tauchn.: ἐγίγνοντο scribit Frank.   6. δὲ αἱ] δε κα b † non tanquam δέκα pro certo
scribere voluerit †: δέκα tamen habent el, δὲ k, δὴ αἱ marg. n, quod haud absurdum.
ἐν δὲ τῇ] 'Imo ἐν τῇ' Frank. Post δόγμα legebatur τῇ ὀγδόῃ ἐπὶ δέκα, quod post ἐκκλησιῶν ponunt ekl; itaque tanquam glossema omittebat Taylor, uncis inclusit Bekk., ejecerunt
recentiores.   14. ἀναγεγράφθαι] ἀναγεγράφεσθαι l, ἀναγράφεσθαι ek, quod mavolt
Frank. Sed ut magis in promptu, ita eo ipso minus probabile videtur.   16. πρῶτον μὲν]
Ita bekl: ceteri πρῶτον μὲν οὖν.   17. γενέσθαι παρασκευάζοντες] παραγενέσθαι κατασκευάζοντες ekl: κατασκευάζοντες praeterea habet pr. b.

the case where, as here, the pronoun is used
of the Athenian nation. Here all the MSS.
have ἡμᾶς (except a few that omit it), but
the Aldine ed. ὑμᾶς, and it is clearly necessary to have either the first or second person
throughout. Some MSS. read ἡμᾶς, ἡμετέρας κ.τ.λ. consistently; but Aldus is entitled
to at least as much respect as they.

§ 69. They voted that you should treat for
peace, tacitly censuring the proposal to treat
for alliance;

5. ἐπειδὴ τοίνυν .. ἀνεγνώσθη δόγμα.
In a sentence of this type it is hard to determine with which of the dependent clauses
the apodosis begins, or whether it be not
truer to say that the apodosis is suppressed.
Here ἐν δὲ τῇ προτέρᾳ κ.τ.λ. is the apodosis
so far as sense goes; but the construction is
rather, 'When the feast was past, and the
assemblies had come on, and a resolution of
the allies was read to the assembly, then
[note our respective conduct];' the real apo-

dosis being §§ 71 sq., and οὗ τὰ κεφάλαια ..
ἀκούσαντες μαθήσεσθε a virtual parenthesis.
Cp. ad D. de Cor. § 161.

10. ἀναγκαιοτέραν ἢ καλλίω. While
we should say 'rather necessary than honourable,' the Greek allows a more developed
contrast, without sacrificing terseness. The
full force of the phrase is, that necessity pre-
dominated over honour rather than honour
over necessity.

11. ἀπήντησαν ὀρθῶς ἰασόμενοι τὸ
Δημοσθένους δωροδόκημα. Note the
freedom of construction. Thucydides would
have written τῷ δωροδοκήματι ἀπήντησαν
ἰασόμενοι.

§ 70. And provided that any Greek might
claim the benefit of the treaty within three
months.

14. μετ᾽ Ἀθηναίων. 'With Athens, on
the same pillar.' Of course μετ᾽ Ἀθηναίων
is in no sense the definition or complement
of τὴν αὐτήν.

ἔπειτα τὴν τῶν Ἑλλήνων εὔνοιαν τῇ πόλει μετὰ κοινοῦ συνεδρίου κτώμενοι, ἵν᾽ εἰ παραβαίνοιντο αἱ συνθῆκαι, μὴ μόνοι
μηδ᾽ ἀπαράσκευοι πολεμήσαιμεν, ἃ νῦν ἡμῖν παθεῖν συνέβη διὰ
Δημοσθένην. ὅτι δ᾽ ἀληθῆ λέγω, ἐξ αὐτοῦ τοῦ δόγματος
5 ἀκούσαντες μαθήσεσθε.

ΔΟΓΜΑ ΣΥΜΜΑΧΩΝ.

Τούτῳ τῷ δόγματι συνειπεῖν ὁμολογῶ, καὶ πάντες οἱ ἐν 71
τῇ προτέρᾳ τῶν ἐκκλησιῶν δημηγοροῦντες· καὶ ὁ δῆμος ἀπ-
ῆλθε τοιαύτην τινὰ δόξαν εἰληφώς, ὡς ἔσται μὲν ἡ εἰρήνη, περὶ
10 δὲ συμμαχίας οὐκ ἄμεινον εἴη διὰ τὴν τῶν Ἑλλήνων παράκλησιν βουλεύσασθαι, ἔσται δὲ κοινῇ μετὰ τῶν Ἑλλήνων ἁπάντων. νὺξ ἐν μέσῳ, καὶ παρῆμεν τῇ ὑστεραίᾳ εἰς τὴν ἐκκλησίαν.
ἐνταῦθα δὴ προκαταλαμβάνων Δημοσθένης τὸ βῆμα, οὐδενὶ
τῶν ἄλλων παραλιπὼν λόγον, οὐδὲν ὄφελος ἔφη τῶν χθὲς
15 εἰρημένων εἶναι λόγων, εἰ ταῦθ᾽ οἱ Φιλίππου μὴ συμπεισθή-
σονται πρέσβεις, οὐδὲ γιγνώσκειν ἔφη τὴν εἰρήνην ἀπούσης

---

3. ἡμῖν] Sic *gmnk*: ceteri libri ὑμῖν.   11. κοινῇ] *κοινὴ gmnkl.*   13. Δημοσθένης
τὸ βῆμα] *τὸ βῆμα Δημοσθένης ekl* et marg., quod mavolt Frank.

---

1. μετὰ κοινοῦ συνεδρίου. 'In conjunction with a common congress' of signa'ories to
the treaty, which, it was hoped, might meet
from time to time to maintain it.

3. ἃ νῦν .. διὰ Δημοσθένην. νῦν is
equivalent to 'as it was,' rather than 'as it
is.' Aeschines is not saying that a larger or
more stable confederacy might have been
formed in 346 than was formed in 339.

§. 71. *I supported the negotiations in this
sense: the general feeling was to conclude
peace and defer alliance.*

7. καὶ πάντες οἱ .... δημηγοροῦντες.
Probably in the nominative only by attraction or parallelism to the first clause, συνειπεῖν ὁμολογῶ; but Aeschines may mean to
assert, 'neither I nor anyone else are now
ashamed of our conduct.' Cp. Ae. de F. L.
§ 64, p. 36.

10. οὐκ ἄμεινον. 'That it was *better not*
to ..:' as in the common formula of ora-
cles, οὐ γὰρ ἄμεινον.

διὰ τὴν τῶν Ἑλλήνων παράκλησιν.
'On account of the (pending) appeal to the
Greeks.'

11. ἔσται .. εἴη .. ἔσται. The majority
believed as a matter of fact that peace would
come, and that the alliance (if concluded
later) would include the whole of Greece:
they believed as a matter of opinion and
inference, that it would be better not to dis-

cuss the alliance until the ambassadors returned.

13. ἐνταῦθα δὴ κ.τ.λ. Yet Aeschines
asserts (de F. L. §§ 67 sqq. p. 36) that no
speaking was allowed on the second day.
Demosthenes is said to have introduced a
motion for including alliance in the negotiations, but to have given it to the Proedri
without any speech, beyond a private colloquy
with one Amyntor.

οὐδενὶ τῶν ἄλλων παραλιπὼν λόγον.
This is probably, in some way or other, a
reference to the prohibition of speaking in
this assembly. Demosthenes was clearly
not Proedros (as in the later one), so cannot
have had the opportunity to make a few remarks from the chair. Perhaps the most
probable reconciliation of Aeschines' discordant statements is, to suppose that the facts
are more correctly stated in the earlier
speech; that then it was more important
to prove that he had not himself made the
speech attributed to him by Demosthenes,
while here, long after the event, he ventures
to set Demosthenes' own conduct in a more
invidious light, by calling his informal remarks to Amyntor a speech from the Bema.
Demosthenes' own charge against Aeschines
(D. de F. L. § 17, p. 345) may perhaps
have the same amount of foundation.

16. οὐδὲ γιγνώσκειν .. τῆς εἰρήνης τὴν

72 συμμαχίας. οὐ γὰρ ἔφη δεῖν, καὶ γὰρ τὸ ῥῆμα μέμνημαι ὡς
εἶπε, διὰ τὴν ἀηδίαν τοῦ λέγοντος ἅμα καὶ τοῦ ὀνόματος, ἀπορ-
ρῆξαι τῆς εἰρήνης τὴν συμμαχίαν, οὐδὲ τὰ τῶν Ἑλλήνων ἀνα-
μένειν μελλήματα, ἀλλ᾽ ἢ πολεμεῖν αὐτοὺς ἢ τὴν εἰρήνην ἰδίᾳ
ποιεῖσθαι. καὶ τελευτῶν ἐπὶ τὸ βῆμα παρακαλέσας Ἀντί- 5
πατρον ἐρώτημά τι ἠρώτα, προειπὼν μὲν ἃ ἐρήσεται, προ-
διδάξας δὲ ἃ χρὴ κατὰ τῆς πόλεως ἀποκρίνασθαι. καὶ τέλος
ταῦτ᾽ ἐνίκα, τῷ μὲν λόγῳ προβιασαμένου Δημοσθένους, τὸ δὲ
73 ψήφισμα γράψαντος Φιλοκράτους. ὃ δὲ ἦν ὑπόλοιπον αὐτοῖς,
Κερσοβλέπτην καὶ τὸν ἐπὶ Θρᾴκης τόπον ἔκδοτον ποιῆσαι, 10
καὶ τοῦτ᾽ ἔπραξαν ἕκτῃ φθίνοντος τοῦ ἐλαφηβολιῶνος, πρὶν
ἐπὶ τὴν ὑστέραν ἀπαίρειν πρεσβείαν τὴν ἐπὶ τοὺς ὅρκους Δη-
μοσθένην· ὁ γὰρ μισαλέξανδρος καὶ μισοφίλιππος ὑμῖν οὑτοσὶ
ῥήτωρ δὶς ἐπρέσβευσεν ἐν Μακεδονίᾳ, ἐξὸν μηδὲ ἅπαξ, ὁ νυνὶ
κελεύων τῶν Μακεδόνων καταπτύειν. εἰς δὲ τὴν ἐκκλησίαν, 15

3. τὰ τῶν Ἑλλήνων] τὰ om. fcd † pr. b †. 4. μελλήματα] μελήματα d † pr. b †,
μελετήματα el. 5. παρακαλέσας] κἀλέσας fcdb. 6. ἐρήσεται] αἱρήσεται f, αἱρήσεται pr. b † mox corr. †, εἰρήσεται gmn. ᾽ 8. προβιασαμένου] Malunt Reisk. et Frank.
προσβιασαμένου. Δημοσθένους] τοῦ Δημοσθένους fcd pr. b: † articulum expunxit
corr. b †. 11. ἐλαφηβολιῶνος] Addebatur usque ad Bekk. μηνός: om. agmn B. et S.
Frank. 13. οὑτοσὶ] Sic agmn: ceteri οὗτος. 14. ἐν Μακεδονίᾳ] εἰς Μακεδονίαν
ekl Bekk.: idque Frankius restitui jubet, quia 'sic Aeschines semper.' Eam causam fuisse
credo, cur aliqui hic habeant, cum hic semel non ita scripserit.

συμμαχίαν. 'He said he did not understand what peace would mean without
alliance; for he said there must be no *disruption* of the peace from the alliance. I
remember the very words, because of the
offensiveness both of the speaker and of the
phrase.' This is certainly lying with a circumstance, if no such speech was made
either privately or publicly.

§ 72. *Demosthenes, by an understanding
with the ambassadors, carried both:*
2. διὰ τὴν ἀηδίαν. Vid. inf. § 166, for
a similar criticism on Demosthenes' inelegant
language, and so repeatedly in Ae. de F. L.
It is possible that his speeches were less perfect (though, by all accounts, not less effective) to hear than to read, not only from
his natural weakness of voice, but that in
extempore speaking he may have used
vigorous but harsh similes, such as those
attributed to him, which on reflection he
would soften in the written speech.
6. προειπὼν μὲν ..... ἀποκρίνασθαι.
'Having told him beforehand what he
meant to ask, and instructed him (to give)
the answer that would damage the city
most.' Since question and answer are
naturally regarded as contrasted, the two

clauses are opposed with a μὲν and δὲ,
though here (where both question and
answer proceed from the same person) they
are successive parts of the same action.
8. ταῦτ᾽ ἐνίκα. 'This *was* carried,' an
intransitive parallel to the transitive and
personal construction noted above on § 63,
and possibly rather commoner. Cp. Soph.
Ant. 274.
§ 73. *And betrayed Cersobleptes (before
that second embassy, which since his change
of policy he finds it convenient to forget),*
10. τὸν ἐπὶ Θρᾴκης τόπον. Best translated 'the Thracian border.' It practically
includes the whole coast, east from and
including Chalcidice. In Thucydides τἀπὶ
Θρᾴκης is especially the district between
Chalcidice and Amphipolis inclusive, which
was already in Philip's hands.
14. διὰ ἐπρέσβευσεν. Demosthenes asserts (de F. L. §§ 188-9, pp. 394-5) that
the second time he went against his will,
having already discovered his colleagues'
treason, but being still obliged to accom-
pany them on account of some Athenian
prisoners whom he had promised to ransom.
15. εἰς δὲ τὴν ἐκκλησίαν. 'He went
down to the Assembly and took the chair,

τὴν τῇ ἕκτῃ λέγω, καθεζόμενος βουλευτὴς ὢν ἐκ παρασκευῆς,
ἔκδοτον Κερσοβλέπτην μετὰ Φιλοκράτους ἐποίησε. λανθάνει 74
γὰρ ὁ μὲν Φιλοκράτης ἐν ψηφίσματι μετὰ τῶν ἄλλων γραμμάτων παρεγγράψας, ὁ δ᾽ ἐπιψηφίσας, Δημοσθένης, ἐν ᾧ γέ-
5 γραπται "ἀποδοῦναι δὲ τοὺς ὅρκους τοῖς πρέσβεσι τοῖς παρὰ
Φιλίππου ἐν τῇδε τῇ ἡμέρᾳ τοὺς συνέδρους τῶν συμμάχων."
παρὰ δὲ Κερσοβλέπτου σύνεδρος οὐκ ἐκάθητο· γράψας δὲ τοὺς
συνεδρεύοντας ὀμνύναι τὸν Κερσοβλέπτην οὐ συνεδρεύοντα ἐξέ-
κλησε τῶν ὅρκων. ὅτι δ᾽ ἀληθῆ λέγω, ἀνάγνωθί μοι, τίς ἦν ὁ
10 ταῦτα γράψας καὶ τίς ὁ ταῦτα ἐπιψηφίσας.

ΨΗΦΙΣΜΑ. ΠΡΟΕΔΡΟΣ.

Καλὸν, ὦ Ἀθηναῖοι, καλὸν ἡ τῶν δημοσίων γραμμάτων φυ- 75
λακή· ἀκίνητον γάρ ἐστι καὶ οὐ συμμεταπίπτει τοῖς αὐτομο-
λοῦσιν ἐν τῇ πολιτείᾳ, ἀλλ᾽ ἐπέδωκε τῷ δήμῳ, ὁπόταν βού-
15 ληται, συνιδεῖν τοὺς πάλαι μὲν πονηρούς, ἐκ μεταβολῆς δ᾽
ἀξιοῦντας εἶναι χρηστούς.

1. λέγω, καθεζόμενος] καθεζόμενος λέγω ag γρ. m, καθεζόμενος n. Vide ne λέγω, βουλευτὴς ὢν, sit antiquom glossema pro καθεζόμενος. 4. ἐν ᾧ γέγραπται] Omitti jubent
Markl. Baiter. Frank. 5. ἀποδοῦναι δὲ] † Om. pr. h †: mox ἀποδοῦναι a m. sec.
restitutum, sed δὲ omissum, quod so'i habent ekl. Post Bekk., δὲ est a plerisque omissum :
sed vid. annot. ad loc. 10. ἐπιψηφίσας] Addebatur πρόεδρος. Delevimus jubente
Frankio, cum pekl et pr. h: † nam in h manus secunda inseruit †. 11. ΠΡΟΕΔΡΟΣ]
Om. a: πρόεδροι dek † πρόεδρων λείπει h, omisso ΨΗΦΙΣΜΑ. † Fortasse πρόεδρος verum;
neque enim solus πρόεδρος Demosthenes fuit 12. γραμμάτων] Sic kl et superscr. in h :
ceteri πραγμάτων. 13. συμμεταπίπτει] μεταπίπτει agmn ekl. 14. ἐπέδωκε] ἀπέδωκε
ekl B. et S. Frank. Vid. annot. ad loc.

having got into the Senate on purpose,' that
whenever his turn for presiding came, Philocrates might with safety bring on his most
unpopular motion. For we cannot suppose
that Demosthenes calculated beforehand the
course of events, and timed his own tenure
of office accordingly.

§ 74. *By a stipulation that only the allies
then represented should be included in the
oaths.*

2. λανθάνει γὰρ κ.τ.λ. 'No one detected
how one partner, Philocrates, had inserted
this clause among others, and the other,
Demosthenes, had put it to the vote.' λανθάνει refers especially to Philocrates: the
clause escaped notice, as well as his motive
for it. The secret thing as regards Demosthenes was, not his act, but its significance
when it concerned Philocrates. That ὁ μὲν
and ὁ δὲ are not mere articles, but emphatic
as rendered above, is plain from the order in
the second clause.

5. ἀποδοῦναι δέ. The best MSS. omit
δὲ, but the form of verbatim quotation is
likelier to have occurred to Aeschines, who
had the whole text of the decree before him,
than to a copyist who had not.

7. παρὰ δὲ Κερσοβλέπτου κ.τ.λ. Vid.
Ae. de F. L. § 88, p. 39.

§ 75. *Happily the state records remain to
convict Demosthenes of this.*

12. καλὸν, ὦ Ἀθηναῖοι. Observe Aeschines' habit of going off into commendation
of the details of the constitution.

14. ἐπέδωκε. The force of the aorist
is maintained amid the presents : 'instead
of keeping pace with every shift of
political turncoats, it occurs once for all.'
Al. leg. ἀπέδωκε : the force of one reading
would be, ' secures to the nation its
right ;' of the other, ' secures the incidental gain' when, as now, we want it,
which seems to suit the use of the tense
better.

76 Ὑπόλοιπον δέ μοι ἐστὶ τὴν κολακείαν αὐτοῦ διεξελθεῖν.
Δημοσθένης γὰρ ἐνιαυτὸν βουλεύσας οὐδεμίαν πώποτε φανεῖται
πρεσβείαν εἰς προεδρίαν καλέσας, ἀλλὰ τότε μόνον καὶ πρῶτον πρέσβεις εἰς προεδρίαν ἐκάλεσε καὶ προσκεφάλαια ἔθηκε
καὶ φοινικίδας περιεπέτασε καὶ ἅμα τῇ ἡμέρᾳ ἡγεῖτο τοῖς 5
πρέσβεσιν εἰς τὸ θέατρον, ὥστε καὶ συρίττεσθαι διὰ τὴν ἀσχη-
μοσύνην καὶ κολακείαν. καὶ ὅτ᾽ ἀπῄεσαν, ἐμισθώσατο αὐτοῖς
τρία ζεύγη ὀρικὰ καὶ προὔπεμψεν εἰς Θήβας, καταγέλαστον
τὴν πόλιν ποιῶν. ἵνα δ᾽ ἐπὶ τῆς ὑποθέσεως μείνω, λαβέ μοι
τὸ ψήφισμα τὸ περὶ τῆς προεδρίας. 10

ΨΗΦΙΣΜΑ.

77 Οὗτος τοίνυν, ὦ Ἀθηναῖοι, ὁ τηλικοῦτος τὸ μέγεθος κόλαξ
πρῶτος διὰ τῶν κατασκόπων τῶν παρὰ Χαριδήμου πυθόμενος
τὴν Φιλίππου τελευτὴν τῶν μὲν θεῶν συμπλάσας ἑαυτῷ ἐνύπνιον κατεψεύσατο, ὡς οὐ παρὰ Χαριδήμου τὸ πρᾶγμα πεπυ- 15
σμένος, ἀλλὰ παρὰ τοῦ Διὸς καὶ τῆς Ἀθηνᾶς, οὓς μεθ᾽ ἡμέραν
ἐπιορκῶν νύκτωρ φησὶν ἑαυτῷ διαλέγεσθαι καὶ τὰ μέλλον-
78 τα ἔσεσθαι προλέγειν, ἑβδόμην δ᾽ ἡμέραν τῆς θυγατρὸς αὐτῷ

---

1. δέ μοι ἐστὶ] δ᾽ ἐστί μοι ekl Bekk. 2. γὰρ] γὰρ, ὦ ἄνδρες Ἀθηναῖοι, ekl Bekk.
φανεῖται] φανήσεται ekl Bremi. 3. μόνον καὶ πρῶτον] πρῶτον καὶ μόνον ekl Bekk.
7. Post ἀπῄεσαν, addebatur εἰς Θήβας: post alterum καὶ, τοὺς πρέσβεις: utrumque primus
omittebat Taylor. Statim post Θήβας, καταγέλαστον .. ποιῶν ponit a. 12. ὦ Ἀθηναῖοι]
Post κόλαξ ponit z. 18. ἑβδόμην δ᾽ ἡμέραν] ἑβδόμῃ δ᾽ ἡμέρᾳ fcd † pr. b †.

§ 76. *Demosthenes courted the ambassadors publicly and privately.*

1. τὴν κολακείαν. Cp. D. de F. L. §
268, p. 414, de Cor. § 35.

3. μόνον καὶ πρῶτον. So most and best
MSS.; but there is something in Bremi's
remark, that his and Bekker's reading, πρῶτον καὶ μόνον, gives more of a climax.

6. ὥστε καὶ συρίττεσθαι. An ordinary
embassy from a Greek state would probably
receive the compliment of προεδρία, on the
motion of an avowed sympathiser, and not
be treated with much further ceremony. It
very likely was thought invidious to receive
the envoys of a semi-barbarian despot with
greater state; while to Demosthenes, who
had seen the Macedonian court, and had a
failure there to atone for, it might seem a fit
thing to be done, and a useful one for him
to do.

8. καταγέλαστον τὴν πόλιν ποιῶν. For
if it was proper or usual for such extravagant
courtesy to be shown to ambassadors, it was
the city's business to provide for it, instead
of leaving it to an individual.

9. ἵνα δ᾽ ἐπὶ τῆς ὑποθέσεως μείνω. For

though the motion of προεδρία was a public
act, the other compliments to the ambassadors were private ones, and so count among
the follies and extravagance which Aeschines
affects not to describe.

§ 77. *Yet after all this flattery to Philip,
he claimed a revelation of his death, and
offered sacrifices of thanksgiving while in
mourning for his only daughter—heartless as
he is ungenerous, and therefore untrustworthy.*

16. οὓς μεθ᾽ ἡμέραν κ.τ.λ. 'He learns to
profane them by fiction, because he is in the
habit of profaning them by perjury.' If the
point were, 'he is a truly pious man, likely
to be favoured with visions,' a more forcible
construction would be οὓς φησιν ἑαυτῷ νύκτωρ διαλέγεσθαι τῷ μεθ᾽ ἡμέραν ἐπιορ-
κοῦντι.

18. ἑβδόμην δ᾽ ἡμέραν. Vid. sup. ad §
51. In Plutarch the comment is made that
would naturally occur to a modern—that
private sorrow might well give place to
national joy, if legitimate; but that the
nation had no right to rejoice at what was
no triumph of their own. But the act of

τετελευτηκυίας, πρὶν πενθῆσαι καὶ τὰ νομιζόμενα ποιῆσαι, στε-
φανωσάμενος καὶ λευκὴν ἐσθῆτα λαβὼν ἐβουθύτει καὶ παρενόμει,
τὴν μόνην ὁ δείλαιος καὶ πρώτην αὐτὸν πατέρα προσειποῦσαν
ἀπολέσας. καὶ οὐ τὸ δυστύχημα ὀνειδίζω, ἀλλὰ τὸν τρόπον
5 ἐξετάζω. ὁ γὰρ μισότεκνος καὶ πατὴρ πονηρὸς οὐκ ἄν ποτε
γένοιτο δημαγωγὸς χρηστός, οὐδὲ ὁ τὰ φίλτατα καὶ οἰκειό-
τατα σώματα μὴ στέργων οὐδέποθ᾽ ὑμᾶς περὶ πλείονος ποιήσεται τοὺς ἀλλοτρίους, οὐδέ γε ὁ ἰδίᾳ πονηρὸς οὐκ ἂν γένοιτο
δημοσίᾳ χρηστός, οὐδ᾽ ὅστις ἐστὶν οἴκοι φαῦλος, οὐδέποτ᾽ ἦν
10 ἐν Μακεδονίᾳ κατὰ τὴν πρεσβείαν καλὸς κἀγαθός· οὐ γὰρ τὸν
τρόπον, ἀλλὰ τὸν τόπον μόνον μετήλλαξεν.

Πόθεν οὖν ἐπὶ τὴν μεταβολὴν ἦλθε τῶν πραγμάτων, οὗτος 79
γάρ ἐστιν ὁ δεύτερος καιρός, καὶ τί ποτ᾽ ἐστὶ τὸ αἴτιον, ὅτι
Φιλοκράτης μὲν ἀπὸ τῶν αὐτῶν πολιτευμάτων Δημοσθένει φυ-
15 γὰς ἀπ᾽ εἰσαγγελίας γεγένηται, Δημοσθένης δὲ ἐπέστη τῶν
ἄλλων κατήγορος, καὶ πόθεν ποθ᾽ ἡμᾶς εἰς τὰς ἀτυχίας ὁ μιαρὸς ἄνθρωπος ἐμβέβληκε, ταῦτ᾽ ἤδη διαφερόντως ἄξιόν ἐστιν
ἀκοῦσαι. ὡς γὰρ τάχιστα εἴσω Πυλῶν Φίλιππος παρῆλθε 80
καὶ τάς τε ἐν Φωκεῦσι πόλεις παραδόξως ἀναστάτους ἐποίησε,

---

2. λαβὼν] βαλὼν *d* et pr. *b* : † λαβὼν corr. *b* †.   παρενόμει] Sic *gmnfck* : ceteri et
superscr. *g* παρηνόμει.   4. ἀπολέσας] Om. *afb* : in *γρ.* habet *b*.   6. τὰ] Om. pr. *f* †
pr. *b* †.   7. πλείονος ποιήσεται] πολλοῦ ποιήσαιτο *ekl*, † πλείονος ποιήσηται pr. *b* †.
8. ἂν] ἄν ποτε *fcdh* Bekk.   10. κατὰ τὴν πρεσβείαν] Om. *p c* : quorum major fuisset
auctoritas, nisi *c* verba ὅστις .. καλὸς κἀγαθός, tum hic tum post δημαγωγὸς χρηστὸς posu-.
isset ; posteroque loco ea verba scripsisset. Omissa probat Bekk.   11. μόνον] Om. *el*
Cobet.   19. τάς τε] τὰς μὲν Reisk.

Pausanias would probably strike the countrymen of Harmodius as a glorious tyrannicide,
though no doubt wrongly, as Philip was a
legitimate monarch, and there was no likelihood or design that his death should over-
throw the monarchy. See Rawlinson, ad
Hdt. 8. 142.

3. τὴν μόνην. Vid. inf. ad § 174.

5. ὁ γὰρ μισότεκνος .. δημοσίᾳ χρηστός. The same statement in three forms
of growing abstraction, and therefore growing certainty, which is indicated by the γε
which introduces the third and most abstract
form.

9. οὐδ᾽ ὅστις .. μετήλλαξεν. Cp. Ae.
de F. L. § 152. After pointing out the
contrast in Demosthenes' attitude between
shameful servility and shameless hostility,
he argues that the change on the second
embassy was not due to an honest change of
conviction. One MS. transposes the two
clauses οὐδέ γε ὁ ἰδίᾳ .. χρηστὸς and οὐδ᾽
ὅστις .. καλὸς κἀγαθός, and it and one other
omit κατὰ τὴν πρεσβείαν—' quibus facile

careas' Bekk. But the order of the text
gives the best sense, though even so the
rhythm is overloaded.

§ 79. *The explanation of Demosthenes'
impunity, as well as of his change of policy,
is this.*

12. οὗτος γάρ. The first period is that
when Demosthenes acted in Philip's interest,
the three others that of his renewed opposition to him ; the second, therefore,
may be called the period of his change of
party.

15. τῶν ἄλλων κατήγορος. The most
definite allusion made by Aeschines in this
speech to Demosthenes' unsuccessful prosecution of him, thirteen years before.

This paragraph contains by implication
four distinct questions : Why Demosthenes
and Philocrates differed ? Why their success
differed ? What were the motives of Demosthenes' pernicious policy ? and What were
the causes of his pernicious influence ?

§ 80. *At the time of the invasion of Phocis, Demosthenes was in danger,*

Θηβαίους δὲ, ὡς τόθ' ὑμῖν ἐδόκει, περαιτέρω τοῦ καιροῦ καὶ
τοῦ ὑμετέρου συμφέροντος ἰσχυροὺς κατεσκεύασεν, ὑμεῖς δὲ ἐκ
τῶν ἀγρῶν φοβηθέντες ἐσκευαγωγήσατε, ἐν ταῖς μεγίσταις δ'
ἦσαν αἰτίαις οἱ πρέσβεις οἱ περὶ τῆς εἰρήνης πρεσβεύσαντες,
πολὺ δὲ τῶν ἄλλων διαφερόντως Φιλοκράτης καὶ Δημοσθένης 5
διὰ τὸ μὴ μόνον πρεσβεύειν, ἀλλὰ καὶ τὰ ψηφίσματα γεγρα-
81 φέναι, συνέβη δ' ἐν τοῖς αὐτοῖς χρόνοις διαφέρεσθαί τι Δημοσθένην καὶ Φιλοκράτην σχεδὸν ὑπὲρ τούτων, ὑπὲρ ὧν καὶ ὑμεῖς
αὐτοὺς ὑπωπτεύσατε διενεχθῆναι, τοιαύτης δὲ ἐμπιπτούσης
ταραχῆς μετὰ τῶν συμφύτων νοσημάτων αὐτῷ ἤδη τὰ μετὰ 10
ταῦτα ἐβουλεύετο, μετὰ δειλίας καὶ τῆς πρὸς Φιλοκράτην ὑπὲρ
τῆς δωροδοκίας ζηλοτυπίας, καὶ ἡγήσατο, εἰ τῶν συμπρεσβευ-
όντων καὶ τοῦ Φιλίππου κατήγορος ἀναφανείη, τὸν μὲν Φιλοκράτην προδήλως ἀπολεῖσθαι, τοὺς δὲ ἄλλους συμπρέσβεις
κινδυνεύσειν, αὐτὸς δ' εὐδοκιμήσειν καὶ προδότης ὢν τῶν φίλων 15
82 καὶ πονηρὸς πιστὸς τῷ δήμῳ φανήσεσθαι. κατιδόντες δ' αὐτὸν
οἱ τῇ τῆς πόλεως προσπολεμοῦντες ἡσυχίᾳ ἄσμενοι παρεκάλουν
ἐπὶ τὸ βῆμα, τὸν μόνον ἀδωροδόκητον ὀνομάζοντες τῇ πόλει·
ὁ δὲ παριὼν ἀρχὰς αὐτοῖς ἐνεδίδου πολέμου καὶ ταραχῆς.

---

1. τοῦ καιροῦ] καιροῦ *fdb* Bekk.   2. ὑμεῖς δὲ] ὑμεῖς τε vel τ' omnes praeter *cd*.
6. τὰ ψηφίσματα] Art. om. libri praeter *ekl*.   7. Δημοσθένην] τὸν Δημοσθένην *afcdb*
B. et S.   11. πρὸς Φιλοκράτην] † πρὸς Φιλοκράτους pr. *b* †.   12. δωροδοκίας ζηλο-
τυπίας] ζηλοτυπίας δωροδοκίας *agmn*: μετὰ δειλίας .. ζηλοτυπίας deleri volunt nonnulli.
14. συμπρέσβεις] πρέσβεις *fed* pr. *b*: † συμπρέσβεις corr. *b* †.   15. κινδυνεύσειν] Sic
k et superscr. in quibusdam aliis : ceteri κινδυνεύειν.   τῶν φίλων] Om. pr. *f* † pr. *b* †.
17. οἱ τῇ .. ἡσυχίᾳ] Sic post Reiskium editores omnes: codicum proxime accedit γρ. *b*,
ubi πολεμοῦντες legitur, cetera ut in volgato. τῇ om. *agmnp*, *fcdb*: προπολεμοῦντες *afcdb* pr. *n* et
cd et Ald., ἡσυχῇ vel -χῇ *fcdb* Ald. οἱ προσπολεμοῦντες τῇ τῆς πόλεως ἡσυχίᾳ *zekl*.

---

1. ὡς τόθ' ὑμῖν ἐδόκει. 'For that was
before Demosthenes had persuaded you to
fall down and worship Thebes.' Aeschines,
after the subjugation of Greece, still affects
to regret the abandonment of the old policy
of keeping a balance of power between
Greek states, and depressing the nearest and
most formidable.

3. ἐν ταῖς μεγίσταις κ.τ.λ. See Ae. de
F. L. §§ 152 sqq., p. 47, for an apparent
admission that general opinion condemned
the ambassadors.

§ 81. *And had quarreled with Philocrates, and therefore tried accusing Philip,*
and

8. ὑπὲρ τούτων κ.τ.λ. Explained below,
τῆς πρὸς Φιλοκράτην ὑπὲρ τῆς δωροδοκίας
ζηλοτυπίας.

15. κινδυνεύσειν. The reading of most
MSS., κινδυνεύειν, may be defended by com-

paring Aeschines' admission above, that they
were ἐν ταῖς μεγίσταις αἰτίαις: 'Philocrates
would be ruined (being, as his accomplice
knew, guilty) ; his colleagues *were already*
in danger (and might take their chance as to
escaping or not) ; he himself *would* get
credit (while at present he at best shared
their danger).'

προδότης ὢν .. πιστὸς τῷ δήμῳ φανήσεσθαι. Demosthenes thought the people incapable of grasping the principle Aeschines had laid down, sup. § 78, οὐδέ γε ὁ
ἰδίᾳ πονηρὸς οὐκ ἄν ποτε γένοιτο δημαγωγὸς
χρηστός.

§ 82. *He was taken up by the war party,
and began to manufacture grievances.*

16. κατιδόντες. Almost 'sighted him,'
as a useful booty.

19. ἐνεδίδου. 'Was always giving them
room to begin.'

οὗτός ἐστιν, ὦ Ἀθηναῖοι, ὁ πρῶτος ἐξευρὼν Σέρρειον τεῖχος
καὶ Δορίσκον καὶ Ἐργίσκην καὶ Μυρτίσκην καὶ Γάνος καὶ
Γανίδα, χωρία, ὧν οὐδὲ τὰ ὀνόματα ᾔδειμεν πρότερον. καὶ
εἰς τοῦτο φέρων περιέστησε τὰ πράγματα, ὥστ᾽ εἰ μὲν μὴ
5 πέμποι Φίλιππος πρέσβεις, καταφρονεῖν αὐτὸν ἔφη τῆς πόλεως, εἰ δὲ πέμποι, κατασκόπους πέμπειν, ἀλλ᾽ οὐ πρέσβεις.
εἰ δὲ ἐπιτρέπειν ἐθέλοι πόλει τινὶ ἴσῃ καὶ ὁμοίᾳ περὶ τῶν 83
ἐγκλημάτων, οὐκ εἶναι κριτὴν ἴσον ἡμῖν ἔφη καὶ Φιλίππῳ.
Ἁλόννησον ἐδίδου· ὁ δ᾽·ἀπηγόρευε μὴ λαμβάνειν, εἰ δίδωσιν,
10 ἀλλὰ μὴ ἀποδίδωσι, περὶ συλλαβῶν διαφερόμενος. καὶ τὸ
τελευταῖον στεφανώσας τοὺς μετὰ Ἀριστοδήμου εἰς Θετταλίαν καὶ Μαγνησίαν παρὰ τὰς τῆς εἰρήνης συνθήκας ἐπιστρα-
τεύσαντας τὴν μὲν εἰρήνην διέλυσε, τὴν δὲ συμφορὰν καὶ τὸν
πόλεμον παρεσκεύασεν.

1. Σέρρειον] Hic libri Σέρριον habent. 2. Μυρτίσκην] Sic z k, Μυργίσκην fcdb: καὶ
Μυργίσκην om. agmnpel, volgo et Bekk. Μουργίσκην. † Et καὶ Μυργίσκην et καὶ Γανίδα
lineola subscripta notavit cod. b corrector. † Ceterum Μυρτηνὸν est in D. de Cor. § 34,
Μυρτανὸν scribit Harpocr. Γάνος καὶ Γανίδα] καὶ Γανίδα om. agmn, Γάνον pro Γάνος
habet p, Δάνδα pro Γανίδα el. Γάνον καὶ Γανίδα legisse videtur Harpocr. Vid. annot.
7. ἐθέλοι] ἐθέλει agmdbl. 9. Ἁλόννησον] Sic b et corr. dni, ἀλλόννησον cf:
ceteri Ἀλόννησον. 12. τῆς εἰρήνης] περὶ τῆς εἰρήνης fcdb ekl. ἐπιστρατεύσαντας]
πρεσβεύσαντας ekl Tauchn. Bakius.

1. ὁ πρῶτος ἐξευρών. Literally of course
'the first who discovered;' but Aeschines
does not mean to impose on his hearers'
ignorance, by saying that there were no such
places known to geographers, but only that
Demosthenes was the first person to suggest
the paradox, that it was a serious wrong to
Athens for Philip to occupy these remote
and barbarous places. The author of the
Fourth Philippic says the same as Aeschines,
§ 89, p. 123.

2. Μυρτίσκην. Most MSS. omit this
name, and the common reading was Μουργίσκην; but among the real names of the
places was Μυρτηνὸν (D. de Cor. § 34), and
it is probable that Aeschines means this,
while he puts it in a ludicrous light by the
assonances and diminutive terminations.
Some MSS. omit both Μυρτίσκην and Γανίδα,
probably from hypercriticism : they suppose
a copyist to have done accidentally what
Aeschines did by design.

4. φέρων περιέστησε τὰ πράγματα.
φέρων implies chiefly violence, or at least
rapidity in the movement effected; and,
secondarily, that the thing removed is carried
off as booty. Thus we might almost translate, 'ran away with the state's interest, till
he brought it to the point that ...' Cp. inf.
§ 90, ὑπέβαλλεν ἑαυτὸν φέρων Θηβαίοις.

6. κατασκόπους πέμπειν ἀλλ᾽ οὐ πρέσβεις. The usual Greek construction; we
should say either 'not ambassadors, but
spies,' or 'spies, not ambassadors,' omitting
the but.

§ 83. And repulsed Philip's attempts at
conciliation.

8. οὐκ εἶναι κριτὴν ἴσον ἡμῖν ἔφη καὶ
Φιλίππῳ. 'He said that there was no
judge impartial between us and Philip.'
ἴσον has its sense determined by the collocation ἴσῃ καὶ ὁμοίᾳ just before, like ἴσος
καὶ κοινός in D. de Cor. § 8, ubi vide. Else
one might have fancied that ἴσον included
equality of power with the parties to the
dispute, for a small state called upon to
arbitrate between two great ones, might be
tempted to decide in favour of the one that
seemed stronger, for fear of consequences to
itself.

9. Ἁλόννησον ἐδίδου .... ἀποδίδωσι.
The same line is taken in the extant speech
on Halonnesus, printed among the works of
Demosthenes, but really by Hegesippus. The
island had been seized by a pirate; Philip
conquered it, and offered to present it to the
Athenians. Demosthenes and his party insisted that he should restore it, acknow-
ledging their right not to have been for-
feited.

84 Ναὶ, ἀλλὰ χαλκοῖς καὶ ἀδαμαντίνοις τείχεσιν, ὡς αὐτός φησι,
τὴν χώραν ἡμῶν ἐτείχισε, τῇ τῶν Εὐβοέων καὶ Θηβαίων συμμαχίᾳ. ἀλλ᾽, ὦ Ἀθηναῖοι, περὶ ταῦτα τρία μέγιστα ἠδικήσθε
καὶ μάλιστα ἠγνοήκατε. σπεύδων δ᾽ εἰπεῖν περὶ τῆς θαυμα-
στῆς συμμαχίας τῆς τῶν Θηβαίων, ἵν᾽ ἐφεξῆς εἴπω, περὶ τῶν 5
Εὐβοέων πρῶτον μνησθήσομαι.

85 Ὑμεῖς γὰρ, ὦ Ἀθηναῖοι, πολλὰ καὶ μεγάλα ἠδικημένοι ὑπὸ
Μνησάρχου τοῦ Χαλκιδέως, τοῦ Καλλίου καὶ Ταυροσθένους
πατρὸς, οὓς οὗτος νυνὶ μισθὸν λαβὼν Ἀθηναίους εἶναι τολμᾷ
γράφειν, καὶ πάλιν ὑπὸ Θεμίσωνος τοῦ Ἐρετριέως, ὃς ἡμῶν 10
εἰρήνης οὔσης Ὠρωπὸν ἀφείλετο, τούτων ἑκόντες ἐπιλαθόμενοι,
ἐπειδὴ διέβησαν εἰς Εὔβοιαν Θηβαῖοι καταδουλώσασθαι τὰς
πόλεις πειρώμενοι, ἐν πέντε ἡμέραις ἐβοηθήσατε αὐτοῖς καὶ
ναυσὶ καὶ πεζικῇ δυνάμει, καὶ πρὶν τριάκονθ᾽ ἡμέρας διελθεῖν
ὑποσπόνδους Θηβαίους ἀφήκατε, κύριοι τῆς Εὐβοίας γενόμενοι, 15
καὶ τάς τε πόλεις αὐτὰς καὶ τὰς πολιτείας ἀπέδοτε ὀρθῶς
καὶ δικαίως τοῖς παρακαταθεμένοις, οὐχ ἡγούμενοι δίκαιον εἶναι
86 τὴν ὀργὴν ἀπομνημονεύειν ἐν τῷ πιστευθῆναι. καὶ τηλικαῦθ᾽ ὑφ᾽
ὑμῶν εὖ πεπονθότες οἱ Χαλκιδεῖς οὐ τὰς ὁμοίας ὑμῖν ἀπέδοσαν

3. τρία μέγιστα] καὶ μέγιστα ekl : † τρία vel omisit pr. b, vel in aliud nescio quid muta-
vit, sed τρία habet corr. †   4. ἠγνοήκατε] † ἠγνοήκατε corr. b †.   θαυμαστῆς] Sic
ekl Bekk. Frank.: ceteri, B. et S., μεγίστης.   5. συμμαχίας] συμπαθείας f pr. b † volg.
restituit corr. b †.   περὶ τῶν Εὐβοέων] περὶ τῆς τῶν Εὐβοέων ekl.   10. ἡμῶν] ὑμῶν
z, ἡμῖν d.   11. ἐπιλαθόμενοι] Sic agmnp † corr. b †: ceteri et Bekk. ἐπιλανθανόμενοι.
12. Θηβαῖοι] † οἱ Θηβαῖοι b †.   14. πεζικῇ] πεζῇ ekl Bekk.: quod restitui nunc volt
Frankius.   16. τάς τε πόλεις] τὰς πόλεις fed † pr. b †.   18. ὑφ᾽ ὑμῶν] ὑφ᾽ om.
agmiu, utrumque om. pr. f, post πεπονθότες ponit b.

§ 84. About the Theban alliance he cheated
you thrice; but I must first explain his vil-
lany in Euboea.

1. χαλκοῖς καὶ ἀδαμαντίνοις τείχεσιν.
Cp. D. de Cor. § 370 sq., to which there is
no doubt a reference. The meaning of
what Demosthenes is supposed to say is,
'walls of bronze and steel,' i. e. armed men.
Aeschines' comment on it is, that the fortifications actually supplied were something
much less concrete—an alliance upon paper.

4. μάλιστα ἠγνοήκατε. Because this
part of Demosthenes' policy was most unas-
sailable, Aeschines says that the Athenians
were peculiarly blind to its villainy.

§ 85. In spite of your grievances against
the rulers of Chalcis and Eretria, you delivered Euboea from Thebes.

11. ἀφείλετο. The special force of the
middle has disappeared. Oropus was annexed to Thebes, not to Eretria.

15. κύριοι τῆς Εὐβοίας γενόμενοι.
Markland wanted to put καὶ before this

clause—'and, having thereby become masters
of Euboea, you then honourably restored ...'
Otherwise it is impossible to take κύριοι ..
γενόμενοι in the most forcible and appropriate sense, of having Euboea at their mercy
and being able to appropriate it but for their
honour's sake. It must refer to a mere military occupation : 'you made yourselves masters of the country, and sent them out of it.'
It seems quite impossible to take the aorist
participle as expressing a result of the action
of the verb, not a condition precedent to it.

17. τοῖς παρακαταθεμένοις gives the
rhetorical reason for ὀρθῶς καὶ δικαίως. The
reading of most MSS., αὐτοῖς παρακαταθέμενοι, seems to require an inadmissible sense
for the participle.

§§ 86–88. Yet in spite of these services, on
your second expedition Callias betrayed you
at Tamynae, and you were in danger of the
disgrace of defeat by an inferior antagonist.

19. ὑμῖν probably goes with ἀπέδοσαν.
It would be forcible, but hardly like Greek

χάριτας, ἀλλ' ἐπειδὴ τάχιστα διέβητε εἰς Εὔβοιαν Πλου-
τάρχῳ βοηθήσοντες, τοὺς μὲν πρώτους χρόνους ἀλλ' οὖν προσ-
εποιοῦνθ' ὑμῖν εἶναι φίλοι, ἐπειδὴ δὲ τάχιστα εἰς Ταμύνας
παρήλθομεν καὶ τὸ Κοτύλαιον ὀνομαζόμενον ὄρος ὑπερεβάλ-
5 λομεν, ἐνταῦθα Καλλίας ὁ Χαλκιδεὺς, ὃν Δημοσθένης μισθὸν
λαβὼν ἐνεκωμίαζεν, ὁρῶν τὸ στρατόπεδον τὸ τῆς πόλεως εἰς 87
τινας δυσχωρίας κατακεκλειμένον, ὅθεν μὴ νικήσασι μάχην οὐκ
ἦν ἀναχώρησις οὐδὲ βοηθείας ἐλπὶς οὔτ' ἐκ γῆς οὔτ' ἐκ θαλάττης, συναγείρας ἐξ ἁπάσης τῆς Εὐβοίας στρατόπεδον καὶ παρὰ
10 Φιλίππου δύναμιν προσμεταπεμψάμενος, ὅ τ' ἀδελφὸς αὐτοῦ
Ταυροσθένης, ὁ νυνὶ πάντας δεξιούμενος καὶ προσγελῶν, τοὺς
Φωκικοὺς ξένους διαβιβάσας, ἦλθον ἐφ' ἡμᾶς ὡς ἀναιρήσοντες.
καὶ εἰ μὴ πρῶτον μὲν θεῶν τις ἔσωσε τὸ στρατόπεδον, ἔπειθ' 88
οἱ στρατιῶται οἱ ὑμέτεροι καὶ πεζοὶ καὶ ἱππεῖς ἄνδρες ἀγαθοὶ
15 ἐγένοντο καὶ παρὰ τὸν ἱππόδρομον τὸν ἐν Ταμύναις ἐκ παρατάξεως μάχῃ κρατήσαντες ἀφεῖσαν ὑποσπόνδους τοὺς πολεμίους, ἐκινδύνευσεν ἂν ἡ πόλις αἴσχιστα παθεῖν· οὐ γὰρ τὸ
δυστυχῆσαι κατὰ πόλεμον μέγιστόν ἐστι κακόν, ἀλλ' ὅταν τις
πρὸς ἀνταγωνιστὰς ἀναξίους αὐτοῦ διακινδυνεύων ἀποτύχῃ, δι-

---

4. ὑπερεβάλλομεν] ὑπερεβάλομεν ekl. 5. μισθὸν λαβὼν] μισθαρνῶν ekl Bekk.
6. ἐνεκωμίαζεν] Sic pzek, ἐνεγκωμίαζεν facili errore l, ἐνεχυρίαζεν ceteri. ' Videtur men-
dum subesse' Frank. 7. τινὰς] δεινὰς ekl. δυσχωρίας] δυσχερείας f pr. b † volg.
restituit corr. b †. κατακεκλειμένον] Sic ac Bekk. B. et S.: κατακεκλημένον mn, unde
vel potius ex vua doctrina κατακεκλημένον Frank.: κατακεκλειαμένον ceteri. 8. οὐδὲ]
Libri οὔτε: correxit Bekk. 12. ἡμᾶς] Sic ael; ceteri ὑμᾶς, prorsus obliti quod ei pugnae
interfuisset Aeschines. 16. μάχῃ] † quod post κρατήσαντες in b ut in f addebatur, a m.
sec. deleta est †. ἀφεῖσαν ὑποσπόνδους] ὑποσπόνδους ἀφεῖσαν ekl: ἀφίεσαν ὑποσπόνδους ceteri et B. et S. Sed imperfectum vix salvo sensu stare potest. 17. ἡ πόλις] ἡμῶν
ἡ πόλις gmnp Bekk., ὑμῶν ἡ πόλις ekl. 19. αὐτοῦ] Sic z B. et S. Frank.: αὐτοῦ agmned:
ceteri ἑαυτοῦ.

---

thought, to take it with ὁμοίας, ' you had
returned them good for evil, but they, unlike
you, returned evil for good.'
2. ἀλλ' οὖν introduces the apodosis to a
suppressed protasis, [if they made no value-
able return] 'at any rate they did profess,'
_etc.
4. παρήλθομεν. Aeschines uses the first
person, so as to remind the court of his own
honourable share in the battle (Ae. de F. L.
§ 180, p. 50): it is creditable to his modesty,
or at least to his taste, that he says nothing
more directly on the subject. Just above
he had said διῆλθετε, 'you, the Athenian
nation, made the expedition.'
6. ἐνεκωμίαζεν. 'Was in the habit of
praising' at the time. It can hardly be a
mere repetition of νῦν μισθὸν λαβὼν 'Αθη-
ναίους εἶναι τολμᾶ γράφειν.
12. ἐφ' ἡμᾶς. Most MSS. read ὑμᾶς,

but the correction seems necessary. It would
be harsh to identify the court with the army
in the field, though they might be identified,
as in the preceding section, with the nation
that sent out the army.
13. πρῶτον μὲν .. ἔπειθ'. Perhaps not
only that the gods are the first cause, and
human merit the second, of all blessings,
but that the two stand first and second in
order of time, as well as of importance. A
god saved the army from the panic that
would have been the natural result of a sudden attack from an allied force; then the
men, having the chance given them of using
their courage, used it with good effect.
Thus ἐκ παρατάξεως is almost epexegetical
of ἔπειτα, .' as soon as they were in line,'
before which time nothing but a special
providence could save them.
19. πρὸς ἀνταγωνιστὰς ἀναξίους goes

πλασίαν εἰκὸς εἶναι τὴν συμφοράν. ἀλλ' ὅμως ὑμεῖς τοιαῦτα
89 πεπονθότες πάλιν διελύσασθε πρὸς αὐτούς. τυχὼν δὲ παρ'
ὑμῶν συγγνώμης Καλλίας ὁ Χαλκιδεὺς μικρὸν διαλιπὼν χρόνον
πάλιν ἧκε φερόμενος εἰς τὴν ἑαυτοῦ φύσιν, Εὐβοϊκὸν μὲν τῷ
λόγῳ συνέδριον εἰς Χαλκίδα συνάγων, ἰσχυρὰν δὲ τὴν Εὔβοιαν 5
ἐφ' ὑμᾶς ἔργῳ παρασκευάζων, ἐξαίρετον δ' αὐτῷ τυραννίδα περι-
ποιούμενος. καὶ ταύτης ἐλπίζων συναγωνιστὴν Φίλιππον λήψεσθαι ἀπῆλθεν εἰς Μακεδονίαν καὶ περιῄει μετὰ Φιλίππου,
90 καὶ τῶν ἑταίρων εἷς ὠνομάζετο. ἀδικήσας δὲ Φίλιππον κἀκεῖθεν ἀποδρὰς ὑπέβαλλεν ἑαυτὸν φέρων Θηβαίοις. ἐγκαταλιπὼν 10
δὲ κἀκείνους, καὶ πλείους τραπόμενος τροπὰς τοῦ Εὐρίπου, παρ'
ὃν ᾤκει, εἰς μέσον πίπτει τῆς τε Θηβαίων ἔχθρας καὶ τῆς
Φιλίππου. ἀπορῶν δ', ὅ τι χρήσαιτο αὐτῷ, καὶ παραγγελλο-
μένης ἐπ' αὐτὸν ἤδη στρατείας, μίαν ἐλπίδα λοιπὴν κατεῖδε
σωτηρίας ἔνορκον λαβεῖν τὸν Ἀθηναίων δῆμον, σύμμαχον ὀνο- 15
μασθέντα, βοηθήσειν, εἴ τις ἐπ' αὐτὸν ἴοι· ὃ πρόδηλον ἦν

2. παρ' ὑμῶν συγγνώμης] συγγνώμης παρ' ὑμῶν ekl Bekk.   3. διαλιπὼν] Om. pr.
f † pr. b †.   10. ὑπέβαλλεν] Sic amnb: ceteri et Bekk. ὑπέβαλεν.   15. τὸν Ἀθηναίων δῆμον] τὸν δῆμον τὸν Ἀθηναίων Bekk., ex ekl qui τὸν δῆμον τῶν Ἀθηναίων habent.

closely with διακινδυνεύων. The disgrace
is to contend on the defensive with unworthy
antagonists: to be defeated by them is a
yet further climax of disgrace.

§ 89. *Callias being again forgiven, under
the plea of uniting Euboea, set about arming
it against you. He offered himself first to
Philip;*

4. ἧκε φερόμενος. Almost 'flew back
with a run;' used of a scale kicking the
beam in D. de Pace, p. 60, § 12. There is,
however, no necessary metaphor in the
Greek expression.

τῷ λόγῳ .. ἔργῳ. The presence and
omission of the article are not accidental: the contrast is not between profession and fact, but between *his* profession and
fact.

6. ἐξαίρετον. As in its technical meaning, Aesch. Ag. 954, etc. Various advantages
were to be secured for Euboea generally, at
the expense of Athens. Of these, the rule
of his own city was specially reserved to
himself.

§ 90. *Then, rejected by him, to Thebes:
then, having deserted them, had no resource
but to try you again.*

10. ὑπέβαλλεν ἑαυτὸν φέρων. 'He
took and subjected himself.' The φέρων
instead of φερόμενος is partly accounted for
by the verb being transitive instead of

neuter; but it brings in (coupled with the
reflexive construction) a further touch of
contempt. Callias was both dealer and com-
modity—a deliberate agent, and the goods
he carried about with him. So below ὅ τι
χρήσαιτο αὐτῷ, 'to what use to turn himself next,' as if he were fit for nothing but a
tool in any case.

ἐγκαταλιπών. Exactly 'left in the
lurch.'

11. Εὐρίπου. The tides in the Medi-
terranean being of uncertain occurrence, and
so slight as only to be perceptible in land-
locked creeks, the Greeks had very vague
notions as to the possible laws of their appearance; and in the Euripus especially,
where they were unusually evident, and
therefore evidently variable, it was fancied
that they changed seven times a day. The
proverbial simile is common enough, e. g.
Ar. Eth. 9 (6). 3.

12. εἰς μέσον. Like Εὐρίπου, παρ' ὃν
ᾤκει, the description of his political situation
is pointed by an analogy with his geogra-
phical.

15. ἔνορκον λαβεῖν. Almost 'entrap
Athens into an oath,' λαβεῖν implying 'to
catch' instantaneously and by surprise, by
force of the tense. Contrast sup. ὑπέβαλλεν
(si vera l.), and at any rate περιῄει and ὠνομάζετο.

ἐσόμενον, εἰ μὴ ὑμεῖς κωλύσαιτε. ταῦτα δὲ διανοηθεὶς ἀπο- 91
στέλλει δεῦρο πρέσβεις Γλαυκέτην καὶ Ἐμπέδωνα καὶ Διόδωρον
τὸν δολιχοδρομήσαντα, φέροντας τῷ μὲν δήμῳ ἐλπίδας κενὰς,
Δημοσθένει δ᾽ ἀργύριον καὶ τοῖς περὶ αὐτόν. τρία δ᾽ ἦν ἃ
5 ἅμα ἐξωνεῖτο, πρῶτον μὲν μὴ διασφαλῆναι τῆς πρὸς ὑμᾶς
συμμαχίας· οὐδὲν γὰρ ἦν τὸ μέσον, εἰ μνησθεὶς τῶν προτέρων
ἀδικημάτων ὁ δῆμος μὴ προσδέξαιτο τὴν συμμαχίαν, ἀλλ᾽
ὑπῆρχεν αὐτῷ ἢ φεύγειν ἐκ Χαλκίδος ἢ τεθνάναι ἐγκαταλη-
φθέντι· τηλικαῦται δυνάμεις ἐπ᾽ αὐτὸν ἐπεστράτευον, ἥ τε Φι-
10 λίππου καὶ Θηβαίων. δεύτερον δ᾽ ἦκον οἱ μισθοὶ τῷ γράψαντι
τὴν συμμαχίαν ὑπὲρ τοῦ μὴ συνεδρεύειν Ἀθήνησι Χαλκιδέας,
τρίτον δὲ ὥστε μὴ τελεῖν συντάξεις. καὶ τούτων τῶν προαιρέ- 92
σεων οὐδεμιᾶς ἀπέτυχε Καλλίας, ἀλλ᾽ ὁ μισοτύραννος Δημοσθένης, ὡς αὐτὸς προσποιεῖται, ὅν φησι Κτησιφῶν τὰ βέλτιστα
15 λέγειν, ἀπέδοτο μὲν τοὺς καιροὺς τοὺς τῆς πόλεως, ἔγραψε δ᾽
ἐν τῇ συμμαχίᾳ βοηθεῖν ἡμᾶς Χαλκιδεῦσι, ῥῆμα μόνον ἀντι-

---

1. κωλύσαιτε] Sic marg. Bern. et post Markland. editi plerique: ἐκωλύσατε b et γρ. gm: ceteri et Brem. κωλύσετε, quod haud scio an stare possit.   8. ἐγκαταληφθέντι] Sic gnmfc: ceteri ἐγκαταλειφθέντι, satis frequenti errore.   10. καὶ Θηβαίων] καὶ ἡ Θηβαίων Steph. B. et S.   12. συντάξεις] φόρους pr. b.   14. ὄν] † ὅς pr. b †.

§ 91. *So he came here to buy a treaty from Demosthenes, whereby he both saved himself and withdrew Chalcis and the tribute from Athens.*

3. τὸν δολιχοδρομήσαντα. As an athlete he would be known and popular (cp. Thuc. 4. 121); possibly at Athens considered a credit to them, as from a kindred state.

6. οὐδὲν γὰρ ἦν τὸ μέσον κ.τ.λ. 'There was no middle term for him .. he might depend either on being constrained to fly from Chalcis, or killed if caught there,' or 'caught there and killed,' the Greek idiom in the last clause expressing both—that his being caught was certain, and would certainly end in the other.

9. τηλικαῦται. Not a very common construction in Attic, but exactly like the Homeric use of τοῖος.

10. ἦκον οἱ μισθοί. The pay for moving an alliance at all has been mentioned above; now he says, 'there was next the pay for the proposer of the alliance to release Chalcis from attendance on the Athenian conference; and, thirdly, for the *condition* (a common use of ὥστε) that they were released from their contribution.' The symmetry of the sentence is disturbed, in order to reiterate the charge of bribery.

12. συντάξεις. φόρους, the original

reading of one MS (*b*), is hardly likely to be accidental. σύνταξις was the term adopted on the re-organization of the Athenian confederacy, in place of the older φόρος, which had become invidious; but it is not impossible that Aeschines casually used the older word (note that he is speaking of the tribute as a clear gain to Athens, not as carrying costly federal duties with it), and that his copyists altered it to the officially correct one, which he uses afterwards repeatedly.

§ 92. *Demosthenes sold him a one-sided alliance, such as he wanted,*

15. ἀπέδοτο μὲν τοὺς καιρούς. 'Sold the opportunity' of insisting on good terms for Athens, which might easily have been secured of Callias in his distress.

16. ῥῆμα μόνον ἀντικαταλλαξάμενος ἀντὶ τούτων. 'Stipulating for this a merely verbal equivalent, viz. that for the sake of appearances he added, that if any one,' etc. The punctuation of the text seems better than Bekker's, with the comma after ἀντικαταλλαξάμενος instead of after τούτων. The equivalent was merely verbal, (1) because the Chalcidians were in imminent danger, the Athenians not, (2) because the Chalcidians were impotent allies in case the danger became real.

καταλλαξάμενος ἀντὶ τούτων, εὐφημίας ἕνεκα προσγράψας Χαλ-
93 κιδέας βοηθεῖν, ἐάν τις ἴῃ ἐπ᾽ Ἀθηναίους· τὰς δὲ συνεδρίας καὶ
τὰς συντάξεις, ἐξ ὧν ἰσχύσειν ὁ πόλεμος ἤμελλεν, ἄρδην ἀπέδοτο, καλλίστοις ὀνόμασιν αἰσχίστας πράξεις γράφων καὶ τῷ
λόγῳ προσβιβάζων ὑμᾶς, τὰς μὲν βοηθείας ὡς δεῖ τὴν πόλιν 5
πρότερον ποιεῖσθαι τοῖς ἀεὶ δεομένοις τῶν Ἑλλήνων, τὰς δὲ
συμμαχίας ὑστέρας μετὰ τὰς εὐεργεσίας. ἵνα δ᾽ εὖ εἰδῆτε, ὅτι
ἀληθῆ λέγω, λαβέ μοι τὴν Καλλίου γραφὴν καὶ τὴν συμμαχίαν, καὶ ἀνάγνωθι τὸ ψήφισμα.

ΨΗΦΙΣΜΑ. 10

94 Οὔπω τοίνυν τοῦτ᾽ ἐστὶ δεινόν, εἰ καιροὶ πέπρανται τηλικοῦτοι καὶ συνεδρίαι καὶ συντάξεις, ἀλλὰ πολὺ τούτου δεινό-
τερον ὑμῖν φανήσεται ὃ μέλλω λέγειν. εἰς γὰρ τοῦτο προήχθη
Καλλίας μὲν ὁ Χαλκιδεὺς ὕβρεως καὶ πλεονεξίας, Δημοσθένης
δέ, ὃν ἐπαινεῖ Κτησιφῶν, δωροδοκίας, ὥστε τὰς ἐξ Ὠρεοῦ συν- 15
τάξεις καὶ τὰς ἐξ Ἐρετρίας, τὰ δέκα τάλαντα, ὁρώντων φρονούντων βλεπόντων ἔλαθον ὑμῶν ὑφελόμενοι, καὶ τοὺς ἐκ τῶν

1. προσγράψας] προγράψας agmn fdb, προσέγραψε el. εὐφημίας ἕνεκα προσγράψας
om. z　　Χαλκιδέας] καὶ Χαλκιδέας zekl et marg. Steph.: fortasse rectius.　　2. συνε-
δρίας] προεδρίας agmn cd pr. b.　　5. τὰς μὲν βοηθείας ὡς δεῖ τὴν πόλιν] ὡς δεῖ τὴν
πόλιν τὰς μὲν βοηθείας fcdb ekl Bekk.　'Latet hic aliquid viti' Frank.　　7. ὑστέρας]
ὑστέρας ποιεῖσθαι agmn fcdb.　　10. † Post ΨΗΦΙΣΜΑ b add. λείπει †　　11. εἰ
καιροὶ] εἰ οἱ καιροὶ agmn fcb Tauchn.　　πέπρανται τηλικοῦτοι] τηλικοῦτοι πεπραμένοι
τυγχάνουσιν ekl: quod certe elegantius, efficitque ut articulus superiore loco forsitan ferri
possit.　　12. τούτου] τοῦτο agmn el et corr. b.　　15. ἐξ] † om. pr. b †.　　17. ὑμῶν]
ὑμᾶς el pr. b: † ut volg. corr. b †.

§ 93. *And cajoled you into sacrificing
substantial advantages to a sentiment.*

2. **συνεδρίας.** The best MSS. have
προεδρίας. Can this mean 'your presidency in the congress,' i. e. their belonging
to a congress under your presidency, instead
of having a separate independent one of
their own?

4. **τῷ λόγῳ προσβιβάζων ὑμᾶς.** 'Bringing you up to the point with the argument ...' It is no more than one might
expect, that some MSS. should read προβι-
βάζων; if right, it would mean 'forcing you
on and on.'

5. **τὰς μὲν βοηθείας ὡς δεῖ τὴν πόλιν.**
So the best group of MSS.; and it is perhaps
likelier to have occurred to Aeschines than
to a transcriber, to have made a harsh inver-
sion for the sake of symmetrical parallelism
with the next clause.

6. **τὰς δὲ συμμαχίας.** Obviously Demosthenes had argued that it was urgent to
support and strengthen Callias, and that the

arrangements between Athens and Euboea
could wait. μετὰ τὰς εὐεργεσίας looks as
though he had been thinking of Thuc. 2.
40, where it is asserted that to act thus is
characteristic of Athens.

8. **τὴν Καλλίου γραφήν.** As we say,
'the paper' of Callias.

§. 94. *Moreover, he actually made you
give up not only Chalcis, but also Eretria
and Oreus.*

11. **εἰ καιροὶ κ.τ.λ.** 'If he has been
selling opportunities, alliances, and contributions on this scale,' τηλικοῦτοι having a
double force, 'as great as this,' but also 'no
greater,' while something greater is to follow.

15. **ὃν ἐπαινεῖ Κτησιφῶν.** Such re-
minders are put in from time to time, in
both speeches, as apologies for irrelevance.

16. **ὁρώντων φρονούντων βλεπόντων
ἔλαθον ὑμῶν ὑφελόμενοι.** 'They stole
from you .., and you, with the power of
sight and sense, with your very eyes on it,

πόλεων τούτων συνέδρους παρ᾽ ἡμῶν μὲν ἀνέστησαν, πάλιν δὲ
εἰς Χαλκίδα καὶ τὸ καλούμενον Εὐβοϊκὸν συνέδριον συνήγαγον.
ὃν δὲ τρόπον καὶ δι᾽ οἵων κακουργημάτων, ταῦτ᾽ ἤδη ἄξιόν
ἐστιν ἀκοῦσαι. ἀφικνεῖται γὰρ πρὸς ὑμᾶς οὐκέτι δι᾽ ἀγγέλων, 95
5 ἀλλ᾽ αὐτὸς ὁ Καλλίας, καὶ παρελθὼν εἰς τὴν ἐκκλησίαν λόγους
διεξῆλθε κατεσκευασμένους ὑπὸ Δημοσθένους. εἶπε γὰρ, ὡς
ἥκοι ἐκ Πελοποννήσου νεωστὶ σύνταγμα συντάξας εἰς ἑκατὸν
ταλάντων πρόσοδον ἐπὶ Φίλιππον, καὶ διελογίζετο, ὅσον ἑκάστους ἔδει συντελεῖν, Ἀχαιοὺς μὲν πάντας καὶ Μεγαρέας ἑξή-
10 κοντα τάλαντα, τὰς δ᾽ ἐν Εὐβοίᾳ πόλεις ἁπάσας τετταρά-
κοντα· ἐκ δὲ τούτων τῶν χρημάτων ὑπάρξειν καὶ ναυτικὴν καὶ 96
πεζικὴν δύναμιν· εἶναι δὲ πολλοὺς ἄλλους τῶν Ἑλλήνων, οὓς
βούλεσθαι κοινωνεῖν τῆς συντάξεως, ὥστε οὔτε χρημάτων οὔτε
στρατιωτῶν ἔσεσθαι ἀπορίαν. καὶ ταῦτα μὲν τὰ φανερά· ἔφη
15 δὲ καὶ πράξεις πράττειν ἑτέρας δι᾽ ἀπορρήτων, καὶ τούτων
εἶναί τινας μάρτυρας τῶν ἡμετέρων πολιτῶν, καὶ τελευτῶν ὀνο-

[notes omitted]

97 μαστὶ παρεκάλει Δημοσθένην καὶ συνειπεῖν ἠξίου. ὁ δὲ σεμνῶς
πάνυ παρελθὼν τόν τε Καλλίαν ὑπερεπήνει τό τε ἀπόρρητον
προσεποιήσατο εἰδέναι· τὴν δ᾽ ἐκ Πελοποννήσου πρεσβείαν,
ἣν ἐπρέσβευσε, καὶ τὴν ἐξ Ἀκαρνανίας ἔφη βούλεσθαι ὑμῖν
ἀπαγγεῖλαι. ἦν δ᾽ αὐτῷ κεφάλαιον τῶν λόγων πάντας μὲν 5
Πελοποννησίους ὑπάρχειν, πάντας δ᾽ Ἀκαρνᾶνας συντεταγμένους ἐπὶ Φίλιππον ὑφ᾽ ἑαυτοῦ, εἶναι δὲ τὸ σύνταγμα χρημάτων μὲν εἰς ἑκατὸν νεῶν ταχυναυτουσῶν πληρώματα καὶ εἰς
98 πεζοὺς στρατιώτας μυρίους καὶ ἱππεῖς χιλίους, ὑπάρξειν δὲ πρὸς
τούτοις καὶ τὰς πολιτικὰς δυνάμεις, ἐκ Πελοποννήσου μὲν πλεί- 10
ονας ἢ δισχιλίους ὁπλίτας, ἐξ Ἀκαρνανίας δὲ ἑτέρους τοσού-
τους· δεδόσθαι δὲ ἀπὸ πάντων τούτων τὴν ἡγεμονίαν ὑμῖν·
πραχθήσεσθαι δὲ αὐτὰ οὐκ εἰς μακρὰν, ἀλλ᾽ εἰς τὴν ἕκτην ἐπὶ
δέκα τοῦ ἀνθεστηριῶνος μηνός· εἰρῆσθαι γὰρ ἐν ταῖς πόλε-
σιν ὑφ᾽ ἑαυτοῦ καὶ παρηγγέλθαι πάντας ἥκειν συνεδρεύσοντας 15

2. τό τε] καὶ τὸ fcdb.	3. ἐκ Πελοποννήσου] εἰς Πελοπόννησον fcdb.	9. ἱππεῖς]
ἱππέας ekl Bekk. Frank.	10. πλείοναϛ] πλέον ekl, πλείους g : alterutrum legi volt
Frank.	12. ἀπὸ πάντων] Sic libri praeter el qui ἀπάντων habent : ὑπὸ πάντων voluerunt
Bekk. Brem. Cobet.	Vid. annot. ad loc.	ὑμῖν] Om. an et pr. gmf.	13. αὐτὰ]
Sic agmndbq : ceteri et Bekk. ταῦτα.	15. ὑφ᾽ ἑαυτοῦ] Sic ekl : ceteri ὑπ᾽ αὐτοῦ.

§. 97. *Demosthenes being appealed to,
confirmed him on both points, and reported
successful embassies of his own:*

6. ὑπάρχειν. Opposed to ὑφ᾽ ἑαυτοῦ:
the Peloponnesians he had found ready;
the Acarnanians he had persuaded to join
the confederation. συντεταγμένους, as συντάξεως before, means 'enrolled' in the alliance in the general sense, but with special
reference to the money contribution. So
σύνταγμα includes contributions of money
and contingents of men, but the former are
ranked first.

9. στρατιώτας. Perhaps already beginning to be used of mercenaries, 'professional
soldiers,' exclusively, as in Ar. Eth. 3. 8. 6,
9; 9. 6, and so opposed to the πολιτικὰς
δυνάμεις, as l.c. 8. 9 to τὰ πολιτικὰ in the
same sense.

§ 98. *That were to give us an army in-
vincible on paper, numbers and dates all
specified,*

10. ἐκ Πελοποννήσου μὲν πλείοναϛ ἢ
δισχιλίους. Note that the Spartans are
clearly not included, though *all* the Peloponnesians are said to be ready to join.
Sparta had too high a prestige, in other
men's eyes as well as her own, to be counted
only as one of the Peloponnesian states,
even after Epaminondas' victories.

12. ἀπὸ πάντων. So all MSS. but two

bad ones, which have ἀπάντων. Either that
or ὑπὸ πάντων (once adopted by Bekker
and Bremi) is an easy correction, but the
text is right. The ἡγεμονία is like a sort
of ἔρανος : each of the states contributes
their own share in the joint enterprise, their
own right to a voice in the council of
war, and the collective supremacy of the
federation is 'offered from all of them to
Athens.'

13. ἕκτην ἐπὶ δέκα. The full moon
would fall on the 15th. Demosthenes
allowed one day, either for accidents or
for variations in local calendars. Or
perhaps the official representatives (συνεδρεύσοντας) would be ready for business
as soon as they arrived, while one day more
might be wanted for the mustering of the
troops.

14. ἀνθεστηριῶνος μηνός. Being the
earliest period when the weather would
allow of military operations. See Mr. F.
Parker's 'Light upon Thucydides,' for a
collection of evidence as to the practical
seasons of ancient Greece, and for some
arguments (stronger than those for his
strange scheme of general chronology) for
supposing that this month is the one designated by Thuc. 2. 2 as ἅμα ἦρι ἀρχο-
μένῳ, in the account of the surprise of
Plataea.

Ἀθήναζε εἰς τὴν πανσέληνον. καὶ γὰρ τοῦτο ἄνθρωπος ἴδιον καὶ 99
οὐ κοινὸν ποιεῖ. οἱ μὲν γὰρ ἄλλοι ἀλαζόνες ὅταν τι ψεύδων-
ται, ἀόριστα καὶ ἀσαφῆ πειρῶνται λέγειν, φοβούμενοι τὸν
ἔλεγχον· Δημοσθένης δ' ὅταν ἀλαζονεύηται, πρῶτον μὲν μεθ'
5 ὅρκου ψεύδεται, ἐξώλειαν ἐπαρώμενος ἑαυτῷ, δεύτερον δέ, ἃ εὖ
οἶδεν οὐδέποτε ἐσόμενα, τολμᾷ λέγειν ἀριθμῶν εἰς ὁπότ' ἔσται,
καὶ ὧν τὰ σώματα οὐχ ἑώρακε, τούτων τὰ ὀνόματα λέγει, κλέπτων τὴν ἀκρόασιν καὶ μιμούμενος τοὺς τἀληθῆ λέγοντας. διὸ
καὶ μάλιστα ἄξιός ἐστι μισεῖσθαι, ὅτι πονηρὸς ὢν καὶ τὰ τῶν
10 χρηστῶν σημεῖα διαφθείρει. ταῦτα δ' εἰπὼν δίδωσιν ἀναγνῶ- 100
ναι ψήφισμα τῷ γραμματεῖ μακρότερον μὲν τῆς Ἰλιάδος, κε-
νότερον δὲ τῶν λόγων, οὓς εἴωθε λέγειν, καὶ τοῦ βίου, ὃν

1. πανσέληνον] σελήνην Tauchn.   ἄνθρωπος] Sic Dind. jubentibus Markl. et B. et S.
Habent agmn ἀνθρώπων, ceteri libri ἄνθρωπος.   5. ἐπαρώμενος] ἐπαρωσάμενος c, † ἐπα-
ρασάμενος b †.   ἑαυτῷ] Sic ne: ceteri αὐτῷ.   6. ἀριθμῶν] Om. gmn ekl.   9. μά-
λιστα] σφόδρα ekl Bekk.   ὅτι] εἰ vel ᾗ pr. f, † εἰ, ut videbatur, pr. b †.   11. κενό-
τερον] Sic n † et superscr. in b †: καινότερον agmpfdk pr. b, ceteri, Bekk., B. et S. κενώ-
τερον.   12. ὃν] † οὗ pr. b, sed corr. eadem manu †.

§ 99. *According to Demosthenes' extra-*
ordinary habit of lying with a circum-
stance.
1. καὶ γὰρ τοῦτο κ.τ.λ. The same
charge is made in similar words Ἀε. de F. L.
§ 162, p. 48, in reference to the story of
the Olynthian prisoner, the invention or
sanction of which is the worst thing proved
against Demosthenes' honour. Here the
point seems to be, that Demosthenes was
under the necessity of performing (in modern
language) the functions of a war minister,
without executive power. He enumerates
large forces of all arms, but either cannot
get the resolution carried for embodying
them (as that in the First Philippic, §§ 16
sqq., p. 44), or the Athenian people and
officials neglect their duty (as described in
Olynth. 3, §§ 4, 5, 14), or the allies are
slack and behindhand, even if the Athenians
do their part. If we had an authentic text
of Demosthenes' decrees, we should probably find more instances than in his speeches
of what Aeschines ridicules.
ἄνθρωπος. A nearly certain correction of the MS. reading ἄνθρωπος. If the
original reading had been ὁ ἄνθρωπος (as
Markland) it is less likely that it would
have been altered. The best group of MSS.
have ἀνθρώπων, which seems unlikely. If
genuine, it must be taken as a hyperbaton,
or rather zeugma, 'peculiar to himself among
men, not common to men generally.'
4. μεθ' ὅρκου ψεύδεται. Besides Ae. de
F. L. l.c., cp. Vit. X. Orat. Dem. p. 845 B,
for a remark on Demosthenes' habit of

swearing. A passage is quoted from a comic
poet (Antiphanes or Timocles), μὰ γῆν, μὰ
κρήνας, μὰ ποταμούς, μὰ νάματα, that appears to have been in ridicule of his style,
but that seems rather to refer to such rhetorical oaths as de Cor. § 263, than to
serious imprecations such as Aeschines speaks
of. But Demosthenes is perhaps more ad-
dicted than most orators to merely conversational μὰ Δία᾽s and the like; while in
Aeschines they are very rare, except in the
Timarchus, where perhaps they are meant
for moral earnestness.
6. εἰς ὁπότ'. A colloquialism not common in early Greek; but εἰς τότε is found
in Plat. Leg. 8, p. 845. εἰς ὅ τε in Od. 2.
99, which is also quoted by Bremi, is different in principle.
9. πονηρὸς ὢν καὶ τὰ κ.τ.λ. 'Besides
being a villain himself, he makes it impossible to tell honest men from villains.'
§§ 100–102. *So be produced a long windy*
decree, that pretended to give you a vast
army, and really robbed you of a vast reve-
nue.
11. μακρότερον τῆς Ἰλιάδος. Several
commentators identify this decree with the
one given in D. de Cor. §§ 232 sqq., and
the unquestionable 'length and verbiage' of
that document look almost as though its
compiler shared the belief. But Aeschines is
still speaking of the Euboic alliance, and
that is concerned with the Theban. And
his objection is not to rhodomontade of
style, such as appears there, but to vain and
false overstatements of resources.

βεβίωκε, μεστὸν δ' ἐλπίδων οὐκ ἐσομένων καὶ στρατοπέδων
οὐδέποτε συλλεγησομένων. ἀπαγαγὼν δ' ὑμᾶς ἄπωθεν ἀπὸ
τοῦ κλέμματος καὶ ἀνακρεμάσας ἀπὸ τῶν ἐλπίδων, ἐνταῦθα δὴ
συστρέψας γράφει κελεύων ἑλέσθαι πρέσβεις εἰς Ἐρέτριαν,
οἵτινες δεήσονται τῶν Ἐρετριέων, πάνυ γὰρ ἔδει δεηθῆναι, μη- 5
κέτι διδόναι τὴν σύνταξιν ὑμῖν, τὰ πέντε τάλαντα, ἀλλὰ Καλ-
λίᾳ, καὶ πάλιν ἑτέρους αἱρεῖσθαι εἰς Ὠρεὸν πρὸς τοὺς Ὠρείτας
πρέσβεις, οἵτινες δεήσονται τὸν αὐτὸν Ἀθηναίοις φίλον καὶ
101 ἐχθρὸν νομίζειν εἶναι. ἔπειτα ἀναφαίνεται περὶ ἅπαντ' ὧν ἐν
τῷ ψηφίσματι πρὸς τῷ κλέμματι, γράψας "καὶ τὰ πέντε τά- 10
λαντα τοὺς πρέσβεις ἀξιοῦν τοὺς Ὠρείτας" μὴ ὑμῖν, ἀλλὰ "Καλ-
λίᾳ διδόναι." ὅτι δ' ἀληθῆ λέγω, ἀφελὼν τὸν κόμπον καὶ τὰς
τριήρεις καὶ τὴν ἀλαζονείαν ἀνάγνωθι καὶ τοῦ κλέμματος ἅψαι,
ὃ ὑφείλετο ὁ μιαρὸς καὶ ἀνόσιος ἄνθρωπος, ὅν φησι Κτησιφῶν
καὶ ἐν τῷδε τῷ ψηφίσματι διατελεῖν λέγοντα καὶ πράττοντα 15
τὰ ἄριστα τῷ δήμῳ τῶν Ἀθηναίων.

ΨΗΦΙΣΜΑ.

102 Οὐκοῦν τὰς μὲν τριήρεις καὶ τὴν πεζὴν στρατιὰν καὶ τὴν

2. ἄπωθεν] Sic af: ceteri et Bekk. ἄποθεν.　　4. κελεύων] καὶ κελεύει ekl, deleri jubet
Frankius, collato Ae. de F. L. § 19, p. 30.　　5. οἵτινες δεήσονται .. νομίζειν εἶναι] Post
δεήσονται, αὐτοῖς inserunt agmn fcdb, αὐτοῖς B. et S., καὶ αὐτοὶ p Reisk.　Mox Ἀθηναίους
agm et corr. b: καὶ ante φίλον add. ekl, εἶναι delent Taylor. Cobet.　Frankio locus usque
a καὶ πάλιν ἑτέρους corruptus videtur.　　9. ἅπαντ' ὧν] Sic post Sauppium Frank.: libri
ἁπάντων, nisi quod ekl πάντων habent.　Mox pro ἐν libri habent ἐπί, praeter eosdem.
10. καὶ] Om. adf † pr. b † B. et S. Frank.　　11. ἀξιοῦν] Sic ekl, corr. b, marg. gm:
ceteri ἀξιῶν.　ὑμῖν] Libri ἡμῖν, sed vid. Plin. Ep. 9. 26.　　13. Post ἀλαζονείαν addebatur cum fcdb ἐκ τοῦ ψηφίσματος.　τοῦ κλέμματος] ἀπὸ τοῦ κλέμματος c ekl pr. b †
hic quidem ab eadem, ut videbatur, manu correctus.†　Fortasse αὐτοῦ τοῦ.　18. στρα-
τιὰν] στρατείαν agmn fcdb.

4. συστρέψας. 'Gathering himself up,'
as Plat. Rep. 1, p. 336 B; or perhaps simply 'coming to the point.'

5. πάνυ γὰρ ἔδει δεηθῆναι. For the
Eretrians themselves had bribed Demosthenes to make such an arrangement.

8. τὸν .. νομίζειν. The exact equivalent
of this formula was employed by the Romans to mark their relation to the Samnites
when completely subdued. In fact the proposal was to exchange the contributions paid
by the Euboeans as members of a confederacy
with limited objects, for a complete control
over their foreign policy.

9. περὶ ἅπαντ' ὧν. So Sauppe and
Franke, omitting the καὶ after γράψας.
The reading of most MSS., ἀναφαίνεται
περὶ ἁπάντων .. γράψας, καὶ τὰ πέντε τάλαντα τοὺς πρέσβεις ἀξιῶν τοὺς Ὠρείτας,
would have to mean either, 'Besides the
trick that pervades the whole decree, it is

proved how he moved a resolution, calling
on the Oreites,' as Bremi, which seems to
suit the order ill; or, 'Then it is proved how
every item in his motion is drawn up for
the cheat, and how he calls upon the Oreites,'
etc., an impossible sense for πρὸς τῷ κλέμματι, while ὧν πρὸς κλέμματι is a familiar
construction enough; 'it is proved that at
each point in his resolution his mind was set
on cheating, since he moved, moreover, that
the ambassadors shall request the Oreites
to give the five talents' (not to you, but) 'to
Callias.' καὶ certainly might, as B. and S.
think, have got in to harmonise with the
reading ἀξιῶν, and several respectable MSS.
omit it; but it seems likelier that its omission is due to wrong criticism, and that like
the δὲ above, § 74, it is a verbatim quotation
of one of the items of the resolution.

12. ἀφελὼν τὸν κόμπον κ.τ.λ.　Of
course any diplomatic measure might be

E

πανσέληνον καὶ τοὺς συνέδρους λόγῳ ἠκούσατε, τὰς δὲ συντάξεις τῶν συμμάχων, τὰ δέκα τάλαντα, ἔργῳ ἀπωλέσατε.

Ὑπόλοιπον δέ μοι ἐστὶν εἰπεῖν, ὅτι λαβὼν τρία τάλαντα 103
μισθὸν τὴν γνώμην ταύτην ἔγραψε Δημοσθένης, τάλαντον μὲν
5 ἐκ Χαλκίδος παρὰ Καλλίου, τάλαντον δ' ἐξ Ἐρετρίας παρὰ
Κλειτάρχου τοῦ τυράννου, τάλαντον δὲ ἐξ Ὠρεοῦ, δι' ὃ καὶ
καταφανὴς ἐγένετο, δημοκρατουμένων τῶν Ὠρειτῶν καὶ πάντα
πραττόντων μετὰ ψηφίσματος. ἐξανηλωμένοι γὰρ ἐν τῷ πολέμῳ καὶ παντελῶς ἀπόρως διακείμενοι πέμπουσι πρὸς αὐτὸν
10 Γνωσίδημον τὸν Χαριγένους υἱὸν τοῦ δυναστεύσαντός ποτε ἐν
Ὠρεῷ, δεησόμενον αὐτοῦ τὸ μὲν τάλαντον ἀφιέναι τῇ πόλει,
ἐπαγγελλόμενον δ' αὐτῷ χαλκῆν εἰκόνα σταθήσεσθαι ἐν Ὠρεῷ.
ὁ δὲ ἀπεκρίνατο τῷ Γνωσιδήμῳ, ὅτι ἐλαχίστου χαλκοῦ οὐδὲν 104
δέοιτο, τὸ δὲ τάλαντον διὰ τοῦ Καλλίου εἰσπράττειν. ἀναγ-
15 καζόμενοι δὲ οἱ Ὠρεῖται καὶ οὐκ εὐποροῦντες ὑπέθεσαν αὐτῷ
τοῦ ταλάντου τὰς δημοσίας προσόδους, καὶ τόκον ἤνεγκαν Δημοσθένει τοῦ δωροδοκήματος δραχμὴν τοῦ μηνὸς τῆς μνᾶς, ἕως
τὸ κεφάλαιον ἀπέδοσαν. καὶ πάντ' ἐπράχθη μετὰ ψηφίσματος
τοῦ δήμου. ὅτι δὲ τἀληθῆ λέγω, λαβέ μοι τὸ ψήφισμα τῶν
20 Ὠρειτῶν.

ΨΗΦΙΣΜΑ.

Τοῦτ' ἐστὶ τὸ ψήφισμα, ὦ Ἀθηναῖοι, αἰσχύνη μὲν τῆς 105
πόλεως, ἔλεγχος δὲ οὐ μικρὸς τῶν Δημοσθένους πολιτευμάτων,
φανερὰ δὲ κατηγορία τοῦ Κτησιφῶντος· τὸν γὰρ οὕτως αἰσ-

3. τρία] δέκα agmn. 6. δι' ὃ] Sic z Brem. B. et S. Frank.: διὸ cum ceteris libris
Bekk., δι' οὗ H. Wolf. 10. δυναστεύσαντός] † δυναστεύοντός pr. b †. 11. ἀφιέναι]
ἀφεῖναι ekl Bekk. Frank. 12. ἐπαγγελλόμενον] ἐπαγγελόμενον mnd, unde fortasse
ortum, quod Stephanus ἐπαγγελούμενον habet, quem sequitur Bekk. 14. εἰσπράττειν]
εἰσέπραττεν ekl. 18. πάντ'] ταῦτ' fdb Bekk. 24. τοῦ] Om. fcdb ekl Bekk.

discredited by such treatment—quoting its
concessions and omitting the considerations
for them: but Aeschines affects to say that
here the concessions were real, the considerations, being fictitious, not worth recording.

§ 103. *For this job he had a talent from
each city in Euboea: at Oreus the city archives
prove it,*

7. **δημοκρατουμένων τῶν Ὠρειτῶν** corresponds to παρὰ Καλλίου and παρὰ Κλειτάρχου τοῦ τυράννου: he got the money
(sent) *from* each of the three cities (ἐκ); but
while in the two first cases it *came from* an
individual ruler (παρὰ), in the third it was the
city's act to send it.

πάντα πραττόντων μετὰ ψηφίσματος.
Opposed to despots who could keep their
own counsel.

§ 104. *And there he meanly screwed the
money out of their poverty.*

13. **ἐλαχίστου χαλκοῦ οὐδὲν δέοιτο.**
'He did not want a scrap of bronze.' It is
really a double negative. A bronze was the
least thing he cared about; he did not care
for it at all.

§ 105. *One job like this proves a man
unworthy of praise like Ctesiphon's.*

23. **ἔλεγχος.** For it may be presumed
that at home, and in dealings with states
whose proceedings were less public, his conduct was as unprincipled, though this is the
only instance where he was so plainly convicted.

24. **οὕτως αἰσχρῶς δωροδοκοῦντα.** For

χρῶς δωροδοκοῦντα οὐκ ἔστιν ἄνδρα γεγονέναι ἀγαθὸν, ἃ τετόλ-
μηκεν οὗτος γράψαι ἐν τῷ ψηφίσματι.

106 Ἐνταῦθ᾽ ἤδη τέτακται καὶ ὁ τρίτος τῶν καιρῶν, μᾶλλον δ᾽
ὁ πάντων πικρότατος χρόνος, ἐν ᾧ Δημοσθένης ἀπώλεσε τὰς
τῶν Ἑλλήνων καὶ τῆς πόλεως πράξεις ἀσεβήσας μὲν εἰς τὸ 5
ἱερὸν τὸ ἐν Δελφοῖς, ἄδικον δὲ καὶ οὐδαμῶς ἴσην τὴν πρὸς
Θηβαίους συμμαχίαν γράψας. ἄρξομαι δὲ ἀπὸ τῶν εἰς τοὺς
θεοὺς αὐτοῦ πλημμελημάτων λέγειν.

107 Ἔστι γὰρ, ὦ Ἀθηναῖοι, τὸ Κιρραῖον ὠνομασμένον πεδίον
καὶ λιμὴν ὁ νῦν ἐξάγιστος καὶ ἐπάρατος ὠνομασμένος. ταύτην 10
ποτὲ τὴν χώραν κατῴκησαν Κιρραῖοι καὶ Ἀκραγαλλίδαι, γένη
παρανομώτατα, οἳ εἰς τὸ ἱερὸν τὸ ἐν Δελφοῖς καὶ [περὶ] τὰ
ἀναθήματα ἠσέβουν, ἐξημάρτανον δὲ καὶ εἰς τοὺς Ἀμφικτύονας.
ἀγανακτήσαντες δ᾽ ἐπὶ τοῖς γενομένοις μάλιστα μὲν, ὡς λέγεται,
οἱ πρόγονοι οἱ ὑμέτεροι, ἔπειτα δὲ καὶ οἱ ἄλλοι Ἀμφικτύονες 15

---

1. ἔστιν] ἔνεστιν *g mnf ekl.*   ἃ] ὃ *pc* et marg. Steph.   10. ταύτην] καὶ ταύτην
g mn.   11. Ἀκραγαλλίδαι] Ἀκραγγαλλίδαι *b*, Ἀκραγαλίδαι *t*, Κραγαλίδαι B. et S.
passim.   12. περὶ] Om. *a m nfdb* Bekk. B. et S. Frank.   Vid. annot.   13. Post
Ἀμφικτύονας addit *g* γυναῖκας δὲ ἥρπαζον καὶ † ἤσθιον †: *b m* in margine habent (ut *g*
teste Bekk.) γυναῖκας .. καὶ ἐλήστευον.   14. γενομένοις] γεγενημένοις *a*, γινομένοις
pekl Bekk.   λέγεται] Sic *a m np* : † λέγηται pro λέγεται *g* † : ceteri et Bekk. λέγονται,
et parum abest quin nos id restituamus.   15. οἱ πρόγονοι οἱ ὑμέτεροι] οἱ πρόγονοι οἱ
ἡμέτεροι *fcd*, οἱ ἡμέτεροι πρόγονοι *b*, οἱ πρόγονοι *a*.   δὲ] Accessit ex *ag mnp* : om. Bekk.

---

the question how far such conduct was regarded as criminal, see Mitford, c. 41, § 5
(vol. vii. p. 97, ed. 1829).

§ 106. *In the third and worst period, he
sinned against gods and men alike*:

3. ἐνταῦθ᾽ ἤδη. ἐνταῦθα is used rather
than ἐντεῦθεν, because the alliance with
Euboea was not followed by, but *was* the
beginning of the war. The transition is
more abrupt than in §§ 79 or 159, because
the next stage of the narrative is especially
important, so that the speaker desires to
arouse special attention on approaching it.

5. ἀσεβήσας .. ἄδικον are in a way
opposed to each other as correlatives, like
contra fas et jus: he sacrificed the rights of
the God and the rights of the City equally.

§ 107. *Against God, in the matter of the
Cirrhaean plain, whose old inhabitants for
their violence*

9. ἔστι γὰρ κ.τ.λ. 'For there is, men
of Athens, the plain that is called the plain
of Cirrha, and the harbour that is now
called polluted and accursed.' We should
say, 'There is *a* plain and *a* harbour called'
so and so; the Greeks say, 'There is (such a
thing as) the plain and the harbour.'

12. [περὶ]. Has been omitted by Bekker and subsequent editors. The best MSS.
omit it : but, while its omission was easy, its
presence is due to a refinement as likely to
have occurred to Aeschines as to a copyist.
The temple is, and the gold of the temple is
not, a sacred thing in itself: 'they trespassed
against the temple, and *in the matter* of the
offerings there.'

13. ἐξημάρτανον. The use of so mild a
word requires accounting for. It may be
only to heighten the horror of ἠσέβουν ; or
we may distinguish, that ἠσέβουν is of *malum
per se*, ἐξημάρτανον of *malum probibitum*,
'transgressed against the Amphictyons,'
whose conventions enforced the natural
obligations of piety. The addition of two
or three MSS., γυναῖκας δὲ ἥρπαζον καὶ
ἐλήστευον, as it can be no part of the text,
so is not a very appropriate gloss, though
no doubt embodying a tradition.

14. ἐπὶ τοῖς γενομένοις. Four MSS.
have γινομένοις, 'at what was going on;'
which might be adopted if there were better
authority, as suiting the sense at least as
well, and being a less common phrase and
so less likely to be altered.

E 2

μαντείαν ἐμαντεύσαντο παρὰ τῷ θεῷ, τίνι χρὴ τιμωρίᾳ τοὺς
ἀνθρώπους τούτους μετελθεῖν. καὶ αὐτοῖς ἀναιρεῖ ἡ Πυθία 108
πολεμεῖν Κιρραίοις καὶ Ἀκραγαλλίδαις πάντ' ἤματα καὶ πάσας
νύκτας, καὶ τὴν χώραν αὐτῶν ἐκπορθήσαντας καὶ αὐτοὺς ἀνδρα-
5 ποδισαμένους ἀναθεῖναι τῷ Ἀπόλλωνι τῷ Πυθίῳ καὶ Ἀρτέμιδι
καὶ Λητοῖ καὶ Ἀθηνᾷ Προναίᾳ ἐπὶ πάσῃ ἀεργίᾳ, καὶ ταύτην
τὴν χώραν μήτ' αὐτοὺς ἐργάζεσθαι μήτ' ἄλλον ἐᾶν. λαβόντες
δὲ τὸν χρησμὸν οἱ Ἀμφικτύονες ἐψηφίσαντο Σόλωνος εἰπόντος Ἀθηναίου τὴν γνώμην, ἀνδρὸς καὶ νομοθετῆσαι δυνατοῦ
10 καὶ περὶ ποίησιν καὶ φιλοσοφίαν διατετριφότος, ἐπιστρατεύειν
ἐπὶ τοὺς ἐναγεῖς κατὰ τὴν μαντείαν τοῦ θεοῦ· καὶ συναθροί- 109
σαντες δύναμιν ἱκανὴν τῶν Ἀμφικτυόνων ἐξηνδραποδίσαντο τοὺς
ἀνθρώπους καὶ τὸν λιμένα ἔχωσαν καὶ τὴν πόλιν αὐτῶν κατέ-

4. Post αὐτῶν καὶ τὴν πόλιν add. *ekl.* 5. τῇ ante Ἀρτέμιδι add. *fcdb.* 6. καὶ ante
Προναίᾳ add. *a* hic et § 110, fin. Προναίᾳ] Sic videtur Harpocratio legisse, idque verum
erat deae Delphicae nomen. Libri Προνοίᾳ passim, et sic Bekk. Frank. Ut nos B. et S.
Vid. annot. 8. Post χρησμὸν, τοῦτον add. *bekl.* 12. ἱκανὴν τῶν Ἀμφικτυό-
νων] πολλὴν pro ἱκανὴν *ekl*, ἐκ ante τῶν *fcdb.* 13. τὸν λιμένα] τοὺς λιμένας omnes
praeter *ekl*, atque ita Tauchn.

1. τοὺς ἀνθρώπους. Perhaps with a
notion of horror, like Ar. Eth. 7. 5. 2 ἡ
ἄνθρωπος, 'the creature.' More commonly
the sense is compassionate.
§ 108. *Were, by command of the oracle,
and the counsel of Solon,*
3. πάντ' ἤματα. Cp. Hdt. 4. 163 for
a similar quotation or paraphrase from an
oracle, with the metre destroyed, yet shewing fragmentary traces of the poetic diction.
Here, as Aeschines is not quoting *verbatim*,
it is perhaps no wonder that the traces of
rhythm are not more marked: else one
might suspect that the Pythia, or the priests
who put her utterances into shape, were
sometimes too much in earnest to round
their hexameters properly.
4. τὴν χώραν αὐτῶν has a double government, depending equally on ἐκπορθήσαντας
and ἀναθεῖναι. Its connection with the last
is obscured by the clause καὶ αὐτοὺς ἀνδρα-
ποδισαμένους, which is almost parenthetical ;
for though ἀναθεῖναι might conceivably include αὐτοὺς (that they were to become ἱερό-
δουλοι), ἐπὶ πάσῃ ἀεργίᾳ would prevent it.
6. Προναίᾳ. So Harpocration ; who,
however, hesitates about the etymology.
Franke restores the MS. reading Προνοίᾳ:
and so inf. passim. Πρόνοια was certainly
an ancient and genuine title of Athena : vid.
Orat. c. Aristog. p. 784, § 42. But this
seems to have been an exclusively Attic
devotion, and the Delphic Athena was

Προναία, because her temple stood before
the great one of Apollo (Προνηίη, Hdt.
1. 92, etc.: she is always Προναία in inscriptions.) All that can be said is, it is uncertain
how early the error arose ; it is possible that
Athenians, as early as Aeschines' time, had
confused the two similar titles, but it seems
safer to credit Aeschines, a zealous and
ritualistic religionist, with accuracy in the
use of a religious term.
8. Σόλωνος εἰπόντος Ἀθηναίου. 'Upon
the motion of Solon of Athens.' Aeschines
purposely puts his name in the bald form in
which it would occur in the official records,
for to those who knew Solon's fame Ἀθηναίου would be redundant. He aims at
producing the rhetorical effect, 'Solon of
Athens moved it, and you Athenians know
what manner of man Solon of Athens was,
what greatness is implied in that name.'
But it is very characteristic of him that he
does not know when to stop, and gives the
panegyric which it was the object of the
designation to supersede.
§ 109. *Enslaved, and their land devoted
to perpetual desolation.*
13. τὸν λιμένα. Most MSS. have τοὺς
λιμένας, but the recent editors are unanimous in reading as in the text. Only the
one harbour of Cirrha is known, to which
the story should apply. Bremi thinks the
plural is used vaguely ; but his instances are
only of abstract nouns.

σκάψαν καὶ τὴν χώραν αὐτῶν καθιέρωσαν κατὰ τὴν μαντείαν·
καὶ ἐπὶ τούτοις ὅρκον ὤμοσαν ἰσχυρὸν μήτ' αὐτοὶ τὴν ἱερὰν
γῆν ἐργάσεσθαι μήτ' ἄλλῳ ἐπιτρέψειν, ἀλλὰ βοηθήσειν τῷ
θεῷ καὶ τῇ γῇ τῇ ἱερᾷ καὶ χειρὶ καὶ ποδὶ [καὶ φωνῇ] καὶ
110 πάσῃ δυνάμει. καὶ οὐκ ἀπέχρησεν αὐτοῖς τοῦτον μόνον τὸν 5
ὅρκον ὀμόσαι, ἀλλὰ καὶ προστροπὴν καὶ ἀρὰν ἰσχυρὰν ὑπὲρ
τούτων ἐποιήσαντο. γέγραπται γὰρ οὕτως ἐν τῇ ἀρᾷ, "εἴ
τις τάδε" φησὶ "παραβαίνοι ἢ πόλις ἢ ἰδιώτης ἢ ἔθνος, ἐναγὴς" φησὶν "ἔστω τοῦ Ἀπόλλωνος καὶ τῆς Ἀρτέμιδος καὶ
111 Λητοῦς καὶ Ἀθηνᾶς Προναίας." καὶ ἐπεύχεται αὐτοῖς μήτε 10
γῆν καρποὺς φέρειν, μήτε γυναῖκας τέκνα τίκτειν γονεῦσιν ἐοικότα, ἀλλὰ τέρατα, μηδὲ βοσκήματα κατὰ φύσιν γονὰς ποιεῖσθαι, ἥτταν δὲ αὐτοῖς εἶναι πολέμου καὶ δικῶν καὶ ἀγορῶν, καὶ
ἐξώλεις εἶναι καὶ αὐτοὺς καὶ οἰκίας καὶ γένος τὸ ἐκείνων. "καὶ
μήποτε" φησὶν "ὁσίως θύσαιεν τῷ Ἀπόλλωνι μηδὲ τῇ Ἀρτέ- 15
μιδι μηδὲ τῇ Λητοῖ μηδ' Ἀθηνᾷ Προναίᾳ, μηδὲ δέξαιντο αὐτῶν τὰ
112 ἱερά." ὅτι δ' ἀληθῆ λέγω, ἀνάγνωθι τὴν τοῦ θεοῦ μαντείαν.

---

3. ἐργάσεσθαι] Sic, ut videtur, ed: ἐργάσασθαι agmnfb: ἐργάζεσθαι et mox ἐπιτρέπειν
ekl: ut nos editi.　　4. καὶ φωνῇ] ex simili loco § 120 addiderunt B. et S.　　10. μήτε]
μηδὲ mnfd.　　12. μηδὲ] Sic a † g † mfcdbekl: ceteri et Bekk. μήτε. Quae sit ratio
mutatae conjunctionis, in annot. explicatur.　　15. θύσαιεν] θύσαι n, θύσειεν bel, pro
θύσειαν, quod habet Frank.　　16. αὐτῶν] Sic agncekl: ceteri et Bekk. αὐτοῖς. Vid.
annot.

---

4. [καὶ φωνῇ]. Added by B. and S., and
adopted by Franke, from the parallel passage
in § 120. It is likely enough to have been
used in the formula, but if it were not, Aeschines is as likely to have incorporated it,
when he was actually exerting his *voice* in
the cause, but had not yet made sure of his
hands and feet to help him.

§§ 110–112. *And an oath and terrible
curse binds all Amphictyonic states to enforce
that sentence for ever.*

5. καὶ οὐκ ἀπέχρησεν αὐτοῖς κ.τ.λ.
The oath could only bind the generation
that took it; accordingly they turned themselves to the gods (προστροπήν), and impre-
cated a curse on all who should transgress it.

8. φησὶ .. φησὶν .. ἐπεύχεται. Grammatically ἡ ἀρὰ is the subject, but it is
hardly to be called a personification. It is
more like our impersonal ' it says,' i. e. the
words are found.

11. τέκνα .. τέρατα. It is almost a definition of τέρας not to be γονεῦσιν ἐοικός:
cp. Plat. Crat. 393 B, ἐὰν ὥσπερ τέρας γένηται ἐξ ἵππου ἄλλο τι ἢ ἵππος. τέρατα is
an exception to the rule of the Atticists,
that would make the plural τέρα: perhaps,

like ἐοικότα, it is a semi-poetical form.

12. μηδὲ βοσκήματα. So almost all
MSS. for μήτε. It is a branch of the curse
on births, not an independent curse.

16. δέξαιντο αὐτῶν. The reading αὐτοῖς
is not to be despised, being less obvious, and
at least as good sense; for it may be regarded as a favour to the worshipper for the
God to accept his gifts. But αὐτῶν has the
best MS. authority, so may be left in the
text. Below, § 121, the MSS. are unanimous for it.

§ 112. There is a good deal of confusion in
the MSS. as regards the titles and order of
the documents. It has been proposed to
arrange them thus: ἀνάγνωθι τὴν τοῦ θεοῦ
μαντείαν. MANTEIA. ἀκούσατε τῆς δρᾶς.
APA. ἀναμνήσθητε τῶν ὅρκων, οὓς .. συνώμοσαν. ΟΡΚΟΙ. The transposition of
the oracle is plausible, since the change of
number and subject between ἀνάγνωθι and
ἀκούσατε is harsh; but it ruins the passage
to spoil the asyndeton, ἀκούσατε, ἀναμνήσθητε, which is a burst of vigorous and no
doubt earnest warning, of the best sort of
eloquence Aeschines could attain.

As to the oracle itself, it is given by Pau-

ἀκούσατε τῆς ἀρᾶς, ἀναμνήσθητε τῶν ὅρκων, οὓς ὑμῶν οἱ πρόγονοι μετὰ τῶν Ἀμφικτυόνων συνώμοσαν.

ΜΑΝΤΕΙΑ.

[Οὐ πρὶν τῆσδε πόληος ἐρείψετε πύργον ἑλόντες,
5   πρίν γε θεοῦ τεμένει κυανώπιδος Ἀμφιτρίτης
κῦμα ποτικλύζῃ κελαδοῦν ἱεραῖσιν ἐπ' ἀκταῖς.]

ΟΡΚΟΙ. ΑΡΑ.

Ταύτης τῆς ἀρᾶς καὶ τῶν ὅρκων καὶ τῆς μαντείας γενο- 113
μένης, ἀναγεγραμμένων ἔτι καὶ νῦν, οἱ Λοκροὶ οἱ Ἀμφισσεῖς,
10 μᾶλλον δὲ οἱ προεστηκότες αὐτῶν, ἄνδρες παρανομώτατοι, ἐπειρ-
γάζοντο τὸ πεδίον, καὶ τὸν λιμένα τὸν ἐξάγιστον καὶ ἐπάρατον
πάλιν ἐτείχισαν καὶ συνῴκισαν, καὶ τέλη τοὺς καταπλέοντας
ἐξέλεγον, καὶ τῶν ἀφικνουμένων εἰς Δελφοὺς πυλαγόρων ἐνίους
χρήμασι διέφθειραν, ὧν εἷς ἦν Δημοσθένης. χειροτονηθεὶς γὰρ 114
15 ὑφ' ὑμῶν πυλαγόρας λαμβάνει δισχιλίας δραχμὰς παρὰ τῶν

4. Versus omittit n, et tres titulos continuos habent nonnulli alii.   8. γενομένης] γε
agmn : † volgatum habet corr. g †.   14. ἦν] Om. gmn.   15. πυλαγόρας] πυλάγορος
pr. f.   Vid. annot.   δισχιλίας] Sic bekl cett. χιλίας.

sanias, and perhaps inserted here on his authority. If it is really the one referred to by Aeschines, the sanction it gave to the proceedings of the Amphictyons must have been extracted by this reasoning : ' You will not take the city till the sea comes up to the god's domain ;' ' Then we will extend the god's domain down to the sea.' In any case it is no doubt a genuine prophecy (for if written to suit the place, it would suit it better than it does), and one of the common type of
  ' Till Birnam Wood shall come to Dunsinane.'
§ 113. In spite of all these, the Locrians of Amphissa encroached on the devoted plain, cultivated it, and restored the harbour,
  8. γενομένης, ἀναγεγραμμένων. It is easier to feel than to explain why the former word agrees with the nearest substantive only, while the latter is put in the plural to agree with all : ' When this curse, oath, and oracle had been delivered, all of which are still extant in the inscription.' One might say that the stop after γενομένης accounts for it. It is probably owing to a sense of this difficulty, that the best group of MSS. read καὶ τῆς μαντείας γενομένης.
  10. μᾶλλον δὲ οἱ προεστηκότες. Did

Philip get the people to desert their leaders ? In any case, it is plain that the occupation was not of immemorial standing, accomplished and subsisting unquestioned, as supposed by Grote. The mention of the exiles in § 129 proves that it was only effected after a party struggle in Amphissa itself, and that, no doubt, within the current generation. And if it had not been very recent, what would have been the risk, worth a bribe to prevent, of an Athenian Pylagoras denouncing them ? Demosthenes does not assert more than that the Amphissians had a case : D. de Cor. § 191.
  12. συνῴκισαν. Made it their port ; took it into their own commonwealth as part of Amphissa.
  14. χρήμασι διέφθειραν. That is, no doubt, they engaged him as their Proxenus, with a fee which a very honourable statesman would have felt called upon to refuse. Vid. sup. ad § 105.
  § 114. And bribed Demosthenes to protect them, both from the Amphictyons and the Athenians—a bad protector, who ruins all that come near him.
  15. πυλαγόρας. The authority is for using this form in the singular, πυλάγοροι in the plural.

Ἀμφισσέων ὑπὲρ τοῦ μηδεμίαν μνείαν περὶ αὐτῶν ἐν τοῖς Ἀφικτύοσι ποιήσασθαι. διωμολογήθη δ' αὐτῷ καὶ εἰς τὸν λοιπὸν χρόνον ἀποσταλήσεσθαι Ἀθήναζε τοῦ ἐνιαυτοῦ ἑκάστου μνᾶς εἴκοσι τῶν ἐξαγίστων καὶ ἐπαράτων χρημάτων, ἐφ' ᾧτε βοηθήσειν τοῖς Ἀμφισσεῦσιν Ἀθήνησι κατὰ πάντα πρόπον· ὅθεν 5 μᾶλλον ἢ πρότερον συμβέβηκεν αὐτῷ, ὅτου ἂν προσάψηται ἀνδρὸς ἰδιώτου ἢ δυνάστου ἢ πόλεως δημοκρατουμένης, τούτων 115 ἑκάστους ἀνιάτοις κακοῖς περιβάλλειν. σκέψασθε δὴ τὸν δαίμονα καὶ τὴν τύχην, ὡς περιεγένετο τῆς τῶν Ἀμφισσέων ἀσεβείας. ἐπὶ γὰρ Θεοφράστου ἄρχοντος, ἱερομνήμονος ὄντος 10 Διογνήτου Ἀναφλυστίου, πυλαγόρους ὑμεῖς εἵλεσθε Μειδίαν τε ἐκεῖνον τὸν Ἀναγυράσιον, ὃν ἐβουλόμην ἂν πολλῶν ἕνεκα ζῆν, καὶ Θρασυκλέα τὸν ἐξ Οἴου καὶ τρίτον δὲ μετὰ τούτων ἐμέ. συνέβη δ' ἡμῖν ἀρτίως μὲν εἰς Δελφοὺς ἀφῖχθαι, παραχρῆμα δὲ τὸν ἱερομνήμονα Διόγνητον πυρέττειν· τὸ δ' αὐτὸ τοῦτο 15 συνεπεπτώκει καὶ τῷ Μειδίᾳ. οἱ δ' ἄλλοι συνεκάθηντο Ἀμφικ- 116 τύονες. ⊽ ἐξηγγέλλετο δ' ἡμῖν παρὰ τῶν βουλομένων εὔνοιαν

1. ὑπὲρ] Om. *bekl* Bekk.　5. Post ὅθεν *fcbekl* add ἔτι.　7. ἀνδρὸς ἰδιώτου] Sic *agmufd*: ἀνδρὸς ἢ ἰδιώτου Bekk. et, ut videtur, *c*, ἢ ἀνδρὸς ἢ ἰδιώτου *bekl*.　9. ὡς] ὅσῳ *bekl* Bekk., ᾧ ὅσω *c*, ᾧ *fd*.　11. Διογνήτου Ἀναφλυστίου] ' Malim Διογνήτου τοῦ 'Ἀναφλυστίου.' Bait.　12. ἕνεκα] ἕνεκεν *agm* B. et S. Frank.; sed hunc poenitet de non volgatum restituisse.　13. ἐξ Οἴου] Sic *bekl* Bekk.: ceteri Λέσβιον, unde F. A. Wolf. Λέκκιον, idque receperunt B. et S. et Frank.　15. τὸν] Om. *agmn*.　16. συνεπεπτώκει] συμπεπτώκει *bel* Bekk.

5. ὅθεν μᾶλλον ἢ πρότερον. It was one of Aeschines' main points against Demosthenes, that besides his crimes and blunders, his ill-luck contributed to the city's disasters; to which the splendid passage De Cor. §§ 314 sqq. is a reply. He here says, 'Always an unlucky man by nature, he brought a fresh curse on himself, and all his enterprises and associates, by sharing in sacrilege.'

7. ἀνδρὸς ἰδιώτου ἢ δυνάστου ἢ πόλεως δημοκρατουμένης. This reading, or that of some MSS. with ἢ inserted before ἀνδρὸς, would make the antithesis between a private individual and a government, despotic and republican. The reading ἀνδρὸς ἢ ἰδιώτου would make it between an individual, subject or ruler, and a commonwealth.

§ 115. Now when Midias and I served as Pylagori,

9. τὴν τύχην. ' Fortune' in the abstract, almost synonymous with δαίμονα, not Demosthenes' fortune, though that was one element that contributed to the general result.

12. ἐκεῖνον. A half jesting allusion to Midias' not very reputable celebrity. So, again, ὃν ἐβουλόμην κ.τ.λ. 'We all knew him, and he was really useful, to do the rough work on the right side.' See Dem. in

Mid. pp. 580–581, where it appears that, like Aeschines, he was a friend and partisan of Eubulus.

13. † ἐξ Οἴου †. So Bekker, with one group of MSS.: the rest have Λέσβιον, which cannot be right. F. A. Wolf corrected Λέκκιον, which is adopted by B. and S. and Franke. It seems safer to follow what some MSS. actually say than what more and better ones possibly mean. Moreover, there were, according to Harpocr., two of these *lonely* Demi, one in the tribe Leontis and the other in the Hippothoontis, besides Οἴα in the tribe Pandionis, whose members were said to be Οἰῆθεν: so that the odds are two to one in their favour as against Leccum.

14. συνέβη δ' ἡμῖν κ.τ.λ. So that I was left almost the only representative of Athenian interests.

§ 116. The Amphissians brought a charge against Athens in the Theban interest,

17. ἐξηγγέλλετο δ' ἡμῖν. Apparently in the absence of its head, the whole legation had stayed away; which is to be understood from οἱ δ' ἄλλοι συνεκάθηντο Ἀμφικτύονες, ' every state had its representatives there but Athens.'

ἐνδείκνυσθαι τῇ πόλει, ὅτι οἱ Ἀμφισσεῖς ὑποπεπτωκότες τότε
καὶ δεινῶς θεραπεύοντες τοὺς Θηβαίους εἰσέφερον δόγμα κατὰ
τῆς ὑμετέρας πόλεως, πεντήκοντα ταλάντοις ζημιῶσαι τὸν δῆμον
τῶν Ἀθηναίων, ὅτι χρυσᾶς ἀσπίδας ἀνέθηκεν πρὸς τὸν καινὸν
5 νεὼν πρὶν ἐξαράσασθαι, καὶ ἐπεγράψαμεν τὸ προσῆκον ἐπίγραμμα "Ἀθηναῖοι ἀπὸ Μήδων καὶ Θηβαίων, ὅτε τἀναντία
τοῖς Ἕλλησιν ἐμάχοντο." μεταπεμψάμενος δέ με ὁ ἱερο-
μνήμων ἠξίου εἰσελθεῖν εἰς τὸ συνέδριον καὶ εἰπεῖν τι πρὸς τοὺς
Ἀμφικτύονας ὑπὲρ τῆς πόλεως, καὶ αὐτὸν οὕτω προῃρημένον.
10 ἀρχομένου δέ μου λέγειν καὶ προθυμότερον πως εἰσεληλυθότος 117
εἰς τὸ συνέδριον, τῶν ἄλλων πυλαγόρων μεθεστηκότων, ἀναβοή-
σας τις τῶν Ἀμφισσέων, ἄνθρωπος ἀσελγέστατος καί, ὡς ἐμοὶ
ἐφαίνετο, οὐδεμιᾶς παιδείας μετεσχηκώς, ἴσως δὲ καὶ δαιμονίου
τινὸς ἐξαμαρτάνειν αὐτὸν προαγομένου, "ἀρχὴν δέ γε" ἔφη

---

3. ὑμετέρας] † ἡμετέρας g †.   4. τῶν Ἀθηναίων] τὸν Ἀθηναῖον f et, ut semper,
Bekker.   Neque hujusmodi locos amplius notabimus.   τὰς ante χρυσᾶς inserunt fcd et
γρ. mb.   ἀνέθηκεν] Sic Harpocr., et ἀνέθεκεν habet l : ceteri ἀνέθεμεν, quod propter
sequens ἐπεγράψαμεν prave mutatum videtur. Vid. annot.   5. ἐξαράσασθαι] Sic el
Harpocr., ἐξαρέσασθαι k, ἐξάρασθαι b, ἐξαρᾶσθαι schol. alter, alter ἐξειργάσθαι, volg. et Bekk.
ἐξειργάσθαι.   7. δέ με] Sic cbekl † et corr. g † : δὲ ceteri, δ' ἐμὲ Bekk.   11. μεθε-
στηκότων] † μετεσχηκότων, ut videbatur, pr. g † : καθεστηκύτων bl, corr. g et γρ. m.
13. οὐδεμιᾶς] † οὐδένος pr. g †.

---

1. τότε. After Philip's crusade in alliance
with Thebes.
4. ἀνέθηκεν. So Harpocration, and it is
better than ἀνέθεμεν, the MS. reading.
πεντήκοντα ταλάντοις . . Ἀθηναίων, ὅτι χρυσᾶς ἀσπίδας ἀνέθηκεν κ.τ.λ. are the actual
words of the Amphissian proposal : Aeschines
adds his own comment in the first person,
καὶ ἐπεγράψαμεν κ.τ.λ., 'the real grievance
was, that we put the proper inscription on
them.'
ϛ. ἐξαράσασθαι. So Harpocr. and two
MSS.; while others point to the same or
ἐξαρᾶσθαι. If we read ἐξειργάσθαι (and the
reading is at least old), the point must be
the same, 'before the temple was finished,'
and therefore before it was consecrated, and
the proper ceremonies performed to fit it to
receive offerings. Probably the Athenians
had tried to steal a march upon the other
members of the Amphictyony, who would
not have permitted the insult to Thebes if
the restoration of the offering had been
proposed to be made in the regular manner.
§ 117. As soon as I began to reply, a
vulgar Amphissian wanted to condemn us
unheard;
10. ἀρχομένου κ.τ.λ. 'As I was beginning to speak (I had come in rather hastily,

and the other Pylagori had made way for
me), one of the Amphissians burst out—a
most scurrilous fellow, that never, as I think,
had had a chance of learning decency; may
be, too, some destiny drove him on to folly—
and said, "If you were wise, men of Greece,
you would not have the name of the people
of Athens in your mouths this day, but
would have driven them out of the holy
place, for the curse is on them long ago."'
11. τῶν ἄλλων πυλαγόρων μεθεστηκότων. Sometimes taken as though the Hie-
romnemones only were present, Aeschines
being there only as representative of the
absent Diognetus. But more probably as
above, the point being that the slight disturbance roused the Amphissians' attention
and his anger.
13. παιδείας. Cp. the last section of
this speech, and Demosthenes' comment on
it, De Cor. § 162. There is some truth in
the criticism there : Aeschines seems to
have been one of the people who are near
enough to having a gentleman's spirit to
wish they had it, and therefore to be always
talking about it.
14. ἀρχὴν δέ γε. 'A question about the
Athenians would never even have arisen at
all,' much less have advanced so far that
they should be allowed a reply.

"ὦ ἄνδρες Ἕλληνες, εἰ ἐσωφρονεῖτε, οὐδ᾽ ἂν ὠνομάζετο τοὔνομα τοῦ δήμου τῶν Ἀθηναίων ἐν ταῖσδε ταῖς ἡμέραις, ἀλλ᾽
118 ὡς ἐναγεῖς ἐξήγετε ἐκ τοῦ ἱεροῦ." ἅμα δὲ ἐμέμνητο τῆς τῶν
Φωκέων συμμαχίας, ἣν ὁ Κρωβύλος ἐκεῖνος ἔγραψε, καὶ ἄλλα
πολλὰ καὶ δυσχερῆ κατὰ τῆς πόλεως διεξῄει λέγων, ἃ ἐγὼ 5
οὔτε τότ᾽ ἐκαρτέρουν ἀκούων οὔτε νῦν ἡδέως μέμνημαι αὐτῶν.
ἀκούσας δὲ οὕτω παρωξύνθην, ὡς οὐδεπώποτ᾽ ἐν τῷ ἐμαυτοῦ βίῳ.
καὶ τοὺς μὲν ἄλλους λόγους ὑπερβήσομαι· ἐπῆλθε δέ μοι ἐπὶ
τὴν γνώμην μνησθῆναι τῆς τῶν Ἀμφισσέων περὶ τὴν γῆν τὴν
ἱερὰν ἀσεβείας, καὶ αὐτόθεν ἑστηκὼς ἐδείκνυον τοῖς Ἀμφικτύο- 10
σιν· ὑπόκειται γὰρ τὸ Κιρραῖον πεδίον τῷ ἱερῷ καὶ ἔστιν
119 εὐσύνοπτον. "ὁρᾶτ᾽," ἔφην ἐγώ, "ὦ ἄνδρες Ἀμφικτύονες,
ἐξειργασμένον τοῦτο τὸ πεδίον ὑπὸ τῶν Ἀμφισσέων καὶ κεραμεῖα ἐνῳκοδομημένα καὶ αὔλια· ὁρᾶτε τοῖς ὀφθαλμοῖς τὸν ἐξάγιστον καὶ ἐπάρατον λιμένα τετειχισμένον· ἴστε τούτους αὐτοί, 15

1. ὠνομάζετο] Sic agmn: ὀνομάζετε e, ceteri et Bekk. ὠνομάζετε.   3. ἐξήγετε]
ἐξείργετ᾽ ἂν bekl Bekk., ἐξήγετε g.   Vid. annot.   4. Κρωβύλος] Sic gn pr. k corr. b,
Κρώβυλος, ut videtur, amfcd et Bekk.: ceteri corrupti. Nimirum κρωβύλος appellative,
nomen proprium προπαροξύτονον esse debere videbatur.   7. † Post ἀκούσας δὲ, ἐγὼ add.
g †.   8. δέ μοι] δ᾽ οὖν μοι fcdbekl Bekk.   9. περὶ] Ita bekl: ceteri ἐπί. τὴν
γῆν τὴν ἱερὰν] τὴν ἱερὰν γῆν fcd bekl.   11. ὑπόκειται] ὑπέκειτο gmnf.   13. τοῦτο]
τουτὶ ekl corr. b Bekk.

1. ὠνομάζετο. The best reading, being
that of the best group of MSS., and the -τε
being easy to account for by the assonance
of ἐσωφρονεῖτε and ἐξήγετε. But the sense
is probably as above rendered, and so the
same as that of ὠνομάζετε, rather than 'You
would not allow any one to speak of or for
Athens' as Aeschines is now doing.
   2. ἐν ταῖσδε ταῖς ἡμέραις. Exactly our
colloquial phrase 'at this time of day;' but
the Amphissian, though vulgar, is not speaking colloquially.
   3. ἐξήγετε. So most MSS. Volg. ἐξείρ-
γετε, Bekk. ἐξείργετ᾽ ἄν. B and S. compare δίκη ἐξαγωγῆς for the strong sense of
ἐξάγειν, 'to drive out,' not 'to lead out.'
   § 118. Bringing up all the charges Demosthenes' party have laid us open to: which
provoked me to remember the heavy guilt
lying upon them:
   4. ὁ Κρωβύλος ἐκεῖνος. ἐκεῖνος no
doubt in a bad sense, since Hegesippus was
a partisan of Demosthenes. The meaning
of his nickname has been much disputed;
but the simplest view is the likeliest, that he
did wear his hair in a κρωβύλος, whether as
an affectation of old fashion, or for mere
dandyism. Perhaps the latter is the likelier,
from the character Aeschines gives of his
brother Hegesander.

6. ἐκαρτέρουν ἀκούων does not mean
that Aeschines interrupted the Amphissian
who had interrupted him (which would
have been οὐκ ἀνειχόμην ἀκούειν, not
ἀκούων—καρτερεῖν is not used with the
infin., and is excluded by διεξῄει), but that
the speech was too much for his feelings:
he could not stand it.
   8. ἐπῆλθε .. γνώμην. Most MSS. have
ἐπῆλθε δ᾽ οὖν; perhaps it is one of the cases
where Baiter and Sauppe omit too readily.
'Verbis ἐπὶ τὴν γνωμὴν facile caruerim,'
Bait.; but it is like Aeschines to use redundant words.
   9. περὶ τὴν γὴν. ἐπί does not appear to be
used with ἀσεβεῖν and correlative words; its
occurrence here in most MSS. is easily accounted for, by its presence in the preceding line.
   10. αὐτόθεν ἑστηκώς. As I stood, from
the place where I stood.
   § 119. Pointing to the scene before them,
and reading to them the sentence passed ;
   13. κεραμεῖα ἐνῳκοδομημένα καὶ αὔλια.
Both signs of irregular occupation of waste
land, and coinciding with μᾶλλον δὲ οἱ προεστηκότες, above, § 113.
   15. ἴστε τούτους αὐτοί. Because many
of them, especially Peloponnesian deputies,
would have arrived by sea, and so had to
pay the port dues.

καὶ οὐδὲν ἑτέρων δεῖσθε μαρτύρων, τέλη πεπραχότας καὶ χρήματα λαμβάνοντας ἐκ τοῦ ἱεροῦ λιμένος." ἅμα δὲ ἀναγιγνώ-
σκειν ἐκέλευον αὐτοῖς τὴν μαντείαν τοῦ θεοῦ, τὸν ὅρκον τῶν
προγόνων, τὴν ἀρὰν τὴν γενομένην, καὶ διωριζόμην, ὅτι " ἐγὼ 120
5 μὲν ὑπὲρ τοῦ δήμου τοῦ Ἀθηναίων καὶ τοῦ σώματος καὶ τῶν
τέκνων καὶ οἰκίας τῆς ἐμαυτοῦ βοηθῶ κατὰ τὸν ὅρκον καὶ τῷ
θεῷ καὶ τῇ γῇ τῇ ἱερᾷ καὶ χειρὶ καὶ ποδὶ καὶ φωνῇ καὶ πᾶσιν
οἷς δύναμαι, καὶ τὴν πόλιν τὴν ἡμετέραν τὰ πρὸς τοὺς θεοὺς
ἀφοσιῶ· ὑμεῖς δ' ὑπὲρ ὑμῶν αὐτῶν ἤδη βουλεύεσθε. ἐνῆρκται
10 μὲν τὰ κανᾶ, παρέστηκε δὲ τοῖς βωμοῖς τὰ θύματα, μέλλετε
δ' αἰτεῖν τοὺς θεοὺς τἀγαθὰ καὶ κοινῇ καὶ ἰδίᾳ. σκοπεῖτε δὲ, 121
ποίᾳ φωνῇ, ποίᾳ ψυχῇ, ποίοις ὄμμασι, τίνα τόλμαν κτησάμενοι τὰς ἱκεσίας ποιήσεσθε, τούτους παρέντες ἀτιμωρήτους
τοὺς ἐναγεῖς καὶ ταῖς ἀραῖς ἐνόχους. οὐ γὰρ δι' αἰνιγμάτων,
15 ἀλλ' ἐναργῶς γέγραπται ἐν τῇ ἀρᾷ κατά τε τῶν ἀσεβησάντων, ἃ χρὴ παθεῖν αὐτούς, καὶ κατὰ τῶν ἐπιτρεψάντων, καὶ
τελευταῖον ἐν τῇ ἀρᾷ γέγραπται, μηδ' ὁσίως θύσειαν οἱ μὴ
τιμωροῦντες, φησί, τῷ Ἀπόλλωνι μηδὲ τῇ Ἀρτέμιδι μηδὲ τῇ
Λητοῖ μηδ' Ἀθηνᾷ Προναίᾳ, μηδὲ δέξαιντο αὐτῶν τὰ ἱερά."
20 τοιαῦτα καὶ πρὸς τούτοις ἕτερα πολλὰ διεξελθόντος ἐμοῦ, 122
ἐπειδή ποτε ἀπηλλάγην καὶ μετέστην ἐκ τοῦ συνεδρίου, κραυγὴ

---

5. τοῦ Ἀθηναίων] τῶν Ἀθηναίων *fcd.*
12. φωνῇ et ψυχῇ inverso ordine ponit *a.*
rectius. Neque enim tragica verbi forma hoc loco inepta est, et certe minus usitata.
μηδ'] Ita Bekk. : μήποθ' *d,* μηθ' ceteri.
18. μηδὲ .. μηδὲ] Ita libri fere omnes : μήτε habet Ald. et volg. ante Bekk.

11. σκοπεῖτε δὲ] σκοπεῖτε δὴ *fcd k* Bekk.
14. αἰνιγμάτων] αἰνιγμῶν *ekl,* quod fortasse
17. ἐν
τῇ ἀρᾷ γέγραπται] Haec verba omitti voluit Baiter, cum de tribus prioribus praeivisset Markl.
θύσειαν] Ita *f* : ceteri plerique θύσαιεν.

---

4. **διωριζόμην.** Drew a line between our
case and theirs; cut ourselves off from fel-
lowship with their guilt.

§ 120. *And proclaiming that I had done
my duty, and Athens was clear.*

5. **τῶν τέκνων καὶ οἰκίας.** Aeschines is
rather fond of these appeals to domestic
sentiment. Cp. above, § 78.

9. **ἐνῆρκται.** Cp. Eur. El. 1141: the
Latin *inchoo* of Aen. 6. 252 is exactly
similar. One might compare Ar. Pax 948,
949, for a similar description of the pre-
liminaries of a sacrifice.

§ 121. *' But how can you,' I asked, ' hope
to be accepted by the God, if you tolerate this
profanation ?'*

12. **ποίᾳ φωνῇ.** He begins with the
voice, as easiest to command; for the transposition of φωνῇ and ψυχῇ in one good MS.
is doubtless accidental.

**ποίοις ὄμμασι, τίνα τόλμαν κτησά-
μενοι** are not coordinate clauses, but mu-

tually explanatory; ' how will you gain the
courage to look the God in the face?'

15. **κατά τε τῶν ἀσεβησάντων .. καὶ
κατὰ τῶν ἐπιτρεψάντων.** ' As well against
those who tolerate as against those who
commit the sacrilege.' τε .. καὶ is not often
so emphatic, but it is natural in Greek that
the clause to be especially emphasised is put
second.

§ 122. *This diverted the assembly's attention from the charge against us ; and they resolved to act on my suggestion.*

21. **μετέστην.** The point of his withdrawal probably is to emphasise what he
had said in § 120, ὑμεῖς ὑπὲρ ὑμῶν αὐτῶν
βουλεύεσθε. Some suppose that it was
always a point of etiquette for a speaker
to leave the assembly as soon as he had
finished, to avoid the appearance of dicta-
tion; comparing ἀπεληλυθότος ἐμοῦ below,
§ 126; but this seems unproved and improbable.

πολλὴ καὶ θόρυβος ἦν τῶν Ἀμφικτυόνων, καὶ λόγος ἦν οὐκέτι
περὶ τῶν ἀσπίδων, ἃς ἡμεῖς ἀνέθεμεν, ἀλλ᾽ ἤδη περὶ τῆς τῶν
Ἀμφισσέων τιμωρίας. ἤδη δὲ πόρρω τῆς ἡμέρας οὔσης προελθὼν ὁ κῆρυξ ἀνεῖπε, Δελφῶν ὅσοι ἐπὶ διετες ἡβῶσι, καὶ δούλους καὶ ἐλευθέρους, ἥκειν ἅμα τῇ ἡμέρᾳ ἔχοντας ἅμας καὶ δικέλ- 5
λας πρὸς τὸ Θύστιον ἐκεῖ καλούμενον· καὶ πάλιν ὁ αὐτὸς κῆρυξ
ἀνηγόρευε τοὺς ἱερομνήμονας καὶ πυλαγόρους ἥκειν εἰς τὸν αὐτὸν
τόπον βοηθήσοντας τῷ θεῷ καὶ τῇ γῇ τῇ ἱερᾷ· " ἥτις δ᾽ ἂν
μὴ παρῇ πόλις, εἴρξεται τοῦ ἱεροῦ καὶ ἐναγὴς ἔσται καὶ τῇ
123 ἀρᾷ ἔνοχος." τῇ δὲ ὑστεραίᾳ ἤκομεν ἕωθεν εἰς τὸν προειρη- 10
μένον τόπον, καὶ κατέβημεν εἰς τὸ Κιρραῖον πεδίον, καὶ τὸν
λιμένα κατασκάψαντες καὶ τὰς οἰκίας ἐμπρήσαντες ἀνεχωροῦμεν. ταῦτα δὲ ἡμῶν πραττόντων οἱ Λοκροὶ οἱ Ἀμφισσεῖς,
ἑξήκοντα στάδια ἄπωθεν οἰκοῦντες Δελφῶν, ἧκον πρὸς ἡμᾶς
μεθ᾽ ὅπλων πανδημεί· καὶ εἰ μὴ δρόμῳ μόλις ἐξεφύγομεν εἰς 15
124 Δελφούς, ἐκινδυνεύσαμεν ἀπολέσθαι. τῇ δὲ ἐπιούσῃ ἡμέρᾳ

---

1. λόγος] ὁ λόγος bekl Bekk.　　　3. οὔσης] 'Immo ὄντος.' Hamak. Vid. annot.
προελθὼν] προσελθὼν libri.　　5. ἅμας] Ita z et editi recentiores : volg. ἅμας.　　6. Θύ-
στιον] Sic Harpocr. s. v.: volg. Θυτεῖον.　　7. ἀνηγόρευε] ἀναγορεύει bekl.　　14. πρὸς
ἡμᾶς] ἐφ᾽ ἡμᾶς bekl Bekk.　　15. μόλις] 'Cum d omiserim.' Frank.　　16. ἐκινδυνεύ-
σαμεν] ἐκινδυνεύσαμεν ἂν bekl Bekk. B. et S.　　Vid. annot.

3. ἤδη δὲ πόρρω τῆς ἡμέρας οὔσης.
'And as the day was far gone by then,'
giving the reason why execution was deferred till next morning, ἅμα τῇ ἡμέρᾳ.
The construction πόρρω εἶναι, 'to be far
advanced,' does not seem to occur elsewhere, and perhaps could not have been
used except in the genitive, which connects
it with such phrases as πρόσω τῆς νυκτὸς
Hdt. 2. 121. 4. Indeed, it might be suspected that this is the construction here,
οὔσης being feminine only by a sort of attraction, 'it being far on in the day.' See
Plat. Protag. 310 C.
4. ὅσοι ἐπὶ διετες ἡβῶσι. The sense of
this phrase has been much disputed, from
Harpocration's time onward : some take it
of youths from 16 to 18, others from 18 to
20, others of all above 18. It is now established that at Athens at any rate only
those between 16 and 18 were said ἡβᾶν, at
18 they were said ἐφηβεῦσαι, were sworn at
the temple of Aglauros, and declared of full
age for citizenship, after which they acted
for two years as Περίπολοι τῆς χώρας, and
then probably for the first time entered upon
the enjoyment of full civic rights.
6. Θύστιον. So Harpocr., followed by
B. and S.: the MSS. give Θυτεῖον. Whichever is read, it must be a dialectical form
(ἐκεῖ καλούμενον) for the ' place of sacri-

fice :' καλούμενον is always used of a significant proper name. The temple was
perhaps hardly in use ; or this may have
been the site of the altar just outside it.
9. μὴ παρῇ. Almost ' put in an appearance,' by its legation.
§ 123. Next day, therefore, we went and
destroyed the buildings on the devo'ed land,
and were assailed by the Amphissians.
10. ἤκομεν .. καὶ κατέβημεν. ' We were
ready at the appointed place, and came
down.' The proper sense of ἥκω, and the
proper force of the imperfect, are both preserved.
12. κατασκάψαντες. Destroying and
throwing into the water an embankment of
earth is probably meant. The case with
which the destruction was effected seems to
shew that ἐτείχισαν in § 113, τετειχισμένον
in § 119, are not to be pressed in the sense
of 'fortified,' but simply describe the works
necessary to counteract the effect of ἔχωσαν,
§ 109.
ἀνεχωροῦμεν. 'Started homewards;'
the imperfect, because they were attacked
before they got back.
16. ἐκινδυνεύσαμεν is in itself a conditional word, which accounts for the omission
of ἂν ; for an overwhelming balance of MSS.
do omit it. Or one might otherwise express
it, their danger was an actual fact, though

Κόττυφος ὁ τὰς γνώμας ἐπιψηφίζων ἐκκλησίαν ἐποίει τῶν Ἀμ-
φικτυόνων· ἐκκλησίαν γὰρ ὀνομάζουσιν, ὅταν μὴ μόνον τοὺς πυλαγόρους καὶ τοὺς ἱερομνήμονας συγκαλέσωσιν, ἀλλὰ καὶ τοὺς
συνθύοντας καὶ χρωμένους τῷ θεῷ. ἐνταῦθ᾽ ἤδη πολλαὶ μὲν
5 ἐγίγνοντο τῶν Ἀμφισσέων κατηγορίαι, πολὺς δ᾽ ἔπαινος ἦν
κατὰ τῆς ἡμετέρας πόλεως· τέλος δὲ παντὸς τοῦ λόγου ψηφί-
ζονται ἥκειν τοὺς ἱερομνήμονας πρὸ τῆς ἐπιούσης πυλαίας ἐν
ῥητῷ χρόνῳ εἰς Πύλας, ἔχοντας δόγμα, καθ᾽ ὅ τι δίκας δώσουσιν οἱ Ἀμφισσεῖς ὑπὲρ ὧν εἰς τὸν θεὸν καὶ τὴν γῆν τὴν ἱερὰν
10 καὶ τοὺς Ἀμφικτύονας ἐξήμαρτον. ὅτι δὲ ἀληθῆ λέγω, ἀναγνώσεται ὑμῖν ὁ γραμματεὺς τὸ ψήφισμα.

ΨΗΦΙΣΜΑ.

Τοῦ δόγματος οὖν τούτου ἀποδοθέντος ὑφ᾽ ἡμῶν ἐν τῇ βουλῇ 125
καὶ πάλιν ἐν τῇ ἐκκλησίᾳ τῷ δήμῳ, καὶ τὰς πράξεις ἡμῶν ἀποδεξα-
15 μένου τοῦ δήμου καὶ τῆς πόλεως πάσης προαιρουμένης εὐσεβεῖν,
καὶ Δημοσθένους ὑπὲρ τοῦ μεσεγγυήματος τοῦ ἐξ Ἀμφίσσης

2. ὅταν μὴ μόνον .. συγκαλέσωσιν] ὅταν τις μὴ μόνον συγκαλέσῃ bekl. Bekk.
5. ἐγίγνοντο τῶν Ἀμφισσέων] τῶν Ἀμφισσέων ἐγίνοντο fcd bekl Bekk.   13. οὖν]
Om. afd bekl.   ἐν τῇ βουλῇ] τῇ βουλῇ bekl Bekk.   14. τῷ δήμῳ] Om. a B. et S.
Frank.   16. ὑπὲρ] † ὑπο g †.

their running away prevented their destruction ; so that he might have said εἰ μὴ δρόμῳ μόλις ἐξεφύγομεν εἰς Δελφοὺς, ἀπωλό-
μεθ᾽ ἄν, but not ἐκινδυνεύσαμεν ἄν, for
ἐκινδυνεύσαμεν, even as it was.

§ 124. *The day after, it was resolved in
full assembly to hold an extraordinary Amphictyonic meeting to judge the case of the
Amphissians.*

2. ἐκκλησίαν γὰρ ὀνομάζουσιν. This
form of Assembly recalls the Homeric Agora,
and is identical in constitution with the Assembly of the Achaian League, which con-
sisted of the delegates of the several states
and all members of the League present in the
city where the congress happened to be held.

7. ἐν ῥητῷ χρόνῳ. So § 126 fin., δς ἐξ
ἀνάγκης πρὸ τοῦ καθήκοντος ἔμελλε χρόνου
γίγνεσθαι. The 'necessity' is not apparent,
and Aeschines seems to admit that the irregularity was a serious one, requiring considerable apology. Probably the exclusion
of the Phocians and destruction of their
cities (in direct violation of the primitive
Amphictyonic league, Ae. de F. L. § 121,
p. 43) had demoralised the Assembly, and
destroyed any religious veneration that it
may ever have commanded, except in the
mind of bigots like Aeschines. Cp. D. de
Pace, fin.

8. ἔχοντας δόγμα. 'With instructions;'

'bringing a decision with them' from their
respective states. At first the Amphictyons
had simply cleared the holy ground from
profane occupatiqn ; as the Amphissians per-
sisted in the profanation, it was necessary to
consult the states upon ulterior measures,
which would require their support.

δίκας δώσουσιν. So most and best
MSS.: Franke δίκην. The sense is not ' to
be punished,' but ' to be judged,' and therefore δίκας is right. The question was, in
the first instance, what issue should be
placed before what court. Incidentally, no
doubt, the Amphictyons in deciding this
would decide the penalty.

11. ὁ γραμματεύς. Some suspect this as
a gloss: cp. ad § 15. But it is foolish to
assume such absolute uniformity in expression.

§ 125. *The Amphictyons' resolution was
approved at Athens ; but Demosthenes' intrigues*

14. ἀποδεξαμένου. Note the vagueness
of the word : the report was ' favourably received,' but he cannot pretend that any
action was taken on it.

16. μεσεγγυήματος τοῦ ἐξ Ἀμφίσσης.
The sum placed in his hands by the Amphissians : above, § 114. Strictly, a pledge de-
posited by a party to a suit in the hands of
a third party, something like the Roman
sacramentum; here nearly = 'a retaining fee.'

ἀντιλέγοντος καὶ ἐμοῦ φανερῶς ἐναντίον ὑμῶν ἐξελέγχοντος, ἐπειδὴ ἐκ τοῦ φανεροῦ τὴν πόλιν ἄνθρωπος οὐκ ἐδύνατο σφῆλαι,
εἰσελθὼν εἰς τὸ βουλευτήριον καὶ μεταστησάμενος τοὺς ἰδιώτας
ἐκφέρεται προβούλευμα εἰς τὴν ἐκκλησίαν, προσλαβὼν τὴν τοῦ
126 γράψαντος ἀπειρίαν· τὸ δ᾽ αὐτὸ τοῦτο καὶ ἐν τῇ ἐκκλησίᾳ διε- 5
πράξατο ἐπιψηφισθῆναι καὶ γενέσθαι δήμου ψήφισμα ἤδη
ἐπαναστάσης τῆς ἐκκλησίας, ἀπεληλυθότος ἐμοῦ, οὗ γὰρ ἄν
ποτε ἐπέτρεψα, καὶ τῶν πολλῶν δὲ ἀφειμένων· οὗ τὸ κεφάλαιόν
ἐστι "τὸν δὲ ἱερομνήμονα" φησὶ "τῶν Ἀθηναίων καὶ τοὺς
πυλαγόρους τοὺς ἀεὶ πυλαγοροῦντας πορεύεσθαι εἰς Πύλας καὶ 10
εἰς Δελφοὺς ἐν τοῖς τεταγμένοις χρόνοις ὑπὸ τῶν προγόνων,"
εὐπρεπῶς γε τῷ ὀνόματι, ἀλλὰ τῷ ἔργῳ αἰσχρῶς· κωλύει γὰρ
εἰς τὸν σύλλογον τὸν ἐν Πύλαις ἀπαντᾶν, ὃς ἐξ ἀνάγκης πρὸ
127 τοῦ καθήκοντος ἔμελλε χρόνου γίγνεσθαι. καὶ πάλιν ἐν τῷ

2. ἄνθρωπος] ἄνθρωπος libri.　　6. δήμου ψήφισμα] Baitero et Sauppio ' δήμου
glossema videtur esse,' Frankio ' certe τοῦ δήμου ψήφισμα scribendum.' τοῦ δήμου τὸ ψήφισμα habent fcd : δήμου non glossema esse, sed πάντων ἐμφατικώτατον, pro certo habe-
mus.　　ἤδη ἐπαναστάσης] ἐπ᾽ ἀναστάσει bekl, haud absurde. Probat Hamaker, modo
post ἐκκλησίας addatur οὔσης : quod certe elegantius.　　8. δὲ ἀφειμένων] Ita fcd Frank.:
ceteri διαφειμένων.　　9. τὸν δὲ ἱερομνήμονα] δὲ om. agmnbekl B. et S.

2. ἄνθρωπος. An easy and probable correction, though denounced as childish by
Reiske and Bremi : cp. ad § 98. But ἄνθρωπος is not impossible, ' finding the city
too wise for one fellow to ruin it,' he tried
to make many fools do the work one knave
could not.

3. εἰσελθὼν εἰς τὸ βουλευτήριον. Was
he a senator again (cp. §§ 3, 73, which
make it not unlikely that tricks in the lottery
were winked at, to secure the presence of
experienced statesmen), or was he, as a
Past Member or as an important person,
admitted to confer with the Senate? μεταστησάμενος τοὺς ἰδιώτας proves that he
went in some official capacity ; but for the
presence of ἰδιῶται cp. D. de F. L. § 19,
p. 346.

4. ἐκφέρεται κ.τ.λ. ' Comes down with
a draught decree, got by availing himself of
the inexperience of the mover :' προσλαβὼν,
' taking it as an ally.' The fact that he did
not move it himself seems to indicate that
he was not a member. ἐκφέρειν is the technical word for ' bringing down' a προβούλευμα to the ἐκκλησία : cp. Orat. in Neaer.
p. 1346, § 4. Here the middle is used, because Demosthenes ' gets the motion brought
down' by the original mover, instead of
bringing it down himself, as Apollodorus did
l. c., who was himself a senator.

§ 126. Carried in disguise a resolution
not to send representatives to the extraordinary Amphictyonic meeting.

6. καὶ γενέσθαι δήμου ψήφισμα. Instead of a προβούλευμα binding on nobody,
and for which the mover might he held responsible. The point is, that though the
people were not fairly consulted on the
question, yet Demosthenes managed to get
them involved in at least material, if not
formal sacrilege ; a point that would be
heightened if we read τοῦ δήμου τὸ ψήφισμα, with one group of MSS.

8. ἀφειμένων, or διαφειμένων, whichever
we read, is ambiguous, like ἀποδεξαμένου.
For Aeschines cannot mean that the assembly was dismissed, because he says τῶν πολλῶν. He can only mean, they had dispersed
with a clear conscience, thinking business
was over. If we had any evidence of semi-
official party ' whips' at Athens, one might
conclude that these had given leave to go.
Demosthenes asserts that Aeschines' own
election as Pylagoras was similarly managed,
De Cor. § 189.

9. τὸν δὲ ἱερομνήμονα. Cp. sup. ad § 74.
τοὺς πυλαγόρους τοὺς ἀεὶ πυλαγοροῦντας. ' The Pylagori for the time being,'
opposed to the Hieromnemon, who held
office for life.

12. κωλύει γὰρ might be quasi-impersonal, or refer to τὸ ψήφισμα ; but from the
following γράφει and φησὶ of the next section, it seems likelier that the subject is the
same as that of διεπράξατο.

§ 127. And even denounced it in terms, or,
in other words, defied the God and the curse.

αὐτῷ ψηφίσματι πολὺ καὶ σαφέστερον καὶ πικρότερον σύγ-
γραμμα γράφει " τὸν ἱερομνήμονα " φησὶ " τῶν Ἀθηναίων καὶ
τοὺς πυλαγόρους τοὺς ἀεὶ πυλαγοροῦντας μὴ μετέχειν τοῖς ἐκεῖ
συλλεγομένοις μήτε λόγων μήτε ἔργων μήτε δογμάτων μήτε
5 πράξεως μηδεμιᾶς.᾽ τὸ δὲ μὴ μετέχειν τί ἐστι; πότερα τἀληθὲς εἴπω ἢ τὸ ἥδιστον ἀκοῦσαι; τὸ ἀληθὲς ἐρῶ· τὸ γὰρ ἀεὶ
πρὸς ἡδονὴν λεγόμενον οὑτωσὶ τὴν πόλιν διατέθεικεν. οὐκ ἐᾷ
μεμνῆσθαι τῶν ὅρκων, οὓς ἡμῶν οἱ πρόγονοι ὤμοσαν, οὐδὲ τῆς
ἀρᾶς οὐδὲ τῆς τοῦ θεοῦ μαντείας.
10 Ἡμεῖς μὲν οὖν, ὦ Ἀθηναῖοι, κατεμείναμεν διὰ τοῦτο τὸ 128
ψήφισμα, οἱ δ᾽ ἄλλοι Ἀμφικτύονες συνελέγησαν εἰς Πύλας
πλὴν μιᾶς πόλεως, ἧς ἐγὼ οὔτ᾽ ἂν τοὔνομα εἴποιμι, μήθ᾽ αἱ
συμφοραὶ παραπλήσιοι γένοιντο αὐτῆς μηδενὶ τῶν Ἑλλήνων.
καὶ συνελθόντες ἐψηφίσαντο ἐπιστρατεύειν ἐπὶ τοὺς Ἀμφισ-
15 σέας, καὶ στρατηγὸν εἵλοντο Κόττυφον τὸν Φαρσάλιον τὸν
τότε τὰς γνώμας ἐπιψηφίζοντα, οὐκ ἐπιδημοῦντος ἐν Μακεδονίᾳ Φιλίππου, ἀλλ᾽ οὐδ᾽ ἐν τῇ Ἑλλάδι παρόντος, ἀλλ᾽ ἐν
Σκύθαις οὕτω μακρὰν ἀπόντος· ὃν αὐτίκα μάλα τολμήσει λέγειν
Δημοσθένης ὡς ἐγὼ ἐπὶ τοὺς Ἕλληνας ἐπήγαγον. καὶ παρελ- 129
20 θόντες τῇ πρώτῃ στρατείᾳ καὶ μάλα μετρίως ἐχρήσαντο τοῖς
Ἀμφισσεῦσιν· ἀντὶ γὰρ τῶν μεγίστων ἀδικημάτων χρήμασιν
αὐτοὺς ἐζημίωσαν, καὶ ταῦτ᾽ ἐν ῥητῷ χρόνῳ προεῖπον τῷ θεῷ
καταθεῖναι, καὶ τοὺς μὲν ἐναγεῖς καὶ τῶν πεπραγμένων αἰτίους

---

1. σύγγραμμα] πρόσταγμα *hekl*, γρ. *gm*.   3. ἐκεῖ] ἐκεῖσε *hekl* Bekk. : idque nunc
probat Frankius.   Mox pro primo μήτε *agmufcd* habent μή.   6. τὸ ἀληθὲς] τἀληθὲς
restitui Frankius jubet : quod librorum solus habet *e*.   7. λεγόμενον] ' Nescio an corrup-
tum sit.' Frank.   διατέθεικεν] διέθηκεν *agmn*.   18. τολμήσει] τολμήσειε *agmn*.

---

7. οὑτωσὶ τὴν πόλιν διατέθεικεν. 'Has
brought the city to its present state.'
Though claiming to be a personal friend of
Alexander, Aeschines does not refuse to
regret the subjection of Athens to him.
   οὐκ ἐᾷ. If taken in the ordinary sense,
'it bids you not remember,' the subject
must be τὸ ψήφισμα rather than τὸ μὴ μετέχειν : if the latter is the real subject, οὐκ ἐᾷ
must be in the literal sense, 'it cuts you off
from remembering.'
   § 128. *So the synod met, without us or
the Thebans; and marched on the Amphissians, without Philip.*
   12. πλὴν μιᾶς πόλεως. Thebes,—being
grateful for the subservience of the Amphissians. That they would co-operate with
Athens against the Amphictyons was not yet
certain.

14. ἐψηφίσαντο ἐπιστρατεύειν. This
went beyond the resolution of the preceding
synod ; which may be explained by the absence of Thebes.
   16. τότε. 'On the former occasion.'
   οὐκ ἐπιδημοῦντος κ.τ.λ. (This was
not, as Demosthenes will insinuate, at Philip's
instigation, since) 'he was not at home in
Macedonia, but had not come down into
Greece either ; he was in Scythia, all that
way off.' If Philip had been at home he
might have instigated the Amphictyonic
execution, if he had been in Greece he
might even have shared in it ; as it was,
the charge against me of bringing him into
Greece is absurd.
   § 129. *They at first inflicted the mildest
penalty possible; but the Amphissians being
still refractory, they had to invoke Philip.*

μετεστήσαντο, τοὺς δὲ δι᾽ εὐσέβειαν φυγόντας κατήγαγον. ἐπειδὴ δὲ οὔτε τὰ χρήματα ἐξέτινον τῷ θεῷ τούς τ᾽ ἐναγεῖς κατήγαγον καὶ τοὺς εὐσεβεῖς κατελθόντας διὰ τῶν Ἀμφικτυόνων
ἐξέβαλον, οὕτως ἤδη τὴν δευτέραν ἐπὶ τοὺς Ἀμφισσέας στρατείαν ἐποιήσαντο, πολλῷ χρόνῳ ὕστερον, ἐπανεληλυθότος Φιλίπ- 5
που ἐκ τῆς ἐπὶ τοὺς Σκύθας στρατείας, τῶν μὲν θεῶν τὴν ἡγεμονίαν τῆς εὐσεβείας ἡμῖν παραδεδωκότων, τῆς δὲ Δημοσθένους
δωροδοκίας ἐμποδὼν γεγενημένης.

130   Ἀλλ᾽ οὐ προὔλεγον, οὐ προεσήμαινον ἡμῖν οἱ θεοὶ φυλάξασθαι, μόνον γε οὐκ ἀνθρώπων φωνὰς προσκτησάμενοι; οὐδε- 10
μίαν τοι πώποτε ἔγωγε μᾶλλον πόλιν ἑώρακα ὑπὸ μὲν τῶν
θεῶν σωζομένην, ὑπὸ δὲ τῶν ῥητόρων ἐνίων ἀπολλυμένην. οὐχ
ἱκανὸν ἦν τὸ τοῖς μυστηρίοις φανὲν σημεῖον φυλάξασθαι, ἢ τῶν
μυστῶν τελευτή; οὐ περὶ τούτων Ἀμεινιάδης μὲν προὔλεγεν
εὐλαβεῖσθαι καὶ πέμπειν εἰς Δελφοὺς ἐπερησομένους τὸν θεόν, 15
ὅ τι χρὴ πράττειν, Δημοσθένης δὲ ἀντέλεγε φιλιππίζειν τὴν Πυ-
θίαν φάσκων, ἀπαίδευτος ὢν καὶ ἀπολαύων καὶ ἐμπιπλάμενος

---

1. φυγόντας] φεύγοντας bekl Cobet., probante Frankio.   2. οὔτε] οὐδὲ agmnfcd.
4. ἐξέβαλον] Ita abekl : ἐξέβαλον εἰς Χερόνειαν g; ceteri ἐξέβαλλον.   ἐπὶ τοὺς Ἀμ-
φισσέας] Post στρατείαν ponunt agmn : 'puto glossema esse' Spp. Ἀμφισσεῖς scribunt
agmnzfcd B. et S.   10. μόνον γε οὐκ] μόνον οὐκ agmnfd B. et S. Frank.   13 φανὲν]
† φάμεν pr. g †.   φυλάξασθαι] 'Malim abesse' Bait., idemque censent Scheib. et
Hamaker.

---

1. μετεστήσαντο. Perhaps a euphemism
for ἐξήλασαν ; perhaps it is meant that they
withdrew without waiting for a sentence.
In Orat. c. Aristog. 2, § 7, p. 802, it is
used of ostracism.
  τοὺς δι᾽ εὐσέβειαν φυγόντας. The
anti-Theban party, we may presume,—expelled after the sacrilege.
  5. πολλῷ χρόνῳ ὕστερον. Measured
by the next words, ἐπανεληλυθότος Φιλίππου κ.τ.λ.
  6. τῶν μὲν θεῶν .. ἡμῖν παραδεδωκότων.
Not only had Solon of old, and Aeschines
now, taken the lead in denouncing the
sacrilege, but while Philip was absent, and
Thebes recusant, Athens would have been
the most powerful state in the confederacy.
  § 130. Thus Demosthenes led us on, in
spite of the warnings of the Gods,
  10. μόνον γε οὐκ. B. and S. and Franke
omit γε, with most MSS. But μόνον οὐκ is
such a common expression, that the omission
of γε in the middle of it is an easier error
than its insertion, while here it has a peculiar force. The sense is not merely ' having
all but taken a human voice to tell you,' but
' having done everything to warn you, ex-

cept gain men to speak on their side.' This
gives a good meaning to προσκτησάμενοι
(which Bekker and one or two other editors
wish to correct to προηγκάμενοι, a rare though
not impossible form), and harmonises better
with the next words.
  13. φυλάξασθαι. ' Malim abesse,' Baiter,
followed by several other critics ; and it
does look like a weak repetition from the
first clause of the section. If genuine, it
depends on σημεῖον rather than ἱκανόν ; 'was
not that enough as a sign to be careful,
which was shewn us at the Mysteries ?'
  ἡ τῶν μυστῶν τελευτή. One or two
of them were seized by a shark, while puri-
fying themselves in the sea.
  16. φιλιππίζειν. Formed on the analogy
of Μηδίζειν, Λακωνίζειν, Βοιωτιάζειν, etc.
There is no previous case of such a verb
formed from a personal name, except Κυψελ-
λίζειν in Theognis, 890. It occurs two or
three times in Demosthenes, e. g. De Cor.
§ 226.
  17. ἀπαίδευτος. The insinuation is,
' never taught to say his prayers.'
  ἀπολαύων καὶ ἐμπιπλάμενος. ' Glut-
ting himself with the enjoyment of the
licence you gave him.'

τῆς διδομένης ὑφ᾽ ὑμῶν αὐτῷ ἐξουσίας ; οὐ τὸ τελευταῖον 131
ἀθύτων καὶ ἀκαλλιερήτων τῶν ἱερῶν ὄντων ἐξέπεμψε τοὺς στρατιώτας ἐπὶ τὸν πρόδηλον κίνδυνον ; καίτοι γε πρῴην ἀπετόλ-
μησε λέγειν, ὅτι παρὰ τοῦτο Φίλιππος οὐκ ἦλθεν ἡμῶν ἐπὶ
5 τὴν χώραν, ὅτι οὐκ ἦν αὐτῷ καλὰ τὰ ἱερά. τίνος οὖν ζημίας
ἄξιος εἰ τυχεῖν, ὦ τῆς Ἑλλάδος ἀλιτήριε ; εἰ γὰρ ὁ μὲν κρατῶν
οὐκ ἦλθεν εἰς τὴν τῶν κρατουμένων χώραν, ὅτι οὐκ ἦν αὐτῷ
καλὰ τὰ ἱερά, σὺ δ᾽ οὐδὲν προειδὼς τῶν μελλόντων ἔσεσθαι
πρὶν καλλιερῆσαι τοὺς στρατιώτας ἐξέπεμψας, πότερον στεφα-
10 νοῦσθαί σε δεῖ ἐπὶ ταῖς τῆς πόλεως ἀτυχίαις ἢ ὑπερωρίσθαι ;

Τοιγάρτοι τί τῶν ἀνελπίστων καὶ ἀπροσδοκήτων ἐφ᾽ ἡμῶν 132
οὐ γέγονεν ; οὐ γὰρ βίον γε ἡμεῖς ἀνθρώπινον βεβιώκαμεν,
ἀλλ᾽ εἰς παραδοξολογίαν τοῖς ἐσομένοις μεθ᾽ ἡμᾶς ἔφυμεν. οὐχ
ὁ μὲν τῶν Περσῶν βασιλεύς, ὁ τὸν Ἄθω διορύξας, ὁ τὸν Ἑλλή-
15 σποντον ζεύξας, ὁ γῆν καὶ ὕδωρ τοὺς Ἕλληνας αἰτῶν, ὁ τολμῶν ἐν ταῖς ἐπιστολαῖς γράφειν, ὅτι δεσπότης ἐστὶν ἁπάντων
ἀνθρώπων ἀφ᾽ ἡλίου ἀνιόντος μέχρι δυομένου, νῦν οὐ περὶ τοῦ
κύριος ἑτέρων εἶναι διαγωνίζεται, ἀλλ᾽ ἤδη περὶ τῆς τοῦ σώ-

---

1. διδομένης] δεδομένης g, superscr. m, et bekl.   2. τῶν ἱερῶν ὄντων] ὄντων τῶν
ἱερῶν bekl Bekk.   ἐξέπεμψε] ἐξέπεμπε gmn.   4. ἐπὶ τὴν χώραν] εἰς τὴν χώραν bkl
Bekk. Vid. annot.   5. ζημίας ἄξιος εἰ] εἰ σὺ ζημίας ἄξιος bekl Bekk.   13. ἐσο-
μένοις] Post ἡμᾶς poiunt bkl et (qui ἐσόμενοι scribit) e : omitti volt Cobet.   14. Ἄθω]
Ἄθων b Bekk.   18. ἑτέρων] Om. agmn B. et S.

---

§ 131. *Even as at Chaeroneia he courted
defeat by defying the omens, while Philip
obeyed them after victory.*

2. ἀθύτων καὶ ἀκαλλιερήτων. The
second as a consequence of the first. If
something interrupted the proper oblation of
the sacrifices (e. g. if the offerings would
not burn) they would be ἀκαλλιέρητα.

3. πρῴην. Perhaps at some time when
the difficulties of Alexander's position (cp.
below, §§ 163 sqq.) had encouraged him to
depreciate the strength of Macedon. Else
we might suppose that Demosthenes retorted
on the party who boasted of Philip's clem-
ency, or depreciated his own works of defence, ' Oh, of course he was too pious to
attack us when the sacrifices were against us.'

4. ἐπὶ τὴν χώραν. Volg. et Bekk. εἰς ;
a more natural expression in general, but the
MS. reading suits the actual circumstances
better. The battle was not on the Athenian
frontier, so that it was open to the victor to
march *into* Attica, but so far off that it was
a question whether to march *upon* Attica.

6. τῆς Ἑλλάδος ἀλιτήριε. ' With the
blood of Greece upon thy head.'

8. σὺ δ᾽ οὐδὲν προειδώς. Whereas
Philip after the battle might calculate that

the chances against him were exhausted.

10. ἢ ὑπερωρίσθαι. ' Or to have been
carried beyond our borders *long ago*,' as an
unclean thing (ἀλιτήριος). Cp. § 245.

§ 132. *Therefore the Gods have turned
everything upside down : the great king is
a fugitive, overthrown by the champion of
religion,*

11. τοιγάρτοι. ' Therefore,' i. e. as this
was not done ; or, generally, as no regard
was paid to the warnings of the Gods.

12. ἀνθρώπινον. With limited and cal-
culable chances.

14. ὁ τὸν Ἄθω .. αἰτῶν. The king is
treated as a *perpetua persona,* and both the
individual acts (διορύξας, ζεύξας) of Xerxes,
and the permanent policy (αἰτῶν) of Darius
and his son, the permanent style (τολμῶν) of
all the kings, are ascribed to the unlucky
Codomannus.

18. ἑτέρων. Necessary to the sense, but
omitted by Baiter and Sauppe, in accordance
with their canon, that an interpolation is
always to be suspected rather than an accidental omission in any decent MS.

ἀλλ᾽ ἤδη περὶ τῆς .. σωτηρίας. In
fact he was probably already dead, though
it was not known at Athens.

ματος σωτηρίας; καὶ τοὺς αὐτοὺς ὁρῶμεν τῆς τε δόξης ταύτης
καὶ τῆς ἐπὶ τὸν Πέρσην ἡγεμονίας ἠξιωμένους, οἳ καὶ τὸ ἐν
133 Δελφοῖς ἱερὸν ἠλευθέρωσαν; Θῆβαι δέ, Θῆβαι, πόλις ἀστυγεί-
τῶν, μεθ' ἡμέραν μίαν ἐκ μέσης τῆς Ἑλλάδος ἀνήρπασται, εἰ
καὶ δικαίως, περὶ τῶν ὅλων οὐκ ὀρθῶς βουλευσάμενοι, ἀλλὰ 5
τήν γε θεοβλάβειαν καὶ τὴν ἀφροσύνην οὐκ ἀνθρωπίνως, ἀλλὰ
δαιμονίως κτησάμενοι. Λακεδαιμόνιοι δ' οἱ ταλαίπωροι, προσαψάμενοι μόνον τούτων τῶν πραγμάτων ἐξ ἀρχῆς περὶ τὴν
τοῦ ἱεροῦ κατάληψιν, οἱ τῶν Ἑλλήνων ποτὲ ἀξιοῦντες ἡγεμόνες εἶναι, νῦν ὁμηρεύσοντες καὶ τῆς συμφορᾶς ἐπίδειξιν ποιη- 10
σόμενοι μέλλουσιν ὡς Ἀλέξανδρον ἀναπέμπεσθαι, τοῦτο πει-
σόμενοι καὶ αὐτοὶ καὶ ἡ πατρίς, ὅ τι ἂν ἐκείνῳ δόξῃ, καὶ ἐν τῇ
134 τοῦ κρατοῦντος καὶ προηδικημένου μετριότητι κριθήσονται. ἡ
δ' ἡμετέρα πόλις, ἡ κοινὴ καταφυγὴ τῶν Ἑλλήνων, πρὸς ἣν
ἀφικνοῦντο πρότερον ἐκ τῆς Ἑλλάδος αἱ πρεσβεῖαι, κατὰ 15
πόλεις ἕκαστοι παρ' ἡμῶν τὴν σωτηρίαν εὑρησόμενοι, νῦν οὐκέτι περὶ τῆς τῶν Ἑλλήνων ἡγεμονίας ἀγωνίζεται, ἀλλ' ἤδη
περὶ τοῦ τῆς πατρίδος ἐδάφους. καὶ ταῦθ' ἡμῖν συμβέβηκεν

---

3. Θῆβαι alterum om. *afcd.*
etiam Herodian. et Longinus.
κριθήσονται] κριθησόμενοι *bekl* Bekk.:
14. τῶν Ἑλλήνων] † in *g* erasa sunt †.
ὑμῖν *agmnfd.*

4. μεθ' ἡμέραν μίαν] Om. Demetr., μίαν om.
13. κρατοῦντος καὶ] † in *g* erasum est †.
† in *g* lineola per literas -σονται ducta est †.
16. ἡμῶν] ὑμῶν *ekl.*   18. ἡμῖν]
vulgate κριθησόμενοι.

1. τῆς τε δόξης ταύτης refers back to
§ 129, τῶν μὲν θεῶν τὴν ἡγεμονίαν κ.τ.λ.
§ 133. *Thebes for their sacrilege blotted
out from the map of Greece, Sparta ruined
for their slight share in it,*
5. περὶ τῶν ὅλων. The general interest
of Greece; also the whole course of their
policy.
6. οὐκ ἀνθρωπίνως. Their punishment
came by the heaven-sent madness that made
them rebel against Alexander: their guilt
was in their aid and comfort to the sacrilegious Amphissians. It is also probably
meant, that this guilt came from a heaven-
sent infatuation: for it was unlike their old
policy; they had resisted and avenged the
sacrilege of the Phocians, and prospered in
so doing.
7. προσαψάμενοι μόνον. ' Though they
did but touch...' As they owed 1000
talents to the Amphictyons for their treacherous attack on the Cadmea, they had supported Phocis at the beginning of the war,
and aided them, like the Athenians, to the
extent of purely defensive measures. Aeschines intimates in the next section, that
Athens was guilty to the same slight extent.
13. κριθήσονται. So most MSS. for the

The sense has a
shade of difference, the indic. implying more
decidedly than the partic. would, that they
will get the benefit of Alexander's merciful
disposition.
§ 134. *We deprived of everything but our
independence for ours: all during Demosthenes' career.*
14. ἡ κοινὴ καταφυγή. Having sheltered
the Heraclids, and the Ionians of Peloponnesus after them : having freed the Greeks
from both Persian and Spartan tyranny in
the days of Aristides. It is hardly likely
that Aeschines refers (as Demosthenes does,
De Cor. § 121) to the way that Athens
interposed to save Thebes from Sparta in
the campaign of Leuctra, and Sparta from
Thebes in that of Mantinea; it is characteristic of his mind to recur rather to mythical
or semi-mythical illustrations than to recent
historical ones.
18. καὶ ταῦθ' ἡμῖν. Most MSS. have
ὑμῖν, but no editor appears to have accepted
it. It would be rather offensive in point of
taste; instead of expressing sympathy with
his country's misfortunes, he would seem to
taunt his countrymen, 'It serves you right
for trusting Demosthenes.' But it is not

F

ἐξ ὅτου Δημοσθένης πρὸς τὴν πολιτείαν προσελήλυθεν. εὖ
γὰρ περὶ τῶν τοιούτων Ἡσίοδος ὁ ποιητὴς ἀποφαίνεται. λέγει γάρ που, παιδεύων τὰ πλήθη καὶ συμβουλεύων ταῖς πόλεσι
τοὺς πονηροὺς τῶν δημαγωγῶν μὴ προσδέχεσθαι. λέξω δὲ
5 κἀγὼ τὰ ἔπη· διὰ τοῦτο γὰρ οἶμαι παῖδας ὄντας ἡμᾶς τὰς 135
τῶν ποιητῶν γνώμας ἐκμανθάνειν, ἵν' ἄνδρες ὄντες αὐταῖς χρώ-
μεθα.

πολλάκι δὴ ξύμπασα πόλις κακοῦ ἀνδρὸς ἀπηύρα,
ὅς κεν ἀλιτραίνῃ καὶ ἀτάσθαλα μηχανάαται.
10 τοῖσιν δ' οὐρανόθεν μέγ' ἐπήγαγε πῆμα Κρονίων, ,
λιμὸν ὁμοῦ καὶ λοιμόν, ἀποφθινύθουσι δὲ λαοί·
ἢ τῶν γε στρατὸν εὐρὺν ἀπώλεσεν ἢ ὅ γε τεῖχος,
ἢ νέας ἐν πόντῳ ἀποτίνυται εὐρύοπα Ζεύς.

ἐὰν δὲ περιελόντες τοῦ ποιητοῦ τὸ μέτρον τὰς γνώμας ἐξετά- 136
15 ζητε, οἶμαι ὑμῖν δόξειν οὐ ποιήματα Ἡσιόδου εἶναι, ἀλλὰ
χρησμὸν εἰς τὴν Δημοσθένους πολιτείαν· καὶ γὰρ ναυτικὴ καὶ
πεζὴ στρατιὰ καὶ πόλεις ἄρδην εἰσὶν ἀνηρπασμέναι ἐκ τῆς
τούτου πολιτείας.

10. μέγ' ἐπήγαγε πῆμα] μέγα πῆμα ἔδωκε teste Bekk. ekl, testibus nobis etiam g.
μέγα πῆμα δῶκε amn (hic quidem verbo supra addito) fcdq et teste Bekk. g. μεγ' ἐπήγαγε
πῆμα b, Ald., codd. Hesiodi secuti : μέγ' ἐπήλασε πῆμα Plut. πῆμα μέγα δῶκε p : 'Fort.
δῶκεν μέγα πῆμα' Spp. 11. Post λαοί b add. οὐδὲ γυναῖκες τίκτουσιν, μινύθουσι δὲ
οἶκοι, [Ζηνὸς φρασμοσύνῃσιν Ὀλυμπίου, ἄλλοτε δ' αὖτε, e textu Hesiodi. 13. ἢ ..
πόντῳ] ἢ νῆας ἐν πόντῳ teste Bekk. ae, testibus nobis etiam g, ἢ νῆας ἐνὶ πόντῳ ceteri
scripti et Bekk. Aldina pro toto versu habet ἢ νέας ἐν πόντῳ Κρονίδης ἀποτίνυται αὐτῶν, ut
legitur in textu Hesiodi. ἀποτίνυται εὐρύοπα Ζεὺς B. et S. In pb τίννυται scriptum est,
in ekl τείνυται, in ceteris τίνυται.

certain that Aeschines was incapable of this
fault. If ἡμῖν be read, it will mean not
'Athens,' but 'the present generation.'

2. λέγει γάρ που. 'Works and Days,'
vv. 245 sqq.

3. τὰ πλήθη. Aeschines treats the poet
as if he had written in reference to a state
of things like that of his own age. But
Hesiod's political philosophy (if it may be
called so) is addressed to corrupt oligarchies,
not misguided democracies; and his notion
of the dangerous citizen is rather the oppressive and unjust lord than the unprincipled demagogue.

§§ 135, 136. Demosthenes is the sinner
whom Hesiod describes as the bane of a state.

4. λέξω δὲ κἀγὼ κ.τ.λ. Aeschines seems
to apologise for reciting the passage himself,
instead of letting it be read by the scribe;
while at the same time he fishes for a compliment to his powers of memory and apt
quotation, and no doubt to his fine recital
also. Apparently Lycurgus recites himself

the long and miscellaneous extracts in his
speech against Leocrates, with the same object, of representing himself as the champion
of the wisdom of the ancients. In the
Timarchus, Aeschines had been content to
have Homer read.

One might take κἀγὼ as pointing a parallel
to λέγει γάρ που, 'in Hesiod's words, which
I will make my own.' The two first verses
are quoted by Aeschines also in De F. L.
§ 168, p. 49.

The third and last lines of the extract are
corrupt. The reading of the text for the
former is that of one MS., the Aldine edition, and of the known text of Hesiod; and
is preferred because the common reading of
the MSS. here, μέγα πῆμα δῶκε, will not
scan. As to the latter, the text is the nearest
to the MS. reading, ἢ νῆας ἐνὶ πόντῳ τίννυται εὐρύοπα Ζεύς, that will scan decently.

14. περιελόντες .. τὸ μέτρον. One does
not see why this should be necessary. Would
not the oracle have been in hexameters?

137 Ἀλλ', οἶμαι, οὔτε Φρυνώνδας οὔτε Εὐρύβατος οὔτ' ἄλλος
οὐδεὶς πώποτε τῶν πάλαι πονηρῶν τοιοῦτος μάγος καὶ γόης
ἐγένετο, ὅς, ὦ γῆ καὶ θεοὶ καὶ δαίμονες καὶ ἄνθρωποι, ὅσοι
βούλεσθε ἀκούειν τἀληθῆ, τολμᾷ λέγειν βλέπων εἰς τὰ πρόσωπα τὰ ὑμέτερα, ὡς ἄρα Θηβαῖοι τὴν συμμαχίαν ὑμῖν ἐποιή- 5
σαντο οὐ διὰ τὸν καιρόν, οὐ διὰ τὸν φόβον τὸν περιστάντα
αὐτούς, οὐ διὰ τὴν ὑμετέραν δόξαν, ἀλλὰ διὰ τὰς Δημοσθέ-
138 νους δημηγορίας. καίτοι πολλὰς μὲν πρότερον πρεσβείας ἐπρέ-
σβευσαν εἰς Θήβας οἱ μάλιστα οἰκείως ἐκείνοις διακείμενοι, πρῶτος μὲν Θρασύβουλος ὁ Κολλυτεύς, ἀνὴρ ἐν Θήβαις πιστευθεὶς 10
ὡς οὐδεὶς ἕτερος, πάλιν Θράσων ὁ Ἐρχιεύς, πρόξενος ὢν Θη-
139 βαίοις, Λεωδάμας ὁ Ἀχαρνεύς, οὐχ ἧττον Δημοσθένους λέγειν
δυνάμενος, ἀλλ' ἔμοιγε καὶ ἡδίων, Ἀρχέδημος ὁ Πήληξ, καὶ
δυνατὸς εἰπεῖν καὶ πολλὰ κεκινδυνευκὼς ἐν τῇ πολιτείᾳ διὰ Θηβαίους, Ἀριστοφῶν ὁ Ἀζηνιεύς, πλεῖστον χρόνον τὴν τοῦ 15

2. πάλαι] Om. agmn. 5. ὑμέτερα] ἡμέτερα ekl, et mox ὑμῖν pz. Dind. pro
volgato ἡμῖν. 9. Post πρῶτος μὲν volg. ante Bekk. addebatur οὗτος στρατηγός:
om. agmn, οὖν στρατηγὸς b. 11. Ἐρχιεύς] Ἀρχιεὺς afcde, ἀρχιερεὺς pr. b l, ceteri
Ἐρχιεύς. 13. Post ἡδίων addebatur ῥήτωρ καὶ οὗτος: quod si genuinum esset, post
ῥήτωρ fuisset interpungendum. Om. agmn: † in b καὶ οὗτος a sec. m. subscripta lineola
notatum est †. 14. καὶ πολλά] ὡς πολλὰ agm, ὃς πολλὰ n. 15. Ante Ἀριστοφῶν addebatur δημαγωγός, ante Πύρανδρος ῥήτωρ. Prius habent libri omnes, alterum om.
agmn bekl. Quattuor glossemata manifesta (nam ῥήτωρ καὶ οὗτος, quamvis per se probabile,
cum ceteris cadit) uncis inclusit Bekk., ejecerunt B. et S.

§ 137. *Then, more scandalously yet, be
pretends to have secured the Theban alliance
by his unaided eloquence:*
1. Φρυνώνδας .. Εὐρύβατος. The first
of these worthies is unknown : for the second, cp. D. de Cor. § 29.
2. μάγος καὶ γόης. The second of these
words is commoner in the moral or metaphorical sense ; it is also a shade more contemptuous. μάγος is the recognised counterpart in the Persian religion at once of
ἱερεὺς and μάντις : he is only suspicious to a
Greek as outlandish. γόης is a mere vulgar
enchanter, without a place in any recognised
religious system, but the parasite of all.
3. ὦ γῆ καὶ θεοί would have been ordinarily sufficient to relieve the speaker's feelings, as D. de Cor. § 363. But Aeschines
wishes to make the point καὶ ἄνθρωποι ὅσοι
βούλεσθε κ.τ.λ., so he introduces the δαίμονες as well, to soften the transition from
heaven to earth.
7. Δημοσθένους. Not αὐτοῦ, that the
name may be said with a sneer. The rhetorical force is something like Αἰσχίνης Δημοσθένους in D. de Cor. § 251.
§ 138. *While many leading politicians*

had before him tried to effect that alliance,
10. Θρασύβουλος. A companion of Thrasybulus the Stirian at Phyle and at Piraeus .
He commanded in Thrace in B.C. 389.
11. Θράσων. Endeavoured to obtain
the restitution of the Cadmea.
12. Λεωδάμας. A pupil of Isocrates.
§ 139. *Though without success, which was
not their fault.*
15. Ἀριστοφῶν. See D. de Cor. § 207.
Aeschines did not admire him : cp. below,
§ 195. And long before, he had made against
Demosthenes the same αἰτίαν τοῦ βοιωτιάζειν, Ae. de F. L. § 112, p. 42. Most MSS.
insert before the name of Thrasybulus οὗτος
στρατηγός; before that of Archedemus, ῥήτωρ καὶ οὗτος; before Aristophon's, δημαγωγὸς (he is so called instead of ῥήτωρ, on
the strength of Aeschines' censure, l.c.); and
ῥήτωρ before Pyrrhander's. All are manifest
glosses but the second, which *can* be punc-
tuated ἀλλ' ἔμοιγε καὶ ἡδίαν ῥήτωρ· καὶ
οὗτος Ἀριστοφῶν. But the best MSS. omit
it, as well as οὗτος στρατηγός. The fact
that they do not omit the two glosses in the
next section proves that all four are old,
while MSS. existed late without them.

F 2

βοιωτιάζειν ὑπομείνας αἰτίαν, Πύρρανδρος ὁ Ἀναφλύστιος, ὃς
ἔτι καὶ νῦν ζῇ. ἀλλ᾽ ὅμως οὐδεὶς πώποτε αὐτοὺς ἐδυνήθη προ-
τρέψασθαι εἰς τὴν ὑμετέραν φιλίαν. τὸ δ᾽ αἴτιον οἶδα μέν,
λέγειν δ᾽ οὐδὲν δέομαι διὰ τὰς ἀτυχίας αὐτῶν. ἀλλ᾽, οἶμαι, 140
5 ἐπειδὴ Φίλιππος αὐτῶν ἀφελόμενος Νίκαιαν Θετταλοῖς παρέ-
δωκε, καὶ τὸν πόλεμον, ὃν πρότερον ἐξήλασεν ἐκ τῆς χώρας
τῆς τῶν Βοιωτῶν, τοῦτον πάλιν τὸν αὐτὸν πόλεμον ἐπήγαγε διὰ
τῆς Φωκίδος ἐπ᾽ αὐτὰς τὰς Θήβας, καὶ τὸ τελευταῖον Ἐλάτειαν καταλαβὼν ἐχαράκωσε καὶ φρουρὰν εἰσήγαγεν, ἐνταῦθ᾽
10 ἤδη, ἐπεὶ τὸ δεινὸν αὐτῶν ἥπτετο, μετεπέμψαντο Ἀθηναίους,
καὶ ὑμεῖς ἐξήλθετε καὶ εἰσῄειτε εἰς τὰς Θήβας ἐν τοῖς ὅπλοις
διεσκευασμένοι, καὶ οἱ ἱππεῖς καὶ οἱ πεζοί, πρὶν περὶ συμμαχίας μίαν μόνην συλλαβὴν γράψαι Δημοσθένην. ὁ δ᾽ εἰσάγων 141
ἦν ὑμᾶς εἰς τὰς Θήβας καιρὸς καὶ φόβος καὶ χρεία συμμαχίας,
15 ἀλλ᾽ οὐ Δημοσθένης, ἐπεὶ περί γε ταύτας τὰς πράξεις τρία τὰ
πάντων μέγιστα Δημοσθένης εἰς ὑμᾶς ἐξημάρτηκε, πρῶτον μέν,
ὅτι Φιλίππου τῷ μὲν ὀνόματι πολεμοῦντος ὑμῖν, τῷ δ᾽ ἔργῳ

1. Πύρρανδρος] Ita hic *agmne*, et bis libri omnes ad A. in Tim. p. 11, § 84. Legebatur
Πύρανδρος. 7. τῆς τῶν] τῶν *gmnf*, τῆς *apc* B. et S. 8. Θήβας] πόλεις *gmn*: † in
g volgatum restituitur a m. sec. †. 12. καὶ οἱ ἱππεῖς καὶ οἱ πεζοί] καὶ οἱ πεζοὶ καὶ
οἱ ἱππεῖς *bekl* Bekk.

3. τὸ δ᾽ αἴτιον κ.τ.λ. It would be invidious to say that it was their pride and steady
malice, when their malice had been renounced
under duress, and their pride had such a
fatal fall.
§ 140. But Philip's advance as Amphictyonic general left them no alternative but
recourse to you.
4. ἀλλ᾽ οἶμαι. The connection is,
'Whatever the cause, it was of a nature
to cease when Philip ...'
7. τοῦτον πάλιν τὸν αὐτὸν πόλεμον.
Viz. an Amphictyonic war, or (if the former
one could hardly be called so) a sacred war
on behalf of Delphi.
11. ἐξήλθετε refers, apparently, to the
march to Eleusis recommended by Demosthenes, De Cor. § 227. But it seems incredible that the Athenians can have been
invited to the alliance then, though Demosthenes had knowledge (ibid. 224 sqq.) of
an Athenian party at Thebes. Probably
his account of these events is much truer
than Aeschines'.
εἰσῄειτε. 'Were moving into Thebes.'
The change of tense from ἐξήλθετε is intentional.
12. πρὶν περὶ συμμαχίας. If this statement is to be believed or reconciled with

Demosthenes', we must take it to mean
merely, that Demosthenes had proposed that
an alliance should be concluded, and gone
himself to negotiate it, but not yet sent back
a draught treaty for ratification.
§ 141. Demosthenes' share in the business
was confined to three wrongs to you, as if
you instead of Thebes had needed aid:
15. τρία τὰ πάντων μέγιστα. Recurring to the topic started but postponed at
§ 84.
16. πρῶτον μέν. Not answered till the
δεύτερον δέ of § 145; the first charge is
subdivided into two branches, and the second
of these into two again. 'He concealed
from you that Philip's real object of assault
was Thebes, not you (ταῦτα μὲν .. πρεσβείας), and so (I.) persuaded you to give him
extravagant powers (πρῶτον μὲν συνέπεισε
.. εἰ γίγνεται), which he used (τοῦτο δὲ
προλαβὼν (II.) I. to surrender Boeotia to
Thebes (ἔκδοτον μὲν .. ἀγανακτήσοντας),
2. to surrender Athens to Thebes also. The
sentence, though somewhat involved, is perfectly symmetrical.
17. τῷ μὲν ὀνόματι πολεμοῦντος ὑμῖν.
Since the relief of Byzantium, the war between Philip and Athens may only have
existed on paper. The Greeks, moreover,

πολὺ μᾶλλον μισοῦντος Θηβαίους, ὡς αὐτὰ τὰ πράγματα δε-
δήλωκε, καὶ τί δεῖ τὰ πλείω λέγειν; ταῦτα μὲν τὰ τηλικαῦτα
τὸ μέγεθος ἀπεκρύψατο, προσποιησάμενος δὲ μέλλειν τὴν συμμαχίαν γενήσεσθαι οὐ διὰ τοὺς καιρούς, ἀλλὰ διὰ τὰς αὐτοῦ
142 πρεσβείας πρῶτον μὲν συνέπεισε τὸν δῆμον μηκέτι βουλεύεσθαι, 5
ἐπὶ τίσι δεῖ ποιεῖσθαι τὴν συμμαχίαν, ἀλλ' ἀγαπᾶν μόνον, εἰ
γίγνεται, τοῦτο δὲ προλαβὼν ἔκδοτον μὲν τὴν Βοιωτίαν πᾶσαν
ἐποίησε Θηβαίοις, γράψας ἐν τῷ ψηφίσματι, ἐάν τις ἀφιστῆ-
ται πόλις ἀπὸ Θηβαίνω, βοηθεῖν Ἀθηναίους Βοιωτοῖς τοῖς ἐν
Θήβαις, τοῖς ὀνόμασι κλέπτων καὶ μεταφέρων τὰ πράγματα, 10
ὥσπερ εἴωθεν, ὡς τοὺς Βοιωτοὺς ἔργῳ κακῶς πάσχοντας τὴν
τῶν ὀνομάτων σύνθεσιν τῶν Δημοσθένους ἀγαπήσοντας, ἀλλ'
143 οὐ μᾶλλον ἐφ' οἷς κακῶς πεπόνθεσαν ἀγανακτήσοντας· δεύτερον
δὲ τῶν εἰς τὸν πόλεμον ἀναλωμάτων τὰ μὲν δύο μέρη ὑμῖν
ἀνέθηκεν, οἷς ἦσαν ἀπωτέρω οἱ κίνδυνοι, τὸ δὲ τρίτον μέρος 15
Θηβαίοις, δωροδοκῶν ἐφ' ἑκάστοις τούτων, καὶ τὴν ἡγεμονίαν
τὴν μὲν κατὰ θάλατταν ἐποίησε κοινήν, τὸ δ' ἀνάλωμα ἴδιον

6. ποιεῖσθαι] ποιήσασθαι bekl Bekk.   7. πᾶσαν] Sic agmn : ceteri et Bekk. ἅπασαν.
13. πεπόνθεσαν] ἐπεπόνθεσαν ekl, idque legi volt Frankius.   17. μὲν] Post prius τὴν
ponit g, post utrumque bl.   θάλατταν] θάλασσαν gmn fcd.

did not think much of a war that did not
involve an invasion : see Thuc. 5. 25, ἐπὶ
ἐξ ἔτη μὲν καὶ δέκα μῆνας ἀπέσχοντο μὴ
ἐπὶ τὴν ἑκατέρων γῆν στρατεῦσαι .. ἔπειτα
μέντοι καὶ ἀναγκασθέντες λῦσαι τὰς .. σπον-
δὰς αὖθις ἐς πόλεμον φανερὸν κατέστη-
σαν.
1. ὡς αὐτὰ .. τὰ πλείω λίγειν. Parenthetical, 'as the facts proved, and why need
I add more?' τὰ πλείω almost = τὰ λοιπά,
the long story that could be made to explain
the situation.
§ 142. First, he made Thebes mistress of
Boeotia under our guarantee,
5. συνέπεισε. 'Persuaded the people
and carried them with him,' unless the point
be, that Demosthenes cannot claim the exclusive credit even of the pernicious measures.
9. Βοιωτοῖς τοῖς ἐν Θήβαις. The Boeotian synod held in Thebes, and thus no
doubt under Theban control.
10. τοῖς ὀνόμασι κ.τ.λ. The charge is,
that Demosthenes affected to consider Theban
supremacy in Boeotia as not a tyranny of
one city over the rest, but an equal federation of all. It sounded less invidious to
secure the right to prevent secession to the
latter than the former; but, says Aeschines,
what was called a federation was really an
empire : it was absurd to suppose that the
subjects of it would be happier for a verbal

recognition of their rights that was the means
of perpetuating their wrongs.
11. ὡς τοὺς Βοιωτοὺς κ.τ.λ. In the
accusative, as being (in a vague sense) part
of Demosthenes' proposition, being in fact
part of his thought. Cp. D. de Cor. § 157 ;
below, § 190.
§ 143. Gave us the greater share of the
expense by land with no share in the command, the whole expense by sea with only an
equal share in the command,
14. τὰ μὲν δύο μέρη κ.τ.λ. It is not
clear how far this, or indeed any other of
the items censured by Aeschines, are articles
expressly contained in the treaty, how far
Aeschines' own deductions as to the practical effect the treaty would have. Perhaps
the charge of unequal division of expense is
not distinct from what is repeated in the
next clause. Athens was to bear the whole
expense by sea and divide the command, to
share the expense by land and practically
resign the command. The latter may rest
on what is said in § 145, that the Athenian
generals acted, not independently, but in
council of war at Thebes, which would give
Thebes a veto on all movements of the
allies. Or it may have been specified, that
the nation in whose country the battle was
fought should have the command : cp. Thuc.
5. 67.

ὑμέτερον, τὴν δὲ κατὰ γῆν, εἰ μὴ δεῖ ληρεῖν, ἄρδην φέρων
ἀνέθηκε Θηβαίοις, ὥστε παρὰ τὸν γενόμενον πόλεμον μὴ κύριον
γενέσθαι Στρατοκλέα τὸν ἡμέτερον στρατηγὸν βουλεύσασθαι
περὶ τῆς τῶν στρατιωτῶν σωτηρίας. καὶ ταῦτ' οὐκ ἐγὼ μὲν 144
5 κατηγορῶ, ἕτεροι δὲ παραλείπουσιν, ἀλλὰ κἀγὼ λέγω καὶ πάντες ἐπιτιμῶσι καὶ ὑμεῖς σύνιστε καὶ οὐκ ὀργίζεσθε. ἐκεῖνο γὰρ
πεπύνθατε πρὸς Δημοσθένην· συνείθισθε ἤδη τἀδικήματα [τὰ]
τούτου ἀκούειν, ὥστε οὐ θαυμάζετε. δεῖ δὲ οὐχ οὕτως, ἀλλ'
ἀγανακτεῖν καὶ τιμωρεῖσθαι, εἰ χρὴ τὰ λοιπὰ τῇ πόλει καλῶς
10 ἔχειν.

Δεύτερον δὲ καὶ πολὺ τούτου μεῖζον ἀδίκημα ἠδίκησεν, ὅτι 145
τὸ βουλευτήριον τὸ τῆς πόλεως καὶ τὴν δημοκρατίαν ἄρδην
ἔλαθεν ὑφελόμενος καὶ μετήνεγκεν εἰς Θήβας εἰς τὴν Καδμείαν,
τὴν κοινωνίαν τῶν πράξεων τοῖς Βοιωτάρχαις συνθέμενος· καὶ
15 τηλικαύτην αὐτὸς αὑτῷ δυναστείαν κατεσκεύασεν, ὥστ' ἤδη παριὼν ἐπὶ τὸ βῆμα πρεσβεύσειν μὲν ἔφη ὅπου ἂν αὐτῷ δοκῇ,

7. τὰ τούτου] τούτου *agmnpr*, αὐτοῦ ceteri. Articulum τὰ inseruerunt B. et S. Vid.
annot.   16. ὅπου] Sic *agmnp bel* : ὅποτ' *fcd*, ὅποι *k* et editi plerique.

1. **εἰ μὴ δεῖ ληρεῖν.** 'If we are to speak
practically,' 'to say what is really meant,'
'to call things by their right names.' So D.
de Cor. § 367, and so in a noble fragment of
Hegesippus : καί τις ἀναστὰς εἶπε, 'πόλεμον
εἰσάγεις, Κρωβύλε·' καὶ ὅς· 'οὐ μόνον γε,'
ἔφη, 'πόλεμον, ἀλλὰ καὶ θανάτους δώρους,
καὶ μέλανα ἱμάτια, καὶ δημοσίας ταφὰς, καὶ
λόγους ἐπιταφίους, εἴ γε βούλεσθε μὴ ληρεῖν
(if you are willing to look facts in the face),
ἀλλὰ τοὺς Ἕλληνας ἐλευθερῶσαι, καὶ κτή-
σασθαι πάλιν αὖ τὴν πατρῴαν ἡγεμονίαν.'
3. **Στρατοκλέα.** Chares and Lysicles
were, by all accounts, the commanders at
Chaeronea itself; Stratocles perhaps in the
earlier and successful part of the campaign.
The change in the command seems an additional reason for the view, that the fighting
in Boeotia lasted during part of two seasons.
περὶ τῆς τῶν στρατιωτῶν σωτηρίας looks as
though Aeschines had no fault to find with
the operations in which Stratocles took part,
except that his men were sacrificed, i. e. exposed to more than their fair share of loss,
in what were actual successes of the allies.
It is hardly likely that Stratocles is the same
as the orator, whom we hear of later with a
very unfavourable character.
§ 144. *As is notorious, but too little
noticed.*
4. **καὶ ταῦτ' οὐκ ἐγὼ κ.τ.λ.** 'This is
not a charge made by me and omitted by
others, but a fact mentioned by me and condemned by all.' There is a climax in πάντες

after ἕτεροι, and a designed anti-climax in
λέγω after κατηγορῶ.
7. **τἀδικήματα [τὰ] τούτου.** The best
MSS. have τούτου, the rest αὐτοῦ ; none τὰ,
which was inserted by Baiter and Sauppe.
They adduce a number of passages from
Isaeus to prove that the repetition of the
article is required before the genitive of any
pronoun not strictly personal ; and would,
therefore, correct Isaeus 9. 10, οἱ ἀναγκαῖοι
[οἱ] ἐκείνου, where the vulgate has the same
construction as here, and where, as here,
the article was liable to be lost by the homoeoteleuton.
9. **εἰ χρὴ τὰ λοιπὰ τῇ πόλει καλῶς
ἔχειν.** The occurrence of iambic verses in
prose is not uncommon, but they rarely
form, as here, clauses complete in sense.
Such a line as this would probably be considered a fault by a Greek rhetorician (see
Dionys. de Comp. Verb. p. 196), as certainly
by Cicero (Orat. c. 56).
§ 145. *Secondly, he contrived to subordinate our lawful government to himself sitting
at Thebes.*
11. **ὅτι τὸ βουλευτήριον .. συνθέμενος.**
He did this by getting it agreed that everything should be done in common with the
Boeotarchs, which implied that he was to do
it : it was he, not Stratocles, who exercised
sovereign functions at the Cadmea : 'he and
the Boeotarchs managed everything between
them.'
16. **ὅπου.** So all the best MSS. ; some

146 κἂν μὴ ὑμεῖς ἐκπέμπητε, εἰ δέ τις αὐτῷ τῶν στρατηγῶν ἀντεί-
ποι, καταδουλούμενος τοὺς ἄρχοντας καὶ συνεθίζων μηδὲν αὐτῷ
ἀντιλέγειν διαδικασίαν ἔφη γράψειν τῷ βήματι πρὸς τὸ στρα-
τήγιον· πλείω γὰρ ὑμᾶς ἀγαθὰ ὑφ' ἑαυτοῦ ἔφη ἀπὸ τοῦ βήματος πεπονθέναι ἢ ὑπὸ τῶν στρατηγῶν ἐκ τοῦ στρατηγίου. 5
μισθοφορῶν δ' ἐν τῷ ξενικῷ κεναῖς χώραις, καὶ τὰ στρατιωτικὰ
χρήματα κλέπτων, καὶ τοὺς μυρίους ξένους ἐκμισθώσας Ἀμφισ-
σεῦσι πολλὰ διαμαρτυρομένου καὶ σχετλιάζοντος ἐν ταῖς ἐκκλησίαις ἐμοῦ, προσέμιξε φέρων ἀναρπασθέντων τῶν ξένων τὸν
147 κίνδυνον ἀπαρασκεύῳ τῇ πόλει.   τί γὰρ ἂν οἴεσθε Φίλιππον ἐν 10
τοῖς τότε καιροῖς εὔξασθαι; οὐ χωρὶς μὲν πρὸς τὴν πολιτικὴν
δύναμιν, χωρὶς δ' ἐν Ἀμφίσσῃ πρὸς τοὺς ξένους διαγωνίσασθαι,
ἀθύμους δὲ τοὺς Ἕλληνας λαβεῖν τηλικαύτης πληγῆς προγεγε-
νημένης; καὶ τηλικούτων κακῶν αἴτιος γεγενημένος Δημοσθένης οὐκ
ἀγαπᾷ, εἰ μὴ δίκην δέδωκεν, ἀλλ' εἰ μὴ καὶ χρυσῷ στεφάνῳ στε- 15
φανωθήσεται, ἀγανακτεῖ· οὐδ' ἱκανόν ἐστιν αὐτῷ ἐναντίον ὑμῶν
κηρύττεσθαι, ἀλλ' εἰ μὴ τῶν Ἑλλήνων ἐναντίον ἀναρρηθήσεται,

---

2. αὐτῷ] Ita B. et S., cum *e* et pr. z ἑαυτῷ habeant, ceteri αὐτῷ.   3. στρατήγιον]
Ita *amubekl*: ceteri et volgo -γεῖον.   Mox στρατηγίου iidem praeter *mb*: † στρατήγαιου
g †.   6. κεναῖς] καιναῖς *amubekl*.   9. ἀναρπασθέντων τῶν ξένων] Sic *agmn*:
ceteri ἐκ τῶν ἀναρπασθέντων ξένων.   13. προγεγενημένης] Sic *agmn*: ceteri et Bekk.
γεγενημένης.

---

have ὅποτε, only one bad one the common
reading ὅποι. ὅπου is of course an inaccu-
racy, but one that is natural in all languages,
and common in most: rare in good Greek;
but cp. Isaeus 9. 14.

§§ 146, 147. *Whereby he was emboldened
to insult our generals, plunder our funds,
and divide our forces:*

1. **εἰ δέ τις αὐτῷ τῶν στρατηγῶν ἀντεί-
ποι.** Demosthenes had (D. de Cor. § 228)
carried a resolution that the ambassadors
should be free to undertake any mission in
concert with the generals: when the generals
hesitated to grant their sanction, Demosthenes, it seems, threatened to go without.

3. **διαδικασίαν.** A suit for precedence ;
probably Demosthenes had used the word in
a context that worked out the metaphor
more fully, a suit between the Bema and
the Strategion for the possession of (perhaps)
the people's gratitude.

6. **μισθοφορῶν .. κεναῖς χώραις.** Of
course in concert with their commander.
The use of χώραις, exactly as we say 'empty
places,' is not common ; but the use of ἐν
χώρᾳ or ἐπὶ χώρας, 'at one's post,' may be
reckoned as an approximation to it.

7. **ἐκμισθώσας.** Perhaps Aeschines feels
safe in imputing bad motives for a blunder :
perhaps Demosthenes advocated sending the
mercenaries as a financial measure. It doubtless was a blunder in a military sense, though
without the misconduct (Dinarchus seems to
impute treachery, c. Demosth. p. 99, § 74)
of their commander it might not have been
a fatal one ; and Demosthenes may be held
to repudiate responsibility for it in such passages as De Cor. § 305. Probably the mercenary commander was really beyond the
control of the government: possibly political
considerations might justify the rash strategy.

8. **διαμαρτυρομένου.** Exactly 'protest-
ing' in the etymological sense: σχετλιάζοντος, 'insisting how hard it was,' almost
'grumbling,' only without vulgar association.

13. **τοὺς Ἕλληνας.** Almost 'the confederacy.' The loss of the ξένοι was a common loss, and a greater blow than if one
state had suffered to the same extent in its
πολιτικὴ δύναμις. Note the vagueness of
the words τηλικαύτης πληγῆς: Aeschines
habitually prefers to allude to the national
misfortunes caused by Demosthenes, rather
than to specify them.

τοῦτ᾽ ἤδη ἀγανακτεῖ. οὕτως, ὡς ἔοικε, πονηρὰ φύσις μεγάλης
ἐξουσίας ἐπιλαβομένη δημοσίας ἀπεργάζεται συμφοράς.
Τρίτον δὲ καὶ τῶν προειρημένων μέγιστόν ἐστιν ὃ μέλλω 148
λέγειν. Φιλίππου γὰρ οὐ καταφρονοῦντος τῶν Ἑλλήνων, οὐδ᾽
5 ἀγνοοῦντος, οὐ γὰρ ἦν ἀσύνετος, ὅτι περὶ τῶν ὑπαρχόντων
ἀγαθῶν ἐν ἡμέρας μικρῷ μέρει διαγωνιεῖται, καὶ διὰ ταῦτα βουλομένου ποιήσασθαι τὴν εἰρήνην καὶ πρεσβείας ἀποστέλλειν
μέλλοντος, καὶ τῶν ἀρχόντων τῶν ἐν Θήβαις φοβουμένων τὸν
ἐπιόντα κίνδυνον, εἰκότως· οὐ γὰρ ῥήτωρ ἀστράτευτος καὶ λιπὼν
10 τὴν τάξιν αὐτοὺς ἐνουθέτησεν, ἀλλ᾽ ὁ Φωκικὸς πόλεμος δεκαε-
τὴς γεγονὼς ἀείμνηστον παιδείαν αὐτοὺς ἐπαίδευσε, τούτων δὲ 149
ἐχόντων οὕτως αἰσθόμενος Δημοσθένης, καὶ τοὺς Βοιωτάρχας

---

1. ἤδη] Sic bekl Bekk.; ceteri et B. et S. om. 4. Ἑλλήνων] † Aliter, ut visum est,
in g scriptum fuit; nos autem ejus lectionem perspicere non potuimus †. 6. μικρῷ] Ita
bk et edd. recentiores: ceteri et Bekk. σμικρῷ. 7. τὴν] In g erasum est.

---

1. **τοῦτ᾽ ἤδη ἀγανακτεῖ.** 'Goes so far
as to complain of *that*.' ἤδη is omitted by
the best MSS., and by B. and S. and later
editors. But it seems hardly like a gloss;
Aeschines would hardly have written the two
successive and parallel clauses ending ἀγανακτεῖ and τοῦτ᾽ ἀγανακτεῖ without something to emphasise the climax; and if he had
done so, an editor who wanted to improve
him would more readily have written καὶ
τοῦτ᾽ than τοῦτ᾽ ἤδη. At the same time
one may remember, that τοῦτ᾽ may have
been so *delivered* as to emphasise the climax
sufficiently by the voice alone.

οὕτως. Almost = ἐπὶ τούτοις, 'this is
the price we have to pay an evil nature in
high authority to work out the ruin of the
state.'

§ 148. *And thirdly, be violently repulsed
Philip's offers of negotiation,*

3. **τῶν προειρημένων μέγιστον** may be
explained as the ordinary Greek idiom, 'the
goodliest of men since born;' but as that
idiom is generally where the superlative is of
a large and indefinite class, and would here
have to mean only 'greater than the *two* I
have named,' it seems easier to make προειρημένων refer back to § 141, 'greatest of
the three that I named,' treating this as
named already, having been included in the
number given.

6. **ἐν ἡμέρας μικρῷ μέρει.** To be taken
quite literally. A pitched battle between
two Greek armies must have been, as a rule,
decided in a very few minutes from its actual
commencement, though manœuvring and
skirmishing might go on for any time before
the serious fighting began.

7. **τὴν εἰρήνην.** 'Wishing to make *the*
peace' he spoke of; being sincere in his offers.

9. **οὐ γὰρ ῥήτωρ κ.τ.λ.** Giving the reason for εἰκότως, not for φοβούμενοι: 'they
had a better teacher than the cowardice of
Demosthenes.' He, having never seen service, but deserted when he ought to have,
did not know what war was like; but they
did. ἀστράτευτος is the exact reverse of
the French *aguerri*, and, so far as we know,
would strictly apply to Demosthenes. λιπὼν
τὴν τάξιν is a stock charge against him,
founded on his return to Athens for the
Dionysia, from the expedition to Euboea,
where he seems to have been acting strictly
within his duty as Choragus. The phrase
is an unvarying one: λιπὼν τὰς τάξεις, the
reading of a few MSS., is clearly wrong.

10. **δεκαετής.** The proper accentuation
of this word is disputed. Ammonius says
that the compounds of ἔτος are oxytone
when marking age, and barytone when
duration; but this distinction is not supported
by MSS. Göttling makes all adjectives
oxytone, and the neuters used adverbially
barytone. But there seems not sufficient
certainty to justify a change of the ordinary
writing where, as here, the MSS. conform to
it.

§ 149. *For fear the Boeotarchs might
get more bribes than be;*

12. **οὕτως.** Viz. with a mutual disposition to treat, Philip feeling the risk of attempting too much, and the Thebans fearing
war after their experience of it. τούτων
ἐχόντων is probably rather a gen. abs. than
dependent on αἰσθόμενος.

ὑποπτεύσας μέλλειν εἰρήνην ἰδίᾳ ποιεῖσθαι χρυσίον ἄνευ αὐτοῦ
παρὰ Φιλίππου λαβόντας, ἀβίωτον ἡγησάμενος εἶναι, εἴ τινος
ἀπολειφθήσεται δωροδοκίας, ἀναπηδήσας ἐν τῇ ἐκκλησίᾳ, οὐδενὸς ἀνθρώπων λέγοντος οὔθ' ὡς δεῖ ποιεῖσθαι πρὸς Φίλιππον
εἰρήνην οὔθ' ὡς οὐ δεῖ, ἀλλ' ὡς ᾤετο, τοῦτο κήρυγμά τι τοῖς 5
Βοιωτάρχαις προκηρύττων ἀναφέρειν αὐτῷ τὰ μέρη τῶν λημ-
150 μάτων, διώμνυτο τὴν Ἀθηνᾶν, ἣν, ὡς ἔοικε, Φειδίας ἐνεργολα-
βεῖν εἰργάσατο καὶ ἐνεπιορκεῖν Δημοσθένει, ἦ μὴν, εἴ τις ἐρεῖ,
ὡς χρὴ πρὸς Φίλιππον εἰρήνην ποιήσασθαι, ἀπάξειν εἰς τὸ
δεσμωτήριον ἐπιλαβόμενος τῶν τριχῶν, ἀπομιμούμενος τὴν Κλεο- 10
φῶντος πολιτείαν, ὃς ἐπὶ τοῦ πρὸς Λακεδαιμονίους πολέμου, ὡς
λέγεται, τὴν πόλιν ἀπώλεσεν. ὡς δ' οὐ προσεῖχον αὐτῷ οἱ
ἄρχοντες οἱ ἐν ταῖς Θήβαις, ἀλλὰ καὶ τοὺς στρατιώτας τοὺς
ὑμετέρους πάλιν ἀνέστρεψαν ἐξεληλυθότας, ἵνα βουλεύσησθε
151 περὶ τῆς εἰρήνης, ἐνταῦθα παντάπασιν ἔκφρων ἐγένετο, καὶ 15

5. τοῦτο κήρυγμά τι] κήρυγμά τι τοῦτο z: atque id sane facilius et elegantius.
6. αὐτῷ] Ita B. et S.: αὐτῷ agmnfd. Legebatur ἑαυτῷ.　　　14. βουλεύσησθε] 'Fort.
βουλεύσαισθε' Spp.　　　15. ἐνταῦθα] ἐνταῦθ' ἤδη bekl Bekk.

1. ἰδίᾳ. It is extraordinary that Aeschines
should not see, that whatever Demosthenes'
faults, he was right in preventing Thebes
from making a separate peace, which would
have enabled Philip to enter Attica at once.
The statement at the end of the next section, τοὺς στρατιώτας .. ἀνέστρεψαν, would
go far to justify, not only his policy, but his
violence of language in enforcing it.

2. ἀβίωτον ἡγησάμενος. Cp. above,
§ 81, ὑπὲρ τῆς δωροδοκίας ζηλοτυπίας.

3. ἐν τῇ ἐκκλησίᾳ. Apparently at
Thebes, not at Athens.

οὐδενὸς ἀνθρώπων κ.τ.λ. 'Not that
any one was speaking on the question of
peace, but to give notice, as he thought, in
this way to the Boeotarchs to hand over
his share of the spoils.' He thought that
they would know him well enough to guess
what he wanted ; but in fact they took no
notice of him at first, and then, when his
violence forced them, took him at his word
and dropped the negotiations. Accepting Aeschines' statement of facts, his imputation of motives is extraordinary : this
is unquestionably the weakest part of his
case.

§ 150. And so, like Cleophon, led us on
to our ruin,

7. ἣν, ὡς ἔοικε κ.τ.λ. 'Whom, as it
seems, Phidias made for Demosthenes to
traffic in perjury thereby.' τὴν Ἀθηνᾶν, by
force of the article, will be Ἀθηνᾶ πολιοῦ-

χος, Athena as tutelary goddess of Athens,
and so identified with her statue in the
Acropolis.

11. ὡς λέγεται. Aeschines' views of history were sufficiently vague (De F. L. §§
183 sqq., p. 51), but he speaks more confi-
dently of the story of Cleophon in the same
speech, § 80. It seems not clear whether he
repeated the same policy after Arginusae as
after Cyzicus : but the parallel seems to
imply that Aeschines admits the successes of
the allies in the first campaign.

12. ὡς δ' οὐ προσεῖχον κ.τ.λ. 'As the
Boeotarchs, instead of taking him into their
counsels, and sharing their profits with him,
actually went on negotiating, and sent your
troops home, to decide whether you would
negotiate too.' For the Athenian troops in
Boeotia were citizens, and therefore the people could hardly hold an assembly to make
peace in their absence ; while, on the other
hand, when they were at home all chance of
a favourable peace was lost, as Demosthenes
saw. He might, in concert with the Boeotarchs, have negotiated a peace on behalf of
the whole confederacy ; but if the allies
negotiated separately, they lost the benefit
of the alliance in case the negotiations failed,
and gave Philip a strong temptation to
break them off.

§ 151. Violently denouncing the Boeotarchs for treating, and forcing them to continue the war.

παρελθὼν ἐπὶ τὸ βῆμα προδότας τῶν Ἑλλήνων τοὺς Βοιωτάρχας ἀπεκάλεσε, καὶ γράψειν ἔφη ψήφισμα ὁ τοῖς πολεμίοις
οὐδέποτ' ἀντιβλέψας πέμπειν ὑμᾶς πρέσβεις εἰς Θήβας αἰτή-
σοντας Θηβαίους δίοδον ἐπὶ Φίλιππον. ὑπεραισχυνθέντες δὲ
5 οἱ ἐν Θήβαις ἄρχοντες, μὴ δόξωσιν ὡς ἀληθῶς εἶναι προδόται
τῶν Ἑλλήνων, ἀπὸ μὲν τῆς εἰρήνης ἀπετρέποντο, ἐπὶ δὲ τὴν
παράταξιν ὥρμησαν.

Ἔνθα δὴ καὶ τῶν ἀγαθῶν ἀνδρῶν ἄξιόν ἐστιν ἐπιμνησθῆναι, 152
οὓς οὗτος ἀθύτων καὶ ἀκαλλιερήτων ὄντων τῶν ἱερῶν ἐκπέμψας
10 ἐπὶ τὸν πρόδηλον κίνδυνον ἐτόλμησε τοῖς δραπέταις ποσὶ καὶ
λελοιπόσι τὴν τάξιν ἀναβὰς ἐπὶ τὸν τάφον τῶν τετελευτηκότων ἐγκωμιάζειν τὴν ἐκείνων ἀρετήν. ὦ πρὸς μὲν τὰ μεγάλα
καὶ σπουδαῖα πάντων ἀνθρώπων ἀχρηστότατε, πρὸς δὲ τὴν ἐν
τοῖς λόγοις τόλμαν θαυμασιώτατε, ἐπιχειρήσειν ἐθελήσεις αὐ-
15 τίκα μάλα, βλέπων εἰς τὰ τούτων πρόσωπα, λέγειν, ὡς δεῖ
σε ἐπὶ ταῖς τῆς πόλεως συμφοραῖς στεφανοῦσθαι; ἐὰν δ' οὗτος
λέγῃ, ὑμεῖς ὑπομενεῖτε, καὶ συναποθανεῖται τοῖς τελευτήσασιν,
ὡς ἔοικε, καὶ ἡ ὑμετέρα μνήμη; γένεσθε δή μοι μικρὸν χρόνον 153

5. ἄρχοντες] Om. z.   6. ἀπετρέποντο] ἀπετράποντο bekl Bekk.   8. τῶν ἀγαθῶν ἀνδρῶν] τῶν ἀνδρῶν τῶν ἀγαθῶν bekl Bekk.   11. τῶν τετελευτηκότων] Habet k
τὸν τῶν τελευτησάντων, τελευτησάντων etiam bel. Et articulum et aoristum servabat Bekk.
13. σπουδαῖα πάντων ἀνθρώπων] σπουδαῖα τῶν πραγμάτων ἀπάντων fcd σπουδαῖα τῶν
ἀνθρώπων amn, μεγάλα τῶν ἔργων ἀπάντων vel ἔργων τὰ μεγάλα ἀπάντων Alexander,
Zonaras, etc. 'Fort. μεγάλα καὶ σπουδαῖα τῶν ἔργων ἀπάντων' Spp.   14. ἐπιχειρήσειν ἐθελήσεις] Ita libri plerique, ἐπιχειρήσειν ἐθέλεις bel, ἐπιχειρήσεις Reisk. B. et S. Vid.
annot.

2. ὁ τοῖς πολεμίοις οὐδέποτ' ἀντιβλέψας. Our phrase 'to look a man in the
face' covers the distinct meanings of two
Greek ones: ἀντιβλέπειν with dat. (as here),
with εἰς or πρὸς and accus., or, in late writers,
with accus. only, is 'to look in the face with
proper courage;' βλέπειν εἰς τὸ πρόσωπον
with a gen. is 'to look in the face without
shame,' i. e. often (according to the context)
with exceptional impudence; as in the next
section.

5. ὡς ἀληθῶς. Perhaps Aeschines means
to admit, that Greece would have been really
ruined if Athens had fought alone: perhaps
he wishes only to emphasise δόξωσιν, 'lest
it should be thought Demosthenes' charge
was true.' But the last sense would probably
have been expressed by ἀληθῶς simply, not
by ὡς ἀληθῶς.

§ 152. Then, when he had led our brave
men to their death, he had the impudence to
pronounce their funeral oration; and now to
ask for a crown for killing them.

9. ἀθύτων .. κίνδυνον. Repeated almost
verbatim from § 131. It is strange that
glossematum venatores like Baiter and Sauppe
have not suspected that some words, in one
or other place, have stolen in from the
parallel passage.

10. δραπέταις. That had fled at Chaeronea, as well as deserted before danger approached in Euboea.

14. ἐπιχειρήσειν ἐθελήσεις. So, practically, all the MSS. As some grammarians
insisted that the future infin. ought not to
be used with verbs of volition, B. and S. following Reiske read ἐπιχειρήσεις. But the
periphrasis, though hard to justify logically,
is natural: one might compare it with the
passive form coeptus used with passive verbs;
and the objections to it are probably grounded
on logic, not on usage.

αὐτίκα μάλα seems to ignore the long
interval between the facts and the trial.

§ 153. Imagine the scene in the theatre
when the crown should be given.

τὴν διάνοιαν μὴ ἐν τῷ δικαστηρίῳ, ἀλλ' ἐν τῷ θεάτρῳ, καὶ
νομίσαθ' ὁρᾶν προϊόντα τὸν κήρυκα καὶ τὴν ἐκ τοῦ ψηφίσματος ἀνάρρησιν μέλλουσαν γίγνεσθαι, καὶ λογίσασθε, πό-
τερ' οἴεσθε τοὺς οἰκείους τῶν τελευτησάντων πλείω δάκρυα ἀφή-
σειν ἐπὶ ταῖς τραγῳδίαις καὶ τοῖς ἡρωικοῖς πάθεσι τοῖς μετὰ 5
154 ταῦτ' ἐπεισιοῦσιν ἢ ἐπὶ τῇ τῆς πόλεως ἀγνωμοσύνῃ. τίς γὰρ
οὐκ ἂν ἀλγήσειεν ἄνθρωπος Ἕλλην ἢ καὶ παιδευθεὶς ἐλευθέρως,
ἀναμνησθεὶς ἐν τῷ θεάτρῳ ἐκεῖνό γε, εἰ μηδὲν ἕτερον, ὅτι ταύτῃ
ποτὲ τῇ ἡμέρᾳ μελλόντων ὥσπερ νυνὶ τῶν τραγῳδῶν γίνεσθαι,
ὅτ' εὐνομεῖτο μᾶλλον ἡ πόλις καὶ βελτίοσι προστάταις ἐχρῆτο, 10
προελθὼν ὁ κῆρυξ καὶ παραστησάμενος τοὺς ὀρφανούς, ὧν οἱ
πατέρες ἦσαν ἐν τῷ πολέμῳ τετελευτηκότες, νεανίσκους πανοπλίᾳ κεκοσμημένους, ἐκήρυττε τὸ κάλλιστον κήρυγμα καὶ προ-
τρεπτικώτατον πρὸς ἀρετήν, ὅτι τούσδε τοὺς νεανίσκους, ὧν οἱ
πατέρες ἐτελεύτησαν ἐν τῷ πολέμῳ ἄνδρες ἀγαθοὶ γενόμενοι, 15
μέχρι μὲν ἥβης ὁ δῆμος ἔτρεφε, νυνὶ δὲ καθοπλίσας τῇδε τῇ
πανοπλίᾳ ἀφίησιν ἀγαθῇ τύχῃ τρέπεσθαι ἐπὶ τὰ ἑαυτῶν, καὶ
155 καλεῖ εἰς προεδρίαν. τότε μὲν ταῦτ' ἐκήρυττεν, ἀλλ' οὐ νῦν,
ἀλλὰ παραστησάμενος τὸν τῆς ὀρφανίας τοῖς παισὶν αἴτιον τί
ποτ' ἀνερεῖ ἢ τί φθέγξεται; καὶ γὰρ ἐὰν αὐτὰ διεξίῃ τὰ ἐκ 20

---

1. τὴν διάνοιαν] 'Malim τῇ διανοίᾳ' Bait. : idque habet Reiski marg. Bern., et Frankius,
ut videtur, Baitero assentit. Vide vero annot. 7. ἢ καὶ] Sic *agmnfsd* : ceteri et volg.
καί. Mox ἐλευθερίως mavolt Cobet. 8. ταύτῃ τῇ ἡμέρᾳ] 'Scribe ἐν ταύτῃ' Frank.
9. γίνεσθαι] γενέσθαι *agmn*, 'sed vid. Frank. ad I (Timarch) § 117' B. et S. 11. προ-
ελθὼν] Sic *k*, παρελθὼν *bel*, ceteri προσελθών. 14. πρὸς ἀρετὴν] εἰς ἀρετὴν *gmn*.
20. ἀνερεῖ] Sic corr. *n* et post Bekkerum editi. Legebatur ἂν ἐρεῖ. ἢ τί φθέγξεται]
Delet Cobet. ἐὰν] Sic *ae* et post Bekk. editi. Ceteri et Ald. ἄν.

---

1. τὴν διάνοιαν. Cp. Tim. § 179, p. 25,
ἐπειδὰν .. τὰς ψυχὰς ἐφ' ἑτέρων γένησθε, an
exactly parallel construction. Baiter, and
even Franke, would like to correct the accusatives in both passages to datives, like τῇ
διανοίᾳ or ταῖς διανοίαις in §§ 157, 187 inf.
But the construction is not exactly the same:
'be in such a place *mentally*' is one thing,
'go to such a place' or '*look* at such an object *with* your mind' is another. The in-
strumental case is proper in the latter sense,
not in the former.

§ 154. Contrast the old custom, of bringing to the theatre the orphans of your brave
citizens in full arms,

7. ἢ καί. So the best MSS. ; but ἢ has
been omitted by previous editors. It seems
to heighten the sense a little, 'any man who
had the generous nature of a Greek, or even
the generous education of a freeman.' Can
the point be intended, 'A Greek would be
ashamed, and Demosthenes, Scythian as he
is, ought to be'?

10. ὅτ' εὐνομεῖτο μᾶλλον ἢ πόλις.
Probably before the disastrous close of the
Peloponnesian war : at all events before the
general employment of mercenaries made
the deaths of citizens in battle rarer.

11. προελθὼν must be right, though
found only in one bad MS. Its congeners
read παρελθὼν, the good ones keep traces of
the right reading in προσελθών.

§ 155. With Ctesiphon's decree, bringing
at the same time and place their murderer to
be crowned.

19. τί ποτ' ἀνερεῖ. An apparently necessary correction (supported by one MS.)
for the vulgate ἂν ἐρεῖ. There seems no
proof that τί ποτ' ἂν had ever so much run
into one word that the common construction of ἂν was lost. ἀνερεῖ and φθέγξεται
are not quite synonymous : 'What will his
proclamation be, or for what words will he
find voice ? Even if he succeeds in reciting
the mere words prescribed by the decree,'
that will not hide the difficulty.

τοῦ ψηφίσματος προστάγματα, ἀλλ' οὐ τό γ' ἐκ τῆς ἀληθείας αἰσχρὸν σιωπηθήσεται, ἀλλὰ τἀναντία δόξει τῇ τοῦ κήρυκος φωνῇ φθέγγεσθαι, ὅτι τόνδε τὸν ἄνδρα, εἰ δὴ καὶ οὗτος
ἀνήρ, στεφανοῖ ὁ δῆμος τῶν Ἀθηναίων ἀρετῆς ἕνεκα τὸν κάκι-
5 στον καὶ ἀνδραγαθίας ἕνεκα τὸν ἄνανδρον καὶ λελοιπότα τὴν
τάξιν. μὴ πρὸς τοῦ Διὸς καὶ τῶν ἄλλων θεῶν, ἱκετεύω ὑμᾶς, 156
ὦ Ἀθηναῖοι, μὴ τρόπαιον ἵστατε ἀφ' ὑμῶν αὐτῶν ἐν τῇ τοῦ
Διονύσου ὀρχήστρᾳ, μηδ' αἱρεῖτε παρανοίας ἐναντίον τῶν Ἑλλήνων τὸν δῆμον τῶν Ἀθηναίων, μηδ' ὑπομιμνήσκετε τῶν ἀνιά-
10 των καὶ ἀνηκέστων κακῶν τοὺς ταλαιπώρους Θηβαίους, οὓς φυγόντας διὰ τοῦτον ὑποδέδεχθε τῇ πόλει, ὧν ἱερὰ καὶ τέκνα καὶ
τάφους ἀπώλεσεν ἡ Δημοσθένους δωροδοκία καὶ τὸ βασιλικὸν
χρυσίον· ἀλλ' ἐπειδὴ τοῖς σώμασιν οὐ παρεγένεσθε, ἀλλὰ ταῖς 157
γε διανοίαις ἀποβλέψατ' αὐτῶν εἰς τὰς συμφορὰς, καὶ νομίσαθ'
15 ὁρᾶν ἁλισκομένην τὴν πόλιν, τειχῶν κατασκαφὰς, ἐμπρήσεις
οἰκιῶν, ἀγομένας γυναῖκας καὶ παῖδας εἰς δουλείαν, πρεσβύτας
ἀνθρώπους, πρεσβύτιδας γυναῖκας, ὀψὲ μεταμανθάνοντας τὴν

---

4. τῶν Ἀθηναίων] Sic αgmnp Ald.: ὁ fcd Bekk.: artic. om. bekl.   5. Prius καὶ] Om.
bekl Bekk.   6. τῶν ἄλλων] Om. bekl.   Mox μὴ oin. bekl Cobet.   7. ἀφ'] καθ'
superscr. in gmb.   'Neutro opus est' Bait.: vid. annot.   10. φυγόντας] 'Imo φεύγοντας' Frank., collato § 129: sed hic nihil variant codd.: neque sensus est 'in exilio degentes'
sed 'in exilium actos.'

1. οὐ τό γ' ἐκ τῆς ἀληθείας κ.τ.λ. 'The
disgrace that truth establishes against him
will not be unheard, but will seem to utter a
voice contradicting his,' by a running commentary such as he goes on to give; ἄνδρα,
ἀρετῆς, ἀνδραγαθίας are all the exact reverse
of the truth, and to hear them said of Demosthenes is only to obtrude the truth upon
the audience. σιωπηθήσεται does not balance δόξει φθέγγεσθαι perfectly, and some
MSS., and editors before Bekker, read σιω-
πήσεται, 'will not be silent, but seem to
speak.' Perhaps the true subject to δόξει
φθέγγεσθαι is not τὸ αἰσχρὸν but ἡ ἀλήθεια,
so that ἐκ τῆς ἀληθείας σιωπηθήσεται is
almost = ὑπὸ τῆς ἀληθείας, only with the
personification less marked.
3. εἰ δὴ καὶ οὗτος ἀνήρ. Cp. Ae. in
Tim. § 131, p. 18. The point must be
different from the ἄνανδρον καὶ λελοιπότα
τὴν τάξιν that follows.
§ 156. Do not be mad enough, thus to
disgrace yourselves and insult the Thebans.
7. ἀφ' ὑμῶν αὐτῶν. 'Do not set up a
trophy won from yourselves.' The ordinary
construction, like triumphare de in Latin:
commoner than the more logical κατά which
some MSS. would introduce here, or the
simple genitive which Baiter inclines to.

8. μηδ' αἱρεῖτε παρανοίας κ.τ.λ. 'Do
not convict the people of Athens of insanity
in the eyes of the Greeks'—perhaps one
should say 'of decrepitude,' as the γραφὴ
παρανοίας was ordinarily against a father in
his dotage. As αἱρεῖν strictly applies to the
prosecutor only, the point of ἐναντίον τῶν
Ἑλλήνων is not that they are unnaturally
exposing their country's shame, but that the
Greeks are a court, which the acquittal of
Ctesiphon would compel to pronounce Athens
mad. Or else we must assume a little confusion in the metaphor.
12. ἡ Δημοσθένους δωροδοκία καὶ τὸ
βασιλικὸν χρυσίον. The charge here is,
that Demosthenes ruined Thebes by his
general venality, while the king sent money
to stir up strife in Greece. Afterwards, in
§ 241, there is a more definite charge not
very consistent with this, that Demosthenes
received money from the king with which
to support the Theban revolt, and did not
do it.
§ 157. Imagine the misery of their en-
slavement, their indignation against the cause
of it.
17. μεταμανθάνοντας τὴν ἐλευθερίαν.
'Learning to forget their free estate,' a rather
uncommon usage of the word, as the object

ἐλευθερίαν, κλαίοντας, ἱκετεύοντας ὑμᾶς, ὀργιζομένους οὐ τοῖς
τιμωρουμένοις, ἀλλὰ τοῖς τούτων αἰτίοις, ἐπισκήπτοντας μηδενὶ
τρόπῳ τὸν τῆς Ἑλλάδος ἀλιτήριον στεφανοῦν, ἀλλὰ καὶ τὸν
δαίμονα καὶ τὴν τύχην τὴν συμπαρακολουθοῦσαν τῷ ἀνθρώπῳ
158 φυλάξασθαι. οὔτε πόλις γὰρ οὔτ᾽ ἰδιώτης ἀνὴρ οὐδεὶς πώποτε 5
καλῶς ἀπήλλαξε Δημοσθένει συμβούλῳ χρησάμενος. ὑμεῖς δ᾽,
ὦ Ἀθηναῖοι, οὐκ αἰσχύνεσθε, εἰ ἐπὶ μὲν τοὺς πορθμέας τοὺς
εἰς Σαλαμῖνα πορθμεύοντας νόμον ἔθεσθε, ἐάν τις αὐτῶν ἄκων
ἐν τῷ πόρῳ πλοῖον ἀνατρέψῃ, τούτῳ μὴ ἐξεῖναι πάλιν πορθ-
μεῖ γενέσθαι, ἵνα μηδεὶς αὐτοσχεδιάζῃ εἰς τὰ τῶν Ἑλλήνων 10
σώματα, τὸν δὲ τὴν Ἑλλάδα καὶ τὴν πόλιν ἄρδην ἀνατετρο-
φότα, τοῦτον ἐάσετε πάλιν ἐπευθύνειν τὰ κοινά;
159 Ἵνα δ᾽ εἴπω καὶ περὶ τοῦ τετάρτου καιροῦ καὶ τῶν νυνὶ
καθεστηκότων πραγμάτων, ἐκεῖνο ὑμᾶς ὑπομνῆσαι βούλομαι, ὅτι
Δημοσθένης οὐ τὴν ἀπὸ στρατοπέδου μόνον τάξιν ἔλιπεν, ἀλλὰ 15
καὶ τὴν ἐκ τῆς πόλεως, τριήρη προσλαβὼν ὑμῶν, καὶ τοὺς Ἕλληνας ἠργυρολόγησε. καταγαγούσης δ᾽ αὐτὸν εἰς τὴν πόλιν

5. πόλις γὰρ] γὰρ πόλις bekl Bekk., et mox ἀνὴρ ἰδιώτης iidem.   11. ἀνατετρο-
φότα] ἀνατετραφότα gfdek Bekk.   12. ἐπευθύνειν] ἀπευθύνειν del pr. b Bekk.
16. Post πόλεως Reiskio videbatur aliquid deesse: Bakiusque e § 254 δὲ τότ᾽ ἀπέδρα supplevit.

is generally (if expressed) a neutral one, applicable to both the old and new knowledge,
as ὕμνον in Aesch. Ag. 709, γλῶσσαν in
Hdt. I. 57. The nearest approach to this
is perhaps Plat. Rep. p. 413 A, ἐκουσίως
μὲν ἡ ψευδὴς [δόξα ἐξίεται ἐκ διανοίας] τοῦ
μεταμανθάνοντος.

4. τῷ ἀνθρώπῳ. 'The wretch,' with a
mixture of pity and horror: cp. sup. ad §
107. It is doubtful whether the καὶ goes
more closely with τὸν δαίμονα or with φυλάξασθαι: it depends on which of these sen-
timents predominates. Either 'do not crown
him, for he is a villain: even avoid having
anything to do with him, for a curse is on
him,' or 'do not crown him, for he is a villain: avoid having anything to do with him,
for he is unlucky also.' For τὸν δαίμονα
καὶ τὴν τύχην, cp. above, § 115.

§ 158. One accident disqualifies a boat-
man : does not Demosthenes' whole career
disqualify him for steering the state?
7. ἐπὶ τοὺς πορθμέας. Almost 'against
the ferrymen,' because the law, though not
intended to injure them, injured those it
affected. As is not wonderful, this is the
only passage where the law is mentioned.
10. αὐτοσχεδιάζῃ εἰς. The construction
is not a common one, though the sense of
the verb is exactly the same as usual. 'Make
experiments upon' is perhaps the nearest

English idiom, though not exactly equivalent
to the Greek.
12. ἐπευθύνειν. With more or less notion of setting right after the upset: so still
more if ἀπευθύνειν were read.

§ 159. In the fourth period, he first bid
himself and got money away from Athens,
then stayed at home in obscurity :
15. τὴν ἀπὸ στρατοπέδου .. τὴν ἐκ τῆς
πόλεως. 'Deserted not only from the
army, but from his country.' The common
explanation of the position of the article
before these prepositions, 'left his post in
the army by going from it,' seems hardly
satisfactory. If the phrase occurred with
ἐκ only, one might explain it 'on the side
of,' the sense of motion, if any, being supplied by the verb. Here it might be enough
to say, that τὴν τάξιν λιπεῖν is almost one
verb, 'to desert.'
16. τριήρη προσλαβὼν ὑμῶν. 'Not
only did he go off, but he took a trireme of
yours into the bargain.' A very ingenious
turn to give to the fact that he went with a
public commission.
17. καταγαγούσης κ.τ.λ. When the
treaty was concluded, not only was Demosthenes comparatively safe at Athens, but it
was unnecessary to levy contributions from
the few remaining dependencies.

τῆς ἀπροσδοκήτου σωτηρίας τοὺς μὲν πρώτους χρόνους ὑπό-
τρομος ἦν ἄνθρωπος, καὶ παριὼν ἡμιθνὴς ἐπὶ τὸ βῆμα εἰρηνο-
φύλακα ὑμᾶς αὐτὸν ἐκέλευε χειροτονεῖν· ὑμεῖς δὲ κατὰ μὲν τοὺς
πρώτους χρόνους οὐδ' ἐπὶ τὰ ψηφίσματα εἴᾱτε τὸ Δημοσθέ-
5 νους ἐπιγράφειν ὄνομα, ἀλλὰ Ναυσικλεῖ τοῦτο προσετάττετε·
νυνὶ δ' ἤδη καὶ στεφανοῦσθαι ἀξιοῖ. ἐπειδὴ δ' ἐτελεύτησε Φί- 180
λιππος, 'Αλέξανδρος δ' εἰς τὴν ἀρχὴν κατέστη, πάλιν αὖ τερατευόμενος ἱερὰ μὲν ἱδρύσατο Παυσανίου, εἰς αἰτίαν δὲ εὐαγγελίων θυσίας τὴν βουλὴν κατέστησεν, ἐπωνυμίαν δ' 'Αλεξάνδρῳ
10 Μαργίτην ἐτίθετο, ἀπετόλμα δὲ λέγειν, ὡς οὐ κινηθήσεται ἐκ
Μακεδονίας· ἀγαπᾶν γὰρ αὐτὸν ἔφη ἐν Πέλλῃ περιπατοῦντα
καὶ τὰ σπλάγχνα φυλάττοντα. καὶ ταῦτα λέγειν ἔφη οὐκ
εἰκάζων, ἀλλ' ἀκριβῶς εἰδώς, ὅτι αἵματός ἐστιν ἡ ἀρετὴ ὠνία,
αὐτὸς οὐκ ἔχων αἷμα καὶ θεωρῶν τὸν 'Αλέξανδρον οὐκ ἐκ τῆς
15 'Αλεξάνδρου φύσεως, ἀλλ' ἐκ τῆς ἑαυτοῦ ἀνανδρίας, ἤδη δ' 161

2. ἄνθρωπος] Libri ἄνθρωπος, ὁ ἄνθρωπος Markl. Aut hoc aut nostrum (quod habent
Dind. Frank.) recipi volunt B. et S. Minus tamen certa videtur correctio. 3. αὐτὸν
ἐκέλευε] αὐτὸν ἐκέλευε libri plerique, ἐκέλευε ε, ἐκέλευεν αὐτὸν cdl et volg. ante Bekk. ἐκέλευεν αὐτὸν Bekk. 6. Post ἐτελεύτησε μὲν add bekl Bekk.: idque probat Frank.
8. Post εὐαγγελίων καὶ add agmn. 9. δ'] Om. agmfcd. 10. ἐτίθετο] ἔθετο
Harpocr. Suid. 12. ταῦτα] Sic agmn: ceteri ταυτί.

4. οὐδ' ἐπὶ τὰ ψηφίσματα κ.τ.λ. According to Plutarch, the arrangement was
due to the shame or timidity of Demosthenes
himself; a much more probable view. Aeschines, in attributing it to the indignation
of Athens, seems to have in his mind something like Ae. in Tim. §§ 180, 181, p. 25.
§ 160. When Philip was dead, he ridiculed Alexander as a timid school-boy,
7. πάλιν αὖ τερατευόμενος. 'He turned
round, and went in again for the prodigious.'
It may mean that his conduct was prodigious, but far more probably refers to the
story in §§ 77, 78.
8. ἱερὰ μὲν ἱδρύσατο Παυσανίου. Con-
sisting of an altar with a crowned statue,
like those of the native tyrannicides.
εἰς αἰτίαν δὲ κ.τ.λ. 'Made the senate
responsible' to Alexander 'for a sacrifice for
glad tidings.'
10. Μαργίτην. Who πόλλ' ἠπίστατο
ἔργα, κακῶς δ' ἠπίστατο πάντα. There is a
sneer at Alexander as a carefully educated
and universally accomplished school-boy;
perhaps also especially at his desire to emu-
late Achilles. 'There is another hero of
Homer's,' says Demosthenes, 'whom he resembles more.'
11. περιπατοῦντα continues the same
sneer, whether the precise allusion be to the
pupil of Aristotle or to the steady young man

who took regular exercise. From Plut. Vit.
Alex. 7. 2, the former seems likely; but the
two may be combined, as the object of Aristotle's open-air discourses was no doubt (in
part sanitary. Cp. Plat. Phaedr. p. 227 A.
12. τὰ σπλάγχνα φυλάττοντα. Another sneer of Demosthenes at the piety
of the Macedonian princes, which their
partisans boasted of. As regular attendance on sacrifices was really a characteristic
habit of Alexander's, and it harmonises
with the preceding ridicule, it seems better to take the words thus, not as 'keeping a whole skin,' as Bremi suggests on the
analogy of a popular proverb in Italy and a
vulgar one in Germany. Besides, after
Chaeronea it would have been hard to say
that Alexander was a coward, though it
might not be known that he was a hero.
14. οὐκ ἔχων αἷμα. Demosthenes was
a water drinker (D. de F. L. § 51, p. 355,
etc.), and not a man of robust health, so had
a double right to paleness. Cp. Eth. Nic. 3.
8; 4. 9. 2, for the contemporary Greek
opinion as to the connection of courage and
bodily temperament.
§ 166. But was afraid to go near him at
Thebes; and rewarded your misplaced generosity
15. ἤδη ἐψηφισμένων Θετταλῶν. The
Athenians were uncertain whether the expe-

ἐψηφισμένων Θετταλῶν ἐπιστρατεύειν ἐπὶ τὴν ὑμετέραν πόλιν,
καὶ τοῦ νεανίσκου τὸ πρῶτον παροξυνθέντος εἰκότως, ἐπειδὴ
περὶ Θήβας ἦν τὸ στρατόπεδον, πρεσβευτὴς ὑφ᾽ ὑμῶν χειρο-
τονηθείς, ἀποδρὰς ἐκ μέσου τοῦ Κιθαιρῶνος ἧκεν ὑποστρέψας,
οὔτ᾽ ἐν εἰρήνῃ οὔτ᾽ ἐν πολέμῳ χρήσιμον ἑαυτὸν παρέχων. καὶ 5
τὸ πάντων δεινότατον, ὑμεῖς μὲν τοῦτον οὐ προὔδοτε, οὐδ᾽ εἰά-
σατε κριθῆναι ἐν τῷ τῶν Ἑλλήνων συνεδρίῳ, οὗτος δ᾽ ὑμᾶς νῦν
162 προδέδωκεν, εἴπερ ἀληθῆ ἐστιν ἃ λέγεται. ὡς γάρ φασιν οἱ
Πάραλοι καὶ οἱ πρεσβεύσαντες πρὸς Ἀλέξανδρον, καὶ τὸ πρᾶγμα εἰκότως πιστεύεται, ἔστι τις Ἀριστίων Πλαταϊκός, ὁ τοῦ 10
Ἀριστοβούλου τοῦ φαρμακοπώλου υἱός, εἴ τις ἄρα καὶ ὑμῶν
γιγνώσκει. οὗτός ποτε ὁ νεανίσκος ἑτέρων τὴν ὄψιν διαφέρων
γενόμενος ᾤκησε πολὺν χρόνον ἐν τῇ Δημοσθένους οἰκίᾳ· ὅ τι
δὲ πράττων ἢ πάσχων, ἀμφίβολος ἡ αἰτία καὶ τὸ πρᾶγμα
οὐδαμῶς εὔσχημον ἐμοὶ λέγειν. οὗτος, ὡς ἐγὼ ἀκούω, ἠγνοη- 15
μένος ὅστις καὶ πῶς ποτ᾽ ἐστὶ βεβιωκώς, τὸν Ἀλέξανδρον
ὑποτρέχει καὶ πλησιάζει ἐκείνῳ. διὰ τούτου γράμματα πέμψας ὡς Ἀλέξανδρον ἄδειάν τινα εὕρηται καὶ διαλλαγὰς καὶ
163 πολλὴν κολακείαν πεποίηται. ἐκεῖθεν δὲ θεωρήσατε, ὡς ὅμοιόν

---

1. ὑμετέραν] ἡμετέραν gbekl.　　9. Πάραλοι] Sic amn † et corr. g †: ceteri
παράλιοι.　　13. γενόμενος] Om. d, abesse malit Frank.　　16. ὅστις καὶ
πῶς ποτ᾽ ἐστὶ] ὅστις ποτ᾽ ἐστὶ καὶ πῶς bekl et corr. g m et volg.　　17. Post πέμψας
Δημοσθένης add. fcd et volg. ante Bekk.

dition of Alexander was against Thebes only
or against themselves also: the decree of
his allies threw an alarming light upon the
question.

4. ἐκ μέσου τοῦ Κιθαιρῶνος. When
half-way across the border.

7. ἐν τῷ τῶν Ἑλλήνων συνεδρίῳ. The
Amphictyonic council according to Bremi,
who compares D. de Cor. § 396 init. But
perhaps rather the synod of Greeks under
Alexander's supremacy.

οὗτος δ᾽ ὑμᾶς νῦν προδέδωκεν. The
argument to prove this is weak : ' he has
made his peace with Alexander, and he has
let opportunities pass for injuring him : he
therefore must have bargained to keep you
quiet, as the price of his own safety.'

§ 162. *By bargaining for his safety
through a worthless boy, at a price which
may be guessed*

10. Πλαταϊκός. Not Πλαταιεὺς, though
that is also used of status, not birth, in Ar.
Ran. 694. Aristion was, according to some
of Harpocration's authorities, a Samian ;
whence the charitable may conjecture that
he was a relation of Demosthenes' wife,

who according to Plutarch was also from
Samos.

11. καὶ ὑμῶν. As well as of those who
had seen him at Alexander's court.

12. ἑτέρων τὴν ὄψιν διαφέρων. Apparently a rather contemptuous description of
good looks : cp. Ae. in Tim. § 75, p. 11.
'γενόμενος cum d abesse malim' Franke ;
but, being a stock phrase, it might be used
with another participle as if it were an
adjective. Vid. Bremi ad § 10 of this
speech.

16. ὅστις καὶ πῶς ποτ᾽ ἐστὶ βεβιωκώς.
So the best MSS. : volg. ὅστις ποτ᾽ ἐστὶ καὶ
πῶς βεβιωκώς : the text is rather more forcible, as well as less obvious.

17. ὑποτρέχει. We should say, ' crept
up his sleeve,' 'slunk up to him,' 'wormed
himself into his favour ;' the Greek word
expresses something of surprise. According
to Harpocr., he made interest with Hephae-
stion.

§ 163. *From the way in which, while
professing to be Alexander's enemy, he has
lost three good chances of injuring him : first
at his entrance into Asia,*

ἐστι τὸ πρᾶγμα τῇ αἰτίᾳ. εἰ γάρ τι τούτων ἐφρόνει Δημοσθένης καὶ πολεμικῶς εἶχεν, ὥσπερ καὶ φησὶ, πρὸς Ἀλέξανδρον, τρεῖς αὐτῷ καιροὶ κάλλιστοι παραγεγόνασιν, ὧν οὐδενὶ
φαίνεται κεχρημένος. εἰς μὲν ὁ πρῶτος, ὅτ᾽ εἰς τὴν ἀρχὴν οὐ
5 πάλαι καθεστηκὼς Ἀλέξανδρος ἀπαρασκεύων αὐτῷ τῶν ἰδίων
ὄντων εἰς τὴν Ἀσίαν διέβη, ἤκμαζε δ᾽ ὁ τῶν Περσῶν βασιλεὺς καὶ ναυσὶ καὶ χρήμασι καὶ πεζῇ στρατιᾷ, ἄσμενος δ᾽ ἂν
ὑμᾶς εἰς τὴν συμμαχίαν προσεδέξατο διὰ τοὺς ἐπιφερομένους
αὐτῷ κινδύνους. εἶπάς τινα ἐνταῦθα λόγον, Δημόσθενες, ἢ
10 ἔγραψάς τι ψήφισμα; βούλει σε θῶ φοβηθῆναι καὶ χρήσασθαι τῷ αὑτοῦ τρόπῳ; καίτοι ῥητορικὴν δειλίαν δημόσιος καιρὸς οὐκ ἀναμένει. ἀλλ᾽ ἐπειδὴ πάσῃ τῇ δυνάμει Δαρεῖος κατε-164
βεβήκει, ὁ δ᾽ Ἀλέξανδρος ἦν ἀπειλημμένος ἐν Κιλικίᾳ πάντων
ἐνδεής, ὡς ἔφησθα σύ, αὐτίκα μάλα δ᾽ ἤμελλεν, ὡς ἦν ὁ παρὰ
15 σοῦ λόγος, συμπατηθήσεσθαι ὑπὸ τῆς Περσικῆς ἵππου, τὴν δὲ
σὴν ἀηδίαν ἡ πόλις οὐκ ἐχώρει καὶ τὰς ἐπιστολὰς, ἃς ἐξηρτημένος ἐκ τῶν δακτύλων περιῄεις, ἐπιδεικνύων τισὶ τὸ ἐμὸν πρόσωπον ὡς ἐκπεπληγμένου καὶ ἀθυμοῦντος, καὶ χρυσόκερων ἀπο-

5. ἀπαρασκεύων] ἀκατασκεύων bkl Bekk.   αὐτῷ] αὐτῷ sine caussa B. et S.   7. δ᾽
ἂν] ἂν δ᾽ agm. Statim ἡμᾶς ekl Bekk.   9. αὐτῷ] Ita B. et S., cum afcd αὐτῷ habeant,
ceteri et Bekk. ἑαυτῷ.   10. Ante φοβηθῆναι καὶ inserunt fcd.   11. αὑτοῦ] Ita
B. et S., cum pro volgato ἑαυτοῦ am † et pr. g † habeant αὐτοῦ, pl αὑτῷ, σαυτοῦ ze et corr.
gb. 'Vide tamen, ne σαυτοῦ praestet' Frank.: idque receperat Bekk.   12. κατεβεβή-
κει] Ita amnk; ceteri et Bekk. καταβεβήκει.   13. ἀπειλημμένος] ἀπειλημένος g.
14. μάλα δὲ] δὲ μάλα bekl Bekk.

1. τὸ πρᾶγμα τῇ αἰτίᾳ. As we should
say, 'the facts look very like this charge.'
3. παραγεγόνασιν = 'have come and
passed.'
5. ἀπαρασκεύων. 'Before he had everything ready at home.' Bekker's reading
ἀκατασκεύων would suit the sense much
better, 'while everything at home was un-
settled;' but the MS. authority against it is
too great.
7. ἄσμενος δ᾽ ἂν κ.τ.λ. Cp. below, §
239 sq.
11. ῥητορικὴν δειλίαν might be simply
'cannot wait for a cowardly orator,' but
better, 'cannot wait as long as it takes an
orator's cowardice to screw itself up to
action.'
§ 164. Then before Issus, when Demosthenes ostentatiously proclaimed his case
desperate,
12. πάσῃ τῇ δυνάμει. Opposed to the
small force that fought at the Granicus.
13. ἀπειλημμένος ἐν Κιλικίᾳ refers to
Alexander's position before the manœuvres

that led to the battle of Issus. He had
already carried one pass by strategical skill,
before fighting the battle.
16. ἃς ἐξηρτημένος κ.τ.λ. Each letter
being tied up with a string, and he carrying
a letter hanging by its string from each
finger. The passage is repeated almost
verbally by Dinarchus, c. Dem. § 36, p. 94
fin.
18. χρυσόκερων .. κατεστέφθαι. 'If
any misfortune happens to Alexander, Aeschines had already got his horns gilded and
his garlands on, ready to be sacrificed.' There
may be an allusion to the oracle said to have
been given to Philip while meditating the
expedition into Asia, ἔσεπται μὲν ὁ ταῦρος,
ἔχει τέλος, ἔστιν ὁ θύσων; it was no doubt
meant to be ambiguous, and was applied to
his own approaching death. Demosthenes
may have proposed the further interpretation, 'The bull is Alexander's friends in
Greece.' There may also be an allusion to
'Macedonian gold,' as having only served to
deck the receiver for the slaughter.

καλῶν καὶ κατεστέφθαι φάσκων, εἴ τι πταῖσμα συμβήσεται
Ἀλεξάνδρῳ, οὐδ᾽ ἐνταῦθα ἔπραξας οὐδὲν, ἀλλ᾽ εἴς τινα καιρὸν
165 ἀνεβάλλου καλλίῳ. ὑπερβὰς τοίνυν ἅπαντα ταῦτα ὑπὲρ τῶν
νυνὶ καθεστηκότων λέξω. Λακεδαιμόνιοι μὲν καὶ τὸ ξενικὸν
ἐπέτυχον μάχῃ καὶ διέφθειραν τοὺς περὶ Κόρραγον στρατιώ- 5
τας, Ἠλεῖοι δ᾽ αὐτοῖς συμμετεβάλοντο καὶ Ἀχαιοὶ πάντες
πλὴν Πελληναίων καὶ Ἀρκαδία πᾶσα πλὴν Μεγάλης πόλεως,
αὕτη δὲ ἐπολιορκεῖτο καὶ καθ᾽ ἑκάστην ἡμέραν ἐπίδοξος ἦν
ἁλῶναι, ὁ δ᾽ Ἀλέξανδρος ἔξω τῆς ἄρκτου καὶ τῆς οἰκουμένης
ὀλίγου δεῖν πάσης μεθειστήκει, ὁ δὲ Ἀντίπατρος πολὺν χρόνον 10
συνῆγε στρατόπεδον, τὸ δ᾽ ἐσόμενον ἄδηλον ἦν. ἐνταῦθ᾽ ἡμῖν
ἀπόδειξιν ποίησαι, Δημόσθενες, τί ποτ᾽ ἦν ἃ ἔπραξας ἢ τί
ποτ᾽ ἦν ἃ ἔλεγες· καὶ εἰ βούλει, παραχωρῶ σοι τοῦ βήματος,
166 ἕως ἂν εἴπῃς. ἐπειδὴ δὲ σιγᾷς, ὅτι μὲν ἀπορεῖς, συγγνώμην
ἔχω σοι, ἃ δὲ τότ᾽ ἔλεγες, ἐγὼ νῦν λέξω.· οὐ μέμνησθε αὐτοῦ 15
τὰ μιαρὰ καὶ ἀπίθανα ῥήματα, ἃ πῶς ποθ᾽ ὑμεῖς, ὦ σιδηροῖ,

---

5. μάχῃ] μάχης g.　　6. συμμετεβάλοντο] Sic ekl et editi : συνεπιβάλλοντο
rec. marg. t, συνεπελάβοντο Flor. pr. z, 'quod praetulerim' Frank. et habet Schultz.; συμμετεβάλοντο ceteri.　　7. Πελληναίων] Imo Πελληνέων, Cobet. Frank. Schultz.
12. Δημόσθενες] Om. e : ὦ Δημόσθενες kl Bekk.　　ἤ] Sic agmnpr : ceteri et Bekk.
καί.　　15. νῦν] νυνὶ bekl Bekk.　　16. ὦ σιδηροῖ] ὦ σιδήρεοι libri, nisi quod
ὧς habent bekl, iidemque in voce subsequenti temere nonnihil variant.

---

3. ἀνεβάλλου. The middle is used by
the orators of delay by which a man cheats
himself, the active of delay by which he
cheats his neighbours.

§ 165. And, lastly, when the Spartans
had a fair prospect of victory,
ὑπὲρ τῶν νυνὶ καθεστηκότων. He
reckons the situation as unchanged in the
whole period after Issus; as, in regard to
the state of Athens particularly, after Chaeronea (§§ 55, 159).

4. τὸ ξενικόν. The mercenaries sent
over after Issus.

5. τοὺς περὶ Κόρραγον στρατιώτας.
The construction is rarely used of the relation of soldiers to their general, oftener of
partisans to their chief. Probably we are
to take στρατιώτας as meaning mercenaries,
who would be spoken of as fellow-adven-
turers or personal adherents of their commander. It is very unlikely that the name
of a place should be used in this construction.

9. ἔξω τῆς ἄρκτου καὶ τῆς οἰκουμένης.
Whether the former phrase means 'beyond
the pole' the other side of the Bear, or ' beyond the tropics' where the Bear is lost
sight of, may be doubted: perhaps Aeschines
himself conceived the matter vaguely. 'Out
of our hemisphere' is the sense in either

case. τῆς οἰκουμένης may mean 'the world
of known civilization,' like the well-known
later usage of the Roman empire; but perhaps is rather to be taken literally, ' out of
the habitable world,' into desert and half-
mythical countries.

10. πολὺν χρόνον συνῆγε στρατόπεδον.
So that Athens had plenty of time to move.

12. τί ποτ᾽ ἦν ἃ ἔλεγες. One might
translate 'What did what you said come to?'
but for what follows, which shows that the
point is, ' You cannot point to anything you
did : I will point to things ridiculous as well
as disloyal that you said.'

13. παραχωρῶ σοι τοῦ βήματος. Cp.
sup. ad § 55, D. de Cor. 176. Probably
the usage of the court was too uniform to
make such appeals more than a matter of
form.

§ 166. You, instead of doing anything,
gave us obscure and nasty metaphors as reasons for doing nothing.

16. ἀπίθανα. Implying that his violence
defeated his object.

ὦ σιδηροῖ. Meant probably for a
left-handed compliment: 'You must have
had a marvellous constitution to endure the
disgust, which I will not insult you by doubt-
ing that you felt.' Aeschines in every other
passage uses the contracted forms of the

ἐκαρτερεῖτε ἀκροώμενοι ; ὅτ᾽ ἔφη παρελθὼν "ἀμπελουργοῦσί
τινες τὴν πόλιν, ἀνατετμήκασί τινες τὰ κλήματα τοῦ δήμου,
ὑποτέτμηται τὰ νεῦρα τῶν πραγμάτων, φορμορραφούμεθα ἐπὶ
τὰ στενά, τινὲς πρῶτον ὥσπερ τὰς βελόνας διείρουσι." ταῦτα 167
5 δὲ τί ἐστιν, ὦ κίναδος ; ῥήματα ἢ θαύματα ; καὶ πάλιν ὅτε
κύκλῳ περιδινῶν σεαυτὸν ἐπὶ τοῦ βήματος ἔλεγες ὡς ἀντιπράτ-
των Ἀλεξάνδρῳ "ὁμολογῶ τὰ Λακωνικὰ συστῆσαι, ὁμολογῶ
Θετταλοὺς καὶ Περραιβοὺς ἀφιστάναι." [σὺ Θετταλοὺς ἀφι-

3. ὑποτέτμηται] † ὑποτέτμητε in litura g †.   φορμορραφούμεθα] Statim post hanc
vocem interpungunt Dionys. B. et S., mox omisso πρῶτον.   4. τὰς βελόνας] τοὺς βελῶνας † g † bel, τὰς βελῶνας Vat.   5. τί] Sic bekl et editi : ceteri τίνος.   6. ἀντι-
πράττων] † ἐναντιούμενος corr. g †.

metallic adjectives : Phrynichus states the
rule as universal in Attic, and Cobet and
Franke follow him. Libri et volgo σιδήρεοι ;
but the MSS. of Aeschines are not infallible
on a point of grammatical criticism, even
when unanimous, and here there is a little
confusion in some.

1. ἀμπελουργοῦσί τινες κ.τ.λ. For
τινὲς, see on § 1. Here they must mean
Aeschines and his friends : Demosthenes
does commonly avoid naming political opponents. He would have named Alexander,
had he been the man intended. It seems
just possible to explain all the metaphors,
except perhaps ὑποτέτμηται τὰ νεῦρα τῶν
πραγμάτων, of vine-dressing : 'certain men
have cut back the shoots of democracy : the
main fibres of our fortunes are cut through :
we are being stitched with matting into a
corner: some people are getting their needles
threaded to begin with.' On the whole,
perhaps this would give the best meaning to
the difficult words φορμορραφούμεθα ἐπὶ τὰ
στενά, which might be a description of a
process intended to keep a vine from spread-
ing over the ground. It is hard to believe
that at his harshest Demosthenes mixed up
two metaphors in defiance of logic, and
meant, 'We have no more room to turn
than if we were sewn up in matting like a
mummy' (it is hardly necessary to mention
Wunderlich's unpleasant emendation for
πρῶτον, which would continue that image :
yet cp. Ae. de F. L. p. 31, § 22). Any
way, the first two clauses must be understood
as implying that Athens was to be kept sub-
servient rather than exactly mutilated : it
was to be trained and trimmed, not allowed
to grow its own way. It is as hard to accept
the last words, as they stand, of the section
as genuine, as it is to suggest any probable
correction. The reading of Dionysius,
adopted by B. and S., φορμορραφούμεθα, ἐπὶ

τὰ στενά τινες ὥσπερ κ.τ.λ., would mean,
'we are being dragged through a needle's
eye,' which makes sense at the expense of
introducing a third metaphor, but fails entirely to account for the insertion of πρῶτον.
πρῶτον is probably right, for 'threading a
needle' is a natural prelude to φορμορραφούμεθα. But an accusative seems to be wanted,
to be illustrated by ὥσπερ τὰς βελόνας, if it
means 'some people are first of all threading
[their instruments] like needles ;' if we take
it 'some people are as it were passing needles
through [us] first of all,' we lose the only
possible force of πρῶτον, and still want the
remoter object of διείρουσι to be expressed.
No reading has yet been extracted from the
fact, that four MSS. have τοὺς βελώνας.

§ 167. Claiming all the credit for what
other people were doing—things which you
have never the heart to do, but always the
face to ask to be paid for.

5. ῥήματα ἢ θαύματα. Aeschines is
rather fond of these imperfect assonances :
one might translate 'metaphors or mon-
sters?'

καὶ πάλιν ὅτε. Exactly like vel quom
in Aen. 11. 406. Had Virgil this passage in
his head? since the idiom is noted as strange
in Latin.

7. ὁμολογῶ. Demosthenes was alter-
nately taunted as a coward and a firebrand ;
his reply to the second class of charges was to
boast of what he was accused of doing. Aeschines presses the first class, to shew the
emptiness of the boast.

8. [Σὺ Θετταλοὺς ἀφιστάναι]. We
bracket these words because other editors
have not adopted them, rather than because
we doubt their genuineness. The MSS.
exhibit marks of confusion, some omitting
this clause and some the next ; but there is
hardly better authority for omitting one
than the other, and it is clear that, from the

στάναι ;] σὺ γὰρ ἂν κώμην ἀποστήσειας; σὺ γὰρ ἂν προσέλ-
θοις μὴ ὅτι πρὸς πόλιν, ἀλλὰ πρὸς οἰκίαν, ὅπου κίνδυνος πρόσεστιν; ἀλλ᾽ εἰ μέν που χρήματα ἀναλίσκεται, προσκαθίσεις,
πρᾶξιν δὲ ἀνδρὸς οὐ πράξεις· ἐὰν δ᾽ αὐτόματόν τι συμβῇ, προσ-
ποιήσει καὶ σαυτὸν ἐπὶ τὸ γεγενημένον ἐπιγράψεις· ἂν δ᾽ 5
ἔλθῃ φόβος τις, ἀποδράσει· ἐὰν δὲ θαρρήσωμεν, δωρεὰς αἰτή-
σεις καὶ χρυσοῖς στεφάνοις στεφανοῦσθαι.

168 Ναὶ, ἀλλὰ δημοτικός ἐστιν. ἐὰν μὲν τοίνυν πρὸς τὴν εὐφημίαν αὐτοῦ τῶν λόγων ἀποβλέπητε, ἐξαπατηθήσεσθε, ὥσπερ
καὶ πρότερον, ἐὰν δ᾽ εἰς τὴν φύσιν καὶ τὴν ἀλήθειαν, οὐκ 10
ἐξαπατηθήσεσθε. ἐκείνως δὲ ἀπολάβετε παρ᾽ αὐτοῦ τὸν λόγον.

1. σὺ .. ἀποστήσειας] σὺ † Θετταλίαν † ἀφιστάναι; σὺ γαρ ἂν κώμην ἀποστῆσαις;
marg. g (cum a pr. m. omissum esset σὺ Θετταλοὺς ἀφιστάναι), σὺ Θετταλοὺς ἀφιστάναι;
σὺ γὰρ κ.τ.λ. marg. m (itaque teste Bekk. marg. g), σὺ Θετταλοὺς ἀποστήσειας; σὺ γὰρ
κ.τ.λ. c, σὺ Θετταλοὺς ἀφιστάναι; οὐ γὰρ ἂν κώμην ἀποστήσειας; bk σὺ Θετταλοὺς ἀφιστάναι; οὐ γὰρ ἂν κώμην ἀποστῆσαις e, οὐ Θετταλοὺς ἀφιστάναι σὺ γὰρ ἂν κώμην ἀποστήσειας
Flor. l, σὺ Θετταλους ἀποστήσειας f, σὺ Θετταλοὺς ἀφιστήσειας d. σὺ γὰρ ἂν κώμην ἀπο-
στήσαις an pr. gm et editi. ἀποστήσειας mavolt Frank., habet Schultz. 3. προσκα-
θίσεις] προσκαθιζήσει post Lobeck. editi, habetque προσκαθίσεις z, προσκαθίζεις εἰς k, προ-
σκαθίζειν εἰς bel, quae pro προσκαθιζήσει posita esse probabile est. προκαθιστήση fd,
ceteri προσκαθεσθήση. 8. πρὸς] εἰς be Cobet. 9. αὐτοῦ τῶν λόγων] τῶν
λόγων αὐτοῦ agmnp: vid. annot.

similarity of their beginning and end, either
was very likely to be omitted accidentally.
And the vigorous scorn of the question, and
the climax of the next, are too like Aeschines' best manner to have been forced on
him by a copyist. The true reading of one
MS. (marg. g.) may perhaps be thought to
throw a little doubt on the subject, as proving some uncertainty in the body of the
clause. But perhaps Θετταλίαν may be
right: it would be an abbreviated expression,
including the two nations of Thessalians and
Perrhaebians. Note the change of tense
from ἀφιστάναι to ἀποστήσειας : ' I confess
that I am getting up a revolt in Thessaly.'
' You get up a revolt in Thessaly! Could
you bring a single village to the point of
revolting?' and be there, as the next clause
proves, at the time of the outbreak, to see
that your work prospered.
3. προσκαθίσεις. This reading is now
found in one good MS., and, considering
that another group seem to point to προσκαθίζεις, has as fair a chance of probability as
the vulgate προσκαθιζήσει, itself a correction
of Lobeck's for the reading of most MSS.,
προσκαθεσθήση. The last is, according to
Phrynichus, a post-classical form: Demosthenes uses προσκαθεδεῖται, Olynt. 1, § 18,
p. 24. And, moreover, the metaphor, 'you
will besiege, blockade it,' seems violent.

προσκαθίσεις would mean no more than
' you will sit by, watching for something to
turn up,' like a beggar, or at best a Micawber.
5. σαυτὸν .. ἐπιγράψεις. Perhaps simply claim credit for it in a fussy, self-import-
ant speech, as described above; perhaps
more definitely, ' move a decree in your
own name,' which your partisans can quote
as having produced what had happened already; as, according to Aeschines, in the
case of the Theban alliance.
§ 168. Then he calls himself a friend to
the Constitution. But is he?
8. τὴν εὐφημίαν αὐτοῦ τῶν λόγων. So
Bekker. B. and S. and later editors transpose τῶν λόγων αὐτοῦ; but the old reading
is less like late Greek, and gives a more
forcible sense, ' His delicacy, which stops at
words.' εὐφημία, as usual, implies negative
rather than positive commendation: ' There
is nothing to offend in his language, he
speaks like a sober incorruptible man.' We
should have a specimen of εὐφημία in Demosthenes' constant affectation of reserve on
personal matters which he contrasts with
the ribaldry of Aeschines.
11. ἐκείνως. Rarely thus used of what
is immediately to be explained, like ὧδε :
cp. Dem. Lept. § 69, p. 475. The distinction between the two adverbs is probably
that ὧδε means merely 'in the way I am

ἐγὼ μὲν μεθ' ὑμῶν λογιοῦμαι, ἃ δεῖ ὑπάρξαι ἐν τῇ φύσει τῷ
δημοτικῷ ἀνδρὶ καὶ σώφρονι, καὶ πάλιν ἀντιθήσω, ποῖόν τινα
εἰκός ἐστιν εἶναι τὸν ὀλιγαρχικὸν ἄνθρωπον καὶ φαῦλον· ὑμεῖς
δ' ἀντιθέντες ἑκάτερα τούτων θεωρήσατ' αὐτὸν, μὴ ὁποτέρου
5 τοῦ λόγου, ἀλλ' ὁποτέρου τοῦ βίου ἐστίν. οἶμαι τοίνυν ἅπαν- 169
τας ἂν ὁμολογήσειν ὑμᾶς τάδε δεῖν ὑπάρξαι τῷ δημοτικῷ,
πρῶτον μὲν ἐλεύθερον αὐτὸν εἶναι καὶ πρὸς πατρὸς καὶ πρὸς
μητρός, ἵνα μὴ διὰ τὴν περὶ τὸ γένος ἀτυχίαν δυσμενὴς ᾖ τοῖς
νόμοις, οἳ σώζουσι τὴν δημοκρατίαν, δεύτερον δ' ἀπὸ τῶν προ-
10 γόνων εὐεργεσίαν τινὰ αὐτῷ πρὸς τὸν δῆμον ὑπάρχειν, ἢ τό γ'

6. ἂν] 'Deletum malim' Frank.: namque ὁμολογήσειν habent omnes praeter *bekl*. ὁμολογήσειν ὑμᾶς habent *agmnp* Vat. Laur., ὑμᾶς ὁμολογῆσαι *bekl* Bekk. ceteri ὑμᾶς ὁμολογήσειν. 7. ἐλεύθερον αὐτὸν] αὐτὸν ἐλεύθερον *fcdekl*, αὐτῷ ἐλεύθερον *d*. πρὸς]
ante μητρὸs om. *agmnfcdq* Vat. Barb. Flor.: mox πρὸς pro περὶ ponunt *agmnz* Laur. Flor. *cd*.

going to tell you;' ἐκείνως has the further
force 'in the way you never have yet,' or
'the reverse way to that which he suggests
to you.' Perhaps the article with λόγον,
'the account he invites you to scrutinise,'
marks the latter sense as most prominent.

1. τῷ δημοτικῷ ἀνδρὶ καὶ σώφρονι.
Democracy, being so long established at
Athens, had all the respectable and conservative associations which we, an1 most
Greeks likewise, connect rather with aristocracy. The democrat is a sober man of
assured position; the oligarch a dangerous
adventurer and revolutionist. Such was the
universal Athenian sentiment, strengthened
and largely justified by reminiscences of the
Four Hundred and of the Thirty; but cosmopolitan thinkers like Socrates and his dis-
ciples fell in rather with the general view,
which saw in Sparta the best type of a strong
legitimate government. The great speech
of Pericles is almost the only work of any
speculative depth that attempts to justify
the affection felt by every loyal Athenian for
his own constitution.

4. μὴ ὁποτέρου τοῦ λόγου κ.τ.λ. 'To
which party he belongs, not by profession
but by action,' lit. 'to which life he belongs,
not to which profession.' ὁ δημοτικὸς βίος
and ὁ ὀλιγαρχικὸς βίος are contrasted, being
identified with ὁ σώφρων and ὁ φαῦλος βίος
respectively: the contrast between 'popular
professions' and 'oligarchic professions' is
more easily translatable.

§ 169. To prove himself so, a man should
be a true-born citizen, or he will hate the
constitution that excludes him: a man whose
ancestors have been the city's friends, or he
will keep up the feud against the city:

7. ἐλεύθερον αὐτὸν εἶναι. It is probable

that there were many men allowed to pass
as citizens, but known to have very doubtful
claims. The διαψήφισις seems to have commanded little respect (vid. ad D. de Cor. §
168), and it was invidious to appeal to it
(Ae. de F. L. § 193): while the fact that
accusations of civil illegitimacy could be
bandied about as they are by Demosthenes
and Aeschines, or introduced quite paren-
thetically and jestingly, as by Demosthenes
against the aristocratic Midias, suggests that
there must have been a vague and uncomfortable suspicion, that if the matter were
pressed, no one would be safe.

πρὸς μητρὸς .. περὶ τὸ γένος. Most
good MSS. omit πρὸς before μητρὸς, and
substitute it for περὶ afterwards: the first
is probably an error and the cause of the
other, which if it stood alone might be defended.

10. εὐεργεσίαν .. πρὸς τὸν δῆμον. It
would be just possible to translate, 'that he
should have from his ancestors some benefit
(received from the people) binding him to
gratitude to the people.' This suits the
context and the parallelism of clauses, but
the sense it requires for πρὸς is a very forced
one; had it been meant, Aeschines would
have written πρὸς τοῦ δήμου. We must
therefore translate the natural way, 'that he
should have some good deed to shew done by
his ancestors to the people, or at least no
enmity' between them and it: εὐεργεσία
being conceived as implying mutual good
will, as ἔχθρα naturally does mutual ill will.
It is assumed that if his fathers have done
the state some service, the state will know
it, and will have rewarded them and trust
him. The assumption is aided by the lati-
tude of meaning of χάρις.

ἀναγκαιότατον μηδεμίαν ἔχθραν, ἵνα μὴ βοηθῶν τοῖς τῶν πρυ-
170 γόνων ἀτυχήμασι κακῶς ἐπιχειρῇ ποιεῖν τὴν πόλιν. τρίτον
σώφρονα καὶ μέτριον χρὴ πεφυκέναι αὐτὸν πρὸς τὴν καθ' ἡμέραν
δίαιταν, ὅπως μὴ διὰ τὴν ἀσέλγειαν τῆς δαπάνης δωροδοκῇ κατὰ
τοῦ δήμου, τέταρτον εὐγνώμονα καὶ δυνατὸν εἰπεῖν· καλὸν γὰρ 5
τὴν μὲν διάνοιαν προαιρεῖσθαι τὰ βέλτιστα, τὴν δὲ παιδείαν
τὴν τοῦ ῥήτορος καὶ τὸν λόγον πείθειν τοὺς ἀκούοντας· εἰ δὲ
μὴ, τήν γ' εὐγνωμοσύνην ἀεὶ προτακτέον τοῦ λόγου. πέμπτον
ἀνδρεῖον εἶναι τὴν ψυχὴν, ἵνα μὴ παρὰ τὰ δεινὰ καὶ τοὺς πο-
λέμους ἐγκαταλείπῃ τὸν δῆμον.   τὸν δ' ὀλιγαρχικὸν πάντα 10
δεῖ τἀναντία τούτων ἔχειν· τί γὰρ δεῖ πάλιν διεξιέναι; σκέψασθε δὴ, τί τούτων ὑπάρχει Δημοσθένει· ὁ δὲ λογισμὸς ἔστω
ἐπὶ πᾶσι δικαίοις.

171   Τούτῳ πατὴρ μὲν ἦν Δημοσθένης ὁ Παιανιεύς, ἀνὴρ ἐλεύ-
θερος· οὐ γὰρ δεῖ ψεύδεσθαι· τὰ δ' ἀπὸ τῆς μητρὸς καὶ τοῦ 15
πάππου τοῦ πρὸς μητρὸς πῶς ἔχει αὐτῷ; ἐγὼ φράσω. Γύλων
ἦν ἐκ Κεραμέων. οὗτος προδοὺς τοῖς πολεμίοις Νύμφαιον τὸ
ἐν τῷ Πόντῳ, τότε τῆς πόλεως ἐχούσης τὸ χωρίον τοῦτο, φυγὰς ἐκ τῆς πόλεως ἐγένετο θανάτου καταγνωσθέντος αὐτοῦ,

9. πολέμους] κινδύνους bekl corr. g Bekk.   10. ἐγκαταλείπῃ] Sic agmnp : ceteri
et Bekk. -λίπῃ.   14. ἦν] Om. p Vat. Laur.   17. Post Κεραμέων ἀπόδημος
add. g et marg. mb.   18. τῷ Πόντῳ] Ita gmnpfcdb et duo codd. Harpocrationis :
ceteri articulum omittunt.   Post φυγὰς ἀπ' εἰσαγγελίας add. cekl et marg. gmf,
ἀπὸ ἀγγελίας pr. g, ἐπ' εἰσαγγελίας p. 'Glossema g § 79 irrepsit' B. et S. Bakio θανάτου
καταγνωσθέντος αὐτοῦ ejiciendum esse videbatur : facilius fuisset θάνατον γὰρ .. κατέγνωτε
in proximo § ejicere, ut glossema videlicet hinc desumptum.

§ 170. A man of virtuous private life, or
he will take bribes to support his profligacy :
a sound thinker and, if possible, a trained
speaker : and last not least, a brave and
high-minded man.
4. κατὰ τοῦ δήμου. Not τῆς πόλεως,
because it is ὁ δημοτικὸς not ὁ εὔνους πολίτης that is under discussion.
5. εὐγνώμονα would naturally coincide
with the intellectual side only of the ambiguous εὖ φρονεῖν ; but, being explained by
τὴν μὲν διάνοιαν προαιρεῖσθαι τὰ βέλτιστα,
it gains something of the notion of good
will, while this explanation itself includes
something of good judgment. Some take
διάνοιαν and παιδείαν καὶ λόγον as subjects
to the infinitives : better as accusatives of
respect. Note that he conceives oratorical
ability as depending entirely on παιδεία.
9. παρὰ τὰ δεινά. Perhaps 'at the time
of,' rather than 'by reason of :' at any rate
it illustrates the origin of the latter sense.
13. ἐπὶ πᾶσι δικαίοις. 'Be made on
the fairest terms,' 'under conditions of the
most perfect justice.'

§ 171. Now Demosthenes' father was a
real citizen : his mother the daughter of Gylon who betrayed Nymphaeum,
15. οὐ γὰρ δεῖ ψεύδεσθαι. Probably 'I
will not tell lies about his father, as he does
about mine.' But if we admit the genuineness of the exquisite fragments of speeches
by Demades preserved in Tzetzes, it will appear that Demosthenes the elder, though a
wealthy man, was not thought well-connected
enough to justify his son's claim to honour
and thorough respectability : and then the
point might be, 'a free man certainly—but
an utter snob.' Those who heard the speech
would know which was meant.
16. Γύλων ἦν ἐκ Κεραμέων. 'There
was one Gylon .. :' he begins at the beginning. Some MSS. add ἀπόδημος, probably
a corruption of a gloss explaining that ἐκ
Κεραμέων meant ἀπὸ δήμου Κεραμέων.
19. θανάτου καταγνωσθέντος αὐτοῦ.
Apparently he had really been sentenced on
some criminal charge. Demosthenes only
confesses to a fine, which he asserts had been
paid before his death : D. in Aph. 2. ad init.

τὴν κρίσιν οὐχ ὑπομείνας, καὶ ἀφικνεῖται εἰς Βόσπορον, κἀκεῖ 172
λαμβάνει δωρεὰν παρὰ τῶν τυράννων τοὺς ὠνομασμένους Κή-
πους, καὶ γαμεῖ γυναῖκα πλουσίαν μὲν νὴ Δία καὶ χρυσίον ἐπιφερομένην πολύ, Σκύθιν δὲ τὸ γένος, ἐξ ἧς γίγνονται αὐτῷ
5 θυγατέρες δύο, ἃς ἐκεῖνος δεῦρο μετὰ πολλῶν χρημάτων ἀποστείλας συνῴκισε τὴν μὲν ἑτέραν ὁτῳδήποτε, ἵνα μὴ πολλοῖς
ἀπεχθάνωμαι· τὴν δ᾽ ἑτέραν ἔγημε παριδὼν τοὺς τῆς πόλεως
νόμους Δημοσθένης ὁ Παιανιεύς, ἐξ ἧς ὑμῖν ὁ περίεργος καὶ
συκοφάντης Δημοσθένης γεγένηται. οὐκοῦν ἀπὸ μὲν τοῦ πάπ-
10 που τοῦ πρὸς μητρὸς πολέμιος ἂν εἴη τῷ δήμῳ, θάνατον γὰρ
αὐτοῦ τῶν προγόνων κατέγνωτε, τὰ δ᾽ ἀπὸ τῆς μητρὸς Σκύ-
θης, βάρβαρος ἑλληνίζων τῇ φωνῇ· ὅθεν καὶ τὴν πονηρίαν οὐκ
ἐπιχώριός ἐστι. περὶ δὲ τὴν καθ᾽ ἡμέραν δίαιταν τίς ἐστιν; 173
ἐκ τριηράρχου λογογράφος ἀνεφάνη, τὰ πατρῷα καταγελά-

---

6. στείλας] ἀποστείλας *fcdbekl* et volg. usque ad Bekk.   9. Δημοσθένης γεγένη-
ται] Δημοσθένης γεγέννηται *pe*, γεγένηται Δημοσθένης *gmnfd* Bekk.   10. τοῦ πρὸς
μητρὸς] Om. *bekl*.

§ 172. By a Scythian woman whom he
married in exile: so Demosthenes is by descent a barbarian and a traitor.
3. ἐπιφερομένην. As Lys. pro bonis
Aristoph. 14.
4. Σκύθιν δὲ τὸ γένος. No doubt she
was practically a Greek ; but Aeschines uses
even stronger language about her barbarism
in De F. L. § 82, p. 38, ἐκ τῶν νομάδων
Σκυθῶν τὸ πρὸς μητρὸς γένος ὤν.
6. συνῴκισε would cover both the case
of legitimate marriage, and of what passed
as such but was not.
ὁτῳδήποτε. Demochares: D. in Aph.
2. § 4, p. 836. See the whole passage,
which tells strongly against the truth of this
story. If Cleobule had been no true Athenian, Aphobus would have been certain to
plead the fact as a reason for not marrying
her ; instead of the very lame defence which
he appears to have made, that the elder Demosthenes purposely left his accounts in dis-
order, lest he should be called upon for his
father-in-law's fine. This Demochares, Demosthenes' *uncle*, seems to be sometimes
confounded with his namesake, Demosthenes'
nephew, an orator and historian.
10. τοῦ πρὸς μητρός is omitted by one
group of MSS., and looks very like a gloss :
besides that, it makes τοῦ πάππου a weak as
well as formally a false antithesis to τὰ δ᾽
ἀπὸ μητρὸς below. The next clause, θάνατον .. κατέγνωτε, also looks like a gloss,
τῶν προγόνων being especially suspicious, and
though all MSS. have the words and it is
one of the commonest faults of Aeschines'

style to put glosses on his own sentences, it
is more certain that he ought not to have
written these words than that he wrote
them.
11. τὰ δ᾽ ἀπὸ μητρός. As we say, ' in
the female line ;' his mother's mother was a
Scythian, his grandfather (who can, as his
wife cannot, be spoken of as Demosthenes'
direct relation) being a traitor.
12. βάρβαρος ἑλληνίζων τῇ φωνῇ. 'A
Scythian' in the fullest sense (not merely a
Greek of one of the colonies on the Pontic
coast), ' a barbarian with nothing Greek
about him, but that he has learnt the language.'
οὐκ ἐπιχώριος. Not only ' *too* wicked
to be like an Athenian,' but ' with something outlandish even in his style of wickedness' as well as his language.
§ 173. *As to his daily life, he ruined a
good fortune by extravagance, and had to
make another by betraying first his clients and
then his country. By the latter he has succeeded—for the present only.*
14. ἐκ τριηράρχου λογογράφος ἀνεφάνη.
' He sank as a trierarch to rise as a petti-
fogger.' The position of the συνήγορος was
honourable, like that of the Roman *patronus*,
but.the λογογράφος was a mere tradesman
who dealt in speeches—different, also, from
the λογοποιὸς or composer of shew declamations.
τὰ πατρῷα καταγελάστως προέμενος.
One might be tempted to take this of the
way in which, apparently, Demosthenes
compromised his lawsuit with his guardians,

στως· προέμενος· ἄπιστος δὲ καὶ περὶ ταῦτα δόξας εἶναι καὶ
τοὺς λόγους ἐκφέρων τοῖς ἀντιδίκοις ἀνεπήδησεν ἐπὶ τὸ βῆμα·
πλεῖστον δ᾽ ἐκ τῆς πόλεως εἰληφὼς ἀργύριον ἐλάχιστα περι-
εποιήσατο νῦν μέντοι τὸ βασιλικὸν χρυσίον ἐπικέκλυκε τὴν δα-
πάνην αὐτοῦ, ἔσται δ᾽ οὐδὲ τοῦθ᾽ ἱκανόν· οὐδεὶς γὰρ πώποτε 5
πλοῦτος τρόπου πονηροῦ περιεγένετο· καὶ τὸ κεφάλαιον, τὸν
βίον οὐκ ἐκ τῶν ἰδίων προσόδων πορίζεται, ἀλλ᾽ ἐκ τῶν ὑμε-
174 τέρων κινδύνων. περὶ δ᾽ εὐγνωμοσύνην καὶ λόγου δύναμιν πῶς
πέφυκε; δεινὸς λέγειν, κακὸς βιῶναι. οὕτω γὰρ κέχρηται καὶ
τῷ ἑαυτοῦ σώματι καὶ παιδοποιίᾳ ὥστ᾽ ἐμὲ μὴ βούλεσθαι λέγειν 10

3. πόλεως] πολιτείας bekl et marg. gm Bekk.   9. βιῶναι] ἴσως βιων marg. ghm.
10. ὥστ᾽ ἐμὲ μή] Ita Bekk., cum bekl ὥστε μή με habeant, n ὥστε μή, ceteri ὥστε με μή.

accepting (or at least being only able to get)
a much smaller sum than he had claimed
(Mid. p. 565, § 200). But this would not
harmonise with the tone taken by Aeschines
elsewhere in speaking of Demosthenes' conduct in that matter: see Ae. de F. L. § 105,
p. 41, where he treats the prosecution as
unnatural and fraudulent. And besides it
does not suit the context: the imputation is
not that he was a bad man of business, but
that he was a man of expensive tastes, which
he gratified at any cost. καταγελάστως is
a word of serious censure, 'contemptibly,'
perhaps 'in low pleasures': cp. Ae. in Tim.
§ 76, p. 11.

1. ἄπιστος .. καὶ τοὺς λόγους ἐκφέρων
τοῖς ἀντιδίκοις. The same charge is made
in Ae. de F. L. § 176, p. 50, with a specification of the case of Phormion and Apollodorus. Now we know that, in the series of
lawsuits that arose in Pasion's family, Demosthenes wrote a speech on each side at different stages of the process: and that is
perhaps the whole foundation for this charge.
If so, it is very inaccurately put: Demosthenes' conduct might bear a bad colour,
though probably it would not be proscribed
by modern professional honour; but it was
not fraudulent on the surface. For the construction, both ἄπιστος and ἐκφέρων depend
on δόξας εἶναι. As it is rather unusual in
Greek to put a participle in this construction
like an adjective and coordinate with one
(but cp. sup. ad § 162), there is a temptation either to strike out καὶ before τοὺς λόγους, or to suppose a slight breach of grammatical continuity; so that τοὺς λόγους ἐκφέρων .. ἀνεπήδησεν ἐπὶ τὸ βῆμα should be
parallel to ἐκ τριηράρχου λογογράφος ἀνεφάνη. 'Opening life as a man of independent property, he ran through his fortune
and had to turn legal hack. Having a new

opening in this lower character, he lost even
that (καὶ περὶ ταῦτα) by dishonesty, and
had to turn statesman,' as 'the last refuge of
a scoundrel.' In any case, the two are probably so far parallel, that both ἀνεφάνη and
ἀνεπήδησεν are meant to imply a certain
Jack-in-the-box vehemence and indecorum
in his behaviour, both as a legal and a political speaker; the latter, also, of the suddenness of his appearance as a politician.

3. ἐκ τῆς πόλεως.   πολιτείας, false as a
reading, is right as a gloss. He has got his
money 'out of (his connection with) the city,'
not, all of it, from public funds.

4. ἐπικέκλυκε. 'Has come like a flood
over his extravagance,' so that he is afloat
again, and the money he spends is but a drop
in the ocean of the money he has got. The
point is not that Demosthenes ran into debt
by his extravagance, but that he earned
money by treason to meet it : else we might
translate, 'has passed a sponge over his extravagance.'

§ 174. As to sound judgment and eloquence, his clever speaking disguises scanda-
lous profligacy.

10. τῷ ἑαυτοῦ σώματι καὶ παιδοποιίᾳ.
According to a tradition general among later
rhetoricians, he had two illegitimate sons;
and is described, on his trial in the matter of
Harpalus, as bringing them into court, but
not their mother, from a regard to decorum.
But Plutarch knows nothing of this story,
which is very hard to reconcile with § 78
above, where we read of his only child,
clearly legitimate. Besides, if this were all
alluded to, it would be hard to say that it
was too disgusting to mention directly :
though this view may gain some support
from Ae. de F. L. § 188, p. 52. But more
probably, σώματι is an insinuation like Ae. in
Tim. § 151, p. 18; de F. L. § 105, p. 41,

ἃ τούτῳ πέπρακται· ἤδη γάρ ποτε εἶδον μισηθέντας τοὺς
τὰ τῶν πλησίον αἰσχρὰ λίαν σαφῶς λέγοντας. ἔπειτα τί
συμβαίνει τῇ πόλει; οἱ μὲν λόγοι καλοί, τὰ δ' ἔργα φαῦλα.
πρὸς δὲ ἀνδρίαν βραχύς μοι λείπεται λόγος. εἰ μὲν γὰρ 175
5 ἠρνεῖτο μὴ δειλὸς εἶναι ἢ ὑμεῖς μὴ συνῄδειτε, διατριβὴν ὁ
λόγος ἄν μοι παρέσχεν· ἐπειδὴ δὲ καὶ αὐτὸς ὁμολογεῖ ἐν ταῖς
ἐκκλησίαις καὶ ὑμεῖς σύνιστε, λοιπὸν ὑπομνῆσαι τοὺς περὶ τούτων κειμένους νόμους. ὁ γὰρ Σόλων ὁ παλαιὸς νομοθέτης ἐν
τοῖς αὐτοῖς ἐπιτιμίοις ᾤετο δεῖν ἐνέχεσθαι τὸν ἀστράτευτον
10 καὶ τὸν λελοιπότα τὴν τάξιν καὶ τὸν δειλὸν ὁμοίως· εἰσὶ γὰρ
καὶ δειλίας γραφαί. καίτοι θαυμάσειεν ἄν τις ὑμῶν, εἰ εἰσὶ
φύσεως γραφαί. εἰσίν. τίνος ἕνεκα; ἵν' ἕκαστος ἡμῶν τὰς ἐκ
τῶν νόμων ζημίας φοβούμενος μᾶλλον ἢ τοὺς πολεμίους ἀμείνων ἀγωνιστὴς ὑπὲρ τῆς πατρίδος ὑπάρχῃ. ὁ μὲν τοίνυν νομο- 176
15 θέτης τὸν ἀστράτευτον καὶ τὸν δειλὸν καὶ τὸν λιπόντα τὴν
τάξιν ἔξω τῶν περιρραντηρίων τῆς ἀγορᾶς ἐξείργει, καὶ οὐκ
ἐᾷ στεφανοῦσθαι οὐδ' εἰσιέναι εἰς τὰ ἱερὰ τὰ δημοτελῆ· σὺ
δὲ τὸν ἀστεφάνωτον ἐκ τῶν νόμων κελεύεις ἡμᾶς στεφανοῦν,
καὶ τῷ σαυτοῦ ψηφίσματι τὸν οὐ προσήκοντα εἰσκαλεῖς τοῖς
20 τραγῳδοῖς εἰς τὴν ὀρχήστραν, εἰς τὸ ἱερὸν τοῦ Διονύσου τὸν
τὰ ἱερὰ διὰ δειλίαν προδεδωκότα.

---

4. ἀνδρίαν] † ἀνδρείαν pr. g †.   5. Post συνῄδειτε αὐτῷ add. fcd et pr. b et Bekk.
6. παρέσχεν] παρεῖχεν bekl Bekk.   11. καίτοι .. γραφαί] Om. ekl.   12. ἡμῶν]
ὑμῶν agmnfcd.   14. ὑπάρχῃ] γίγνηται bekl Flor., ὑπάρχοι a Vat. Laur. fc et superscr.
Barb.

and παιδοποιίᾳ refers to the story in Ae. de
F. L. § 158, p. 48, of which that in Din. in
Dem. § 71, p. 99 is probably a variant form.
The contrast with Ctesiphon's πορνοβοσκία,
below, § 215, makes it, perhaps, unlikely
that the charge is of personal profligacy. If,
as Plutarch says, his wife was a Samian,
there may have been doubts as to her legitimate status that would account for both
forms of the scandal.

1. ἤδη γάρ ποτε. When I prosecuted
Timarchus.

2. ἔπειτα .. φαῦλα, i. e. a man cannot
be εὐγνώμων—well-meaning and well-judg-
ing on behalf of Athens—when all she gets
out of him is fair words and foul deeds. The
assumption is, that an honourable policy
cannot be carried out at the suggestion of a
man who leads a dishonourable life.

§§ 175-176. *As for courage, he admits
he has none—which Solon treats as a crime
in itself, not an apology for the further crime
of desertion. Is a man like this a friend to
the Constitution?*

6. ὁμολογεῖ: Ae. de F. L. § 106, p. 42.

8. ἐν τοῖς αὐτοῖς .. δειλίας γραφαί.
'Thought there ought to be just the same
penalties to bind the coward as the man who
refuses to serve, or the man who quits his
post: for the law recognises prosecutions for
cowardice,' as well as for the other two
crimes, of which, he would insinuate, Demosthenes is also guilty.

11. θαυμάσειεν ἄν τις κ.τ.λ. One might
have thought, 'A man cannot help constitutional timidity: if he is φύσει δειλός, it is
hard that he should be prosecuted for it.'
'But the Law,' says Aeschines, 'does provide prosecution for it; for, if it cannot
change the man's nature, it can give him
something else to fear, so that he may be
depended on' (ὑπάρχῃ) 'to serve his country
in battle,' and at least not *act* like a coward.
Some MSS. omit this clause, no doubt accidentally, from its homoioteleuton with the
preceding.

16. ἔξω τῶν περιρραντηρίων τῆς ἀγορᾶς. Cp. Aristoph. Eccl. 379.

20. τὸν τὰ ἱερὰ κ.τ.λ. The point may
be only 'Demosthenes' cowardice placed all

"Ινα δὲ μὴ ἀποπλανῶ ὑμᾶς ἀπὸ τῆς ὑποθέσεως, ἐκεῖνο μέμνησθε, ὅταν φῇ δημοτικὸς εἶναι· θεωρεῖτ' αὐτοῦ μὴ τὸν λόγον,
ἀλλὰ τὸν βίον, καὶ σκοπεῖτε, μὴ τίς φησιν εἶναι, ἀλλὰ τίς
ἐστιν.

177 Ἐπεὶ δὲ στεφάνων ἀνεμνήσθην καὶ δωρεῶν, ἕως ἔτι μέμνη- 5
μαι, προλέγω ὑμῖν, ἄνδρες Ἀθηναῖοι, εἰ μὴ καταλύσετε τὰς
ἀφθόνους ταύτας δωρεὰς καὶ τοὺς εἰκῆ διδομένους στεφάνους,
οὔθ' οἱ τιμώμενοι χάριν ὑμῖν εἴσονται οὔτε τὰ τῆς πόλεως
πράγματα ἐπανορθωθήσεται· τοὺς μὲν γὰρ πονηροὺς οὐ μή
ποτε βελτίους ποιήσετε, τοὺς δὲ χρηστοὺς εἰς τὴν ἐσχάτην 10
ἀθυμίαν ἐμβαλεῖτε. ὅτι δ' ἀληθῆ λέγω, μεγάλα τούτων οἶμαι
178 σημεῖα δείξειν ὑμῖν. εἰ γάρ τις ὑμᾶς ἐρωτήσειε, πότερον ὑμῖν
ἐνδοξοτέρα δοκεῖ ἡ πόλις ἡμῶν εἶναι ἐπὶ τῶν νυνὶ καιρῶν ἢ ἐπὶ
τῶν προγόνων, ἅπαντες ἂν ὁμολογήσαιτε, ἐπὶ τῶν προγόνων.
ἄνδρες δὲ πότερον τότε ἀμείνους ἦσαν ἢ νυνί; τότε μὲν δια- 15
φέροντες, νυνὶ δὲ πολλῷ καταδεέστεροι. δωρεαὶ δὲ καὶ στέφανοι καὶ κηρύγματα καὶ σιτήσεις ἐν πρυτανείῳ πότερον τότε

---

9. γὰρ] Om. gmnbekl.   10. ποιήσετε] ποιήσητε fcd.   13. ἡμῶν] ὑμῶν k,
om. fcdbl B. et S. Schultz.   ἐπὶ] ὅτι ἐπὶ b Bekk.   17. σιτήσεις] σιτίσεις azp
et Schultziani.

our temples at the mercy of the enemy,' but
as no actual profanation followed, and as τὰ
ἱερὰ comes immediately after the name of
Dionysus, it is likelier that the allusion is to
the abandoning the charge of impiety against
Midias. As the charge of abandoning the
proceedings from cowardice is not very consistent with that already made, of abandoning them for a bribe, can Aeschines mean
that he ought to have killed Midias on the
spot? which he takes great credit to himself, as a law-abiding citizen, for not doing.
(Mid. § 96, p. 538.)

1. ἵνα δὲ μὴ ἀποπλανῶ. By insisting
on his cowardice, which may be thought
chiefly a technical disqualification.

§ 177. In fact, it is a common fault in
our generation to be too lavish of crowns
and public honours.

5. ἕως ἔτι μέμνημαι. An affectation of extempore delivery not uncommon in the orators; though it is not unlikely that Aeschines'
speech as delivered was not as entirely pre-
composed as the one we read. He probably
was less dependent on premeditation than
Demosthenes, as we may guess from the
way he tells the story in De F. L. §§ 37 sq.,
pp. 32 sq., especially the words τῶν γεγραμμένων διεσφάλη.

9. τοὺς μὲν γὰρ πονηροὺς κ.τ.λ. 'You
will not reform the rogues while you reward
them, and while you reward them, you will

discourage the honest men.'

11. ὅτι δ' ἀληθῆ λέγω κ.τ.λ. He has
asserted two things, (A) 'those you honour
will be ungrateful,' (B) 'your affairs will not
recover.' As a sign of the truth of the first,
he points out that when honours were scarce
great men were plentiful: as a sign of the
second, that when honours were scarce
Athens flourished more. The arrangement
of clauses is governed by the principle of
Chiasmus, thus : (a) οὔθ' οἱ τιμώμενοι χάριν
ὑμῖν εἴσονται, (b) οὔτε τὰ τῆς πόλεως πράγματα ἐπανορθωθήσεται, (b b)εἰ γάρ τις ὑμᾶς
ἐρωτήσειε .. ὁμολογήσαιτε, ἐπὶ τῶν προγόνων, (a a) ἄνδρες δὲ πότερον .. καταδεέστεροι.

§ 178. The city is worse off than in past
ages, and the citizens less meritorious, yet
public rewards are now a matter of course
that then were rare.

14. ἐπὶ τῶν προγόνων. Bekker with
one MS. read ὅτι ἐπὶ, which is a more
common construction. It is likelier that
the word was introduced into one MS. by
criticism, than that it should have fallen
by accident out of all, easy as the latter
would have been, from the resemblance of
the characters of ὅτι and ἐπὶ.

17. σιτήσεις ἐν πρυτανείῳ. Several good
MSS. have σιτίσεις, which may be only the
common blunder of itacism, but if genuine
would affect the sense. σίτησις is the privi-

ἦσαν πλείους ἢ νυνί; τότε μὲν ἦν σπάνια τὰ καλὰ παρ' ἡμῖν
καὶ τὸ τῆς ἀρετῆς ὄνομα τίμιον· νῦν δ' ἤδη καταπέπλυται τὸ
πρᾶγμα, καὶ τὸ στεφανοῦν ἐξ ἔθους, ἀλλ' οὐκ ἐκ προνοίας
ποιεῖσθε. οὐκ οὖν ἄτοπον οὑτωσὶ διαλογιζομένοις τὰς μὲν 179
5 δωρεὰς νῦν πλείους εἶναι, τὰ δὲ πράγματα τῆς πόλεως τότε
μᾶλλον ἢ νῦν ἰσχύειν, καὶ τοὺς ἄνδρας νῦν μὲν χείρους εἶναι,
τότε δ' ἀμείνους; ἐγὼ δὲ τοῦθ' ὑμᾶς ἐπιχειρήσω διδάσκειν.
οἴεσθ' ἄν ποτε, ὦ Ἀθηναῖοι, ἐθελῆσαί τινα ἐπασκεῖν εἰς τὰ
Ὀλύμπια ἢ εἰς ἄλλον τινὰ τῶν στεφανιτῶν ἀγώνων παγκρά-
10 τιον ἢ καὶ ἄλλο τι τῶν βαρυτέρων ἄθλων, εἰ ὁ στέφανος
ἐδίδοτο μὴ τῷ κρατίστῳ, ἀλλὰ τῷ διαπραξαμένῳ; οὐδεὶς ἄν
ποτ' ἠθέλησεν ἐπασκεῖν. νῦν δ', οἶμαι, διὰ τὸ σπάνιον καὶ τὸ
περιμάχητον καὶ τὸ καλὸν καὶ τὸ ἀείμνηστον ἐκ τῆς νίκης ἐθέ-
λουσί τινες τὰ σώματα παρακαταθέμενοι καὶ τὰς μεγίστας
15 ταλαιπωρίας ὑπομείναντες διακινδυνεύειν. ὑπολάβετε τοίνυν 180
ὑμᾶς αὐτοὺς εἶναι ἀγωνοθέτας πολιτικῆς ἀρετῆς, κἀκεῖνο ἐκλο-
γίσασθε, ὅτι, ἐὰν μὲν τὰς δωρεὰς ὀλίγοις καὶ ἀξίοις καὶ κατὰ
τοὺς νόμους διδῶτε, πολλοὺς ἀγωνιστὰς ἕξετε τῆς ἀρετῆς, ἐὰν

---

1. καλὰ] ἆθλα Markl.   4. διαλογιζομένοις] † Aliter, ut videbatur, in g scriptum erat †.
6. ἢ νῦν] Om. bekl Bekk. Cobet. Schultz.   8. οἴεσθ' ἄν ποτε] οἴεσθέ ποτε agmnιfcd.

lege of taking meals, σίτισις the act of giving a meal: hence only the ἀείσιτοι could be said strictly speaking to have σίτησις, while σίτισις would cover the case of ambassadors and others invited for one occasion only. But σίτισις apparently never occurs except as a v. l. for σίτησις, while the latter is an unquestioned word, e. g. below, § 197.

2. καταπέπλυται τὸ πρᾶγμα. By a Chiasmus similar to that noted just above, this clause answers to τὸ τῆς ἀρετῆς ὄνομα τίμιον. In the first half of the sentence he puts the fact first and its consequence second, in the latter half the effect first and its cause second, because he wishes them from the effect to infer the tendency of the cause. The metaphor in καταπέπλυται is apparently 'the thing has all the colour washed out of it,' or possibly, 'is knocked to pieces at the wash,' and so 'is hackneyed, grown stale.' The use of πλύνω in the sense of laver la tête, 'give one a dressing,' implies more active vilification than is appropriate here.

3. ἐξ ἔθους, ἀλλ' οὐκ ἐκ προνοίας. This statement receives some support from Demosthenes' assertion (De F. L. § 35, p. 350) that it was unheard of for an embassy not to be invited to the Prytaneum on its return: however foolish may be the pedantry, rather characteristic of Aeschines, which attributes the decline of the state to no deeper cause.

§ 179. And these two facts tend to perpetuate each other: just as no one would train for the Olympia if the prize went by intrigue, &c.

7. ἐγὼ δὲ τοῦθ' ὑμᾶς ἐπιχειρήσω διδάσκειν. 'I will try to explain the fact to you' seems to be the force rather than 'I will prove that it is absurd.' The explanation is, that by making honours cheap, they make it cease to be worth while to pay the cost of deserving them.

11. κρατίστῳ. Not necessarily 'strongest,' but 'best' in the matter of strength.

14. τὰ σώματα .. διακινδυνεύειν. They trust their bodies to the judges, leave it to rest with them that their trouble shall not be in vain; and then, as they can trust them, endure the certainty of suffering for the chance of winning.

§ 180. So you must be no less careful to give no prize except to surpassing merit, or you will destroy the competition.

16. ἀγωνοθέτας. The Agonothetae were probably the most incorruptible court in Greece, and nearly the only one whose decisions were universally respected. It is remarkable, that when he speaks of the more intellectual trial of the Dionysia, Aeschines thinks it necessary to apologise for the comparison: below, § 233.

δὲ τῷ βουλομένῳ καὶ τοῖς διαπραξαμένοις χαρίζησθε, καὶ τὰς
181 ἐπιεικεῖς φύσεις διαφθερεῖτε. ὅτι δὲ ὀρθῶς λέγω, ἔτι μικρῷ
σαφέστερον ὑμᾶς βούλομαι διδάξαι. πότερον ὑμῖν ἀμείνων ἀνὴρ
εἶναι δοκεῖ Θεμιστοκλῆς ὁ στρατηγήσας, ὅτ᾽ ἐν τῇ [περὶ]
Σαλαμῖνι ναυμαχίᾳ τὸν Πέρσην ἐνικᾶτε, ἢ Δημοσθένης ὁ τὴν 5
τάξιν λιπών; Μιλτιάδης δὲ ὁ τὴν ἐν Μαραθῶνι μάχην τοὺς
βαρβάρους νικήσας, ἢ οὗτος; ἔτι δ᾽ οἱ ἀπὸ Φυλῆς φεύγοντα
τὸν δῆμον καταγαγόντες; Ἀριστείδης δ᾽ ὁ δίκαιος, ὁ τὴν
182 ἀνόμοιον ἔχων ἐπωνυμίαν Δημοσθένει; ἀλλ᾽ ἔγωγε μὰ τοὺς
θεοὺς τοὺς Ὀλυμπίους οὐδ᾽ ἐν ταῖς αὐταῖς ἡμέραις ἄξιον ἡγοῦμαι 10
μεμνῆσθαι τοῦ θηρίου τούτου καὶ ἐκείνων τῶν ἀνδρῶν. ἐπιδειξάτω

---

4. ὅτ᾽ ἐν] ὅτε *fed* Ald. B. et S.   περὶ Σαλαμῖνι] Sic az Laur. Flor. Barb. *fed*, Σαλαμῖνι *p* Vat. B. et S. Schultz., παρὰ Σαλαμῖνι *gmn* παρὰ Σαλαμῖνα *bekl* et teste Bekk. *f* : vid
Annot.   Certe ἐν Σαλαμῖνι et Μαραθῶνι usitatior est formula; sed iis qui et hic et infra ea
reponi jubent non est cur assentiamus.   8. Post δίκαιος ἐπικαλούμενος add. omnes
praeter *agmn*.   11. καὶ ἐκείνων] κἀκείνων *c* Bekk.: idque reponi volt Frank.

1. χαρίζησθε in sense belongs more
appropriately to τῷ βουλομένῳ than to τοῖς
διαπραξαμένοις : in fact in the latter would be
better away. Aeschines' argument is, ' You
ought to give crowns only to rare merit :
by lavishing them τῷ βουλομένῳ, you make
them accessible τοῖς διαπραξαμένοις,' i. e. by
giving them recklessly to men who have perhaps done some *slight* service, you make it
easy for a traitor like Demosthenes to get
them by intrigue. But he is so anxious to
say that Demosthenes has got them by intrigue, that he inserts the statement against
him where he ought to keep to the general
principle. The rhetorical symmetry, however, is not sacrificed, even if the sense be
confused : τῷ βουλομένῳ answers to ὀλίγοις,
τοῖς διαπραξαμένοις to ἀξίοις.
§ 181. *Compare then Demosthenes with
the great men of old.*
2. μικρῷ σαφέστερον. Almost ' in more
detail,' with concrete instances, instead of in
general terms.
4. Θεμιστοκλῆς. His subsequent treason
being conveniently ignored.
[περὶ] Σαλαμῖνι. Most MSS. have
the dative, and nearly all have either περὶ or
παρά. παρὰ with the dative is hardly possible, while περὶ with the dative might have
seemed strange to a copyist, and so have
furnished a motive for altering either the
preposition or the case. περὶ Σαλαμῖνι
would be much like περὶ τῇ Σικελίᾳ in Thuc.
6. 34, very nearly identical with the Homeric
usage of fighting *over* a dead man. The
local sense predominates, ' fighting *off* Salamis,' but fighting ' for Salamis ' also enters
into the idea. And considering how far the

line of ships must have reached, especially
after the Persians were broken, περὶ would
be the most accurate word that could be
used. The simple Σαλαμῖνι is less accurately descriptive : we should say, ' Nelson
commanded at Trafalgar,' but only because
the name suggests to us the battle rather
than the cape. If we wished to describe
the locality, we should say ' off Trafalgar,'
and similarly in Greek (though ἐν Σαλαμῖνι
came to be familiarised in usage) Σαλαμῖνι
would be harsh. παρὰ Σαλαμῖνα would describe the scene of action almost as well as
the text, but the authority is against it.
8. ὁ τὴν ἀνόμοιον ἔχων ἐπωνυμίαν Δημοσθένει. ' Whose surname is such a contrast to the character of Demosthenes.'
§ 182. *Nay, he is not comparable with
them : yet they, true patriots as they were,
were never crowned.*
10. ἐν ταῖς αὐταῖς ἡμέραις : cp. ad §
117. This phrase is exactly like ours, ' not
fit to be named in the same day with them ;'
but the Greek assumes that there would be
many days on which they would be spoken
of, and expresses that on any of those days
it would be a shame to speak of Demosthenes.
11. θηρίου seems to have been almost a
nickname of Demosthenes, who had attained
a distinction that made even his enemies
concede the *oderint dum metuant* test of
greatness. Here the antithesis to ἀνδρῶν is
almost too pointed for good effect. Note
also how ἐκείνων, opposed to τούτου, comes
to express eminence, ' the *great* men of the
good *old* times,' contrasted with the scoun-
drels who pass for great men now.

τοίνυν Δημοσθένης ἐν τῷ αὐτοῦ λόγῳ, εἴ που γέγραπταί
τινα τῶν ἀνδρῶν τούτων στεφανῶσαι. ἀχάριστος ἄρ᾽ ἦν
ὁ δῆμος; οὔκ, ἀλλὰ μεγαλόφρων, κἀκεῖνοί γε οἱ μὴ τετιμη-
μένοι τῆς πόλεως ἄξιοι· οὐ γὰρ ᾤοντο δεῖν ἐν τοῖς γράμμασι
5 τιμᾶσθαι, ἀλλ᾽ ἐν τῇ μνήμῃ τῶν εὖ πεπονθότων, ἣ ἀπ᾽ ἐκείνου
τοῦ χρόνου μέχρι τῆσδε τῆς ἡμέρας ἀθάνατος οὖσα διαμένει.
δωρεὰς δὲ τίνας ἐλάμβανον; ὧν ἄξιόν ἐστι μνησθῆναι.

Ἦσάν τινες κατὰ τοὺς τότε καιρούς, οἳ πολὺν ὑπομείναντες 183
πόνον καὶ μεγάλους κινδύνους ἐπὶ τῷ Στρυμόνι ποταμῷ
10 ἐνίκων μαχόμενοι Μήδους· οὗτοι δεῦρο ἀφικόμενοι τὸν δῆμον

2. τῶν ἀνδρῶν τούτων] Sic *agmnp* Vat. Laur. Flor.: ceteri et volg. τούτων τῶν ἀνδρῶν.
3. κἀκεῖνοί] κἀκεῖνό *amn* et teste Bekk. *g*: † nisi mea vox legentis fratrem fefellit, *g*
κἀκείνῳ a m. pr. habet, quod verum esse credimus †.   οἱ μὴ] εἰ μὴ a, οἱ μὲν *n*, οἱ μὴ
οὕτω *fcdq* Barb. Reisk.   Hoc sane glossema videtur esse: nec tamen est cur οἱ μὴ τετιμη-
μένοι cum Hamakero et Frankio deleamus.   4. ἄξιοι] ἀνάξιοι *fcd*.   7. ὦν] Om.
fcd et volg. ante Bekk.   Veterem lectionem (δωρεὰς .. ἐλάμβανον, ἄξιον κ.τ.λ.) restitui
jubent Bak. Cobet. Frank.   ἐστι μνησθῆναι] † ἔτι μέμνησθαι pr. *g* †.   8. Post
ἦσαν δὲ add. *gmn*.   Post τινες ὦ ἄνδρες ᾽Αθηναῖοι add. *bekl* Eekk.   πολὺν
ὑπομείναντες πόνον] πολὺν πόνον ὑπομείναντες Bekk. Schultz.: πόνον ὑπομείναντες χρόνον
teste illo habent *agmn*, etiam Laur.: † nobis videbatur *g* a pr. m. habuisse πόνον ὑπομεί-
ναντας, a secunda ὑπομείναντες χρόνον, denique χρόνον subscriptis punctis notatum esse,
profecto ut vetus scriptura restitueretur †; ὑπομείναντες χρόνον habent Vat. *pfcdq* Barb.

3. κἀκεῖνοί γε .. ἄξιοι. Reading as in
the text, which no doubt is the easiest and
perhaps as likely as any, τῆς πόλεως ἄξιοι
will mean 'they were μεγαλόφρονες too,'
and their preferring the honour of memorials
in men's hearts to those of decrees or inscriptions is given as a proof of it. The reading
κἀκεῖνό γε of the best MSS. is probably to
be explained as an error for κἀκείνῳ γε, the
way it is written in one at least of them:
'and through that very fact, those who received no honour became worthy of the
city,' i. e. because the city did not lavish
petty rewards for petty services, they were
forced to the true nobleness that wins en-
during honour. Another group of MSS. has
ἀνάξιοι for ἄξιοι, which must be either a
genuine reading, or a literary correction.
'And were they, who received no honour,
unworthy of the city? Nay, they thought
it right to win honour, not in ...' Reading
ἀνάξιοι, it would still be an improvement to
have ἐκείνῳ, 'But did that fact,' viz. their
receiving no honour, 'make them unworthy
of the city?' The *objection* to the reading
ἀνάξιοι is, that it would seem to necessitate
the change of γε into δέ, for which there is
no MS. authority. The *advantage* of it
would be, that the passage would be more
symmetrical. Reading as we do below, in
the sentence δωρεὰς δὲ .. μνησθῆναι, we
should thus have *three* questions and answers,
(1) ἀχάριστος .. μεγαλόφρων, (2) κἀκείνῳ

γε (or κἀκεῖνοί γε) .. διαμένει, (3) δωρεὰς ..
μνησθῆναι, only the second of which is of any
length. As it is, we have one question with
a very long answer, followed by a very short
one. But it is remarkable that the MSS.
which read ἀνάξιοι here are the *same* that
omit ὦν. κἀκείνῳ we believe to be right:
but one is afraid to trust one's own eyes
against Bekker's. Vid. Conspectus Codicum.
7. δωρεὰς δὲ .. μνησθῆναι. 'But what
kind of gifts did they receive?' (lit. 'what
gifts was it *usual* for them to receive?')
'Gifts that it will be worth while to specify,'
viz. such as those mentioned below, as given
to the captors of Eion. Bekker with the
great majority of MSS. read as in the text:
but some editors desire to return to the old
reading δωρεὰς δὲ τίνας ἐλάμβανον, ἄξιόν
ἐστι μνησθῆναι. The MS. reading is less
obvious, and for reasons given in the last
note perhaps more forcible.
§§ 183–186. *The conquerors of Eion
were rewarded by an inscription not giving
their names, but ascribing the glory of their
deed to the nation.*
10. ἐνίκων μαχόμενοι. In fact the place
was reduced by famine, as is admitted in the
first inscription: and the siege seems on the
whole to have been one from which the
besiegers reaped less glory than the defenders.
See Hdt. 7. 107, Thuc. 1. 98.
τὸν δῆμον ᾔτησαν δωρεάν. If we
compare this, and the request of Miltiades

ἤτησαν δωρεὰν, καὶ ἔδωκεν αὐτοῖς ὁ δῆμος τιμὰς μεγάλας, ὡς
τότ᾽ ἐδόκει, τρεῖς λιθίνους Ἑρμᾶς στῆσαι ἐν τῇ στοᾷ τῇ τῶν
Ἑρμῶν, ἐφ᾽ ᾧτε μὴ ἐπιγράφειν τὰ ὀνόματα τὰ ἑαυτῶν, ἵνα
μὴ τῶν στρατηγῶν, ἀλλὰ τοῦ δήμου δοκῇ εἶναι τὸ ἐπίγραμμα.
184 ὅτι δ᾽ ἀληθῆ λέγω, ἐξ αὐτῶν πῶν ποιημάτων εἴσεσθε. ἐπιγέ- 5
γραπται γὰρ ἐπὶ τῷ μὲν πρώτῳ τῶν Ἑρμῶν

  ἦν ἄρα κἀκεῖνοι ταλακάρδιοι, οἵ ποτε Μήδων
  παισὶν ἐπ᾽ Ἠϊόνι, Στρυμόνος ἀμφὶ ῥοὰς,
  λιμόν τ᾽ αἴθωνα κρατερόν τ᾽ ἐπάγοντες Ἄρηα
  πρῶτοι δυσμενέων εὗρον ἀμηχανίην.   10

185 ἐπὶ δὲ τῷ δευτέρῳ

  ἡγεμόνεσσι δὲ μισθὸν Ἀθηναῖοι τάδ᾽ ἔδωκαν
  ἀντ᾽ εὐεργεσίης καὶ μεγάλης ἀρετῆς.
  μᾶλλόν τις τάδ᾽ ἰδὼν καὶ ἐπεσσομένων ἐθελήσει
  ἀμφὶ ξυνοῖσι πράγμασι μόχθον ἔχειν.   15

186 ἐπὶ δὲ τῷ τρίτῳ ἐπιγέγραπται Ἑρμῇ

  ἔκ ποτε τῆσδε πόληος ἅμ᾽ Ἀτρείδῃσι Μενεσθεὺς
  ἡγεῖτο ζάθεον Τρωικὸν ἂμ πεδίον,
  ὅν ποθ᾽ Ὅμηρος ἔφη Δαναῶν πύκα χαλκοχιτώνων
  κοσμήτορα μάχης ἔξοχον ἄνδρα μολεῖν.   20

3. ἐφ᾽ ᾧτε] ἔφητε gamnc, ἔφηντε α, ἔφησε fd.   6. τῷ μὲν] Sic amn Vat. Laur.
χάριτος
Barb.: ceteri μὲν τῷ, itaque volg. usque ad Bekk.   13. ἀρετῆς] ἀμοιβῆς α.
15. ἀμφὶ ξυνοῖσι] ἀμφὶ περὶ ξυνοῖς Anthol. Gr. Plut. in vit. Cimon. c. 7, B. et S. Schultz.
19. χαλκοχιτώνων] περ φρονεόντων α, θωρηκτάων (ut Plut. l. c.) narg. Bern. et super
versum ginb. Vid. annot.   20. κοσμήτορα] Ita Vat. Barb. bekl: ceteri κοσμήτορα
vel. -τωρα.

mentioned below, which was categorically
refused, with the arrogant inscription of Pausanias (Thuc. I. 132), and with the general
tone of Pindar's heroes, it seems likely
enough that there was a real collision between the ambition of Cimon and the
jealousy of Athenian democracy.

3. ἵνα μὴ τῶν στρατηγῶν. Almost 'in
order that the inscription might *belong to*
the people, not the generals,' that it might
be an ἀνάθημα of the nation's, not of theirs.
Putting it up was a national act: the nation
reserved jealously to itself the honour of
it.

9. λιμόν τ᾽ αἴθωνα. It is noted that the
Germans have exactly the same idiom, *ein
brennender Hunger*.

10. ἀμηχανίην. Commonly taken, 'found
means of bringing the foe to helplessness.'
But perhaps the sense is, 'they were the
first Greeks to find a Persian army at their
mercy,' as Herodotus remarks that the
Athenians at Marathon were the first to

meet a Persian army in the field without
dishonour (6. 112 fin.) The superstitious
horror of the Persians which was felt to the
last, seems as though the superstitious terror
there mentioned had been a reality: and the
capitulation of Eion may have been a moral
surprise like that of Sphacteria.

19. Ὅμηρος: Il. 2. 553. The commendation of Menestheus was declared by some
to be an Athenian interpolation.

πύκα χαλκοχιτώνων. A meaningless
phrase: in Homer we have constantly πύκα
θωρηκτάων, and that is the text of this inscription as given by Plutarch. Some MSS.
correct the text accordingly: but Aeschines,
quoting from memory, is likelier to have
made the blunder than either the epigram-
matist or copyist. πύκα περ φρονεόντων,
the reading of one of the best MSS. known,
is not impossible, 'wise as all Greeks are, he
surpassed them in skill:' i. e. if Aeschines
blundered, he is likelier to have fallen into a
blunder that was not nonsensical.

οὕτως οὐδὲν ἀεικὲς Ἀθηναίοισι καλεῖσθαι
κοσμητὰς πολέμου τ' ἀμφὶ καὶ ἠνορέης.
ἔστι που τὸ τῶν στρατηγῶν ὄνομα; οὐδαμοῦ, ἀλλὰ τὸ τοῦ
δήμου.

5 Προέλθετε δὴ τῇ διανοίᾳ καὶ εἰς τὴν στοὰν τὴν ποικίλην· 187
ἁπάντων γὰρ ὑμῖν τῶν καλῶν ἔργων τὰ ὑπομνήματα ἐν τῇ
ἀγορᾷ ἀνάκειται. τί οὖν ἐστιν, ὦ Ἀθηναῖοι, ὃ ἐγὼ λέγω;
ἐνταῦθα ἡ ἐν Μαραθῶνι μάχη γέγραπται. τίς οὖν ἦν ὁ
στρατηγός; οὑτωσὶ μὲν ἐρωτηθέντες ἅπαντες ἀποκρίναισθε ἄν,
10 ὅτι Μιλτιάδης, ἐκεῖ δὲ οὐκ ἐπιγέγραπται. πῶς; οὐκ ᾔτησε
τὴν δωρεὰν ταύτην; ᾔτησεν, ἀλλ' ὁ δῆμος οὐκ ἔδωκεν, ἀλλ'
ἀντὶ τοῦ ὀνόματος συνεχώρησεν αὐτῷ πρώτῳ γραφῆναι, παρα-
καλοῦντι τοὺς στρατιώτας. ἐν τοίνυν τῷ μητρῴῳ παρὰ τὸ 188
βουλευτήριον, ἣν ἔδοτε δωρεὰν τοῖς ἀπὸ Φυλῆς φεύγοντα τὸν
15 δῆμον καταγαγοῦσιν, ἔστιν ἰδεῖν. ἣν μὲν γὰρ ὁ τὸ ψήφισμα
γράψας καὶ νικήσας Ἀρχῖνος ὁ ἐκ Κοίλης, εἷς τῶν καταγαγόντων τὸν δῆμον, ἔγραψε δὲ πρῶτον μὲν αὐτοῖς εἰς θυσίαν
καὶ ἀναθήματα δοῦναι χιλίας δραχμάς, καὶ τοῦτ' ἐστὶν ἔλαττον ἢ δέκα δραχμαὶ κατ' ἄνδρα ἕκαστον, ἔπειτα κελεύει στε-
20 φανοῦσθαι θαλλοῦ στεφάνῳ αὐτῶν ἕκαστον, ἀλλ' οὐ χρυσῷ·
τότε μὲν γὰρ ἦν ὁ τοῦ θαλλοῦ στέφανος τίμιος, νυνὶ δὲ καὶ
ὁ χρυσοῦς καταπεφρόνηται. καὶ οὐδὲ τοῦτο εἰκῇ πρᾶξαι κε-

5. προέλθετε] Sic Barb. ƒᵈᵍ bekl Bak. Cobet.: ceteri et Schultz. προσέλθετε   9. ἀπο-
κρίναισθε] ἀποκρίνεσθε pr. g, -νεῖσθε corr. id., † mox deleto ἄν·†. ἀποκρίνεσθε ἄν ρᵍ Vat.
Laur. Barb. ƒ, ἀποκρίνασθε ἄν n, ἀποκρίνασθε ἄν m, ἀποκρινεῖσθε bel, ἂν ἀποκρινεῖσθε k.
19. στεφανοῦσθαι] στεφανῶσαι bekl Bekk.

§ 187. *So in the painting of Marathon, you see Miltiades' figure, but not his unforgotten name:* that *was refused to him.*

6. ἁπάντων γὰρ gives the reason for the preceding καὶ: 'You have only to turn from the Portico of the Hermae to the Portico of the Pictures: your country is not ungrateful, all the achievements of her children are on record in the market-place.' This sense gives force to the reading προέλθετε, 'go on a little further:' volgo προσέλθετε.

9. οὑτωσί. 'When a man asks you as I ask you now;' when he appeals to your general knowledge, to which the picture would add nothing.

ἀποκρίναισθε ἄν. We have to choose between this reading and ἀποκρίνεσθε, to which several MSS. point. 'I know you *will* answer' is harsh, but perhaps with a harshness more like the effort of an author than the error of a transcriber: however, we follow the balance of authority.

12. πρώτῳ. 'In the foremost place,' at the head of the troops.

§ 188. *The restorers of the democracy were crowned—with olive, not with gold: in those days the other was thought honour enough—but only after a rigid proof of their services.*

13. ἐν τῷ μητρῴῳ. The temple of Cybele built by Phidias, to expiate the slaughter of a μητραγύρτης who had initiated the women of Attica. In Pausanias' time the building was extant, and still used as a record office. παρὰ τὸ βουλευτήριον is suspected as a gloss by many critics, not unreasonably.

14. τοῖς ἀπὸ Φυλῆς .. καταγαγοῦσιν. 'To the men from Phyle who brought back the Commons.'

22. καὶ οὐδὲ τοῦτο κ.τ.λ. 'And even this moderate honour was not allowed to be given carelessly, but only after the Senate had determined the true list of those actually

λεύει, ἀλλ' ἀκριβῶς τὴν βουλὴν σκεψαμένην, ὅσοι αὐτῶν ἐπὶ
Φυλῇ ἐπολιορκήθησαν, ὅτε Λακεδαιμόνιοι καὶ οἱ τριάκοντα
προσέβαλλον τοῖς καταλαβοῦσι Φυλήν, οὐχ ὅσοι τὴν τάξιν
ἔλιπον ἐν Χαιρωνείᾳ τῶν πολεμίων ἐπιόντων. ὅτι δ' ἀληθῆ
λέγω, ἀναγνώσεται ὑμῖν τὸ ψήφισμα.   5

ΨΗΦΙΣΜΑ ΠΕΡΙ ΔΩΡΕΑΣ ΤΟΙΣ ΑΠΟ ΦΥΛΗΣ.

189 Παρανάγνωθι καὶ ὃ γέγραφε Κτησιφῶν Δημοσθένει τῷ τῶν
μεγίστων κακῶν αἰτίῳ.

ΨΗΦΙΣΜΑ.

Τούτῳ τῷ ψηφίσματι ἐξαλείφεται ἡ τῶν καταγαγόντων 10
τὸν δῆμον δωρεά. εἰ τοῦτ' ἔχει καλῶς, ἐκεῖνο αἰσχρῶς· εἰ
ἐκεῖνοι κατ' ἀξίαν ἐτιμήθησαν, οὗτος ἀνάξιος ὢν στεφανοῦται.

190 Καίτοι πυνθάνομαί γ' αὐτὸν μέλλειν λέγειν, ὡς οὐ δίκαια

2. Φυλῇ] Φυλῆ agmn B. et S., qui conferunt Lys. 12, § 52. Volg. et Bekk. Φυλῆς.
Ante Λακεδαιμόνιοι οἱ add. z.   7. Post παρανάγνωθι δὴ add. z.

engaged in the defence of Phyle.' No one
who had not been there, or had not done his
duty, was to be allowed a chance of getting
in by mistake: much less was a man who
had done the reverse of his duty to be treated
better than they were. For the construction, τὴν βουλὴν is of course the subject of
πρᾶξαι, and the object of κελεύει, but it is
an afterthought to express it, as in both
relations it might have been omitted. τὴν
βουλὴν, without further designation, usually
means the Five Hundred: else the investigation is a business of a kind that was usually
referred to the Areopagus.

1. ἐπὶ Φυλῇ. So the best MSS.: volg.
ἐπὶ Φυλῆς. B. and S. compare Lys. 12, §
52.

3. οὐχ ὅσοι τὴν τάξιν κ.τ.λ. The symmetry of the clauses is rather a fictitious
one, but the object of it is to imply what is
stated below, § 245, 'if you ask what are
Demosthenes' qualifications for a crown, you
can only say, His vices.'

§ 189. *You bear what was done for them
—a disgracefully mean reward, if Ctesiphon
be right.*

10. ἐξαλείφεται. It ceases to be a δωρεά
worth mentioning : it becomes a fact, that
the people ungratefully gave no reward to
the restorers of their liberty, if a man who
had done so little service to the state—in
fact, less than none—received a reward such
as Ctesiphon proposed.

12. στεφανοῦται. In an imperfect sense,

'it is proposed to crown him.' But there
are occasional indications, that Aeschines
felt as he went on that his case was hopeless,
and this perhaps is one of them : he admits
that Demosthenes is in a fair way to get the
crown, but can only protest that he does not
deserve it.

§ 190. *Then he pretends that he ought to
be compared with his contemporaries only.
But no one deserves a crown unless he can
afford to be compared with the highest standard of absolute merit.*

13. πυνθάνομαί γ' αὐτὸν μέλλειν λέγειν
κ.τ.λ. The illustration does actually occur
in Demosthenes' speech as we have it, § 392.
There is no difficulty in supposing that the
whole of this section was added in preparing
the speech for publication, or rather for use
in Aeschines' school of rhetoric. And although Aeschines may have guessed the line
of Demosthenes' argument, or even have
had intelligence of the concrete shape it
would take (neither Demosthenes in describing his intended point, nor the reporter in
telling Aeschines, was likely to omit the
vivid details which made it telling and easy
to remember), it is hardly likely that Demosthenes would have repeated his illustration
unaltered after this attempt to mar its point.
φησὶ (volgo φήσει) is to be referred to Demosthenes' habitual language about the trial,
though it would suit the point of view
of a man with Demosthenes' speech before
him.

ποιῶ παραβάλλων αὐτῷ τὰ τῶν προγόνων ἔργα· οὐδὲ γὰρ
Φιλάμμωνά φησι τὸν πύκτην Ὀλυμπίασι στεφανωθῆναι νικήσαντα Γλαῦκον τὸν παλαιὸν ἐκεῖνον πύκτην, ἀλλὰ τοὺς καθ᾽
ἑαυτὸν ἀγωνιστὰς, ὥσπερ ὑμᾶς ἀγνοοῦντας, ὅτι τοῖς μὲν πύκ-
5 ταις ἐστὶν ὁ ἀγὼν πρὸς ἀλλήλους, τοῖς δ᾽ ἀξιοῦσι στεφανοῦσθαι πρὸς αὐτὴν τὴν ἀρετὴν, ἧς καὶ ἕνεκα στεφανοῦνται. δεῖ
γὰρ τὸν κήρυκα ἀψευδεῖν, ὅταν τὴν ἀνάρρησιν ἐν τῷ θεάτρῳ
ποιῆται πρὸς τοὺς Ἕλληνας. μὴ οὖν ἡμῖν, ὡς Παταικίωνος
ἄμεινον πεπολίτευσαι, διέξιθι, ἀλλ᾽ ἐφικόμενος τῆς ἀνδραγα-
10 θίας, οὕτω τὰς χάριτας τὸν δῆμον ἀπαίτει.
    Ἵνα δὲ μὴ ἀποπλανῶ ὑμᾶς ἀπὸ τῆς ὑποθέσεως, ἀναγνώσεται 191
ὑμῖν ὁ γραμματεὺς τὸ ἐπίγραμμα, ὃ ἐπιγέγραπται τοῖς ἀπὸ
Φυλῆς τὸν δῆμον καταγαγοῦσιν.

ΕΠΙΓΡΑΜΜΑ.

15   Τούσδ᾽ ἀρετῆς ἕνεκα στεφάνοις ἐγέραιρε παλαίχθων
    δῆμος Ἀθηναίων, οἵ ποτε τοὺς ἀδίκοις
    δεσμοῖς ἄρξαντας πρῶτοι πόλεως καταπαύειν
    ἦρξαν, κίνδυνον σώμασιν ἀράμενοι.

    Ὅτι τοὺς παρὰ τοὺς νόμους ἄρξαντας κατέλυσαν, διὰ τοῦτ᾽ αὖ-192
20 τούς φησιν ὁ ποιητὴς τιμηθῆναι. ἔναυλον γὰρ ἦν ἔτι τότε πᾶσιν,

2. φησὶ] Sic agmnk Vat. Laur. Flor., φασὶ b, φασὶ el: volgo φήσει. Vid. annot.
4. ὑμᾶς] ἡμᾶς fcdbekl.   5. ὁ ἀγὼν] ἀγὼν fcdq: 'scrib. opinor ἀγὼν' Frank.
9. ἐφικόμενος] καταλαμβάνων coit. g.   17. πρῶτοι πόλεως] πόλιος πρῶτοι bk
Bckk., πόλιος πρῶτοι el. 'Scribe πόλεως πρῶτοι' Frank.   20. ἔτι] Om. a et fortasse
per incuriam Frank.

4. ὥσπερ ὑμᾶς ἀγνοοῦντας. The accusative by a kind of attraction to Φιλάμμωνα
.. στεφανωθῆναι νικήσαντα: what Demosthenes thought is expressed in the same construction as what he said.
6. δεῖ γὰρ τὸν κήρυκα κ.τ.λ. Half
ironical: 'if you are vain enough to require
that your virtue shall be proclaimed to all
Greece in spite of the law, you ought at least
to let the virtue be real.'
8. Παταικίωνος. According to Suidas,
he traded upon quarrels with young men of
rank and character: but the context here
would lead us to think of political rather
than private rascality.
10. οὕτω. Almost equivalent to εἶτα,
'first attain to virtue, and then ask to be
thanked for it.' Only οὕτω does not emphasise the idea of time: it is 'when you are in
that state,' not, 'afterwards, when you have
done that.'
§ 191. But consider the spirit of those
men, the restorers of the democracy.
11. ἵνα δὲ μὴ .. ὑποθέσεως. He con-

cludes the digression about the comparative
frequency of crowns in old and recent times,
but from the mention of the restorers of the
democracy he passes back to the subject of
τὸ παρανόμον gradually.
15. παλαίχθων δῆμος. With special reference to the autochthonous character of
the nation, and its antiquity, Thuc. 2. 36.
The word παλαίχθων also occurs in Aesch.
S. c. T. 105 παλαίχθων Ἄρης, where the
sense is very similar. Ares was the father of
Harmonia, the ancestress of the royal line:
and the Sparti were descended from his
sacred dragon.
§ 192. In those days (I heard it from my
father, who shared in them) men knew what
it was for Law to be overthrown:
20. ἔναυλον γὰρ .. πᾶσιν. 'At that
time every one had it, dinned into their ears,'
because the Four Hundred had abolished
the γραφὴ παρανόμων as the first step in
their revolution: of which that of the Thirty
was considered the natural sequel. τινὲς
will probably mean the Four Hundred.

ὅτι τηνικαῦτα ὁ δῆμος κατελύθη, ἐπειδή τινες τὰς γραφὰς τῶν
παρανόμων ἀνεῖλον. καὶ γάρ τοι, ὡς ἐγὼ τοῦ πατρὸς τοῦ
ἐμαυτοῦ ἐπυνθανόμην, ὃς ἔτη βιοὺς ἐνενήκοντα καὶ πέντε ἐτελεύ-
τησεν, ἁπάντων μετασχὼν τῶν πόνων τῇ πόλει, ὃς πολλάκις
πρὸς ἐμὲ διεξῄει ἐπὶ σχολῆς· ἔφη γάρ, ὅτε ἀρτίως κατελη- 5
λύθει ὁ δῆμος, εἴ τις εἰσίοι γραφὴν παρανόμων εἰς δικαστήριον,
εἶναι ὅμοιον τὸ ὄνομα καὶ τὸ ἔργον. τί γάρ ἐστιν ἀνοσιώτε-
193 ρον ἀνδρὸς παράνομα λέγοντος καὶ πράττοντος; καὶ τὴν ἀκρόασιν, ὡς ἐκεῖνος ἀπήγγελλεν, οὐ τὸν αὐτὸν τρόπον ἐποιοῦντο,
ὥσπερ νῦν γίγνεται, ἀλλ' ἦσαν πολὺ χαλεπώτεροι οἱ δικασταὶ 10
τοῖς τὰ παράνομα γράφουσιν αὐτοῦ τοῦ κατηγόρου, καὶ πολλάκις ἀνεπόδιζον τὸν γραμματέα καὶ ἐκέλευον πάλιν ἀναγιγνώ-
σκειν τοὺς νόμους καὶ τὸ ψήφισμα, καὶ ἡλίσκοντο οἱ παράνομα γράφοντες, οὐκ εἰ πάντας παραπηδήσειαν τοὺς νόμους,
ἀλλ' εἰ μίαν μόνον συλλαβὴν παραλλάξειαν. τὸ δὲ νυνὶ γιγ- 15
νόμενον πρᾶγμα ὑπερκαταγέλαστόν ἐστιν· ὁ μὲν γὰρ γραμματεὺς ἀναγιγνώσκει τὸ παράνομον, οἱ δὲ δικασταὶ ὥσπερ ἐπῳδὴν

---

4. ὅς] Vid. annot.   Mox Frank. διεξῄειν scribi jubet.   6. γραφὴν] γραφὴ q.
11. τὰ] Om. fed bekl Bekk.   12. ἀνεπόδιζον] ἐνεπόδιζον b, corr. g, et marg. m.
16. γὰρ] Om. gmekl.

---

2. τοῦ πατρὸς τοῦ ἐμαυτοῦ: cp. Ae. de
F. L. p. 38, § 82. Aeschines knew the
discreditable stories about his father's origin
and, it appears, could afford to notice them
as there, or to treat them as beneath notice,
as here.

3. ἐνενήκοντα καὶ πέντε: cp. Ae. de F.
L. fin. He therefore died the year after his
son's acquittal.

4. ὃς πολλάκις. As the repetition of
the relative, after ὃς ἔτη βιοὺς κ.τ.λ., is
clumsy, one is tempted to adopt Markland's
conjecture οὕς. Taylor's, ὡς, is exposed to
just the same objection as the text.

5. διεξῄει ἐπὶ σχολῆς. 'Used to tell
me all about it.'

ἔφη γὰρ resumes καὶ γάρ τοι, and gives
the reason of ἔναυλον ἦν. The form of the
paragraph is lively and ungrammatical: we
should have expected ὅμοιον ἦν, to complete
ὡς .. ἐπυνθανόμην, instead of ἔφη .. εἶναι
ὅμοιον.

6. εἰσίοι γραφήν. Volg. ante Bekk.
γραφή: the only attraction of which is the
occurrence of the phrase below, § 198.
Only one MS. has it.

7. εἶναι ὅμοιον τὸ ὄνομα καὶ τὸ ἔργον.
'The thing was treated in fact as it was in
theory,' the trial in name was a trial indeed;
'and reason good; for what is more abom-
inable than a man who breaks the law in

word and deed?' The antithesis of the
last clause is a temptation to take that of
the former as parallel to it, so that τὸ ὄνομα
καὶ τὸ ἔργον should balance λέγοντος καὶ
πράττοντος. But τὸ ὄνομα then would
have to mean 'his proposition,' which is
hardly possible; if it were, the point would
be 'a mover of illegal resolutions is as bad
as a law-breaker in action,' a common criminal. It would be a bad commendation to
say, 'when a man was brought to trial for
an unconstitutional law, men were as indig-
nant at hearing the name as at the thing
itself,' i. e. they started with a prejudice
against the prisoner, thinking that to be
even suspected of such a crime was a crime
in itself. But Aeschines does sometimes
pay such doubtful compliments.

§ 193. The court attended to the legal
details, and punished the slightest irregularity; now they do not attend to the laws,
but only to the speeches.

11. πολλάκις. Probably 'often' in
every trial, not merely 'in many trials.'

12. ἀνεπόδιζον. 'Pulled him up,' made
him go over the ground again: explained by
the next clause.

17. ἐπῳδήν. A magical formula, that
had to be gone through before the trial
could legitimately commence, but which no
one was expected to understand.

H

ἢ ἀλλότριόν τι πρᾶγμα ἀκροώμενοι πρὸς ἑτέρῳ τινὶ τὴν
γνώμην ἔχουσιν. ἤδη δ' ἐκ τῶν τεχνῶν τῶν Δημοσθένους αἰσ- 194
χρὸν ἔθος ἐν τοῖς δικαστηρίοις παραδέχεσθε. μετενήνεκται
γὰρ ὑμῖν τὰ τῆς πόλεως δίκαια· ὁ μὲν γὰρ κατήγορος ἀπολο-
5 γεῖται, ὁ δὲ φεύγων τὴν γραφὴν κατηγορεῖ, οἱ δὲ δικασταὶ
ἐνίοτε ὧν μέν εἰσι κριταὶ ἐπιλανθάνονται, ὧν δ' οὐκ εἰσὶ δικασταί, περὶ τούτων ἀναγκάζονται τὴν ψῆφον φέρειν. λέγει δὲ
ὁ φεύγων, ἂν ἄρα ποθ' ἅψηται τοῦ πράγματος, οὐχ ὡς ἔννομα
γέγραφεν, ἀλλ' ὡς ἤδη ποτὲ καὶ πρότερον ἕτερος τοιαῦτα
10 γράψας ἀπέφυγεν. ἐφ' ᾧ καὶ νυνὶ μέγα φρονεῖν ἀκούω Κτησιφῶντα. ἐτόλμα δ' ἐν ὑμῖν ποτε σεμνύνεσθαι Ἀριστοφῶν 195
ἐκεῖνος ὁ Ἀζηνιεὺς λέγων, ὅτι γραφὰς παρανόμων πέφευγεν
ἑβδομήκοντα καὶ πέντε. ἀλλ' οὐχὶ ὁ Κέφαλος ὁ παλαιὸς

4. ὑμῖν] Ita Markl. Bekk. Frank. Schultz: ἡμῖν bek, ceteri ὑμῶν, unde ὑφ' ὑμῶν Reisk.:
om. B. et S.   11. Ἀριστοφῶν] † ὁ Ἀριστοφῶν g †.   12. πέφευγεν] ἀπέφυγεν
bekl Cobet.   13. ὁ Κέφαλος] Κέφαλος z.

1. πρὸς ἑτέρῳ τινί. Perhaps he means,
that they do not attend to the trial at all
during the reading of the impeached resolution and the παραγεγραμμένοι νόμοι. He
does not mean that they are inattentive to
the trial *throughout*, but the ἤδη δὲ of the
next sentence makes it unlikely that he here
introduces the charge, which follows there,
of deciding the trial on a false issue. Here
the point seems to be, 'they form their
opinion of the illegality, not from the laws but
from the speeches;' then he goes on to say,
'they often come to decide without regarding the question of illegality at all.'
§ 194. *And since Demosthenes has influ-
enced the courts, often decide on a totally
irrelevant issue, because the speeches are about
one.*
2. ἤδη .. παραδέχεσθε. 'It has come
to this, through the arts of Demosthenes,
that you habitually tolerate a shameful custom in the courts:' the force of the present
is fixed by μετενήνεκται.
4. ὁ μὲν γὰρ .. κατηγορεῖ: cp. Ae. in
Tim. p. 25, § 175, which proves that ascribing the custom to Demosthenes is not a
meaningless invective. Here the moral is,
'If you had attended to the technicalities I
began with, you would have voted right:
as it is, I have to defend myself against
Demosthenes' stock accusations, and you
will vote on the general merits of our respective policy.'
5. οἱ δὲ δικασταὶ .. κριταὶ .. δικασταί.
'The *judges in the court* forget the questions
they have to *decide*, and have to vote on
questions that are not *before the court*,' even

supposing it is the judges' business, as individual citizens, to have an opinion on them,
δικασταὶ being the more technical word.
Cobet and Schultz would omit the second
δικασταί, but the above point seems to
justify its retention.
7. ἀναγκάζονται. They are forced to
decide the issue they have allowed to be
raised.
10. ἐφ' ᾧ καὶ κ.τ.λ. The argument is
actually brought forward, D. de Cor. § 281:
cp. ibid. §§ 103 sq., 145 sqq. Of course a
modern court would consider the defence a
good one: it is the only technical weakness
of Aeschines' case.
§ 195. *In consequence of this change of
spirit, Aristophon prides himself on his skill
in getting off charges, which Cephalus prided
himself on never incurring.*
11. Ἀριστοφῶν: cp. sup. ad § 139.
13. Κέφαλος. Sometimes confounded,
even by ancient writers, with the friend of
Pericles, and interlocutor in Plato's Republic.
But he was a Syracusan, and never was
admitted to Athenian citizenship, and so
cannot have proposed resolutions in the Assembly. This Cephalus was a demagogue
of rather later date, one of those who over-
threw the Thirty (by which time his namesake was dead). He is mentioned by Aristophanes in Eccles. 248, as one of the
speakers Praxagora will find it hardest to
reply to: but whether we are to understand
from that passage that the author thought
him a scurrilous debater or a steady friend to
the constitution is not clear. Modern writers have assumed the former.

ἐκεῖνος, ὁ δοκῶν δημοτικώτατος γεγονέναι, οὐχ οὕτως, ἀλλ᾽ ἐπὶ
τοῖς ἐναντίοις ἐφιλοτιμεῖτο, λέγων, ὅτι πλεῖστα πάντων γεγραφὼς ψηφίσματα οὐδεμίαν πώποτε γραφὴν πέφευγε παρανόμων,
καλῶς, οἶμαι, σεμνυνόμενος. ἐγράφοντο γὰρ ἀλλήλους παρανόμων οὐ μόνον οἱ διαπολιτευόμενοι, ἀλλὰ καὶ οἱ φίλοι τοὺς φίλους, 5
196 εἴ τι ἐξαμαρτάνοιεν εἰς τὴν πόλιν. ἐκεῖθεν δὲ τοῦτο γνώσεσθε.
Ἀρχῖνος γὰρ ὁ ἐκ Κοίλης ἐγράψατο παρανόμων Θρασύβου-
λον τὸν Στειριᾶ [γράψαντά τι παρὰ τοὺς νόμους], ἕνα τῶν
συγκατελθόντων αὐτῷ ἀπὸ Φυλῆς, καὶ εἶλε νεωστὶ γεγενημένων
αὐτῷ τῶν εὐεργεσιῶν, ἃς οὐχ ὑπελογίσαντο οἱ δικασταί· ἡγοῦντο 10
γάρ, ὥσπερ τότε αὐτοὺς φεύγοντας ἀπὸ Φυλῆς Θρασύβουλος
κατήγαγεν, οὕτω νῦν μένοντας ἐξελαύνειν παρὰ τοὺς νόμους
197 γράφοντά τι. ἀλλ᾽ οὐ νῦν, ἀλλ᾽ ἅπαν τοὐναντίον γίγνεται·
οἱ γὰρ ἀγαθοὶ στρατηγοὶ ὑμῖν καὶ τῶν τὰς σιτήσεις τινὲς
εὑρημένων ἐν τῷ πρυτανείῳ ἐξαιτοῦνται τὰς γραφὰς τῶν παρα- 15
νόμων, οὓς ὑμεῖς ἀχαρίστους εἶναι δικαίως ἂν ὑπολαμβάνοιτε·
εἰ γάρ τις ἐν δημοκρατίᾳ τετιμημένος, ἐν τοιαύτῃ πολιτείᾳ,
ἣν οἱ θεοὶ καὶ οἱ νόμοι σώζουσι, τολμᾷ βοηθεῖν τοῖς παράνομα γράφουσι, καταλύει τὴν πολιτείαν, ὑφ᾽ ἧς τετίμηται.

---

3. πέφευγε] ἔφευγε *bekl*, ἔφυγε Cobet.　　8. ἕνα] στεφανοῦν ἕνα libri praeter *fdq*
Barb.: vid. annot.　Paullo supra γράψαντα .. νόμους omitti jubent Hamak. Frank. Schultz.
12. παρὰ τοὺς νόμους γράφοντά τι] γράφοντά τι παρὰ τοὺς νόμους *bekl* Bekk.
13. ἀλλ᾽ ἅπαν] ἀλλὰ πᾶν Vat. *bekl* Bekk. Schultz.　　14. ὑμῖν] Sic *ek* Bekk. Frank.
ἡμῖν *bl*, ὑμῶν ceteri, om. B. et S.

5. **οἱ διαπολιτευόμενοι.** Just equivalent
to the Latin ' *de republica* dissentire,' which
implies the previous possibility of agreement,
and explains the distinction of Ammonius,
διαπολιτεύεσθαι λέγουσι τοὺς ἐκ τῆς αὐτῆς
πόλεως· ἀντιπολιτεύεσθαι δὲ τοὺς ἐξ ἑτέρας
δι᾽ ἑτέρας ἀντιδιαστατοῦντας ἀλλήλοις. E.g.
Demosthenes would be said διαπολιτεύεσθαι
Αἰσχίνει, but ἀντιπολιτεύεσθαι would be
applied to his debate with Philip's ambassadors at Thebes.

§ 196. *Thrasybulus did not escape for his
services: Archinus himself did not hesitate to
prosecute him: for his services were the restoration of law, and law overrides friendship.*

6. **ἐκεῖθεν.** Much like ἐκείνως above,
§ 168. So D. de Cor. § 192.

8. **[γράψαντα .. νόμους].** Naturally suspected as a gloss by Hamaker. The proposal
was to confer citizenship on Lysias for his
services against the Thirty, without the necessary προβούλευμα.

ἕνα τῶν κ.τ.λ. The story is given in
Ps. Plut. Vit. X. Orat. Lysias, p. 835 fin :
from the form of his sentence, Orelli (ap.
Brenni ad hunc loc.) conjectures that he read

ἐνί. which to be a curicus *dativus com-
modi*. If we retain the clause γράψαντα ..
νόμους, we must take the two accusatives as
qualifications, in different senses, of Θρασύ-
βουλον, ' *because* he proposed .., though he
was one .. :' not as though ἕνα τῶν referred
to Lysias, and were a double accusative after
γράψαντα. But probably the latter view
was taken by the author of the gloss στεφανοῦν found in nearly all MSS. before ἕνα, as
well as by those who read ἐνί.

12. **μένοντας ἐξελαύνειν.** Compare the
expression in the Heliastic Oath (given ap.
Dem. in Timocr. pp. 746, 747) οὐδὲ τοὺς
μένοντας ἐξελῶ παρὰ τοὺς νόμους τοὺς κειμένους κ.τ.λ.

§ 197. *Now men, themselves good and
honoured public servants, turn against the
public service in cases like this.*

15. **ἐξαιτοῦνται τὰς γραφάς.** The common sense of ἐξαιτεῖσθαι is to withdraw by
entreaty, whether from judgment or from
vengeance. Hence it can be used with an
accusative either of the criminal, as Dem.
Mid. p. 426, § 27, or of the crime, as Eur.
Andr. 53-55, or of the case, as here.

18. **οἱ θεοὶ καὶ οἱ νόμοι** : cp. above, § 6.

τίς οὖν ἀποδέδεικται λόγος ἀνδρὶ δικαίῳ συνηγόρῳ καὶ σώ- 198
φρονι; ἐγὼ λέξω. εἰς τρία μέρη διαιρεῖται ἡ ἡμέρα, ὅταν
εἰσίῃ γραφὴ παρανόμων εἰς τὸ δικαστήριον. ἐγχεῖται γὰρ
τὸ μὲν πρῶτον ὕδωρ τῷ κατηγόρῳ καὶ τοῖς νόμοις καὶ τῇ δη-
5 μοκρατίᾳ, τὸ δὲ δεύτερον ὕδωρ τῷ τὴν γραφὴν φεύγοντι καὶ
τοῖς εἰς αὐτὸ τὸ πρᾶγμα λέγουσιν· ἐπειδὰν δὲ τῇ πρώτῃ
ψήφῳ μὴ λυθῇ τὸ παράνομον, ἤδη τὸ τρίτον ὕδωρ ἐγχεῖται
τῇ τιμήσει καὶ τῷ μεγέθει τῆς ὀργῆς τῆς ὑμετέρας. ὅστις 199
μὲν οὖν ἐν τῇ τιμήσει τὴν ψῆφον αἰτεῖ, τὴν ὀργὴν τὴν ὑμε-
10 τέραν παραιτεῖται· ὅστις δ' ἐν τῷ πρώτῳ λόγῳ τὴν ψῆφον
αἰτεῖ, ὅρκον αἰτεῖ, νόμον αἰτεῖ, δημοκρατίαν αἰτεῖ, ὧν οὔτε
αἰτῆσαι οὐδὲν ὅσιον οὐδενὶ οὔτ' αἰτηθέντα ἑτέρῳ δοῦναι. κε-
λεύσατε οὖν αὐτούς, ἐάσαντας ὑμᾶς τὴν πρώτην ψῆφον κατὰ
τοὺς νόμους διενεγκεῖν, ἀπαντᾶν εἰς τὴν τίμησιν. ὅλως δ' 200
15 ἔγωγε, ὦ Ἀθηναῖοι, ὀλίγου δέω εἰπεῖν, ὡς καὶ νόμον δεῖ τεθῆ-
ναι ἐπὶ ταῖς γραφαῖς μόνον τῶν παρανόμων, μὴ ἐξεῖναι μήτε

1. ἀνδρὶ δικαίῳ συνηγόρῳ καὶ σώφρονι] Ita *afcd*: ἀνδρὶ συνηγόρῳ δικαίῳ καὶ
σώφρονι *gmn* B. et S.: ἀνδρὶ δικαίῳ συνηγόρῳ *bekl*. Vid. annot.   7. μὴ] Om.
bekl.   10. παραιτεῖται] αἰτεῖται *gmn*.   11. ὅρκον αἰτεῖ] Om. *agmn*, post
νόμον αἰτεῖ ponunt z Flor. *bekl*, post τὴν ψῆφον αἰτεῖ Vat. *p*.   14. ἀπαντᾶν] ἔπειτα
ἀπαντᾶν *p*. Reisk.   16. ταῖς .. τῶν] ταῖς *b* Bekk., ceteri τῶν.

§ 198. *The right thing for a man to do
in defence of such a case is to speak only in
mitigation of penalty:*

1. ἀνδρὶ δικαίῳ συνηγόρῳ καὶ σώφρονι.
So most MSS.; B. and S. and others transpose συνηγόρῳ δικαίῳ. As a matter of taste,
it is hard to say which order is preferable:
'what is a man to say who wishes to be
loyal to his client, without transgressing his
duty to the state?' is the sense in either
case. To express this, it is more obvious to
couple δικαίῳ καὶ σώφρονι immediately together; but, some may think, less artistic.

2. ὅταν εἰσίῃ γραφὴ παρανόμων. The
arrangement was common to all public prosecutions.

4. τῷ κατηγόρῳ .. δημοκρατίᾳ. Aeschines does not quite assume that the accused is guilty, but does assume that the
accuser has no motive but loyalty for the
prosecution.

6. εἰς αὐτὸ τὸ πρᾶγμα. To prove that
the decree is consistent with the letter of the
law.

§ 199. *Then, and then only, are appeals
to your favour admissible without treason.*

9. τὴν ψῆφον αἰτεῖ. 'Asks for your
vote as a favour,' instead of attempting to
convince you that the vote favourable to
him will be *right*.

10. παραιτεῖται. ' Tries by his entrea-

ties to *turn aside* your anger' is the force of
the preposition: 'to beg off' in English
covers the sense both of παραιτεῖσθαι and
ἐξαιτεῖσθαι.

11. ὅρκον αἰτεῖ, νόμον αἰτεῖ, δημοκρατίαν αἰτεῖ. This figure ἐπιμονή, which produces its effect by dwelling on a subject
through a juxtaposition of equivalent clauses
in *crescendo*, is characteristic of Aeschines,
as polysyndeton is of Demosthenes. Cp.
above, §§ 24, 25, 94; below, §§ 201 fin. 203.

13. αὐτούς. The συνήγοροι whom Aeschines feels obliged to treat without abuse.
It is not known who they were: one might
almost guess Phocion, from his known indifference to party ties, and Aeschines' deprecatory respect. But in § 230, it seems hinted
the general engaged was no speaker.

§§ 200, 201. *In fact, I wish that in these
trials advocates were not allowed at all, to
obscure the simple legal issue.*

16. μόνον. In other public trials, there
will ordinarily be room for differences of
opinion, either as to the facts or the merits
of the case (ἀόριστον τὸ δίκαιον): in these
the thing to be done is simply to compare
the texts of two documents. Of course Aeschines exaggerates the simplicity of the
latter problem; perhaps honestly, because,
having himself a lawyer's intellect, *he* found
it easy.

τῷ κατηγόρῳ συνηγόρους παρασχέσθαι μήτε τῷ τὴν γραφὴν
τῶν παρανόμων φεύγοντι. οὐ γὰρ ἀόριστόν ἐστι τὸ δίκαιον,
ἀλλ᾽ ὡρισμένον τοῖς νόμοις τοῖς ὑμετέροις. ὥσπερ γὰρ ἐν τῇ
τεκτονικῇ, ὅταν εἰδέναι βουλώμεθα τὸ ὀρθὸν καὶ τὸ μή, τὸν
201 κανόνα προσφέρομεν, ᾧ διαγιγνώσκεται, οὕτω καὶ ἐν ταῖς γρα- 5
φαῖς τῶν παρανόμων παράκειται κανὼν τοῦ δικαίου τουτὶ τὸ
σανίδιον καὶ τὸ ψήφισμα καὶ οἱ παραγεγραμμένοι νόμοι.
ταῦτα συμφωνοῦντα ἀλλήλοις ἐπιδείξας κατάβαινε· καὶ τί δεῖ
σε Δημοσθένην παρακαλεῖν; ὅταν δ᾽ ὑπερπηδήσας τὴν δικαίαν
ἀπολογίαν παρακαλῇς κακοῦργον ἄνθρωπον καὶ τεχνίτην λόγων, 10
κλέπτεις τὴν ἀκρόασιν, βλάπτεις τὴν πόλιν, καταλύεις τὴν
δημοκρατίαν.

202 Τίς οὖν ἐστιν ἀποτροπὴ τῶν τοιούτων λόγων; ἐγὼ ἐρῶ.
ἐπειδὰν προσελθὼν ἐνταυθοῖ Κτησιφῶν διεξέλθῃ πρὸς ὑμᾶς
τοῦτο δὴ τὸ συντεταγμένον αὐτῷ προοίμιον, ἔπειτ᾽ ἐνδιατρίβῃ 15
καὶ μὴ ἀπολογῆται, ὑπομνήσατ᾽ αὐτὸν ἄνευ θορύβου τὸ σανίδιον λαβεῖν καὶ τοὺς νόμους τῷ ψηφίσματι παραναγνῶναι.
ἐὰν δὲ μὴ προσποιῆται ὑμῶν ἀκούειν, μηδὲ ὑμεῖς ἐκείνου ἐθέλετε

---

6. τῶν] ταῖς τῶν *k* Bekk.　Mox ‘καὶ ante τὸ ψήφισμα puto delendum esse’ Saupp.
14. προσελθών] προελθὼν *ekl.*

6. **τουτὶ τὸ σανίδιον** is the whole, τὸ
ψήφισμα and οἱ παραγεγραμμένοι νόμοι the
parts, the two written in parallel columns on
the tablet, for comparison and contrast.

9. **ὑπερπηδήσας.** ‘ Overleaping the
limits:’ cp. above, § 12. The word is
chosen to express the extent, the easy
magnificence, so to speak, of Ctesiphon’s
contempt for law.

10. **κακοῦργον.** Fitted to carry you
through in setting aside the constitution by
violence : **τεχνίτην λόγων**, fitted to disguise
the true nature of your attempt. **τεχνίτην
λόγων** of Demosthenes also in Ae. in Tim.
p. 24, § 170.

11. **κλέπτεις τὴν ἀκρόασιν**: cp. above,
§ 99, which seems to indicate that the sense
is rather ‘playing tricks with the ears’ of the
courts, ‘taking in those who allow you a
hearing,’ than ‘gaining a hearing under false
pretences,’ the most obvious sense here.

§ 202. *It rests with you, judges, to remove these abuses, by refusing Ctesiphon a
hearing except when speaking in the point :*

15. **τοῦτο δὴ τὸ συντεταγμένον αὐτῷ
προοίμιον.** ‘The introductory remarks,
which you will of course regard as assigned
to him by Demosthenes.’ The ablest orator
on the side seems to have undertaken the
conduct of the defence generally, and to

have assigned to each of the συνήγοροι
their respective parts ; it does not follow
that Ctesiphon’s speech is supposed to have
been *written* by Demosthenes, but only so
arranged by him as to serve as a προοίμιον
to his own.

ἔπειτ᾽ ἐνδιατρίβῃ. ‘And then begins
making a delay, instead of proceeding with
his defence.’ Having said a few things calculated to introduce Demosthenes’ speech,
he goes on for a little while, lest curtness
should seem disrespectful to the court; but
never gets beyond his exordium, and then,
apologising for his inexperience in speaking,
asks to be allowed to entrust his cause to
Demosthenes.

16. **ἄνευ θορύβου** goes with ὑπομνήσατ᾽
αὐτὸν, and is answered by μηδὲ ὑμεῖς ἐκείνου
ἐθέλετε ἀκούειν. For the danger of the
court scraping a man down, and the use of
θορυβεῖν in the technical sense of refusing
him a hearing by such means, cp. Plat. Apol.
p. 20 E, Andoc. Alcib. p. 30, init. § 4, the
latter in a context somewhat like this.

18. **ἐὰν δὲ μὴ προσποιῆται.** ‘If he
pretends not to hear you.’ The pretence
would not be absurd, as 500 men could
hardly cry out in perfect unison, even if
unanimous in making the demand Aeschines
suggests.

ἀκούειν· οὐ γὰρ τῶν φευγόντων τὰς οὐ δικαίας ἀπολογίας εἰσεληλύθατε ἀκροασόμενοι, ἀλλὰ τῶν ἐθελόντων δικαίως
ἀπολογεῖσθαι. ἐὰν δ᾽ ὑπερπηδήσας τὴν δικαίαν ἀπολογίαν 203
Δημοσθένην παρακαλῇ, μάλιστα μὲν μὴ προσδέχεσθε κακοῦρ-
5 γον ἄνθρωπον, οἰόμενον ῥήμασι τοὺς νόμους ἀναιρήσειν, μηδ᾽
ἐν ἀρετῇ τοῦθ᾽ ὑμῶν μηδεὶς καταλογιζέσθω, ὃς ἂν ἐπανερομέ-
νου Κτησιφῶντος, εἰ καλέσῃ Δημοσθένην, πρῶτος ἀναβοήσῃ
"κάλει, κάλει." ἐπὶ σαυτὸν καλεῖς, ἐπὶ τοὺς νόμους καλεῖς,
ἐπὶ τὴν δημοκρατίαν καλεῖς. ἂν δ᾽ ἄρα ὑμῖν δόξῃ ἀκούειν,
10 ἀξιώσατε τὸν Δημοσθένην τὸν αὐτὸν τρόπον ἀπολογεῖσθαι,
ὅνπερ κἀγὼ κατηγόρηκα. ἐγὼ δὲ πῶς κατηγόρηκα; ἵνα καὶ
ὑπομνήσω ὑμᾶς. οὔτε τὸν ἴδιον βίον τὸν Δημοσθένους πρό- 204
τερον διεξῆλθον οὔτε τῶν δημοσίων ἀδικημάτων οὐδενὸς πρότερον ἐμνήσθην, ἄφθονα δήπου καὶ πολλὰ ἔχων λέγειν, ἢ πάν-
15 των γ᾽ ἂν εἴην ἀπορώτατος· ἀλλὰ πρῶτον μὲν τοὺς νόμους
ἐπέδειξα ἀπαγορεύοντας μὴ στεφανοῦν τοὺς ὑπευθύνους, ἔπειτα
τὸν ῥήτορα ἐξήλεγξα γράψαντα Δημοσθένην ὑπεύθυνον ὄντα

---

1. Alterum οὐ om. Flor. Hamaker.   2. τῶν ἐθελόντων] τὰς τῶν ἐθελόντων volg.
ante Bekk., sine librorum auctoritate.   4. 'Verba κακοῦργον .. ἀναιρήσειν Bakius ut
ex § 16 repetita delet:' atque ex eodem loco z iis σοφιστὴν praeponit.   7. εἰ καλέσῃ]
εἰ καλέσω agmnr Joan. Sicul, εἰ καλέσει fcdηz, εἰ καλέσειε bekl, εἰ καλέσοι Ald. Reisk. ἢ
καλέσω B. et S.   11. ὅνπερ .. πῶς] ὅνπερ κἀγώ. ὧδέ πως fcd Barb.   13. οὐδενὸς
πρότερον] πρότερον οὐδένος a.

2. ἀκροασόμενοι. Perhaps with the
notion of 'listening for entertainment.'

§ 203. And by refusing Demosthenes a
bearing at all, except on condition of following the order of my speech:

3. ὑπερπηδήσας ..ἀπολογίαν. It is
hard to avoid thinking that some of these
words are a repetition from § 201. Similarly
those that follow, κακοῦργον .. ἀναιρήσειν,
are repeated from § 16, with only the substitution of ἄνθρωπον for σοφιστήν : and
one good MS. puts σοφιστὴν before κακοῦργον here.

5. μηδ᾽ ἐν ἀρετῇ κ.τ.λ. 'Let none of
you make it a merit, if he is the first,
when Ctesiphon asks if he shall call Demosthenes, to cry out "Call him."' ἐν
ἀρετῇ, 'as a proof of kindness :' cp. Thuc.
2. 40.

7. εἰ καλέσῃ. Bekker compares Ae. de
F. L. p. 36, §§ 67 fin., 71, for εἰ with a
deliberative conjunctive : in the former passage
there are traces of a v.l. with the future.
The best group of MSS., with Joannes Sicel-
iota, here read εἰ καλέσω ; whence B. and S.
ἢ καλέσω, which may be right, and in any
case is what Ctesiphon would actually say.
But the variations of the MSS. suggest the

view that they are all conjectural emenda-
tions of the text.

8. κάλει, κάλει. Repeated, in a good-
natured eagerness to give the man on his
trial every chance.

11. ὅνπερ κἀγώ. The force of καὶ is 'to
submit to the same restrictions in his defence
to which I have submitted in my accusation,'
trying to disguise the fact, that his demand
deprives his enemy of a liberty which he
himself has used. Demosthenes naturally
refuses this demand at the outset, De Cor.
§ 15.

§ 204. First I alleged the law against
crowning accountable officials, and proved
that Ctesiphon violated it openly ; replying to
objections.

12. οὔτε τὸν ἴδιον βίον κ.τ.λ. According to the hackneyed custom of vulgar orators (followed even by Cicero). Demosthenes does not begin with attacks on Aeschines' private life, and De Cor. § 13 may
be held to refer to this passage : whence it
appears that here Aeschines has not altered
the speech since delivery.

15. ἀπορώτατος. 'Most helpless,' unable to avail myself of an extensive choice
(εὐπορία) of topics.

στεφανοῦν οὐδὲν προβαλλόμενον, οὐδὲ προσεγγράψαντα "ἐπειδὰν δῷ τὰς εὐθύνας," ἀλλὰ παντελῶς καὶ ὑμῶν καὶ τῶν νόμων
καταπεφρονηκότα· καὶ τὰς ἐσομένας πρὸς ταῦτα προφάσεις
205 εἶπον, ας ἀξιῶ καὶ ὑμᾶς διαμνημονεύειν. δεύτερον δ' ὑμῖν διεξῆλθον τοὺς περὶ τῶν κηρυγμάτων νόμους, ἐν οἷς διαρρήδην 5
ἀπείρηται τὸν ὑπὸ τοῦ δήμου στεφανούμενον μὴ κηρύττεσθαι
ἔξω τῆς ἐκκλησίας· ὁ δὲ ῥήτωρ ὁ φεύγων τὴν γραφὴν οὐ τοὺς
νόμους μόνον παραβέβηκεν, ἀλλὰ καὶ τὸν καιρὸν τῆς ἀναρρήσεως καὶ τὸν τόπον, κελεύων οὐκ ἐν τῇ ἐκκλησίᾳ, ἀλλ' ἐν τῷ
θεάτρῳ τὴν ἀνάρρησιν γίγνεσθαι, οὐδ' ἐκκλησιαζόντων Ἀθη- 10
ναίων, ἀλλὰ μελλόντων τραγῳδῶν εἰσιέναι· ταῦτα δ' εἰπὼν
μικρὰ μὲν περὶ τῶν ἰδίων εἶπον, τὰ δὲ πλεῖστα περὶ τῶν δη-
206 μοσίων ἀδικημάτων λέγω. οὕτω δὴ καὶ τὸν Δημοσθένην ἀξιώσατε ἀπολογεῖσθαι πρὸς τὸν τῶν ὑπευθύνων νόμον πρῶτον καὶ
τὸν περὶ τῶν κηρυγμάτων δεύτερον, τρίτον δὲ τὸ μέγιστον 15
λέγω, ὡς οὐδὲ ἄξιός ἐστι τῆς δωρεᾶς. ἐὰν δ' ὑμῶν δέηται

---

1. προβαλλόμενον] προβαλόμενον Steph. Bekk., idque mavolt Frank.   προσεγ-
γράψαντα] προσγράψαντα *bʃ*.   3. ταῦτα] ταύτας *agmnʃc*.   13. λέγω] Om. *ʃcdq*
B. et S. Schultz.   15. τὸ μέγιστον] τὸν μέγιστον *a*: 'malim *b*' Bekk.   16. οὐδὲ
ἄξιός] οὐδὲν ἀνάξιός *bel* γρ. *g*, οὐδὲ ἀνάξιός *k*, οὐκ ἀνάξιός *f*; quae omnia fortasse ex οὐδὲν
ἄξιος nata sint. Durum est ὡς οὐκ ἀνάξιος cum ἀπολογεῖσθαι construere.

---

1. **οὐδὲν προβαλλόμενον.** So the MSS.,
B. and S., and Franke in his text. Bekker,
and Franke in his second edition, follow
Stephanus in reading προβαλόμενον. The
aorist is of course more symmetrical with
προσεγγράψαντα ; on the other hand, the
present may have a distinctive force, 'he has
moved to crown Demosthenes .., without
attempting a disguise, and without having
used the *specific* precaution of a clause . . .'

2. **παντελῶς.** Such a saving clause
would have been a sign, not of respect, but
of incomplete contempt. Cp. § 11 sq.

§ 205. *Then I proved that the manner of
the proclamation was as illegal as the time
of the gift : lastly, I said a little about Demosthenes' private vices, and a good deal
about his political treasons.*

7. **ὁ δὲ ῥήτωρ** : cp. ad § 31. The designation ὁ φεύγων τὴν γραφὴν is required,
lest ὁ ῥήτωρ by itself should seem to mean
Demosthenes.

**τοὺς νόμους .. τὸν καιρὸν .. καὶ τὸν
τόπον.** We have had a similar false antithesis in § 34, ubi vide. Note the χιασμὸς
in the next clause, οὐκ ἐν τῇ ἐκκλησίᾳ ἀλλ'
ἐν τῷ θεάτρῳ answering to τὸν τύπον, and
οὐδ' ἐκκλησιαζόντων.. εἰσιέναι to τὸν καιρόν.

13. **λέγω.** B. and S. omit this word, as

suggested by Markland and supported by
one group of MSS. But Aeschines means
to imply, 'I have continued that subject
down to this moment,' according to the
common Greek idiom. Strictly, Aeschines
had continued the subject until his digressions on the degeneracy of Athens, as shewn
first by recklessness in the bestowal of public
honours, and then by disregard of illegal
propositions. If λέγω be not genuine, it
must be a gloss, to give the sense of Reiske's
punctuation περὶ τῶν δημοσίων, ἀδικημάτων
λέγω, which Bremi calls *miram rationem*.

§ 206. *Keep him to the same order : if
he tries to transgress it, be sure that his object is to evade the legal point altogether.*

15. **τὸ μέγιστον.** If δ were read, λέγω
would be superfluous : with τὸ, it is not
necessary but idiomatic.

16. **οὐδὲ ἄξιος.** 'Not worthy of the gift
either,' even if the gift were one that might
lawfully be given to a worthy man. Some
MSS. have ἀνάξιος, the negative being in one
οὐκ and in another οὐδὲν instead of οὐδέ.
These may be merely traces of a reading
οὐδὲν ἄξιος ; or may be corrections on the
hypothesis that the clause describes, as
formally it ought, the most important part
of *Demosthenes'* case, not of Aeschines'.

συγχωρῆσαι αὐτῷ περὶ τῆς τάξεως τοῦ λόγου, κατεπαγγελλόμενος, ὡς ἐπὶ τῇ τελευτῇ τῆς ἀπολογίας λύσει τὸ παράνομον,
μὴ συγχωρεῖτε, μηδ᾽ ἀγνοεῖθ᾽, ὅτι πάλαισμα τοῦτ᾽ ἐστὶ δικα-
στηρίου· οὐ γὰρ εἰσαῦθίς ποτε βούλεται πρὸς τὸ παράνομον
5 ἀπολογεῖσθαι, ἀλλ᾽ οὐδὲν ἔχων δίκαιον εἰπεῖν ἑτέρων παρεμ-
βολῇ πραγμάτων εἰς λήθην ὑμᾶς βούλεται τῆς κατηγορίας
ἐμβαλεῖν. ὥσπερ οὖν ἐν τοῖς γυμνικοῖς ἀγῶσιν ὁρᾶτε τοὺς 207
πύκτας περὶ τῆς στάσεως ἀλλήλοις διαγωνιζομένους, οὕτω καὶ
ὑμεῖς ὅλην τὴν ἡμέραν ὑπὲρ τῆς πόλεως περὶ τῆς τάξεως αὐτῷ
10 τοῦ λόγου μάχεσθε, καὶ μὴ ἐᾶτε αὐτὸν [εἰς τοὺς] ἔξω τοῦ
παρανόμου λόγους περιίστασθαι, ἀλλ᾽ ἐγκαθήμενοι καὶ ἐνεδρεύ-
οντες ἐν τῇ ἀκροάσει εἰσελαύνετε αὐτὸν εἰς τοὺς τοῦ πράγματος
λόγους, καὶ τὰς ἐκτροπὰς αὐτοῦ τῶν λόγων ἐπιτηρεῖτε. ἀλλ᾽ 208
ἃ δὴ συμβήσεται ὑμῖν, ἐὰν τοῦτον τὸν τρόπον τὴν ἀκρόασιν

---

4. βούλεται] βούλοιτ᾽ ἂν γρ. g.   8. ἀλλήλοις] Ita B. et S., Frankium in Quaest.

Aeschin. apud Act. Soc. Gr. secuti.   ἀλλήλους habent *ann*, ἀλλήλους *b* : volgo πρὸς ἀλλήλους.   10. ἔξω τοῦ παρανόμου] εἰς τοὺς ἔξω τοῦ παρανόμου λόγους *bekl* Bekk. († εἰς
τοὺς delevit corr. *b* †) : ἔξω τοῦ παρανόμου λόγους *agmnpr* B. et S., ἔξω τοῦ παρανόμου
λόγου *fdq*, εἰς τοὺς τοῦ παρανόμου λόγους Plin. Ep. 9. 26. λόγους sive λόγου ejiciebat Frank.,
collato Ae. in Tim. p. 25, § 176 : idque om. Vat. Laur.   12. ἀκροάσει] ἐκκλησία pr.
bekl Plin. l. c., et mox παρανόμου pro πράγματος iidem.   14. ἐàν] ἐὰν μὴ Taylor.
post Lambinum, idque probat Frank. Vid. annot.

But Aeschines brings in the assertion ὡς οὐδὲ
ἄξιός ἐστι, where he ought to have quietly
asked Demosthenes to prove ὡς οὐκ ἀνάξιός
ἐστιν. Though a fault, it is more in his
own manner than a copyist's.

1. κατεπαγγελλόμενος. The word is
used by Aeschines also in Tim. §§ 117, 173,
pp. 16, 24 : below, § 224 ubi vide. In all
of these passages the κατὰ seems to have its
proper force, either 'promising' one person
something 'to the detriment' of another, or
making a deceitful promise, and so 'promising to the detriment' of the recipient of
the promise. Here the reference, if to any
definite passage in Demosthenes' speech, is
to § 71 : but it is not likely that this passage is added after delivery. For Demosthenes does not either promise or give the
legal argument at the end of his speech, but
in the middle, §§ 140 sqq., as a parenthesis
in the political one—κακοὺς ἐς μέσσον ἐλάσ-
σας, as the writer of the anonymous Hypothesis remarks.

3. πάλαισμα .. δικαστηρίου. As we
should say, 'a lawyer's trick of fence.' Cp.
ad § 28 : the almost tropical use of this
word suggests the metaphor that follows.

§ 207. *Do not allow him to fight on his
own ground :*

10. [εἰς τοὺς] ἔξω τοῦ παρανόμου λό-

γους περιίστασθαι. Franke's omission of
λόγους is now supported by two good MSS.,
but if retained, its retention appears necessarily
to involve that of εἰς τοὺς, though against the
balance of MS. authority. περιίστασθαι does
not appear to be ever used transitively, like
προίστασθαι, in the sense of 'surrounding
oneself with' a thing. With either Bekker's
reading or Franke's, the sense will be 'to
work his way, shift his ground, off the subject of the breach of law ;' with that of B.
and S., we must give it this unusual sense,
'entrench himself in arguments outside the
question of illegality.' περίστημι, in both
its transitive and intransitive forms, has
generally the sense of changing a position
for the worse. ἐγκαθήμενοι and ἐνεδρεύ-
οντες, and perhaps ἐκτροπὰς, continue the
metaphor of the Palaestra : mild as the
metaphor is, ἐν τῇ ἀκροάσει and τῶν λόγων
are introduced to soften it.

§ 208. *Else I will warn you of the consequences. Demosthenes will arise, and identify
loyalty to the state with loyalty to his party.*

14. τοῦτον τὸν τρόπον. As ἐκείνως in
§ 168 meant 'in the way I tell you, which is
not your way,' so this must mean 'in your
natural way, which I am warning you
against,' i.e. if you let Ctesiphon call Demosthenes, and Demosthenes argue his own

ποιῆσθε, ταῦθ' ὑμῖν ἤδη δίκαιός εἰμι προειπεῖν. ἐπεισάξει γὰρ
τὸν γόητα καὶ βαλαντιοτόμον καὶ διατετμηκότα τὴν πολιτείαν.
οὗτος κλαίει μὲν ῥᾷον ἢ ἄλλοι γελῶσιν, ἐπιορκεῖ δὲ πάντων
προχειρότατα· οὐκ ἂν θαυμάσαιμι δέ, εἰ μεταβαλλόμενος τοῖς
ἔξω περιεστηκόσι λοιδορήσεται, φάσκων τοὺς μὲν ὀλιγαρχι- 5
κοὺς ὑπ' αὐτῆς τῆς ἀληθείας διηριθμημένους ἥκειν πρὸς τὸ τοῦ
κατηγόρου βῆμα, τοὺς δὲ δημοτικοὺς πρὸς τὸ τοῦ φεύγοντος.
209 ὅταν δὴ ταῦτα λέγῃ, πρὸς μὲν τοὺς στασιαστικοὺς λόγους
ἐκεῖνο αὐτῷ ὑποβάλλετε· "ὦ Δημόσθενες, εἰ σοὶ ἦσαν ὅμοιοι
οἱ ἀπὸ Φυλῆς φεύγοντα τὸν δῆμον καταγαγόντες, οὐκ ἄν ποθ' 10
ἡ δημοκρατία κατέστη. νῦν δὲ ἐκεῖνοι μὲν μεγάλων κακῶν
συμβάντων ἔσωσαν τὴν πόλιν τὸ κάλλιστον ἐκ παιδείας ῥῆμα
φθεγξάμενοι, μὴ μνησικακεῖν· σὺ δὲ ἑλκοποιεῖς, καὶ μᾶλλόν
σοι μέλει τῶν αὐθημερὸν λόγων ἢ τῆς σωτηρίας τῆς πόλεως."

3. ῥᾷον] ῥᾳδίως agmnpfcd Ald., ῥᾴδιον Scheib.   4. Post προχειρότατα ἀνθρώπων
add. fcd.   8. ταῦτα] τὰ τοιαῦτα bekl Bekk.   9. ὑποβάλλετε] Volg. ὑποβάλλετε
ὅτι: ὅτι om. agmnp B. et S.   14. αὐθημερὸν] αὐθημέρων fcel pr. b, corr. k.

way. If this sense of τοῦτον τὸν τρόπον
seems forced, it is a yet greater difficulty
how else to find a suitable subject for ἐπεισάξει. If it were permissible to speculate on
confusions that may have arisen from successive redactions of the speech, one might
be tempted to make the connection as follows: 'If you hold Ctesiphon to the point
of law, he will bring in Demosthenes to save
him by rhetoric,' treating all after ἐπὶ τὴν
δημοκρατίαν καλεῖς in § 203 as an afterthought. But this seems precluded by Demosthenes' reference to Aeschines dictating
to him the order of topics. Some editors
in despair propose to read ἐὰν μὴ τούτον,
which of course cuts the knot.

1. δίκαιός εἰμι. 'I may be allowed to
warn you,' affecting a disregard, for himself
personally, of the consequences of the court
deciding wrongly: he only is determined to
do his duty to them. So ἤδη, 'having told
you not to do it, I am not afraid to say
what will happen if you do.'

2. διατετμηκότα τὴν πολιτείαν. Probably simply 'who has mutilated and paralysed the city's life,' broken its backbone, as
we should say. διατετμηκότα πολιτείαν
cannot mean the same as διατετμηκότα πόλιν, 'divides the city into two hostile parties,' and can hardly mean 'has made political life sectional,' though either of these
would suit the next sentence, describing
what Aeschines calls his στασιαστικοὺς λόγους; and would be fairly justified by facts,
in the sense that Demosthenes had managed
to introduce something like the modern
'government by party,' without the modern

assumption that 'his majesty's opposition'
were as loyal to King Demos as the mini-
stry.

4. οὐκ ἂν θαυμάσαιμι. There is no
such passage in Demosthenes, and the form
of this sentence looks as though it were
composed really before he heard his speech.
Yet ὑπ' αὐτῆς τῆς ἀληθείας διηριθμημένους,
'told off by the simple force of facts,' looks
like a quotation. The party of Aeschines is
stigmatised as oligarchical, not that of the
prosecutor generally.

§ 209. To his appeals to the Constitution,
reply that it would never have existed if our
statesmen had always been like him: to his
oaths, that you and the Gods know him too
well to trust him:

12. τὸ κάλλιστον ἐκ παιδείας ῥῆμα
φθεγξάμενοι. 'Giving utterance to that
noble lesson' may express the sense. But
in the comprehensive sense of the word
παιδεία (a favourite of Aeschines, vid. al
§ 117), it almost corresponds to 'civility' in
its eighteenth century use, for which John-
son thought 'civilisation' a needless barbarism. ἀπαιδευσία at any rate is exactly
'incivility' in that sense.

13. ἑλκοποιεῖς. As we speak of 'estab-
lishing a raw.'

14. αὐθημερὸν λόγων. Plin. Ep. 9. 26
quotes the passage with the reading αὐθημέρων; and most MSS. give that form, at least
as an alternative. The adjective is very rare
in Attic: if genuine, the sense is not 'extempore speeches,' which Demosthenes' were
not, but 'speeches that are spoken one day
and done with,' the same as -ρον.

ὅταν δ᾽ ἐπίορκος ὢν εἰς τὴν διὰ τῶν ὅρκων πίστιν καταφυγ-
γάνῃ, ἐκεῖνο ἀπομνημονεύσατε αὐτῷ, ὅτι τῷ πολλάκις μὲν ἐπιορ-
κοῦντι, ἀεὶ δὲ μεθ᾽ ὅρκων ἀξιοῦντι πιστεύεσθαι δυοῖν θάτερον
ὑπάρξαι δεῖ, ὧν οὐδέτερόν ἐστι Δημοσθένει ὑπάρχον, ἢ τοὺς
5 θεοὺς καινοὺς ἢ τοὺς ἀκροατὰς μὴ τοὺς αὐτούς. περὶ δὲ τῶν 210
δακρύων καὶ τοῦ τόνου τῆς φωνῆς, ὅταν ὑμᾶς ἐπερωτᾷ "ποῖ
φύγω, ἄνδρες Ἀθηναῖοι; περιγράψατέ με ἐκ τῆς πολιτείας·
οὐκ ἔστιν ὅποι ἀναπτήσομαι," ἀνθυποβάλλετε αὐτῷ "ὁ δὲ
δῆμος ὁ Ἀθηναίων ποῖ καταφύγῃ, Δημόσθενες; ἢ πρὸς ποίαν
10 συμμάχων παρασκευήν; πρὸς ποῖα χρήματα; τί προβαλλόμενος ὑπὲρ τοῦ δήμου πεπολίτευσαι; ἃ μὲν γὰρ ὑπὲρ σεαυτοῦ
βεβούλευσαι, ἅπαντες ὁρῶμεν. ἐκλιπὼν μὲν τὸ ἄστυ οὐκ οἰ-
κεῖς, ὡς δοκεῖς, ἐν Πειραιεῖ, ἀλλ᾽ ἐξορμεῖς ἐκ τῆς πόλεως,

---

3. πρὸς τοὺς αὐτούς, quod post ἀεὶ δὲ legebatur, deleri voluit Dobr., delevit Frank.
7. φύγω] Ita agmnp B. et S. Frank. ceteri καταφύγω.   περιγράψατέ] περιεγράψατέ
bk, περιεγράψατέ el: mox hi omnes om. ἐκ τῆς πολιτείας: (id vero supplevit corr. b) εἰ περιγράψετε cum marg. Bern. Reisk. Bakius.   8. ὅποι] ὅπῃ Bekk.   9. ἢ πρὸς] Ita
agmnz Flor. fcdq Barb.   11. πεπολίτευσαι] τί πεπολίτευσαι f bekl.

---

1. ἐπίορκος ὤν one is tempted to suspect as a gloss, but it is one of Aeschines' own. πρὸς τοὺς αὐτούς however, which follows after ἀεὶ δὲ in the MSS., suits neither the sense nor construction, and seems rightly omitted. The first insertion at worst is otiose, the second makes one of the alternatives in the apodosis unmeaning.

5. καινούς. That one group of MSS. has κενούς is nothing remarkable; but that two other copies *correct* to κενούς cannot be accidental. 'Imaginary gods,' or 'gods powerless to avenge his perjuries,' would avoid the objection that the antithesis to μὴ τοὺς αὐτούς is merely verbal. But the point of the whole sentence seems to be best sustained by the vulgate: and the antithesis is no worse than § 214 below, ἀληθεῖς .. οὐ ψευδεῖς.

§ 210. *To his appeals to compassion, that he is in less danger than the city is through him.*

6. δακρύων. We cannot doubt that Aeschines was fatally disappointed; for, after the modest exordium, there is nothing deprecatory or timid in Demosthenes' speech: see especially § 330.

τοῦ τόνου τῆς φωνῆς. So, again, in the next section. The point corresponds to Demosthenes' of φωνασκία, D. de Cor. §§ 345, 381. Demosthenes had a bad voice, and had to study how to use it (cp. Ae. de F. L. p. 49, § 167); Aeschines had a fine one, and practised to keep it in good condition.

7. περιγράψατέ με. 'Shut me out from

public life' (cp. below, § 227, συκοφαντηθέν-τας ἐκ τῆς πολιτείας, 'slandered out of public life,' 'and then I have nowhere to go: ') εἰ περιγράψετε is therefore a gloss. Above, we have not restored καταφύγω for φύγω, though καταφύγῃ follows in the parallel clause. The people can 'fly for refuge' in distress, but does not want a *place* to flee to actually: Demosthenes is supposed to say that he does want such a place, and finds none.

8. ἀναπτήσομαι. A metaphor of a bird surrounded by snares, and rising into the open air.

9. ἢ πρός. We have inserted ἢ with the best MSS., as there seemed no tempta-tion to a copyist to insert it, and the temp-tation of seeming symmetry to omit it. In truth, it does not damage the symmetry to say 'Where? or to what resources?' break-ing up the latter into several subordinate questions, while all together are coordinate with the first.

10. τί προβαλλόμενος. Referring to Demosthenes' constant boasts of the bul-warks with which he had surrounded Athens, above, § 84, D. de Cor. § 370. As the change of person is a little abrupt, one might read σὺ πεπολίτευσαι in place of the τί πε-πολίτευσαι of one group of MSS.

12. ἐκλιπὼν κ.τ.λ. 'You have left the City, not to take a house in the harbour quarter, as you would have it thought, but to be *in* the harbour,' ready to sail off at a moment's notice.

ἐφόδια δὲ πεπόρισαι τῇ σαυτοῦ ἀνανδρίᾳ τὸ βασιλικὸν χρυ-
211 σίον καὶ τὰ δημόσια δωροδοκήματα." ὅλως δὲ τί τὰ δάκρυα;
τίς ἡ κραυγή; τίς ὁ τόνος τῆς φωνῆς; οὐχ ὁ μὲν τὴν γραφὴν
φεύγων ἐστὶ Κτησιφῶν, ὁ δ' ἀγὼν οὐκ ἀτίμητος, σὺ δ' οὔτε
περὶ τῆς οὐσίας οὔτε περὶ τοῦ σώματος οὔτε περὶ τῆς ἐπιτι- 5
μίας ἀγωνίζει; ἀλλὰ περὶ τίνος ἐστὶν αὐτῷ ἡ σπουδή; περὶ
χρυσῶν στεφάνων καὶ κηρυγμάτων ἐν τῷ θεάτρῳ παρὰ τοὺς
212 νόμους· ὃν ἐχρῆν, εἰ καὶ μανεὶς ὁ δῆμος ἢ τῶν καθεστηκότων
ἐπιλελησμένος ἐπὶ τοιαύτης ἀκαιρίας ἐβούλετο στεφανοῦν αὐτὸν,
παρελθόντα εἰς τὴν ἐκκλησίαν εἰπεῖν· "ἄνδρες Ἀθηναῖοι, τὸν 10
μὲν στέφανον δέχομαι, τὸν δὲ καιρὸν ἀποδοκιμάζω, ἐν ᾧ τὸ
κήρυγμα γίγνεται· οὐ γὰρ δεῖ, ἐφ' οἷς ἡ πόλις ἐπένθησε καὶ
ἐκείρατο, ἐπὶ τούτοις ἐμὲ στεφανοῦσθαι." ἀλλ' οἶμαι, ταῦτα
μὲν ἂν εἴποι ἀνὴρ ὄντως βεβιωκὼς μετ' ἀρετῆς· ἃ δὲ σὺ λέξεις,
213 εἴποι ἂν κάθαρμα ζηλοτυποῦν ἀρετήν. οὐ γὰρ δὴ μὰ τὸν 15
Ἡρακλέα τοῦτό γε ὑμῶν οὐδεὶς φοβήσεται, μὴ ὁ Δημοσθένης,
ἀνὴρ μεγαλόψυχος καὶ τὰ πολεμικὰ διαφέρων, ἀποτυχὼν τῶν

---

12. ἐπένθησε καὶ ἐκείρατο] ἐκείρετο καὶ ἐπένθησεν bekl.   16. φοβήσεται] Sic
afcdbekl : ceteri φοβηθήσεται.

§ 211. *Indeed, it is absurd for him to
ask for pity for not getting a crown* :
3. ὁ μέν. Answered by ὁ δ' ἀγὼν and
σὺ δέ, in different relations. (1) Technically,
'The defendant is Ctesiphon, and the trial
one where the penalty rests with the court,'
so that there is a chance of a mild sentence,
and you need not excite yourself on his account ; (2) personally, 'It is Ctesiphon that
is on his trial, and *you* risk neither person,
civil rights, nor property.'
§ 212. *He ought to be ashamed to take
one, even if you were mad enough to give it* :
8. μανείς. They must have been mad
to crown him at all, but, in the case supposed, the crown would have been given
under lawful conditions of time and place.
ἐπὶ τοιαύτης ἀκαιρίας is clearly 'on such an
inauspicious occasion,' and this fixes the
sense of τὸν δὲ καιρὸν ἀποδοκιμάζω, which
else one might have thought the same as
τὸν καιρὸν τῆς ἀναρρήσεως in § 205. Note
that the decree was as yet only a προβούλευμα, so that Aeschines could still assume
that the people would never vote it, even if
it was fit to come before them.
12. ἐπένθησε καὶ ἐκείρατο. One group
of MSS. transposes these verbs; which, if of
any significance, points to καὶ ἐπένθησε being
a gloss. For ἐκείρατο is certainly meant to
be emphatically opposed to στεφανοῦσθαι,
the thought being something like St. Paul's,
Ad Cor. I. 11. 6.

14. ἃ δὲ σὺ λέξεις. The connection
with what follows is 'You will pretend to
treat the conviction of Ctesiphon as an intolerable affront ;' but it will be a pretence,
'for you will not kill yourself, like Ajax.'
15. ζηλοτυποῦν ἀρετήν. Commonly
taken, 'pretending to virtue,' which seems a
frigid even if a possible sense of the word.
Better as Harpocr., 'in jealous mockery of
virtue,' which he cannot or will not imitate :
Bremi compares Cic. Tusc. 4. 8. 18 for this
force of ζηλοτυπία = *obtrectatio* as distinct
from *aemulatio*. And perhaps better still in
the ordinary sense of the word, in this construction with an accusative of a *person* :
ὄντως βεβιωκὼς μετ' ἀρετῆς being a metaphor
from an honourable and recognised marriage,
κάθαρμα ζηλοτυποῦν ἀρετὴν from an absurd
jealousy of an unattainable mistress.
§ 213. *Nor is he so high-spirited as to be
likely to kill himself for honour, though
ready enough to wound himself for money.*
μὰ τὸν Ἡρακλέα. As patron of ἄνδρες
μεγαλόψυχοι καὶ τὰ πολεμικὰ διαφέροντες :
cp. ad § 99, for the comparative seriousness
of meaning in Aeschines' rhetorical oaths.
17. ἀποτυχὼν τῶν ἀριστείων. Of course
the comparison suggested is with Ajax, ὃς
ἄριστος ἔην εἶδός τε δέμας τε, so that part
of the point may be that Demosthenes was
ugly—his face disfigured by dishonourable
wounds—as well as feeble in body and
cowardly in spirit.

ἀριστείων οἴκαδε ἐπανελθὼν ἑαυτὸν διαχρήσηται· ὃς τοσοῦτον
καταγελᾷ τῆς πρὸς ὑμᾶς φιλοτιμίας, ὥστε τὴν μιαρὰν κεφαλὴν ταύτην καὶ ὑπεύθυνον, ἣν οὗτος παρὰ τοὺς νόμους γέγραφε
στεφανῶσαι, μυριάκις κατατέτμηκε καὶ τούτων μισθοὺς εἴληφε
5 τραύματος ἐκ προνοίας γραφὰς γραφόμενος, καὶ κατακεκονδύλισται, ὥστε αὐτὸν οἶμαι τὰ τῶν κονδύλων ἴχνη τῶν Μειδίου
ἔχειν ἔτι φανερά· ὁ γὰρ ἄνθρωπος οὐ κεφαλήν, ἀλλὰ πρόσοδον κέκτηται.

Περὶ δὲ Κτησιφῶντος τοῦ γράψαντος τὴν γνώμην βραχέα 214
10 βούλομαι εἰπεῖν, τὰ δὲ πολλὰ ὑπερβήσομαι, ἵνα καὶ πεῖραν
[ὑμῶν] λάβω, εἰ δύνασθε τοὺς σφόδρα πονηροὺς, κἂν μή τις
προείπῃ, διαγιγνώσκειν· ὃ δ᾽ ἐστὶ κοινὸν καὶ δίκαιον κατ᾽ ἀμφοτέρων αὐτῶν ἀπαγγεῖλαι πρὸς ὑμᾶς, τοῦτ᾽ ἐρῶ. περιέρ-
χονται γὰρ τὴν ἀγορὰν ἀληθεῖς κατ᾽ ἀλλήλων ἔχοντες δόξας
15 καὶ λόγους οὐ ψευδεῖς λέγοντες. ὁ μὲν γὰρ Κτησιφῶν οὐ τὸ 215

3. παρὰ τοὺς νόμους] παρὰ πάντας τοὺς νόμους Bekk. cum libris praeter *agmnp*.
7. πρόσοδον] πρόσωδον *d*. De Toupi, Orelli, Westermanni, et Franki conjecturis, vid.
annot.   10. ἵνα καὶ πεῖραν λάβω] ὑμῶν post ἵνα ponunt *bekl*, post λάβω *gmn*, post
πεῖραν ceteri: ejecerunt B. et S.   14. τὴν ἀγορὰν] κατὰ τὴν ἀγορὰν *be*, idque mavolt
Frank.

2. καταγελᾷ .... φιλοτιμίας. He dis-
honours his own head, so he cannot think
much of the proposal that you should honour
it.
4. μυριάκις κατατέτμηκε. The reference is to the story told in § 51 : κατατέτμηκε is a stronger word than the ἐπιτομὴ
there used, because the point there is 'he
gave himself a slight wound to substantiate a
false charge of assault,' here 'he has not
spared himself a serious injury, when he
could make money by it.' If we once begin
suspecting glosses, one would be inclined to
omit καὶ τούτων .. γραφόμενος : μυριάκις
κατατέτμηκε καὶ κατακεκονδύλισται would
be a less violent exaggeration of two stories
than μυριάκις κατατέτμηκε of one.
7. οὐ κεφαλήν, ἀλλὰ πρόσοδον. Toup
conjectured that πρόσοδον is a gloss for κεφάλαιον, 'a capital' to secure πρόσοδον 'a
revenue :' improved by Westermann into οὐ
κεφαλὴν ἀλλὰ κεφάλαιον, οὐ πρόσωπον ἀλλὰ
πρόσοδον κέκτηται ; for which he finds support in the reading πρόσωδον of one indifferent
MS. Orelli ap. Brem. suggests οὐ κεφαλὴν
κεφαλὴν, which is approved by Franke with
the necessary correction οὐ κεφαλὴν τὴν κεφαλήν: in that form, it perhaps improves the
style a little, but is not necessary. Of Westermann's reading the only thing one can say
is, that it is a great pity that Aeschines did
not write it: Toup's pun very likely was

present to his mind and to his hearers'.
§ 214. *Of Ctesiphon I will say little harm,
leaving it to your own knowledge and to Demosthenes :*
10. ἵνα καὶ πεῖραν [ὑμῶν] λάβω. ὑμῶν
is placed by one group of MSS. immediately
after ἵνα, by *most* of another after λάβω, by
the rest (on the whole the best) here ; but
from the variations, B. and S. and Franke
have been led to exclude it. The clause
seems a little bald without it: perhaps the
likeliest place is after ἵνα, as best accounting
for the transposition, while yet most like Aeschines' style: cp. annot. crit. ad § 3. The force
of καὶ may be '(both to spare you fatigue),
and to prove you for my own satisfaction,'
the former clause being suggested by τὰ δὲ
πολλὰ ὑπερβήσομαι alone: or rather 'though
I have told you he is a rascal, I should like
also to see if you would know it without
telling:' or perhaps, ' though I have told you
Demosthenes is a rascal, I should like to
leave you to find it out for yourselves in
the case of Ctesiphon.' The last interpretation is favoured by what follows, 'I will not
say much harm of Ctesiphon apart from
Demosthenes, only that which is common to
both, viz. that each is afraid of the other.'
§ 215. *Who owns to Ctesiphon's private
vices making him as hard to defend as Ctesiphon says his public corruption makes him to
commend.*

καθ' ἑαυτόν φησι φοβεῖσθαι, ἐλπίζειν γὰρ δόξειν ἰδιώτης εἶναι,
ἀλλὰ τὴν τοῦ Δημοσθένους ἐν τῇ πολιτείᾳ δωροδοκίαν φησὶ
φοβεῖσθαι καὶ τὴν ἐμπληξίαν καὶ δειλίαν· ὁ δὲ Δημοσθένης
εἰς αὑτὸν μὲν ἀποβλέπων θαρρεῖν φησιν, τὴν δὲ τοῦ Κτησιφῶντος πονηρίαν καὶ πορνοβοσκίαν ἰσχυρῶς δεδιέναι. τοὺς 5
δὲ δὴ κατεγνωκότας ἀλλήλων ἀδικεῖν μηδαμῶς ὑμεῖς οἱ κοινοὶ
κριταὶ τῶν ἐγκλημάτων ἀπολύσητε.

216 Περὶ δὲ τῶν εἰς ἐμαυτὸν λοιδοριῶν βραχέα βούλομαι προειπεῖν. πυνθάνομαι γὰρ λέξειν Δημοσθένην, ὡς ἡ πόλις ὑπ'
αὐτοῦ μὲν ὠφέληται πολλά, ὑπ' ἐμοῦ δὲ καταβέβλαπται, καὶ 10
τὸν Φίλιππον καὶ τὸν Ἀλέξανδρον καὶ τὰς ἀπὸ τούτων αἰτίας
ἀνοίσειν ἐπ' ἐμέ. οὕτω γάρ ἐστιν, ὡς ἔοικε, δεινὸς δημιουργὸς
λόγων, ὥστε οὐκ ἀπόχρη αὐτῷ, εἴ τι πεπολίτευμαι παρ' ὑμῖν
217 ἐγὼ ἢ εἴ τινας δημηγορίας εἴρηκα, τούτων κατηγορεῖν, ἀλλὰ
καὶ τὴν ἡσυχίαν μου τοῦ βίου διαβάλλει καὶ τῆς σιωπῆς μου 15
κατηγορεῖ, ἵνα μηδεὶς αὐτῷ τόπος ἀσυκοφάντητος παραλείπηται,
καὶ τὰς ἐν τοῖς γυμνασίοις μετὰ τῶν νεωτέρων μου διατριβὰς

---

5. τοὺς δὲ δὴ] Ita *agm*, τοὺς δὲ *n*, τοὺς δὴ ceteri.   8. προειπεῖν] προσειπεῖν *gmnxz*
ekl.   15. τὴν ἡσυχίαν μου] τὴν ἡσυχίαν αὑτὴν *fcd*.   16. παραλείπηται] παρα-
λίπηται *agmncdh* Flor. corr. z.

1. ἐλπίζειν γὰρ κ.τ.λ. 'For, he says, he
hopes that no one will take him for a politician.' According to Breni, there is a
kind of pun in the use of ἰδιώτης : Ctesiphon means it as above, while Aeschines,
quoting him, implies 'they will take him for
an ἰδιώτης indeed, i. e. an idiot.' But though,
from the sense of 'not professionally skilled,'
ἰδιώτης and the cognate words tend to mean
'unskilful,' it does not appear that in so early
Greek it can be used *absolutely*, for 'a fool.'
3. ἐμπληξία. Strictly the condition of
the ἔμπληκτος or ἐμβρόντητος (D. de Cor.
§ 303), the man who has been unhinged by
a *shock*. Hence it appears to indicate an
insane and inconsistent violence—vehement
sometimes one way, sometimes the other—
which is well consistent with δειλία.
4. ἀποβλέπων. Here the preposition
has more of its proper force than usual,
'fixing his eyes on his own case,' to the exclusion of Ctesiphon.
5. πορνοβοσκίαν. A meaner vice than
παιδοποιεῖσθαι ἐξ ἑταιρῶν, even if that refers
to Demosthenes. Vid. ad § 174.
6. οἱ κοινοὶ κριταί. 'Who have no
interest in clearing one at the expense of the
other,' as each of them has in clearing himself.
§§ 216-218. Then *Demosthenes will attack my character ;—my political action, my
political inaction, my private pursuits. I
am ashamed of none.*

8. περὶ δὲ τῶν εἰς ἐμαυτὸν λοιδοριῶν.
This looks almost like an answer to Demosthenes, written after he had heard what the
λοιδορίαι were. But it is impossible to say
that any part of the paragraph is added later
than § 219, which is actually quoted by Demosthenes, de Cor. § 102.
11. τὰς ἀπὸ τούτων αἰτίας. 'Any
charge to which they give occasion.'
12. οὕτω γάρ ἐστιν κ.τ.λ. γὰρ gives the
reason for what is not expressed : ' he charges
me with having done [no good like himself, in
fact] harm.' Or, perhaps, 'he will have it
that I have done harm, when the worst he
can say of me is that I have done nothing.'
15. ἡσυχίαν .. σιωπῆς : cp. D. de Cor.
§§ 253, 379 fin., etc.
17. τὰς ἐν τοῖς γυμνασίοις .. διατριβάς.
See the Life of Aeschines for one interpretation—almost ' my employment of schoolmaster.' Perhaps the order of words is
favourable to it, for μου would naturally be
taken with νεωτέρων, 'my young people :'
and the use of διατριβὰς is illustrated by Ae.
in Tim. p. 25, § 175, ἐν τῇ τῶν μειρακίων
διατριβῇ. Else one might connect it with
ibid. p. 19, § 135, that Demosthenes remarked on his spending his time at the
Gymnasia at his rather advanced age (cp.
Plat. Rep. 5, p. 452 B, which seems to shew
that this was odd though not discreditable),
and imputed motives.

καταμέμφεται, καὶ κατὰ τῆσδε τῆς κρίσεως εὐθὺς ἀρχόμενος
τοῦ λόγου φέρει τινὰ αἰτίαν, λέγων, ὡς ἐγὼ τὴν γραφὴν οὐχ
ὑπὲρ τῆς πόλεως ἐγραψάμην, ἀλλ' ἐνδεικνύμενος Ἀλεξάνδρῳ
διὰ τὴν πρὸς αὐτὸν ἔχθραν. καὶ νὴ Δί', ὡς ἐγὼ πυνθάνο-
5 μαι, μέλλει με ἀνερωτᾶν, διὰ τί τὸ μὲν κεφάλαιον τῆς πολιτείας αὐτοῦ ψέγω, τὰ δὲ καθ' ἕκαστα οὐκ ἐκώλυον οὐδ' ἐγ-
ραφόμην, ἀλλὰ διαλιπὼν καὶ πρὸς τὴν πολιτείαν οὐ πυκνὰ
προσιὼν ἀπήνεγκα τὴν γραφήν. ἐγὼ δὲ οὔτε τὰς Δημοσθένους 218
διατριβὰς ἐζήλωκα, οὔτ' ἐπὶ ταῖς ἐμαυτοῦ αἰσχύνομαι, οὔτε
10 τοὺς εἰρημένους ἐν ὑμῖν λόγους ἐμαυτῷ ἀρρήτους εἶναι βουλοίμην, οὔτε τὰ αὐτὰ τούτῳ δημηγορήσας ἐδεξάμην ἂν ζῆν.
τὴν δ' ἐμὴν σιωπήν, ὦ Δημόσθενες, ἡ τοῦ βίου μετριότης παρε- 219
σκεύασεν· ἀρκεῖ γάρ μοι μικρὰ καὶ μειζόνων αἰσχρῶς οὐκ
ἐπιθυμῶ, ὥστε καὶ σιγῶ καὶ λέγω βουλευσάμενος, ἀλλ' οὐκ
15 ἀναγκαζόμενος ὑπὸ τῆς ἐν τῇ φύσει δαπάνης. σὺ δ', οἶμαι,
λαβὼν μὲν σεσίγηκας, ἀναλώσας δὲ κέκραγας. λέγεις δὲ οὐχ
ὁπόταν σοι δοκῇ οὐδ' ἃ βούλει, ἀλλ' ὁπόταν οἱ μισθοδόται
σοι προστάττωσιν· οὐκ αἰσχύνῃ δὲ ἀλαζονευόμενος, ἃ παρα-

6. ἕκαστα] Ita Vat. Laur. ρzfη Flor. Barb.: volgo ἕκαστον.   10. βουλοίμην] Vid.
annot.   Mox ταὐτὰ scribi jubet Frank.

3. ἐνδεικνύμενος differs from ἐπιδεικνύμενος (cp. D. de Cor. § 345, ἐπίδειξιν), 'letting a man see' from 'making a display to
him.'
4. διὰ τὴν πρὸς αὐτὸν ἔχθραν. 'Because of his (Alexander's) enmity to him
(Demosthenes).'
καὶ νὴ Δι' κ.τ.λ.: cp. D. de Cor. §§
241 sqq., 282 sqq. Perhaps § 285 is as
much meant as any one passage of the
actual speech.   In truth, the complaint is
unfairly worded by Aeschines: the contrast
is not between denouncing offences singly
and in the lump, but between denouncing
pernicious counsels, or suggesting better
ones, at the time of action, and making
criminal charges when the time for action is
past.
8. ἐγὼ δὲ οὔτε .. ἐζήλωκα. Whatever
be the sense of διατριβὰς, one point will be
' my young friends turn out better than Demosthenes', alluding perhaps especially to
Aristarchus: cp. Ae. in Tim. p. 24, §§ 170
sqq., de F. L. p. 50, § 177; and a further
one, on the one view, 'My steady professional rise is more creditable than his multi-
farious devices for money-making,' on the
other, ' My open-air flirtations are more
honourable than his secret intrigues,' above,
§ 162.

10. βουλοίμην. 'Deest ἂν,' says Bekker,
meaning probably that it ought to be inserted.   But no one can find a place for it
without hurting the cadence : and all later
editors have agreed that, for this reason,
Aeschines left it to be supplied from the
next clause.
§ 219. I speak when I have something to
say, not, like you, because I am short of
money : and hence I speak less often.
12. ἡ τοῦ βίου μετριότης. Answered
by Demosthenes, § 380, in a deprecatory
tone which looks as though this passage had
told, or might be expected to tell, on the
sympathies of the court.
14. ὥστε .. βουλευσάμενος. 'So that I
can afford to make up my mind beforehand
whether to speak or not to speak.'
15. σὺ δ', οἶμαι κ.τ.λ.: D. de Cor. §
102.
17. ἀλλ' ὁπόταν. One MS. adds καὶ ἅ,
which was approved by Taylor; but it
probably only shews that the copyist felt
the same desire as Bremi for the antithesis
to run on all fours, but was less exigent as
to the two pairs of legs matching.
18. οὐκ αἰσχύνῃ κ.τ.λ. Having put
one charge in a telling form, he does not
let his hearers dwell on it, but hurries them
back to another.

220 χρῆμα ἐξελέγχῃ ψευδόμενος. ἀπηνέχθη γὰρ ἡ κατὰ τοῦδε
τοῦ ψηφίσματος γραφὴ, ἣν οὐχ ὑπὲρ τῆς πόλεως, ἀλλ᾽ ὑπὲρ
τῆς εἰς Ἀλέξανδρον ἐνδείξεώς με φῇς ἀπενεγκεῖν, ἔτι Φιλίππου
ζῶντος, πρὶν Ἀλέξανδρον εἰς τὴν ἀρχὴν καταστῆναι, οὔπω
σοῦ τὸ περὶ Παυσανίαν ἐνύπνιον ἑωρακότος οὐδὲ πρὸς τὴν 5
Ἀθηνᾶν καὶ τὴν Ἥραν νύκτωρ διειλεγμένου. πῶς ἂν οὖν ἐγὼ
προενεδεικνύμην Ἀλεξάνδρῳ; εἴ γε μὴ ταὐτὸν ἐνύπνιον ἐγὼ καὶ
221 Δημοσθένης εἴδομεν. ἐπιτιμᾷς δέ μοι, εἰ μὴ συνεχῶς, ἀλλὰ
διαλείπων πρὸς τὸν δῆμον προσέρχομαι, καὶ τὴν ἀξίωσιν ταύτην οἴει λανθάνειν μεταφέρων οὐκ ἐκ δημοκρατίας, ἀλλ᾽ ἐξ 10
ἑτέρας πολιτείας. ἐν μὲν γὰρ ταῖς ὀλιγαρχίαις οὐχ ὁ βουλόμενος, ἀλλ᾽ ὁ δυναστεύων κατηγορεῖ, ἐν δὲ ταῖς δημοκρατίαις
ὁ βουλόμενος καὶ ὅταν αὐτῷ δοκῇ. καὶ τὸ μὲν διὰ χρόνου
λέγειν σημεῖόν ἐστιν ἐπὶ τῶν καιρῶν καὶ τοῦ συμφέροντος

---

1. ἐξελέγχῃ] ἐξελεγχθήσῃ bekl et γρ. gm. 3. εἰς] πρὸς bekl Bekk. 7. ταὐτὸν] Hoc volunt Cobet. et Frank. : volg. ταὐτό. 10. Post λανθάνειν addebatur ἡμᾶς. Om. ann B. et S. 12. κατηγορεῖ] De Bekkeri conjectura δημηγορεῖ vid. annot. 13 δοκῇ] Ita apbekl: ceteri et volg. usque ad Bekk. δόξῃ.

§ 220. *The present prosecution was commenced in Philip's lifetime, not to please his successor.*

1. ἀπηνέχθη γὰρ κ.τ.λ. But probably Aeschines was responsible for having let the case lie dormant for eight years : and the practical question was not his motive in bringing the charge, but in calling it on for trial.

5. πρὸς τὴν Ἀθηνᾶν καὶ τὴν Ἥραν. In § 77 it is παρὰ τοῦ Διὸς καὶ τῆς Ἀθηνᾶς: probably Athena was especially mentioned, and other gods and goddesses spoken of vaguely, in Demosthenes' own story.

7. εἴ γε μή. 'Nisi forte:' a contemptuous adjunct to a contemptuous question. It does not at all support Böhnecke's theory, that the trial must have been commenced only just before Philip's death, or indeed after it happened but before it was known.

§ 221. *In prosecuting now and not sooner, I use my discretion like a free citizen.*

8. ἐπιτιμᾷς δέ μοι κ.τ.λ. He returns to the charge of intermittent political activity, seeking to obscure that of inconsistency in his intermittent prosecution of Ctesiphon, by confusing it with the more general one. 'You attribute to me,' he says, ' the responsibilities of an oligarchical statesman as well as his power. In a democracy every citizen is free to act; and, as a consequence, to choose his time.'

12. ὁ δυναστεύων κατηγορεῖ. So the MSS. : Dindorf, Franke, and Schultz adopt Bekker's conjecture δημηγορεῖ. Orelli ap. Brem. observes, that there would be little or no δημηγορία in an oligarchy, where there was no ἰσηγορία: and suggests, more questionably, that there may be a brachylogy, ' in oligarchia potentissimus quisque *judicia exercet*, in democratia quicunque vult adversario *diem dicit*.' Is it incredible, that in an average Greek oligarchy no one could bring a criminal action, except through a party from belonging to the privileged classes? A μέτοικος needed a προστάτης at Athens, and the typical oligarchy would be one where the μέτοικοι had become a *plebs*, and the full citizens an aristocracy. At any rate, none but one of the ruling body would have any interest in bringing a *public* accusation.

ἐν δὲ ταῖς δημοκρατίαις. A nearer approach than is often avowed to Mitford's view of the cherished rights of a free Athenian.

13. καὶ τὸ μὲν κ.τ.λ. ' And to take time before speaking is a note of a man with a policy adapted to circumstances and to the public interest : but to speak every day, and miss none, is a note of a trader and a hireling' ἀνδρὸς πολιτευομένου are, from their position, both emphatic—' a man, with a policy,' both worthy of the name : and thus balance ἐργαζομένου καὶ μισθαρνοῦντος.

ἀνδρὸς πολιτευομένου, τὸ δὲ μηδεμίαν παραλιπεῖν ἡμέραν
ἐργαζομένου καὶ μισθαρνοῦντος. ὑπὲρ δὲ τοῦ μηδέπω κεκρί- 222
σθαι ὑπ᾽ ἐμοῦ μηδὲ τῶν ἀδικημάτων τιμωρίαν ὑποσχεῖν, ὅταν
καταφεύγῃς ἐπὶ τοὺς τοιούτους λόγους, ἢ τοὺς ἀκούοντας ἐπι-
5 λήσμονας ὑπολαμβάνεις ἢ σαυτὸν παραλογίζῃ. τὰ μὲν γὰρ
περὶ τοὺς Ἀμφισσέας ἠσεβημένα σοι καὶ τὰ περὶ τὴν Εὔβοιαν
δωροδοκηθέντα, χρόνων ἐγγεγενημένων ἐν οἷς ὑπ᾽ ἐμοῦ φανερῶς
ἐξηλέγχου, ἴσως ἐλπίζεις τὸν δῆμον ἀμνημονεῖν· τὰ δὲ περὶ 223
τὰς τριήρεις καὶ τοὺς τριηράρχους ἁρπάγματα τίς ἂν ἀποκρύ-
10 ψαι χρόνος δύναιτ᾽ ἄν, ὅτε νομοθετήσας περὶ τῶν τριακοσίων
καὶ σαυτὸν πείσας Ἀθηναίους ἐπιστάτην τάξαι τοῦ ναυτικοῦ,
ἐξηλέγχθης ὑπ᾽ ἐμοῦ ἑξήκοντα καὶ πέντε νεῶν ταχυναυτουσῶν τριηράρχους ὑφῃρημένος, πλέον τῆς πόλεως ἡμῶν ἀφανίζων

---

1. παραλιπεῖν] Ita *agmn fcd* Ald.: ceteri et edd. plerique παραλείπειν. Vid. annot.
2. μηδέπω] Sic *agmnc*: ceteri et Bekk. μήπω. 10. τριακοσίων] Legebatur τριακοσίων νεῶν: om. *agmnpb* B. et S. Frank. 13. πλέον] Sic *anpz* Vat. Laur. Barb. Flor.
Ald.: ceteri πλεῖον. ἡμῶν] Om. *bekl* Bekk. Mox pro ὅτε, ὅτῳ conj. Cobetus.

---

1. παραλιπεῖν. So all the best MSS.
and the Aldine edition: volg. -λείπειν.
'Not to let a single day pass' is equivalent to
a permanent habit, but 'to let a single day
pass' would be an individual act: ard thus
the aorist is quite intelligible. It would be
more strictly correct, if Aeschines had said
μηδέποτε μίαν ἡμέραν παραλιπεῖν.

§ 222. *You say I have never prosecuted
you, when I exposed your sacrilege at Amphissa, your treachery in Euboea,*
3. ὅταν καταφεύγῃς κ.τ.λ.: D. de Cor.
§ 313. The argument is an *ignoratio elen-
chi:* Demosthenes says, 'You never brought
me to trial;' Aeschines says, 'I denounced
you.' In § 224, he accounts for his failure
to prosecute, in the only case where he had
attempted it.

5. τὰ μὲν γὰρ περὶ .. δωροδοκηθέντα.
These charges we have had already, above,
§§ 91-105, 114, 125 sqq. In § 125 Aeschines asserts, as here, that he denounced
Demosthenes' conduct at the time.

§ 223. *And notably your frauds in the
naval department.*
10. περὶ τῶν τριακοσίων. νεῶν, omitted
by the best MSS., is a gloss, or rather a correction arising from ignorance. Οἱ τριακόσιοι are the same as in D. de Cor. § 221:
perhaps the authors of the reading thought
that Demosthenes reduced the strength of
the fleet from 365 ships to 300—the same
number as before the Peloponnesian war.

12. ἐξηλέγχθης κ.τ.λ In this matter
we very likely have simply the two sides of

the shield. Under the old law the trierarchical body were liable for fitting out 65
more ships than under the new, but under
the new levy the liability was more equit-
ably divided, and so much more certainly
enforced. See D. de Cor. § 136. Else
Demosthenes says, ibid. § 385 fin., that Aeschines had not only opposed his trierarchic
law, but had spoilt it, i. e. carried some
modifications, which Demosthenes did not
accept as improvements, though content
with the success of his measure as a whole.
And Aeschines may refer to these amend-
ments, as proving that the original scheme
was treasonable. It is hard to see how it
can even have appeared corrupt, when the
measure was against the interests of the
rich: Demosthenes' assertion (De Cor. §
129), that he had large bribes offered him
to abandon it, is perfectly credible, and his
charge against Aeschines of being paid for
his opposition to it not unlikely. B. and S.
compare Hyperides ap. Harpocr. p. 172. 14,
Dinarchus in Demosth. p. 95, § 42.

13. πλέον τῆς πόλεως ἡμῶν ἀφανίζων
ναυτικόν. 'Making away with a larger
Athenian fleet than that which fought at
Naxos.' It may be doubted whether ἡμῶν
goes with πόλεως, 'a fleet of our city,' or
whether it can possibly depend on ἀφανίζων,
'withdrawing from our eyes.' There is no
good authority for omitting it, with Bekker
and B. and S.; but it is rather otiose on the
former and more obvious view. ἀφανίζων
in any case is a technical word, especially

ναυτικὸν, ἢ ὅτε Ἀθηναῖοι τὴν ἐν Νάξῳ ναυμαχίαν Δακεδαιμο-
224 νίους καὶ Πόλλιν ἐνίκησαν; οὕτω δὲ ταῖς αἰτίαις ἐνέφραξας τὰς
κατὰ σαυτοῦ τιμωρίας, ὥστε τὸν κίνδυνον εἶναι μὴ σοὶ τῷ ἀδι-
κήσαντι, ἀλλὰ τοῖς ἐπεξιοῦσι, πολὺν μὲν τὸν Ἀλέξανδρον καὶ
Φίλιππον ἐν ταῖς διαβολαῖς φέρων, αἰτιώμενος δέ τινας ἐμπο- 5
δίζειν τοὺς τῆς πόλεως καιρούς, ἀεὶ τὸ παρὸν λυμαινόμενος, τὸ
δὲ μέλλον κατεπαγγελλόμενος. οὐ τὸ τελευταῖον εἰσαγγελ-
λεσθαι μέλλων ὑπ' ἐμοῦ, τὴν Ἀναξίνου σύλληψιν τοῦ Ὠρείτου
225 κατασκευάσας, τοῦ τὰ ἀγοράσματα Ὀλυμπιάδι ἀγοράζοντος,
καὶ τὸν αὐτὸν ἄνδρα δὶς στρεβλώσας τῇ σαυτοῦ χειρί, ἔγραψας 10
αὐτὸν θανάτῳ ζημιῶσαι; καὶ παρὰ τῷ αὐτῷ ἐν Ὠρεῷ κατήγου,
καὶ ἀπὸ τῆς αὐτῆς τραπέζης ἔφαγες καὶ ἔπιες καὶ ἔσπεισας,
καὶ τὴν δεξιὰν ἐνέβαλες ἄνδρα φίλον καὶ ξένον ποιούμενος.
καὶ τοῦτον ἀπέκτεινας, καὶ περὶ τούτων ἐν ἅπασιν Ἀθηναίοις

---

5. Ante **Φίλιππον τὸν** inserunt *behl* Bekk.　9. **κατασκευάσας .. δὶς στρεβλώσας ..**
ἔγραψας] Sic *agm*, et (nisi quod διαστρεβλώσας habet) Vat. et **κατασκευάσας** habent *phk*,
διαστρεβλώσας *p*, δὶς στρεβλώσας *n*, ἔγραψας *np*, cum in ceteris volgato κατεσκεύασας .. διε-
στρέβλωσας .. γράψας consentiunt.

applicable to the loss of *ships* (e. g. Thuc.
8. 38 init.): one might almost translate
'sending to the bottom of the Aegaean,'
while its more general sense would make
the construction suggested possible.

§ 224. *I have not formally prosecuted
you, because you had taken good care to
make it unsafe:*

2. **ταῖς αἰτίαις .. τιμωρίας**: cp. above,
§ 194.

4. **πολὺν μὲν τὸν κ.τ.λ.** 'Making a
great deal of Alexander and Philip in your
accusations,' inserting their names in them
frequently: perhaps making their actions a
reproach to those who had nothing to do
with them.

6. **λυμαινόμενος.** Just as we say 'vili-
fying,' 'reviling the present situation.'

7. **κατεπαγγελλόμενος.** 'Discounting'
in the American sense, exhausting in promises. Vid. ad § 206.

εἰσαγγέλλεσθαι. On account of intrigues with Persia.

8. **Ἀναξίνου**: D. de Cor. § 174. It
would seem that Aeschines was unable to
deny the assertion there made of his private
interview with this man, or the fact that he
was in some sense an agent of the Macedonian court. Hence he confesses that he
suffered so much in credit, that it was hopeless to bring an action against his rival.
Yet as Athens was then in theory the ally
of Alexander, it is hard to see how his conduct was criminal, or what was the crime
even of Anaxinus.

9. **κατασκευάσας.** So the best MSS.,

and two even of those that have διεστρέ-
βλωσας in the next section.

§ 225. *You murdered your old host
Anaxinus to escape from one prosecution:*

ἀγοράσματα. Especially of *small*
goods : Aeschines tries to extenuate the
importance of his commission from Macedon to the utmost. It is scarcely necessary
to notice Bishop Thirlwall's extraordinary
translation of the passage, 'on mercantile
business, connected with the Olympic festival
of the year!' This is worthier of Mr. Grote
than of the author.

10. **δὶς στρεβλώσας τῇ σαυτοῦ χειρί,
ἔγραψας.** So the best group of MSS., one
having διαστρεβλώσας, which Franke adopts.
Volg. et Bekk. διεστρεβλώσας .. γράψας.
If the latter reading be right, the sting of
the charge will be, 'You tortured him, not
before conviction to ascertain whether he
was guilty, but after sentence, out of mere
cruelty.' In either case, τῇ σαυτοῦ χειρὶ
must go with στρεβλώσας. Aeschines can
hardly mean that Demosthenes worked the
rack, but he says it: he can hardly mean
merely, 'You put your own hand to the
motion for his torture,' but that Demosthenes
was present at the torture, as commissioner
to take down his disclosures; so that it
would be a slight hyperbole to speak of him
as the actual torturer.

11. **παρὰ τῷ αὐτῷ.** Correlative to τὸν
αὐτὸν ἄνδρα just before. In Latin, *idem* in
the second clause would have been enough.

14. **περὶ τούτων.** Aeschines being unable, it would seem, to assert that Anaxinus

ἐξελεγχθεὶς ὑπ' ἐμοῦ καὶ κληθεὶς ξενοκτόνος οὐ τὸ ἀσέβημα
ἠρνήσω, ἀλλ' ἀπεκρίνω, ἐφ' ᾧ ἀνεβόησεν ὁ δῆμος καὶ ὅσοι
ξένοι περιέστασαν τὴν ἐκκλησίαν· ἔφησθα γὰρ τοὺς τῆς πόλεως ἅλας περὶ πλείονος ποιήσασθαι τῆς ξενικῆς τραπέζης.
5 ἐπιστολὰς δὲ σιγῶ ψευδεῖς καὶ κατασκόπων συλλήψεις καὶ βα- 226
σάνους ἐπ' αἰτίαις ἀγενήτοις, ὡς ἐμοῦ μετά τινων ἐν τῇ πόλει
νεωτερίζειν βουλομένου. ἔπειτα ἐπερωτᾶν με, ὡς ἐγὼ πυνθάνομαι, μέλλει, τίς ἂν εἴη τοιοῦτος ἰατρός, ὅστις τῷ νοσοῦντι
μεταξὺ μὲν ἀσθενοῦντι μηδὲν συμβουλεύοι, τελευτήσαντος δὲ
10 αὐτοῦ ἐλθὼν εἰς τὰ ἔνατα διεξίοι πρὸς τοὺς οἰκείους, ἃ ἐπιτη-
δεύσας ὑγιὴς ἂν ἐγένετο. σαυτὸν δ' οὐκ ἀντερωτᾷς, τίς ἂν εἴη 227
δημαγωγὸς τοιοῦτος, ὅστις τὸν μὲν δῆμον θωπεῦσαι δύναιτο,
τοὺς δὲ καιροὺς, ἐν οἷς ἦν σῴζεσθαι τὴν πόλιν, ἀποδοῖτο,
τοὺς δ' εὖ φρονοῦντας κωλύοι διαβάλλων συμβουλεύειν, ἀπο-
15 δρὰς δ' ἐκ τῶν κινδύνων καὶ τὴν πόλιν ἀνηκέστοις κακοῖς περι-
βαλὼν ἀξιοῖ στεφανοῦσθαι ἐπ' ἀρετῇ, ἀγαθὸν μὲν πεποιηκὼς

---

4. ποιήσασθαι] ποιεῖσθαι bkl Schultz.
ceteri ἔνναται.

10. ἔνατα] Sic azdqe Laur. Flor., ἔνατα f:

was not a spy, produced minute proofs of
the hospitality received from him by Demosthenes; and urged the point so eloquently,
that the people were shocked when Demosthenes admitted the fact. Cp. sup. ad § 52.
3. τοὺς τῆς πόλεως ἅλας. A favourite
phrase of Demosthenes: Ae. de F. L. p. 31,
§ 24.
§ 226. *You have invented plenty of false
charges to evade others: yet you expect me to
have had my remedy ready before the disease,*
5. ἐπιστολὰς .. ψευδεῖς. False accusations of intrigues with Macedon, alleged to
come from foreign correspondents. Letters
in the name of Aeschines or his partisans
would have been hard to forge and, probably, easy to detect.
κατασκόπων συλλήψεις. Besides
Anaxinus, we have the story of one Antiphon told by Demosthenes, de Cor. § 168
sq., where he says that Aeschines then also
denounced his conduct, and was publicly
censured for so doing.
6. ἐπ' αἰτίαις ἀγενήτοις. 'To discover
their share in crimes never committed,' a
supposed conspiracy of Aeschines and his
party in the Macedonian interest.
7. ἔπειτα. 'After this,' when you have
behaved in this fashion. Though this passage must, like § 190, have been inserted
after hearing Demosthenes' speech (§ 303),
it is far more artistically worked into the
context than that. τὸ πάντων τελευταῖον
in the beginning of § 228, is perhaps a trace

of the way the sentence ran before the insertion: the reading ἀποκρίνοντο may *possibly*
be another.
10. ἔνατα. Commonly explained as a
sacrifice the *ninth* day from the funeral.
The custom cannot be denied, and may be
connected with the notion of 9 as a number
of the dead, in the ninefold Styx, the nine
worlds of Hel, the nine circles of Dante's
Inferno, and perhaps the nine lives (Plat.
Phaedr. p. 248, Rep. 9, p. 387) of a human
soul, and even of the proverbial cat, herself
a magical, electrical, and perhaps infernal
animal. Yet it seems a question, whether
the word itself should not be rather connected with ἔνος (implied in ἔνη καὶ νέα), to
which it would bear the same relation as
the musical term νεάτη does to νέος: so that
ἔνατα should mean ' the last offices '= τὰ νομιζόμενα in the parallel passage in Demosthenes.
It should always be written with one ν: so
it is in the best MSS. of each group here.
§ 227. *As if I were responsible for not
stopping it, not you for causing it.*
14. κωλύοι .. συμβουλεύειν .. συκοφαντηθέντας ἐκ τῆς πολιτείας are nearly synonymous clauses, giving (from his own
point of view) the true explanation of his
inactivity, viz. that during Demosthenes'
ascendancy he had no chance of a hearing.
For ἐκ τῆς πολιτείας, vid. ad § 210.
16. ἐπ' ἀρετῇ, ἀγαθόν. Virtually correlative words, though not etymologically
cognate, as if he had said ' to be crowned

μηδέν, πάντων δὲ τῶν κακῶν αἴτιος γεγονώς, ἐπερωτῴη δὲ
τοὺς συκοφαντηθέντας ἐκ τῆς πολιτείας ἐπ' ἐκείνων τῶν καιρῶν,
ὅτ' ἐνῆν σώζεσθαι, διὰ τί αὐτὸν οὐκ ἐκώλυσαν ἐξαμαρτάνειν,
228 ἀποκρύπτοιτο δὲ τὸ πάντων τελευταῖον, ὅτι τῆς μάχης ἐπιγε-
νομένης οὐκ ἐσχολάζομεν περὶ τὴν σὴν εἶναι τιμωρίαν, ἀλλ' 5
ὑπὲρ τῆς σωτηρίας τῆς πόλεως ἐπρεσβεύομεν· ἐπειδὴ δὲ οὐκ
ἀπέχρη σοι δίκην μὴ δεδωκέναι, ἀλλὰ καὶ δωρεὰς αἰτεῖς καταγέλαστον ἐν τοῖς Ἕλλησι τὴν πόλιν ποιῶν, ἐνταυθ' ἐνέστην
καὶ τὴν γραφὴν ἀπήνεγκα.
229 Καὶ νὴ τοὺς θεοὺς τοὺς Ὀλυμπίους, ὧν ἐγὼ πυνθάνομαι 10
Δημοσθένην λέξειν, ἐφ' ᾧ νυνὶ μέλλω λέγειν ἀγανακτῶ μάλιστα.

4. ἀποκρύπτοιτο] ἀποκρίνοιντο *nfcd* Reisk. 10. ὧν] ὡς *agnfc bekl*. 11. ἀγανακτῶ μάλιστα] Sic Laur. Flor. et a m. pr. corr. z, et μάλιστα ἀγανακτῶ *l*: μάλιστα ἀγανακτῶν *bek*, ἀγανακτῶν μάλιστα ceteri.

for goodness, when you have done no good,
but only harm.'

2. ἐπ' ἐκείνων .. σώζεσθαι. Most naturally taken with what goes before: but it is
not unlike Aeschines' style to have put διὰ
τί .. ἐξαμαρτάνειν after it, if he meant it to
be taken with it.

§ 228. *Besides, Chaeronea gave us other
things to think of more important than
you.*

4. ἀποκρύπτοιτο. A brilliant conjecture
of Stephanus for ἀποκρίνοιντο, disapproved
of by Reiske, but universally received since
Bekker proved it to have the immense balance of MS. authority. ἀποκρίνοιντο would
have to mean 'a popular leader who should
.. ask the victims of his arts ..', while they
would have the answer..,' which could
hardly stand without ἐκεῖνοι δ' ἂν ἀποκρίνοιντο. See on § 226.

6. ἐπρεσβεύομεν. It was Demades who
negotiated the peace (D. de Cor. § 352);
but Aeschines either accompanied him, or
went on an independent mission to Philip:
ibid. § 347.

ἐπειδὴ δὲ proves that Ctesiphon's motion was after Chaeronea, which has been
questioned.

8. ἐνέστην. 'Stood up in the way:'
exactly the sense in which it is used in later
Greek, as i.q. *intercedo*, of the Roman tri-
bunes.

§ 229. *Then he compares the charm of my
eloquence to that of the Sirens' songs:*
This illustration does not, like the last,
occur in Demosthenes' speech as we have it.
It seems hardly possible to believe, with
Dindorf, that all these illustrations were
taken *bona fide* from rumours of what Demosthenes meant to say, and sometimes did

say and sometimes not. From Ae. in Tim.
p. 25, § 175, we must suppose that even
Demosthenes' friends and pupils did not
know until afterwards even the general line
he intended to take in a difficult case. Yet
we must either assume this, or suppose that
Demosthenes suppressed the passage afterwards; which points to Dissen's opinion,
that neither orator had *read* the other's
speech when he retouched his own, but only
heard it. It could hardly, with Aeschines'
speech before them, have been cut out by
the critics, like the passage in D. de Cor.
§ 324, quoted by Hermogenes.

The reading of the first sentence is doubtful. Nearly all MSS. have ὡς for ὧν, and
ἀγανακτῶν for ἀγανακτῶ. It would be just
possible to construe this, making ἀφομοιοῖ
γὰρ .. τῶν ἀκουόντων a sort of parenthesis,
with only colons before and after it; and
supposing that when the thread of the sentence is resumed by καίτοι τὸν λόγον τοῦτον
κ.τ.λ., there is an anacoluthon or modification of the sense to suit the parenthesis, and
that the object to λέξειν is omitted, having
been virtually expressed. One would then
translate, 'As I hear that Demosthenes will
urge a point (with more indignation at
hearing of that point than of any other),
comparing me to the Sirens.., yet' that
illustration I am not afraid of, for the cap
does not fit me, and Demosthenes is not
the man to put it on me if it did: καίτοι
introducing the apodosis to ὡς. But it is
far likelier that ὧν is right and ὡς a corrupt
repetition from ὡς ἐγὼ πυνθάνομαι in § 226:
and as for ἀγανακτῶ, two or three good
MSS. have it, and so has one indifferent
one, of the group that transposes μάλιστα
ἀγανακτῶ.

I 2

ἀφομοιοῖ γάρ μου τὴν φύσιν ταῖς Σειρῆσιν, ὡς ἔοικε. καὶ
γὰρ ὑπ᾽ ἐκείνων οὐ κηλεῖσθαί φησι τοὺς ἀκροωμένους, ἀλλ᾽
ἀπόλλυσθαι, διόπερ οὐκ εὐδοκιμεῖν τὴν τῶν Σειρήνων μουσικήν·
καὶ δὴ καὶ τὴν τῶν [ἐμῶν] λόγων ἐμπειρίαν καὶ τὴν φύσιν
5 μου γεγενῆσθαι ἐπὶ βλάβῃ τῶν ἀκουόντων. καίτοι τὸν λόγον
τοῦτον ὅλως μὲν ἔγωγε οὐδενὶ πρέπειν ἡγοῦμαι περὶ ἐμοῦ λέ-
γειν· τῆς γὰρ αἰτίας αἰσχρὸν τὸν αἰτιώμενόν ἐστι τὸ ἔργον
μὴ ἔχειν ἐπιδεῖξαι· εἰ δ᾽ ἦν ἀναγκαῖον ῥηθῆναι, οὐ Δημοσθένους 230
ἦν ὁ λόγος, ἀλλ᾽ ἀνδρὸς στρατηγοῦ μεγάλα μὲν τῇ πόλει
10 κατειργασμένου, λέγειν δὲ ἀδυνάτου καὶ τὴν τῶν ἀντιδίκων διὰ
τοῦτο ἐζηλωκότος φύσιν, ὅτι σύνοιδεν ἑαυτῷ μὲν οὐδὲν ὧν δια-
πέπρακται δυναμένῳ φράσαι, τὸν δὲ κατήγορον ὁρᾷ δυνάμενον

1. ὡς ἔοικε] Post φύσιν ponunt bekl, quasi illorum scriptores tanquam glossema intellex-
issent. 3. οὐκ] οὐδ᾽ Vat. pn bekl Bekk. B. et S. Schultz. Σειρήνων] εἰρημένων
ηfdq Barb. Ald.: vid. annot. 4. ἐμῶν] Ejecit Sauppius: ἐμὴν volunt Bakius et
Hamaker. Mox ἐμπειρίαν] ἀπορίαν a, εὐπορίαν bekl (qui ante λόγων ponunt)
et γρ. gm. 9. τῇ πόλει] τὴν πόλιν bekl Bekk.

1. ἀφομοιοῖ.. ὡς ἔοικε. 'He compares
my nature, it appears, to the Sirens.' If it
were necessary to logic to say 'to that of
the Sirens,' one might illustrate from the
Homeric κόμαι Χαρίτεσσιν ὅμοιαι. 'ὡς
ἔοικε malim abesse,' says Baiter. One group
of MSS. puts it before ταῖς Σειρῆσιν, which
looks as though it were understood as a
gloss, 'that it is like them.'
2. κηλεῖσθαι. Especially of the charms
of music.
3. διόπερ οὐκ εὐδοκιμεῖν looks like a
direct quotation from Demosthenes. Bekker
and B. and S. have οὐδ᾽ εὐδοκιμεῖν, which is
more elegant, but most of the best MSS.
have οὐκ: and the δ might have got there
from the next syllable.
τὴν τῶν Σειρήνων μουσικήν. Volg.
ante Bekk. τῶν εἰρημένων, which is very
flat, in fact probably post-classical. Some
MSS. have it, including the oldest known,
and one not of the same family with it; so
the reading must be old: and in fact it is
not unlikely that τῶν εἰρημένων is the original gloss, and τῶν Σειρήνων a not unintelligent correction of it: for the repetition
of the name is harsh, though less flat than
the pronominal phrase.
4. τὴν τῶν [ἐμῶν] λόγων ἐμπειρίαν.
So most MSS.: one group has εὐπορίαν λόγων, and one or two others mention or point
towards that word, without noticing the
transposition. εὐπορίαν suits rather better
with what Demosthenes does say (de Cor.
§ 381) of the character of Aeschines' eloquence; but no doubt he is trying to get a
higher compliment out of the comparison
than was intended or expressed. ἐμῶν is

in all the MSS., and we do not venture to
omit it with B. and S. and Franke: 'the
abundance of my words,' or even 'the skil-
fulness of my speaking,' is not a very harsh
phrase. Or had Demosthenes said, it was
better to stop your ears like Ulysses' men
than to be ἔμπειροι τῶν ἐκείνου λόγων?
As for the correction τὴν ἐμὴν τῶν λόγων
ἐμπειρίαν, that would have been much easier
for Aeschines to have written—much likelier, also, to have been put down as a gloss.
6. ὅλως μὲν οὐδενὶ answers to εἰ δ᾽ ἦν
ἀναγκαῖον ῥηθῆναι, οὐ Δημοσθένους ἦν ὁ
λόγος.
7. τῆς αἰτίας .. τὸ ἔργον. 'The fact
which corresponds to his charge:' it is a
shame to say my eloquence is pernicious,
when you cannot point to the harm it has
done.
§ 230. Though Demosthenes is the last
person who should talk of the mischief of
seductive eloquence.
8. εἰ δ᾽ ἦν ἀναγκαῖον ῥηθῆναι. If my
enemies could not do without the illustration, they should have put it in somebody
else's mouth. ἦν without ἄν will probably
mean, 'The topic did not belong to Demosthenes,' and should not have been given to
him when Ctesiphon's σύνδικοι were arrang-
ing their parts: cp. ad § 202. One of them
was a general, § 197: can Aeschines, who
could not venture to attack his character,
intend a sneer at his abilities?
9. τῇ πόλει. One group of MSS. has
τὴν πόλιν—a correction after their manner,
to correspond with the commoner Attic
usage.
12. δυνάμενον. One is almost tempted

καὶ τὰ μὴ πεπραγμένα ὑφ᾿ αὐτοῦ παριστάναι τοῖς ἀκούουσιν
ὡς διώκηκεν. ὅταν δ᾿ ἐξ ὀνομάτων συγκείμενος ἄνθρωπος, καὶ·
τούτων πικρῶν καὶ περιέργων, ἔπειτα ἐπὶ τὴν ἁπλότητα καὶ
τὰ ἔργα καταφεύγῃ, τίς ἂν ἀνάσχοιτο; οὗ τὴν γλῶτταν ὥσπερ τῶν αὐλῶν ἐάν τις ἀφέλῃ, τὸ λοιπὸν οὐδέν ἐστιν. 5
231 Θαυμάζω δ᾿ ἔγωγε ὑμῶν, ὦ Ἀθηναῖοι, καὶ ζητῶ, πρὸς τί
ἂν ἀποβλέποντες ἀποψηφίσαισθε τὴν γραφήν. πότερον ὡς
τὸ ψήφισμά ἐστιν ἔννομον; ἀλλ᾿ οὐδεμία πώποτε γνώμη
παρανομωτέρα γεγένηται. ἀλλ᾿ ὡς ὁ τὸ ψήφισμα γράψας
οὐκ ἐπιτήδειός ἐστι δίκην δοῦναι; οὐκ ἄρ᾿ εἰσὶ παρ᾿ ὑμῖν εὔθυ- 10
ναι βίου, εἰ τοῦτον ἀφήσετε. ἐκεῖνο δ᾿ οὐ λυπηρὸν, εἰ πρότερον μὲν ἐνεπίμπλατο ἡ ὀρχήστρα χρυσῶν στεφάνων, οἷς ὁ
δῆμος ἐστεφανοῦτο ὑπὸ τῶν Ἑλλήνων, διὰ τὸ ξενικοῖς στεφάνοις ταύτην ἀποδεδόσθαι τὴν ἡμέραν, ἐκ δὲ τῶν Δημοσθένους
πολιτευμάτων ὑμεῖς μὲν ἀστεφάνωτοι καὶ ἀκήρυκτοι γίγνεσθε, 15
232 οὗτος δὲ κηρυχθήσεται; καὶ εἰ μέν τις τῶν τραγικῶν ποιητῶν τῶν
μετὰ ταῦτα ἐπεισαγόντων ποιήσειεν ἐν τραγῳδίᾳ τὸν Θερσίτην
ὑπὸ τῶν Ἑλλήνων στεφανούμενον, οὐδεὶς ἂν ὑμῶν ὑπομείνειεν,
ὅτι φησὶν Ὅμηρος ἄνανδρον αὐτὸν εἶναι καὶ συκοφάντην·

6. Post ζητῶ, πυθέσθαι add. fcd.　　7. ἂν ἀποβλέποντες] ἀναβλέψαντες bkl.
ἀποψηφίσαισθε] Sic Steph., z Flor., et si ex Bekkeri silentio fas est conjectare c:
ἀποψηφίσεσθαι a, -σεσθε gmnfe, -σησθε Vat. p, -σασθε k, -σασθαι l, ἀπεψηφίσασθε b, ἀποψη-
φίζεσθαι d.　　πότερον] πότερ᾿ bekl Bekk.　　10. οὐκ] Om. a.　　12. ἐνεπίμ-
πλατο] ἐνεπίπλατο acd.　　οἷς] οὓς bekl, quod fortasse verum.

to put a comma after this word, so as to
complete the sense, and make what fills up
the sentence a more forcible climax: 'but
he sees the accuser can, and can even ascribe
to him ...'

3. πικρῶν. Aeschines is not saying, as
Dionysius (περὶ τῆς λεκτικῆς Δημοσθένους
δεινότητος, c. 55 sq.) supposes, that πικρότης
is a fault in an orator. He says that Demosthenes, a man of words (aye, and bitter
artificial words), has no right to assume the
tone of an honest man of action.

4. τὴν γλῶτταν, ὥσπερ τῶν αὐλῶν
either was a proverb, or, from a vague recollection of this passage, was ascribed to Demades as a description of the Athenians.

§ 231. How can you absolve an unlawful
decree, moved by a scoundrel, to crown a
man who has discrowned the nation?

6. ζητῶ. Volg. ante Bekk. added the
gloss πυθέσθαι, with one group of MSS.

7. ἀποψηφίσαισθε. Most MSS. have
ἀποψηφίσεσθε, or what seems to be meant
for it, but only one MS. omits ἂν (three
confuse it with the next word), so it is no
doubt a mere phonetic corruption of -σαισθε.

Moreover, had Aeschines meant to use the
future, he would have written ἀποψηφεῖσθε.

10. οὐκ ἐπιτήδειός ἐστι δίκην δοῦναι.
'Not a suitable person to select to make an
example of,' i. e. that though Ctesiphon has
broken the law, one would sooner strain a
point than punish so upright a man. There
is an exactly similar sentiment in Demosth.
Androt. p. 610, § 57, ἐπιτήδειαι ἐκεῖναι (αἱ
πόρναι as here ὁ πορνοβοσκὸς) παθεῖν κακά.

13. διὰ τὸ ξενικοῖς κ.τ.λ. Aeschines
recurs to his own interpretation of the law
(above, § 41 sqq.); strengthening his argument, it seems, by the assertion that the law
had been acted on in that sense.

§ 232. How can you give Demosthenes
an honour in the theatre, which he deserves
no better than Thersites, without making the
state answerable for the evil deeds of the
citizens, not for the good?

17. ἐπεισαγόντων. Not elsewhere used
absolutely in this sense; but exactly correlative to ἐπεισιοῦσιν in § 153, of the actors:
so that perhaps one should rather supply
τοὺς τραγῳδοὺς or τοὺς χόρους than τὰ
δράματα.

αὐτοὶ δ' ὅταν τὸν τοιοῦτον ἄνθρωπον στεφανῶτε, οὐκ οἴεσθε
ἐν ταῖς τῶν Ἑλλήνων δόξαις συρίττεσθαι; οἱ μὲν γὰρ πατέρες ὑμῶν τὰ ἔνδοξα καὶ λαμπρὰ τῶν πραγμάτων ἀνετίθεσαν τῷ δήμῳ, τὰ δὲ ταπεινὰ καὶ καταδεέστερα εἰς τοὺς ῥή-
5 τορας τοὺς φαύλους ἔτρεπον· Κτησιφῶν δ' ὑμᾶς οἴεται δεῖν
ἀφελόντας τὴν ἀδοξίαν ἀπὸ Δημοσθένους περιθεῖναι τῷ δήμῳ.
καὶ φατὲ μὲν εὐτυχεῖς εἶναι, ὡς καὶ ἐστὲ καλῶς ποιοῦντες, ψη-233
φιεῖσθε δ' ὑπὸ μὲν τῆς τύχης ἐγκαταλελεῖφθαι, ὑπὸ Δημοσθένους δὲ εὖ πεπονθέναι; καὶ τὸ πάντων ἀτοπώτατον, ἐν τοῖς
10 αὐτοῖς δικαστηρίοις τοὺς μὲν τὰς τῶν δώρων γραφὰς ἁλισκομένους ἀτιμοῦτε, ὃν δ' αὐτοὶ μισθοῦ πολιτευόμενον σύνιστε,
στεφανώσετε; καὶ τοὺς μὲν κριτὰς τοὺς ἐκ τῶν Διονυσίων,
ἐὰν μὴ δικαίως τοὺς κυκλίους χοροὺς κρίνωσι, ζημιοῦτε· αὐτοὶ
δὲ οὐ κυκλίων χορῶν κριταὶ καθεστηκότες, ἀλλὰ νόμων καὶ
15 πολιτικῆς ἀρετῆς, τὰς δωρεὰς οὐ κατὰ τοὺς νόμους οὐδ' ὀλίγοις
καὶ τοῖς ἀξίοις, ἀλλὰ τῷ διαπραξαμένῳ δώσετε; ἔπειτ' ἔξεισιν 234
ἐκ τοῦ δικαστηρίου ὁ τοιοῦτος κριτὴς ἑαυτὸν μὲν ἀσθενῆ πε-

---

3. τὰ ἔνδοξα] τὰ μὲν ἔνδοξα. Vat. *pz fqt* Laur. Flor. Schultz. 12. τῶν] Ante
Διονυσίων om. Bekk. cum codd. praeter *a* Laur. 14. κριταί] Om. *mfcd* B. et S.,
post καθεστηκότες ponunt *bekl* Bekk.

3. ἀνετίθεσαν. The reference is to §
186 fin. Bremi is wrong in thinking there
is a metaphor, of 'dedicating' an honour like
a votive offering: ἀνατίθημι is constantly
no more than 'to ascribe' a thing to a person.
There is perhaps here something of a play on
the word περιθεῖναι in the next sentence.

4. τὰ δὲ ταπεινὰ κ.τ.λ. He asserts,
truly, no doubt, that the spirit of the old
times was always to hold that there must be
some individual traitor responsible for the
national ill success : in the next section, he
goes on to denounce Demosthenes' common-
sense view, that failure in an honourable
cause was a misfortune, not a fault of either
the nation or an individual.

§ 233. *Can the gods' blessing on Athens
have failed, rather than a man have been in
fault? or will you give a false judgment in law
and politics, when you punish one at the games?*

7. καὶ φατὲ μὲν εὐτυχεῖς εἶναι : cp. D. de
Cor. § 316 sqq., which are probably meant to
reply to this passage, as well as to § 114. etc.

καλῶς ποιοῦντες. One might translate
'as you are *when* you act rightly,' but since
the argument is 'King Demos can do no
wrong. nor has he bad luck,' it seems better
to take it in the common sense, almost equivalent to ἀγαθῇ τύχῃ, 'you have good fortune, and much good may it do you!'
Bremi thinks that these phrases have usually
a slight irony—as have our equivalent ones.

11. ὃν δ' αὐτοὶ .. σύνιστε. He appeals,
as in the Timarchus, pp. 11, 13, §§ 78 sqq.,
92, to the personal extra-judicial knowledge
of the court: not very consistently with
§ 59, above. αὐτοὶ σύνιστε is thus opposed
to ἁλισκομένους, convicted on investigation.

13. κυκλίους χορούς. Dithyrambic
choruses, as opposed to dramatic: not =
ἐγκύκλιοι, 'yearly choruses,' as F. A. Wolf
and Bremi. It appears from Ar. Nub. 333,
that they were not very respectable, from
Ran. 365, that they were not always in the
theatre : hence, when they were performed
at the Dionysia, it would perhaps be thought
the least serious part of the judges' business
to decide on them, as compared with the
tragic or even comic.

14. κυκλίων χορῶν κριταὶ. B. and S.
omit κριταὶ with four respectable MSS.: but
though the sense is clear enough for a copyist
not to feel the want, it is not likely that
Aeschines would have ventured to write
such an elliptical sentence.

15. ὀλίγοις .. διαπραξαμένῳ. 'Not to
rare cases of desert, but to mere intrigue.'

§ 234. *If you do, you will have sold your
constitutional freedom, and incurred the
curse of perjury. for nothing.*

16. ἔπειτ'. 'And then,' besides the ab-
surdities pointed out above.

17. ὁ τοιοῦτος κριτής. 'The man who
decides on such principles,' τὰς δωρεὰς .. τῷ

ποιηκὼς, ἰσχυρὸν δὲ τὸν ῥήτορα. ἀνὴρ γὰρ ἰδιώτης ἐν πόλε.
δημοκρατουμένῃ νόμῳ καὶ ψήφῳ βασιλεύει· ὅταν δ' ἑτέρῳ
ταῦτα παραδῷ, καταλέλυκεν αὐτὸς τὴν αὐτοῦ δυναστείαν.
ἔπειθ'
ὁ μὲν ὅρκος, ὃν ὀμωμοκὼς δικάζει, συμπαρακολουθῶν αὐτὸν λυ-
πεῖ· δι' αὐτὸν γάρ, οἶμαι, γέγονε τὸ ἁμάρτημα· ἡ δὲ χάρις 5
πρὸς ὃν ἐχαρίζετο ἄδηλος γεγένηται· ἡ γὰρ ψῆφος ἀφανὴς
φέρεται.

235 Δοκοῦμεν δ' ἔμοιγε, ὦ Ἀθηναῖοι, ἀμφότερα καὶ κατορθοῦν
καὶ παρακινδυνεύειν εἰς τὴν πολιτείαν οὐ σωφρονοῦντες. ὅτι
μὲν γὰρ ἐπὶ τῶν νῦν καιρῶν οἱ πολλοὶ τοῖς ὀλίγοις προΐεσθε 10
τὰ τῆς δημοκρατίας ἰσχυρά, οὐκ ἐπαινῶ· ὅτι δ' οὐ γεγένηται
φορὰ καθ' ἡμᾶς ῥητόρων πονηρῶν ἅμα καὶ πολμηρῶν, εὐτυ-
χοῦμεν. πρότερον μὲν γὰρ τοιαύτας φύσεις ἤνεγκε τὸ δημόσιον, αἳ ῥᾳδίως οὕτω κατέλυσαν τὸν δῆμον· ἔχαιρε γὰρ κολα-
κευόμενος, ἔπειτ' αὐτὸν οὐχ οὓς ἐφοβεῖτο, ἀλλ' οἷς ἑαυτὸν 15
236 ἐνεχείριζε, κατέλυσαν· ἔνιοι δὲ καὶ αὐτοὶ τῶν τριάκοντα ἐγένοντο, οἳ πλείους ἢ χιλίους καὶ πεντακοσίους τῶν πολιτῶν
ἀκρίτους ἀπέκτειναν πρὶν καὶ τὰς αἰτίας ἀκοῦσαι, ἐφ' αἷς ἔμελλον ἀποθνήσκειν, καὶ οὐδ' ἐπὶ τὰς ταφὰς καὶ ἐκφορὰς τῶν
τελευτησάντων εἴων τοὺς προσήκοντας παραγενέσθαι. οὐκ ὑφ' 20
ὑμῖν αὐτοῖς ἕξετε τοὺς πολιτευομένους; οὐ ταπεινώσαντες ἀποπέμψετε τοὺς νῦν ἐπηρμένους; οὐ μέμνησθ', ὅτι οὐδεὶς πώποτε

---

3. αὐτὸς τὴν] τὴν αὐτὸς bekl Bekk.
volgo πρίν.   20. παραγενέσθαι] Sic
Om. a Vat. p pr. Laur.

18. πρὶν καὶ] Sic agm et supra versum b :
aufcd : ceteri et Bekk. παραγίγνεσθαι.   ὑφ']

διαπραξαμένῳ διδοὺς, so far as any special
words are referred to.
5. δι' αὐτὸν γάρ. As the words stand,
they can only mean, 'For his offence is committed because of the oath,' i. e. the wrong
vote is a crime, because it is a perjury. One
or two MSS. have αὐτοῦ, which shews that
the writers felt a difficulty. It would be
easy to read αὐτὸν, and perhaps possible to
find a meaning for it : 'he himself will suffer
from the guilt of perjury (and it was to
benefit himself that he incurred it), while the
other man' (Demosthenes or Ctesiphon),
'whose favour he hoped to secure, cannot
thank him if he would.' Or one might
transpose δι' αὐτὸν .. ἁμάρτημα and ἡ δὲ
χάρις πρὸς ὃν ἐχαρίζετο, and translate, 'and
the favour done to the person favoured (for
it is for his benefit that he has done the
wrong) has passed unknown and unthanked,
since the vote is given in secret.' The argument of the worthlessness of χάρις was a
commonplace with orators : cp. Dem. Mid.
pp. 575, 582, §§ 188, 212.

§ 235. In truth, whether we are fortunate
or no, we are doing nothing to deserve it : it is mere
good fortune
8. δοκοῦμεν δ' ἔμοιγε κ.τ.λ. 'It seems
to me, Athenians, that there is no sense
either in the hazards or in the successes of
our policy.' Both the clauses in the next
sentence are proofs of this want of sense : in
a clever nation, there would have been
plenty of orators to profit by the supineness
of the Assembly.
11. τὰ τῆς δημοκρατίας ἰσχυρά. Especially the γραφὴ παρανόμων, as in § 5.
§ 236. That our demagogues are not in
the position of the Thirty, who began in the
same way.
18. πρὶν τὰς αἰτίας .. ἀποθνήσκειν. A
climax upon ἀκρίτους, not only without
giving them a chance of proving their innocence, but without letting them or others
know the real or pretended crime.
20. παραγενέσθαι. So perhaps the best
MSS. : al. παραγίγνεσθαι. Cp. ad § 221
for the rationale of either tense.

ἐπέθετο πρότερον τῇ τοῦ δήμου καταλύσει, πρὶν ἂν μεῖζον
τῶν δικαστηρίων ἰσχύσῃ;
     Ἡδέως δ᾽ ἂν ἔγωγε, ὦ ᾽Αθηναῖοι, ἐναντίον ὑμῶν ἀναλογι- 237
σαίμην πρὸς τὸν γράψαντα τὸ ψήφισμα, διὰ ποίας εὐεργε-
5 σίας ἀξιοῖ Δημοσθένην στεφανῶσαι. εἰ μὲν γὰρ λέγεις, ὅθεν
τὴν ἀρχὴν τοῦ ψηφίσματος ἐποιήσω, ὅτι τὰς τάφρους τὰς
περὶ τὰ τείχη καλῶς ἐτάφρευσε, θαυμάζω σου. τοῦ γὰρ
ταῦτ᾽ ἐξεργασθῆναι καλῶς τὸ γεγενῆσθαι τούτων αἴτιον μεῖζω
κατηγορίαν ἔχει· οὐ γὰρ περιχαρακώσαντα χρὴ τὰ τείχη οὐδὲ
10 τὰς δημοσίας τάφας ἀνελόντα τὸν ὀρθῶς πεπολιτευμένον δωρεὰς αἰτεῖν, ἀλλ᾽ ἀγαθοῦ τινος αἴτιον γεγενημένον τῇ πόλει.
εἰ δὲ ἥξεις ἐπὶ τὸ δεύτερον μέρος τοῦ ψηφίσματος, ἐν ᾧ τε- 238
τόλμηκας γράφειν, ὡς ἔστιν ἀνὴρ ἀγαθὸς καὶ διατελεῖ λέγων
καὶ πράττων τὰ ἄριστα τῷ δήμῳ τῶν ᾽Αθηναίων, ἀφελὼν τὴν
15 ἀλαζονείαν καὶ τὸν κόμπον τοῦ ψηφίσματος ἅψαι τῶν ἔργων,
ἐπίδειξον ἡμῖν ὅ τι λέγεις. τὰς μὲν γὰρ περὶ τοὺς ᾽Αμφισ-

---

1. μεῖζον] μείζω *agmηſcde.*   3. ἀναλογισαίμην] ὁμολογησαίμην Vat. Laur. *agmp*
B. et S. Frank.: vid. annot.   8. ἐξεργασθῆναι] ἐξείργασθαι *k,* ἐξεργάσασθαι el Bekk.,
ἐξεργάσασθαι *b.*   14. τῶν ᾽Αθηναίων] τῷ ᾽Αθηναίων *nf* et, ut semper, Bekk.

---

1. ἐπέθετο. Exactly as we say ' set upon
putting down democracy.'
     πρὶν ἂν .. ἰσχύσῃ. ' No one ever yet
set upon putting down democracy, before he
makes himself stronger:' the sentiment being
general, the conjunctive is used in the dependent clause, as a present would be.
     § 237. *What are Demosthenes' merits?*
that he prepared the City for a siege he tried
to bring upon it?
     3. ἀναλογισαίμην. ' I should like to
examine the account,' to go *over again* the
sum that Ctesiphon has done, whereby he
seeks to prove that Demosthenes has a
balance due from the city. The reading
ὁμολογησαίμην, ' came to an understanding
with you,' is a stranger sense of the word,
and seems less appropriate: the middle form,
also, is rare, but it has rather the better
authority. ἀναλογίζομαι appears always to
refer to this deliberate afterthought: e. g.
Thuc. 5. 7 init. ἀναλογιζομένων δὲ τὴν
ἐκείνου ἡγεμονίαν, πρὸς οἵαν ἐμπειρίαν καὶ
τόλμαν μετὰ οἵας ἀνεπιστημοσύνης καὶ μα-
λακίας γενήσοιτο, ' when the thought grew
upon them,' though at first they may have
trusted Cleon like their fellow-citizens who
elected him.
     6. τάφρους .. ἐτάφρευσε : vid. ad § 95.
τὰς περὶ τὰ τείχη makes it likely that they
were still in existence, as a permanent addition to the fortifications.

7. τοῦ γὰρ ταῦτ᾽ κ.τ.λ. ' For to have
performed this well is nothing to the blame
of having made it necessary :' lit. ' there is
more blame in having made this necessary
than (credit) in having done it well.'
     9. περιχαρακώσαντα is contemptuous ;
there were the walls, what were a few stakes
more or less ?
     10. τὰς δημοσίας τάφας ἀνελόντα is
invidious. We must suppose that the en-
trenchments ran over the site of the tombs
in the Ceramicus ; possibly also the monu-
ments were used for materials, as in the
original fortification of the city (Thuc. 1.
93): the precedent would prevent objections
like Aeschines' being raised until the danger
was past. (See Lyc. in Leocr. p. 153, § 44,
where ' the dead' are said to ' offer their
tombs' to the work of defence, while though
Demosthenes is not named, his services are
unmistakably alluded to.) Demosthenes
having claimed credit for his munificence,
both the participles are meant to point to
the shabby, patchwork character of the repairs.
     § 238. *Or on his general high character*
and services? The less you say about Am-
phissa or Euboea the better, as for Thebes,
will you credit him at the expense of Athens?
     14. ἀφελὼν κ.τ.λ. : cp. § 101.
     16. τὰς μὲν γὰρ .. δωροδοκίας. A sort
of sneer παρὰ προσδοκίαν, ' his alleged ser-

σέας καὶ τοὺς Εὐβοᾶς δωροδοκίας παραλείπω· ὅταν δὲ τῆς
πρὸς Θηβαίους συμμαχίας τὰς αἰτίας ἀνατιθῆς Δημοσθένει,
τοὺς μὲν ἀγνοοῦντας ἐξαπατᾶς, τοὺς δ᾽ εἰδότας καὶ αἰσθανο-
μένους ὑβρίζεις. ἀφελὼν γὰρ τὸν καιρὸν καὶ τὴν δόξαν τὴν
τούτων, δι᾽ ἢν ἐγένετο ἡ συμμαχία, οἴει λανθάνειν ἡμᾶς τὸ τῆς 5
239 πόλεως ἀξίωμα Δημοσθένει περιτιθείς. ἡλίκον δ᾽ ἐστὶ τὸ ἀλα-
ζόνευμα τοῦτο, ἐγὼ πειράσομαι μεγάλῳ σημείῳ διδάξαι. ὁ
γὰρ τῶν Περσῶν βασιλεὺς οὐ πολλῷ πρότερον χρόνῳ πρὸ
τῆς Ἀλεξάνδρου διαβάσεως εἰς τὴν Ἀσίαν κατέπεμψε τῷ
δήμῳ καὶ μάλα ὑβριστικὴν καὶ βάρβαρον ἐπιστολὴν, ἐν ᾗ τά 10
τε δὴ ἄλλα καὶ μάλ᾽ ἀπαιδεύτως διελέχθη, καὶ ἐπὶ τελευτῆς
ἐνέγραψεν ἐν τῇ ἐπιστολῇ, "ἐγὼ" φησὶν "ὑμῖν χρυσίον οὐ
240 δώσω· μή με αἰτεῖτε· οὐ γὰρ λήψεσθε." οὗτος μέντοι ὁ αὐτὸς ἐγκαταληφθεὶς ὑπὸ τῶν νυνὶ παρόντων αὐτῷ κινδύνων, οὐκ
αἰτούντων Ἀθηναίων, αὐτὸς ἑκὼν κατέπεμψε τριακόσια τάλαντα 15
τῷ δήμῳ, ἃ σωφρονῶν οὐκ ἐδέξατο. ὁ δὲ κομίζων ἦν τὸ χρυσίον καιρὸς καὶ φόβος καὶ χρεία συμμάχων. τὸ δὲ αὐτὸ τοῦτο καὶ τὴν Θηβαίων συμμαχίαν ἐξειργάζετο. σὺ δὲ τὸ μὲν
τῶν Θηβαίων ὄνομα καὶ τὸ τῆς δυστυχεστάτης συμμαχίας ἐνο-
χλεῖς ἀεὶ λέγων, τὰ δ᾽ ἑβδομήκοντα τάλαντα ὑποσιωπᾷς, ἃ 20
241 προλαβὼν τοῦ βασιλικοῦ χρυσίου ἀπεστέρησας. οὐ δι᾽ ἔνδειαν

---

5. οἴει λανθάνειν] λανθάνειν οἴει bekl Bekk.　　8. πρότερον] Om. bekl.　　12. ἐν
τῇ ἐπιστολῇ] Om. Hamak. Schultz.　　15. τριακόσια] πεντήκοντα a, τριάκοντα gmbekl.
16. Post σωφρονῶν ὁ δῆμος add. bekl Bekk.　　18. ἐξειργάζετο] ἐξειργάσατο bekl,
quod mavolt Frank., habetque Frank.

---

vices in the Euboean and Amphissian affairs
I need not mention: he was paid for what
he did, so it must have been bad,' is the
argument, but it is expressed 'I need not
speak of the bribes he took in the Euboean
and Amphissian affairs.'

5. τὸ τῆς πόλεως ἀξίωμα Δημοσθένει
περιτιθείς. 'You think that we shall not
see how you clothe Demosthenes in the
majesty that belongs to Athens;' the clause
is correlative to ἀφελὼν γὰρ .. τούτων, and
the object is almost the same; τὴν δόξαν
τὴν τούτων = τὸ τῆς πόλεως ἀξίωμα. Aeschines had named before the same motives
as inducing the Thebans to join Athens,
§ 137 : Ctesiphon attributed their action to
Demosthenes.

§ 239. *Just as the King insolently refused
us money before Alexander's invasion,*

12. φησίν. Pleonastically to mark a
verbatim quotation, though ἐνέγραψεν has
been expressed already.

χρυσίον οὐ δώσω .. οὐ γὰρ λήψεσθε.
One cannot help comparing Ar. Ach. 104.

It is scarcely possible that Aeschines is imitating it; but that is an imitation, this perhaps
a real quotation, of the bald style of a communication meant to be dictatorial, and perhaps the more wordy through imperfect translation. It is this fault of style
which Aeschines characteristically attributes
to ἀπαιδευσία as well as ὕβρις.

§ 240. *But prayed us in vain to take it
after, so was it with Thebes joining us :
which Demosthenes is always talking of,
while afterwards he ruined them by keeping
back the King's money :*

17. καιρὸς καὶ φόβος καὶ χρεία συμμάχων. Exactly the same as with the Thebans,
§ 137 : only with him the need of *any* allies,
with them the need of *so powerful* allies, was
what determined their application to Athens.

21. ἀπεστέρησας. 'You embezzled;'
a technical term, used in just the same way,
Ae. de F. L. p. 50, § 177. The story was,
that Demosthenes had 70 talents (300 according to Dinarchus, in Dem. p. 92, § 18)
from the King to administer at his discre-

μὲν χρημάτων, ἕνεκα πέντε ταλάντων οἱ ξένοι τοῖς Θηβαίοις
τὴν ἄκραν οὐ παρέδοσαν; διὰ ἐννέα δὲ τάλαντα ἀργυρίου πάντων Ἀρκάδων ἐξεληλυθότων καὶ τῶν ἡγεμόνων ἑτοίμων ὄντων
βοηθεῖν ἡ πρᾶξις οὐ γεγένηται; σὺ δὲ πλουτεῖς καὶ ταῖς ἡδο-
5 ναῖς ταῖς σαυτοῦ χορηγεῖς. καὶ τὸ κεφάλαιον, τὸ μὲν βασιλικὸν χρυσίον παρὰ τούτῳ, οἱ δὲ κίνδυνοι παρ᾽ ὑμῖν.

Ἄξιον δ᾽ ἐστὶ καὶ τὴν ἀπαιδευσίαν αὐτῶν θεωρῆσαι. εἰ γὰρ 242
τολμήσει Κτησιφῶν μὲν Δημοσθένην παρακαλεῖν λέξοντα εἰς
ὑμᾶς, οὗτος δ᾽ ἀναβὰς ἑαυτὸν ἐγκωμιάσει, βαρύτερον τῶν ἔρ-
10 γων ὧν πεπόνθατε τὸ ἀκρόαμα γίγνεται. ὅπου γὰρ δὴ τοὺς
μὲν ὄντως ἄνδρας ἀγαθούς, οἷς πολλὰ καὶ καλὰ σύνισμεν ἔργα,
ἐὰν τοὺς καθ᾽ ἑαυτῶν ἐπαίνους λέγωσιν, οὐ φέρομεν· ὅταν δὲ
ἄνθρωπος αἰσχύνη τῆς πόλεως γεγονὼς ἑαυτὸν ἐγκωμιάζῃ, τίς
ἂν τὰ τοιαῦτα καρτερήσειεν ἀκούων;

15 Ἀπὸ μὲν οὖν τῆς ἀναισχύντου πραγματείας, ἐὰν σωφρονῇς, 243
ἀποστήσει, ποίησαι δέ, ὦ Κτησιφῶν, διὰ σαυτοῦ τὴν ἀπολο-

1. μὲν] Dubitasse videntur codd. nonnulli, utrum hoc omittendum esset.　　2. διὰ
ἐννέα δὲ] Frankio Bekkerus visus est referre, codd. aliquot qui διὰ δὲ ἐννέα habent, διὰ δὲ
ἐννέα δὲ habere. Unde in Quaest. Aeschin. ipse διὰ δέκα δὲ conjecit: in editione sua
meliore consilio rem omnino siluit.　　8. τολμήσει] τολμήσειε agmn fcd.　　9. οὗτος]
αὐτὸς g.　　10. δὴ] Sic agmp Vat. Laur.: ceteri et Bekk. om.　　12. δὲ] Om. p
Markl.　　14. ἀκούων] Om. Vat. Laur. Flor. gmpzbkl.　　16. ποίησαι] ' Malim
ποίησῃ, sive ποιήσει ' Bekk.: malitque Cobet. -σει.

tion, and refused to spend any: no doubt he
took, and was expected to take, a considerable commission.

§ 241. *When five talents would have given
them the Cadmea, and nine the Arcadian
alliance.*

δι᾽ ἔνδειαν μὲν χρημάτων, ἕνεκα πέντε
ταλάντων. 'Was it not because money
failed, in fact for a matter of five talents,
that the mercenaries did not give up the
Citadel to the Thebans?' This seems more
forcible than to make ἕνεκα πέντε ταλάντων merely a specification of the χρήματα,
for want of which the scheme failed: we put
a comma after χρημάτων to mark this view
of the construction.

2. διὰ ἐννέα δέ. So the best MSS. for
διὰ δὲ ἐννέα: it seems to be rather characteristic of Aeschines to put particles and
enclitics as late in the sentence as they will
go. The sum of *ten* talents is mentioned by
Dinarchus (in Dem. p. 92, § 20), where the
story is told more fully: and Franke once
imagined there were traces of the reading
δέκα here; but no doubt the details varied
of a story that was left as a subject of gossip,
without judicial investigation.

§ 242. *Consider the bad taste of self-praise,
and that from a rascal.*

8. τολμήσει. So Bekker and most edi-

tors since, though the old reading τολμήσειε
has much better MS. authority. But it
seems hard to give a meaning to the change
of mood between τολμήσειε and ἐγκωμιάσει.
Demosthenes, if called on to speak, is sure
to praise himself, so that the two verbs are
of just the same degree of certainty: it is
considered as bad taste in Ctesiphon to call
on him, as in him to rise. Demosthenes
apologises for the necessity of self-praise, in
De Cor. §§ 4 sq.

10. ὅπου γὰρ .. ὅταν δέ. It seems truer
to say that the sentence is irregular—constructed on two different plans, ὅπου implying one with protasis and apodosis, δὲ one
with thesis and antithesis—than that δὲ introduces the apodosis. It is idle to wish to
omit δέ, though one good MS. does so.

§ 243. *You had much better speak for yourself, Ctesiphon: favour the Court with the eloquence and pathos that served for Cleopatra.*

16. ποίησαι. 'Malim ποιήσῃ sive ποιήσει' Bekk. But the change of construction
is too little obvious to be due to a copyist.
If Ctesiphon had any sense or taste, he
would abstain from calling on Demosthenes,
but it is not sense or taste that will make
him speak for himself. Perhaps if he had a
little more he would say nothing, but throw
himself on the mercy of the Court.

γίαν. οὐ γὰρ δή που τοῦτό γε σκήψει, ὡς οὐ δυνατὸς εἶ
λέγειν. καὶ γὰρ ἄτοπόν σοι συμβαίνει, εἰ πρῴην μέν ποθ'
ὑπέμεινας πρεσβευτὴς ὡς Κλεοπάτραν τὴν Φιλίππου θυγατέρα
χειροτονεῖσθαι συναχθεσθησόμενος ἐπὶ τῇ τοῦ Μολοττῶν βασιλέως Ἀλεξάνδρου τελευτῇ, νυνὶ δὲ οὐ φήσεις δύνασθαι λέγειν. 5
ἔπειτα γυναῖκα μὲν ἀλλοτρίαν πενθοῦσαν δύνασαι παραμυθεῖ-
244 σθαι, γράψας δὲ μισθοῦ ψήφισμα οὐκ ἀπολογήσει; ἢ τοιοῦτός
ἐστιν ὃν γέγραφας στεφανοῦσθαι, οἷος μὴ γιγνώσκεσθαι ὑπὸ
τῶν εὖ πεπονθότων, ἂν μή τις σοι συνείπῃ; ἐπερώτησον δὴ
τοὺς δικαστάς, εἰ ἐγίγνωσκον Χαβρίαν καὶ Ἰφικράτην καὶ Τι- 10
μόθεον, καὶ πυθοῦ παρ' αὐτῶν, διὰ τί τὰς δωρεὰς αὐτοῖς ἔδοσαν καὶ τὰς εἰκόνας ἔστησαν. ἅπαντες γὰρ ἅμα σοι ἀποκρι-
νοῦνται, ὅτι Χαβρίᾳ μὲν διὰ τὴν περὶ Νάξον ναυμαχίαν, Ἰφι-
κράτει δέ, ὅτι μόραν Λακεδαιμονίων ἀπέκτεινε, Τιμοθέῳ δὲ
διὰ τὸν περίπλουν τὸν εἰς Κέρκυραν, καὶ ἄλλοις, ὧν ἑκάστῳ 15
245 πολλὰ καὶ καλὰ κατὰ πόλεμον ἔργα πέπρακται. Δημοσθένει

2. συμβαίνει] Sic agm Laur. Flor., et ἂν om. z: ceteri et Schultz. καὶ γὰρ ἂν ἄτοπόν σοι
συμβαίνοι. 4. συναχθεσθησόμενος] συναχθησόμενος gq, -χθεσόμενος Cobet.
14. μόραν] Ita Vat. Flor. z, hic in rasura: ceteri μοῖραν. Correxit H. Wolf. 16. Δημοσθένει δ' κ.τ.λ.] Δημοσθένει δ' ἀντερῶ διὰ τί δώσετε bekl Bekk.: post οὐ δώσετε, φήσετε add. pc, et teste Bekk. f: Δημοσθένει δ' ἐάν τις ἐρωτᾷ διὰ τί; ὅτι κ.τ.λ. B. et S.

2. καὶ γὰρ ἄτοπόν σοι συμβαίνει. 'For
your case is really ridiculous,' the indicative
affecting to conceive the alleged excuse as
possibly true. But see the critical note.
πρῴην. In the course of the previous
year, when he had been killed, and his army
destroyed, in his expedition to aid Tarentum
against the Bruttians.
3. ὑπέμεινας. A sarcastic word, almost
'were not too shy;' perhaps also it has the
same point as τὴν Φιλίππου θυγατέρα certainly has, 'With all your hatred for Macedon, you could bring yourself to be civil to
a Macedonian princess; so do the same for
the law of your country.'
6. ἀλλοτρίαν. Answered by γράψας
μισθοῦ: he had a personal interest in the
defence of a mercenary decree.
§ 244. Or is Demosthenes' fame so obscure,
that his praise cannot be justified without an
elaborate panegyric? He is not like our
real great men, if so.
8. οἷος μὴ γιγνώσκεσθαι. We should
say, 'not the sort of man to be known.'
9. ἂν μή τις σοι συνείπῃ. 'Except
you have a speaker to support you;' τις,
because it is on the supposition that Demosthenes comes, not to defend himself personally, but to supply to Ctesiphon professional aid and skilled eloquence, so that any
other practised orator would do as well.

The argument is, 'Real merit is always ap-
preciated at Athens;' Demosthenes answers
(De Cor. § 390), 'Yes, sooner or later,' but
the συνήγορος is wanted to counteract the
συκοφάντης, during the great man's lifetime. But Aeschines says, ἐπερώτησον .. εἰ
ἐγίγνωσκον, 'ask whether they knew' the
heroes, while they were still alive, the judges
being old enough to remember them. Timotheus, at least, is a strange instance to quote
to prove that public gratitude was unfailing.
14. ἀπέκτεινε. A rather curious word to
use of slaughtering a body of men. Iphicrates'
exploit is usually described by κατέκοψε.
§ 245. But Demosthenes' only claim to be
known is for his vices: the dumb instruments
of murder are unclean.
16. Δημοσθένει .. οὐ δώσετε. The best
MSS. read as in the text, but the sense is
rather awkward: for Demosthenes might
say, like Phocion, that Aeschines con-
fessed that men would rather ask why he
had not a crown than why he had. But
Aeschines probably began meaning to say
διὰ τί δώσετε, and puts in the negative παρ'
ὑπόνοιαν, meaning to imply, 'You will not
do so really,' and forgetting the more logical
inference. The various readings, Δημοσθένει δ' ἀντερῶ διὰ τί δώσετε, and φήσετε
added after δώσετε, are both probably conjectures; the first meant to clear up the

δ᾽ ἐάν τις ἐρωτᾷ διὰ τί οὐ δώσετε; ὅτι δωροδόκος, ὅτι δειλὸς,
ὅτι τὴν τάξιν ἔλιπε. καὶ πότερον τοῦτον τιμήσετε, ἢ ὑμᾶς
αὐτοὺς ἀτιμάσετε καὶ τοὺς ὑπὲρ ὑμῶν ἐν τῇ μάχῃ τελευτήσαντας; οὓς νομίζεθ᾽ ὁρᾶν σχετλιάζοντας, εἰ οὗτος στεφανω-
5 θήσεται. καὶ γὰρ ἂν εἴη δεινὸν, ὦ Ἀθηναῖοι, εἰ τὰ μὲν ξύλα
καὶ τοὺς λίθους καὶ τὸν σίδηρον, τὰ ἄφωνα καὶ τὰ ἀγνώμονα,
ἐάν τῳ ἐμπεσόντα ἀποκτείνῃ, ὑπερορίζομεν, καὶ ἐάν τις αὐτὸν
διαχρήσηται, τὴν χεῖρα τὴν τοῦτο πράξασαν χωρὶς τοῦ σώματος θάπτομεν, Δημοσθένην δὲ, ὦ Ἀθηναῖοι, τὸν γράψαντα 246
10 μὲν τὴν πανυστάτην ἔξοδον, προδόντα δὲ τοὺς στρατιώτας,
τοῦτον ὑμεῖς τιμήσετε. οὐκοῦν ὑβρίζονται μὲν οἱ τελευτή-
σαντες, ἀθυμότεροι δὲ οἱ ζῶντες γίγνονται ὁρῶντες τῆς ἀρετῆς
ἆθλον τὸν θάνατον κείμενον, τὴν δὲ μνήμην ἐπιλείπουσαν. τὸ
δὲ μέγιστον, ἐὰν ἐπερωτῶσιν ὑμᾶς οἱ νεώτεροι, πρὸς ποῖον χρὴ
15 παράδειγμα αὐτοὺς τὸν βίον ποιεῖσθαι, τί κρινεῖτε; εὖ γὰρ 247
ἴστε, ὅτι οὐχ αἱ παλαῖστραι οὐδὲ τὰ διδασκαλεῖα οὐδ᾽ ἡ μουσικὴ μόνον παιδεύει τοὺς νεωτέρους, ἀλλὰ πολὺ μᾶλλον τὰ
δημόσια κηρύγματα. κηρύττεταί τις ἐν τῷ θεάτρῳ, ὅτι στεφανοῦται ἀρετῆς ἕνεκα καὶ ἀνδραγαθίας καὶ εὐνοίας, ἄνθρωπος
20 ἀσχημονῶν τῷ βίῳ καὶ βδελυρός· ὁ δέ γε νεώτερος ταῦτ᾽ ἰδὼν
διεφθάρη. δίκην τις δέδωκε πονηρὸς καὶ πορνοβοσκὸς, ὥσπερ
Κτησιφῶν· οἱ δέ γε ἄλλοι πεπαίδευνται. τἀναντία τις ψη-

---

2. ἔλιπε] λέλοιπε z.   3. ἀτιμάσετε] Ita n: ἀτιμωρήτους ἐάσετε bekl: ceteri ἀτι-
μώσετε.   4. νομίζεθ᾽] νομίσαθ᾽ bekl Bekk.   6. Alterum τὰ om. fdk.   16. Post
ἴστε ὦ ἄνδρες Ἀθηναῖοι add. bekl Bekk.   20. ἀσχημονῶν] Ita agekl: ceteri et Bekk.
ἀσχήμων ὤν.

confusion of the thought, the second a gloss
to develope the sense of the text. Τὸ ἀντε-
ροῦ there is an objection, that unless the
speaker turns from Ctesiphon to the Court,
δώσετε has no proper subject: one can
hardly make it mean 'ask why *you and your
countrymen* are going to give it.' To omit
οὐ δώσετε with B. and S. is cutting the knot.

3. ἀτιμάσετε. So Franke from one MS. It
seems to suit the sense better, and ἀτιμοῦν
being so common a word in the orators, perhaps is the likelier of the two to have got in
by an error: else one is tempted to credit Aeschines with the strong image 'deprive yourself and the dead of the name of Athenians.'

4. οὓς νομίζεθ᾽ ὁρᾶν. So below, § 258.

8. τὴν χεῖρα .. θάπτομεν. Probably to
prevent the corpse becoming a vampire, like
the stake through the body in modern times.
So murderers were mutilated, and mutilated
their victims (ἠκρωτηρίαζον) after death.
Josephus, mentioning the custom, gives the
sentimental reason, that the hand was considered alien to the body; which was prob-

ably a real Greek sentiment, but an afterthought. From Ar. Eth. 5. 11. 3, it appears
there was felt to be an ethical meaning in
the posthumous treatment of suicides.

§ 246. *And is not Demosthenes more than
a murderer?*

10. προδόντα δὲ τοὺς στρατιώτας. The
allusion is chiefly to § 146 sq.: also perhaps
to § 152.

15. τί κρινεῖτε. i. q. 'what answer will
your decision give?'

§ 247. *Above all, consider the moral
effect, for good or evil, which public proclamations and trials produce.*

16. παλαῖστραι .... διδασκαλεῖα correspond to γυμναστικὴ and γράμματα, and so,
without being too formally coordinate with
μουσικὴ, exhaust, together with it, the
items of the common Greek curriculum.

22. τἀναντία τις κ.τ.λ. 'Let a man go
home to educate his son, after recording a
vote against virtue and justice, the son has
reason to be unbelieving: here we are come to
a fair case for calling admonition molestation.'

φισάμενος τῶν καλῶν καὶ δικαίων ἐπανελθὼν οἴκαδε παιδεύει
τὸν υἱόν· ὁ δέ γε εἰκότως οὐ πείθεται, ἀλλὰ τὸ νουθετεῖν
248 ἐνταῦθα ἐνοχλεῖν ἤδη καὶ δικαίως ὀνομάζεται. ὡς οὖν μὴ μόνον
κρίνοντες, ἀλλὰ καὶ θεωρούμενοι, οὕτω τὴν ψῆφον φέρετε, εἰς
ἀπολογισμὸν τοῖς νῦν μὲν οὐ παροῦσι τῶν πολιτῶν, ἐπερησο- 5
μένοις δὲ ὑμᾶς, τί ἐδικάζετε. εὖ γὰρ ἴστε, ὦ Ἀθηναῖοι, ὅτι
τοιαύτη δόξει ἡ πόλις εἶναι, ὁποῖός τις ἂν ᾖ ὁ κηρυττόμενος·
ἔστι δὲ ὄνειδος μὴ τοῖς προγόνοις ἡμᾶς, ἀλλὰ τῇ Δημοσθένους
ἀνανδρίᾳ προσεικασθῆναι. πῶς οὖν ἄν τις τὴν τοιαύτην αἰσχύ-
249 νην ἐκφύγοι; ἐὰν τοὺς προκαταλαμβάνοντας τὰ κοινὰ καὶ 10
φιλάνθρωπα τῶν ὀνομάτων, ἀπίστους ὄντας τοῖς ἤθεσι, φυλά-
ξησθε. ἡ γὰρ εὔνοια καὶ τὸ τῆς δημοκρατίας ὄνομα κεῖται
μὲν ἐν μέσῳ, φθάνουσι δ᾽ ἐπ᾽ αὐτὰ καταφεύγοντες τῷ λόγῳ
250 ὡς ἐπὶ πολὺ οἱ τοῖς ἔργοις πλεῖστον ἀπέχοντες. ὅταν οὖν
λάβητε ῥήτορα ξενικῶν στεφάνων καὶ κηρυγμάτων ἐν τοῖς Ἕλ- 15
λησιν ἐπιθυμοῦντα, ἐπανάγειν αὐτὸν κελεύετε τὸν λόγον, ὥσπερ

---

1. παιδεύει] παιδεύειν pr. g.   2. νουθετεῖν] παιδεύειν agm.   3. ἐνταῦθα
ἐνοχλεῖν] Ita agmn: ceteri et Schultz. ἐνοχλεῖν ἐνταῦθ'.   καὶ] Sic ag: ceteri et Bekk.
om.   4. εἰς ἀπολογισμὸν κ.τ.λ.] 'Haec cum superioribus male cohaerent, ita ut ante
ea excidisse quaedam videantur' B. et S.   8. ἡμᾶς] ἡμῶν g, ὑμῶν b, ὑμᾶς e Bekk.:
om. m B. et S.   14. πολὺ] τὸ πολὺ fdq.   16. τὸν λόγον] Ita agmpb: καὶ τῶν
λόγων nfc dekl Ald. ceteri τῶν λόγων.

§ 248. Vote now so that the City may be
clear from Demosthenes' shame;

3. μὴ μόνον .. θεωρούμενοι. Having
not only a judge's responsibility to abstract
truth, but a public officer's to his country
and to the world.

4. εἰς ἀπολογισμόν. He hints as strongly
as he can without offence, that they are
themselves on their trial: possibly he may
have meant to put ἀλλὰ καὶ κρινόμενοι in
the first clause, or at least to suggest it by
the form of the contrast.

9. προσεικασθῆναι. Perhaps the preposition may have the force, not so much of
' being thought like Demosthenes' cowardice'
as 'being judged of by the standard of Demosthenes' cowardice;' which would imply
being actually on a lower moral level than
Demosthenes, since he was their great man.
But the usage of the word supports the more
obvious view, though the etymology would
suit the other at least as well.

§ 249. As it will be if you distrust the
fine names he appeals to,

10. τοὺς προκαταλαμβάνοντας κ.τ.λ.
refers to such arguments as are anticipated
in § 208, etc.: Demosthenes and his party
are the first to call themselves friends to
democracy, and so beg the question whether
they or their opponents are the truer friends.

In the published form, at least, of Demosthenes' speech, we do not find such claptrap
arguments to any considerable extent.

12. ἡ γὰρ εὔνοια κ.τ.λ. 'It is equally
easy for everybody to call himself a patriot
and a democrat : but the first (φθάνουσι) to
screen themselves under such professions are
often those whose conduct is most exactly
opposite to them,' unpatriotic and oligarchical.

§ 250. And require him to give evidence
of respectability, before you leave the Constitution in his power.

15. ξενικῶν στεφάνων can hardly bear a
different sense from that in § 231. The
crown Demosthenes wanted is called a foreign
crown, because given when foreign crowns
ought to be.

16. ἐπανάγειν αὐτὸν κελεύετε τὸν λόγον.
The simplest reading, and also that of the
best group of MSS. The rest have καὶ
τῶν λόγων instead of τὸν λόγον: Bekker
reads καὶ τὸν λόγον, B. and S. τῶν λόγων.
One group of MSS. omit καὶ before τὰs
βεβαιώσεις, where though convenient it
is not necessary : perhaps the doubt about
it there led to confusion above. The genitive λόγων, if right, must be by a kind of
attraction, to form a parallelism with κτημάτων.

καὶ τὰς βεβαιώσεις τῶν κτημάτων ὁ νόμος κελεύει ποιεῖσθαι,
εἰς βίον ἀξιόχρεων καὶ τρόπον σώφρονα. ὅτῳ δὲ ταῦτα μὴ
μαρτυρεῖται, μὴ βεβαιοῦτε αὐτῷ τοὺς ἐπαίνους, καὶ τῆς δημοκρατίας ἐπιμελήθητε ἤδη διαφευγούσης ὑμᾶς. ἢ οὐ δεινὸν δοκεῖ 251
5 ὑμῖν εἶναι, εἰ τὸ μὲν βουλευτήριον καὶ ὁ δῆμος παρορᾶται, αἱ
δ' ἐπιστολαὶ καὶ πρεσβεῖαι ἀφικνοῦνται εἰς ἰδιωτικὰς οἰκίας,
οὐ παρὰ τῶν τυχόντων ἀνθρώπων, ἀλλὰ παρὰ τῶν πρωτευόν-
των ἐν τῇ Ἀσίᾳ καὶ τῇ Εὐρώπῃ; καὶ ἐφ' οἷς ἐστιν ἐκ τῶν
νόμων ζημία θάνατος, ταῦτά τινες οὐκ ἐξαρνοῦνται πράττειν,
10 ἀλλ' ὁμολογοῦσιν ἐν τῷ δήμῳ, καὶ τὰς ἐπιστολὰς ἀλλήλοις
παραναγιγνώσκουσιν, καὶ παρακελεύονται οἱ μὲν ὑμῖν βλέπειν
εἰς τὰ ἑαυτῶν πρόσωπα ὡς φύλακες τῆς δημοκρατίας, ἕτεροι
δ' αἰτοῦσι δωρεὰς ὡς σωτῆρες τῆς πόλεως ὄντες. ὁ δὲ δῆμος 252
ἐκ τῆς ἀθυμίας τῶν συμβεβηκότων ὥσπερ παραγεγηρακὼς ἢ
15 παρανοίας ἑαλωκὼς αὐτὸ μόνον τοὔνομα τῆς δημοκρατίας περι-
ποιεῖται, τῶν δ' ἔργων ἑτέροις παρακεχώρηκεν. ἔπειτ' ἀπέρ-
χεσθε ἐκ τῶν ἐκκλησιῶν οὐ βουλευσάμενοι, ἀλλ' ὥσπερ ἐκ τῶν
ἐράνων, τὰ περιόντα νειμάμενοι. ὅτι δ' οὐ ληρῶ, ἐκεῖθεν τὸν 253
λόγον θεωρήσατε. ἐγένετό τις, ἄχθομαι δὲ πολλάκις μεμνη-

---

1. καὶ] Om. fcd Bekk. 3. μαρτυρεῖται] ·ρεῖτε bel: 'Fort. μαρτυρεῖ' Saupp.
4. δοκεῖ ὑμῖν εἶναι] Ita agmz: ὑμῖν εἶναι δοκεῖ bekl: ceteri et Bekk. ὑμῖν δοκεῖ εἶναι.
5. εἰ] ὅτι ηfcekl Bekk. 6. πρεσβεῖαι] αἱ πρεσβεῖαι Bekk. cum omnibus praeter
agmp. 11. οἱ μὲν ὑμῖν] ὑμῖν οἱ μὲν fcdgekl, οἱ μὲν ὑμᾶς b: 'Fort. ὑμῖν delendum'
Spp., et delet Schultz. 19. πολλάκις μεμνημένος] μεμνημένος πολλάκις bekl Bekk.

---

1. τὰς βεβαιώσεις. Where the vendor's
title was disputed, it would often be alleged
that he was a mere colourable owner, and
then the question of his way of living would
be relevant.

§ 251. Is it not shameful, for private
men to assume the dignity and power of the
state,

6. πρεσβεῖαι.. οἰκίας. He is no doubt
thinking of the story told by Dinarchus in
Dem. p. 92, § 92: whatever were the facts
as to Demosthenes' refusal of the application, there seems no room to doubt that it
was made. The Theban envoys will thus
be οἱ πρωτεύοντες ἐν τῇ Εὐρώπῃ, the Asia-
tics, of course, are the Persian court.

8. ἐφ' οἷς ἐστὶν κ.τ.λ. Taking bribes
from foreign powers; while Demosthenes
claimed credit for having money from Persia to administer.

10. τὰς ἐπιστολὰς.. παραναγιγνώσκουσιν must describe Demosthenes and a partisan
each reading a letter from abroad, the information of one supplementing that of the
other. We cannot tell what exact story is

alluded to, but it is probably a case of the
ἐπιστολὰς ψευδεῖς of § 225.

§ 252. While the state, like a father in
his dotage, is content to be superseded in its
lifetime?

14. παραγεγηρακώς. 'Having fallen
into dotage' gradually and naturally, so that
it was not παρανοίας ἑαλωκὼς by one definite act, but the undutiful heir stepped into
possession with his father's impotent acquiescence.

18. τὰ περιόντα νειμάμενοι. The politicians divided the substantial proceeds of
their policy : out of the surplus, they found
funds to pay the citizens, who then went
away satisfied.

§ 253. While law was regarded, the fugi-
tives after Chaeronea were punished :

19. ἐγένετό τις. We do not know his
name: Lycurgus (in Leocr. p. 154, § 52)
says that several persons were put to death
by the Areopagus on the charge. From
his tone in the passage, it is clear that the
people were shocked at their act, at least
when the danger was over; especially, no

μένος τὰς ἀτυχίας τῆς πόλεως, ἐνταῦθ᾽ ἀνὴρ ἰδιώτης, ὃς ἐκπλεῖ
μόνον εἰς Σάμον ἐπιχειρήσας ὡς προδότης τῆς πατρίδος αὐθημερὸν ὑπὸ τῆς ἐξ Ἀρείου πάγου βουλῆς θανάτῳ ἐζημιώθη.
ἕτερος δ᾽ ἰδιώτης ἐκπλεύσας εἰς Ῥόδον, ὅτι τὸν φόβον ἀνάν-
δρως ἤνεγκε, πρώην ποτὲ εἰσηγγέλθη καὶ ἴσαι αἱ ψῆφοι αὐτῷ 5
ἐγένοντο· εἰ δὲ μία μόνον μετέπεσεν, ὑπερώριστ᾽ ἂν ἢ ἀπέ-
254 θανεν. ἀντιθῶμεν δὴ τὸ νῦν γιγνόμενον. ἀνὴρ ῥήτωρ, ὁ πάντων τῶν κακῶν αἴτιος, ἔλιπε μὲν τὴν ἀπὸ στρατοπέδου τάξιν,
ἀπέδρα δ᾽ ἐκ τῆς πόλεως· οὗτος στεφανοῦσθαι ἀξιοῖ καὶ κηρύττεσθαι οἴεται δεῖν. οὐκ ἀποπέμψετε τὸν ἄνθρωπον ὡς κοινὴν 10
τῶν Ἑλλήνων συμφοράν; ἢ συλλαβόντες ὡς λῃστὴν τῶν πραγμάτων, ἐπ᾽ ὀνομάτων διὰ τῆς πολιτείας πλέοντα, τιμωρήσεσθε;
255 καὶ τὸν καιρὸν μὴν μνήσθητε, ἐν ᾧ τὴν ψῆφον φέρετε. ἡμερῶν μὲν ὀλίγων μέλλει τὰ Πύθια γίγνεσθαι καὶ τὸ συνέδριον
τὸ τῶν Ἑλλήνων συλλέγεσθαι· διαβέβληται δ᾽ ἡμῶν ἡ πόλις ἐκ 15
τῶν Δημοσθένους πολιτευμάτων περὶ τοὺς νῦν καιρούς· δόξετε δ᾽,
ἐὰν μὲν τοῦτον στεφανώσητε, ὁμογνώμονες εἶναι τοῖς παραβαίνουσι

2. μόνον] Ita Taylor. et fortasse k : om. fdq B. et S.: ceteri μόνος.   4. ἰδιώτης
ἐκπλεύσας] πλεύσας ἰδιώτης Harpocr.: ἐκπλεύσας ἰδιώτης bekl B. et S. ἰδιώτης om. Schultz. :
ceteri libri et Bekk. ἰδιώτης ἐκπλεύσας.   5. Post πρώην μὲν add. Harpocr. Phot.
Suid.   αἱ ψῆφοι αὐτῷ] αὐτῷ αἱ ψῆφοι bekl Bekk.   6. μόνον] ψῆφος Harpocr.
'Fortasse utrumque glossatoribus debetur' B. et S.   7. νῦν] νυνὶ bekl Bekk.   13. μὴν
μνήσθητε ..] μὴ μνήσθητε agm Vat. bekl, μὴν μνήσθητε p Bekk., μὴν μέμνησθε Ald. B.
et S., ceteri et Schultz. μέμνησθε: 'fort. μὴ οὐ μνήσθητε' Saupp.   15. ἡμῶν] Om.
bekl Bekk. B. et S.

doubt, in the case of Autolycus, who only sent
away his wife and children. From ἐκπλεῖν
μόνον (si vera l.) ἐπιχειρήσας, one might
suppose that it is he whom Aeschines means.

4. ἕτερος δ᾽ ἰδιώτης. Leocrates : vid.
Lyc. in Leocr. passim. ἰδιώτης twice over,
opposed to Demosthenes, whose public character laid on him especial obligations to
remain.

5. πρώην ποτέ. Less than a year before,
for Lycurgus' speech (p. 153, § 45) was
delivered eight years after his flight.

6. εἰ δὲ μία κ.τ.λ. The process can
hardly have been ἀτίμητος, but we know
from the case of Socrates that a small
majority for condemnation did not always
involve a mild assessment of penalty.

§ 254. Will you acquit Demosthenes for
the same conduct, and thereby declare him to
be above law?

8. ἔλιπε μὲν .. πόλεως: cp. above, § 159.

10. οἴεται δεῖν. A climax of irony after
ἀξιοῖ, which has come to mean no more
than 'claims.' 'He puts in a claim to a
crown, and thinks it proper and necessary
that he should have a proclamation.'

ἀποπέμψετε. i. q. ἀποπομπὴν ποιή-

σεσθε, 'velut piaculi et monstri,' Orelli ap.
Brem. ad loc.: it includes no doubt the
literal local sense = ὑπερώρισθαι, above, § 245.

11. ἢ συλλαβόντες κ.τ.λ. 'Or take
him up and punish him for a rover upon the
sea of politics, who rigs his bark with words
and makes prize of things.' ἐπ᾽ ὀνομάτων,
more literally, 'embarked on a bottom of
words.' For the metaphor, cp. Plat. Phaed.
p. 85 D.

§ 255. Will you let Athens be committed
to Demosthenes' policy, before the assembly of
Greece at the Pythian games?

13. ἡμερῶν μὲν ὀλίγων. They were
held, it appears, early in the spring.

14. τὸ συνέδριον. Usually interpreted of
the ἱαρινὴ Πυλαία of the Amphictyons : perhaps merely of the πανήγυρις of spectators.

15. διαβέβληται. In consequence of
his correspondence with Persia, when the
anti-Persian feeling was at its height, and
centred in Alexander's person.

17. τοῖς παραβαίνουσι .. εἰρήνην. Especially the Greeks in the Persian service,
who were formally traitors to their own
governments, these having submitted to
Macedon.

τὴν κοινὴν εἰρήνην, ἐὰν δὲ τοὐναντίον τούτου πράξητε, ἀπολύσετε
τὸν δῆμον τῶν αἰτιῶν.

Μὴ οὖν ὡς ὑπὲρ ἀλλοτρίας, ἀλλ᾽ ὡς ὑπὲρ οἰκείας τῆς πό- 256
λεως βουλεύεσθε, καὶ τὰς φιλοτιμίας μὴ νέμετε, ἀλλὰ κρίνετε,
5 καὶ τὰς δωρεὰς εἰς βελτίω σώματα καὶ ἄνδρας ἀξιολογωτέρους
ἀπόθεσθε, καὶ μὴ μόνον τοῖς ὠσὶν, ἀλλὰ καὶ τοῖς ὄμμασι δια-
βλέψαντες εἰς ὑμᾶς αὐτοὺς βουλεύσασθε, τίνες ὑμῶν εἰσιν οἱ
βοηθήσοντες Δημοσθένει, πότερον οἱ συγκυνηγέται, ἢ οἱ συγ-
γυμνασταὶ αὐτοῦ, ὅτ᾽ ἦν ἐν ἡλικίᾳ. ἀλλὰ μὰ τὸν Δία τὸν
10 Ὀλύμπιον οὐχ ὗς ἀγρίους κυνηγετῶν οὐδὲ τῆς τοῦ σώματος
εὐεξίας ἐπιμελόμενος, ἀλλ᾽ ἐπασκῶν τέχνας ἐπὶ τοὺς τὰς οὐσίας
κεκτημένους διαγεγένηται. ἀλλ᾽ εἰς τὴν ἀλαζονείαν ἀποβλέ- 257
ψαντες, ὅταν φῇ Βυζαντίους μὲν ἐκ τῶν χειρῶν πρεσβεύσας
ἐξελέσθαι τοῦ Φιλίππου, ἀποστῆσαι δὲ Ἀκαρνᾶνας, ἐκπλῆξαι
15 δὲ Θηβαίους δημηγορήσας· οἴεται γὰρ ὑμᾶς εἰς τοσοῦτον εὐη-
θείας ἤδη προβεβηκέναι, ὥστε καὶ ταῦτα ἀναπεισθήσεσθαι, ὥσπερ
Πειθὼ τρέφοντας, ἀλλ᾽ οὐ συκοφάντην ἄνθρωπον ἐν τῇ πόλει.
ὅταν δ᾽ ἐπὶ τελευτῆς ἤδη τοῦ λόγου συνηγόρους τοὺς κοινωνοὺς 258
τῶν δωροδοκημάτων αὐτῷ παρακαλῇ, ὑπολαμβάνετε ὁρᾶν ἐπὶ

5. ἄνδρας ἀξιολογωτέρους] ἀξιολογωτέρους ἄνδρας agmnfed.   11. ἐπιμελόμενος]
Sic ak: ceteri ἐπιμελούμενος. Statim διατελέλεκεν addunt agmnc, διατετέληκεν p Vat.
Laur. Flor. Barb.   Inter §§ 256–257, Frankio 'nonnulla excidisse videntur.'   14. τοῦ
Φιλίππου] τῶν Φιλίππου nfk Bekk.   17. τῇ] Om. z.

§ 256. *Think seriously of your duties:
look at the appearance of Demosthenes and
his supporters as an index of their habits:*
4. **καὶ τὰς φιλοτιμίας μὴ νέμετε, ἀλλὰ
κρίνετε.** 'Make the objects of ambition a
prize and not a lottery.' νέμειν is to give
away indiscriminately to the first applicant.
5. **εἰς βελτίω σώματα.** 'Do not give
them except to some one who is more of a
man.' Whether the bodily feebleness of
Demosthenes' supporters, as well as his own,
is intended, will depend on the range of
meaning of ὑμᾶς αὐτούς. Probably it includes the whole audience, or even the whole
nation: the thought is, 'Sift Demosthenes'
defenders by their looks as well as their
words. They do not *look* like the companions of his youthful sports: they are in
fact (§ 258) οἱ κοινωνοὶ τῶν δωροδοκημάτων.' If ὑμᾶς αὐτοὺς and ὑμῶν mean the
judges only, the point must be 'Do not
vote for Demosthenes, unless he has an
honourable personal claim on any of you.'
9. **ἀλλὰ μὰ τὸν Δία κ.τ.λ.** Demosthenes'
unmanly habits in youth seem unquestionable: his own explanation (Ae. in Tim. p.
17, § 126) of the nickname Βάταλος or
Βάτταλος, suggests that they arose rather

from his being brought up by women than
from weak health.
11. **ἐπασκῶν τέχνας κ.τ.λ.:** cp. Ae. in
Tim. p. 24, §§ 170 sq.
§ 257. *Think of his boastfulness, almost
blasphemous:*
12. Franke thinks some words are lost
before the beginning of this sentence —
whether because there is no apodosis to
ἀποβλέψαντες, or for want of connection
with the former section, is not stated. The
latter is not a good reason, for the sentence
is parallel in form with those before and
after, and so is not to be expected to start
from a point of intersection: and the former
is not a decisive one, as the parenthesis οἴεται
γὰρ might break the intended construction.
Instead of the inference from his ἀλαζονεία,
we have an aggravated instance of it.
17. **συκοφάντην ἄνθρωπον.** Opposed
to the eloquent goddess.
§ 258. *Think his array of corrupt supporters met by Solon, defending his own laws,*
18. See the Life of Aeschines for the
rhetorical point of this appeal.
19. **ἐπὶ τοῦ βήματος, οὗ νῦν κ.τ.λ.**
With a reference to what Demosthenes is
supposed to say in § 208.

τοῦ βήματος, οὗ νῦν ἑστηκὼς ἐγὼ λέγω, ἀντιπαρατεταγμένους
πρὸς τὴν τούτων ἀσέλγειαν τοὺς τῆς πόλεως εὐεργέτας, Σόλωνα
μὲν τὸν καλλίστοις νόμοις κοσμήσαντα τὴν δημοκρατίαν, ἄνδρα
φιλόσοφον καὶ νομοθέτην ἀγαθόν, σωφρόνως, ὡς προσῆκεν αὐτῷ,
δεόμενον ὑμῶν μηδενὶ τρόπῳ τοὺς Δημοσθένους λόγους περὶ 5
259 πλείονος ποιήσασθαι τῶν ὅρκων καὶ τῶν νόμων, Ἀριστείδην
δὲ τὸν τοὺς φόρους τάξαντα τοῖς Ἕλλησιν, οὗ τελευτήσαντος
τὰς θυγατέρας ἐξέδωκεν ὁ δῆμος, σχετλιάζοντα ἐπὶ τῷ τῆς
δικαιοσύνης προπηλακισμῷ καὶ ἐπερωτῶντα, εἰ οὐκ αἰσχύνεσθε,
εἰ οἱ μὲν πατέρες ὑμῶν Ἄρθμιον τὸν Ζελείτην κομίσαντα εἰς 10
τὴν Ἑλλάδα τὸ ἐκ Μήδων χρυσίον, ἐπιδημήσαντα εἰς τὴν
πόλιν, πρόξενον ὄντα τοῦ δήμου τῶν Ἀθηναίων, παρ' οὐδὲν
μὲν ἦλθον ἀποκτεῖναι, ἐξεκήρυξαν δ' ἐκ τῆς πόλεως καὶ ἐξ
ἁπάσης ἧς Ἀθηναῖοι ἄρχουσιν, ὑμεῖς δὲ Δημοσθένην, οὐ κομίσαντα τὸ ἐκ Μήδων χρυσίον, ἀλλὰ δωροδοκήσαντα καὶ ἔτι καὶ 15
νῦν κεκτημένον, χρυσῷ στεφάνῳ μέλλετε στεφανοῦν. Θεμι-
στοκλέα δὲ καὶ τοὺς ἐν Μαραθῶνι τελευτήσαντας καὶ τοὺς ἐν
Πλαταιαῖς καὶ αὐτοὺς τοὺς τάφους τοὺς τῶν προγόνων οὐκ
οἴεσθε στενάξειν, εἰ ὁ μετὰ τῶν βαρβάρων ὁμολογῶν τοῖς
Ἕλλησιν ἀντιπράττειν στεφανωθήσεται ; 20
260 Ἐγὼ μὲν οὖν, ὦ γῆ καὶ ἥλιε καὶ ἀρετὴ καὶ σύνεσις καὶ

---

10. εἰ] ὅτι bekl.　12. τῶν Ἀθηναίων] τοῦ Vat. mz Flor. Barb. cdk et teste Schultz f.
19. οἴεσθε στενάξειν] Ita Flor. bekl Frank., ἂν οἴεσθε στενάξειν e, ἂν οἴεσθε ἀναστενάξαι n
Laur. Barb. fcdq, οἴεσθε στενάξαι agm z Vat., ἂν οἴεσθε στενάξαι B. et S. Schultz.

2. πρὸς τὴν τούτων ἀσέλγειαν. Several
of Demosthenes' partisans were open to
attack for personal profligacy : Hyperides
and Chares, as well as Ctesiphon.

Σόλωνα κ.τ.λ. He is conceived rather
as having provided the democracy with a
good code against it arose, than as having
founded it : but cp. ad § 38. For the second
rather frigid clause of the panegyric, cp.
above, § 108 : for σωφρόνως ὡς προσῆκεν
αὐτῷ, Ae. in. Tim. p. 4, § 25.

§ 259. By Aristides in the name of justice, by the heroes of the Persian war in that
of Hellas.

9. εἰ οὐκ αἰσχύνεσθε, εἰ. The archetype
of one group of MSS., being offended by the
double εἰ, altered the second to ὅτι. The
first would be better worth altering, and as
that cannot be altered, we must suppose
that Aeschines did not feel it as a fault.

10. Ἄρθμιον τὸν Ζελείτην: cp. Demosth.
Phil. 3, p. 119, § 42 sqq.

12. παρ' οὐδὲν μὲν ἦλθον. 'Came

within a hair's breadth of killing him,' lit.
' within a nothing.'

13. ἐξεκήρυξαν. In terms (Demosth.
l. c.) amounting to a sentence of death.

14. οὐ κομίσαντα κ.τ.λ. The point is,
' Arthmius brought the money for the
nation : Demosthenes kept it for himself.'

18. οὐκ οἴεσθε στενάξειν. All the best
MSS. read στενάξαι or ἀναστενάξαι, with or
without ἄν. Hence there is something to be
said for Bremi's view, that ἂν στενάξαι and
στενάξειν are rival conjectures, for a harsh
but genuine reading οὐκ οἴεσθε ἀναστενάξαι.
But the future seems really required by the
sense.

19. τοῖς Ἕλλησιν. He regards Alexander as the head of a bona fide Greek
federation, as Isocrates had wished to make
Philip.

§ 260. I at least have done my duty to
the cause of virtue and culture.

21. ὦ γῆ καὶ ἥλιε κ.τ.λ. Ridiculed by
Demosthenes, De Cor. § 162.

K

παιδεία, ᾗ διαγιγνώσκομεν τὰ καλὰ καὶ τὰ αἰσχρὰ, βεβοήθηκα καὶ εἴρηκα. καὶ εἰ μὲν καλῶς καὶ ἀξίως τοῦ ἀδικήματος
κατηγόρηκα, εἶπον ὡς ἐβουλόμην, εἰ δὲ ἐνδεεστέρως, ὡς ἐδυνάμην. ὑμεῖς δὲ καὶ ἐκ τῶν εἰρημένων λόγων καὶ ἐκ τῶν παρα-
5 λελειμμένων αὐτοὶ τὰ δίκαια καὶ τὰ συμφέροντα ὑπὲρ τῆς πόλεως ψηφίσασθε.

4. **παραλελειμμένων**] παραλειπομένων f Barb. *bekl* Bekk.

1. **βεβοήθηκα.** 'I have done my duty
to you,' to the more abstract, at least, of
the deities invoked. As Demosthenes charges
him with roaring out these words as if he
were on the stage, Reiske conjectured βε-
βόηκα : which is found in three MSS., and
is not absurd, as Demosthenes uses the word
for 'lifting up the voice in a protest,' De
Cor. § 183.   But it is no doubt a mere

conjecture, from unfamiliarity with βοηθεῖν
used absolutely.

2. **καὶ εἰ μὲν καλῶς.** A rhetorical commonplace reproduced by the writer of the
Second Book of Maccabees, 15. 38.

5. **αὐτοί.** Especially correlative to τῶν
παραλελειμμένων, ' supplying from your
own knowledge any point that I have left
out.'

ΔΗΜΟΣΘΕΝΟΥΣ

ΥΠΕΡ ΚΤΗΣΙΦΩΝΤΟΣ ΠΕΡΙ ΤΟΥ ΣΤΕΦΑΝΟΥ ΛΟΓΟΣ.

ΔΗΜΟΣΘΕΝΟΥΣ

ΥΠΕΡ ΚΤΗΣΙΦΩΝΤΟΣ ΠΕΡΙ ΤΟΥ
ΣΤΕΦΑΝΟΥ ΛΟΓΟΣ.

ΛΙΒΑΝΙΟΥ ΥΠΟΘΕΣΙΣ.

Τεῖχος μὲν ὁ ῥήτωρ ὑπὲρ Ἀθηναίων προὐβάλετο τῶν συνήθων τούτων καὶ χειροποιήτων ἀρραγέστερόν τε καὶ βέλτιον, τήν τε εἰς τὴν πόλιν εὔνοιαν καὶ περὶ λόγους δεινότητα, ὡς αὐτὸς εἴρηκεν " οὐ λίθοις καὶ πλίνθοις τὰς Ἀθήνας ὠχύρωσα, ἀλλὰ μεγάλαις δυνάμεσι καὶ πολλῇ τινὶ συμμαχίᾳ, τῇ μὲν ἐκ γῆς, τῇ δὲ ἐκ θαλάττης·" οὐ μὴν ἀλλὰ καὶ εἰς τὸν χειροποίητον περίβολον οὐ μικρὰ τῇ πόλει συνεβάλετο. πεπονηκότος γὰρ κατὰ πολλὰ μέρη τοῦ τείχους τοῖς Ἀθηναίοις, ἐπειδὴ ἔδοξεν ἀνορθοῦν αὐτό, ᾑρέθησαν ἐπὶ τὸ ἔργον ἄνδρες δέκα, φυλῆς ἑκάστης εἷς, οὓς ἔδει τὴν ἐπιμέλειαν παρέχεσθαι ψιλήν· τὸ γὰρ ἀνάλωμα δημόσιον. εἷς τοίνυν τούτων καὶ ὁ ῥήτωρ γενόμενος οὐχ ὁμοίως τοῖς ἄλλοις τὴν ἐπιμέλειαν μόνην εἰσήνεγκε τῇ χρείᾳ, ἀλλὰ τὸ μὲν ἔργον ἀμέμπτως ἀπετέλεσε, τὰ δὲ χρήματα ἔδωκεν οἴκοθεν τῇ πόλει. ἐπήνεσεν αὐτοῦ τὴν εὔνοιαν ταύτην ἡ βουλή, καὶ τὴν προθυμίαν ἡμείψατο στεφάνῳ χρυσῷ· ἕτοιμοι γὰρ Ἀθηναῖοι πρὸς τὰς χάριτας τῶν εὖ ποιούντων. Κτησιφῶν δὲ ἦν ὁ τὴν γνώμην εἰπὼν ὡς δεῖ στεφανῶσαι τὸν Δημοσθένην, ἐν μὲν καιρῷ τοῖς Διονυσίοις, ἐν δὲ τόπῳ τῷ τοῦ Διονύσου θεάτρῳ, ἐν δὲ θεαταῖς πᾶσι τοῖς Ἕλλησιν, οὓς ἡ πανήγυρις συνήγιγε· καὶ τούτων ἐναντίον ἀνειπεῖν τὸν κήρυκα ὅτι στεφανοῖ Δημοσθένην Δημοσθένους Παιανιέα ἡ πόλις ἀρετῆς συμπάσης ἕνεκα καὶ εὐνοίας τῆς πρὸς αὐτήν. ἣν οὖν πανταχόθεν ἡ τιμὴ θαυμαστή· διὸ καὶ φθόνος αὐτῆς ἥψατο, καὶ τοῦ ψηφίσματος ἀπηνέχθη παρανόμων γραφή. Αἰσχίνης γὰρ ἐχθρὸς ὢν τοῦ Δημοσθένους ἀγῶνα παρανόμων ἐπήγγειλε Κτησιφῶντι, λέγων ἄρχοντα γεγονότα τὸν Δημοσθένην καὶ μὴ δόντα λόγον ὑπεύθυνον εἶναι, νόμον δὲ κελεύειν τοὺς ὑπευθύνους μὴ στεφανοῦν, καὶ πάλιν νόμου παρεχόμενος τὸν κελεύοντα, ἐὰν μέν τινα ὁ δῆμος ὁ Ἀθηναίων στεφανοῖ, ἐν τῇ ἐκκλησίᾳ τὸν στέφανον ἀναγορεύεσθαι, ἐὰν δὲ ἡ βουλή, ἐν τῷ βουλευτηρίῳ, ἀλλαχόθι δὲ μὴ ἐξεῖναι. φησὶ δὲ καὶ τοὺς ἐπαίνους εἶναι τοὺς ἐπὶ τῷ Δημοσθένει ψευδεῖς· μὴ γὰρ πεπολιτεῦσθαι καλῶς τὸν ῥήτορα, ἀλλὰ καὶ δωροδόκον εἶναι καὶ πολλῶν κακῶν αἴτιον τῇ πόλει. καὶ τάξει γε ταύτῃ τῆς κατηγορίας Αἰσχίνης κέχρηται, πρῶτον εἰπὼν περὶ τοῦ τῶν ὑπευθύνων νόμου καὶ δεύτερον περὶ τοῦ τῶν κηρυγμάτων καὶ τρίτον περὶ τῆς πολιτείας· ἠξίωσε δὲ καὶ τὸν Δημοσθένην τὴν αὐτὴν τάξιν ποιήσασθαι. ὁ δὲ ῥήτωρ καὶ ἀπὸ τῆς πολιτείας τὴν ἀρχὴν ἐποιήσατο καὶ πάλιν εἰς ταύτην τὸν λόγον κατέστρεψε, τεχνικῶς ποιῶν· δεῖ γὰρ ἄρχεσθαί τε ἀπὸ τῶν ἰσχυροτέρων καὶ λήγειν εἰς ταῦτα· μέσα δὲ τέθεικε τὰ περὶ τῶν νόμων, καὶ τῷ μὲν περὶ τῶν ὑπευθύνων ἀντιτίθησι διανοίας, τῷ δὲ περὶ τῶν κηρυγμάτων νόμον ἕτερον ἤτοι νόμου μέρος, ὥς φησιν αὐτός, ἐν ᾧ συγκεχώρηται καὶ ἐν τῷ θεάτρῳ κηρύττειν, ἐὰν ὁ δῆμος ἢ ἡ βουλὴ τοῦτο ψηφίσηται.

ΕΤΕΡΑ ΥΠΟΘΕΣΙΣ.

Ἀθηναῖοι καὶ Θηβαῖοι πολεμοῦντες πρὸς Φίλιππον ἐν Χαιρωνείᾳ, πόλει τῆς Βοιωτίας, ἡττήθησαν. ἐπικρατήσας οὖν ὁ Μακεδὼν φρουρὰν μὲν εἰς τὰς Θήβας ἐνέβαλε, καὶ εἶχεν ὑπὸ χεῖρα δουλεύουσαν. ἐλπίσαντες οὖν τὸ αὐτὸ παθεῖν Ἀθηναῖοι καὶ ὅσον οὐδέπω κατ' αὐτῶν ἥξειν προσδοκῶντες τὸν τύραννον, ἐσκέψαντο τὰ πεπονηκότα μέρη τῷ χρόνῳ τοῦ τείχους ἐπανορθώσασθαι, καὶ δὴ ἀφ' ἑκάστης φυλῆς τειχοποιοὶ προεβλήθησαν. τοιόνδε καὶ ἡ Πανδιονὶς ἐξ ἑαυτῆς εἵλετο πρὸς τὴν χρείαν τὸν ῥήτορα. τῆς τοίνυν ἐργασίας ἐν χερσὶν οὔσης, προσδεηθεὶς ἔτι χρημάτων μετὰ τὰ δεδομένα ὑπὸ τῆς πόλεως, ὁ ῥήτωρ ἐκ τῶν ἰδίων ἐδαπάνησε, καὶ οὐκ ἐλογίσατο αὐτὰ τῇ πόλει, ἀλλὰ καὶ ἐχαρίσατο. ταύτην ἀφορμὴν ὁ Κτησιφῶν, εἰς τῶν πολιτευομένων, δεξάμενος εἰσήνεγκε γνώμην ἐν τῇ βουλῇ περὶ αὐτοῦ τοιαύτην, "ἐπειδὴ διατελεῖ Δημοσθένης ὁ Δημοσθένους παρ' ὅλον τὸν βίον εὔνοιαν εἰς τὴν πόλιν ἐπιδεικνύμενος, καὶ νῦν δὲ τειχοποιὸς ὢν καὶ προσδεηθεὶς χρημάτων οἴκοθεν παρέσχε καὶ ἐχαρίσατο, διὰ τοῦτο δεδόχθαι τῇ βουλῇ καὶ τῷ δήμῳ στεφανοῦσθαι αὐτὸν χρυσῷ στεφάνῳ, ἐν τῷ θεάτρῳ, τραγῳδιῶν ἀγομένων καινῶν," ἴσως ὅτε πλήθη συντρέχει ἐπιθυμοῦντα καινὰ δράματα βλέπειν. εἰσαγομένου τοίνυν καὶ εἰς τὸν δῆμον τοῦ προβουλεύματος, ἐφίσταται τοῦ Κτησιφῶντος κατήγορος Αἰσχίνης ἐκ τῆς πολιτείας ὑπάρχων ἐχθρὸς, παράνομον εἶναι φάσκων πρὸς τρεῖς νόμους τὸ ψήφισμα, ἕνα μὲν τὸν κελεύοντα τὸν ὑπεύθυνον μὴ στεφανοῦσθαι, πρὶν ἂν δῷ τὰς εὐθύνας· οὔπω δὲ ταύτας, φησὶν, ὁ Δημοσθένης ἐδεδώκει καὶ τὰ θεωρικὰ διοικῶν καὶ τειχοποιῶν, καὶ ἔδει ἀναμεῖναι καὶ ἐπισχεῖν τὸ γέρας, ἕως ἂν ὀφθῇ καθαρὸς ἐξετασθείς. δεύτερον δὲ ἀναγινώσκει νόμον τὸν κελεύοντα ἐν πυκνὶ στεφανοῦσθαι, ἐν τῇ ἐκκλησίᾳ, διαβάλλων τοὺς πολίτας τοὺς δεξαμένους ἐν τῷ θεάτρῳ ἀναγορευθῆναι τοῦ Δημοσθένους τὸν στέφανον. ὁ δὲ τρίτος νόμος εἰς τὴν ὅλην ὁρᾷ τοῦ βίου καὶ τῆς πολιτείας ἐξέτασιν· κελεύει γὰρ μηδέποτε ψευδῆ γράμματα εἰς τὸ Μητρῷον εἰσάγειν, ἔνθα ἐστὶν ὅλα τὰ δημόσια γράμματα. ἐψεύσατο δὲ, φησὶν, εὔνοιαν καὶ σπουδὴν μαρτυρήσας τῷ Δημοσθένει· κακόνους γὰρ μᾶλλον καὶ πολέμιος εὑρίσκεται τῇ πατρίδι. τούτου τοῦ νόμου χρησίμου τυγχάνοντος, τοῦ τρίτου, ἀντιλαβόμενος ὥσπερ τινὸς ἀγκύρας ὁ ῥήτωρ κατεπάλαισε τὸν ἀντίδικον, μεθόδῳ

δεινοτάτη καὶ σοφωτάτη τῇ περὶ τοῦ κατηγόρου χρησάμενος· ἐκεῖθεν γὰρ ἔσχι
λαβὴν ἑλεῖν καὶ καταγωνίσασθαι τὸν πολέμιον. τοὺς μὲν γὰρ ἄλλους δύο νόμους, τόν τε τῶν ὑπευθύνων καὶ τὸν τοῦ κηρύγματος, εἰς τὸ μέσον τοῦ λόγου
ἀπέρριψε, στρατηγικῶς κακοὺς εἰς μέσον ἐλάσας, τῷ δὲ ἰσχυροτάτῳ εἰς τὰ ἄκρα
προσκέχρηται, τὸ σαθρὸν τῶν ἄλλων ἐξ ἑκατέρου ῥωννύς. ἔοικε δὲ καὶ διοικεῖν
πρὸς τὸ συμφέρον τὸν λόγον, καὶ οὐ σφόδρα ἀναιδῶς τὴν τέχνην ἐπιδεικνύμενος.
δοκῶν γὰρ ἐν πρώτοις ὑπερβαίνειν τὸ νόμιμον, ἑτέρῳ τρόπῳ τῷ νομίμῳ προσ-
κέχρηται· καὶ γὰρ νόμον ἀνέγνω Αἰσχίνης τὸν περὶ τῶν στεφάνων ψευδῆ, πρὸς
ὃν ὁ ῥήτωρ ἀποκρινόμενος εὗρε καιρὸν εἰς μέσον ἀγαγεῖν τὰ ἑαυτοῦ πολιτεύματα,
ὡς νομίμῳ μαχόμενος. καὶ ἡ μὲν διοίκησις τοῦ λόγου τοιαύτη, κεφάλαιον δὲ
ἰσχυρὸν τῷ μὲν Αἰσχίνῃ τὸ νόμιμον, τῷ δὲ ῥήτορι τὸ δίκαιον, κοινὸν δὲ ἀπὸ τοῦ
ἴσου τὸ συμφέρον, οὐκ ἔχον φανερὰν τὴν ἐξέτασιν. ἡ στάσις ἔγγραφος πραγ-
ματική· περὶ ῥητοῦ γὰρ τὸ ψήφισμα.

Τῆς δὲ γραφῆς ἔτι Φιλίππου ζῶντος ἀποτεθείσης, ἐπὶ Ἀλεξάνδρου διαδεξα-
μένου τὴν ἀρχὴν ὁ λόγος ἐστὶ καὶ ἡ κρίσις. ὡς γὰρ ἀπέθανε Φίλιππος καὶ τὴν
φρουρὰν οἱ Θηβαῖοι τεθαρσηκότες ἐξέβαλον, ὁ μὲν Ἀλέξανδρος ὡς καταφρονηθεὶς
τὰς Θήβας κατέσκαψεν, εἶτα μεταγνοὺς ἐπὶ τῷ πεπραγμένῳ ἐξεχώρησε τῆς Ἑλλάδος αἰσχυνόμενος καὶ κατὰ τῶν βαρβάρων ἐστράτευσεν, οἱ δὲ Ἀθηναῖοι καιρὸν
ἔχειν ἐνόμισαν κρίσει παραδοῦναι τοὺς προδότας τοὺς τὴν Ἑλλάδα ἀδικήσαντας,
καὶ οὕτω συνεκροτήθη τὸ δικαστήριον.

1   Πρῶτον μὲν, ὦ ἄνδρες Ἀθηναῖοι, τοῖς θεοῖς εὔχομαι πᾶσι
καὶ πάσαις, ὅσην εὔνοιαν ἔχων ἐγὼ διατελῶ τῇ τε πόλει καὶ
πᾶσιν ὑμῖν, τοσαύτην ὑπάρξαι μοι παρ᾽ ὑμῶν εἰς τουτονὶ τὸν
ἀγῶνα, ἔπειθ᾽ ὅπερ ἐστὶ μάλισθ᾽ ὑπὲρ ὑμῶν καὶ τῆς ὑμετέρας
εὐσεβείας τε καὶ δόξης, τοῦτο παραστῆσαι τοὺς θεοὺς ὑμῖν, μὴ 5
τὸν ἀντίδικον σύμβουλον ποιήσασθαι περὶ τοῦ πῶς ἀκούειν
ὑμᾶς ἐμοῦ δεῖ (σχέτλιον γὰρ ἂν εἴη τοῦτό γε), ἀλλὰ τοὺς
νόμους καὶ τὸν ὅρκον, ἐν ᾧ πρὸς ἅπασι τοῖς ἄλλοις δικαίοις
2 καὶ τοῦτο γέγραπται, τὸ ὁμοίως ἀμφοῖν ἀκροάσασθαι. τοῦτο

9. ἀκροάσασθαι] Ita Σ: ceteri ἀκροᾶσθαι.

§§ 1, 2. *I pray first that I may be rewarded for my good will to you, next that
you may have grace to keep your oath, and
allow me to arrange my defence as I like;
you are sworn to give both sides an equal
hearing, but if the accuser is to dictate the
line of the defence, where is the equality?*
2. ἐγὼ answers to παρ᾽ ὑμῶν: in earlier
writers the antithesis would have been more
symmetrical and emphatic.
4. ὅπερ .. ὑμῖν. 'That the Gods may
put in your heart what is most profitable for
you and for your piety and your honour.'

μάλιστα does not imply that the second
part of the prayer concerns them principally,
but that it contains the best gift he can ask
for them. His first prayer was for a favourable hearing: his second is for simple impartiality.
§ 2. 'This means, not only to have no
foregone conclusion, nor yet to render good
will to both equally, but also to let the arrangement and the defence be taken in the
order that each party has chosen and preferred.' Demosthenes is stating a general
principle for his own benefit, and therefore

δ᾽ ἐστὶν οὐ μόνον τὸ μὴ προκατεγνωκέναι μηδέν, οὐδὲ τὸ τὴν
εὔνοιαν ἴσην ἀμφοτέροις ἀποδοῦναι, ἀλλὰ καὶ τὸ τῇ τάξει καὶ
τῇ ἀπολογίᾳ, ὡς βεβούληται καὶ προῄρηται τῶν ἀγωνιζομένων
ἕκαστος, οὕτως ἐᾶσαι χρήσασθαι.

5 Πολλὰ μὲν οὖν ἔγωγ᾽ ἐλαττοῦμαι κατὰ τουτονὶ τὸν ἀγῶνα 3
Αἰσχίνου, δύο δ᾽, ὦ ἄνδρες Ἀθηναῖοι, καὶ μεγάλα, ἓν μὲν ὅτι
οὐ περὶ τῶν ἴσων ἀγωνίζομαι· οὐ γάρ ἐστιν ἴσον νῦν ἐμοὶ τῆς
παρ᾽ ὑμῶν εὐνοίας διαμαρτεῖν καὶ τούτῳ μὴ ἑλεῖν τὴν γραφήν,
ἀλλ᾽ ἐμοὶ μὲν—οὐ βούλομαι δὲ δυσχερὲς εἰπεῖν οὐδὲν ἀρχό- 4
10 μενος τοῦ λόγου, οὗτος δ᾽ ἐκ περιουσίας μου κατηγορεῖ. ἕτερον
δ᾽, ὃ φύσει πᾶσιν ἀνθρώποις ὑπάρχει, τῶν μὲν λοιδοριῶν καὶ
τῶν κατηγοριῶν ἀκούειν ἡδέως, τοῖς ἐπαινοῦσι δ᾽ αὐτοὺς ἄχθε-

---

2. ἀμφοτέροις] Om. pr. Σ.

---

states it in the form which shews its bearing
on his own case: hence, while τῇ τάξει includes Aeschines, it is coupled not with a
general word like ἀποδείξει, but one which
applies to Demosthenes exclusively. The
phrase cannot be explained as a mere hendiadys = τῇ τάξει τῆς ἀπολογίας, for the
sense is, 'Your oath requires that, as Aeschines has put his accusation in the order
which suited him, so I should be equally
free to arrange my defence,' instead of being
bound over to follow his order as he had
demanded (In Ctes. § 203).

§ 3. *Aeschines starts at an advantage. I
have more to lose by your censure than Aeschines by simply failing to get a conviction.*
§ 3. After saying that he only asks equality, he suggests his need of favour, by saying that Aeschines cannot but have an advantage. 'I know, indeed, that in this
contest Aeschines has many advantages over
me: he has two great advantages, men of
Athens.'
5. ἔγωγε. I, whatever be the case with
other defendants: tr. 'A man like me.'
7. οὐ γάρ ἐστιν ἴσον. Contrast below,
§ 330, where Aeschines is threatened with
ruin by the failure of the prosecution (as
actually happened); while Demosthenes says
he has nothing to lose, only the crown to
gain by success. Perhaps his confidence rose
in the course of the speech as he watched its
effect upon the court (cp. § 64, ἀκούεις ἃ
λέγουσιν, if the words were spoken): perhaps this *timidum submissumque principium*
(Quinct. 11. 3. 97) is merely intended to
disarm criticism.
νῦν. 'Now,' after my long services,
after your long gratitude.
§§ 4, 5. *Also it is always pleasanter to*

listen to detraction than to self-laudation;
yet some measure of self-laudation is forced
upon me.
10. οὗτος δὲ answers in a manner to ἐμοὶ
μέν; but the latter clause is modified because
the former is left incomplete. Demosthenes
intended to say, 'I have a great position to
lose, he has none:' he does say, 'I have—
I won't say what; but he can well afford to
accuse me.' δυσχερὲς seems to mean 'offensive' rather than 'ominous:' the offensiveness may be either in Demosthenes' praising
himself or in the contrast he was going to
draw.
ἐκ περιουσίας. 'Risking nothing,'
nothing beyond his spare resources, nothing
that he cannot afford to lose : the words can
scarcely mean 'wantonly,' 'ex mera inso-
lentia,' and in Plat. Theaet. p. 154 D, which
is quoted in support of this sense, there is no
difficulty in explaining the phrase in its usual
and etymological sense, 'with our spare
mental energy' which we can devote to
mental luxuries: the things spoken of are
not necessaries.
11. ὃ is in construction a pronoun, probably with ἕτερον as its antecedent; in trans-
lating it would be best expressed by an
adverb, like ὅτι which it balances here, or
the Latin *quod.* The construction is, 'The
second [difficulty is] the tendency innate in
all men to hear with pleasure,' etc.; the
rhetorical effect is, 'The second, that whereas
it is human nature to like abuse of others
and dislike self-praise, the first falls to Aeschines, the second to me.' For the sentiment, cp. Thuc. 2. 35. 4, 5, where Pericles
dilates on the natural reluctance of men to
hear the praise of others; without apologising,
like Demosthenes, for what he imputes.

σθαι· τούτων τοίνυν ὃ μέν ἐστι πρὸς ἡδονήν, τούτῳ δέδοται,
ὃ δὲ πᾶσιν ὡς ἔπος εἰπεῖν ἐνοχλεῖ, λοιπὸν ἐμοί. κἂν μὲν
εὐλαβούμενος τοῦτο μὴ λέγω τὰ πεπραγμένα ἐμαυτῷ, οὐκ ἔχειν
ἀπολύσασθαι τὰ κατηγορημένα δόξω οὐδ᾽ ἐφ᾽ οἷς ἀξιῶ τιμᾶ-
5 σθαι δεικνύναι· ἐὰν δ᾽ ἐφ᾽ ἃ καὶ πεποίηκα καὶ πεπολίτευμαι 5
βαδίζω, πολλάκις λέγειν ἀναγκασθήσομαι περὶ ἐμαυτοῦ. πειράσομαι μὲν οὖν ὡς μετριώτατα τοῦτο ποιεῖν· ὅ τι δ᾽ ἂν τὸ
πρᾶγμα αὐτὸ ἀναγκάζῃ, τούτου τὴν αἰτίαν οὗτός ἐστι δίκαιος
ἔχειν ὁ τοιοῦτον ἀγῶνα ἐνστησάμενος.
6   Οἶμαι δ᾽ ὑμᾶς, ὦ ἄνδρες Ἀθηναῖοι, πάντας ἂν ὁμολογῆσαι 10
κοινὸν εἶναι τουτονὶ τὸν ἀγῶνα ἐμοί τε καὶ Κτησιφῶντι καὶ
οὐδὲν ἐλάττονος ἄξιον σπουδῆς ἐμοί· πάντων μὲν γὰρ ἀποστερεῖσθαι λυπηρόν ἐστι καὶ χαλεπόν, ἄλλως τε κἂν ὑπ᾽ ἐχθροῦ
τῳ τοῦτο συμβαίνῃ, μάλιστα δὲ τῆς παρ᾽ ὑμῶν εὐνοίας καὶ
φιλανθρωπίας, ὅσωπερ καὶ τὸ τυχεῖν τούτων μέγιστόν ἐστιν. 15
7 περὶ τούτων δ᾽ ὄντος τουτουὶ τοῦ ἀγῶνος, ἀξιῶ καὶ δέομαι
πάντων ὁμοίως ὑμῶν ἀκοῦσαί μου περὶ τῶν κατηγορημένων
ἀπολογουμένου δικαίως, ὥσπερ οἱ νόμοι κελεύουσιν, οὓς ὁ τιθεὶς
ἐξ ἀρχῆς Σόλων, εὔνους ὢν ὑμῖν καὶ δημοτικός, οὐ μόνον τῷ

---

10. Ἀθηναῖοι] Ita Σ et al.: volg. usque ad Bekk. δικασταί.   Statim post πάντας,
ὑμᾶς add. Σ.

3. οὐκ ἔχειν .. δεικνύναι. Aeschines had put forward a double plea to prove the decree unlawful : (*a*) That Demosthenes had done no good ; (*b*) That he had done positive harm. Hence the double position that Demosthenes says he cannot make good without self-praise.

8. τούτου .. ἐνστησάμενος. 'The blame for this ought to rest with him ; he is the man who provoked a contest like this.' The presence of the article is a victory of the rhetorical form over the logical : instead of saying 'he, because he provoked this contest,' Demosthenes points out his opponent twice : οὗτος, 'the man before you ;' ὁ .. ἐνστησάμενος, 'the man that provoked.'

§§ 6-8. *I have a right to take an interest in the suit : for every loss is painful [and I risk losing my crown] : doubly painful if inflicted by an enemy [and Aeschines is mine] : yet more so when the loss is as serious as mine if I lose your favour. Hence I need the impartiality to which you are sworn : and you are sworn in order to counteract the advantage the accuser has in speaking first.*

10. ἄνδρες Ἀθηναῖοι. One would expect this form of address to be used only where there was a distinct political appeal ; but (to take the nearest instances)

in §§ 3 and 10, where Ἀθηναῖοι is used, the appeal seems to be only to their judicial capacity ; and even in §§ 1 and 15, the appeal is quite as much to them as judges as citizens. One of the most elaborate passages in Aeschines (§ 211) is to prove that Demosthenes ought to be neutral : here Demosthenes quietly assumes the contrary.

12. πάντων. 'Anything,' not 'everything.'

17. πάντων ὁμοίως. 'To all alike,' whatever your party or inclination may be.

19. Σόλων probably fixed the constitution of the courts ; though subsequent legislation extended their jurisdiction and stimulated their activity. Of course much was attributed to him that could not possibly be his ; but the *original* form of the oath here appealed to is almost certain to date from his time. It is quoted in full ap. Dem. in Timoc. pp. 746, 747, where we see that it must have been modified in terms to suit the later constitution (τῆς βουλῆς τῶν πεντακοσίαν is on the face of it later than Clisthenes) ; but the oath against abolition of debts and redistribution of lands, seems to point to a time before the judicial and legislative functions of the Ἡλιαία were separated, not to

γράψαι κυρίους ᾤετο δεῖν εἶναι, ἀλλὰ καὶ τῷ τοὺς δικάζοντας
ὑμᾶς ὀμωμοκέναι, οὐκ ἀπιστῶν ὑμῖν, ὥς γ᾽ ἐμοὶ φαίνεται, ἀλλ᾽ 8
ὁρῶν ὅτι τὰς αἰτίας καὶ τὰς διαβολὰς, αἷς ἐκ τοῦ πρότερος
λέγειν ὁ διώκων ἰσχύει, οὐκ ἔνι τῷ φεύγοντι παρελθεῖν, εἰ μὴ
5 τῶν δικαζόντων ἕκαστος ὑμῶν τὴν πρὸς τοὺς θεοὺς εὐσέβειαν
διαφυλάττων καὶ τὰ τοῦ λέγοντος ὑστέρου δίκαια εὐνοϊκῶς
προσδέξεται, καὶ παρασχὼν ἑαυτὸν ἴσον καὶ κοινὸν ἀμφοτέροις
ἀκροατὴν οὕτω τὴν διάγνωσιν ποιήσεται περὶ ἁπάντων.

Μέλλων δὲ τοῦ τε ἰδίου βίου παντὸς, ὡς ἔοικε, λόγον διδό- 9
10 ναι τήμερον καὶ τῶν κοινῇ πεπολιτευμένων, βούλομαι πάλιν
τοὺς θεοὺς παρακαλέσαι, καὶ ἐναντίον ὑμῶν εὔχομαι πρῶτον
μὲν, ὅσην εὔνοιαν ἔχων ἐγὼ διατελῶ τῇ τε πόλει καὶ πᾶσιν
ὑμῖν, τοσαύτην ὑπάρξαι μοι παρ᾽ ὑμῶν εἰς τουτονὶ τὸν ἀγῶνα,
ἔπειθ᾽ ὅ τι μέλλει συνοίσειν καὶ πρὸς εὐδοξίαν κοινῇ καὶ πρὸς
15 εὐσέβειαν ἑκάστῳ, τοῦτο παραστῆσαι τοὺς θεοὺς πᾶσιν ὑμῖν
περὶ ταυτησὶ τῆς γραφῆς γνῶναι.

Εἰ μὲν οὖν περὶ ὧν ἐδίωκε μόνον κατηγόρησεν Αἰσχίνης, 10
κἀγὼ περὶ αὐτοῦ τοῦ προβουλεύματος· εὐθὺς ἂν ἀπελογούμην·
ἐπειδὴ δ᾽ οὐκ ἐλάττω λόγον τἆλλα διεξιὼν ἀνήλωκε καὶ τὰ

6. ὑστέρου] Ita pr. ΣΥ et al. A et socii : ceteri ὕστερον.   10. βούλομαι] Post hoc
addebatur usque ad Bekk. καθάπερ ἐν ἀρχῇ.   Om. ΣΑ et socii.   15. τοὺς θεοὺς] Om. Σ.

mention that such a provision could hardly
have been introduced after the era of the
Pisistratidae, who seem to have left no social
questions open. It may be added that the
archons are mentioned as important magistrates.

εὔνους ὢν ὑμῖν καὶ δημοτικός: cp.
Ar. Nub. 1190, ὁ Σόλων ὁ παλαιὸς ἦν φιλό-
δημος τὴν φύσιν. The clause is inserted to
establish οὐκ ἀπιστῶν .. ἀλλ᾽ ὁρῶν κ.τ.λ.
As a good citizen and your well-wisher he
cannot have distrusted you, but he saw the
temptation to which you were exposed.

6. τὰ τοῦ λέγοντος ὑστέρου δίκαια.
'The pleas of right put forward by the second
speaker.' In this context, δίκαια is always
subjective; not 'rights,' but 'views of right.'

7. ἴσον καὶ κοινόν. 'Indifferent and
impartial.' If the words are to be distinguished, a clue may perhaps be found in the
speech of Prodicus ap. Plat. Prot. p. 337 B,
κοινοὺς μὲν εἶναι, ἴσους δὲ μή, which one
might paraphrase, 'be equally open to the
influence of both sides, but not find the influence of both equally strong.'

§ 9. As the indictment covers my whole
life, public and private, I again pray that
you may bear me as good will as I bear you,
and that you may be guided to such a judg-

ment that each of you may keep his oath, and
all get good report.

13. ὑπάρξαι. 'That I may count on as
much good will from you,' etc. Note that
he varies his prayer a little from its original
form in § 1. Then he prayed for a fair
hearing, now for a right decision; and the
repetition of his appeal to their piety and
honour is enriched by a favourite antithesis
[κοινῇ and ἑκάστῳ].

§ 10. If Aeschines had kept to the illegality, so would I : but most of his speech
was on my general character; so I must
reply, to remove a prejudice which might
affect the special question.

18. τοῦ προβουλεύματος. The motion
made by Ctesiphon in the Senate of Five
Hundred, as a preliminary to bringing it
before the Assembly. Demosthenes' point
is that Aeschines was making a small question into a great one: accordingly he speaks
of the act of Ctesiphon as a mere suggestion, too inchoate to be responsible. The
term is technically accurate; otherwise ψήφισμα would be more natural.

19. ἐπειδὴ δ᾽ .. κατεψεύσατό μου. 'Since
half his speech was a rehearsal of other matters, and most of it lies.' οὐκ ἐλάττω,
strictly 'the better half.'

πλεῖστα κατεψεύσατό μου, ἀναγκαῖον εἶναι νομίζω καὶ δίκαιον
ἅμα βραχέα, ὦ ἄνδρες Ἀθηναῖοι, περὶ τούτων πρῶτον εἰπεῖν,
ἵνα μηδεὶς ὑμῶν τοῖς ἔξωθεν λόγοις ἠγμένος ἀλλοτριώτερον
τῶν ὑπὲρ τῆς γραφῆς δικαίων ἀκούῃ μου.

11 Περὶ μὲν δὴ τῶν ἰδίων ὅσα λοιδορούμενος βεβλασφήμηκε 5
περὶ ἐμοῦ, θεάσασθε ὡς ἁπλᾶ καὶ δίκαια λέγω. εἰ μὲν ἴστε
με τοιοῦτον οἷον οὗτος ᾐτιᾶτο (οὐ γὰρ ἄλλοθί που βεβίωκα
ἢ παρ' ὑμῖν), μηδὲ φωνὴν ἀνάσχησθε, μηδ' εἰ πάντα τὰ κοινὰ
ὑπέρευ πεπολίτευμαι, ἀλλ' ἀναστάντες καταψηφίσασθε ἤδη·
12 εἰ δὲ πολλῷ βελτίω τούτου καὶ ἐκ βελτιόνων, καὶ μηδενὸς τῶν 10
μετρίων, ἵνα μηδὲν ἐπαχθὲς λέγω, χείρονα καὶ ἐμὲ καὶ τοὺς
ἐμοὺς ὑπειλήφατε καὶ γιγνώσκετε, τούτῳ μὲν μηδ' ὑπὲρ τῶν
ἄλλων πιστεύετε (δῆλον γὰρ ὡς ὁμοίως ἅπαντ' ἐπλάττετο),
ἐμοὶ δ', ἣν παρὰ πάντα τὸν χρόνον εὔνοιαν ἐνδέδειχθε ἐπὶ
13 πολλῶν ἀγώνων τῶν πρότερον, καὶ νυνὶ παράσχεσθε. κακοή- 15
θης δ' ὤν, Αἰσχίνη, τοῦτο παντελῶς εὔηθες ᾠήθης, τοὺς περὶ
τῶν πεπραγμένων καὶ πεπολιτευμένων λόγους ἀφέντα με πρὸς
τὰς λοιδορίας τὰς παρὰ σοῦ τρέψεσθαι. οὐ δὴ ποιήσω τοῦτο·
οὐχ οὕτω τετύφωμαι· ἀλλ' ὑπὲρ μὲν τῶν πεπολιτευμένων ἃ
κατεψεύδου καὶ διέβαλλες, αὐτίκα ἐξετάσω, τῆς δὲ πομπείας 20
ταύτης τῆς ἀνέδην οὑτωσὶ γεγενημένης ὕστερον, ἂν βουλομένοις
ἀκούειν ᾖ τουτοισί, μνησθήσομαι.

15. τῶν πρότερον] Post haec addebatur usque ad Bekk. γεγενημένων. Om. ΣΑ et socii.
20. αὐτίκα] Om. ΣΓΥΦ, post ἐξετάσω ponunt nonnulli. 21. οὑτωσὶ] Om. ΣΑ et
socii Bekk.

3. ἵνα μηδείς. 'That none of you may
be led by his irrelevant arguments to listen
with any degree of aversion to what I have
to plead to the indictment,' unless τοῖς ἔξωθεν λόγοις is to be taken generally like τὰ
ἔξωθεν, 'talk outside the matter.'

ἀλλοτριώτερον, lit. 'With more aversion on that account.'

§§ 11, 12. I have a simple reply to his
personal charges. You know me: do not
listen to me if they are true, whatever my
public services: but if I am a better man
than he is, and (to put it mildly) no worse
than any of my respectable neighbours, then
take his imputations against my private life
as a presumption against his public charges;
and shew me the good will you always
shew.

7. οὐ γὰρ ἄλλοθι κ.τ.λ. One of the
principal contrasts between Demosthenes
and Aeschines is, that the latter never identifies or attempts to identify himself with his
audience: as he had done in his own defence,
Ae. de F. L. p. 52, § 193.

12. μηδ' ὑπὲρ τῶν ἄλλων. 'Do not

believe him about the other matters either.'

§ 13. Knave as you are, Aeschines, it
was a fool's thought that I would linger on
my private affairs; they may come after the
public charges if the court cares for them.

15. κακοήθης .. ᾠήθης. A verbal paradox, designedly completed by the assonance
of ᾠήθης. The passage in Aeschines' speech
referred to seems to be § 204.

17. τῶν πεπραγμένων καὶ πεπολιτευμένων. 'My acts and policy,' almost a
hendiadys, 'my public acts,' repeated below,
§ 72, s. v. l., 140.

19. τετύφωμαι. 'Infatuated :' cp. below,
§ 303. ἐμβρόντητε.

ὑπὲρ μὲν .. ἐξετάσω. 'I will examine
at once your calumnies that affect my public
life.'

20. πομπείας. Cp. below, § 159 : also
§ 157, for the parallel expression ὥσπερ ἐξ
ἁμάξης.

21. τῆς ἀνέδην οὑτωσὶ γεγενημένης.
Before discussing these accusations, he intimates that they were made loosely, without
any sense of responsibility.

Τὰ μὲν οὖν κατηγορημένα πολλὰ [καὶ δεινά], καὶ περὶ ὧν 14
ἐνίων μεγάλας καὶ τὰς ἐσχάτας οἱ νόμοι διδόασι τιμωρίας.
τοῦ δὲ παρόντος ἀγῶνος ἡ προαίρεσις αὕτη ἐχθροῦ μὲν ἐπή-
ρειαν ἔχει καὶ ὕβριν καὶ λοιδορίαν καὶ προπηλακισμὸν ὁμοῦ
5 καὶ πάντα τὰ τοιαῦτα· τῶν μέντοι κατηγοριῶν καὶ τῶν αἰτιῶν
τῶν εἰρημένων, εἴπερ ἦσαν ἀληθεῖς, οὐκ ἔνι τῇ πόλει δίκην ἀξίαν
λαβεῖν, οὐδ᾿ ἐγγύς. οὐ γὰρ ἀφαιρεῖσθαι δεῖ τὸ προσελθεῖν 15
τῷ δήμῳ καὶ λόγου τυχεῖν, οὐδ᾿ ἐν ἐπηρείας τάξει καὶ φθόνου
τοῦτο ποιεῖν· οὔτε μὰ τοὺς θεοὺς ὀρθῶς ἔχον οὔτε πολιτικὸν
10 οὔτε δίκαιόν ἐστιν, ὦ ἄνδρες ᾿Αθηναῖοι· ἀλλ᾿ ἐφ᾿ οἷς ἀδικοῦντά
με ἑώρα τὴν πόλιν, οὖσί γε τηλικούτοις ἡλίκα νῦν ἐτραγώδει
καὶ διεξήει, ταῖς ἐκ τῶν νόμων τιμωρίαις παρ᾿ αὐτὰ τἀδικήματα
χρῆσθαι, εἰ μὲν εἰσαγγελίας ἄξια πράττοντα ἑώρα, εἰσαγγέλ- 16
λοντα καὶ τοῦτον τὸν τρόπον εἰς κρίσιν καθιστάντα παρ᾿
15 ὑμῖν, εἰ δὲ γράφοντα παράνομα, παρανόμων γραφόμενον· οὐ

---

1. καὶ δεινά] Om. ΣΑ et socii B. et S.   3. αὕτη] αὐτὴ Σ, αὕτη Φ et al. Bekk.,
ceteri αὐτή.   9. οὔτε μὰ τοὺς κ.τ.λ.] Morelli conjecturam, ὃ οὔτε κ.τ.λ., probat Dind.

§§ 14–16. He says that I have committed capital crimes; and proposes to disfranchise Ctesiphon for spite. He ought to have prosecuted me: he would, if he had thought there was a chance of convicting me; for if he was afraid of me, why is he not afraid to prosecute me under the name of Ctesiphon?

2. μεγάλας καὶ τὰς ἐσχάτας. 'The laws assign a heavy, aye, the heaviest penalty.'

3. τοῦ παρόντος .. αὕτη. 'But this design shewn in the present trial.' The antithesis has four members: 1. (a) The charges; (b) the animus of the trial. 2. (a) The penalties appointed by law; (b) the malice displayed by an individual. There is a reading αὐτὴ, 'the mere scheme of the trial' is enough to condemn it: but αὕτη has the authority of the Paris MS. Σ and several others. Expl. 'the design shewn, being such as it is.'

7. οὐ γὰρ ἀφαιρεῖσθαι κ.τ.λ. The sense is determined by the previous sentence. The connection is, 'The trial is a display of malice, for charges are made of crimes for which the state has no power [as the indictment is framed] of exacting anything like an adequate penalty; for [if the charges were true] the right course would have been not to disfranchise Ctesiphon now, but to have punished me at the time.'

ἀφαιρεῖσθαι is in the middle voice to suggest pleasure in the process, the object is most probably Ctesiphon not Demosthenes, both from the general sense of the passage

and because προσελθεῖν or τῷ δήμῳ points to the Assembly rather than the Court, so that there can scarcely be a reference to Aesch. in Ctes. § 203, where the Court is warned against hearing Demosthenes. Aeschines proposed to disfranchise Ctesiphon by inflicting upon him a fine beyond his means: moreover, it seems that conviction in an indictment for illegal motion would of itself involve the loss of the right to bring forward any motion thereafter, just as Aeschines lost the right of prosecution for illegal motion when the Court acquitted Ctesiphon by a majority of more than four-fifths. The scholiast complains of the obscurity of this whole passage.

9. πολιτικὸν is 'neighbourly' idealised, the way one citizen ought to behave to another; perhaps 'patriotic' is the least objectionable translation.

12. παρ᾿ αὐτὰ τἀδικήματα. 'At the very moment of my crimes,' strictly 'parallel with the course of the crimes,' 'as fast as each was committed.'

15. οὐ γὰρ δήπου κ.τ.λ. The connection is, 'Such was his duty; for the pretence that I terrorised him into silence (in Ctes. § 227) is disproved by the present prosecution. We cannot think that he is equal to prosecuting Ctesiphon and not equal to prosecuting me; we cannot doubt that he would have done so had he thought he had a case.' οὐ of course negatives the whole antithetical sentence, and the second clause more emphatically than the first.

γὰρ δήπου Κτησιφῶντα μὲν δύναται διώκειν δι᾽ ἐμέ, ἐμὲ δ᾽,
17 εἴπερ ἐξελέγξειν ἐνόμιζεν, αὐτὸν οὐκ ἂν ἐγράψατο. καὶ μὴν
εἴ τι τῶν ἄλλων ὧν νυνὶ διέβαλλε καὶ διεξῄει ἢ καὶ ἄλλ᾽ ὁτιοῦν
ἀδικοῦντά με ὑμᾶς ἑώρα, εἰσὶ νόμοι περὶ πάντων καὶ τιμωρίαι
καὶ ἀγῶνες καὶ κρίσεις πικρὰ καὶ μεγάλα ἔχουσαι τἀπιτίμια, 5
καὶ τούτοις ἐξῆν ἅπασι χρῆσθαι, καὶ ὁπηνίκα ἐφαίνετο ταῦτα
πεποιηκὼς καὶ τοῦτον τὸν τρόπον κεχρημένος τοῖς πρὸς ἐμέ,
18 ὡμολογεῖτ᾽ ἂν ἡ κατηγορία τοῖς ἔργοις αὐτοῦ. νῦν δ᾽ ἐκστὰς
τῆς ὀρθῆς καὶ δικαίας ὁδοῦ καὶ φυγὼν τοὺς παρ᾽ αὐτὰ τὰ
πράγματα ἐλέγχους, τοσούτοις ὕστερον χρόνοις αἰτίας καὶ 10
σκώμματα καὶ λοιδορίας συμφορήσας ὑποκρίνεται· εἶτα κατηγορεῖ μὲν ἐμοῦ, κρίνει δὲ τουτονί, καὶ τοῦ μὲν ἀγῶνος ὅλου
τὴν πρὸς ἐμὲ ἔχθραν προΐσταται, οὐδαμοῦ δ᾽ ἐπὶ ταύτην ἀπηντηκὼς ἐμοὶ τὴν ἑτέρου ζητῶν ἐπιτιμίαν ἀφελέσθαι φαίνεται.
19 καίτοι πρὸς ἅπασιν, ὦ ἄνδρες Ἀθηναῖοι, τοῖς ἄλλοις δικαίοις 15
οἷς ἂν εἰπεῖν τις ὑπὲρ Κτησιφῶντος ἔχοι, καὶ τοῦτ᾽ ἔμοιγε
δοκεῖ καὶ μάλ᾽ εἰκότως ἂν λέγειν, ὅτι τῆς ἡμετέρας ἔχθρας
ἡμᾶς ἐφ᾽ ἡμῶν αὐτῶν δίκαιον ἦν τὸν ἐξετασμὸν ποιεῖσθαι, οὐ
τὸ μὲν πρὸς ἀλλήλους ἀγωνίζεσθαι παραλείπειν, ἑτέρῳ δ᾽ ὅτῳ
κακόν τι δώσομεν ζητεῖν· ὑπερβολὴ γὰρ ἀδικίας τοῦτό γε. 20
20 Πάντα μὲν τοίνυν τὰ κατηγορημένα ὁμοίως ἐκ τούτων ἂν

2. ἐξελέγξειν] Ita Ak et superscr. Σ s: ceteri ἐξελέγχειν.   6. χρῆσθαι] Post hoc
addebatur κατ᾽ ἐμοῦ: om. ΣΦΨΩ et al.   7. πρὸς ἐμέ] πρός με Σ.

§§ 17-19. *If he had a case on any point
of his present accusations, there were severe
penalties fixed by law, and his conduct in
prosecuting me would have been in harmony
with his accusations. As it is, he refused a
trial at the time, and (with much parade)
is acting a part now. Moreover, his speech is
against one man and his indictment against
another. It is a sufficient ground for acquitting Ctesiphon, that he ought not to be made
the scapegoat of our enmity.*

5. κρίσεις .. τἀπιτίμια. The severity
of the legal punishment was used (above,
§ 14), to establish that if Aeschines had
believed his charges, he *ought* to have brought
them forward directly: the point here is
that he *would* have brought them against
Demosthenes, if he had believed them; since
his enmity was so keen that he tried to
reach Demosthenes, through Ctesiphon, with
charges which he did not believe.

7. καὶ τοῦτον .. πρὸς ἐμέ. 'Dealing in
this fashion with what he had against me.'

11. ὑποκρίνεται is the real predicate, and
independent of συμφορήσας, 'he has heaped
up cavils and quips and revilings, and all for

a stage display.' The allusion is to his
former profession of actor; so above, § 15,
ἐτραγῴδει.

εἶτα .. φαίνεται. 'Then he accuses
me and prosecutes Ctesiphon: his hatred to
me is in the forefront of the whole trial, yet
it is clear that he has never joined issue on
that in this attempt to disfranchise a third
person.' εἶτα in aggravation; not only is
he acting a part, but an unfair part. For
κατηγορεῖ .. κρίνει, cp. De Fals. Leg. p. 434,
§ 333. προΐσταται. Because Aeschines
claims a right to prosecute Ctesiphon on the
ground of his legitimate hatred to Demosthenes. ἐπὶ ταύτην ἀπηντηκὼς like ἐπὶ δίαιταν ἀπαντᾶν. ἐπὶ διαλύσεις ἀπαντήσεσθαι
Dem. in Phoen. p. 1043, § 14, ἐπὶ denoting
the rendezvous at which the litigants as
enemies are to encounter each other. τὴν
ἑτέρου ἐπιτιμίαν ἀφελέσθαι like ἀφαιρεῖσθαι
τὸ προσελθεῖν κ.τ.λ. above, § 15, of which
it fixes the sense.

19. ἑτέρῳ δ᾽ ὅτῳ. 'To what third person?'

§ 20. *As the prosecution is insincere as a
whole, so it breaks down in every part,*

τις ἴδοι οὔτε δικαίως οὔτ' ἐπ' ἀληθείας οὐδεμιᾶς εἰρημένα· βούλομαι δὲ καὶ καθ' ἓν ἕκαστον αὐτῶν ἐξετάσαι, καὶ μάλισθ'
ὅσα ὑπὲρ τῆς εἰρήνης καὶ τῆς πρεσβείας κατεψεύσατό μου,
τὰ πεπραγμένα ἑαυτῷ μετὰ Φιλοκράτους ἀνατιθεὶς ἐμοί. ἔστι
5 δ' ἀναγκαῖον, ὦ ἄνδρες Ἀθηναῖοι, καὶ προσῆκον ἴσως, ὡς κατ'
ἐκείνους τοὺς χρόνους εἶχε τὰ πράγματα ἀναμνῆσαι ὑμᾶς, ἵνα
πρὸς τὸν ὑπάρχοντα καιρὸν ἕκαστα θεωρῆτε.

Τοῦ γὰρ Φωκικοῦ συστάντος πολέμου, οὐ δι' ἐμὲ (οὐ γὰρ 21
ἔγωγε ἐπολιτευόμην πω τότε), πρῶτον μὲν ὑμεῖς οὕτω διέκεισθε
10 ὥστε Φωκέας μὲν βούλεσθαι σωθῆναι, καίπερ οὐ δίκαια ποιοῦντας ὁρῶντες, Θηβαίοις δ' ὁτιοῦν ἂν ἐφησθῆναι παθοῦσιν, οὐκ
ἀλόγως οὐδ' ἀδίκως αὐτοῖς ὀργιζόμενοι· οἷς γὰρ ηὐτυχήκεσαν
ἐν Λεύκτροις, οὐ μετρίως ἐκέχρηντο· ἔπειθ' ἡ Πελοπόννησος 22
ἅπασα διειστήκει, καὶ οὔθ' οἱ μισοῦντες Λακεδαιμονίους οὕτως

6. ὑμᾶς] Om. Σ.

1. ἐπ' ἀληθείας. Like ἐπὶ μαρτυρίας, ἐπὶ
τῆς ἀληθείας below, § 285. As we say,
'With any truth to go upon.' 'The accusation is made unjustly, with no regard for
truth; and I will prove in detail that it is
false.'

4. ἔστι δ' ἀναγκαῖον .. καὶ προσῆκον
ἴσως. The second clause is added to shew
that the recapitulation of the history is not
a mere argumentative necessity, but has a
moral fitness also : in fact the whole defence
of Demosthenes resolves itself into a proof
that he only acted in the spirit of Athenian
history.

7. πρὸς τὸν ὑπάρχοντα καιρὸν κ.τ.λ.
'That you may judge my several actions by
the opportunities *in my reach* at the time.'
Cp. for the force of ὑπάρχοντα and for the
sentiment, Ar. Eth. Nic. I. 10. 13 τῷ παρόντι
στρατοπέδῳ χρῆσθαι πολεμικώτατα· μετὰ
τῶν δοθέντων σκυτῶν τὸ κάλλιστον ὑπό-
δημα ποιεῖν.

§§ 21-25. *At the outbreak of the Phocian
war (for which I was not responsible) you
were favourable to the Phocians; the Peloponnese was paralysed by internal dissen-
sions and exposed to the intrigues of Philip.
In its course the Thebans would have been
forced to throw themselves on you; to
avoid which, Philip came to help them, and
make peace with you. The peace was accepted, because the other Greeks had never
supported you, in the war you carried on for
the common good. Your disgust at all this,
not my advice, caused the peace: the venality
of Philocrates, Aeschines, and the like-mind-
ed, caused the subsequent calamities.*

8. γάρ. The so-called γὰρ narrativum,

of which this is an instance, is a delicacy of
Greek construction which cannot be exactly
represented in English : our equivalent would
be 'well,' which confesses that the visible
connection is interrupted, while γὰρ narrativum affirms that a latent connection exists.
Here the connection is that the importance
of the circumstances stated above § 20, is
proved by this enumeration of them. The
use of γὰρ after σημεῖον δὲ and the like is
analogous, but less remote from modern
usage.

οὐ γὰρ ἔγωγε. His first public speech
(on Peloponnesian politics) was the year
after its commencement. ἔγωγε of course
contains an insinuation that older politicians (hardly Aeschines himself, who seems
to have taken to politics later than Demosthenes, though some four years older) who
were still active may have caused the mischief.

10. Φωκέας .. Θηβαίοις. When national
names of this kind are used without the
article, they represent units; with the article
they represent complex bodies. The difference is parallel to that between the Thebans
and Thebes, the Phocians and Phocis, the
Romans and Rome. Both in Greek and
English the form without the article gives a
shade more relief to any associations the
names may have : here also the collocation
is emphatic.

11. ἐφησθῆναι. Rather less than 'exult
over,' and rather more than 'be pleased at.'

14. οἱ μισοῦντες Λακεδαιμονίους include both the Theban party in all the cities,
and especially states like Messena and Megalopolis, which leant upon Theban support.

ἴσχυον ὥστε ἀνελεῖν αὐτούς, οὔθ᾽ οἱ πρότερον δι᾽ ἐκείνων ἄρχοντες κύριοι τῶν πόλεων ἦσαν, ἀλλά τις ἦν ἄκριτος καὶ παρὰ
23 τούτοις καὶ παρὰ τοῖς ἄλλοις ἅπασιν ἔρις καὶ ταραχή. ταῦτα
δ᾽ ὁρῶν ὁ Φίλιππος (οὐ γὰρ ἦν ἀφανῆ) τοῖς παρ᾽ ἑκάστοις
προδόταις χρήματα ἀναλίσκων πάντας συνέκρουε καὶ πρὸς αὑ- 5
τοὺς ἐτάραττεν· εἶτ᾽ ἐν οἷς ἡμάρτανον ἄλλοι καὶ κακῶς ἐφρόνουν, αὐτὸς παρεσκευάζετο καὶ κατὰ πάντων ἐφύετο. ὡς δὲ
ταλαιπωρούμενοι τῷ μήκει τοῦ πολέμου οἱ τότε μὲν βαρεῖς,
νῦν δ᾽ ἀτυχεῖς Θηβαῖοι φανεροὶ πᾶσιν ἦσαν ἀναγκασθησόμενοι
καταφεύγειν ἐφ᾽ ὑμᾶς, ὁ Φίλιππος, ἵνα μὴ τοῦτο γένηται μηδὲ 10
συνέλθοιεν αἱ πόλεις, ὑμῖν μὲν εἰρήνην, ἐκείνοις δὲ βοήθειαν
24 ἐπηγγείλατο. τί οὖν συνηγωνίσατο αὐτῷ πρὸς τὸ λαβεῖν
ὀλίγου δεῖν ὑμᾶς ἑκόντας ἐξαπατωμένους; ἡ τῶν ἄλλων Ἑλλήνων, εἴτε χρὴ κακίαν εἴτ᾽ ἄγνοιαν εἴτε καὶ ἀμφότερα ταῦτ᾽
εἰπεῖν, οἳ πόλεμον συνεχῆ καὶ μακρὸν πολεμούντων ὑμῶν, καὶ 15
τοῦτον ὑπὲρ τῶν πᾶσι συμφερόντων, ὡς ἔργῳ φανερὸν γέγονεν,
οὔτε χρήμασιν οὔτε σώμασιν οὔτ᾽ ἄλλῳ οὐδενὶ τῶν ἁπάντων

---

3. παρὰ] Om. ΓΥΦΩ et socii r. Mox Ἕλλησιν post ἅπασιν add. Α et socii Ω et al., † post
ἔρις superscr. Σ †.   6. ἄλλοι] Sic Σ: ceteri et Bekk. οἱ ἄλλοι.   10. γένηται]
Ita pr. Σ, Α et socii et ο: volgo γένοιτο. Vid. annot.   16. τῶν πᾶσι] Ita Σ: volg.
ante Bekk. τῶν κοινῇ πᾶσι.

1. **ὥστε ἀνελεῖν αὐτούς.** While they
continued to exist, they furnished a nucleus
of reaction.

οἱ πρότερον δι᾽ ἐκείνων ἄρχοντες refers not so much to the Lysandrian dec-
archies, which flourished in the Aegean and
Hellespont, as to the *protégés* of Agesilaus,
such as the extreme oligarchical party at
Phlius, whom their patron embodied with
other refugees to the number of 1000 heavy
armed, or the oligarchs of Mantinea, who
acquiesced with growing satisfaction in the
ἀνοικισμὸς enforced by Sparta.

2. **παρὰ τούτοις κ.τ.λ.** 'But they
and every one else were in a state of inde-
cisive contention and confusion.' There
is no need to suppose that the Lacedae-
monian party were divided against themselves.

6. **εἶτ᾽ ἐν οἷς .. ἐφύετο.** 'After that, all
the errors and the malice of others were
opportunities to him, to make ready (against
all) and grow too great for all.'

κακῶς φρονεῖν is always a little ambiguous, being used both of moral and intellectual perversity: but here it is much likelier and more forcible to take κακῶς ἐφρόνουν as complement to ἡμάρτανον than as
a synonym.

10. **ἵνα μὴ .. πόλεις.** Since it is ascer-

tained that Σ had originally γένηται, as well
as the Augsburg MS. and its satellites, there
can be little doubt that it is the true reading, instead of γένοιτο. Cp. ad § 41. αἱ πόλεις is limited to Thebes and Athens by
ὑμῖν μὲν .. ἐκείνοις δέ.

13. **ὀλίγου δεῖν** has become a mere adverb = 'almost :' if it were a verb with λαβεῖν dependent on it, it would have come
immediately after the article. Here the
sense is not that the Athenians were almost
surprised into a dishonourable peace—they
were so surprised: but that they almost
were surprised into a state of wilful self-
deception.

15. **συνεχῆ καὶ μακρόν.** These epithets
suggest, 'You wanted help: they had time
to give it, and could not say you did not deserve it.' The next clause (ὑπὲρ τῶν πᾶσι
συμφερόντων) proves that they not only
might have helped Athens, but ought to
have done so.

17. **οὔτε .. συνελάμβανον.** Mark the
force of the imperfect, '*Shewed no sign* of
helping you with men or money or anything
else.'

ἄλλῳ οὐδενὶ, e. g. by refusing Philip a
market for his prizes in neutral ports, or by
adopting a decided diplomatic attitude in
support of Athens.

συνελάμβανον ὑμῖν· οἷς καὶ δικαίως καὶ προσηκόντως ὀργιζό-
μενοι ἑτοίμως ὑπηκούσατε τῷ Φιλίππῳ. ἡ μὲν οὖν τότε συγ- 25
χωρηθεῖσα εἰρήνη διὰ ταῦτ᾽, οὐ δι᾽ ἐμέ, ὡς οὗτος διέβαλλεν,
ἐπράχθη· τὰ δὲ τούτων ἀδικήματα καὶ δωροδοκήματα ἐν αὐτῇ
5 τῶν νυνὶ παρόντων πραγμάτων, ἄν τις ἐξετάζῃ δικαίως, αἴτια
εὑρήσει. καὶ ταυτὶ πάνθ᾽ ὑπὲρ τῆς ἀληθείας ἀκριβολογοῦμαι 26
καὶ διεξέρχομαι. εἰ γὰρ εἶναί τι δοκοίη τὰ μάλιστα ἐν τούτοις ἀδίκημα, οὐδέν ἐστι δήπου πρὸς ἐμέ, ἀλλ᾽ ὁ μὲν πρῶτος
εἰπὼν καὶ μνησθεὶς ὑπὲρ τῆς εἰρήνης Ἀριστόδημος ἦν ὁ ὑπο-
10 κριτής, ὁ δ᾽ ἐκδεξάμενος καὶ γράψας καὶ ἑαυτὸν μετὰ τούτου
μισθώσας ἐπὶ ταῦτα Φιλοκράτης ὁ Ἁγνούσιος, ὁ σός, Αἰσχίνη,
κοινωνός, οὐχ ὁ ἐμός, οὐδ᾽ ἂν σὺ διαρραγῇς ψευδόμενος, οἱ δὲ
συνειπόντες ὅτου δήποτε ἕνεκα (ἐῶ γὰρ τοῦτό γ᾽ ἐν τῷ παρόντι) Εὔβουλος καὶ Κηφισοφῶν· ἐγὼ δ᾽ οὐδὲν οὐδαμοῦ. ἀλλ᾽ 27

---

7. τι .. ἀδίκημα] Ita Σ: ceteri inepte τινα .. ἀδικήματα.   9. ὑπὲρ] περὶ FΥ p Λ et
socii, † ὑπερ Σ †.   Vid. annot.   12. οὐχ ὁ ἐμός] Ita Σ: ceteri οὐκ ἐμός.

1. **δικαίως καὶ προσηκόντως.** ' As
was right and proper' they deserved your
anger, which became you well.

§§ 26-28. *I have no interest except love
of truth in apologising for the peace. I
neither proposed nor negotiated it. Yet he
pretends that I am to blame for our making
peace, and for our making it without allies.
Did you, Aeschines, ever expose me or oppose
me? No, you never said a word. It was
clear long before that we had no allies: he
has not spoken a word of truth.*

7. **εἰ γὰρ .. ἀδίκημα.** 'For even granting there were the strongest appearance of
some foul play, there is nothing against me.'
πρὸς ἐμέ, like τοῖς πρὸς ἐμέ above, § 17.

9. **μνησθεὶς ὑπέρ.** Several MSS. alter
this to περὶ (cp. Thuc. 8. 47), and the διορ-
θωτὴς of Σ at least wished to do so, in order
to avoid an usage of ὑπέρ, which is exceptional in Attic. The Epic and Ionic usage
as simply equal to 'about' (cp Il. 6. 524;
Hdt. 2. 123), like the Latin *super* Virg. Aen.
1. 750 'Multa super Priamo rogitans, super
Hectore multum,' undoubtedly persists in
Attic. Cp. Soph. O. T. 1444 τί τοῦτο δ᾽
ἄνδρος ἀθλίου πεύσεσθ᾽ ὑπέρ, and Dem. in
Mid. p. 554. 11 ὑπὲρ Ἀριστάρχου τοῦ
Μόσχου, = in re Aristarchi. (The words
are probably Demosthenes' own : see Excursus on the Documents quoted in the Orators.)
Cp. also below, § 39, note. In Polybius
and later Greek this sense of ὑπέρ is common enough, whether as a return to primitive usage or in obedience to the craving for
more emphatic forms which always marks

the decline of a language. Here a pregnant
sense of μνησθεὶς, 'made mention *of* by
speaking *in behalf of*,' would suit the context and preserve a trace of the ordinary
Attic usage of ὑπέρ.

10. **ἐκδεξάμενος.** Not technically 'his
seconder;' but the next to 'take up' his
idea and draw up a motion on it. There is
no reason to suppose that a resolution required a seconder, still less that it ever was
drafted by him. Aristodemus simply recommended negotiation—he did not propose it.

11. **Φιλοκράτης** had been *convicted* of
corruption.

12. **οὐχ ὁ ἐμός.** The other reading. οὐκ
ἐμὸς, would mean 'no partner of mine,' instead of ' your partner, not mine.'

13. **ὅτου δήποτε ἕνεκα.** This hesitating
insinuation of sinister motives was all that
could be ventured against a statesman universally respected like Eubulus, whom Demosthenes himself appeals to (below, § 207)
as an authority in favour of the Theban alliance. Yet they belonged (so far as the
term is not an anachronism) to opposite
parties: Eubulus spoke in defence of Aeschines
at his trial (Aesch. de Fals. Leg. ad fin.), and
he was the author of the law against diver-
sion of surplus revenue from the theoric fund
to military purposes, which gave Demosthenes so much trouble.

14. **ἐγὼ δ᾽ οὐδὲν οὐδαμοῦ.** ' I was
nothing and nowhere,' i. e. I took no part
as suggester or proposer or supporter of any
motion at any stage of the negotiation.

ὅμως, τούτων τοιούτων ὄντων καὶ ἐπ' αὐτῆς τῆς ἀληθείας οὕτω
δεικνυμένων, εἰς τοῦθ' ἧκεν ἀναιδείας ὥστ' ἐτόλμα λέγειν ὡς
ἄρα ἐγὼ πρὸς τῷ τῆς εἰρήνης αἴτιος γεγενῆσθαι καὶ κεκωλυκὼς
εἴην τὴν πόλιν μετὰ κοινοῦ συνεδρίου τῶν Ἑλλήνων αὐτὴν ποιήσασθαι. εἶτ' ὦ—τί ἂν εἰπών σέ τις ὀρθῶς προσείποι; ἔστιν 5
ὅπου σὺ παρὼν τηλικαύτην πρᾶξιν καὶ συμμαχίαν, ἡλίκην νυνὶ
διεξήεις, ὁρῶν ἀφαιρούμενόν με τῆς πόλεως ἠγανάκτησας, ἢ
28 παρελθὼν ταῦτα ἃ νῦν κατηγορεῖς ἐδίδαξας καὶ διεξῆλθες; καὶ
μὴν εἰ τὸ κωλῦσαι τὴν τῶν Ἑλλήνων κοινωνίαν ἐπεπράκειν
ἐγὼ Φιλίππῳ, σοὶ τὸ μὴ σιγῆσαι λοιπὸν ἦν, ἀλλὰ βοᾶν καὶ 10
διαμαρτύρεσθαι καὶ δηλοῦν τουτοισί. οὐ τοίνυν ἐποίησας οὐδαμοῦ τοῦτο, οὐδ' ἤκουσέ σου ταύτην τὴν φωνὴν οὐδείς, εἰκότως·
οὔτε γὰρ ἦν πρεσβεία πρὸς οὐδένας ἀπεσταλμένη τότε τῶν
Ἑλλήνων, ἀλλὰ πάλαι πάντες ἦσαν ἐξεληλεγμένοι, οὔθ' οὗτος
29 ὑγιὲς περὶ τούτων εἴρηκεν οὐδέν. χωρὶς δὲ τούτων καὶ δια- 15
βάλλει τὴν πόλιν τὰ μέγιστα ἐν οἷς ψεύδεται· εἰ γὰρ ὑμεῖς
ἅμα τοὺς μὲν Ἕλληνας εἰς πόλεμον παρεκαλεῖτε, αὐτοὶ δὲ

---

7. διεξήεις] Ante hoc ἐτραγώδεις καὶ add. FΥΩ et al. A et socii.　　　12. εἰκότως]
Om. ΣΓΥΦΩ uv.　　　13. οὐδένας] οὐδένα ΣΓΥΦ et al. : sed vid. annot.　　　17. Ἑλ-
ληνας] ἄλλους Ἑλληνας FΥΦΩ et socii.

2. ὡς ἄρα .. ποιήσασθαι. 'That I forsooth, not content with promoting the peace,
had hindered the city from making it at the
head of a general congress of Greece.' ἄρα,
of a statement (sometimes of a discovery)
incredible or unheard of; so εἰ ἄρα, εἰ μὴ
ἄρα. Lat. si forte, nisi forte. Vid. Buttmann
ad Dem. Mid. n. 45.
5. εἶτ' ὦ—.. τουτοισί. 'Then, you—
what name is there for you strong enough?
You were there; can you shew when you
denounced me, if you saw me shutting out
the city from such an alliance and such an
opportunity as you have just detailed in full
tragic style? when you came forward to expose and unfold the crimes with which
you charge me now? For if I had sold myself to Philip to prevent Greece making
common cause, it was still open to you to
speak—to raise your splendid voice, to protest and inform your countrymen.' πρᾶξιν
καὶ συμμαχίαν, i. e. the noble achievement
of presiding at a general pacification, and
the permanent alliance Athens would gain.
ἐτραγώδεις καὶ are omitted by Σ: but nearly
all the others have them, and they are not
like a copyist's blunder. They occur with
διεξήεις above, § 15, and may have been
hypercritically omitted here by Σ as a needless repetition.
9. τὸ κωλῦσαι .. ἐπεπράκειν. It is to be

noticed that in such contexts we always
speak of the traitor as selling his person or
his country. or some material result of his
treason, never the specific service, as here
and frequently in the Orators.
10. βοᾶν is perhaps most forcible if taken
as an allusion to Aeschines' fine voice and
apparently rather violent manner: cp. below,
§§ 102, 345; De Fals. Leg. § 390, p. 490
fin. On the other hand, we get the same
words in a similar context below, § 183,
of Demosthenes himself.
13. οὔτε γὰρ .. ἀπεσταλμένη. 'There
was no embassy sent out [and not returned,
'en mission'] to any Greek state at the
time.' οὐδένας, 'to any nation,' as ἕκαστοι
and the like are used of collectives, so that
οὐδένα the reading of Σ and others is unnecessary.
§§ 29, 30. His charges are not only
slanders against me, but insults to you.
If you called a congress and acted without
it, you were traitors. But the project was
never entertained: it would have been unmeaning. So far then I am clear.
17. Several MSS. insert ἄλλους before
Ἑλληνας. We need not go beyond the
preceding chapter for justification of the
text; but in § 72 we find Ἑλληνες and Ἑλληνικὰ used of matters affecting Greece
generally, and so opposed to Athens indi-

L.

πρὸς Φίλιππον περὶ εἰρήνης πρέσβεις ἐπέμπετε, Εὐρυβάτου
πρᾶγμα, οὐ πόλεως ἔργον οὐδὲ χρηστῶν ἀνθρώπων διεπράττεσθε. ἀλλ' οὐκ ἔστι ταῦτα, οὐκ ἔστι· τί γὰρ καὶ βουλόμενοι 30
μετεπέμπεσθ' ἂν αὐτοὺς ἐν τούτῳ τῷ καιρῷ; ἐπὶ τὴν εἰρήνην;
5 ἀλλ' ὑπῆρχεν ἅπασιν. ἀλλ' ἐπὶ τὸν πόλεμον; ἀλλ' αὐτοὶ
περὶ εἰρήνης ἐβουλεύεσθε. οὐκοῦν οὔτε τῆς ἐξ ἀρχῆς εἰρήνης
ἡγεμὼν οὐδ' αἴτιος ὢν ἐγὼ φαίνομαι, οὔτε τῶν ἄλλων ὧν κατεψεύσατό μου οὐδὲν ἀληθὲς ὂν δείκνυται.

Ἐπειδὴ τοίνυν ἐποιήσατο τὴν εἰρήνην ἡ πόλις, ἐνταῦθα 31
10 πάλιν σκέψασθε τί ἡμῶν ἑκάτερος προείλετο πράττειν· καὶ
γὰρ ἐκ τούτων εἴσεσθε τίς ἦν ὁ Φιλίππῳ πάντα συναγωνιζό-
μενος, καὶ τίς ὁ πράττων ὑπὲρ ὑμῶν καὶ τὸ τῇ πόλει συμφέρον ζητῶν. ἐγὼ μὲν τοίνυν ἔγραψα βουλεύων ἀποπλεῖν 32
τὴν ταχίστην τοὺς πρέσβεις ἐπὶ τοὺς τόπους ἐν οἷς ἂν ὄντα
15 Φίλιππον πυνθάνωνται, καὶ τοὺς ὅρκους ἀπολαμβάνειν· οὗτοι
δὲ οὐδὲ γράψαντος ἐμοῦ ταῦτα ποιεῖν ἠθέλησαν. τί δὲ τοῦτ'
ἐδύνατο, ἄνδρες Ἀθηναῖοι; ἐγὼ διδάξω. Φιλίππῳ μὲν ἦν συμφέρον ὡς πλεῖστον τὸν μεταξὺ χρόνον γενέσθαι τῶν ὅρκων,

11. πάντα] τε τὴν εἰρήνην Σ: quod fieri potest ut verum sit.   16. οὐδὲ] οὐ pr. Σ.

---

vidually. And it was probably from seeing
that this was the sense here, and not seeing
that Ἕλληνας expressed it adequately, that
ἄλλους came to be introduced.

1. **Εὐρυβάτου πρᾶγμα.** ' A deed for an
Eurybates,' who took Croesus' money to
hire mercenaries against Cyrus, and betrayed
his employers. But Eurybates was the
name of one of the Cecropes : and it is at
least as likely that such a proverb should
allude to a character in popular mythology,
as to one in rather unfamiliar history. The
point of the antithesis between πρᾶγμα and
ἔργον is, that the former is a mere fact, the
latter is the appropriate result of the character of the agent. ' You were doing a deed
for an Eurybates ; what no city and no
honest man should do.' Further, perhaps,
πρᾶγμα is coloured by the use of πράσσω or
underhand transactions, which is certainly
the force of διεπράττεσθε. Note that πόλεως, without any laudatory epithet, balances
χρηστῶν ἀνθρώπων : the city in itself is an
ideal, which excluded such baseness.

5. **ὑπῆρχεν ἅπασιν.** 'They all were at
peace already,' i. e. with Philip.

7. **οὔτε τῶν ἄλλων . . δείκνυται.** ' Nor
is any other of his slanders against me justified by evidence :' it is rather implied than
expressed, that all were refuted.

§ 31. *After the peace, compare my con-*

duct with his, and say which was Philip's
hireling.

10. **καὶ γὰρ ἐκ τούτων.** Demosthenes
had no fault to find with Aeschines' conduct
before the peace : hence the force of καὶ
must be, ' Here as before the facts will acquit
me, and condemn him :' while he disguises
the fact that ' as before' applies to the former
clause only.

§§ 32-34. *I proposed to secure Philip's
ratification without delay ; for it was his
interest to delay it, to give him time for encroachments, which you would endure rather
than lose the peace. In fact he did make
the encroachments which I tried to forestall.*

13. **βουλεύων.** ' At my place in the
senate :' so, again, § 35.

15. **τοὺς ὅρκους ἀπολαμβάνειν.** ' Take
his oath as agreed.' The plural is probably
used as it was a treaty both of peace and
alliance : the present may have a tentative
force, ' take steps to receive.'

16. **τοῦτο,** i. e. ὡς πλεῖστον τὸν μεταξὺ
χρόνον γενέσθαι. The connection is, ' In
your interest, against Philip's, I was anxious
to shorten the interval before his ratification,
for on your side the interval was an armistice, on his side Philip was anxious to pro-
long it, knowing how he could use it.'

18. **τὸν μεταξὺ χρόνον** may be simply
' the interval,' as in Dem. de Fals. Leg. § 181,

33 ὑμῖν δ' ὡς ἐλάχιστον. διὰ τί; ὅτι ὑμεῖς μὲν οὐκ ἀφ' ἧς ὠμόσατε ἡμέρας μόνον, ἀλλ' ἀφ' ἧς ἠλπίσατε τὴν εἰρήνην ἔσεσθαι,
πάσας ἐξελύσασθε τὰς παρασκευὰς τὰς τοῦ πολέμου, ὁ δὲ τοῦτο
ἐκ παντὸς τοῦ χρόνου μάλιστα ἐπραγματεύετο, νομίζων, ὅπερ
ἦν ἀληθὲς, ὅσα τῆς πόλεως προλάβοι πρὸ τοῦ τοὺς ὅρκους
ἀποδοῦναι, πάντα ταῦτα βεβαίως ἕξειν· οὐδένα γὰρ τὴν εἰρή-
34 νην λύσειν τούτων ἕνεκα. ἃ ἐγὼ προορώμενος, ἄνδρες Ἀθηναῖοι, καὶ λογιζόμενος τὸ ψήφισμα τοῦτο γράφω, πλεῖν ἐπὶ
τοὺς τόπους ἐν οἷς ἂν ᾖ Φίλιππος, καὶ τοὺς ὅρκους τὴν ταχίστην ἀπολαμβάνειν, ἵν' ἐχόντων τῶν Θρᾳκῶν, τῶν ὑμετέρων
συμμάχων, ταῦτα τὰ χωρία ἃ νῦν οὗτος διέσυρε, τὸ Σέρρειον
καὶ τὸ Μυρτηνὸν καὶ τὴν Ἐργίσκην, οὕτω γίγνοινθ' οἱ ὅρκοι,
καὶ μὴ προλαβὼν ἐκεῖνος τοὺς ἐπικαίρους τῶν τόπων κύριος
τῆς Θρᾴκης κατασταίη, μηδὲ πολλῶν μὲν χρημάτων, πολλῶν
δὲ στρατιωτῶν εὐπορήσας ἐκ τούτων ῥᾳδίως τοῖς λοιποῖς ἐπι-
35 χειροίη πράγμασιν. εἶτα τοῦτο μὲν οὐχὶ λέγει τὸ ψήφισμα,
οὐδ' ἀναγιγνώσκει· εἰ δὲ βουλεύων ἐγὼ προσάγειν τοὺς πρέσβεις ᤤμην δεῖν, τοῦτό μου διαβάλλει. ἀλλὰ τί ἐχρῆν με

2. **ἡμέρας μόνον**] Sic ΣA et socii: ceteri et Bekk. *μόνον ἡμέρας*. 3. **ἐξελύσασθε**] Id optimum plerisque editoribus videtur, quamvis Σ et al. *ἐξελύσατε* habeant. 11. **ταῦτα τὰ χωρία**] Sic Σ, *τὰ χωρία p*, *τὰ χωρία ταῦτα* ceteri et volg. usque ad Bekk. **Σέρρειον**] Ita hic solus Υ: ceteri plerique *Σέρριον*. Mox Σ, ut Dindorfio videbatur (neque enim nos rem accuratius inspeximus quam ut *Μυρτηνον* in litura esse animadverterimus) primum *μυρρονιν*, mox *μυρ$\overset{\tau\iota}{\tau}$ηνον* sive *μυρ$\overset{\gamma\iota}{\tau}$ηνον* habuit. *Μυρτηνὸν* habent A *k*: vid. ad Ae. in Ct. § 82. Codd. plerique et Bekk. *Μύρτιον*.

p. 393, where the same time is referred to, only there it is defined somewhat differently, *πρὸ τοῦ τοὺς ὅρκους ἀπολαβεῖν*: if so, *τῶν ὅρκων* must mean 'the interval required for the oaths.' Cp. however below, § 33, **ἀφ' ἧς ὠμόσατε ἡμέρας**, which might suggest 'The interval between your oath and Philip's,' but for *ὅρκους* in the plural just above for the oath of one party only.

5. **τῆς πόλεως.** More strictly below, § 34, *τῶν Θρᾳκῶν, τῶν ὑμετέρων συμμάχων*.

10. **ἵν' ἐχόντων κ.τ.λ.** 'That your allies the Thracians might be in possession of the *places* [in the military sense: the commonest meaning of **χωρία**] .. which Aeschines was *disparaging* just now [in Ctes. § 82 *διέσυρε*, lit. pulled to pieces] when the oaths were taken, and that he might not preoccupy every spot of vantage, and so become lord of Thrace, nor have his future undertakings made easy by the large command of men and money that he would gain by holding those posts.'

11. **τὸ Σέρρειον κ.τ.λ.** '*The* Serrium [that he complained of my mentioning].' Our only English equivalent for this ironical use of the article, is to put a word in inverted commas.

§ 35. *I get no credit for this decree, but am accused for trivial courtesies. However, you shall hear the decree.*

17. **εἰ δὲ βουλεύων ἐγὼ .. δεῖν.** 'But if I as senator thought proper to move the introduction of the ambassadors' [instead of leaving it to others who had not urged on the Olynthiac war]. **ἐγὼ** contains the admission of this presumption of impropriety, *βουλεύων* contains the apology. It seems that even such a formal act as granting an audience required the preliminary authorisation of the Senate: so Demosthenes says, 'If I, being a senator, did a senator's business.' See Ae. de F. L. p. 35, § 53.

18. **ἀλλὰ τί .. τοῦτ' ἐγράφη.** 'What was I to do, to move that men who had come for the very purpose of addressing you should not be introduced, that the contractor should not assign them a place? Does he mean that then they must have paid for their seats? Was it for me to secure you an advantage like that, and sell all Athens like him?'

ποιεῖν; μὴ προσάγειν γράψαι τοὺς ἐπὶ τοῦθ' ἥκοντας, ἵν'
ὑμῖν διαλεχθῶσιν; ἢ θέαν μὴ κατανεῖμαι τὸν ἀρχιτέκτονα
αὐτοῖς κελεῦσαι; ἀλλ' ἐν τοῖν δυοῖν ὀβολοῖν ἐθεώρουν ἄν, εἰ
μὴ τοῦτ' ἐγράφη. ἢ τὰ μικρὰ συμφέροντα τῆς πόλεως ἔδει
5 με φυλάττειν, τὰ δ' ὅλα, ὥσπερ οὗτοι, πεπρακέναι; οὐ δήπου.
λέγε τοίνυν μοι τὸ ψήφισμα τουτὶ λαβών, ὃ σαφῶς οὗτος
εἰδὼς παρέβη.

ΨΗΦΙΣΜΑ. 36

[Ἐπὶ ἄρχοντος Μνησιφίλου, ἑκατομβαιῶνος ἕνῃ καὶ νέᾳ, φυλῆς
10 πρυτανευούσης Πανδιονίδος, Δημοσθένης Δημοσθένους Παιανιεὺς
εἶπεν, ἐπειδὴ Φίλιππος ἀποστείλας πρέσβεις περὶ τῆς εἰρήνης ὁμο-
λογουμένας πεποίηται συνθήκας, δεδόχθαι τῇ βουλῇ καὶ τῷ δήμῳ
τῷ Ἀθηναίων, ὅπως ἂν ἡ εἰρήνη ἐπιτελεσθῇ ἡ ἐπιχειροτονηθεῖσα
ἐν τῇ πρώτῃ ἐκκλησίᾳ, πρέσβεις ἑλέσθαι ἐκ πάντων Ἀθηναίων ἤδη
15 πέντε, τοὺς δὲ χειροτονηθέντας ἀποδημεῖν μηδεμίαν ὑπερβολὴν ποι-37
ουμένους, ὅπου ἂν ὄντα πυνθάνωνται τὸν Φίλιππον, καὶ τοὺς ὅρκους
λαβεῖν τε παρ' αὐτοῦ καὶ δοῦναι τὴν ταχίστην ἐπὶ ταῖς ὡμολογη-
μέναις συνθήκαις αὐτῷ πρὸς τὸν Ἀθηναίων δῆμον, συμπεριλαμβάνοντας
καὶ τοὺς ἑκατέρων συμμάχους. πρέσβεις ᾑρέθησαν Εὔβουλος Ἀναφ-
20 λύστιος, Αἰσχίνης Κοθωκίδης, Κηφισοφῶν Ῥαμνούσιος, Δημοκράτης
Φλυεύς, Κλέων Κοθωκίδης.]

Ταῦτα γράψαντος ἐμοῦ τότε καὶ τὸ τῇ πόλει συμφέρον, 38
οὐ τὸ Φιλίππῳ ζητοῦντος, βραχὺ φροντίσαντες οἱ χρηστοὶ
πρέσβεις οὗτοι καθῆντο ἐν Μακεδονίᾳ τρεῖς ὅλους μῆνας, ἕως

---

7. Post παρέβη, λέγε add. omnes praeter Σ.　　15. ὑπερβολὴν] Sic pr. Σ et FΦ:
ceteri ἀναβολήν.　　20. Αἰσχίνης] Om. ΣFΓΦ, Ἀτρομήτου add. rec. Ω.

1. τοὺς ἐπὶ τοῦθ'..διαλεχθῶσιν, though
not exactly parallel in form, balances ἀλλ'
ἐν τοῖν .. τοῦτ' ἐγράφη.

2. τὸν ἀρχιτέκτονα. The fee received
from the spectators, or indirectly from the
State, only covered the expenses of the
maintenance of the fabric (those of the ex-
hibition being borne by the choregi). Hence
the lessee or contractor is called ἀρχιτέκτων.

3. ἐν τοῖν δυοῖν ὀβολοῖν. ' In the two-
penny [more accurately threepenny] seats.'
Two obols were the price of a ticket of admission on both days of the festival to the
worst seats in the theatre : the better were
half-a-drachma for each day.

§§ 36, 37. See Introduction on the Documents.

§§ 38–40. This decree proves my good
faith : they disregarded it, and not only
wasted months which gave Philip time to
reduce Thrace, but were bribed to remain in
his camp till he was ready to march on Phocis; that our return might be too late to give

you warning, and let you stop him at Thermopylae.

22. γράψαντος .. καὶ .. ζητοῦντος. A
convenient illustration of the force of the
aorist, as marking an act isolated by its
completion. One might paraphrase, ' When
I had drawn up this decree in my constant
character of a seeker of the public good.'

23 βραχὺ φροντίσαντες. ' Taking little
heed of that,' viz. the decree.

24. τρεῖς ὅλους μῆνας. This calculation
is repeatedly made, both here and in the De
Falsa Legatione. Nor does Aeschines
seriously deny it, though he tries to prove
that Demosthenes designedly overestimated
the importance of the delay. Accordingly
we must suppose that the statement is a fair
one, i. e. that the time is calculated from the
ratification of the peace by Athens to the
return of the ambassadors. The interval
between their actual departure and their return was only seventy days; the date of
their departure being fixed by the uncon-

ἦλθε Φίλιππος ἐκ Θρᾴκης πάντα καταστρεψάμενος τἀκεῖ, ἐξὸν
ἡμερῶν δέκα, μᾶλλον δὲ τριῶν ἢ τεττάρων, εἰς τὸν Ἑλλήσποντον ἀφῖχθαι καὶ τὰ χωρία σῶσαι, λαβόντας τοὺς ὅρκους πρὶν
ἐκεῖνον ἐξελεῖν αὐτά· οὐ γὰρ ἂν ἥψατ᾽ αὐτῶν παρόντων ἡμῶν,
ἢ οὐκ ἂν ὡρκίζομεν αὐτόν, ὥστε τῆς εἰρήνης ἂν διημαρτήκει 5
καὶ οὐκ ἂν ἀμφότερα εἶχε, καὶ τὴν εἰρήνην καὶ τὰ χωρία.

39   Τὸ μὲν τοίνυν ἐν τῇ πρεσβείᾳ πρῶτον κλέμμα μὲν Φιλίππου, δωροδόκημα δὲ τῶν ἀδίκων τούτων ἀνθρώπων καὶ θεοῖς
ἐχθρῶν τοιοῦτον ἐγένετο· ὑπὲρ οὗ καὶ τότε καὶ νῦν καὶ ἀεὶ
ὁμολογῶ πολεμεῖν καὶ διαφέρεσθαι τούτοις. ἕτερον δ᾽ εὐθὺς 10
40 ἐφεξῆς ἔτι τούτου μεῖζον κακούργημα θεάσασθε. ἐπειδὴ γὰρ
ὡμολόγησε τὴν εἰρήνην ὁ Φίλιππος προλαβὼν τὴν Θρᾴκην διὰ
τούτους οὐχὶ πεισθέντας τῷ ἐμῷ ψηφίσματι, πάλιν ὠνεῖται
παρ᾽ αὐτῶν ὅπως μὴ ἀπίωμεν ἐκ Μακεδονίας, ἕως τὰ τῆς στρατείας τῆς ἐπὶ τοὺς Φωκέας εὐτρεπῆ ποιήσαιτο, ἵνα μή, δεῦρ᾽ 15
ἀπαγγειλάντων ἡμῶν ὅτι μέλλει καὶ παρασκευάζεται πορεύεσθαι, ἐξέλθοιτε ὑμεῖς καὶ περιπλεύσαντες ταῖς τριήρεσιν εἰς

1. τἀκεῖ] Om. pr. Σ: et ante καταστρεψάμενος ponunt nonnulli.   2. μᾶλλον]
ὁμοίως ΣΑ et socii: quod vix stare potest.   8. καὶ θεοῖς ἐχθρῶν] Om. ΣΑ s.
12. ὡμολόγησε] Sic ΣΦΩ uv et superscr. s: ceteri et Bekk. ὤμοσε: quod sane sensui
melius convenit.   14. ἀπίωμεν] Ita Σ pr. F et A et socii: legebatur ἀπίωσιν.
16. ἡμῶν] Ita ΣΝ et socii et γρ. ΕΦ: ceteri et Bekk. αὐτῶν: vid annot.

tested statement of Aeschines (De Fals. Leg.
p. 40, § 93), that of their return by Demosthenes (De Fals. Leg. p. 359, § 65). But
a fortnight passed between the peace and
their departure, making altogether eighty-
four days, which might fairly enough be
called three months. The actual time that
the embassy waited in Macedonia was only
one month, so the force of the words καθῆντο .. μῆνας must be, 'wasted three whole
months through loitering in Macedonia.'
Demosthenes' reason for insisting so repeatedly on 'three whole months,' is that for
this period it was possible to save Phocis:
but all this time was lost through Aeschines.
   5. ἢ introduces an afterthought, ' or if he
had, we should not have sworn him to the
peace.'
   9. ὑπὲρ οὗ κ.τ.λ.   ' Over which, I own
it, I was, I am, I shall be, at strife and variance with them, then, now, and for ever.'
In this context the English preposition 'over'
coincides with the sense of ὑπὲρ and super,
of which examples are given above, §§ 2,
26. The clause is intended to parry a charge
repeatedly made by Aeschines (De Fals. Leg.
p. 30, § 21, etc.), that his antagonism with

him was a mere personal quarrel dating from
this embassy.
   12. ὡμολόγησε.   'Recognised,' 'agreed
to recognise :' he had consented to its terms
long before.
   διὰ τούτους κ.τ.λ.   ' Thanks to these
men and their disobedience to my decree ;'
practically i. q. διὰ τὸ τούτους μὴ πεισθῆ-
ναι.
   14. ἕως .. ποιήσαιτο,   'Till he could
get all ready for his expedition.' Demosthenes intimates that Philip put this forward
as his motive for proposing the bargain.
   16. ἀπαγγειλάντων ἡμῶν is almost certainly right: it is the reading of Σ and other
MSS., the rest having αὐτῶν, not knowing
that Demosthenes himself was on the embassy. They may have been misled either
by the list in § 37, or by οὗτοι above, § 38,
and τούτους below, § 40. So at the end of
this section Σ has ἡμῶν, and one or two
others retain traces of it: the rest have ὑμῖν
τούτων. The force of ἡμῶν is the same in
both places: to report at Athens was part of
the legitimate business of the embassy with
which Demosthenes was willing to associate
himself.

Πύλας ὥσπερ πρότερον κλείσαιτε τὸν πορθμὸν, ἀλλ' ἄμ' ἀκούοιτε ταῦτα ἀπαγγελλόντων ἡμῶν κἀκεῖνος ἐντὸς εἴη Πυλῶν
καὶ μηδὲν ἔχοιθ' ὑμεῖς ποιῆσαι. οὕτω δ' ἦν ὁ Φίλιππος ἐν 41
φόβῳ καὶ πολλῇ ἀγωνίᾳ, μὴ καὶ ταῦτα προειληφότος αὐτοῦ,
5 πρὸ τοῦ τοὺς Φωκέας ἀπολέσθαι ψηφίσησθε βοηθεῖν, καὶ ἐκφύγοι τὰ πράγματ' αὐτὸν, ὥστε μισθοῦται τὸν κατάπτυστον
τουτονὶ, οὐκέτι κοινῇ μετὰ τῶν ἄλλων πρέσβεων, ἀλλ' ἰδίᾳ
καθ' αὑτὸν, τοιαῦτα πρὸς ὑμᾶς εἰπεῖν καὶ ἀπαγγεῖλαι δι' ὧν
ἅπαντ' ἀπώλετο. ἀξιῶ δὲ ὑμᾶς, ὦ ἄνδρες Ἀθηναῖοι, καὶ δέο- 42
10 μαι τοῦτο μεμνῆσθαι παρ' ὅλον τὸν ἀγῶνα, ὅτι μὴ κατηγορή-
σαντος Αἰσχίνου μηδὲν ἔξω τῆς γραφῆς οὐδ' ἂν ἐγὼ λόγοθ
οὐδένα ἐποιούμην ἕτερον, πάσαις δ' αἰτίαις καὶ βλασφημίαις

1. πορθμὸν] τόπον Σ *ks* γρ. ΦΦ.   2. ἡμῶν] Ita solus Σ, sed ὑμῶν *k*, ἡμῶν *s* : ceteri
ὑμῶν τούτων, τούτων Bekk.   4. καὶ πολλῇ ἀγωνίᾳ] Om. nonnulli.   5. πρὸ τοῦ
τοὺς .. ἐκφύγοι] Σ ante haec inserit *εἰ*, mox ante ἐκφύγοι omisso καί : qua de lectione vid.
annot.   Post ἀπολέσθαι, omnes praeter Σ habent ἀκούσαντες : statim ψηφίσησθε ΣΦ *p* A et
socii, ceteri ψηφίσαισθε.   Ante βοηθεῖν, Σ add. τοῖς Φωκεῦσι, post idem αὐτοῖς ceteri omnes
praeter ΓΥΦ.   9. ὑμᾶς] Hic ponunt A *k* Dind., post μεμνῆσθαι libri plerique et Bekk.,
utroque loco om. Σ *s*.

1. ἄμ' ἀκούοιτε .. ποιῆσαι. 'You might
hear of this [his diplomatic victory and
military preparations] and he be inside the
pass, and you be helpless, all at once.' ἐντὸς
is used because Πύλαι being conceived as
literally a gate, so that it is 'going in' to
pass it southwards from the point of view
either of an invader or of a southern Greek.

§ 41. Yet even so Philip feared that you
might march into Phocis. Accordingly he
made a separate bargain with Aeschines, to
keep you quiet by falsehoods.

4. μὴ καὶ ταῦτα .. τὰ πράγματ' αὐτόν.
Σ reads μὴ καὶ ταῦτα προειληφότος αὐτοῦ,
εἰ πρὸ τοῦ τοὺς Φωκέας ἀπολέσθαι ψηφίσησθε τοῖς Φωκεῦσι βοηθεῖν, ἐκφύγοι τὰ
πράγματ' αὐτόν. The others have μὴ καὶ
ταῦτα προειληφότος αὐτοῦ, πρὸ τοῦ τοὺς
Φωκέας ἀπολέσθαι, ἀκούσαντες ψηφίσαισθε
(five retain ψηφίσησθε with Σ) βοηθεῖν (most
add αὐτοῖς) καὶ ἐκφύγοι κ.τ.λ. Both τοῖς
Φωκεῦσι and αὐτοῖς are clearly marginal
glosses, perhaps first added by writers who
knew that Philip called upon the Athenians
as his allies to join him in the Phocian expedition. ἀκούσαντες may well be omitted
on the authority of Σ; but εἰ can scarcely
be retained, for (to say nothing of the irregularity of εἰ with the conjunctive in late
Attic prose) the presence of καί in all the
other MSS. would be wholely unexplained.
But omitting εἰ and reading καὶ ἐκφύγοι,
the conjunctive would be quite intelligible, on
the principle that of two results, one depen-

dent on the other, the first is expressed by
the conjunctive, the second by the optative.
For instances of this, see Thuc. 3. 22. 9; 7.
17. 4, Eur. Hec. 1138-1141 : also Dem. de
F. L. p. 357, § 57, a passage curiously like
this. εἰ is probably a gloss to explain the
relation of ψηφίσησθε to ἐκφύγοι, which
got into the text of the archetype of Σ, and
so caused the omission of καί.

7. οὐκέτι κοινῇ. This is an inference
from the fact, that until Philip was within
the pass, Demosthenes was overruled by the
joint action of his colleagues ; after their return, he was thwarted in the Assembly by
the arguments and promises of Aeschines.

8. τοιαῦτα κ.τ.λ. We should expect, 'Of
such a nature as to forward his [Philip's]
policy ;' instead we have, 'Of such a nature
that they were the ruin of everything.' The
rhetorical effect required the result of Aeschines' treachery, not the purport of Philip's
policy.

§ 42. (This digression must be excused by
the rambling character of the prosecution.)

11. ἔξω τῆς γραφῆς κ.τ.λ. The rhetorical value of this is as a reply to Aeschines'
claim to shut up the defence to the formal
regularity of Ctesiphon's decree, while con-
tending himself that it was not only irregular, but based upon false allegations. Here
Demosthenes assumes that the proofs of his
bad citizenship alleged by Aeschines were at
least as irrelevant as his that Aeschines was
himself a traitor.

ἅμα τούτου κεχρημένου ἀνάγκη κἀμοὶ πρὸς ἕκαστα τῶν κατη-
43 γορημένων μικρὰ ἀποκρίνασθαι. τίνες οὖν ἦσαν οἱ παρὰ τούτου λόγοι τότε ῥηθέντες, καὶ δι᾽ οὓς ἅπαντ᾽ ἀπώλετο ; ὡς οὐ
δεῖ θορυβεῖσθαι τῷ παρεληλυθέναι Φίλιππον εἴσω Πυλῶν· ἔσται
γὰρ ἅπανθ᾽ ὅσα βούλεσθ᾽ ὑμεῖς, ἂν ἔχηθ᾽ ἡσυχίαν, καὶ ἀκού- 5
σεσθε δυοῖν ἢ τριῶν ἡμερῶν, οἷς μὲν ἐχθρὸς ἥκει, φίλον αὐτὸν
γεγενημένον, οἷς δὲ φίλος, τοὐναντίον ἐχθρόν. οὐ γὰρ τὰ
ῥήματα τὰς οἰκειότητας ἔφη βεβαιοῦν, μάλα σεμνῶς ὀνομάζων,
ἀλλὰ τὸ ταὐτὰ συμφέρειν· συμφέρειν δὲ Φιλίππῳ καὶ Φωκεῦσι καὶ ὑμῖν ὁμοίως ἅπασι τῆς ἀναλγησίας καὶ τῆς βαρύ- 10
44 τητος ἀπαλλαγῆναι τῆς τῶν Θηβαίων. ταῦτα δ᾽ ἀσμένως τινὲς
ἤκουον αὐτοῦ διὰ τὴν τόθ᾽ ὑποῦσαν ἀπέχθειαν πρὸς τοὺς Θηβαίους. τί οὖν συνέβη μετὰ ταῦτ᾽ εὐθύς, οὐκ εἰς μακράν ;
τοὺς μὲν Φωκέας ἀπολέσθαι ˙ καὶ κατασκαφῆναι ˙ τὰς πόλεις
αὐτῶν, ὑμᾶς δ᾽ ἡσυχίαν ἀγαγόντας καὶ τούτῳ πεισθέντας μικ- 15
45 ρὸν ὕστερον σκευαγωγεῖν ἐκ τῶν ἀγρῶν, τοῦτον δὲ χρυσίον
λαβεῖν, καὶ ἔτι πρὸς τούτοις τὴν μὲν ἀπέχθειαν τὴν πρὸς
Θηβαίους καὶ Θετταλοὺς τῇ πόλει γενέσθαι, τὴν δὲ χάριν
τὴν ὑπὲρ τῶν πεπραγμένων Φιλίππῳ. ὅτι δ᾽ οὕτω ταῦτ᾽
ἔχει, λέγε μοι τό τε τοῦ Καλλισθένους ψήφισμα καὶ τὴν 20
ἐπιστολὴν τὴν τοῦ Φιλίππου, ἐξ ὧν ἀμφοτέρων ταῦθ᾽ ἅπανθ᾽
ὑμῖν ἔσται φανερά. λέγε.

ΨΗΦΙΣΜΑ.

46 [Ἐπὶ Μνησιφίλου ἄρχοντος, συγκλήτου ἐκκλησίας ὑπὸ στρατηγῶν
καὶ πρυτάνεων [καὶ] βουλῆς γνώμῃ, μαιμακτηριῶνος δεκάτῃ ἀπιόντος, 25

---

1. κατηγορημένων] κατηγορουμένων Σ.   2. ἀποκρίνασθαι] Ita ΣA et socii, ἀπο-
λογήσασθαι ΓΦ γρ. Σ: volg. ante Bekk. ἀποκρίνεσθαι.   9. συμφέρειν] Ita Σ p :
ceteri συμφέρει.   14. Φωκέας] ταλαιπώρους Φωκέας omnes praeter Σ, et edd. usque ad
Bekk.   18. Θηβαίους] Ita Σ p A et socii : ceteri τοὺς Θηβαίους.   21. τὴν τοῦ]
τοῦ Σ p Ω u. Mox ordo verborum ταῦθ᾽ .. ἔσται in variis codd. variat : receptam lectionem
habet Σ.   24. Post στρατηγῶν addebatur γενομένης : om. ΣΓΥΦ, et ante ὑπὸ ponunt
A et socii.

§§ 43-45. Aeschines now pretended that
Philip had a common interest with you in
the ruin of Thebes. He was believed, and
the Phocians were ruined and you terrified.
8. μάλα σεμνῶς ὀνομάζων. 'With a
great display of fine names.'
10. τῆς βαρύτητος : cp. above, § 23, οἱ
τότε μὲν βαρεῖς .. Θηβαῖοι. This is
not a quality, like ἀναλγησία, so much as
the effect produced upon others, by that and
their other qualities.
13. εὐθύς, οὐκ εἰς μακράν. Emphasised,
to exclude the possibility of honest error.
17. τὴν μὲν ἀπέχθειαν κ.τ.λ. 'The

city's share was the ill-will of the Thebans
and Thessalians : their gratitude went to
Philip.' Their feelings are conceived as a
fixed quantity : out of this stock, all that
was good was bestowed upon Philip, all
that was hostile upon Athens ; hence the
articles.
§§ 46-50. This is proved by your decree
and Philip's insolent letter.
24. συγκλήτου. 'A special assembly.'
Several MSS. insert γενομένης after ἐκκλησίας or στρατηγῶν, but Σ and some of the
best of the others omit it. Cp. below, § 90,
for a similar variation.

Καλλισθένης Ἐτεονίκου Φαληρεὺς εἶπε μηδένα Ἀθηναίων μηδεμιᾷ
παρευρέσει ἐν τῇ χώρᾳ κοιταῖον γίγνεσθαι, ἀλλ' ἐν ἄστει καὶ Πειραιεῖ,
ὅσοι μὴ ἐν τοῖς φρουρίοις εἰσὶν ἀποτεταγμένοι· τούτων δ' ἑκάστους ἦν
παρέλαβον τάξιν διατηρεῖν μήτε ἀφημερεύοντας μήτε ἀποκοιτοῦντας.
5 ὃς δ' ἂν ἀπειθήσῃ τῷδε τῷ ψηφίσματι, ἔνοχος ἔστω τοῖς τῆς προδοσίας 47
ἐπιτιμίοις, ἐὰν μή τι ἀδύνατον ἐπιδεικνύῃ περὶ ἑαυτὸν ὄν· περὶ δὲ τοῦ
ἀδυνάτου ἐπικρινέτω ὁ ἐπὶ τῶν ὅπλων στρατηγὸς καὶ ὁ ἐπὶ τῆς διοικήσεως καὶ ὁ γραμματεὺς τῆς βουλῆς. κατακομίζειν δὲ καὶ τὰ ἐκ τῶν
ἀγρῶν πάντα τὴν ταχίστην, τὰ μὲν ἐντὸς σταδίων ἑκατὸν εἴκοσιν εἰς
10 ἄστυ καὶ Πειραιᾶ, τὰ δὲ ἐκτὸς σταδίων ἑκατὸν εἴκοσιν εἰς Ἐλευσῖνα
καὶ Φυλὴν καὶ Ἀφιδναν καὶ Ῥαμνοῦντα καὶ Σούνιον. εἶπε Καλλισθένης Φαληρεύς.]

Ἆρ' ἐπὶ ταύταις ταῖς ἐλπίσι τὴν εἰρήνην ἐποιεῖσθε, ἢ ταῦτ' 48
ἐπηγγέλλεθ' ὑμῖν οὗτος ὁ μισθωτός;
15 Λέγε δὴ τὴν ἐπιστολὴν ἣν δεῦρ' ἔπεμψε Φίλιππος μετὰ
ταῦτα.

ΕΠΙΣΤΟΛΗ.

[Βασιλεὺς Μακεδόνων Φίλιππος Ἀθηναίων τῇ βουλῇ καὶ τῷ δήμῳ 49
χαίρειν. ἴστε ἡμᾶς παρεληλυθότας εἴσω Πυλῶν καὶ τὰ κατὰ τὴν
20 Φωκίδα ὑφ' ἑαυτοὺς πεποιημένους, καὶ ὅσα μὲν ἑκουσίως προσετίθετο
τῶν πολισμάτων, φρουρὰς εἰσαγηοχότας, τὰ δὲ μὴ ὑπακούοντα κατὰ
κράτος λαβόντες καὶ ἐξανδραποδισάμενοι κατεσκάψαμεν. ἀκούων δὲ 50
καὶ ὑμᾶς παρασκευάζεσθαι βοηθεῖν αὐτοῖς γέγραφα ὑμῖν, ἵνα μὴ ἐπὶ
πλέον ἐνοχλῆσθε περὶ τούτων· τοῖς μὲν γὰρ ὅλοις οὐδὲν μέτριόν μοι
25 δοκεῖτε ποιεῖν, τὴν εἰρήνην συνθέμενοι καὶ ὁμοίως ἀντιπαρεξάγοντες,
καὶ ταῦτα οὐδὲ συμπεριειλημμένων τῶν Φωκέων ἐν ταῖς κοιναῖς ἡμῶν
συνθήκαις. ὥστε ἐὰν μὴ ἐμμένητε τοῖς ὡμολογημένοις, οὐδὲν προτερή-
σετε ἔξω τοῦ ἐφθακέναι ἀδικοῦντες.]

Ἀκούετε ὡς σαφῶς δηλοῖ καὶ διορίζεται ἐν τῇ πρὸς ὑμᾶς 51

---

5. ὅν] Ob similitudinem ultimae verbi ἑαυτὸν syllabae, om. ΣΦΥ.   10. εἰς ante
Ἐλευσῖνα om. ΣF et al.   15. δὴ] Ita ΣΦΥ, δ' αὐτὴν A ct socii, ceteri δ' αὖ.
23. ἐπὶ] Om. ΣF et socii.   25. εἰρήνην] εἰρήνην ἣν ΣΥΦ, vix, ut credo, fortuito.

6. τι ἀδύνατον. 'Something *rendering*
it impossible.' Cp. below, § 157, which
looks as if it were a regular legal phrase.

7. ὁ ἐπὶ τῆς διοικήσεως. Perhaps the
compiler thought that, as the board of στρατηγοὶ were the only important body of
executive officers, they divided all depart-
ments of government among themselves. In
fact, the paymaster was an independent officer, otherwise called ὁ ταμίας τῆς διοικήσεως.

21. τὰ δὲ μὴ ὑπακούοντα κ.τ.λ. harmonises very ill with Demosthenes' statement, De F. L. p. 360, § 68.

26. οὐδὲ συμπεριειλημμένων. οὐδὲ is
used because though no treaty could have
justified armed intervention without previous
negotiation, even this excuse was absent.

§§ 51-53. *This insult to you confirmed
his ascendancy over his own allies, and all
this was due to Aeschines.*

29. ἀκούετε .. τοὺς ἑαυτοῦ συμμάχους.
'You see how his letter to you is really addressed to his own allies—to establish a plain
contrast (σαφῶς .. δηλοῖ καὶ διορίζεται) for
their instruction.' The *contrast* is between
Philip's policy and that of Athens : it is explained by Demosthenes' paraphrase of the
sense of the letter, 'You see I have carried
out a policy of benevolence to you in the
teeth of Athens : hence you must count
upon Athenian enmity (τούτους μὲν ἐχθροὺς
ὑπολήψεσθε), and rely upon me [as able and
willing to protect you against Athens, which
I have already humbled].'

ἐπιστολῇ πρὸς τοὺς ἑαυτοῦ συμμάχους, ὅτι " ἐγὼ ταῦτα πεποίηκα ἀκόντων Ἀθηναίων καὶ λυπουμένων, ὥστ᾽ εἴπερ εὖ φρο-
νεῖτε, ὦ Θηβαῖοι καὶ Θετταλοί, τούτους μὲν ἐχθροὺς ὑπολήψεσθε, ἐμοὶ δὲ πιστεύσετε," οὐ τούτοις τοῖς ῥήμασι γράψας,
52 ταῦτα δὲ βουλόμενος δεικνύναι. τοιγαροῦν ἐκ τούτων ᾤχετ᾽ 5
ἐκείνους λαβὼν εἰς τὸ μηδ᾽ ὁτιοῦν προορᾶν τῶν μετὰ ταῦτα
μηδ᾽ αἰσθάνεσθαι, ἀλλ᾽ ἐᾶσαι πάντα τὰ πράγματα ἐκεῖνον ὑφ᾽
ἑαυτῷ ποιήσασθαι· ἐξ ὧν ταῖς παρούσαις συμφοραῖς οἱ ταλαί-
53 πωροι κέχρηνται. ὁ δὲ ταύτης τῆς πίστεως αὐτῷ συνεργὸς
καὶ συναγωνιστὴς καὶ ὁ δεῦρ᾽ ἀπαγγείλας τὰ ψευδῆ καὶ φενα- 10
κίσας ὑμᾶς οὑτοσὶ ὁ τὰ Θηβαίων ὀδυρόμενος νῦν πάθη καὶ
διεξιὼν ὡς οἰκτρά, καὶ τούτων καὶ τῶν ἐν Φωκεῦσι κακῶν καὶ
ὅσ᾽ ἄλλα πεπόνθασιν οἱ Ἕλληνες ἁπάντων αὐτὸς ὢν αἴτιος.
54 δῆλον γὰρ ὅτι σὺ μὲν ἀλγεῖς ἐπὶ τοῖς συμβεβηκόσιν, Αἰσχίνη,
καὶ τοὺς Θηβαίους ἐλεεῖς, κτήματ᾽ ἔχων ἐν τῇ Βοιωτίᾳ καὶ 15
γεωργῶν τὰ ἐκείνων, ἐγὼ δὲ χαίρω, ὃς εὐθὺς ἐξῃτούμην ὑπὸ
τοῦ ταῦτα πράξαντος.

Ἀλλὰ γὰρ ἐμπέπτωκα εἰς λόγους, οὓς αὐτίκα μᾶλλον ἴσως
ἁρμόσει λέγειν. ἐπάνειμι δὴ πάλιν ἐπὶ τὰς ἀποδείξεις, ὡς τὰ
τούτων ἀδικήματα τῶν νυνὶ παρόντων πραγμάτων γέγονεν 20
αἴτια.

8. Extr. ταλαίπωροι κέχρηνται] Post alterum horum, Θηβαῖοι add. omnes praeter Σ.
11. οὑτοσί] οὗτός ἐστιν omnes praeter Σ.   15. κτήματ᾽] κτῆμ᾽ Σ.

5. ᾤχετ᾽ ἐκείνους λαβών. 'Carried them
along with him till they neither foresaw nor
perceived anything that followed.' ᾤχετο
implies further that he got beyond the reach
of control. The force of προορᾶν and αἰσθάνεσθαι is, 'They neither anticipated that his
measures would enslave them, nor realised
that they were enslaved.'

11. ὁ τὰ Θηβαίων κ.τ.λ. Ae. in Ct. §
157, is the passage especially intended.

§ 54. Before narrating the full measure
of these calamities, I will complete the proof
that Aeschines is responsible for them.

16. γεωργῶν τὰ ἐκείνων: cp. D. de F. L.
§§ 158, 360.

17. τοῦ ταῦτα πράξαντος. Alexander,
who destroyed Thebes, which Philip had
before enslaved. Aeschines held Demosthenes
responsible for the ruin of Thebes, on the
ground that he had promoted the revolt:
Demosthenes claims this very fact, attested
by Alexander (ὃς εὐθὺς ἐξῃτούμην ὑπὸ τοῦ
ταῦτα πράξαντος), as a proof of his sympathy with the liberty of Thebes. It does
refute the charge ἐγὼ δὲ χαίρω artfully put

into the mouth of Aeschines, who never said
so.

18. ἀλλὰ γάρ. 'But let me stop,' 'but
let this wait,' a common formula of interruption : cp. below, § 267. Commonly explained as an ellipsis ; 'but [I will stop]
for...' It would be more accurate to say
that the protasis is transposed, than that the
apodosis is suppressed ; e.g. there is here substantially the apodosis required in ἐπάνειμι
δή : and, even where there is no word like
this, to go on with another subject itself expressed that a change of subject is desirable
for the reason alleged. Cp. Soph. Antig.
148, where ἀλλὰ γάρ is followed by the
apodosis ἐκ μὲν δὴ πολέμων κ.τ.λ., while in
the same chorus, l. 155, it has (unless a
line has been lost) no formal apodosis at all.
In Latin sed enim is sometimes used in the
same way to introduce an interruption, sometimes it has an intensive force—to which
the hypothesis of an ellipsis is inapplicable.

αὐτίκα. Exactly the English 'presently :' and like it, has come to be opposed
to its primitive sense 'immediately.'

Ἐπειδὴ γὰρ ἐξηπάτησθε μὲν ὑμεῖς ὑπὸ τοῦ Φιλίππου διὰ 55
τούτων τῶν ἐν ταῖς πρεσβείαις μισθωσάντων ἑαυτοὺς [τῷ Φι-
λίππῳ] καὶ οὐδὲν ἀληθὲς ὑμῖν ἀπαγγειλάντων, ἐξηπάτηντο δὲ
οἱ ταλαίπωροι Φωκεῖς καὶ ἀνῄρηντο αἱ πόλεις αὐτῶν, τί ἐγέ-
5 νετο; οἱ μὲν κατάπτυστοι Θετταλοὶ καὶ ἀναίσθητοι Θηβαῖοι
φίλον, εὐεργέτην, σωτῆρα τὸν Φίλιππον ἡγοῦντο· πάντ' ἐκεῖνος ἦν αὐτοῖς· οὐδὲ φωνὴν ἤκουον, εἴ τις ἄλλο τι βούλοιτο
λέγειν. ὑμεῖς δὲ ὑφορώμενοι τὰ πεπραγμένα καὶ δυσχεραί-
νοντες ἤγετε τὴν εἰρήνην ὅμως· οὐ γὰρ ἦν ὅ τι ἂν ἐποιεῖτε.
10 καὶ οἱ ἄλλοι δὲ Ἕλληνες, ὁμοίως ὑμῖν πεφενακισμένοι καὶ 56
διημαρτηκότες ὧν ἤλπισαν, ἦγον τὴν εἰρήνην ἄσμενοι, καὶ αὐτοὶ
τρόπον τινὰ ἐκ πολλοῦ πολεμούμενοι. ὅτε γὰρ περιιὼν Φίλιππος Ἰλλυριοὺς καὶ Τριβαλλούς, τινὰς δὲ καὶ τῶν Ἑλλήνων
κατεστρέφετο, καὶ δυνάμεις πολλὰς καὶ μεγάλας ἐποιεῖθ' ὑφ'
15 ἑαυτῷ, καί τινες τῶν ἐκ τῶν πόλεων ἐπὶ τῇ τῆς εἰρήνης ἐξουσίᾳ
βαδίζοντες ἐκεῖσε διεφθείροντο, ὧν εἷς οὗτος ἦν, τότε πάντες,
ἐφ' οὓς ταῦτα παρεσκευάζετ' ἐκεῖνος, ἐπολεμοῦντο. εἰ δὲ μὴ 57

---

2. τῷ Φιλίππῳ] Om. A et socii Bekk. Dind. Et certe durum est, cum τοῦ Φιλίππου
praecesserit : sed unde nisi ex veritate accessit ?   11. ἄσμενοι, καὶ] Om. Σ.

§§ 55–57. *After you were cheated and
the Phocians ruined, Philip was strengthened,
and you and the rest of Greece bewildered
and paralysed; so that Philip was ready to
make war upon all, for, through different
causes, none heeded the warnings I gave.*

6. πάντ' ἐκεῖνος ἦν αὐτοῖς: cp. Herod.
I. 122.

11. ὧν ἤλπισαν. The humiliation of
Thebes, which was desired by Sparta and
her old allies, and by the Achaeans.

ἄσμενοι. A predicate, the reason of
which is given by καὶ .. πολεμούμενοι: 'The
treaty was a relief to them, which they enjoyed : for Philip, in a remote kind of a
way, was making war upon them as well as
upon us, until it came.' The clause describing the conduct of the other Greeks is parallel to that describing the conduct of Athens,
so that ὑμεῖς .. ὅμως answers to καὶ οἱ ἄλλοι .. ἄσμενοι, the individual word ὅμως
balances ἄσμενοι, and by consequence οὐ γὰρ
.. ἐποιεῖτε must be balanced by καὶ αὐτοὶ ..
πολεμούμενοι. But for this parallelism, it
would be tempting to say, that the real war
continued in spite of the nominal peace;
and this was obviously the view of the writer
of Σ, who omits ἄσμενοι καί. Nor is the
presence of these words fatal to this interpretation, which would suit the circumstances and the arguments, if it is not at variance with Demosthenes' cast of expression.

12. ἐκ πολλοῦ πολεμούμενοι. Lit.
' from a distance,' so ' indirectly :' for the
passive use of πολεμούμενοι, cp. Thuc. I.
37.

13. τινὰς δὲ καὶ κ.τ.λ. Amphipolis, and
the confederacy of Olynthus.

15. τινές .. ἐκεῖσε. ' Sundry of the visitors from *Greek* states, who went there
freely, for they professed to *be at peace*, or
making peace.' τῶν πόλεων, ' The cities' of
Greece, marked off as a class from ἔθνη, like
Ἰλλυριοὶ or Τριβαλλοί. There is a sort of
zeugma in the words τῆς εἰρήνης. The
phrase includes both the numerous states,
not directly involved in the war ended by
the peace of Philocrates, in which the conquests spoken of were made, and Aeschines
(ὧν εἷς οὗτος ἦν). In the former case ἐπὶ
τῇ τῆς εἰρήνης ἐξουσίᾳ must mean, 'Relying
on the absence of declared hostilities;' in
the latter, ' Authorised by the peace he went
to negotiate:' for we can hardly think of
him as corrupted before the declaration of
the war, since we learn from Dem. de Fals.
Leg. §§ 10–15, that until his first embassy
to Macedonia, Aeschines was an eager opponent of Philip, and that even on his return
his tone was for a time moderate and
patriotic.

17. εἰ δὲ μὴ κ.τ.λ. '[The danger and
the uneasiness were real :] if the cause was
unperceived, that was not my fault.'

ἠσθάνοντο, ἕτερος λόγος οὗτος, οὐ πρὸς ἐμέ. ἐγὼ μὲν γὰρ
προὔλεγον καὶ διεμαρτυρόμην καὶ παρ᾽ ὑμῖν ἀεὶ καὶ ὅποι πεμ-
φθείην· αἱ δὲ πόλεις ἐνόσουν τῶν μὲν ἐν τῷ πολιτεύεσθαι καὶ
πράττειν δωροδοκούντων καὶ διαφθειρομένων ἐπὶ χρήμασι, τῶν
δὲ ἰδιωτῶν καὶ πολλῶν τὰ μὲν οὐ προορωμένων, τὰ δὲ τῇ καθ᾽ 5
ἡμέραν ῥᾳστώνῃ καὶ σχολῇ δελεαζομένων, καὶ τοιουτονί τι
πάθος πεπονθότων ἁπάντων, πλὴν οὐκ ἐφ᾽ ἑαυτοὺς ἑκάστων
οἰομένων τὸ δεινὸν ἥξειν, ἀλλὰ διὰ τῶν ἑτέρων κινδύνων τὰ
58 ἑαυτῶν ἀσφαλῶς σχήσειν, ὅταν βούλωνται. εἶτ᾽ οἶμαι συμβέβηκε τοῖς μὲν πλήθεσιν ἀντὶ τῆς πολλῆς καὶ ἀκαίρου ῥᾳθυ- 10
μίας τὴν ἐλευθερίαν ἀπολωλεκέναι, τοῖς δὲ προεστηκόσι καὶ
τἆλλα πλὴν ἑαυτοὺς οἰομένοις πωλεῖν πρώτους ἑαυτοὺς πεπρακόσιν αἰσθέσθαι· ἀντὶ γὰρ φίλων καὶ ξένων, ἃ τότε ὠνομά-
ζοντο, ἡνίκα ἐδωροδόκουν, νῦν κόλακες καὶ θεοῖς ἐχθροὶ καὶ
59 τἆλλ᾽ ἃ προσήκει πάντ᾽ ἀκούουσιν. εἰκότως· οὐδεὶς γὰρ, ἄν- 15
δρες Ἀθηναῖοι, τὸ τοῦ προδιδόντος συμφέρον ζητῶν χρήματ᾽
ἀναλίσκει, οὐδ᾽ ἐπειδὰν ὧν ἂν πρίηται κύριος γένηται, τῷ προ-
δότῃ συμβούλῳ περὶ τῶν λοιπῶν ἔτι χρῆται· οὐδὲν γὰρ ἂν
ἦν εὐδαιμονέστερον προδότου. ἀλλ᾽ οὐκ ἔστι ταῦτα· πόθεν ;
πολλοῦ γε καὶ δεῖ. ἀλλ᾽ ἐπειδὰν τῶν πραγμάτων ἐγκρατὴς 20
ὁ ζητῶν ἄρχειν καταστῇ, καὶ τῶν ταῦτα ἀποδομένων δεσπότης
ἐστί, τὴν δὲ πονηρίαν εἰδὼς τότε δή, τότε καὶ μισεῖ καὶ ἀπιστεῖ

---

8. ἀλλά] καὶ ΣΥ et al.   9. Post σχήσειν addebatur ante Bekk. ὑπολαμβανόντων:
om. Σ.   15. εἰκότως] Om. ΣF et al.   19. οὐκ ἔστι ταῦτα] Post haec οὐκ ἔστιν
iterant omnes praeter Σ : haud ita inepte.

3. αἱ δὲ πόλεις .. ἥξειν. 'The cities
suffered under the venality and corruption of
their active politicians, and the shortsightedness, the blind love of ease and repose, of
the majority of private citizens: all the states
alike being in this frame of mind, only each
thinking that they were the one beyond the
reach of danger.' πλὴν .. ἥξειν, lit. 'That
it would come, but not as far as themselves.'
πλὴν, because ἑκάστων modifies ἑαυτούς.

§ 58. As a result the many are enslaved ;
their leaders who betrayed them find themselves betrayed.

9. συμβέβηκε. Almost, 'They found it
included in their bargain,' rather as a consequence than a coincidence: though no doubt
the word is meant to remark on the event
being so exactly the reverse of their expecta-
tions.

12. πρώτους must agree with ἑαυτούς, so
that we cannot imagine Demosthenes to
mean, 'Feel the slavery first.' They were
the first thing sold, though perhaps the last

to pass into the purchasers' hands, i. e. the
man who concluded a treacherous bargain,
thereby put himself in the power of his
country's enemy, even before he fulfilled the
bargain by putting his country in his power
too. The force of πεπρακόσιν, moreover,
when used metaphorically of persons, is
always rather 'betrayed' than 'given into
slavery.' Cp. Soph. Phil. 978, Aesch. Cho.
915 ; though in the latter passage there is a
play on the literal sense.

§§ 59, 60. Of course Philip never loved
them : and when he found he no longer
needed them, he cast them off.

16. ζητῶν. The really important predicate: 'No one seeks the traitor's profit, when
he spends his money.'

19. πόθεν. 'It is not so ; why should it
be ?' Tr. 'of course not.'

22. τὴν δὲ .. τότε δή. 'And as he can
afford to discover their villainy then,' having
till then affected to treat them as honest
partisans.

καὶ προπηλακίζει. σκοπεῖτε δέ· καὶ γὰρ εἰ παρελήλυθεν ὁ **60**
τῶν πραγμάτων καιρὸς, ὁ τοῦ γε εἰδέναι τὰ τοιαῦτα καιρὸς
ἀεὶ πάρεστι τοῖς εὖ φρονοῦσι. μέχρι τούτου Λασθένης φίλος
ὠνομάζετο Φιλίππου, ἕως προὔδωκεν Ὄλυνθον· μέχρι τούτου
5 Τιμόλαος, ἕως ἀπώλεσε Θήβας· μέχρι τούτου Εὔδικος καὶ
Σῖμος οἱ Λαρισαῖοι, ἕως Θετταλίαν ὑπὸ Φιλίππῳ ἐποίησαν.
εἶτ' ἐλαυνομένων καὶ ὑβριζομένων καὶ τί κακὸν οὐχὶ πασχόντων
πᾶσα ἡ οἰκουμένη μεστὴ γέγονε προδοτῶν. τί δ' Ἀρίστρατος
ἐν Σικυῶνι, καὶ τί Περίλαος ἐν Μεγάροις; οὐκ ἀπερριμμένοι;
10 ἐξ ὧν καὶ σαφέστατ' ἄν τις ἴδοι ὅτι ὁ μάλιστα φυλάττων τὴν **61**
ἑαυτοῦ πατρίδα καὶ πλεῖστα ἀντιλέγων τούτοις, οὗτος ὑμῖν,
Αἰσχίνη, τοῖς προδιδοῦσι καὶ μισθαρνοῦσι τὸ ἔχειν ἐφ' ὅτῳ
δωροδοκήσετε περιποιεῖ, καὶ διὰ τοὺς πολλοὺς τουτωνὶ καὶ τοὺς
ἀνθισταμένους τοῖς ὑμετέροις βουλήμασιν ὑμεῖς ἐστὲ σῷ καὶ
15 ἔμμισθοι, ἐπεὶ διά γε ὑμᾶς αὐτοὺς πάλαι ἂν ἀπωλώλειτε.

Καὶ περὶ μὲν τῶν τότε πραχθέντων ἔχων ἔτι πολλὰ λέγειν, **62**
καὶ ταῦτα ἡγοῦμαι πλείω τῶν ἱκανῶν εἰρῆσθαι. αἴτιος δ' οὗτος,
ὥσπερ ἑωλοκρασίαν τινά μου τῆς πονηρίας τῆς ἑαυτοῦ καὶ τῶν
ἀδικημάτων κατασκεδάσας, ἣν ἀναγκαῖον ἦν πρὸς τοὺς νεωτέ-
20 ρους τῶν πεπραγμένων ἀπολύσασθαι. παρηνώχλησθε δὲ [καὶ]

---

4. Φιλίππου] Om. ΣΥ, Φιλίππῳ γρ. Σ.   13. τουτωνὶ] Ita Σ, τούτους Bekk., τούτων libri plerique.   17. καὶ] Om. ΣΑ et socii: statim ὑμεῖς om. Σ.

7. εἶτ' ἐλαυνομένων κ.τ.λ. 'Traitors are
over all the world since then, hunted, insulted, wretched every way.'
§ 61. *Aeschines, you have to thank patriots
[like me] that you are still paid to betray your
country: but for them you would have no
country to betray.*
12. Αἰσχίνη. Besides the rhetorical
effect of this 'apostrophe,' the name is
needed to soften the change of person from
τούτοις to ὑμῖν.
13. διὰ τοὺς .. ἀνθισταμένους. 'It is,
thanks to the majority of your countrymen,
and to the men who balk your will.' τουτωνὶ, strictly, of course 'the court and audience.' Here as below, § 345, τὸ ταὐτὰ
προαιρεῖσθαι τοῖς πολλοῖς is the note of good
citizenship.
15. διά γε ὑμᾶς αὐτοὺς in form balances
the clause διὰ τοὺς .. ἀνθισταμένους; but
διὰ is in rather a different sense, like the
Latin *per* in such phrases as *per me licet,
mora nulla per Histrum* (Juv. 12. 111).
§ 62. *I leave the subject of your condition
after the peace of Philocrates, which I should
not have handled unless he had made it a
field for calumny.*

§ 62. These frequent apologies for digression, serve to cover the invidious character of Demosthenes' allusions to his rival's
conduct at a time when his own action was
below his character.
18. ὥσπερ κ.τ.λ. This is a very Greek
way of suggesting a metaphor that it would
be offensive to present in detail. Demosthenes says in effect, that Aeschines has
been drenched with villainy to the last and
nastiest dregs, and now is venting his drunken
vomit upon him; yet the harm done can be
dispelled very simply, no word could be more
neutral or general than ἀπολύσασθαι.
19. τοὺς νεωτέρους τῶν πεπραγμένων.
'Those too young to have taken part in the
events.' The lowest age for jurors was
thirty. The speech was delivered in 330 B.C.,
so the Court may well have contained
several members with only a secondhand
acquaintance with the events of 346 B.C.
20. παρηνώχλησθε. 'You too may
have sustained a little disturbance by the
way.' He does not say that they were perplexed: the word only expresses the vague
annoyance produced by a confident contra-
diction of what we know.

ὑμεῖς ἴσως, οἱ καὶ πρὶν ἐμὲ εἰπεῖν ὁτιοῦν εἰδότες τὴν τούτου
63 τότε μισθαρνίαν. καίτοι φιλίαν γε καὶ ξενίαν αὐτὴν ὀνομάζει,
καὶ νῦν εἶπέ που λέγων " ὁ τὴν Ἀλεξάνδρου ξενίαν ὀνειδίζων
ἐμοί." ἐγώ σοι ξενίαν Ἀλεξάνδρου; πόθεν λαβόντι ἢ πῶς
ἀξιωθέντι; οὔτε Φιλίππου ξένον οὔτ' Ἀλεξάνδρου φίλον εἴποιμ' 5
ἂν ἐγώ σε, οὐχ οὕτω μαίνομαι, εἰ μὴ καὶ τοὺς θεριστὰς καὶ
τοὺς ἄλλο τι μισθοῦ πράττοντας φίλους καὶ ξένους δεῖ καλεῖν
64 τῶν μισθωσαμένων. ἀλλ' οὐκ ἔστι ταῦτα· πόθεν; πολλοῦ
γε καὶ δεῖ. ἀλλὰ μισθωτὸν ἐγώ σε Φιλίππου πρότερον καὶ
νῦν Ἀλεξάνδρου καλῶ, καὶ οὗτοι πάντες. εἰ δ' ἀπιστεῖς, ἐρώ- 10
τησον αὐτούς, μᾶλλον δ' ἐγὼ τοῦθ' ὑπὲρ σοῦ ποιήσω. πότερον ὑμῖν, ἄνδρες Ἀθηναῖοι, δοκεῖ μισθωτὸς Αἰσχίνης ἢ ξένος
εἶναι Ἀλεξάνδρου; ἀκούεις ἃ λέγουσιν.
65 Βούλομαι τοίνυν ἤδη καὶ περὶ τῆς γραφῆς αὐτῆς ἀπολογή-
σασθαι καὶ διεξελθεῖν τὰ πεπραγμέν' ἐμαυτῷ, ἵνα καίπερ εἰδὼς 15
Αἰσχίνης ὅμως ἀκούσῃ δι' ἃ φημι καὶ τούτων τῶν προβεβουλευμένων καὶ πολλῷ μειζόνων ἔτι τούτων δωρεῶν δίκαιος εἶναι
τυγχάνειν. καί μοι λέγε τὴν γραφὴν αὐτὴν λαβών.

ΓΡΑΦΗ.

66　[Ἐπὶ Χαιρώνδου ἄρχοντος, ἐλαφηβολιῶνος ἕκτῃ ἱσταμένου, Αἰσχί- 20
νης Ἀτρομήτου Κοθωκίδης ἀπήνεγκε πρὸς τὸν ἄρχοντα παρανόμων

---

4. πόθεν .. ἀξιωθέντι] Om. Tiberius.
παρανόμων addebatur γραφὴν: om. ΣΓΥΦ.

12. μισθωτὸς] † μίσθωτος Σ †.　　21. Post

§§ 63, 64. *Yet he claims to be a courtier,
mere hireling as he is and you think him.*

2. ξενίαν. 'Guestright,' though somewhat harsh, is perhaps the least inadequate
translation. The relation is φιλία, made
solemn and formal, and so to speak official.
τὴν Ἀλεξάνδρου ξενίαν would be, 'My
guestright with Alexander.'

5. Φιλίππου .. φίλον. He would be
Philip's ξένος in virtue of their friendly intercourse on the embassy, but to Alexander
personally he would only be a φίλος, till he
actually enjoyed his hospitality, though the
relation itself was hereditary.

8. ἀλλ' οὐκ .. δεῖ: verbatim above, § 59.
The motive of these repetitions is to produce the full effect on every hearer. From
this point of view they correspond with an
artifice common in the Republic, where
Socrates puts the proposition to which he
wants Glaucon's assent in several different
forms, before Glaucon admits that he understands it sufficiently to agree with it.

13. ἀκούεις ἃ λέγουσιν. Ulpian mentions a tradition that Demosthenes purposely

misplaced the accent of μισθωτὸς tô get the
audience to correct him, which is valuable as
a proof that in prose the Grammarians supposed accent to have been the predominant
element in pronunciation : Dissen supposes
that the phrase was added on publication,
as Aeschines would have had friends enough
present to make the answer doubtful. Σ
writes μίσθωτος, according to the tradition.

§ 65. *Now I come to the actual charge,
as Aeschines wishes.*

14. τοίνυν. 'Therefore,' as I see. I
need dwell no longer upon the irrelevancies
forced upon me by Aeschines.

16. τῶν προβεβουλευμένων. 'For which
the preliminary decree is passed.' Cp. above,
§ 10, τοῦ προβουλεύματος, note.

§§ 66–68. [*Indictment.*]

21. Σ and some others omit γραφὴν,
commonly added after παρανόμων. It would
be as easy to explain ἀπήνεγκε παρανόμων
as a technical brachylogy, as by imputing
laziness or carelessness to the copyist of the
archetype.

κατὰ Κτησιφῶντος τοῦ Λεωσθένους Ἀναφλυστίου, ὅτι ἔγραψε
παράνομον ψήφισμα, ὡς ἄρα δεῖ στεφανῶσαι Δημοσθένην Δημοσθένους Παιανιέα χρυσῷ στεφάνῳ, καὶ ἀναγορεῦσαι ἐν τῷ θεάτρῳ
Διονυσίοις τοῖς μεγάλοις, τραγῳδοῖς καινοῖς, ὅτι στεφανοῖ ὁ δῆμος 67
5 Δημοσθένην Δημοσθένους Παιανιέα χρυσῷ στεφάνῳ ἀρετῆς ἕνεκα,
καὶ εὐνοίας ἧς ἔχων διατελεῖ εἴς τε τοὺς Ἕλληνας ἅπαντας καὶ τὸν
δῆμον τῶν Ἀθηναίων, καὶ ἀνδραγαθίας, καὶ διότι διατελεῖ πράττων
καὶ λέγων τὰ βέλτιστα τῷ δήμῳ καὶ πρόθυμός ἐστι ποιεῖν ὅ τι
ἂν δύνηται ἀγαθόν, πάντα ταῦτα ψευδῆ γράψας καὶ παράνομα, τῶν 68
10 νόμων οὐκ ἐώντων πρῶτον μὲν ψευδεῖς γραφὰς εἰς τὰ δημόσια
γράμματα καταβάλλεσθαι, εἶτα τὸν ὑπεύθυνον στεφανοῦν (ἔστι δὲ
Δημοσθένης τειχοποιὸς καὶ ἐπὶ τῷ θεωρικῷ τεταγμένος), ἔτι δὲ μὴ
ἀναγορεύειν τὸν στέφανον ἐν τῷ θεάτρῳ Διονυσίοις τραγῳδῶν τῇ
καινῇ, ἀλλ᾽ ἐὰν μὲν ἡ βουλὴ στεφανοῖ, ἐν τῷ βουλευτηρίῳ ἀνει-
15 πεῖν, ἐὰν δὲ ἡ πόλις, ἐν πυκνὶ ἐν τῇ ἐκκλησίᾳ. τίμημα τάλαντα
πεντήκοντα. κλητῆρες Κηφισοφῶν Κηφισοφῶντος Ῥαμνούσιος,
Κλέων Κλέωνος Κοθωκίδης.]

Ἃ μὲν διώκει τοῦ ψηφίσματος, ἄνδρες Ἀθηναῖοι, ταῦτ᾽ 69
ἐστιν. ἐγὼ δ᾽ ἀπ᾽ αὐτῶν τούτων πρῶτον οἶμαι δῆλον ὑμῖν
20 ποιήσειν ὅτι πάντα δικαίως ἀπολογήσομαι· τὴν γὰρ αὐτὴν
τούτῳ ποιησάμενος τῶν γεγραμμένων τάξιν περὶ πάντων ἐρῶ
καθ᾽ ἕκαστον ἐφεξῆς καὶ οὐδὲν ἑκὼν παραλείψω. τοῦ μὲν οὖν 70
γράψαι πράττοντα καὶ λέγοντα τὰ βέλτιστά με τῷ δήμῳ
διατελεῖν καὶ πρόθυμον εἶναι ποιεῖν ὅ τι ἂν δύνωμαι ἀγαθόν,
25 καὶ ἐπαινεῖν ἐπὶ τούτοις, ἐν τοῖς πεπολιτευμένοις τὴν κρίσιν
εἶναι νομίζω· ἀπὸ γὰρ τούτων ἐξεταζομένων εὑρεθήσεται εἴτε
ἀληθῆ περὶ ἐμοῦ γέγραφε Κτησιφῶν ταῦτα καὶ προσήκοντα

---

7. τῶν] τὸν T Bekk, Dind.   11. ἔστι δὲ] ἔστι ΣΥΦΩ et al.: et mox τῶν θεωρικῶν
Ω et al., τῶν θεωριῶν ΣΦΤΦ.   15. ἐν τῇ] τῇ pks.   24. εἶναι] εἶναί μοι Α.

2. ὡς ἄρα: cp. above, § 27, ὡς ἄρα ἐγὼ
.. κεκωλυκὼς εἴην, where the ironical form
is more in place than in a legal document.
It occurs again below, § 90, in the decree
of Eubulus.

15. ἐν πυκνὶ ἐν τῇ ἐκκλησίᾳ. Three
MSS. omit the second ἐν: cp. Ae. in Ct. § 52.

τίμημα τάλαντα πεντήκοντα. The
fine was purposely fixed at a sum too high
to pay, that Ctesiphon might be disfranchised as a state debtor. Hence, in § 18
and elsewhere, Demosthenes dwells on the
danger of his becoming ἄτιμος.

§ 69. *And here I will take the order of
his indictment.*

18. ἃ μὲν answers to ἐγὼ δ᾽. In an
earlier stage of Greek prose the antithesis
would have been more symmetrical, e. g. Ἃ
μὲν διώκει Αἰσχίνης .. ἀπ᾽ αὐτῶν δὲ τούτων
ἐγώ.

19. ἐγὼ .. παραλείψω. Having gained
one rhetorical advantage in the exordium,
by refusing to follow the order of his opponent's speech, he here secures another by
promising to follow the order of the indictment, where of course his opponent had to
follow the order of Ctesiphon's decree. πρῶτον. 'The very first proof of the fairness
of my reply will be found in its arrangement'
[its substance when completed will supply
another].

§ 70. *The first count refers to my policy.*

22. τοῦ μὲν οὖν γράψαι κ.τ.λ. i. e. the
words of the decree and the vote of thanks
must be judged by my public policy.

27. προσήκοντα. The symmetry of the
sentence suggests ἐμοὶ to be supplied from
περὶ ἐμοῦ. Tr. 'If this that Ctesiphon has
written of me is true and fitting.'

71 εἴτε καὶ ψευδῆ· τὸ δὲ μὴ προσγράψαντα "ἐπειδὰν τὰς εὐθύνας δῶ" στεφανοῦν, καὶ ἀνειπεῖν ἐν τῷ θεάτρῳ τὸν στέφανον
κελεῦσαι, κοινωνεῖν μὲν ἡγοῦμαι καὶ τοῦτο τοῖς πεπολιτευμένοις, εἴτε ἄξιός εἰμι τοῦ στεφάνου καὶ τῆς ἀναρρήσεως τῆς ἐν
τούτοις εἴτε καὶ μὴ, ἔτι μέντοι καὶ τοὺς νόμους δεικτέον εἶναί 5
μοι δοκεῖ, καθ' οὓς ταῦτα γράφειν ἐξῆν τούτῳ. οὑτωσὶ μὲν,
ὦ ἄνδρες Ἀθηναῖοι, δικαίως καὶ ἁπλῶς τὴν ἀπολογίαν ἔγνωκα
72 ποιεῖσθαι, βαδιοῦμαι δ' ἐπ' αὐτὰ ἃ πέπρακταί μοι. καί με
μηδεὶς ὑπολάβῃ ἀπαρτᾶν τὸν λόγον τῆς γραφῆς, ἐὰν εἰς Ἑλληνικὰς πράξεις καὶ λόγους ἐμπέσω· ὁ γὰρ διώκων τοῦ ψη- 10
φίσματος τὸ λέγειν καὶ πράττειν τὰ ἄριστά με καὶ γεγραμ-
μένος ταῦτα ὡς οὐκ ἀληθῆ, οὗτός ἐστιν ὁ τοὺς περὶ ἁπάντων
τῶν ἐμοὶ πεπολιτευμένων λόγους οἰκείους καὶ ἀναγκαίους τῇ
γραφῇ πεποιηκώς. εἶτα καὶ πολλῶν προαιρέσεων οὐσῶν τῆς
πολιτείας τὴν περὶ τὰς Ἑλληνικὰς πράξεις εἱλόμην ἐγώ, ὥστε 15
καὶ τὰς ἀποδείξεις ἐκ τούτων δίκαιός εἰμι ποιεῖσθαι.

73 Ἃ μὲν οὖν πρὸ τοῦ πολιτεύεσθαι καὶ δημηγορεῖν ἐμὲ προΰ-
λαβε καὶ κατέσχε Φίλιππος, ἐάσω· οὐδὲν γὰρ ἡγοῦμαι τούτων εἶναι πρὸς ἐμέ· ἃ δ' ἀφ' ἧς ἡμέρας ἐπὶ ταῦτα ἐπέστην
ἐγὼ διεκωλύθη, ταῦτα ἀναμνήσω καὶ τούτων ὑφέξω λόγον, 20
74 τοσοῦτον ὑπειπών. πλεονέκτημα, ὦ ἄνδρες Ἀθηναῖοι, μέγα

2. καὶ] Om. Α. 13. Post πεπολιτευμένων καὶ πεπραγμένων add. omnes praeter
Σ Ω. 20. ἐγώ] ἐγὼ καὶ Σ Β. et S.

1. εἴτε καὶ ψευδῆ. 'Or if it is false' [as
Aeschines says, and is certainly possible].
. § 71. Even the details of the honours
voted to me must be considered with reference to my deserts, though also with reference
to the law.
2. στεφανοῦν is parallel to κελεῦσαι, not
dependent on it, 'to give me a crown without the proviso, when the accounts are
passed.'
3. κοινωνεῖν. 'Has much in common
with.' Both the details of the vote and his
public policy involve a discussion of his
character.
4. τῆς ἐν τούτοις. 'Before your countrymen.' He is addressing Aeschines, and
identifies the Court, which is the people by
representation, with the people assembled
en masse at the Dionysia (cp. below, § 310
fin.), and thereby pointedly replies to Aeschines' taunt, that he preferred a foreign to
an Athenian reputation.
§ 71. It is no digression to recall my
foreign policy: for the vote of thanks is
grounded on my whole career, which has

been spent mainly in foreign affairs.
9. ἀπαρτᾶν. Commonly taken as = dis-
jungere: the lexicographers supply no instance which might not be taken of remote
connection as well as of disconnection. Here
it would be tempting and etymologically
possible to translate, 'Make the indictment
a mere peg for the speech.'
Ἑλληνικὰς opposed to πολιτικὰς, as
foreign to domestic. Cp. below, § 139,
where it is opposed to τὰ κατὰ τὴν πόλιν
πεπολιτεύματα.
13. πεπολιτευμένων. Vide ad § 13.
14. πολλῶν προαιρέσεων κ.τ.λ. 'Whereas there are many lines of pulic life.'
§ 73. My responsibility does not begin
with the beginning of Philip's aggrandisement.
19. ἐπὶ ταῦτα, i. e. ἐπὶ τὸ πολιτεύεσθαι
καὶ δημηγορεῖν.
§ 74. Which was greatly aided by the
corruption of public men.
21. πλεονέκτημα. 'An unfair advantage' when secured, as πλεονεξία is a craving for unfair advantage.

ὑπῆρξε Φιλίππῳ. παρὰ γὰρ τοῖς Ἕλλησιν, οὐ τισὶν, ἀλλὰ
πᾶσιν ὁμοίως, φορὰν προδοτῶν καὶ δωροδόκων καὶ θεοῖς ἐχθρῶν
ἀνθρώπων συνέβη γενέσθαι τοσαύτην ὅσην οὐδείς πω πρότερον
μέμνηται γεγονυῖαν· οὓς συναγωνιστὰς καὶ συνεργοὺς λαβὼν 75
5 καὶ πρότερον κακῶς τοὺς Ἕλληνας ἔχοντας πρὸς ἑαυτοὺς καὶ
στασιαστικῶς ἔτι χεῖρον διέθηκε, τοὺς μὲν ἐξαπατῶν, τοῖς δὲ
διδοὺς, τοὺς δὲ πάντα τρόπον διαφθείρων, καὶ διέστησεν εἰς
μέρη πολλὰ ἑνὸς τοῦ συμφέροντος ἅπασιν ὄντος, κωλύειν ἐκεῖνον μέγαν γίγνεσθαι. ἐν τοιαύτῃ δὲ καταστάσει καὶ ἔτι ἀγνοίᾳ 76
10 τοῦ συνισταμένου καὶ φυομένου κακοῦ τῶν ἁπάντων Ἑλλήνων
ὄντων δεῖ σκοπεῖν ὑμᾶς, ὦ ἄνδρες Ἀθηναῖοι, τί προσῆκον ἦν
ἑλέσθαι πράττειν καὶ ποιεῖν τὴν πόλιν, καὶ τούτων λόγον παρ᾽
ἐμοῦ λαβεῖν· ὁ γὰρ ἐνταῦθα ἑαυτὸν τάξας τῆς πολιτείας εἰμὶ
ἐγώ. πότερον αὐτὴν ἐχρῆν, Αἰσχίνη, τὸ φρόνημα ἀφεῖσαν καὶ 77
15 τὴν ἀξίαν τὴν αὑτῆς ἐν τῇ Θετταλῶν καὶ Δολόπων τάξει συγ-
κατακτᾶσθαι Φιλίππῳ τὴν τῶν Ἑλλήνων ἀρχὴν καὶ τὰ τῶν
προγόνων καλὰ καὶ δίκαια ἀναιρεῖν; ἢ τοῦτο μὲν μὴ ποιεῖν,
δεινὸν γὰρ ὡς ἀληθῶς, ἃ δ᾽ ἑώρα συμβησόμενα, εἰ μηδεὶς κωλύ-
σει, καὶ προῃσθάνεθ᾽, ὡς ἔοικεν, ἐκ πολλοῦ, ταῦτα περιιδεῖν
20 γιγνόμενα ; ἀλλὰ νῦν ἔγωγε τὸν μάλιστα ἐπιτιμῶντα τοῖς 78
πεπραγμένοις ἡδέως ἂν ἐροίμην, τῆς ποίας μερίδος γενέσθαι τὴν
πόλιν ἐβούλετ᾽ ἄν, πότερον τῆς συναιτίας τῶν συμβεβηκότων
τοῖς Ἕλλησι κακῶν καὶ αἰσχρῶν, ἧς ἂν Θετταλοὺς καὶ τοὺς
μετὰ τούτων εἴποι τις, ἢ τῆς περιεορακυίας ταῦτα γιγνόμενα
25 ἐπὶ τῇ τῆς ἰδίας πλεονεξίας ἐλπίδι, ἧς ἂν Ἀρκάδας καὶ Μεσ-
σηνίους καὶ Ἀργείους θείημεν. ἀλλὰ καὶ τούτων πολλοί, μᾶλ- 79

2. θεοῖς ἐχθρῶν, almost exactly equivalent to our 'detestable.' Aristophanes uses
the word lightly; Demosthenes is fond of
using it seriously as a climax in his denun-
ciation of men.

§ 75. By whose aid he was able to aggravate the internal confusion of Greece.

6. στασιαστικῶς includes both party dis-
sensions in the separate states, and the heart-
burning and rivalries of the states with one
another.

§ 76. This imposed a duty on Athens and
on me, for I took up foreign policy.

10. φυομένου. Σ φυρομένου: but cp.
above, § 23, κατὰ πάντων ἐφύετο.

12. πράττειν καὶ ποιεῖν. 'Conduct and
action.' πράττειν has a moral element,
hence Arist. Eth. Nic. 6. 2. 2, says that
animals are incapable of action, and Plato,
Charmid. c. 11, p. 163 D, says Critias has
learnt from Prodicus to define πράξεις as

ποιήσεις τῶν ἀγαθῶν.
τούτων κ.τ.λ. 'And demand from
me an account of these things' (i. e. of conduct and action worthy of Athens), 'hold
me responsible for this.'

§ 77. Was this subservience or neutrality?

19. ὡς ἔοικεν, i. e. as was to be expected
of a wise and powerful state.

§ 78. Those who chose either disgraceful
alternative, suffered more than Athens.

21. μερίδος, related to μέρος, as party to
part.

§ 79. Even if Philip had been satisfied
with victory, it would have been disgraceful
not to oppose him; but as his victory meant
ruin, the resistance of Athens was the more
honourable and necessary.

26. καὶ τούτων. 'Even these' [whose
selfishness was not so shocking as the slavish-
ness of others].

λον δὲ πάντες, χεῖρον ἡμῶν ἀπηλλάχασιν. καὶ γὰρ εἰ μὲν ὡς
ἐκράτησε Φίλιππος ᾤχετ' εὐθέως ἀπιὼν καὶ μετὰ ταῦτ' ἦγεν
ἡσυχίαν, μήτε τῶν αὑτοῦ συμμάχων μήτε τῶν ἄλλων Ἑλλήνων μηδένα μηδὲν λυπήσας, ὅμως ἦν ἄν τις κατὰ τῶν [οὐκ]
ἐναντιωθέντων οἷς ἔπραττεν ἐκεῖνος μέμψις καὶ κατηγορία· εἰ 5
δὲ ὁμοίως ἁπάντων τὸ ἀξίωμα, τὴν ἡγεμονίαν, τὴν ἐλευθερίαν
περιείλετο, μᾶλλον δὲ καὶ τὰς πολιτείας, ὅσων ἐδύνατο, πῶς
οὐχ ἁπάντων ἐνδοξότατα ὑμεῖς ἐβουλεύσασθε ἐμοὶ πεισθέντες;
80 Ἀλλ' ἐκεῖσε ἐπανέρχομαι. τί τὴν πόλιν, Αἰσχίνη, προσῆκε
ποιεῖν ἀρχὴν καὶ τυραννίδα τῶν Ἑλλήνων ὁρῶσαν ἑαυτῷ κατα- 10
σκευαζόμενον Φίλιππον; ἢ τί τὸν σύμβουλον ἔδει λέγειν ἢ
γράφειν τὸν Ἀθήνησιν ἐμὲ (καὶ γὰρ τοῦτο πλεῖστον διαφέρει),
81 ὃς συνῄδειν μὲν ἐκ παντὸς τοῦ χρόνου μέχρι τῆς ἡμέρας ἀφ'
ἧς αὐτὸς ἐπὶ τὸ βῆμα ἀνέβην, ἀεὶ περὶ πρωτείων καὶ τιμῆς
καὶ δόξης ἀγωνιζομένην τὴν πατρίδα, καὶ πλείω καὶ χρήματα 15
καὶ σώματα ἀνηλωκυῖαν ὑπὲρ φιλοτιμίας καὶ τῶν πᾶσι συμφερόντων ἢ τῶν ἄλλων Ἑλλήνων ὑπὲρ αὑτῶν ἀνηλώκασιν ἕκαστοι,
82 ἑώρων δ' αὐτὸν τὸν Φίλιππον, πρὸς ὃν ἦν ἡμῖν ὁ ἀγών, ὑπὲρ
ἀρχῆς καὶ δυναστείας τὸν ὀφθαλμὸν ἐκκεκομμένον, τὴν κλεῖν

---

4. ὅμως] Om. ΣΑ². Mox οὐκ add. unus e Morelli codd. et marg. ΥΩ. 12. ἐμέ]
Om. Σ B. et S.

4. ἦν .. ἐναντιωθέντων. All MSS. but Σ
insert ὅμως before these words: two or three
insert οὐκ before ἐναντιωθέντων. This
reading gives the more vigorous sense, 'Not
to have opposed Philip would have been disgraceful, if it had not been suicidal;' but
the MS. authority is so decidedly against
οὐκ as to make its insertion doubtful. It is
difficult to find a sense for ὅμως without οὐκ,
and this is probably the reason why ὅμως is
omitted in Σ. If οὐκ was not omitted accidentally, the meaning must be, 'They were
to blame after all [in spite of their patriot-
ism].'

6. ἐλευθερία, 'independence;' πολιτεία,
'existence as a civic community.' The two
were separable, e. g. the subject allies of
Athens had πολιτεία but not ἐλευθερία: the
Dii, the Thracian allies of Sitalces, had
ἐλευθερία but not πολιτεία.

§ 80. To waive the question of expediency,
what became the city and her counsellors,

12. ἐμέ. Σ omits this, in which case
τοῦτο .. διαφέρει refers simply to Ἀθήνησιν,
and implies that a public man at Athens had
higher duties than another Greek: otherwise the phrase must point forward also,
and imply, 'I had a special duty, with my

double knowledge of the glory of Athens
and the daring of Philip.'

§ 81. In view of her reputation
15. χρήματα καὶ σώματα. A regular
conjunction, familiarised by the assonance
like our 'money and men.' All the MSS.
but Σ put σώματα first, like our 'men and
money.'

§ 82. And the courage of Philip, which it
would be shameful
19. τὸν ὀφθαλμόν. By an arrow at the
siege of Methone.

τὴν κλεῖν. In the Illyrian war: he
was lamed by a wound in the war with the
Triballi. He was attended after these
wounds by Nicomachus, the father of Aristotle, who we are told in detail, cured his
eye 'citra deformitatem oris,' etc. Philip's
good looks and elegant manners were a
favourite topic with his admirers (see Ae.
de F. L. p. 33, § 45), hence Demosthenes
thinks it worth while to say with a little sarcasm, 'Letting go every part of his body that
fortune might please to take,' on condition
that he might live, all that was left of him,
with honour and reputation. All his great
deeds were only done to glorify a mutilated
trunk.

M

κατεαγότα, τὴν χεῖρα, τὸ σκέλος πεπηρωμένον, πᾶν ὅ τι βου-
ληθείη μέρος ἡ τύχη τοῦ σώματος παρελέσθαι, τοῦτο προϊέ-
μενον, ὥστε τῷ λοιπῷ μετὰ τιμῆς καὶ δόξης ζῆν. καὶ μὴν 83
οὐδὲ τοῦτό γε οὐδεὶς ἂν εἰπεῖν τολμήσαι, ὡς τῷ μὲν ἐν Πέλλῃ
5 τραφέντι, χωρίῳ ἀδόξῳ τότε γε ὄντι καὶ μικρῷ, τοσαύτην
μεγαλοψυχίαν προσῆκεν ἐγγενέσθαι, ὥστε τῆς τῶν Ἑλλήνων
ἀρχῆς ἐπιθυμῆσαι καὶ τοῦτ' εἰς τὸν νοῦν ἐμβαλέσθαι, ὑμῖν δ'
οὖσιν Ἀθηναίοις καὶ κατὰ τὴν ἡμέραν ἑκάστην ἐν πᾶσι καὶ
λόγοις καὶ θεωρήμασι τῆς τῶν προγόνων ἀρετῆς ὑπομνήμαθ'
10 ὁρῶσι τοσαύτην κακίαν ὑπάρξαι ὥστε τῆς τῶν Ἑλλήνων ἐλευθερίας αὐτεπαγγέλτους ἐθελοντὰς παραχωρῆσαι Φιλίππῳ. οὐδ' 84
ἂν εἰς ταῦτα φήσειεν. λοιπὸν τοίνυν ἦν καὶ ἀναγκαῖον ἅμα
πᾶσιν οἷς ἐκεῖνος ἔπραττεν ἀδικῶν ὑμᾶς ἐναντιοῦσθαι δικαίως.
τοῦτ' ἐποιεῖτε μὲν ὑμεῖς ἐξ ἀρχῆς εἰκότως καὶ προσηκόντως,
15 ἔγραφον δὲ καὶ συνεβούλευον καὶ ἐγὼ καθ' οὓς ἐπολιτευόμην
χρόνους. ὁμολογῶ. ἀλλὰ τί ἐχρῆν με ποιεῖν; ἤδη γάρ σ' 85
ἐρωτῶ, πάντα τἄλλ' ἀφεὶς, Ἀμφίπολιν, Πύδναν, Ποτίδαιαν,
Ἀλόννησον· οὐδενὸς τούτων μέμνημαι· Σέρρειον δὲ καὶ Δορίσκον καὶ τὴν Πεπαρήθου πόρθησιν καὶ ὅσ' ἄλλα τοιαῦτα ἡ
20 πόλις ἠδίκητο, οὐδ' εἰ γέγονεν οἶδα. καίτοι σύ γ' ἔφησθά
με ταῦτα λέγοντα εἰς ἔχθραν ἐμβαλεῖν τουτουσί, Εὐβούλου
καὶ Ἀριστοφῶντος καὶ Διοπείθους τῶν περὶ τούτων ψηφισμάτων ὄντων, οὐκ ἐμῶν, ὦ λέγων εὐχερῶς ὅ τι ἂν βουληθῇς.
οὐδὲ νῦν περὶ τούτων ἐρῶ. ἀλλ' ὁ τὴν Εὔβοιαν ἐκεῖνος σφε- 86
25 τεριζόμενος καὶ κατασκευάζων ἐπιτείχισμα ἐπὶ τὴν Ἀττικήν,

---

§ 83. *Not to surpass, having a nobler
past and a better cause.*
4. ἐν Πέλλῃ τραφέντι. Demosthenes
consistently treats Philip as a barbarian,
though his claims to Hellenic descent were
generally recognised ; so here, to disparage
his Hellenic education, he says he was
brought up at Pella, though he spent several
years very profitably as a hostage at Thebes.
11. αὐτεπαγγέλτους ἐθελοντάς. 'Volun-
teer of our own accord to abandon Greek
freedom to Philip.' The two synonyms
differ as 'ultro' and 'sponte.'
§ 84. *Resistance remained : you resisted
even before my advice was given, though I
do not deny that I gave it.* For,
14. ἐξ ἀρχῆς corresponds to καθ' οὓς ἐπολιτευόμην χρόνους.
§ 85. (*I waive diplomatic grievances
urged by other statesmen, though you charge
me with using them to inflame odium ;
but*)
21. Εὐβούλου. In the Athenian As-

sembly, a speech might be made not only
without making a motion, but when no
motion was before the Assembly, so that
this refutation of Aeschines is less complete
than it looks.
24. οὐδὲ νῦν. He implies that he did
not then.
§ 86. *Was not the attempt to control Euboea, Megara, the Hellespont, a casus belli ?*
§ 86. 'But Philip [he, not I, nor even
any Athenian who did make speeches or
motions], the man who tried to appropriate
Euboea . . he was the real aggressor.' The
more obvious order would have been ἐκεῖνος
ὁ τὴν Εὔβοιαν σφετεριζόμενος, but then
ἐκεῖνος would have been the real subject,
and ὁ σφετεριζόμενος almost a mere epithet.
The present order makes ὁ τὴν Εὔβοιαν
σφετεριζόμενος the real subject, while ἐκεῖνος, in its subordinate position, just serves to
mark the antithesis.
25. κατασκευάζων ἐπιτείχισμα. 'Turning it into a post against Attica.'

καὶ Μεγάροις ἐπιχειρῶν, καὶ καταλαμβάνων Ὠρεὸν, καὶ κατα-
σκάπτων Πορθμὸν, καὶ καθιστὰς ἐν μὲν Ὠρεῷ Φιλιστίδην τύραννον, ἐν δ᾽ Ἐρετρίᾳ Κλείταρχον, καὶ τὸν Ἑλλήσποντον
ὑφ᾽ ἑαυτῷ ποιούμενος, καὶ Βυζάντιον πολιορκῶν, καὶ πόλεις
Ἑλληνίδας ἃς μὲν ἀναιρῶν, εἰς ἃς δὲ τοὺς φυγάδας κατάγων, 5
πότερον ταῦτα πάντα ποιῶν ἠδίκει καὶ παρεσπόνδει καὶ ἔλυε
τὴν εἰρήνην ἢ οὔ; καὶ πότερον φανῆναί τινα τῶν Ἑλλήνων
87 τὸν ταῦτα κωλύσοντα ποιεῖν αὐτὸν ἐχρῆν ἢ μή; εἰ μὲν γὰρ
μὴ ἐχρῆν, ἀλλὰ τὴν Μυσῶν λείαν καλουμένην τὴν Ἑλλάδα
οὖσαν ὀφθῆναι ζώντων καὶ ὄντων Ἀθηναίων, περιείργασμαι 10
μὲν ἐγὼ περὶ τούτων εἰπὼν, περιείργασται δ᾽ ἡ πόλις ἡ πει-
σθεῖσα ἐμοὶ, ἔστω δὲ ἀδικήματα πάντα ἃ πέπρακται καὶ ἁμαρ-
88 τήματα ἐμά. εἰ δὲ ἔδει τινὰ τούτων κωλυτὴν φανῆναι, τίνα
ἄλλον ἢ τὸν Ἀθηναίων δῆμον προσῆκε γενέσθαι; ταῦτα τοίνυν ἐπολιτευόμην ἐγώ, καὶ ὁρῶν καταδουλούμενον πάντας ἀνθρώ- 15
πους ἐκεῖνον ἠναντιούμην, καὶ προλέγων καὶ διδάσκων μὴ προΐ-
εσθαι ταῦτα Φιλίππῳ διετέλουν.
89 Καὶ μὴν τὴν εἰρήνην γ᾽ ἐκεῖνος ἔλυσε τὰ πλοῖα λαβὼν, οὐχ
ἡ πόλις, Αἰσχίνη. Φέρε δ᾽ αὐτὰ τὰ ψηφίσματα καὶ τὴν
ἐπιστολὴν τὴν τοῦ Φιλίππου, καὶ λέγε ἐφεξῆς· ἀπὸ γὰρ τού- 20
των ἐξεταζομένων τίς τίνος αἴτιός ἐστι γενήσεται φανερόν.

ΨΗΦΙΣΜΑ.

90 [Ἐπὶ ἄρχοντος Νεοκλέους, μηνὸς βοηδρομιῶνος, ἐκκλησίας συγκλήτου ὑπὸ στρατηγῶν, Εὔβουλος Μνησιθέου Κόπρειος εἶπεν, ἐπειδὴ

10. ζώντων καὶ ὄντων Ἀθηναίων] Ita ΣΑ et socii: ceteri ζώντων Ἀθηναίων καὶ ὄντων.
13. εἰ δὲ ἔδει.. γενέσθαι] εἰ δὲ ἔδει, τίνα τοῦτον ἄλλον ἢ τὸν Ἀθηναίων δῆμον προσῆκε
γενέσθαι γρ. Σ. † Et mihi quidem videbatur, primus quoque hujus cod. auctor inter hanc
lectionem et volgatam haesitasse: nempe primum τοῦτον scripsisse, mox alterum o in ω inter
scribendum mutasse, lineola per medium ducta. Accentus autem acutus in penultima additur,
ita ut τοῦτον non scribenti placuisse certum sit; neque ego fratri persuadere potui, formam
litterae ω non fortuito variatam esse.† τούτων τίνα habent O tu : τινὰ om. FΤΦ pv, τούτων
κωλυτὴν φανῆναι in margine habet A.

§ 87. Was such tyranny not to be resisted
by Greece? If so, Athens was wrong, and
I also.

10. 'If this was wrong, if it was right
that Greece should be seen like the Mysian
booty in the proverb, with Athenians alive
in the world, then it has all been lost labour
for me to speak of this, all lost labour for
the city to listen to me; let all that was
done go for a crime and a blunder, let the
crime and the blunder lie at my door.' ζώντων καὶ ὄντων Ἀθηναίων, more exactly,
'While there were Athenians alive, in fact
while there were Athenians.' ἐμά is em-

phatic by its position, 'A crime and a
blunder of mine' [not of Athens].

§ 88. If not, Athens ought to have stood
in the breach, as it was my policy she should
stand.

§ 89. Yet the first act of hostility came
from him.

18. τὰ πλοῖα λαβών. For this incident,
see Justin, 9. 1. 6.

§§ 90, 91. [Decree of Eubulus.]

24. ὑπὸ στρατηγῶν. A few MSS. add
συναχθείσης.

Εὔβουλος Μνησιθέου Κόπρειος. The
famous Eubulus, who is doubtless meant by

προσήγγειλαν οἱ στρατηγοὶ ἐν τῇ ἐκκλησίᾳ ὡς ἄρα Λεωδάμαντα τὸν
ναύαρχον καὶ τὰ μετ' αὐτοῦ ἀποσταλέντα σκάφη εἴκοσιν ἐπὶ τὴν
τοῦ σίτου παραπομπὴν εἰς Ἑλλήσποντον ὁ παρὰ Φιλίππου στρατηγὸς Ἀμύντας καταγήοχεν εἰς Μακεδονίαν καὶ ἐν φυλακῇ ἔχει, ἐπι- 91
5 μεληθῆναι τοὺς πρυτάνεις καὶ τοὺς στρατηγοὺς ὅπως ἡ βουλὴ συναχθῇ
καὶ αἱρεθῶσι πρέσβεις πρὸς Φίλιππον, οἵτινες παραγενόμενοι διαλέξονται πρὸς αὐτὸν περὶ τοῦ ἀφεθῆναι τὸν ναύαρχον καὶ τὰ πλοῖα καὶ
τοὺς στρατιώτας. καὶ εἰ μὲν δι' ἄγνοιαν ταῦτα πεποίηκεν ὁ Ἀμύντας,
ὅτι οὐ μεμψιμοιρεῖ ὁ δῆμος οὐδὲν αὐτῷ· εἰ δέ τι πλημμελοῦντα παρὰ
10 τὰ ἐπεσταλμένα λαβὼν, ὅτι ἐπισκεψάμενοι Ἀθηναῖοι ἐπιτιμήσουσι
κατὰ τὴν τῆς ὀλιγωρίας ἀξίαν. εἰ δὲ μηδέτερον τούτων ἐστὶν, ἀλλ'
ἰδίᾳ ἀγνωμονοῦσιν ἢ ὁ ἀποστείλας ἢ ὁ ἀπεσταλμένος, καὶ τοῦτο λέγειν,
ἵνα αἰσθανόμενος ὁ δῆμος βουλεύσηται τί δεῖ ποιεῖν.]

Τοῦτο μὲν τοίνυν τὸ ψήφισμα Εὔβουλος ἔγραψεν, οὐκ 92
15 ἐγώ, τὸ δ' ἐφεξῆς Ἀριστοφῶν, εἶθ' Ἡγήσιππος, εἶτ' Ἀριστοφῶν πάλιν, εἶτα Φιλοκράτης, εἶτα Κηφισοφῶν, εἶτα πάντες
οἱ ἄλλοι· ἐγὼ δ' οὐδὲν περὶ τούτων. λέγε.

ΨΗΦΙΣΜΑ.

[Ἐπὶ Νεοκλέους ἄρχοντος, βοηδρομιῶνος ἔνῃ καὶ νέᾳ, βουλῆς γνώ- 93
20 μῃ, πρυτάνεις καὶ στρατηγοὶ ἐχρημάτισαν τὰ ἐκ τῆς ἐκκλησίας ἀνενεγ-
κόντες, ὅτι ἔδοξε τῷ δήμῳ, πρέσβεις ἑλέσθαι πρὸς Φίλιππον περὶ τῆς
τῶν πλοίων ἀνακομιδῆς καὶ ἐντολὰς δοῦναι κατὰ τὰ ἐκ τῆς ἐκκλησίας
ψηφίσματα. καὶ εἵλοντο τούσδε, Κηφισοφῶντα Κλέωνος Ἀναφλύ-
στιον, Δημόκριτον Δημοφῶντος Ἀναγυράσιον, Πολύκριτον Ἀπημάντου

---

5. συναχθῇ] Ita A et socii p: legebatur συναχθῶσι. 18. Post ΨΗΦΙΣΜΑ,
occurrit nota ὅ ▷. διπλῆ: cujus ratio in obscuro est. Nescio an Baitero et Sauppio visum
sit indicare, duo ψηφίσματα legenda esse, ita ut titulus bis repeti debeat : certe ipsi ΨΗΦΙ-
ΣΜΑΤΑ in titulo scripserunt, sine librorum, ut videtur, auctoritate, et pro sententia utique
verborum Demosthenis. Non est prorsus idem signum atque διπλῆ περιστιγμένη, quem
πρὸς τὰς ἐνίων διορθώσεις adscribi monet Diog. Laert. lib. 3, c. 66.

Demosthenes, was really Ἀναφλύστιος, as
he is rightly called above, § 37. Similarly
Aristophon was Ἀζηνιεὺς (below, § 163),
who is called Κολλυτεὺς below, § 93.

2. ναύαρχον. See Introduction on the
Documents for this word and τὰ πλοῖα below,
§ 91, which seem to be used in the late sense
of νῆας.

5. συναχθῇ καὶ αἱρεθῶσι. The old
reading συναχθῶσι would be a very extreme
case of the plural being used with a noun
of multitude. Reiske suggested ἡ βουλὴ
καὶ ὁ δῆμος, but the text is an easier alteration, and has fair MS. authority.

§ 92. This decree and the rest are none of
mine.

§ 92. All the decrees were produced and

quoted on the trial: the compiler only inserts
what purports to be a mere appendix to a
decree already cited.

§ 93. [Decree of Aristophon.]

19. Νεοκλέους. Almost all the MSS. of
any authority except the Munich group read
Νικοκλέους; the text is due to the perverse
acuteness which perceived that the events
belonged to the same year, and not that the
archon was pseudeponymous. Boeckh's
theory of the pseudeponymous archons
would justify the reading of the best
MSS.

23. Κηφισοφῶντα. The Cephisophon
of the preceding section was Κηφισοφῶν
Μενεξένου Παιανιεύς. Of course there may
have been such a person as this.

Κοθωκίδην. πρυτανείᾳ φυλῆς Ἱπποθωντίδος, Ἀριστοφῶν Κολλυτεὺς
πρόεδρος εἶπεν.]

94 "Ὥσπερ τοίνυν ἐγὼ ταῦτα δεικνύω τὰ ψηφίσματα, οὕτω καὶ
σὺ δεῖξον, Αἰσχίνη, ποῖον ἐγὼ γράψας ψήφισμα αἴτιός εἰμι
τοῦ πολέμου. ἀλλ' οὐκ ἂν ἔχοις· εἰ γὰρ εἶχες, οὐδὲν ἂν αὐτοῦ 5
πρότερον νυνὶ παρέσχου. καὶ μὴν οὐδ' ὁ Φίλιππος οὐδὲν
αἰτιᾶται ἐμὲ ὑπὲρ τοῦ πολέμου, ἑτέροις ἐγκαλῶν. Λέγε δ'
αὐτὴν τὴν ἐπιστολὴν τὴν τοῦ Φιλίππου.

ΕΠΙΣΤΟΛΗ.

95 [Βασιλεὺς Μακεδόνων Φίλιππος Ἀθηναίων τῇ βουλῇ καὶ τῷ δήμῳ 10
χαίρειν. παραγενόμενοι πρὸς ἐμὲ οἱ παρ' ὑμῶν πρεσβευταὶ, Κηφισοφῶν καὶ Δημόκριτος καὶ Πολύκριτος, διελέγοντο περὶ τῆς τῶν πλοίων
ἀφέσεως ὧν ἐναυάρχει Λεωδάμας. καθ' ὅλου μὲν οὖν ἔμοιγε φαίνεσθε
ἐν μεγάλῃ εὐηθείᾳ ἔσεσθαι, εἰ οἴεσθ' ἐμὲ λανθάνειν ὅτι ἐξαπεστάλη
ταῦτα τὰ πλοῖα πρόφασιν μὲν ὡς τὸν σῖτον παραπέμψοντα ἐκ τοῦ Ἑλ- 15
λησπόντου εἰς Λῆμνον, βοηθήσοντα δὲ Σηλυβριανοῖς τοῖς ὑπ' ἐμοῦ μὲν
πολιορκουμένοις, οὐ συμπεριειλημμένοις δὲ ἐν ταῖς τῆς φιλίας κοινῇ
96 κειμέναις ἡμῖν συνθήκαις. καὶ ταῦτα συνετάχθη τῷ ναυάρχῳ ἄνευ μὲν
τοῦ δήμου τοῦ Ἀθηναίων, ὑπὸ δέ τινων ἀρχόντων καὶ ἑτέρων ἰδιωτῶν
μὲν νῦν ὄντων, ἐκ παντὸς δὲ τρόπου βουλομένων τὸν δῆμον ἀντὶ τῆς 20
νῦν ὑπαρχούσης πρὸς ἐμὲ φιλίας τὸν πόλεμον ἀναλαβεῖν, πολλῷ μᾶλλον φιλοτιμουμένων τοῦτο συντελεσθαι ἢ τοῖς Σηλυβριανοῖς βοηθῆ-
97 σαι. καὶ ὑπολαμβάνουσιν αὐτοῖς τὸ τοιοῦτο πρόσοδον ἔσεσθαι· οὐ
μέντοι μοι δοκεῖ τοῦτο χρήσιμον ὑπάρχειν οὔθ' ὑμῖν οὔτ' ἐμοί. διόπερ
τά τε νῦν καταχθέντα πλοῖα πρὸς ἡμᾶς ἀφίημι ὑμῖν, καὶ τοῦ λοιποῦ, 25
ἐὰν βούλησθε μὴ ἐπιτρέπειν τοῖς προεστηκόσιν ὑμῶν κακοήθως πολιτεύεσθαι, ἀλλ' ἐπιτιμᾶτε, πειράσομαι κἀγὼ διαφυλάττειν τὴν εἰρήνην.
εὐτυχεῖτε.]

98 Ἐνταῦθ' οὐδαμοῦ Δημοσθένην γέγραφεν, οὐδ' αἰτίαν οὐδεμίαν κατ' ἐμοῦ. τί ποτ' οὖν τοῖς ἄλλοις ἐγκαλῶν τῶν ἐμοὶ 30
πεπραγμένων οὐχὶ μέμνηται; ὅτι τῶν ἀδικημάτων ἂν ἐμέμνητο τῶν αὐτοῦ, εἴ τι περὶ ἐμοῦ ἐγεγράφει· τούτων γὰρ εἰχό-
99 μην ἐγὼ καὶ τούτοις ἠναντιούμην. καὶ πρῶτον μὲν τὴν εἰς

---

13. Λεωδάμας] Σ Λαομενων Λαοδαμων pz, vid. § 90.   22. φιλοτιμουμένων] Σ et
al. φιλοτιμούμενον: Ἴσων φιλοτιμουμένων Schol.

Πελοπόννησον πρεσβείαν ἔγραψα, ὅτε πρῶτον ἐκεῖνος εἰς Πελοπόννησον παρεδύετο, εἶτα τὴν εἰς Εὔβοιαν, ἡνίκ' Εὐβοίας
ἥπτετο, εἶτα τὴν ἐπ' Ὠρεὸν ἔξοδον, οὐκέτι πρεσβείαν, καὶ τὴν
εἰς Ἐρέτριαν, ἐπειδὴ τυράννους ἐκεῖνος ἐν ταύταις ταῖς πόλεσι
5 κατέστησεν. μετὰ ταῦτα δὲ τοὺς ἀποστόλους ἅπαντας ἀπέ-
στειλα, καθ' οὓς Χερρόνησος ἐσώθη καὶ Βυζάντιον καὶ πάντες
οἱ σύμμαχοι. ἐξ ὧν ὑμῖν μὲν τὰ κάλλιστα, ἔπαινοι, δόξαι, 100
τιμαί, στέφανοι, χάριτες παρὰ τῶν εὖ πεπονθότων ὑπῆρχον·
τῶν δ' ἀδικουμένων τοῖς μὲν ὑμῖν τότε πεισθεῖσιν ἡ σωτηρία
10 περιεγένετο, τοῖς δ' ὀλιγωρήσασι τὸ πολλάκις ὧν ὑμεῖς προείπατε μεμνῆσθαι, καὶ νομίζειν ὑμᾶς μὴ μόνον εὔνους ἑαυτοῖς,
ἀλλὰ καὶ φρονίμους ἀνθρώπους καὶ μάντεις εἶναι· πάντα γὰρ
ἐκβέβηκεν ἃ προείπατε. καὶ μὴν ὅτι πολλὰ μὲν ἂν χρήματα 101
ἔδωκε Φιλιστίδης ὥστ' ἔχειν Ὠρεόν, πολλὰ δὲ Κλείταρχος
15 ὥστ' ἔχειν Ἐρέτριαν, πολλὰ δ' αὐτὸς ὁ Φίλιππος ὥστε ταῦθ'
ὑπάρχειν ἐφ' ὑμᾶς αὐτῷ, καὶ περὶ τῶν ἄλλων μηδὲν ἐξελέγ-
χεσθαι μηδ' ἃ ποιῶν ἠδίκει μηδένα ἐξετάζειν πανταχοῦ, οὐδεὶς
ἀγνοεῖ, καὶ πάντων ἥκιστα σύ· οἱ γὰρ παρὰ τοῦ Κλειτάρχου 102
καὶ τοῦ Φιλιστίδου τότε πρέσβεις δεῦρ' ἀφικνούμενοι παρὰ σοὶ
20 κατέλυον, Αἰσχίνη, καὶ σὺ προὐξένεις αὐτῶν· οὓς ἡ μὲν πόλις
ὡς ἐχθροὺς καὶ οὔτε δίκαια οὔτε συμφέροντα λέγοντας ἀπήλασε, σοὶ δ' ἦσαν φίλοι. οὐ τοίνυν ἐπράχθη τούτων οὐδέν,
ὦ βλασφημῶν περὶ ἐμοῦ καὶ λέγων ὡς σιωπῶ μὲν λαβών,
βοῶ δ' ἀναλώσας. ἀλλ' οὐ σύ γε, ἀλλὰ βοᾷς μὲν ἔχων, παύ-

---

8. ὑπῆρχον] Ita ΣΑ et socii: ceteri ἐγίγνοντο. 24. γε] Om. Σ Β. et S.

---

2. παρεδύετο. As we say, 'Was gaining
an influence.'
3. ἥπτετο. 'Was getting a hold.'
ἔξοδον. Not στρατείαν, because Demosthenes wishes to convey that a demonstration in force sufficed : see below, § 124,
where the words are juxtaposed as distinct.
§ 100. *And procured you glory and gratitude.*
7. ἔπαινοι, δόξαι, τιμαί. Formal votes
of commendation, general good repute in
men's minds and talk, privileges and precedence conferred on the representatives or
citizens of the state. In the decree of the
Byzantines we have the ἔπαινος in the exordium, then the τιμαί, ἐπιτιμία, ἐπιγαμία,
ἔγκτησις, etc., and the στέφανοι at the
end. Of course the δόξαι and χάριτες are
not included in formal decrees.
8. ὑπῆρχον. A much better reading than

ἐγίγνοντο, but this has decidedly better
authority. Translate, 'Were secured to
you.'
§ 101. *If I was bribed to defend the Locrians, I might have got as much from Philip's
dependents and Philip not to thwart their
schemes ;*
15. ταῦθ'..αὐτῷ. 'To have these ready
to his hand when he attacked you.'
§ 102. *But their agents came to you, not
to me.*
20. σὺ προὐξένεις. This is put in to
balance Aeschines' point (In Ctes. § 76), of
Demosthenes' civility to the ambassadors
sent to negotiate the peace of Philocrates, as
these had not had their proposals rejected,
the point οὓς ἡ μὲν πόλις .. ἀπήλασε, σοὶ δ'
ἦσαν φίλοι is inserted to prevent the parallel
occurring to anyone as a retort.
23. σιωπῶ μὲν λαβών. Aesch. in Ctes.
§ 219.

σει δὲ οὐδέποτ', ἐὰν μή σε οὗτοι παύσωσιν ἀτιμώσαντες τήμε-
103 ρον. στεφανωσάντων τοίνυν ὑμῶν ἐμὲ ἐπὶ τούτοις τότε, καὶ
γράψαντος Ἀριστονίκου τὰς αὐτὰς συλλαβὰς ἅσπερ οὑτοσὶ
Κτησιφῶν νῦν γέγραφε, καὶ ἀναρρηθέντος ἐν τῷ θεάτρῳ τοῦ
στεφάνου, καὶ δευτέρου κηρύγματος ἤδη μοι τούτου γιγνομέ- 5
νου, οὔτ' ἀντεῖπεν Αἰσχίνης παρὼν οὔτε τὸν εἰπόντα ἐγράψατο. Καί μοι λέγε καὶ τοῦτο τὸ ψήφισμα λαβών.

ΨΗΦΙΣΜΑ.

104 [Ἐπὶ Χαιρώνδου Ἡγήμονος ἄρχοντος, γαμηλιῶνος ἕκτῃ ἀπιόντος,
φυλῆς πρυτανευούσης Λεοντίδος, Ἀριστόνικος Φρεάρριος εἶπεν, ἐπειδὴ 10
Δημοσθένης Δημοσθένους Παιανιεὺς πολλὰς καὶ μεγάλας χρείας παρέ-
σχηται τῷ δήμῳ τῷ Ἀθηναίων καὶ πολλοῖς τῶν συμμάχων καὶ πρότερον, καὶ ἐν τῷ παρόντι καιρῷ βεβοήθηκε διὰ τῶν ψηφισμάτων, καί
τινας τῶν ἐν τῇ Εὐβοίᾳ πόλεων ἠλευθέρωκε, καὶ διατελεῖ εὔνους ὢν
105 τῷ δήμῳ τῷ Ἀθηναίων, καὶ λέγει καὶ πράττει ὅ τι ἂν δύνηται ἀγαθὸν 15
ὑπέρ τε αὐτῶν Ἀθηναίων καὶ τῶν ἄλλων Ἑλλήνων, δεδόχθαι τῇ βουλῇ
καὶ τῷ δήμῳ τῷ Ἀθηναίων ἐπαινέσαι Δημοσθένην Δημοσθένους Παιανιέα καὶ στεφανῶσαι χρυσῷ στεφάνῳ, καὶ ἀναγορεῦσαι τὸν στέφανον
ἐν τῷ θεάτρῳ Διονυσίοις, τραγῳδοῖς καινοῖς, τῆς δὲ ἀναγορεύσεως τοῦ
στεφάνου ἐπιμεληθῆναι τὴν πρυτανεύουσαν φυλὴν καὶ τὸν ἀγωνοθέτην. 20
εἶπεν Ἀριστόνικος ὁ Φρεάρριος.]

106 Ἔστιν οὖν ὅστις ὑμῶν οἶδέ τινα αἰσχύνην τῇ πόλει συμ-
βᾶσαν διὰ τοῦτο τὸ ψήφισμα ἢ χλευασμὸν ἢ γέλωτα, ἃ νῦν

---

21. Ἀριστόνικος] Ἀριστόδημος Σ et al.

---

1. ἀτιμώσαντες. By acquitting Ctesiphon by a four-fifths vote; though Aeschines could have paid the fine of 1000
drachmas, it was pretty certain that he
would not pay without being forced, and
not quite certain that payment would have
rehabilitated him in law, or at any rate
in opinion. One MS. adds περὶ τὸ βῆμα,
which may easily be a gloss; though
Reiske extracted a very brilliant reading
from it, περιυλακτοῦντα τὸ βῆμα, which
would describe exactly the precise degree of
ἀτιμία involved, as below, § 330. See note
on § 15.
§ 103. I received a crown which you did
not oppose.
5. καὶ δευτέρου. 'And though this of
Aristonicus was already the second time I
received a vote of thanks' [so that Aeschines
could see the Athenians were getting into
the habit he disliked] 'he neither spoke
against it nor prosecuted the mover.' This

precedent covers two of the points that Aeschines raises, it affirms that Demosthenes
was a good citizen, and fixes the same time
and place for the proclamation. A conjecture is mentioned by the Scholiast,
that Demosthenes had before this had a
foreign crown so proclaimed: which Aristonicus had treated as a precedent for
his motion, and been allowed to do so
unchallenged: while Demosthenes, knowing his case was weak, does not go into
details.
6. παρών, i. e. He was at Athens, and
might have been at the Assembly; probably
Demosthenes even means, 'He was there.'
Cp. ad § 299.
§§ 104, 105. [Decree of Aristonicus.]
§ 106. This decree exposed you to no
ridicule from foreigners for your confidence
in me.
23. ἃ νῦν. 'Which Aeschines said would
be the result now if I were crowned.'

οὗτος ἔφη συμβήσεσθαι, ἂν ἐγὼ στεφανῶμαι; καὶ μὴν ὅταν
ᾖ νέα καὶ γνώριμα πᾶσι τὰ πράγματα, ἐάν τε καλῶς ἔχῃ,
χάριτος τυγχάνει, ἐάν θ' ὡς ἑτέρως, τιμωρίας. φαίνομαι τοίνυν ἐγὼ χάριτος τετυχηκὼς τότε, καὶ οὐ μέμψεως οὐδὲ τιμω-
5 ρίας.

Οὐκοῦν μέχρι μὲν τῶν χρόνων ἐκείνων, ἐν οἷς ταῦτ' ἐπράχθη, 107
πάντας ἀνωμολόγημαι τοὺς χρόνους τὰ ἄριστα πράττειν τῇ
πόλει, τῷ νικᾶν, ὅτ' ἐβουλεύεσθε, λέγων καὶ γράφων, τῷ κατα-
πραχθῆναι τὰ γραφέντα, καὶ στεφάνους ἐξ αὐτῶν τῇ πόλει
10 καὶ ἐμοὶ καὶ πᾶσιν ὑμῖν γενέσθαι, τῷ θυσίας τοῖς θεοῖς καὶ
προσόδους ὡς ἀγαθῶν τούτων ὄντων ὑμᾶς πεποιῆσθαι.

Ἐπειδὴ τοίνυν ἐκ τῆς Εὐβοίας ὁ Φίλιππος ἐξηλάθη, τοῖς 108
μὲν ὅπλοις ὑφ' ὑμῶν, τῇ δὲ πολιτείᾳ καὶ τοῖς ψηφίσμασι,
κἂν διαρραγῶσί τινες τούτων, ὑπ' ἐμοῦ, ἕτερον κατὰ τῆς πό-
15 λεως ἐπιτειχισμὸν ἐζήτει. ὁρῶν δ' ὅτι σίτῳ πάντων ἀνθρώπων πλείστῳ χρώμεθ' ἐπεισάκτῳ, βουλόμενος τῆς σιτοπομπίας
κύριος γενέσθαι, παρελθὼν ἐπὶ Θρᾴκης Βυζαντίους συμμάχους 109
ὄντας αὐτῷ τὸ μὲν πρῶτον ἠξίου συμπολεμεῖν τὸν πρὸς ὑμᾶς
πόλεμον, ὡς δ' οὐκ ἤθελον οὐδ' ἐπὶ τούτοις ἔφασαν τὴν συμ-
20 μαχίαν πεποιῆσθαι, λέγοντες ἀληθῆ, χάρακα βαλόμενος πρὸς
τῇ πόλει καὶ μηχανήματ' ἐπιστήσας ἐπολιόρκει. τούτων δὲ
γιγνομένων ὅ τι μὲν προσῆκε ποιεῖν ὑμᾶς, οὐκέτ' ἐρωτήσω·
δῆλον γάρ ἐστιν ἅπασιν. ἀλλὰ τίς ἦν ὁ βοηθήσας τοῖς Βυ- 110
ζαντίοις καὶ σώσας αὐτούς; τίς ὁ κωλύσας τὸν Ἑλλήσποντον

---

7. τοὺς χρόνους] In γρ. habet Σ: om. B. et S.   20. χάρακα] Ita Σ Harpocr. :
χαρακώματα FΥΦΩ et al.: legebatur χαράκωμα.

---

1. καὶ μὴν κ.τ.λ., i. e. 'If such a result is
probable now it was certain then,' people
had not had time to misjudge the matter.
§ 107. *But up to that decree my policy
proved best.*
7. τοὺς χρόνους is given as a variant in
Σ, and it would be harsh to supply a substantive from τῶν χρόνων ἐκείνων.
8. τῷ νικᾶν .. πεποιῆσθαι. Here we
have three proofs of the excellence of Demosthenes' policy: it was adopted by Athens:
it was successfully executed to her great
glory: its success was acknowledged by joy-
ful thanksgiving. It is assumed that thanksgiving implies the blessings were not curses.
The same argument recurs below, § 274 sqq.
§ 108. *Philip, failing in Euboea, tried to
deprive you of your corn supplies by getting
the Byzantines'.*
12. τοῖς ὅπλοις .. τῇ πολιτείᾳ. The

article marks the two demands contributing
to the same result, 'The military force being
supplied by you, the statesmanship by me.'
Below, § 155, πολιτεία has the commoner
sense of 'policy.'
§ 109. *When the Byzantines insisted that
he was exceeding the terms of his alliance
with them, he besieged them.*
18. ἠξίου. 'Called upon them,' claimed
it as a right secured to him by the terms of
the alliance: they denied this claim.
20. χάρακα. This reading is recognised
by Harpocration (ap. Suidas), who quotes
Demosthenes for the collective use of the
word, 'Throwing up a palisade against the
city.' The palisade was to support an embankment, as we learn from the next clause
μηχανήματ' ἐπιστήσας.
§ 110. *Your duty was plain. You saved
Byzantium, I was your organ.*

ἀλλοτριωθῆναι κατ᾽ ἐκείνους τοὺς χρόνους ; ὑμεῖς, ὦ ἄνδρες
Ἀθηναῖοι. τὸ δ᾽ ὑμεῖς ὅταν λέγω, τὴν πόλιν λέγω. τίς δ᾽
ὁ τῇ πόλει λέγων καὶ γράφων καὶ πράττων καὶ ἁπλῶς ἑαυτὸν
εἰς τὰ πράγματα ἀφειδῶς διδούς ; ἐγώ. ἀλλὰ μὴν ἡλίκα
111 ταῦτα ὠφέλησεν ἅπαντας, οὐκέτ᾽ ἐκ τοῦ λόγου δεῖ μαθεῖν, 5
ἀλλ᾽ ἔργῳ πεπείρασθε· ὁ γὰρ τότε ἐνστὰς πόλεμος ἄνευ τοῦ
καλὴν δόξαν ἐνεγκεῖν ἐν πᾶσι τοῖς κατὰ τὸν βίον ἀφθονωτέ-
ροις καὶ εὐωνοτέροις διῆγεν ὑμᾶς τῆς νῦν εἰρήνης, ἣν οὗτοι κατὰ
τῆς πατρίδος τηροῦσιν οἱ χρηστοὶ ἐπὶ ταῖς μελλούσαις ἐλπίσιν, ὧν διαμάρτοιεν, καὶ μετάσχοιεν ὧν ὑμεῖς οἱ τὰ βέλτιστα 10
βουλόμενοι τοὺς θεοὺς αἰτεῖτε, μὴ μεταδοῖεν ὑμῖν ὧν αὐτοὶ
προῄρηνται. Λέγε δ᾽ αὐτοῖς καὶ τοὺς τῶν Βυζαντίων στεφάνους καὶ τοὺς τῶν Περινθίων, οἷς ἐστεφάνουν ἐκ τούτων
τὴν πόλιν.

ΨΗΦΙΣΜΑ ΒΥΖΑΝΤΙΩΝ. 15

112　[Ἐπὶ ἱερομνάμονος Βοσπορίχω Δαμάγητος ἐν τᾷ ἁλίᾳ ἔλεξεν, ἐκ
τᾶς βωλᾶς λαβὼν ῥάτραν, ἐπειδὴ ὁ δᾶμος ὁ Ἀθαναίων ἔν τε τοῖς
προγεγεναμένοις καιροῖς εὐνόεων διατελέει Βυζαντίοις καὶ τοῖς συμμάχοις καὶ συγγενέσι Περινθίοις καὶ πολλὰς καὶ μεγάλας χρείας παρέ-
σχηται, ἔν τε τῷ παρεστακότι καιρῷ Φιλίππω τῶ Μακεδόνος ἐπιστρα- 20
τεύσαντος ἐπὶ τὰν χώραν καὶ τὰν πόλιν ἐπ᾽ ἀναστάσει Βυζαντίων καὶ

---

1. ἀλλοτριωθῆναι. By passing under
an alien power.

ὑμεῖς. After ὁ βοηθήσας καὶ σώσας
and ὁ κωλύσας in the singular, this word in
the plural has all the effect of a παρὰ προσδοκίαν. Demosthenes began his sentence to
suggest the answer ἐγώ; ὁ τῶν Ἀθηναίων
δῆμος would complete the sentence logically,
but the form in the text gives more effect to
Demosthenes' disclaimer of this exaggerated
praise. For himself it is enough praise to
have done what he claims in τίς δ᾽ ὁ τῇ
..; ἐγώ. Cp. below, § 159.

2. ὅταν λέγω. So Bekker and Dindorf
from Σ : the other MSS. read ὅταν εἴπω.
The aorist is awkward, and the phrase
could only mean, 'On every occasion of
uttering the word "you," my constant
meaning is the city.'

4. διδούς. So Dindorf and Bekker
against most of the oldest MSS., which
read δούς, which is perhaps more forcible,
though the gain is scarcely enough to
compensate the superior ease and cadence
of διδοὺς, which perhaps suggested the
vulgate.

§ 111. *You bad experience of the advantage of courage.*

5. οὐκέτι, i.e. I have told you of the
facts, I need not tell you of the benefit.

8. διῆγεν ὑμᾶς. As we say, 'Kept you
in all the comforts of life, in greater plenty
and at lower prices.'

9. ἐπὶ ταῖς μελλούσαις ἐλπίσιν. They
hoped to be established by Macedon, in the
position of dynasts ; after the Lamian war
the remaining leaders of the party were not
disappointed.

10. ὧν διαμάρτοιεν .. ... προῄρηνται.
' May their hopes fail, may they lose the
blessings which you, that is the honest men,
pray for, and not make you partakers of the
portion they have chosen.' ὧν προῄρηνται
is not synonymous with ἐλπίσιν ; it is the
actual result of their determination. According to Demosthenes, Macedonian partisans were certain to be sacrificed at the first
moment that they could be spared.

13. καὶ τούς. As this is repeated, it is
clear that there were two separate decrees
from Byzantium and Perinthus.

§§ 112, 113. [*The decrees of the Byzantines.*]

16. τᾷ ἁλίᾳ. Like ἡλιαίᾳ, and probably
closer to the etymology. Most MSS. have
τεαλίᾳ, but the correction is tolerably certain; probably the first a slipped out and e
represents the aspirate.

17. λαβὼν ῥάτραν, i.e. ' Bringing down the
decree from the senate.'

Περινθίων καὶ τὰν χώραν δαίοντος καὶ δενδροκοπέοντος, βοηθήσας
πλοίοις ἑκατὸν καὶ εἴκοσι καὶ σίτῳ καὶ βέλεσι καὶ ὁπλίταις ἐξείλετο
ἀμὲ ἐκ τῶν μεγάλων κινδύνων καὶ ἀποκατέστασε τὰν πάτριον πολιτείαν
καὶ τὼς νόμως καὶ τὼς τάφως, δεδόχθαι τῷ δάμῳ τῷ Βυζαντίων καὶ 113
5 Περινθίων Ἀθαναίοις δόμεν ἐπιγαμίαν, πολιτείαν, ἔγκτασιν γᾶς καὶ
οἰκιᾶν, προεδρίαν ἐν τοῖς ἀγῶσι, πόθοδον ποτὶ τὰν βωλὰν καὶ τὸν
δᾶμον πράτοις μετὰ τὰ ἱερά, καὶ τοῖς κατοικέειν ἐθέλουσι τὰν πόλιν
ἀλειτουργήτοις ἦμεν πασᾶν τᾶν λειτουργιᾶν· στᾶσαι δὲ καὶ εἰκόνας
τρεῖς ἑκκαιδεκαπάχεις ἐν τῷ Βοσπορείῳ, στεφανουμένον τὸν δᾶμον τὸν
10 Ἀθαναίων ὑπὸ τῶ δάμω τῶ Βυζαντίων καὶ Περινθίων· ἀποστεῖλαι δὲ
καὶ θεωρίας ἐς τὰς ἐν τᾷ Ἑλλάδι παναγύριας, Ἴσθμια καὶ Νέμεα καὶ
Ὀλύμπια καὶ Πύθια, καὶ ἀνακαρῦξαι τὼς στεφάνως οἷς ἐστεφάνωται ὁ
δᾶμος ὁ Ἀθαναίων ὑφ᾽ ἡμῶν, ὅπως ἐπιστέωνται οἱ Ἕλλανες τάν τε
Ἀθαναίων ἀρετὰν καὶ τὰν Βυζαντίων καὶ Περινθίων εὐχαριστίαν.]
15 Λέγε καὶ τοὺς παρὰ τῶν ἐν Χερρονήσῳ στεφάνους.   114

ΨΗΦΙΣΜΑ ΧΕΡΡΟΝΗΣΙΤΩΝ.

[Χερρονησιτῶν οἱ κατοικοῦντες Σηστόν, Ἐλεοῦντα, Μάδυτον, Ἀλω-
πεκόννησον, στεφανοῦσιν Ἀθηναίων τὴν βουλὴν καὶ τὸν δῆμον χρυσῷ
στεφάνῳ ἀπὸ ταλάντων ἑξήκοντα, καὶ χάριτος βωμὸν ἱδρύονται καὶ
20 δήμου Ἀθηναίων, ὅτι πάντων μεγίστου ἀγαθῶν παραίτιος γέγονε Χερ-
ρονησίταις, ἐξελόμενος ἐκ τῆς Φιλίππου καὶ ἀποδοὺς τὰς πατρίδας, τοὺς
νόμους, τὴν ἐλευθερίαν, τὰ ἱερά. καὶ ἐν τῷ μετὰ ταῦτα αἰῶνι παντὶ
οὐκ ἐλλείψει εὐχαριστῶν ι.αὶ ποιῶν ὅ τι ἂν δύνηται ἀγαθόν. ταῦτα
ἐψηφίσαντο ἐν τῷ κοινῷ βουλευτηρίῳ.]

25 Οὐκοῦν οὐ μόνον τὸ Χερρόνησον καὶ Βυζάντιον σῶσαι, οὐδὲ 115
τὸ κωλῦσαι τὸν Ἑλλήσποντον ὑπὸ Φιλίππῳ γενέσθαι τότε,
οὐδὲ τὸ τιμᾶσθαι τὴν πόλιν ἐκ τούτων ἡ προαίρεσις ἡ ἐμὴ
καὶ ἡ πολιτεία διεπράξατο, ἀλλὰ καὶ πᾶσιν ἔδειξεν ἀνθρώποις
τήν τε τῆς πόλεως καλοκαγαθίαν καὶ τὴν Φιλίππου κακίαν.
30 ὁ μέν γε φίλος καὶ σύμμαχος ὢν τοῖς Βυζαντίοις πολιορκῶν
αὐτοὺς ἑωρᾶτο ὑπὸ πάντων, οὗ τί γένοιτ᾽ ἂν αἴσχιον ἢ μιαρώ-
τερον; ὑμεῖς δ᾽ οἱ καὶ μεμψάμενοι πολλὰ καὶ δίκαια ἂν ἐκεί- 116
νοις εἰκότως περὶ ὧν ἠγνωμονήκεσαν εἰς ὑμᾶς ἐν τοῖς ἔμπρο-

---

4. τὼς νόμως καὶ τὼς τάφως. The
tombs would naturally be profaned in making
approaches to the city.

8. πασᾶν τὰν λειτουργιᾶν. Reiske
found in his MSS. a reading πασᾶν πρὸς τὰν,
whence he conjectured πασᾶν προστακτᾶν
λειτουργιᾶν, all extraordinary liturgies.

114. [Decree of the people of Cherronese.]
§ 115. Beside these material advantages,
my policy placed before the public a moral
contrast between the generosity of Athens and
the perfidy of Philip. He was the ally of
the Byzantines ;

27. ἡ προαίρεσις. 'My system and
my policy.' For this use of πολιτεία, cp.
Dem. de F. L. p. 343 fin. § 9, εἰς τίνα τάξιν
ἔταξεν ἑαυτὸν ἐν τῇ πολιτείᾳ.

§ 116. You had reason to complain of
them. He would have ruined them; you
saved them : and were crowned, an honour which no other statesman gained for
you.

32. οἱ καὶ μεμψάμενοι, i. e. 'So far from
being bound to them, you had even well-
founded grievances you might fairly have
urged against them.'

σθεν χρόνοις, οὐ μόνον οὐ μνησικακοῦντες οὐδὲ προϊέμενοι τοὺς
ἀδικουμένους, ἀλλὰ καὶ σώζοντες ἐφαίνεσθε, ἐξ ὧν δόξαν, εὔνοιαν, τιμὴν παρὰ πάντων ἐκτᾶσθε. καὶ μὴν ὅτι μὲν πολλοὺς
ἐστεφανώκατ᾽ ἤδη τῶν πολιτευομένων ἅπαντες ἴσασι· δι᾽ ὅντινα
δ᾽ ἄλλον ἡ πόλις ἐστεφάνωται, σύμβουλον λέγω καὶ ῥήτορα, 5
πλὴν δι᾽ ἐμὲ, οὐδ᾽ ἂν εἷς εἰπεῖν ἔχοι.

117   Ἵνα τοίνυν καὶ τὰς βλασφημίας ἃς κατὰ τῶν Εὐβοέων καὶ
τῶν Βυζαντίων ἐποιήσατο, εἴ τι δυσχερὲς αὐτοῖς ἐπέπρακτο
πρὸς ὑμᾶς ὑπομιμνήσκων, συκοφαντίας οὔσας ἐπιδείξω μὴ μόνον
τῷ ψευδεῖς εἶναι (τοῦτο μὲν γὰρ ὑπάρχειν ὑμᾶς εἰδότας ἡγοῦ- 10
μαι), ἀλλὰ καὶ τῷ, εἰ τὰ μάλιστ᾽ ἦσαν ἀληθεῖς, οὕτως ὡς ἐγὼ
κέχρημαι τοῖς πράγμασι συμφέρειν χρήσασθαι, ἐν ἢ δύο βούλομαι τῶν καθ᾽ ὑμᾶς πεπραγμένων καλῶν τῇ πόλει διεξελθεῖν,
καὶ ταῦτ᾽ ἐν βραχέσι· καὶ γὰρ ἄνδρα ἰδίᾳ καὶ πόλιν κοινῇ πρὸς
τὰ κάλλιστα τῶν ὑπαρχόντων ἀεὶ δεῖ πειρᾶσθαι τὰ λοιπὰ 15
118 πράττειν. ὑμεῖς τοίνυν, ὦ ἄνδρες Ἀθηναῖοι, Λακεδαιμονίων
γῆς καὶ θαλάττης ἀρχόντων καὶ τὰ κύκλῳ τῆς Ἀττικῆς κατε-
χόντων ἁρμοσταῖς καὶ φρουραῖς, Εὔβοιαν, Τάναγραν, καὶ Βοιωτίαν ἅπασαν, Μέγαρα, Αἴγιναν, Κλεωνὰς, τὰς ἄλλας νήσους,
οὐ ναῦς, οὐ τείχη τῆς πόλεως τότε κτησαμένης, ἐξήλθετε 20
εἰς Ἁλίαρτον καὶ πάλιν οὐ πολλαῖς ἡμέραις ὕστερον εἰς Κόρινθον, τῶν τότε Ἀθηναίων πόλλ᾽ ἂν ἐχόντων μνησικακῆσαι καὶ
Κορινθίοις καὶ Θηβαίοις τῶν περὶ τὸν Δεκελεικὸν πόλεμον

---

20. οὐ τείχη] οὔτε τείχη Σ, unde οὔτε ναῦς οὔτε τείχη nunc legit Dind.   κτησα-
μένης] Ita Σ: ceteri κεκτημένης.

1. προϊέμενοι. The climax is rather
shadowy. The Athenians were not content
with shewing they bore no malice, which
might have been done by a diplomatic protest, nor with shewing that they did not
abandon the oppressed, which might have
been done by scanty and grudging succours.
Only a vigorous and successful intervention
could content their generosity.

5. σύμβουλον λέγω καὶ ῥήτορα. The
proviso is necessary, for a general in the service of Athens who lent his army to a
foreign power, of course would propitiate
his legitimate employers, by insisting on a
certificate that he had done them credit.

§ 117. *I will prove that this generosity
was politic, however undeserved. I only
proposed you should act up to the precedents
set by your fathers.*

7. τὰς βλασφημίας κ.τ.λ. 'I will prove
that Aeschines' abuse of the Euboeans and
Byzantines, when he twitted you with everything disagreeable they had ever done to you,

was a mass of vexatious calumny not
merely because it was false, I take this for
granted' [inasmuch as Euboea and Byzantium were not then unfriendly], 'but because
if it was true my policy was still right.'

14. πρὸς τὰ κάλλιστα τῶν ὑπαρχόντων.
'According to the most glorious precedents
of her previous history.' Cp. § 126, τῶν
ὑπαρχόντων τῇ πόλει καλῶν.

§ 118. *They assisted Thebes and Corinth,
their ancient enemies, against Sparta at the
height of her power :*

19. τὰς ἄλλας νήσους. As the only
islands mentioned, Euboea and Aegina are
separated from each other, and from this
phrase, by the names of other places to 'the
islands beside.' Cp. Xen. An. I. 5. 5, Soph.
El. 601. The reading ἄλλας νήσους would
imply that Cleonae was an island.

21. εἰς Κόρινθον. The Scholiast remarks
on the force of saying, 'You braved even
defeat, in the cause of freedom and generosity.'

πραχθέντων· ἀλλ' οὐκ ἐποίουν τοῦτο, οὐδ' ἐγγύς. καίτοι τότε 119
ταῦτα ἀμφότερα, Αἰσχίνη, οὔθ' ὑπὲρ εὐεργετῶν ἐποίουν οὔτ'
ἀκίνδυνα ἑώρων. ἀλλ' οὐ διὰ ταῦτα προΐεντο τοὺς καταφεύ-
γοντας ἐφ' ἑαυτούς, ἀλλ' ὑπὲρ εὐδοξίας καὶ τιμῆς ἤθελον τοῖς
5 δεινοῖς αὐτοὺς διδόναι, ὀρθῶς καὶ καλῶς βουλευόμενοι. πέρας 120
μὲν γὰρ ἅπασιν ἀνθρώποις ἐστὶ τοῦ βίου θάνατος, κἂν ἐν
οἰκίσκῳ τις αὐτὸν καθείρξας τηρῇ· δεῖ δὲ τοὺς ἀγαθοὺς ἄνδρας
ἐγχειρεῖν μὲν ἅπασιν ἀεὶ τοῖς καλοῖς, τὴν ἀγαθὴν προβαλλο-
μένους ἐλπίδα, φέρειν δ' ὅ τι ἂν ὁ θεὸς διδῷ γενναίως. ταῦτ' 121
10 ἐποίουν οἱ ὑμέτεροι πρόγονοι, ταῦθ' ὑμῶν οἱ πρεσβύτεροι, οἳ
Λακεδαιμονίους οὐ φίλους ὄντας οὐδ' εὐεργέτας, ἀλλὰ πολλὰ
τὴν πόλιν ἡμῶν ἠδικηκότας καὶ μεγάλα, ἐπειδὴ Θηβαῖοι κρατήσαντες ἐν Λεύκτροις ἀνελεῖν ἐπεχείρουν, διεκωλύσατε, οὐ φοβηθέντες τὴν τότε Θηβαίοις ῥώμην καὶ δόξαν ὑπάρχουσαν, οὐδ'
15 ὑπὲρ οἵα πεποιηκότων ἀνθρώπων κινδυνεύσετε διαλογισάμενοι·
καὶ γάρ τοι πᾶσι τοῖς Ἕλλησιν ἐδείξατε ἐκ τούτων ὅτι κἂν 122
ὁτιοῦν τις εἰς ὑμᾶς ἐξαμάρτῃ, τούτῳ τὴν ὀργὴν εἰς τἄλλα
ἔχετε, ἐὰν δ' ὑπὲρ σωτηρίας ἢ ἐλευθερίας κίνδυνός τις αὐτοὺς
καταλαμβάνῃ, οὔτε μνησικακήσετε οὔθ' ὑπολογιεῖσθε. καὶ οὐκ 123
20 ἐπὶ τούτων μόνων οὕτως ἐσχήκατε, ἀλλὰ πάλιν σφετεριζομένων

---

10. ὑμέτεροι] ἡμέτεροι A et socii.   Mox pro ὑμῶν, ὑμεῖς γρ. ὑμῶν Σ.

§ 119. *They ran a risk to protect those who trusted their honour.*

2. ὑπὲρ εὐεργετῶν. A terse, popular, impolitic common-place often urged by Aeschines, that no state could claim help from a state to which it had given none. Cp. Dem. de F. L. p. 345, § 17. Demosthenes (ib. p. 361, § 73) appeals to the same sentiment, on the positive side.

§ 120. *For all men must die, and brave men die for honour.*

§ 120. 'For at last the life of every man must come to death, even if one should shut himself in a cell and keep close; but brave men ought always to reach out to all things honourable, putting on the breast-plate of good hope, and then bear whatsoever God sends manfully.' According to the Scholiast, οἴκισκος is in Attic 'a bird's nest.'

§ 121. *In this spirit you protected the Spartans against Thebes,*

9. ταῦτ' ἐποίουν. 'And so your ancestors did' [when they assisted Thebes and Corinth], and so did the elder among you. Σ has ὑμεῖς instead of ὑμῶν, which goes rather better with διεκωλύσατε: and οἱ πρεσβύτεροι would be added quite naturally

in epexegesi, though the genitive is of course more familiar.

14. οὐδὲ.. διαλογισάμενοι. 'Not being terrified at the strength and reputation on which Thebes might reckon then, nor discussing the treatment you had received from the men for whom you were to risk so much.' The latter part of the clause is a rather extreme example of the intrusion of oratio recta in dependent sentences.

§ 122. *And proved that you never indulged your just resentment against a state when its freedom and safety were in peril.*

16. κἂν ὁτιοῦν κ.τ.λ. 'Be the offence what it may, you resent it in other things, but when they' [the Greeks or the offenders] 'come in peril of freedom or safety, you will bear no malice [will not take the opportunity of vengeance], nor count up old scores' [as a deduction from the assistance which might otherwise have been given]. κίνδυνος ὑπὲρ σωτηρίας = τὸ ὑπὲρ σωτηρίας κινδυνεύειν.

§ 123. *Further, you protected Euboea from Thebes (as now from Philip). though Euboean leaders had deprived you of Oropus; in this I aided, but I will not speak of this yet.*

Θηβαίων τὴν Εὔβοιαν οὐ περιείδετε, οὐδ᾽ ὧν ὑπὸ Θεμίσωνος
καὶ Θεοδώρου περὶ Ὠρωπὸν ἠδίκησθε ἀνεμνήσθητε, ἀλλ᾽ ἐβοηθήσατε καὶ τούτοις, τῶν ἐθελοντῶν τότε τριηράρχων πρῶτον
γενομένων τῇ πόλει, ὧν εἷς ἦν ἐγώ. ἀλλ᾽ οὔπω περὶ τούτων.

124 καίτοι καλὸν μὲν ἐποιήσατε καὶ τὸ σῶσαι τὴν νῆσον, πολλῷ 5
δ᾽ ἔτι τούτου κάλλιον τὸ καταστάντες κύριοι καὶ τῶν σωμάτων
καὶ τῶν πόλεων ἀποδοῦναι ταῦτα δικαίως αὐτοῖς τοῖς ἐξημαρ-
τηκόσιν εἰς ὑμᾶς, μηδὲν ὧν ἠδίκησθε ἐν οἷς ἐπιστεύθητε ὑπολο-
γισάμενοι. μυρία τοίνυν ἕτερα εἰπεῖν ἔχων παραλείπω, ναυμα-
χίας, ἐξόδους πεζὰς, στρατείας, καὶ πάλαι γεγονυίας καὶ νῦν 10
ἐφ᾽ ὑμῶν αὐτῶν, ἃς ἁπάσας ἡ πόλις τῆς τῶν ἄλλων Ἑλλήνων
125 ἐλευθερίας καὶ σωτηρίας πεποίηται. εἶτ᾽ ἐγὼ τεθεωρηκὼς ἐν
τοσούτοις καὶ τοιούτοις τὴν πόλιν ὑπὲρ τῶν τοῖς ἄλλοις συμφερόντων ἐθέλουσαν ἀγωνίζεσθαι, ὑπὲρ αὐτῆς τρόπον τινὰ τῆς
βουλῆς οὔσης τι ἔμελλον κελεύσειν ἢ τί συμβουλεύσειν αὐτῇ 15
ποιεῖν; μνησικακεῖν νὴ Δία πρὸς τοὺς βουλομένους σῴζεσθαι,
126 καὶ προφάσεις ζητεῖν δι᾽ ἃς ἅπαντα προησόμεθα. καὶ τίς οὐκ
ἂν ἀπέκτεινέ με δικαίως, εἴ τι τῶν ὑπαρχόντων τῇ πόλει καλῶν
λόγῳ μόνον καταισχύνειν ἐπεχείρησα; ἐπεὶ τό γε ἔργον οὐκ
ἂν ἐποιήσαθ᾽ ὑμεῖς, ἀκριβῶς οἶδ᾽ ἐγώ· εἰ γὰρ ἐβούλεσθε, τί ἦν 20
ἐμποδών; οὐκ ἐξῆν; οὐχ ὑπῆρχον οἱ ταῦτ᾽ ἐροῦντες οὗτοι;

3. τῶν ἐθελοντῶν τότε τριηράρχων] Sic Σ: ceteri τῶν τριηράρχων τότε ἐθελοντῶν.
Praeterea, omnes fere libri pravom accentum ἐθελόντων habent.   5. καίτοι] καὶ ΣΦ.
16. μνησικακεῖν] μνησικακήσειν plerique.   19. ἐπεχείρησα] ἐπεχείρησ᾽ ἂν Σ et al.

3. καὶ τούτοις. You aided these, as
well as the other Euboean leaders whom
Aeschines reproaches me with supporting.

4. ἀλλ᾽ οὔπω περὶ τούτων, i. e. it is not
yet time to raise the invidious question of
my personal munificence in the public service.

§ 124. However, your generosity was disinterested.

5. καίτοι. Implying—at the same time
the policy which called out the enthusiasm
of so many citizens and mine was noble,
and still more your conduct when that
policy succeeded.

§ 125. Your generosity imposed a duty
upon me as your adviser.

14. ὑπὲρ αὐτῆς .. τῆς βουλῆς οὔσης.
'When the debate concerned her own interests indirectly.' There were precedents that
would lead Athens to save, first the Euboeans,
and afterwards the Thebans, as a matter of
mere generosity; but when Philip's attacks
on them were merely indirect advances
against Athens, the case was stronger than
in any of the previous instances, because

there were considerations of policy to enforce the dictates of generosity,

16. μνησικακεῖν νὴ Δία. 'Why of
course rake up old grudges with men before
me begging you to save them.' μνησικακήσειν, if right, is attracted by συμβουλεύσειν. Σ and most good MSS. omit the
obvious gloss τὰ συμφέροντα after προησόμεθα.

§ 126. I should have deserved to be
punished for giving ungenerous advice which
you would not have followed.

19. ἐπεχείρησα. Many good MSS. add
ἄν. Is it possible Greek, to say εἰ ἐπεχεί-
ρησ᾽ ἄν for 'if I had wanted to try'?

20. γὰρ gives the reason for ὑμεῖς with
its emphatic position; the sense is, 'You,
being what you are, would not, for you
could, and you had people ready to bear the
personal shame of giving the dishonourable
counsel.'

21. οὗτοι refers to Aeschines himself and
his supporters in court. οἱ ταῦτ᾽ ἐροῦντες is
the regular use of the future participle with
the article, only found after a negative, 'some

Βούλομαι τοίνυν ἐπανελθεῖν ἐφ' ἃ τούτων ἑξῆς ἐπολιτευόμην· 127
καὶ σκοπεῖτε ἐν τούτοις πάλιν αὖ, τί τὸ τῇ πόλει βέλτιστον
ἦν. ὁρῶν γὰρ, ὦ ἄνδρες Ἀθηναῖοι, τὸ ναυτικὸν ὑμῶν κατα-
λυόμενον, καὶ τοὺς μὲν πλουσίους ἀτελεῖς ἀπὸ μικρῶν ἀναλω-
5 μάτων γιγνομένους, τοὺς δὲ μέτρια ἢ μικρὰ κεκτημένους τῶν
πολιτῶν τὰ ὄντα ἀπολλύντας, ἔτι δ' ὑστερίζουσαν ἐκ τούτων
τὴν πόλιν τῶν καιρῶν, ἔθηκα νόμον καθ' ὃν τοὺς μὲν τὰ δίκαια 128
ποιεῖν ἠνάγκασα, τοὺς πλουσίους, τοὺς δὲ πένητας ἔπαυσ' ἀδικουμένους, τῇ πόλει δ' ὅπερ ἦν χρησιμώτατον, ἐν καιρῷ γίγνε-
10 σθαι τὰς παρασκευὰς ἐποίησα. καὶ γραφεὶς τὸν ἀγῶνα τοῦτον
εἰς ὑμᾶς εἰσῆλθον καὶ ἀπέφυγον, καὶ τὸ μέρος τῶν ψήφων ὁ
διώκων οὐκ ἔλαβεν. καίτοι πόσα χρήματα τοὺς ἡγεμόνας τῶν 129
συμμοριῶν ἢ τοὺς δευτέρους καὶ τρίτους οἴεσθέ μοι διδόναι
ὥστε μάλιστα μὲν μὴ θεῖναι τὸν νόμον τοῦτον, εἰ δὲ μὴ, κατα-
15 βαλόντα ἐᾶν ἐν ὑπωμοσίᾳ; τοσαῦτ', ὦ ἄνδρες Ἀθηναῖοι, ὅσα
ὀκνήσαιμ' ἂν πρὸς ὑμᾶς εἰπεῖν. καὶ ταῦτ' εἰκότως ἔπραττον 130
ἐκεῖνοι. ἦν γὰρ αὐτοῖς ἐν μὲν τῶν προτέρων νόμων συνεκκαίδεκα λειτουργεῖν, αὐτοῖς μὲν μικρὰ καὶ οὐδὲν ἀναλίσκουσι, τοὺς

---

5. ἦ] καὶ A et socii, haud absurde.   10. γραφεὶς .. τοῦτον] Post alterum horum
nonnulli addunt παρανόμων.   14. καταβαλόντα] καταβάλλοντα Σ et al. B. et S.
16. πρὸς ὑμᾶς εἰπεῖν] εἰπεῖν πρὸς ὑ̔μᾶς ἐγώ A et socii et al.

---

one to do so and so ;' but here it is defined
and explained by the addition of οὗτοι : cp.
the insertion of ἐκεῖνος above, § 86.

§§ 127, 128. *I return to the next stage of
my policy, my legislation for the maintenance
of your navy in which you sustained.*

4. ἀτελεῖς. The heads of the symmoriae
commonly found a contractor to take the
whole responsibility of the trierarchy for a
fixed sum, generally a trifle under the estimate which they gave to their partners, so
that when the partners had paid their share
of the estimate, the heads of the symmoriae
had recouped their advance to the contractors without any expense to themselves, or
at any rate only paid as much as the poorest.
As the technical privilege of ἀτελεία did not
include exemption from the trierarchy, the
exact force here will be, 'They spent little
or nothing, and were free of all other burdens.'

10. τὰς παρασκευάς. Reiske adds ναυ-
τικὰς, which is given as a γρ. in Σ.

τὸν ἀγῶνα τοῦτον go with εἰσῆλθον,
not with γραφείς. Cp. Aesch. in Ctes. §
192 εἴ τις εἰσίοι γραφήν, and Dem. de Cor.
§ 13 εἰσῆλθον τὴν γράφην.

§§ 129–131. *Here, also, I prove that my*

policy was disinterested ; by pointing to those
who would have paid high to buy me off,
having a strong interest in doing so.

12. καίτοι πόσα χρήματα. Demosthenes returns to the charge of corruption,
evidently one of the strongest parts of Aeschines' case.

13. ἢ τοὺς δευτέρους καὶ τρίτους. These
only paid as much as the poorest, while they
might be almost as rich as the heads of the
partnership, and so were interested in the
existing system almost as much as the heads,
though they had not the same chance as the
latter of recouping themselves entirely.

διδόναι. The infinitive without ἂν
shews that the offer was actually made.

14. καταβαλόντα. The present καταβάλλοντα is harder, and MS. authority is not
very trustworthy in the case of the doubling
of a letter : else authority is for it.

15. ἐὰν ἐν ὑπωμοσίᾳ. 'Let it drop on
affidavit,' by which course Demosthenes
would have escaped the personal consequences
of a conviction on a γραφὴ παρανόμων.

18. μικρὰ καὶ οὐδέν. 'Little or nothing;'
more exactly, 'Little, in fact nothing.' The
logical form is more natural in English, the
rhetorical in Greek.

δ' ἀπόρους τῶν πολιτῶν ἐπιτρίβουσιν, ἐκ δὲ τοῦ ἐμοῦ νόμου τὸ
γιγνόμενον κατὰ τὴν οὐσίαν ἕκαστον τιθέναι, καὶ δυοῖν ἐφάνη
τριήραρχος ὁ τῆς μιᾶς ἕκτος καὶ δέκατος πρότερον συντελής·
οὐδὲ γὰρ τριηράρχους ἔτι ὠνόμαζον ἑαυτούς, ἀλλὰ συντελεῖς.
131 ὥστε δὴ ταῦτα λυθῆναι καὶ μὴ τὰ δίκαια ποιεῖν ἀναγκασθῆναι, 5
οὐκ ἔσθ᾽ ὅ τι οὐκ ἐδίδοσαν. Καί μοι λέγε πρῶτον μὲν τὸ
ψήφισμα καθ᾽ ὃ εἰσῆλθον τὴν γραφήν, εἶτα τοὺς καταλόγους,
τόν τ᾽ ἐκ τοῦ προτέρου νόμου καὶ τὸν κατὰ τὸν ἐμόν. λέγε.

ΨΗΦΙΣΜΑ.

132 [Ἐπὶ ἄρχοντος Πολυκλέους, μηνὸς βοηδρομιῶνος ἕκτῃ ἐπὶ δέκα, 10
φυλῆς πρυτανευούσης Ἱπποθωντίδος, Δημοσθένης Δημοσθένους Παιανιεὺς εἰσήνεγκε νόμον τριηραρχικὸν ἀντὶ τοῦ προτέρου, καθ᾽ ὃν αἱ
συντέλειαι ἦσαν τῶν τριηράρχων· καὶ ἐπεχειροτόνησεν ἡ βουλὴ καὶ
ὁ δῆμος· καὶ ἀπήνεγκε παρανόμων Δημοσθένει Πατροκλῆς Φλυεύς,
καὶ τὸ μέρος τῶν ψήφων οὐ λαβὼν ἀπέτισε τὰς πεντακοσίας δραχμάς.] 15

133 Φέρε δὴ καὶ τὸν καλὸν κατάλογον.

ΚΑΤΑΛΟΓΟΣ.

[Τοὺς τριηράρχους καλεῖσθαι ἐπὶ τὴν τριήρη συνεκκαίδεκα ἐκ τῶν ἐν
τοῖς λόχοις συντελειῶν, ἀπὸ εἴκοσι καὶ πέντε ἐτῶν εἰς τετταράκοντα,
ἐπὶ ἴσον τῇ χορηγίᾳ χρωμένοις.] 20

Φέρε δὴ παρὰ τοῦτον τὸν ἐκ τοῦ ἐμοῦ νόμου κατάλογον.

ΚΑΤΑΛΟΓΟΣ.

134 [Τοὺς τριηάρχους αἱρεῖσθαι ἐπὶ τὴν τριήρη ἀπὸ τῆς οὐσίας κατὰ
τίμησιν, ἀπὸ ταλάντων δέκα· ἐὰν δὲ πλειόνων ἡ οὐσία ἀποτετιμημένη
ᾖ χρημάτων, κατὰ τὸν ἀναλογισμὸν ἕως τριῶν πλοίων καὶ ὑπηρετικοῦ ἡ 25
λειτουργία ἔστω. κατὰ τὴν αὐτὴν δὲ ἀναλογίαν ἔστω καὶ οἷς ἐλάττων
οὐσία ἐστὶ τῶν δέκα ταλάντων, εἰς συντέλειαν συναγομένοις εἰς τὰ
δέκα τάλαντα.]

135 Ἆρά γε μικρὰ βοηθῆσαι τοῖς πένησιν ὑμῶν δοκῶ, ἢ μικρὰ

---

20. χρωμένους] Sic A et socii: ceteri plerique χρώμενον, quod fortasse nonnihil omissum
esse indicat.

7. τοὺς καταλόγους. The lists were
read at full, and the comparative liabilities
of well-known rich men superseded comment, and justified the sarcastic τὸν καλὸν
κατάλογον below, § 133.
§ 132. [Decree.]
§§ 133, 134. [Registers of trierarchs.]

§ 135. *Was my law unimportant to the
poor or to the rich, who might have bought
it off. I may boast of more than my courage
and impunity.*
29. τοῖς πένησιν ὑμῶν. A very adroit
appeal to the selfish interests of the court,
implying that the poorest of the jury were
still liable to serve as trierarchs.

ἀναλῶσαι ἂν τοῦ μὴ τὰ δίκαια ποιεῖν οἱ πλούσιοι; οὐ τοίνυν
μόνον τῷ μὴ καθυφεῖναι ταῦτα σεμνύνομαι, οὐδὲ τῷ γραφεὶς
ἀποφυγεῖν, ἀλλὰ καὶ τῷ συμφέροντα θεῖναι τὸν νόμον καὶ τῷ
πεῖραν ἔργῳ δεδωκέναι. πάντα γὰρ τὸν πόλεμον τῶν ἀπο- 136
5 στόλων γιγνομένων κατὰ τὸν νόμον τὸν ἐμὸν οὐχ ἱκετηρίαν
ἔθηκε τριήραρχος οὐδεὶς πώποθ᾽ ὡς ἀδικούμενος παρ᾽ ὑμῖν, οὐκ
ἐν Μουνυχίᾳ ἐκαθέζετο, οὐχ ὑπὸ τῶν ἀποστολέων ἐδέθη, οὐ
τριήρης οὔτ᾽ ἔξω καταληφθεῖσα ἀπώλετο τῇ πόλει, οὔτ᾽ αὐτοῦ
ἀπελείφθη οὐ δυναμένη ἀνάγεσθαι. καίτοι κατὰ τοὺς προτέ- 137
10 ρους νόμους ἅπαντα ταῦτα ἐγίγνετο. τὸ δ᾽ αἴτιον, ἐν τοῖς
πένησιν ἦν τὸ λειτουργεῖν· πολλὰ δὴ τὰ ἀδύνατα συνέβαινεν.
ἐγὼ δ᾽ ἐκ τῶν ἀπόρων εἰς τοὺς εὐπόρους μετήνεγκα τὰς τριηραρ-
χίας· πάντ᾽ οὖν τὰ δέοντα ἐγίγνετο. καὶ μὴν καὶ κατ᾽ αὐτὸ 138
τοῦτο ἄξιός εἰμι ἐπαίνου τυχεῖν, ὅτι πάντα τὰ τοιαῦτα προῃ-
15 ρούμην πολιτεύματα, ἀφ᾽ ὧν ἅμα δόξαι καὶ τιμαὶ καὶ δυνάμεις
συνέβαινον τῇ πόλει· βάσκανον δὲ καὶ πικρὸν καὶ κακόηθες
οὐδέν ἐστι πολίτευμα ἐμόν, οὐδὲ ταπεινόν, οὐδὲ τῆς πόλεως
ἀνάξιον. ταὐτὸ τοίνυν ἦθος ἔχων ἔν τε τοῖς κατὰ τὴν πόλιν 139
πολιτεύμασι καὶ ἐν τοῖς Ἑλληνικοῖς φανήσομαι· οὔτε γὰρ ἐν
20 τῇ πόλει τὰς παρὰ τῶν πλουσίων χάριτας μᾶλλον ἢ τὰ τῶν
πολλῶν δίκαια εἱλόμην, οὔτ᾽ ἐν τοῖς Ἑλληνικοῖς τὰ Φιλίππου
δῶρα καὶ τὴν ξενίαν ἠγάπησα ἀντὶ τῶν κοινῇ πᾶσι τοῖς Ἕλλησι συμφερόντων.

---

1. ποιεῖν] Sic A et socii : Σ et ceteri plerique ποιεῖν ἐθέλειν, impedito sensu idque receperunt B. et S.   7. ἀποστολέων] ἀποστόλων Ω u idque legisse scholiasta videtur.
8. καταληφθεῖσα] Ita A ' sp : ceteri et B. et S. καταλειφθεῖσα.   11. λειτουργεῖν]
Nonnulli vel ante vel post hoc verbum μὴ δύνασθαι addunt.

§ 136. Of the success of my legislation,
5. ἱκετηρίαν ἔθηκε. Almost 'Set up as
a suppliant,' or ' Take sanctuary in Munychia.' The first clause refers to the privileges of persons complying with certain ceremonies at the hearth or domestic altar of
the person appealed to—in this case, at the
national altar of the Assembly in Pnyx ;
the second to the privileges of the special
shrine of Artemis in Munychia. Cp. Lys.
Cont. Agorat. § 24.
8. ἔξω καταληφθεῖσα. Most MSS.
read καταλειφθεῖσα: ει and η are constantly
interchanged, and Σ, to mend matters, reads
inf. ἀπελήφθη, which is impossible. The
force of either participle would be much the
same, except that καταληφθεῖσα would give
the result. and ἀπολειφθεῖσα the cause. He
means, 'No trireme was in bad condition,
so that it was captured abroad or afraid to

put to sea.'
§ 137. In remedying the old code, which
left the burden on the wrong shoulders;
11. τὰ ἀδύνατα. 'The cases of impos-
sibility.' Cp. ad § 47.
§ 138. Of a constant course of large-
hearted and noble policy,
16. βάσκανον δὲ καὶ πικρὸν καὶ κακόηθες. All these qualities would make Demosthenes justly odious to individual citizens; the two he disclaims in the latter half
of the clause, would offend collective public
sentiment
§ 139. Incorruptible at home and abroad.
19. ἐν τοῖς Ἑλληνικοῖς: cp. above,
§ 72.
21. τὰ Φιλίππου δῶρα καὶ τὴν ξενίαν.
He had as good a claim to the second, and
had had as good a chance of the first, as his
fellow ambassadors.

140 Ἡγοῦμαι τοίνυν λοιπὸν εἶναί μοι περὶ τοῦ κηρύγματος εἰπεῖι
καὶ τῶν εὐθυνῶν· τὸ γὰρ ὡς τὰ ἄριστα τε ἔπραττον καὶ διὰ
παντὸς εὔνους εἰμὶ καὶ πρόθυμος εὖ ποιεῖν ὑμᾶς, ἱκανῶς ἐκ τῶν
εἰρημένων δεδηλῶσθαί μοι νομίζω. καίτοι τὰ μέγιστά γε τῶν
πεπολιτευμένων καὶ πεπραγμένων ἐμαυτῷ παραλείπω, ὑπολαμ- 5
βάνων πρῶτον μὲν ἐφεξῆς τοὺς περὶ αὐτοῦ τοῦ παρανόμου
λόγους ἀποδοῦναί με δεῖν, εἶτα, κἂν μηδὲν εἴπω περὶ τῶν λοιπῶν
πολιτευμάτων, ὁμοίως παρ' ὑμῶν ἑκάστῳ τὸ συνειδὸς ὑπάρχειν
μοι.

141 Τῶν μὲν οὖν λόγων, οὓς οὗτος ἄνω καὶ κάτω διακυκῶν ἔλεγε 10
περὶ τῶν παραγεγραμμένων νόμων, οὔτε μὰ τοὺς θεοὺς ὑμᾶς
οἶμαι μανθάνειν οὔτ' αὐτὸς ἐδυνάμην συνεῖναι τοὺς πολλούς·
142 ἁπλῶς δὲ τὴν ὀρθὴν περὶ τῶν δικαίων διαλέξομαι. τοσούτου
γὰρ δέω λέγειν ὡς οὐκ εἰμὶ ὑπεύθυνος, ὃ νῦν οὗτος διέβαλλε
καὶ διωρίζετο, ὥσθ' ἅπαντα τὸν βίον ὑπεύθυνος εἶναι ὁμολογῶ 15
ὧν ἢ διακεχείρικα ἢ πεπολίτευμαι παρ' ὑμῖν. ὧν μέντοι γε ἐκ
τῆς ἰδίας οὐσίας ἐπαγγειλάμενος δέδωκα τῷ δήμῳ, οὐδεμίαν
ἡμέραν ὑπεύθυνος εἶναί φημι (ἀκούεις Αἰσχίνη;) οὐδ' ἄλλον
143 οὐδένα, οὐδ' ἂν τῶν ἐννέα ἀρχόντων τις ὢν τύχῃ. τίς γάρ

---

11. παραγεγραμμένων] γεγραμμένων A et socii.   14. διέβαλλε] πολλάκις διέβαλλε omnes praeter ΣF.   17. δέδωκα] † In litura habet Σ † ἐπέδωκα (omisso
ἐπαγγειλάμενος) Hermog. Syrian.

§ 140. Only the technical details remain;
yet I omit my greatest merits; but you know
them.

2. τὸ γὰρ κ.τ.λ. 'The clause setting
forth,' etc. The article is to mark the words
that follow as a quotation, though the quotation is not verbatim.

5. πεπολιτευμένων καὶ πεπραγμένων:
cp. above, §§ 13, 72.

8. ὁμοίως. A sort of secondary equivalent for ὅμως, with an additional shade of
meaning. One might say ὅμως answers to
'just the same,' and ὁμοίως to 'equally
well.' ὅμως implies a sharp contrast between the protasis and apodosis, ὁμοίως that
the former is a reserve which does not
really affect the integrity of the latter.

§ 141. Aeschines has confused the matter,
I will put it simply.

10. διακυκῶν. Because Aeschines has
boasted of his arrangement as the only legitimate and reasonable one, Demosthenes
calls it a muddle; perhaps, too, there is a
touch of sarcasm on the very elaborate
manner in which Aeschines goes over the
ground.

11. τῶν παραγεγραμμένων νόμων: cp.
Aesch. in Ctes. § 201. The laws alleged

to be violated were written beside the decree in stating the indictment.

12. μανθάνειν .. συνεῖναι. 'I do not
suppose you could follow what he said, for
my part I could not understand what he
meant.'

§ 142. I admit my perpetual responsibility
for the public money: for my free gifts I am
not responsible an hour.

15. ἅπαντα τὸν βίον. 'All my life,'
even after my accounts are passed; ὧν ἢ
διακεχείρικα ἢ πεπολίτευμαι, 'For all my
acts administrative or political,' though legal
accountability only extends to the first.

17. ἐπαγγειλάμενος. A regular form of
donation in public assemblies. The ἀνελεύ-
θερος of Theophrastus goes out when the
ἐπαγγελίαι, otherwise called ἐπιδόσεις, begin.

18. ἀκούεις Αἰσχίνη. As Aeschines
had dilated, 'If Demosthenes says,' etc.,
when Demosthenes makes the exact statement anticipated, he naturally turns round,
'I say .. you hear I do.'

19. τῶν ἐννέα ἀρχόντων. This office was
the oldest and in a sense the highest, therefore the most strictly responsible.

§ 143. No law would impose such a tyran-
nical responsibility.

178 ΔΗΜΟΣΘΕΝΟΥΣ §§ 144–146.

ἐστὶ νόμος τοσαύτης ἀδικίας καὶ μισανθρωπίας μεστὸς ὥστε
τὸν δόντα τι τῶν ἰδίων καὶ ποιήσαντα πρᾶγμα φιλάνθρωπον
καὶ φιλόδωρον τῆς χάριτος μὲν ἀποστερεῖν, εἰς τοὺς συκοφάντας δ᾽ ἄγειν, καὶ τούτους ἐπὶ τὰς εὐθύνας ὧν ἔδωκεν ἐφιστάναι;
5 οὐδὲ εἷς. εἰ δέ φησιν οὗτος, δειξάτω, κἀγὼ στέρξω καὶ σιω-
πήσομαι. ἀλλ᾽ οὐκ ἔστιν, ὦ ἄνδρες Ἀθηναῖοι, ἀλλ᾽ οὗτος 144
συκοφαντῶν, ὅτι ἐπὶ τῷ θεωρικῷ τότε ὢν ἐπέδωκα τὰ χρήματα, "ἐπήνεσεν αὐτόν," φησὶν, "ἡ βουλὴ ὑπεύθυνον ὄντα."
οὐ περὶ τούτων γε οὐδενός, ὧν ὑπεύθυνος ἦν, ἀλλ᾽ ἐφ᾽ οἷς
10 ἐπέδωκα, ὦ συκοφάντα. ἀλλὰ καὶ τειχοποιὸς ἦσθα, φησί.
καὶ διά γε τοῦτο ὀρθῶς ἐπηνούμην, ὅτι τἀνηλωμένα ἐπέδωκα
καὶ οὐκ ἐλογιζόμην. ὁ μὲν γὰρ λογισμὸς εὐθυνῶν καὶ τῶν
ἐξετασόντων προσδεῖται, ἡ δὲ δωρεὰ χάριτος καὶ ἐπαίνου δικαία
ἐστὶ τυγχάνειν· διόπερ ταῦτ᾽ ἔγραψεν ὁδὶ περὶ ἐμοῦ· ὅτι δ᾽ 145
15 οὕτω ταῦτα οὐ μόνον ἐν τοῖς νόμοις, ἀλλὰ καὶ ἐν τοῖς ὑμετέροις ἤθεσιν ὥρισται, ἐγὼ ῥᾳδίως πολλαχόθεν δείξω. πρῶτον
μὲν γὰρ Ναυσικλῆς στρατηγῶν, ἐφ᾽ οἷς ἀπὸ τῶν ἰδίων προεῖτο,
πολλάκις ἐστεφάνωται ὑφ᾽ ὑμῶν· εἶθ᾽ ὅτε τὰς ἀσπίδας Διότιμος ἔδωκε καὶ πάλιν Χαρίδημος, ἐστεφανοῦντο· εἶθ᾽ οὑτοσὶ
20 Νεοπτόλεμος πολλῶν ἔργων ἐπιστάτης ὤν, ἐφ᾽ οἷς ἐπέδωκε,
τετίμηται. σχέτλιον γὰρ ἂν εἴη τοῦτό γε, εἰ τῷ τινὰ ἀρχὴν 146

3. εἰς τοὺς συκοφάντας δὲ] εἰς δὲ τοὺς συκοφάντας A et socii.   7. ἐπέδωκα] ἔδωκα
ΣA et al.   15. ὑμετέροις] ΣΦ et vulgo ἡμετέροις. Statim pro ἤθεσιν, ἔθεσιν habent
Marcellinus Sopater Dind.   18. ὅτι] Fieri potest, ut scholiasta ὅτι legerit, cum
asserat Charidemum Diotimumque tum demum coronatos esse, cum magistratu se abdica-
vissent. Sed omnes optimi codd. ὅτε habent.   19. οὑτοσὶ] οὗτος ΣΓΥΦΩ uv.

3. εἰς τοὺς συκοφάντας δ᾽ ἄγειν. Because if the accounts of free gifts were
checked, it would be by sycophants.

§ 144. *There is a difference between accounts and generosity,*

7. συκοφαντῶν. 'He is a sycophant
when he says.' One might connect this
perhaps still more closely with οὐκ ἔστιν
(which answers to εἰ δέ φησιν above, not
φησὶν below). Then the sense will be,
'Such a law does not exist; but Aeschines
does exist, he is a sycophant: why, he says,'
etc. If so, there should be a colon instead
of a comma after συκοφαντῶν.

8. ἡ βουλή. He puts Aeschines' conduct in an invidious light, as having attacked
Ctesiphon after the Senate had approved
his motion. So the Scholiast remarks, here
and on § 153.

§ 145. *Which has often been recognised
in the case of others.*

16. ἤθεσιν. So the MSS. Bekker and

Dindorf adopt ἔθεσιν from quotations. Cp.
below, § 339.

17. Ναυσικλῆς was appointed to command the troops sent to Phocis in 352 B.C.,
proposed Aeschines as ambassador to Philip,
and supported him on his trial. Afterwards
he acted with Demosthenes, and lent his
name to the decrees drawn up by the latter
after Chaeronea.

18. Διότιμος. A wealthy and patriotic
citizen, whose surrender was demanded by
Alexander.

19. Χαρίδημος of Oreus, naturalised
at Athens, a condottiere who ultimately
settled in the interest of Athens, or rather
of the enemies of Macedon. He was put
to death by the Persian court, having entered
the service of Darius.

οὑτοσί. As Neoptolemus was present,
the decree in his honour is naturally omitted.

§ 146. *Which proceed on a natural principle, and shall be established by documents.*

ἄρχοντι ἢ διδόναι τῇ πόλει τὰ ἑαυτοῦ διὰ τὴν ἀρχὴν μὴ ἐξέσται, ἢ τῶν δοθέντων ἀντὶ τοῦ κομίσασθαι χάριν εὐθύνας ὑφέξει. Ὅτι τοίνυν ταῦτ' ἀληθῆ λέγω, λέγε τὰ ψηφίσματά μοι τὰ τούτοις γεγενημένα αὐτὰ λαβών. λέγε.

ΨΗΦΙΣΜΑ. 5

147 [Ἄρχων Δημόνικος Φλυεύς, βοηδρομιῶνος ἕκτῃ μετ' εἰκάδα, γνώμῃ βουλῆς καὶ δήμου, Καλλίας Φρεάρριος εἶπεν ὅτι δοκεῖ τῇ βουλῇ καὶ τῷ δήμῳ στεφανῶσαι Ναυσικλέα τὸν ἐπὶ τῶν ὅπλων, ὅτι Ἀθηναίων ὁπλιτῶν δισχιλίων ὄντων ἐν Ἴμβρῳ καὶ βοηθούντων τοῖς κατοικοῦσιν Ἀθηναίων τὴν νῆσον, οὐ δυναμένου Φίλωνος τοῦ ἐπὶ τῆς διοικήσεως 10 κεχειροτονημένου διὰ τοὺς χειμῶνας πλεῦσαι καὶ μισθοδοτῆσαι τοὺς ὁπλίτας, ἐκ τῆς ἰδίας οὐσίας ἔδωκε καὶ οὐκ εἰσέπραξε τὸν δῆμον, καὶ ἀναγορεῦσαι τὸν στέφανον Διονυσίοις τραγῳδοῖς καινοῖς.]

ΕΤΕΡΟΝ ΨΗΦΙΣΜΑ.

148 [Εἶπε Καλλίας Φρεάρριος, πρυτάνεων λεγόντων βουλῆς γνώμῃ, 15 ἐπειδὴ Χαρίδημος ὁ ἐπὶ τῶν ὁπλιτῶν, ἀποσταλεὶς εἰς Σαλαμῖνα, καὶ Διότιμος ὁ ἐπὶ τῶν ἱππέων, ἐν τῇ ἐπὶ τοῦ ποταμοῦ μάχῃ τῶν στρατιωτῶν τινῶν ὑπὸ τῶν πολεμίων σκυλευθέντων, ἐκ τῶν ἰδίων ἀναλωμάτων καθώπλισαν τοὺς νεανίσκους ἀσπίσιν ὀκτακοσίαις, δεδόχθαι τῇ βουλῇ καὶ τῷ δήμῳ στεφανῶσαι Χαρίδημον καὶ Διότιμον χρυσῷ 20 στεφάνῳ, καὶ ἀναγορεῦσαι Παναθηναίοις τοῖς μεγάλοις ἐν τῷ γυμνικῷ ἀγῶνι καὶ Διονυσίοις τραγῳδοῖς καινοῖς· τῆς δὲ ἀναγορεύσεως ἐπιμεληθῆναι θεσμοθέτας, πρυτάνεις, ἀγωνοθέτας.]

149 Τούτων ἕκαστος, Αἰσχίνη, τῆς μὲν ἀρχῆς ἧς ἦρχεν ὑπεύθυνος ἦν, ἐφ' οἷς δ' ἐστεφανοῦτο, οὐχ ὑπεύθυνος. οὐκοῦν οὐδ' 25 ἐγώ· ταὐτὰ γὰρ δίκαιά ἐστί μοι περὶ τῶν αὐτῶν τοῖς ἄλλοις δήπου. ἐπέδωκα· ἐπαινοῦμαι διὰ ταῦτα, οὐκ ὢν ὧν ἐπέδωκα ὑπεύθυνος. ἦρχον· καὶ δέδωκά γε εὐθύνας ἐκείνων, οὐχ ὧν ἐπέδωκα. νὴ Δί', ἀλλ' ἀδίκως ἦρξα; εἶτα παρών, ὅτε με εἰσῆγον οἱ λογισταί, οὐ κατηγόρεις;

30

§ 147. [*Decree in honour of Nausicles.*]
11. μισθοδοτῆσαι. Usually with the dative.
12. οὐκ εἰσέπραξε τὸν δῆμον. As we say, 'Did not get it in from the people.'
§ 148. [*Decree in honour of Charidemus and Diotimus.*]
15. πρυτάνεων .. γνώμῃ: cp. § 46 init.
16. ὁ ἐπὶ τῶν ὁπλιτῶν: cp. § 47, ὁ ἐπὶ τῶν ὅπλων.
22. τῆς δὲ ἀναγορεύσεως ἐπιμεληθῆναι κ.τ.λ. A scarcely credible arrangement, says Dindorf.
§ 149. *Each of these owed account for his official duty: not for his free gifts. Their case is mine. I gave free gifts: I passed*

my accounts unopposed by you.
§ 149. Here Demosthenes' argument really concedes the technical objection urged by Aeschines, that the crown was proposed at a time when the letter of the law forbade him to be crowned. He only replies, the spirit of the law was not violated. I was crowned for matters independent of my accounts: my accounts were all right, as is witnessed by your silence: there is no discredit from them to balance the credit of my free gift. It may be said that καὶ δέδωκά γε κ.τ.λ. is an attempt to make a point from the delay in the action: Aeschines could not deny that the crown would now be legal.

Ἵνα τοίνυν εἰδῆτε ὅτι αὐτὸς οὗτός μοι μαρτυρεῖ ἐφ᾽ οἷς 150 οὐχ ὑπεύθυνος ἦν ἐστεφανῶσθαι, λαβὼν ἀνάγνωθι τὸ ψήφισμα ὅλον τὸ γραφέν μοι. οἷς γὰρ οὐκ ἐγράψατο τοῦ προβουλεύματος, τούτοις ἃ διώκει συκοφαντῶν φανήσεται. λέγε.

5 **ΨΗΦΙΣΜΑ.**

[Ἐπὶ ἄρχοντος Εὐθυκλέους, πυανεψιῶνος ἐνάτῃ ἀπιόντος, φυλῆς 151 πρυτανευούσης Οἰνηΐδος, Κτησιφῶν Λεωσθένους Ἀναφλύστιος εἶπεν, ἐπειδὴ Δημοσθένης Δημοσθένους Παιανιεὺς γενόμενος ἐπιμελητὴς τῆς τῶν τειχῶν ἐπισκευῆς καὶ προσαναλώσας εἰς τὰ ἔργα ἀπὸ τῆς ἰδίας 10 οὐσίας τρία τάλαντα ἐπέδωκε ταῦτα τῷ δήμῳ, καὶ ἐπὶ τοῦ θεωρικοῦ κατασταθεὶς ἐπέδωκε τοῖς ἐκ πασῶν τῶν φυλῶν θεωροῖς ἑκατὸν μνᾶς εἰς 152 θυσίας, δεδόχθαι τῇ βουλῇ καὶ τῷ δήμῳ τῷ Ἀθηναίων ἐπαινέσαι Δημοσθένην Δημοσθένους Παιανιέα ἀρετῆς ἕνεκα καὶ καλοκαγαθίας ἧς ἔχων διατελεῖ ἐν παντὶ καιρῷ εἰς τὸν δῆμον τὸν Ἀθηναίων, καὶ στεφανῶσαι 15 χρυσῷ στεφάνῳ, καὶ ἀναγορεῦσαι τὸν στέφανον ἐν τῷ θεάτρῳ Διονυσίοις τραγῳδοῖς καινοῖς· τῆς δὲ ἀναγορεύσεως ἐπιμεληθῆναι τὸν ἀγωνοθέτην.]

Οὐκοῦν ἃ μὲν ἐπέδωκα, ταῦτ᾽ ἐστίν, ὧν οὐδὲν σὺ γέγραψαι· 153 ἃ δέ φησιν ἡ βουλὴ δεῖν ἀντὶ τούτων γενέσθαι μοι, ταῦτ᾽ ἔσθ᾽ 20 ἃ διώκεις. τὸ λαβεῖν οὖν τὰ διδόμενα ὁμολογῶν ἔννομον εἶναι, τὸ χάριν τούτων ἀποδοῦναι παρανόμων γράφει. ὁ δὲ παμπόνηρος ἄνθρωπος καὶ θεοῖς ἐχθρὸς καὶ βάσκανος ὄντως ποῖός τις ἂν εἴη πρὸς θεῶν; οὐχ ὁ τοιοῦτος;

Καὶ μὴν περὶ τοῦ γ᾽ ἐν τῷ θεάτρῳ κηρύττεσθαι, τὸ μὲν 154 25 μυριάκις μυρίους κεκηρῦχθαι παραλείπω καὶ τὸ πολλάκις αὐτὸς ἐστεφανῶσθαι πρότερον. ἀλλὰ πρὸς θεῶν οὕτω σκαιὸς εἶ καὶ ἀναίσθητος, Αἰσχίνη, ὥστ᾽ οὐ δύνασαι λογίσασθαι ὅτι τῷ μὲν στεφανουμένῳ τὸν αὐτὸν ἔχει ζῆλον ὁ στέφανος, ὅπου ἂν ἀναρρηθῇ, τοῦ δὲ τῶν στεφανούντων ἕνεκα συμφέροντος ἐν τῷ θεά-

---

13. Παιανιέα] Παιανιᾶ Σ Β. et S.   27. δύνασαι] ΣΤΦ krs.

§ 150. *His silence on parts of the decree, proves that he knew what I was crowned for lay outside my accountability.*
3. **οἷς .. φανήσεται.** The clauses in the decree (vide ad § 151 sq.) which he did not prosecute, will prove that those he did prosecute were selected maliciously and captiously. The point, as fairly represented by the compiler of the documents, is that the indictment does not recite anything corresponding to **Δημοσθένης .. θυσίας.**
προβουλεύματος: cp. also § 10 above.
§§ 151, 152. [*Decree in honour of Demosthenes.*]

§ 153. *Is it not execrable to receive a gift, and denounce a grateful return?*
21. **τὸ .. γράφει.** 'He admits that my gifts might be accepted lawfully: it is the expression of gratitude for them which he prosecutes as illegal.'
§ 154. *As to the details I waive precedent; but is the publicity of the reward the interest of the receiver or the giver? Of the latter he wishes to provoke emulation.*
27. **ὥστ᾽ οὐ δύνασαι.** So the best MSS.: volgo δύνασθαι, which arose from homoeoteleuton, and violates the rule of ὥστε with the infinitive taking μή.

τρῳ γίγνεται τὸ κήρυγμα ; οἱ γὰρ ἀκούσαντες ἅπαντες εἰς
τὸ ποιεῖν εὖ τὴν πόλιν προτρέπονται, καὶ τοὺς ἀποδιδόντας
τὴν χάριν μᾶλλον ἐπαινοῦσι τοῦ στεφανουμένου· διόπερ τὸν
155 νόμον τοῦτον ἡ πόλις γέγραφεν. Λέγε δ' αὐτόν μοι τὸν
νόμον λαβών.   5

ΝΟΜΟΣ.

[Ὅσους στεφανοῦσί τινες τῶν δήμων, τὰς ἀναγορεύσεις τῶν στεφάνων ποιεῖσθαι ἐν αὐτοῖς ἑκάστους τοῖς ἰδίοις δήμοις, ἐὰν μή τινας
ὁ δῆμος ὁ τῶν Ἀθηναίων ἢ ἡ βουλὴ στεφανοῖ· τούτους δ' ἐξεῖναι
ἐν τῷ θεάτρῳ Διονυσίοις ἀναγορεύεσθαι.]   10

156 Ἀκούεις, Αἰσχίνη, τοῦ νόμου λέγοντος σαφῶς, πλὴν ἐάν
τινας ὁ δῆμος ἢ ἡ βουλὴ ψηφίσηται· τούτους δὲ ἀναγορευέτω.
τί οὖν, ὦ ταλαίπωρε, συκοφαντεῖς ; τί λόγους πλάττεις ; τί
σαυτὸν οὐκ ἐλλεβορίζεις ἐπὶ τούτοις ; ἀλλ' οὐδ' αἰσχύνει φθόνου δίκην εἰσάγων, οὐκ ἀδικήματος οὐδενός, καὶ νόμους τοὺς 15
μὲν μεταποιῶν, τῶν δ' ἀφαιρῶν μέρη, οὓς ὅλους δίκαιον ἦν
ἀναγιγνώσκεσθαι τοῖς γε ὀμωμοκόσι κατὰ τοὺς νόμους ψηφιεῖ-
157 σθαι ; ἔπειτα τοιαῦτα ποιῶν λέγεις ἃ δεῖ τροσεῖναι τῷ δημοτικῷ, ὥσπερ ἀνδριάντα ἐκδεδωκὼς κατὰ συγγραφήν, εἶτ' οὐκ
ἔχοντα ἃ. προσῆκεν ἐκ τῆς συγγραφῆς κομιζόμενος, ἢ λόγῳ 20
τοὺς δημοτικούς, ἀλλ' οὐ τοῖς πράγμασι καὶ τοῖς πολιτεύμασι
γιγνωσκομένους. καὶ βοᾷς ῥητὰ καὶ ἄρρητα ὀνομάζων, ὥσπερ

---

12. δῆμος] δῆμος ἔληται legisse videtur Schol.; nisi forte id tanquam glossema deduxerit
ex textu legis fortasse accuratiore.   ψηφίσηται] στεφανώσηται in margine habent
nonnulli.   15. τοὺς μὲν] Om. pr. Σ (a m. sec. restitutum) et editi nonnulli.

---

3. τὸν νόμον τοῦτον. The law has been
implicitly referred to already, still we should
have had τόνδε in Thucydides.

§ 155. [Law.]

9. στεφανοῖ. This cannot be reconciled
with the terms in which Aeschines pleads to
the law (in Ctes. § 33) below, § 156. Two
MSS. read στεφανώσηται instead of ψηφίσηται, and the same conjecture is found in the
margin of better MSS.; but the tone of the
discussion shews, if proof were needed, that
στεφανοῖ is too strong.

§ 156. The law is plain, and you are
malicious or mad.

§ 156. You hear, Aeschines, the law
speaks plainly, ' except in the case of a vote
of the senate and people, then proclamation
may be made.' You wretch, where is the
excuse for your calumnies, and all the words
you put together ? Why not take hellebore

after this ? Are you really not ashamed of
bringing an action for pure spite and for no
wrong whatever, of garbling some laws and
mutilating others, though as the court is
sworn to vote according to law, it was but
fair to let them hear the laws at full ?

11. πλὴν .. ὁ δῆμος .. ψηφίσηται. The
Scholiasts are unanimous in regarding Aeschines' interpretation of the law as the
true one.

§ 157. Then you describe the qualifica-
tion of the statesman, and indulge in ribaldry.

19. ὥσπερ .. γιγνωσκομένους. ' As if
you had contracted for a statue, and the
statue sent did not fulfil the conditions of
the contract, or as if statesmen and patriots
could be judged by theory instead of by
their acts.' Cp. Aesch. in Ctes. §§ 168
sqq.: and for the construction, ibid. § 142
fin.

ἐξ ἁμάξης, ἃ σοὶ καὶ τῷ σῷ γένει πρόσεστιν, οὐκ ἐμοί. καίτοι 158
καὶ τοῦτο, ὦ ἄνδρες Ἀθηναῖοι. ἐγὼ λοιδορίαν κατηγορίας
τούτῳ διαφέρειν ἡγοῦμαι, τῷ τὴν μὲν κατηγορίαν ἀδικήματ᾽
ἔχειν, ὧν ἐν τοῖς νόμοις εἰσὶν αἱ τιμωρίαι, τὴν δὲ λοιδορίαν
5 βλασφημίας, ἃς κατὰ τὴν αὐτῶν φύσιν τοῖς ἐχθροῖς περὶ ἀλλήλων συμβαίνει λέγειν. οἰκοδομῆσαι δὲ τοὺς προγόνους ταυτὶ
τὰ δικαστήρια ὑπείληφα οὐχ ἵνα συλλέξαντες ὑμᾶς εἰς ταῦτα
ἀπὸ τῶν ἰδίων κακῶς τὰ ἀπόρρητα λέγωμεν ἀλλήλους, ἀλλ᾽
ἵνα ἐξελέγχωμεν, ἐάν τις ἠδικηκώς τι τυγχάνῃ τὴν πόλιν.
10 ταῦτα τοίνυν εἰδὼς Αἰσχίνης οὐδὲν ἧττον ἐμοῦ πομπεύειν ἀντὶ 159
τοῦ κατηγορεῖν εἵλετο. οὐ μὴν οὐδ᾽ ἐνταῦθα ἔλαττον ἔχων
δίκαιός ἐστιν ἀπελθεῖν. ἤδη δ᾽ ἐπὶ ταῦτα πορεύσομαι, τοσοῦτον αὐτὸν ἐρωτήσας. πότερόν σέ τις, Αἰσχίνη, τῆς πόλεως
ἐχθρὸν ἢ ἐμὸν εἶναι φῇ; ἐμὸν δῆλον ὅτι. εἶτα οὗ μὲν ἦν
15 παρ᾽ ἐμοῦ δίκην κατὰ τοὺς νόμους ὑπὲρ τούτων λαβεῖν, εἴπερ
ἠδίκουν, ἐξέλιπες, ἐν ταῖς εὐθύναις, ἐν ταῖς γραφαῖς, ἐν ταῖς
ἄλλαις κρίσεσιν· οὗ δ᾽ ἐγὼ μὲν ἀθῷος ἅπασι, τοῖς νόμοις, 160
τῷ χρόνῳ, τῇ προθεσμίᾳ, τῷ κεκρίσθαι περὶ πάντων πολλάκις
πρότερον, τῷ μηδεπώποτε ἐξελεγχθῆναι μηδὲν ὑμᾶς ἀδικῶν, τῇ
20 πόλει δ᾽ ἢ πλέον ἢ ἔλαττον ἀνάγκη τῶν γε δημοσίᾳ πεπραγμένων μετεῖναι τῆς δόξης, ἐνταῦθα ἀπήντηκας; ὅρα μὴ τούτων
μὲν ἐχθρὸς ᾖς, ἐμοὶ δὲ προσποιῇ.

22. ἐμοί] Ita ΣΦ pr. F pr γρ. s B. et S. : ceteri ęt volg. ἐμός.

1. ἐξ ἁμάξης. Ribaldry was used at
the Eleusinia and the Anthesteria, also at
the country Dionysia. The allusion to these
and to mysteries of any kind, would be
insulting to Aeschines.

§ 158. Which is irresponsible, as it in-
volves no legal crimes.

καίτοι καὶ τοῦτο. 'Though there is
this to say' [though Aeschines' accusations
are too vague to deserve a reply], 'it is
worth while to point out the difference
there is in my judgment between invective
and impeachment ; the first is the expression
of dislike, the second specifies punishable
breaches of law.

6. συμβαίνει goes with κατὰ τὴν αὐτῶν
φύσιν, as we say, 'What it comes natural
to them to say;' the extent to which they
indulged in such invective, would be measured by their moderation of character.

§ 159. Still it must be met. As my enemy,
not the enemy of Athens, you should have
prosecuted me where I could be punished.

11. οὐ μὴν .. .. ἀπελθεῖν. 'However,
even here I must give him as good as he
brings;' yet, as ἔλαττον ἔχειν is generally

'to have the worst' of a contest, it is possible that here it means, 'Since he has tried to
force me into bad language, he shall have
his will.'

13. πότερον .. εἶναι φῇ. As in § 110,
Demosthenes suggests the answer that he is
leading up to, though he formally declines
to give it at once. Compare also D. de F.
L. p. 405, § 228, Olynth. I. p. 14 extr., §
20.

§ 160. Instead you take an opportunity of
discrediting Athens, where it is impossible to
punish me.

17. τοῖς νόμοις .. τῷ χρόνῳ are the
securities to which Demosthenes is entitled by positive and natural law, τῇ
προθεσμίᾳ is the union of both: yet the
difference between τῷ χρόνῳ and τῇ προθεσμίᾳ is almost slight enough to justify
Reiske's suspicion that the former is a gloss
upon the latter.

19. τῇ πόλει .. ἀπήντηκας, i. e. To
prosecute the mover of a vote of thanks to
me for recommending policy which Athens
adopted, must discredit Athens, yet that is
the ground you choose.

161 Ἐπειδὴ τοίνυν ἡ μὲν εὐσεβὴς καὶ δικαία ψῆφος ἅπασι δε-
δεικται, δεῖ δέ με, ὡς ἔοικε, καίπερ οὐ φιλολοίδορον ὄντα φύσει,
διὰ τὰς ὑπὸ τούτου βλασφημίας εἰρημένας ἀντὶ πολλῶν καὶ
ψευδῶν αὐτὰ τἀναγκαιότατ᾽ εἰπεῖν περὶ αὐτοῦ, καὶ δεῖξαι τίς
ὢν καὶ τίνων ῥᾳδίως οὕτως ἄρχει τοῦ κακῶς λέγειν, καὶ λόγους 5
τίνας διασύρει, αὐτὸς εἰρηκὼς ἃ τίς οὐκ ἂν ὤκνησε τῶν μετρίων
162 ἀνθρώπων φθέγξασθαι;—εἰ γὰρ Αἰακὸς ἢ Ῥαδάμανθυς ἢ Μί-
νως ἦν κατηγορῶν, ἀλλὰ μὴ σπερμολόγος, περίτριμμα ἀγορᾶς,
ὄλεθρος γραμματεύς, οὐκ ἂν αὐτὸν οἶμαι τοιαῦτ᾽ εἰπεῖν οὐδ᾽
ἂν οὕτως ἐπαχθεῖς λόγους πορίσασθαι, ὥσπερ ἐν τραγῳδίᾳ 10
βοῶντα ὦ γῆ καὶ ἥλιε καὶ ἀρετὴ καὶ τὰ τοιαῦτα, καὶ πάλιν
σύνεσιν καὶ παιδείαν ἐπικαλούμενον, ᾗ τὰ καλὰ καὶ τὰ αἰσχρὰ
διαγιγνώσκεται· ταῦτα γὰρ δήπουθεν ἠκούετ᾽ αὐτοῦ λέγοντος·
163 σοὶ δὲ ἀρετῆς, ὦ κάθαρμα, ἢ τοῖς σοῖς τίς μετουσία ; ἢ καλῶν
ἢ μὴ τοιούτων τίς διάγνωσις ; πόθεν ἢ πῶς ἀξιωθέντι ; ποῦ 15
δὲ παιδείας σοι θέμις μνησθῆναι, ἧς τῶν μὲν ὡς ἀληθῶς τετυχη-
κότων οὐδ᾽ ἂν εἷς εἴποι περὶ αὐτοῦ τοιοῦτον οὐδέν, ἀλλὰ κἂν
ἑτέρου λέγοντος ἐρυθριάσειε, τοῖς δ᾽ ἀπολειφθεῖσι μὲν ὥσπερ
σύ, προσποιουμένοις δ᾽ ὑπ᾽ ἀναισθησίας τὸ τοὺς ἀκούοντας
ἀλγεῖν ποιεῖν, ὅταν λέγωσιν, οὐ τὸ δοκεῖν τοιούτοις εἶναι 20
περίεστιν.

164 Οὐκ ἀπορῶν δ᾽ ὅ τι χρὴ περὶ σοῦ καὶ τῶν σῶν εἰπεῖν,
ἀπορῶ τοῦ πρώτου μνησθῶ, πότερ᾽ ὡς ὁ πατήρ σου Τρόμης
ἐδούλευε παρ᾽ Ἐλπίᾳ τῷ πρὸς τῷ Θησείῳ διδάσκοντι γράμματα, χοίνικας παχείας ἔχων καὶ ξύλον, ἢ ὡς ἡ μήτηρ σου 25

---

§ 161. *Aeschines' calumnies compel me to
indicate his character,*

1. ἅπασι. If this is the dative of the
instrument, ' by the whole argument,' if not,
' in all the points raised.'

2. δεῖ δέ με. One MS. alters δὲ to δή,
in order to make the construction consistent:
the truth is that the apodosis is suppressed:
it would virtually be an anticipation of
§ 164 sq. οὐκ ἀπορῶν δὲ κ.τ.λ.

5. ῥᾳδίως. 'Unscrupulously,' as one
who had nothing to lose.

λόγους τίνας διασύρει. Several MSS.
have τινὰς, 'And pulls some phrases (of
mine) to pieces' (Aesch. in Ctes. §§ 72,
166), while he himself has been talking in
the worst taste possible. This is so much
more obvious a reading as to be suspicious,
and τίνας is more forcible in sense, though

irregular in construction. It should strictly
be, τὶς ὧν λόγους τίνας διασύρει or τίνα αὐτὸς
εἰρηκὼς λόγους τίνας διασύρει, tr. 'What
sort of phrases he thinks it safe to mangle,
though he has said,' etc.

§ 162. *For he has brought charges and
made pretensions no man of character would
bring.*

8. περίτριμμα. So περίτριμμα δικῶν
Ar. Nub. 447. 260. Perhaps the rhythm
from σπερμολόγος .. ὄλεθρος may suggest a
quotation from a comedy, if so, γραμματεὺς
would be substituted παρὰ προσδοκίαν for
the close of the line.

§ 163. *You have no right to such pretensions : men who have would not make
them.*

§§ 164. 165. *I shall only disgrace myself
by telling you what you know of his family.*

τοῖς μεθημερινοῖς γάμοις ἐν τῷ κλεισίῳ τῷ πρὸς τῷ καλαμίτῃ
Ἥρῳ χρωμένη τὸν καλὸν ἀνδριάντα καὶ τριταγωνιστὴν ἄκρον
ἐξέθρεψέ σε. ἀλλ᾽ ὡς ὁ τριηραύλης Φορμίων, ὁ Δίωνος τοῦ 165
Φρεαρρίου δοῦλος, ἀνέστησεν αὐτὴν ἀπὸ ταύτης τῆς καλῆς
5 ἐργασίας; ἀλλὰ νὴ τὸν Δία καὶ τοὺς θεοὺς ὀκνῶ μὴ περὶ σοῦ
τὰ προσήκοντα λέγων αὐτὸς οὐ προσήκοντας ἐμαυτῷ δόξω
προῃρῆσθαι λόγους. ταῦτα μὲν οὖν ἐάσω, ἀπ᾽ αὐτῶν δὲ ὧν
αὐτὸς βεβίωκεν ἄρξομαι· οὐδὲ γὰρ ὧν ἔτυχεν ἦν, ἀλλ᾽ οἷς ὁ
δῆμος καταρᾶται. ὀψὲ γάρ ποτε—, ὀψέ λέγω; χθὲς μὲν 166
10 οὖν καὶ πρώην ἅμ᾽ Ἀθηναῖος καὶ ῥήτωρ γέγονε, καὶ δύο συλλαβὰς προσθεὶς τὸν μὲν πατέρα ἀντὶ Τρόμητος ἐποίησεν Ἀτρό-
μητον, τὴν δὲ μητέρα σεμνῶς πάνυ Γλαυκοθέαν ὠνόμασεν, ἣν
Ἔμπουσαν ἅπαντες ἴσασι καλουμένην, ἐκ τοῦ πάντα ποιεῖν καὶ
πάσχειν δηλονότι ταύτης τῆς ἐπωνυμίας τυχοῦσαν· πόθεν γὰρ 167

<hr/>

2. Ἥρῳ] Om. A et socii : ηρωω in Σ superscriptum est. Utrum ι subscribi an adscribi
debeat. vid. annot.   Quod ad calcem hujus § addebatur, ἀλλὰ πάντες ἴσασι ταῦτα, κἂν
ἐγὼ μὴ λέγω, om. ΣΒΦΨΥ *tv* B. et S.   7. οὖν] Om. pr. Σ : ταῦτα μὲν ...ἄρξομαι
post οὐδὲ γάρ .. καταρᾶται ponit Σ.   14. Post πόθεν γὰρ ἄλλοθεν Reiskio videbantur
ea addenda esse quae memoratur Hermogenes, κνάμους ἐφθοὺς βοῶσα κατὰ πᾶν τὸ θέρος
ἐπλανᾶτο. Ex ipsius Hermogenis verbis videri potest ea potius ad § 324 fuisse : sed ibi
minus bene verbis accommodari possunt.

<hr/>

2. Ἥρῳ. A proper name (cp. Demos.
de F. L. p. 419, § 279) to be written thus,
as there the best MSS. give Ἥρω for the
genitive. καλαμίτη is not a proper name,
but a cant word for a surgeon; even apart
from the question of orthography, the position of the article proves that καλαμίτη, not
ἥρωι, is the epithet.

τὸν καλὸν ἀνδριάντα. As we say,
'The fine figure of a man.' There is a
double sneer at Aeschines' good looks and
at his pretensions to be the model statesman : cp. above, § 157, ὥσπερ ἀνδριάντα
ἐκδεδωκώς. For Aeschines' personal appearance, see Life. It may be added that καλὸς
ἀνδριὰς was a common pet name for a child,
'pretty puppet.'

At the end of this section was added ἀλλὰ
πάντες ἴσασι ταῦτα, κἂν ἐγὼ μὴ λέγω.
Most good MSS. omit it : can it be merely
a gloss on the following ἀλλά?

8. οὐδὲ γὰρ κ.τ.λ. This is Demosthenes'
reply to Aeschines' criticism on his maternal
descent as a disqualification for public life
(in Ctes. §§ 168 sqq.) I confine myself to
his personal history, 'for his parentage was
not simply mean, it was infamous;' his
parents belonged to a class which is included
in the solemn public imprecations, and therefore he is naturally disaffected to the public.
It is mentioned in the margin of Σ, that
some proposed to transpose the clauses
ταῦτα .. ἄρξομαι and οὐδὲ .. καταρᾶται.

Some refer ὧν ἔτυχε to ὧν βεβίωκεν, but
this does not explain the genitive.

§ 166. *Whom he has capriciously dignified.*

9. ὀψὲ γάρ. The γὰρ serves merely to
continue the sense, and to introduce the
narrative of Aeschines' life. Its English
equivalent would be, 'Well, after a long
time : a long time do I say, why it was
only yesterday or the day before,' etc. He
interrupts the narrative before it is fairly
begun, to shew that Aeschines had reason to
be ashamed of his family, or at least behaved
as if he was.

10. ἅμ᾽ Ἀθηναῖος καὶ ῥήτωρ γέγονε,
i.e. 'He was never recognised as a citizen
till of age to be an orator.'

12. Γλαυκοθέαν. Her work-a-day name
was Glaucis. Aeschines (De F. L. p. 38, § 78)
mentions her father Glaucus, in a way which
implies that he was a credit to his descendants.

13. Ἔμπουσαν : cp. Ar. Ran. 288 sqq.
The transformations of this bogy or demon
were the most remarkable point in her character, so that Demosthenes is probably
right in his explanation of the nickname,
but the anonymous biographer of Aeschines
and other grammarians suggest, that she
was so called from her ghostly appearance
in the mysteries : vid. ad § 331.

14. καὶ γίγνεσθαι. These words are
added by Σ. They have very little point

ἄλλοθεν; ἀλλ' ὅμως οὕτως ἀχάριστος εἶ καὶ πονηρὸς φύσει
ὥστ' ἐλεύθερος ἐκ δούλου καὶ πλούσιος ἐκ πτωχοῦ διὰ τουτουσὶ
γεγονὼς οὐχ ὅπως χάριν αὐτοῖς ἔχεις, ἀλλὰ μισθώσας σαυτὸν
κατὰ τουτωνὶ πολιτεύει. καὶ περὶ ὧν μὲν ἔστι τις ἀμφισβήτησις, ὡς ἄρα ὑπὲρ τῆς πόλεως εἴρηκεν, ἐάσω· ἃ δ' ὑπὲρ τῶν 5
ἐχθρῶν φανερῶς ἀπεδείχθη πράττων, ταῦτα ἀναμνήσω.

168 Τίς γὰρ ὑμῶν οὐκ οἶδε τὸν ἀποψηφισθέντα Ἀντιφῶντα,
ὃς ἐπαγγειλάμενος Φιλίππῳ τὰ νεώρια ἐμπρήσειν εἰς τὴν πόλιν
ἦλθεν; ὃν λαβόντος ἐμοῦ κεκρυμμένον ἐν Πειραιεῖ καὶ κατα-
στήσαντος εἰς τὴν ἐκκλησίαν βοῶν ὁ βάσκανος οὗτος καὶ 10
κεκραγὼς, ὡς ἐν δημοκρατίᾳ δεινὰ ποιῶ τοὺς ἠτυχηκότας τῶν
πολιτῶν ὑβρίζων καὶ ἐπ' οἰκίας βαδίζων ἄνευ ψηφίσματος,
169 ἀφεθῆναι ἐποίησεν. καὶ εἰ μὴ ἡ βουλὴ ἡ ἐξ Ἀρείου πάγου τὸ
πρᾶγμα αἰσθομένη καὶ τὴν ὑμετέραν ἄγνοιαν ἐν οὐ δέοντι συμ-
βεβηκυῖαν ἰδοῦσα ἐπεζήτησε τὸν ἄνθρωπον καὶ συλλαβοῦσα 15

---

14. ὑμετέραν] In litura habet Σ, et Dind. ἡμετέραν a m. pr. scriptum fuisse perhibet.

---

in reference to Aeschines' mother; but if
it was more natural to speak of Empusa
turning into everything, than doing or
suffering everything, this would account for
the gloss or the afterthought.

§ 167. *I will come to his own ingratitude
and treason.*

πόθεν γὰρ ἄλλοθεν. See the critical
note for the passage which we know from
Hermogenes was suppressed by ancient
critics, about Glaucis 'crying "boiled
beans" all the summer' It is possible
that something may have been retrenched which referred to Aeschines, and
that it was this, which was clenched by
πόθεν γὰρ ἄλλοθεν. If so, ὅμως would be
intended to introduce a contrast to this; if
the text is still as Demosthenes left it, ὅμως
must refer back to ὀψὲ .. γέγονε. Vid. ad
§ 324.

2. διὰ τουτουσί. 'Thanks to your
countrymen.' Through their good nature,
which tolerated your false claims and admitted your pretended services, Demosthenes implies (below, § 385) that Aeschines was already in comfortable circumstances before he had received anything
from Philip.

4. περὶ ὧν μὲν ἔστι τις ἀμφισβήτησις,
e. g. His support of the peace of Philocrates,
which after Aeschines' acquittal Demosthenes
could not, in courtesy to the judges, treat as
manifest treason.

5. εἴρηκεν. Emphatic, opposed to πράτ-

των. In his speeches, he would have to
mask his treasonable designs, so in them it
would be just possible to believe that *after
all* (ἄρα) he had acted honestly. His *acts*
could bear no such interpretation.

§ 168. *You remember how he procured
the discharge of Antiphon, who came back to
burn the arsenal.*

7. ἀποψηφισθέντα. In 346 B.C. a review of the citizens and claimants to citizenship was held : in each Deme the Demotae
voted on the case of every member whose
claims were doubtful, and every one rejected
had an appeal to the Heliaea, but if cast
on appeal he was sold into slavery, while if
he acquiesced in the vote of the Demotae, he
had his choice of leaving Athens or remaining as a denizen. Libanius founded on this
legal device an amusing subject for a rhetorical exercise : ἑάλω ξενίας ὁ Δημοσθένης·
ἔπεμψε Φίλιππος ὠνούμενος αὐτόν· γράφει
Δημάδης διδόναι, Ὑπερείδης δημόσιον εἶναι.
Antiphon had obviously acquiesced, and
elected to leave Athens.

11. τοὺς ἠτυχηκότας τῶν πολι-
τῶν. As Janet in Waverley speaks of the
'misfortune' of her father, who was
hanged for cattle lifting. A man was
considered unfortunate at Athens when
the law was put in force against him,
except to obtain direct redress for a personal injury.

§ 169. *But he got his deserts, thanks to
the Areopagus.*

ἐπανήγαγεν ὡς ὑμᾶς, ἐξήρπαστ' ἂν ὁ τοιοῦτος καὶ τὸ δίκην
δοῦναι διαδὺς ἐξεπέπεμπτ' ἂν ὑπὸ τοῦ σεμνολόγου τουτουί·
νῦν δ' ὑμεῖς στρεβλώσαντες αὐτὸν ἀπεκτείνατε, ὡς ἔδει γε καὶ
τοῦτον. τοιγαροῦν εἰδυῖα ταῦτα ἡ βουλὴ ἡ ἐξ 'Αρείου πάγου 170
5 τότε τούτῳ πεπραγμένα, χειροτονησάντων αὐτὸν ὑμῶν σύνδικον ὑπὲρ τοῦ ἱεροῦ τοῦ ἐν Δήλῳ ἀπὸ τῆς αὐτῆς ἀγνοίας
ἧσπερ πολλὰ προΐεσθε τῶν κοινῶν, ὡς προ[σ]είλεσθε κἀκείνην καὶ τοῦ πράγματος κυρίαν ἐποιήσατε, τοῦτον μὲν εὐθὺς
ἀπήλασεν ὡς προδότην, Ὑπερείδη δὲ λέγειν προσέταξε· καὶ
10 ταῦτα ἀπὸ τοῦ βωμοῦ φέρουσα τὴν ψῆφον ἔπραξε, καὶ οὐδεμία ψῆφος ἠνέχθη τῷ μιαρῷ τούτῳ. Καὶ ὅτι ταῦτ' ἀληθῆ
λέγω, κάλει μοι τούτων τοὺς μάρτυρας.

ΜΑΡΤΥΡΕΣ.

[Μαρτυροῦσι Δημοσθένει ὑπὲρ ἁπάντων οἵδε, Καλλίας Σουνιεὺς, 171
15 Ζήνων Φλυεὺς, Κλέων Φαληρεὺς, Δημόνικος Μαραθώνιος, ὅτι τοῦ
δήμου ποτὲ χειροτονήσαντος Αἰσχίνην σύνδικον ὑπὲρ τοῦ ἱεροῦ τοῦ
ἐν Δήλῳ εἰς τοὺς Ἀμφικτύονας συνεδρεύσαντες ἡμεῖς ἐκρίναμεν
Ὑπερείδην ἄξιον εἶναι μᾶλλον ὑπὲρ τῆς πόλεως λέγειν, καὶ ἀπε-
στάλη Ὑπερείδης.]

20 Οὐκοῦν ὅτε τούτου λέγοντος ἀπήλασεν ἡ βουλὴ καὶ προσ- 172

---

7. ἧσπερ] ἧσπερ ἕνεκα A et socii : sequiores plerique ἀφ' ἧσπερ.   12. μοι] Om.
Σ et al. B. et S.   20. λέγοντος] Ita Σ teste Dind.   Teste Bekk.   Σ habet μέλλοντος,
idque receperunt B. et S.   Volgatum μέλλοντος λέγειν habet Σ a m. sec.   Poenitet quod
nos non animadverteramus, duas inter se collationes discrepare, unde nec utrum verum sit
notavimus, sed Dindorfio potius ut recentiori credimus.

---

1. ὁ τοιοῦτος. We say, 'a man like
that,' the Greeks say, '*the* man of that
character,' as we say '*the* wretch,' '*the* villain,' or any other special definite imputation.

3. νῦν δέ. 'As it was,' the Greeks say,
'as it is.'

στρεβλώσαντες αὐτὸν ἀπεκτείνατε :
cp. Dinarchus in Dem. p. 98, § 64.

§ 170. *Which censured Aeschines by sub-
stituting Hyperides.*

5. σύνδικον. 'As pleader before the
Amphictyons,' to whom the Delians had
appealed on the old standing question,
whether they or the Athenians were entitled to the custody of the temple of Apollo.
Cp. Hdt. 8. 123, and the fragments of Hyp.
Del. Or. There existed anciently a spurious
speech of Aeschines on this occasion ; one
may suppose written as the one he would
have delivered if he had gone. It appears
from inscriptions, that the Athenians must
have made good their claim.

7. ὡς προείλεσθε κἀκείνην. So the MSS.

Wolf proposed προσείλεσθε, which is adopted
by Dindorf and Dissen : the MS. reading
may be due to the previous προίεσθε : it
cannot mean ' preferred their judgment' (to
your own), for this gives no sense to καὶ,
nor can 'chose them previously' be turned
into ' chose them to exercise a choice previous to his actual departure.' The only
way to defend προείλεσθε, would be to
strike out καὶ and ἐποιήσατε. Wolf's emendation would be milder, if not safer, and gives
an admirable sense, ' co-opted them too' into
the body which appointed the advocate.

10. ἀπὸ τοῦ βωμοῦ φέρουσα τὴν ψῆφον contrasts with χειροτονησάντων. The
voting was more deliberate, more free, and
more responsible, against Aeschines than for
him. The Areopagites took their ballots
from the altar one by one to put them into
the urn.

§ 171. [*Depositions*.]

§ 172. *Clearly the substitution was a censure. Here is one point of comparison between him and me.*

ἔταξεν ἑτέρῳ, τότε καὶ προδότην εἶναι καὶ κακόνουν ὑμῖν
ἀπέφηνεν.

"Ἐν μὲν τοίνυν τοῦτο τοιοῦτο πολίτευμα τοῦ νεανίου τούτου,
ὅμοιόν γε, οὐ γάρ; οἷς ἐμοῦ κατηγορεῖ· ἕτερον δὲ ἀναμιμ-
173 νήσκεσθε. ὅτε γὰρ Πύθωνα Φίλιππος ἔπεμψε τὸν Βυζάντιον 5
καὶ παρὰ τῶν αὐτοῦ συμμάχων πάντων συνέπεμψε πρέσβεις,
ὡς ἐν αἰσχύνη ποιήσων τὴν πόλιν καὶ δείξων ἀδικοῦσαν,
τότε ἐγὼ μὲν τῷ Πύθωνι θρασυνομένῳ καὶ πολλῷ ῥέοντι καθ᾽
ὑμῶν οὐχ ὑπεχώρησα, ἀλλ᾽ ἀναστὰς ἀντεῖπον καὶ τὰ τῆς
πόλεως δίκαια οὐχὶ προὔδωκα, ἀλλ᾽ ἀδικοῦντα Φίλιππον ἐξή- 10
λεγξα φανερῶς οὕτως ὥστε τοὺς ἐκείνου συμμάχους αὐτοὺς
ἀνισταμένους ὁμολογεῖν· οὗτος δὲ συνηγωνίζετο καὶ τἀναντία
ἐμαρτύρει τῇ πατρίδι, καὶ ταῦτα ψευδῆ.
174 Καὶ οὐκ ἀπέχρη ταῦτα, ἀλλὰ πάλιν μετὰ ταῦθ᾽ ὕστερον
Ἀναξίνῳ τῷ κατασκόπῳ συνιὼν εἰς τὴν Θράσωνος οἰκίαν ἐλήφθη. 15
καίτοι ὅστις τῷ ὑπὸ τῶν πολεμίων πεμφθέντι μόνος μόνῳ
συνῄει καὶ ἐκοινολογεῖτο, οὗτος αὐτὸς ὑπῆρχε τῇ φύσει κατάσκοπος καὶ πολέμιος τῇ πατρίδι. Καὶ ὅτι ταῦτ᾽ ἀληθῆ λέγω,
κάλει μοι τούτων τοὺς μάρτυρας.

ΜΑΡΤΥΡΕΣ.　20

175　[Τελέδημος Κλέωνος, Ὑπερείδης Καλλαίσχρου, Νικόμαχος Διο-
φάντου μαρτυροῦσι Δημοσθένει καὶ ἐπωμόσαντο ἐπὶ τῶν στρατηγῶν
εἰδέναι Αἰσχίνην Ἀτρομήτου Κοθωκίδην συνερχόμενον νυκτὸς εἰς
τὴν Θράσωνος οἰκίαν καὶ κοινολογούμενον Ἀναξίνῳ, ὃς ἐκρίθη εἶναι
κατάσκοπος παρὰ Φιλίππου. αὗται ἀπεδόθησαν αἱ μαρτυρίαι ἐπὶ 25
Νικίου, ἑκατομβαιῶνος τρίτῃ ἱσταμένου.]

---

3. τοῦ νεανίου τούτου. 'Our hero here.'
This ironical sense is commoner in the deri-
vatives of νεανίας than in the word itself; but
cp. below, § 386.

4. ὅμοιόν γε. 'It resembles,' not my
conduct which he impeaches, but ' his imputations on me,' as Tennyson has it, 'and
impute themselves Lacking the mental
range.'

§ 173. Again, when Python was sent here
by Philip, I confuted him, Aeschines supported him.

8. τῷ Πύθωνι θρασυνομένῳ. Auctor
de Halonneso, p. 81, §§ 21, 22, gives an
outline of a speech which he says was well
received, in which Python throws the whole
blame of the coldness on the unfriendly attitude of Athens under the influence of the
orators of the war party.

§ 174. Not content with this, be held
interviews with Anaxinus the spy.

15. Ἀναξίνῳ. According to Aeschines
(in Ctes. § 224), he was sent to make pur-
chases for Olympias. The passage has little
of the air of an afterthought, though admirably adapted to reply to this.

17. ὑπῆρχε answers to πεμφθέντι. Philip
sent a spy ; he found a spy on the spot bred
to his hand in Aeschines.

§ 175. [Depositions.]

25. αὗται .. Νικίου. Boeckh conjectures that this evidence was taken soon
after the event, in view of a prosecution
of Aeschines, which the senate declined to
press ; but, as Dissen points out, it is strange
that Aeschines does not make a point
against Demosthenes as an unsuccessful
sycophant.

Μυρία τοίνυν ἕτερ' εἰπεῖν ἔχων περὶ αὐτοῦ παραλείπω. καὶ 176
γὰρ οὕτω πως ἔχει. πολλὰ ἂν ἐγὼ ἔτι τούτων ἔχοιμι δεῖξαι,
ὧν οὗτος κατ' ἐκείνους τοὺς χρόνους τοῖς μὲν ἐχθροῖς ὑπηρετῶν,
ἐμοὶ δ' ἐπηρεάζων εὑρέθη. ἀλλ' οὐ τίθεται ταῦτα παρ' ὑμῖν
5 εἰς ἀκριβῆ μνήμην οὐδ' ἣν προσῆκεν ὀργήν, ἀλλὰ δεδώκατε
ἔθει τινὶ φαύλῳ πολλὴν ἐξουσίαν τῷ βουλομένῳ τὸν λέγοντά
τι τῶν ὑμῖν συμφερόντων ὑποσκελίζειν καὶ συκοφαντεῖν, τῆς
ἐπὶ ταῖς λοιδορίαις ἡδονῆς καὶ χάριτος τὸ τῆς πόλεως συμφέρον ἀνταλλαττόμενοι· διόπερ ῥᾷόν ἐστι καὶ ἀσφαλέστερον
10 ἀεὶ τοῖς ἐχθροῖς ὑπηρετοῦντα μισθαρνεῖν ἢ τὴν ὑπὲρ ὑμῶν
ἑλόμενον τάξιν πολιτεύεσθαι.

Καὶ τὸ μὲν δὴ πρὸ τοῦ πολεμεῖν φανερῶς συναγωνίζεσθαι 177
Φιλίππῳ δεινὸν μέν, ὦ γῆ καὶ θεοί, πῶς γὰρ οὔ; κατὰ τῆς
πατρίδος· δότε δ', εἰ βούλεσθε, δότε αὐτῷ τοῦτο. ἀλλ' ἐπειδὴ
15 φανερῶς ἤδη τὰ πλοῖα ἐσεσύλητο, Χερρόνησος ἐπορθεῖτο, ἐπὶ
τὴν Ἀττικὴν ἐπορεύεθ' ἄνθρωπος, οὐκέτ' ἐν ἀμφισβητησίμῳ
τὰ πράγματα ἦν, ἀλλ' ἐνειστήκει πόλεμος, ὅ τι μὲν πώποτ'
ἔπραξεν ὑπὲρ ὑμῶν ὁ βάσκανος οὗτος ἰαμβειογράφος, οὐκ ἂν 178
ἔχοι δεῖξαι, οὐδ' ἔστιν οὔτε μεῖζον οὔτ' ἔλαττον ψήφισμα
20 οὐδὲν Αἰσχίνη ὑπὲρ τῶν συμφερόντων τῇ πόλει. εἰ δέ φησι,
νῦν δειξάτω ἐν τῷ ἐμῷ ὕδατι. ἀλλ' οὐκ ἔστιν οὐδέν. καίτοι

---

9. ἀνταλλαττόμενοι] ἀντικαταλλόμενοι nonnulli.   16. ἄνθρωπος] Ita ΦΦ: ceteri
ἄνθρωπος.   18. ἰαμβειογράφος] Ita Ω τῶν marg. ΣHermog.: ἰαμβιογράφος ΣΦ,
ἰαμβογράφος Α et socii, ἰαμβειομάχος γρ. F ἰαμβοφάγος † γρ. Σ † Etym. M. s. v. et
Zonaras, ἰαμβιοφάγος Scholiasta Hermogenis, ἰαμβειοφάγος γρ. B et Reiski duo codd. Paris-
ienses.   Hoc recepit Reiske, et post eum edd. plerique omnes.   'Fort. ἰαμβειορράφος' conicit Sauppius.   Vid. annot.   20. ὑπὲρ] Ita Σ: ceteri περί.   21. ἐν] ἐπὶ Σ et plerique.

---

§ 176. But I will not dwell on his treasons;
it is safer to serve your enemies than you.
8. ἡδονῆς καὶ χάριτος. 'Pleasure and
gratification,' by denouncing patriotic speakers
the sycophant χαρίζεται.
9. διόπερ .. πολιτεύεσθαι. 'So it is
easier and safer always to serve your enemies like a hireling, than to choose your
side and act like a free statesman.' The
double antithesis is rather frigid in English,
but forcible in Greek.
§ 177. Though not content with siding
with Philip against you during the peace, he
continued to do so during the war, and
13. κατὰ τῆς πατρίδος. Emphatic, and
at once heightens and confirms the force of
δεινόν. Tr. 'And that against his fatherland.'
§ 178. Can shew no service to you. His
neutrality proves my innocence or his dis-
loyalty.

18. ἰαμβειογράφος. So most MSS., with
insignificant variations: γρ. ἰαμβειομάχος,
which may be only a conjecture, and not
such a good one as ἰαμβειοφάγος, which
had got into the text by the time of the
Scholiast on Hermogenes. ἰαμβειογράφος means a writer of lampoons, and is recognised by the grammarians here, who
explain it φιλολοίδορος ὑβριστὴς, which
last explanation is appended by the Scholiast
on Hermogenes to his new reading. Aeschines (in Tim. § 135) speaks of his love
verses, and it is not a great stretch of imagination to suppose that when his attentions
had involved him in a quarrel he retaliated
by a lampoon. If Aeschines' lampoons were
only half as well known as his ill luck on
the stage, an allusion to them would suit
the context better.
21. ἐν τῷ ἐμῷ ὕδατι. ἐπὶ, as Dindorf says,
would require the genitive.

δυοῖν αὐτὸν ἀνάγκη θάτερον, ἢ μηδὲν τοῖς πραττομένοις ὑπ
ἐμοῦ τότ' ἔχοντ' ἐγκαλεῖν μὴ γράφειν παρὰ ταῦθ' ἕτερα, ἢ
τὸ τῶν ἐχθρῶν συμφέρον ζητοῦντα μὴ φέρειν εἰς μέσον τὰ
τούτων ἀμείνω.

179 Ἆρ' οὖν οὐδ' ἔλεγεν, ὥσπερ οὐδ' ἔγραφεν, ἡνίκα ἐργάσασθαί 5
τι δέοι κακόν; οὐ μὲν οὖν ἦν εἰπεῖν ἑτέρῳ. καὶ τὰ μὲν ἄλλα
καὶ φέρειν ἐδύναθ', ὡς ἔοικεν, ἡ πόλις καὶ ποιῶν οὗτος λαν-
θάνειν· ἓν δ' ἐπεξειργάσατο, ὦ ἄνδρες Ἀθηναῖοι, τοιοῦτον ὃ
πᾶσι τοῖς προτέροις ἐπέθηκε τέλος· περὶ οὗ τοὺς πολλοὺς
ἀνάλωσε λόγους, τὰ τῶν Ἀμφισσέων τῶν Λοκρῶν διεξιὼν δόγ- 10
ματα, ὡς διαστρέψων τἀληθές. τὸ δ' οὐ τοιοῦτόν ἐστι. πόθεν;
οὐδέποτ' ἐκνίψει σὺ τἀκεῖ πεπραγμένα σαυτῷ· οὐχ οὕτω πολλὰ
ἐρεῖς.

180 Καλῶ δ' ἐναντίον ὑμῶν, ὦ ἄνδρες Ἀθηναῖοι, τοὺς θεοὺς
πάντας καὶ πάσας, ὅσοι τὴν χώραν ἔχουσι τὴν Ἀττικήν, καὶ 15
τὸν Ἀπόλλω τὸν Πύθιον, ὅς πατρῷός ἐστι τῇ πόλει, καὶ
ἐπεύχομαι πᾶσι τούτοις, εἰ μὲν ἀληθῆ πρὸς ὑμᾶς εἴποιμι καὶ
εἶπον τότ' εὐθὺς ἐν τῷ δήμῳ, ὅτε πρῶτον εἶδον τουτονὶ τὸν
μιαρὸν τούτου τοῦ πράγματος ἁπτόμενον (ἔγνων γὰρ, εὐθέως
ἔγνων), εὐτυχίαν μοι δοῦναι καὶ σωτηρίαν, εἰ δὲ πρὸς ἔχθραν 20
ἢ φιλονεικίας ἰδίας ἕνεκ' αἰτίαν ἐπάγω τούτῳ ψευδῆ, πάντων
τῶν ἀγαθῶν ἀνόνητόν με ποιῆσαι.

181 Τί οὖν ταῦτ' ἐπήραμαι καὶ διετεινάμην οὑτωσὶ σφοδρῶς;

---

6. Post κακὸν in omnibus praeter ΣΦ additur ὑμᾶς.　　7. καὶ ποιῶν οὗτος λανθά-
νειν] Sic pr. Σ: volgo ἃ ποιῶν οὗτος ἐλάνθανεν: ἃ καὶ ποιῶν οὗτος ἐλάνθανεν A et socii.
10. ἀνάλωσε] ἀνήλωσε Σ.　　11. πόθεν] πολλοῦ γέ καὶ δεῖ add. Σ a m. sec. ΩΥ et volg.
23. καὶ] Om. Σ.

καίτοι .. ἀμείνω. This sentence is a
digression from the general argument of this
part of the speech, which is to prove Aeschines a bad citizen. 'His abstinence in
the first stage of the war proves either that
he did not care to help Athens, or, if he did,
was perfectly satisfied with the measures of
Demosthenes.'

§ 179. Especially the latter, for he was
active when there was mischief to do. He
aided Philip in the Amphissian affair.

10. τὰ .. δόγματα. 'The decrees about
the Amphissian Locrians.' Cp. Aesch. in
Ctes. §§ 113, 124; for a similar genitive, τὸ Μεγάρεων ψήφισμα, Thuc. 1.
140. 6.

11. ὡς διαστρέψων τἀληθές. 'As if
the facts were not too strong for him.'

§ 180. I pray heaven to bless me if I

speak true in this, or curse me if the charge
is a calumny.

16. πατρῷος, as the father of Ion, the
national hero. Demosthenes invokes him
especially, in order to mark that he repu-
diates Aeschines' charge of misprision of
sacrilege, as well as his claim to have been
the champion of religion in the affairs of
Amphissa.

17. εἰ μὲν .. εἴποιμι καὶ εἶπον. 'If I
should speak the truth now to you, and
spoke the truth then.' Demosthenes has
not yet told his story of the Amphissian
business, and therefore regards it as something future and uncertain, to which he is
not yet committed.

§ 181. Aeschines is such a paltry traitor,
you may scarcely believe he ruined Greece:
you did not believe he ruined Phocis.

ὅτι καὶ γράμματ᾽ ἔχων ἐν τῷ δημοσίῳ κείμενα, ἐξ ὧν ταῦτ᾽
ἐπιδείξω σαφῶς, καὶ ὑμᾶς εἰδὼς τὰ πεπραγμένα μνημονεύοντας,
ἐκεῖνο φοβοῦμαι, μὴ τῶν εἰργασμένων αὐτῷ κακῶν ὑποληφθῇ
οὗτος ἐλάττων· ὅπερ πρότερον συνέβη, ὅτε τοὺς ταλαιπώρους
5 Φωκέας ἐποίησεν ἀπολέσθαι τὰ ψευδῆ δεῦρ᾽ ἀπαγγείλας· τὸν 182
γὰρ ἐν Ἀμφίσσῃ πόλεμον, δι᾽ ὃν εἰς Ἐλάτειαν ἦλθε Φίλιππος
καὶ δι᾽ ὃν ᾑρέθη τῶν Ἀμφικτυόνων ἡγεμών, ὃς ἅπαντ᾽ ἀνέτρεψε
τὰ τῶν Ἑλλήνων, οὗτός ἐστιν ὁ συγκατασκευάσας καὶ πάντων
εἷς ἀνὴρ τῶν μεγίστων αἴτιος κακῶν. καὶ τότ᾽ εὐθὺς ἐμοῦ 183
10 διαμαρτυρομένου καὶ βοῶντος ἐν τῇ ἐκκλησίᾳ "πόλεμον εἰς τὴν
Ἀττικὴν εἰσάγεις, Αἰσχίνη, πόλεμον Ἀμφικτυονικόν" οἱ μὲν
ἐκ παρακλήσεως συγκαθήμενοι οὐκ εἴων με λέγειν, οἱ δ᾽ ἐθαύ-
μαζον καὶ κενὴν αἰτίαν διὰ τὴν ἰδίαν ἔχθραν ἐπάγειν με ὑπελάμβανον αὐτῷ. ἥτις δ᾽ ἡ φύσις, ὦ ἄνδρες Ἀθηναῖοι, γέγονε 184
15 τούτων τῶν πραγμάτων, καὶ τίνος ἕνεκα ταῦτα συνεσκευάσθη
καὶ πῶς ἐπράχθη, νῦν ἀκούσατε, ἐπειδὴ τότε ἐκωλύθητε· καὶ
γὰρ εὖ πρᾶγμα συντεθὲν ὄψεσθε, καὶ μεγάλα ὠφελήσεσθε
πρὸς ἱστορίαν τῶν κοινῶν, καὶ ὅση δεινότης ἦν ἐν τῷ Φιλίππῳ
θεάσεσθε.

2. μνημονεύοντας] -νεύσοντας ΣΦ B. et S. 3. ὑποληφθῇ οὗτος ἐλάττων] Ita Σ: ceteri οὗτος ἐλάσσων ὑποληφθῇ. 8. Post Ἑλλήνων πράγματα add. ΤΑ et socii. 9. τῶν] Om. ΣΦ. Mox post κακῶν, γενόμενος add. A et socii. 11. εἰσάγεις] ἄγεις ΕΦ et al. 16. ἀκούσατε] ὑπακούσαμε ΣΒΦ B. et S.

1. γράμματα refers to the χρόνοι and
the letter of Philip cited below, §§ 200,
202. His passionate adjuration is provoked
by the prejudice which he expects to be too
strong for his documentary evidence and the
knowledge of the court.

3. τῶν .. ἐλάττων. 'Too insignificant
for the evil he has done,' 'too small to have
been equal to so much mischief.' So below,
§ 246, πάντων τῶν ἄλλων Ἑλλήνων μείζων,
Cp. Juv. 4. 66, 'Privatis majora focis;'
203, 'Lectus erat Codro Procula minor;'
15. 140, 'Et minor igne rogi.'

4. ὅπερ πρότερον συνέβη. When I
brought him to trial and you acquitted
him.

5. τὰ ψευδῆ δεῦρ᾽ ἀπαγγείλας. 'By
his false report to you.' 'The report' already
proved or admitted to be false.

§ 182. Yet the Amphissian war, which
ruined everything, was his work exclusively,

τὸν .. Ἐλάτειαν is a complete hexa-
meter, and the following words supply three
feet of another.

8. πάντων εἷς ἀνὴρ κ.τ.λ. 'It was all
the work of one man, and the most mis-

chievous work that might be.'

§ 183. Accomplished in spite of my protest, which you disregarded.

10. πόλεμον .. εἰσάγεις. Cp. for the
phrase the first fragment of Hegesippus,
quoted on Aesch. in Ctes. § 143.

12. ἐκ παρακλήσεως. 'Those who had
been summoned to support him.' They sat
together in a dense body, not necessarily
with their leader, for he and they had no
fixed places. Cp. παράταξις (Aesch. in
Ctes. § 1), παραγγελία (Dem. de F. L. § 1),
παρακλητῶν δεήσεις (ibid.) Demosthenes
was naturally εὐκατάπληκτος (Lib. Vit.
Dem. p. 4 init.), perhaps from the natural
weakness of his voice: cp. Dem. de F. L. p. 405,
§ 228. The story in Aeschines (De F. L. p.
35, §§ 37, 38 sq.) looks unlike an invention,
and if true would indicate that he was by
no means always secure against his old constitutional failings.

§ 184. Now at least you shall hear the
truth: it will be an useful lesson.

18. πρὸς ἱστορίαν τῶν κοινῶν. Here
almost equivalent to 'history,' though the
sense of investigation has not quite disappeared.

185 Οὐκ ἦν τοῦ πρὸς ὑμᾶς πολέμου πέρας οὐδ᾽ ἀπαλλαγὴ Φιλίππῳ, εἰ μὴ Θηβαίους καὶ Θετταλοὺς ἐχθροὺς ποιήσειε τῇ
πόλει· ἀλλὰ καίπερ ἀθλίως καὶ κακῶς τῶν στρατηγῶν τῶν
ὑμετέρων πολεμούντων αὐτῷ ὅμως ὑπ᾽ αὐτοῦ τοῦ πολέμου καὶ
τῶν λῃστῶν μυρία ἔπασχε κακά. οὔτε γὰρ ἐξήγετο τῶν ἐκ 5
186 τῆς χώρας γιγνομένων οὐδὲν οὔτ᾽ εἰσήγετο ὧν ἐδεῖτ᾽ αὐτῷ· ἦν
δὲ οὔτ᾽ ἐν τῇ θαλάττῃ τότε κρείττων ὑμῶν οὔτ᾽ εἰς τὴν Ἀττικὴν ἐλθεῖν δυνατὸς μήτε Θετταλῶν ἀκολουθούντων μήτε Θηβαίων διιέντων· συνέβαινε δὲ αὐτῷ τῷ πολέμῳ κρατοῦντι τοὺς
ὁποιουσδήποθ᾽ ὑμεῖς ἐξεπέμπετε στρατηγοὺς (ἐῶ γὰρ τοῦτό γε) 10
187 αὐτῇ τῇ φύσει τοῦ τόπου καὶ τῶν ὑπαρχόντων ἑκατέροις κακο-
παθεῖν. εἰ μὲν οὖν τῆς ἰδίας ἕνεκ᾽ ἔχθρας ἢ τοὺς Θετταλοὺς
ἢ τοὺς Θηβαίους συμπείθοι βαδίζειν ἐφ᾽ ὑμᾶς, οὐδένα ἡγεῖτο
προσέξειν αὐτῷ τὸν νοῦν· ἐὰν δὲ τὰς ἐκείνων κοινὰς προφάσεις
λαβὼν ἡγεμὼν αἱρεθῇ, ῥᾷον ἤλπιζε τὰ μὲν παρακρούσεσθαι, τὰ 15
δὲ πείσειν. τί οὖν; ἐπιχειρεῖ, θεάσασθ᾽ ὡς εὖ, πόλεμον ποιῆσαι
τοῖς Ἀμφικτύοσι καὶ περὶ τὴν Πυλαίαν ταραχήν· εἰς γὰρ ταῦτ᾽
188 εὐθὺς αὐτοὺς ὑπελάμβανεν αὐτοῦ δεήσεσθαι· εἰ μὲν τοίνυν τοῦτο

---

1. ὑμᾶς] ἡμᾶς A et socii.   9. συνέβαινε δὲ] συνέβαινέ τε A et socii.   13. οὐδένα
ἡγεῖτο προσέξειν] Ita Aristides: οὐδένα ἡγεῖτο προσέχειν A et socii, οὐδέν᾽ ἂν ἡγεῖτο
προσέξειν Σ et al. B. et S.

§ 185. *Philip needed to set Thebes and Thessaly against you, in order to end the war.*

3. ἀθλίως. 'In sorry sort,' used oftener of moral depravity than of pure stupidity. Plutarch (De Lib. Ed. p. 6 F) has ἄθλιος ζῳγράφος, 'a sorry painter,' which is exactly parallel.

§ 186. *Which crippled his trade and could only end by an invasion, impossible if Thessaly refused a contingent and Thebes a passage.*

8. μήτε Θετταλῶν .. διιέντων. 'While both the Thessalians refused a contingent and the Thebans a passage.' But unfavourable conditions were in fact united, and their union was decisive. He expected more from the Thessalians, for he had the customs of Pagasae, their chief revenue, in his hands, and so could keep them in dependence.

11. αὐτῇ τῇ φύσει τοῦ τόπου. Philip had to supply himself in a poor country from Macedonia, which was not rich; the Athenian condottieri supplied themselves from the rich Aegean and Bosporus.

§ 187. *To obtain either he had to come forward as their chosen champion, though*

already their ally. *Accordingly he availed himself of the imbroglio at Pylae.*

12. εἰ .. συμπείθοι. 'If he were to persuade.'

τῆς ἰδίας .. ἐχθρᾶς. '*His* private enmity,' opposed as well to ἐκείνων as to κοινάς. He wanted an excuse which should concern the Thebans and Thessalians as well as himself, and one which they could join in pressing on others, as being like him Amphictyons.

14. ἐὰν .. αἱρεθῇ. 'If he should be chosen.' The first of a mere supposition, the second of a possible alternative: so below, § 188, εἰ .. εἰσηγοῖτο, ἂν δ᾽ Ἀθηναῖος ᾖ.

15. ῥᾷον ἤλπιζε κ.τ.λ. 'He hoped to succeed better between cajolery and persuasion.'

16. πόλεμον .. ταραχήν: cp. below, § 193, ἐγκλήματα καὶ πόλεμος ἐταράχθη. Here τοῖς Ἀμφικτύοσι and περὶ τὴν Πυλαίαν ταραχὴν may be parallel clauses, dependent on πόλεμον ποιῆσαι, giving the parties for which and the matter on which the war was got up.

§ 188. *Even there be needed an Athenian agent.*

ἢ τῶν παρ' ἑαυτοῦ πεμπομένων ἱερομνημόνων ἢ τῶν ἐκείνου συμμάχων εἰσηγοῖτό τις, ὑπόψεσθαι τὸ πρᾶγμα ἐνόμιζε καὶ τοὺς
Θηβαίους καὶ τοὺς Θετταλοὺς καὶ πάντας φυλάξεσθαι, ἂν δ'
Ἀθηναῖος ᾖ καὶ παρ' ὑμῶν τῶν ὑπεναντίων ὁ τοῦτο ποιῶν,
5 εὐπόρως λήσειν· ὅπερ συνέβη.   πῶς οὖν ταῦτ' ἐποίησεν; μισ- 189
θοῦται τουτονί.   οὐδενὸς δὲ προειδότος, οἶμαι, τὸ πρᾶγμα
οὐδὲ φυλάττοντος, ὥσπερ εἴωθε τὰ τοιαῦτα παρ' ὑμῖν γίγνεσθαι, προβληθεὶς πυλάγορος οὗτος καὶ τριῶν ἢ τεττάρων
χειροτονησάντων αὐτὸν ἀνερρήθη.   ὡς δὲ τὸ τῆς πόλεως ἀξίωμα 190
10 λαβὼν ἀφίκετο εἰς τοὺς Ἀμφικτύονας, πάντα τἆλλ' ἀφεὶς καὶ
παριδὼν ἐπέραινεν ἐφ' οἷς ἐμισθώθη, καὶ λόγους εὐπροσώπους
καὶ μύθους, ὅθεν ἡ Κιρραία χώρα καθιερώθη, συνθεὶς καὶ διεξελ-
θὼν ἀνθρώπους ἀπείρους λόγων καὶ τὸ μέλλον οὐ προορωμέ-
νους, τοὺς ἱερομνήμονας, πείθει ψηφίσασθαι περιελθεῖν τὴν 191
15 χώραν ἣν οἱ μὲν Ἀμφισσεῖς σφῶν αὐτῶν οὖσαν γεωργεῖν
ἔφασαν, οὗτος δὲ τῆς ἱερᾶς χώρας ᾐτιᾶτο εἶναι, οὐδεμίαν δίκην
τῶν Λοκρῶν ἐπαγόντων ἡμῖν, οὐδ' ἃ νῦν οὗτος προφασίζεται,
λέγων οὐκ ἀληθῆ.   γνώσεσθε δ' ἐκεῖθεν.   οὐκ ἐνῆν ἄνευ τοῦ 192
προσκαλέσασθαι δήπου τοῖς Λοκροῖς δίκην κατὰ τῆς πόλεως
20 τελέσασθαι.   τίς οὖν ἐκλήτευσεν ἡμᾶς; ἀπὸ ποίας ἀρχῆς; εἰπὲ

---

2. εἰσηγοῖτό] Sic Υ p A et socii et superscr. F: ceteri εἰσηγεῖτο.   8. πυλάγορος]
Sic pr. Σ: volgo πυλαγόρας.   17. προφασίζεται λέγων] Al. λέγων προφασίζεται.
20. ἀπὸ] ἐπὶ A et socii Dind.

---

1. τῶν παρ' ἑαυτοῦ. He had two votes
as succeeding to the Phocians.
§ 189. He hired Aeschines.
6. τὸ πρᾶγμα. Not so much that he
was going to be proposed, as that he was
going to do mischief in the office. Demosthenes says that no one thought it worth
while to stay to the end of the assembly,
to vote against Aeschines; they treated the
matter as a merely formal nomination to a
merely formal office. This, rather than a
censure, like § 176, is the point of ὥσπερ
εἴωθε τὰ τοιαῦτα παρ' ὑμῖν γίγνεσθαι: cp.
Aesch. in Ctes. § 136.
§ 190. Who was sent with your authority,
and lost no time about beginning Philip's
business.
12. μύθους, ὅθεν. ' Legends of the
grounds on which.'
13. ἀνθρώπους ἀπείρους λόγων. Almost,
' Poor creatures who could not resist fine
talk,' with the usual compassionate sense of
ἀνθρώπους. The Amphictyons originally
were a confederation of the most backward
parts of Greece.
14. τοὺς ἱερομνήμονας. It seems to

have been optional to send Pylagori : yet
the phrase supports the view mentioned on
Ae. in Ctes. § 117.
§ 191. He induced the Amphictyons to
beat the bounds of territory in dispute, though
the Amphissians had given us no offence.
περιελθεῖν. Exactly, ' To beat the
bounds.'
περιελθεῖν .. εἶναι. Demosthenes de-
fends the Amphissians, not by an appeal to
prescription, but by suggesting that the dispute arose about a doubtful question of
boundaries.
16. οὐδεμίαν .. προφασίζεται. 'Bringing no charge against us, nor shewing the
feeling he makes us a pretence of now.'
§ 192. There is no evidence of a citation
from them.
18. οὐκ ἐνῆν .. δήπου. 'Of course it
was out of the question.' All that Aeschines asserts (In Ctes. §§ 117, 118), is
that a complaint was in contemplation, not
that a complaint has been actually laid : and
after all Athens might have been condemned
unheard, as Amphissa was at last.
20. ἀπὸ ποίας ἀρχῆς. 'From whose

τὸν εἰδότα, δεῖξον. ἀλλ' οὐκ ἂν ἔχοις, ἀλλὰ κενῇ προφάσει
193 ταύτῃ κατεχρῶ καὶ ψευδεῖ. περιιόντων τοίνυν τὴν χώραν τῶν
Ἀμφικτυόνων κατὰ τὴν ὑφήγησιν τὴν τούτου, προσπεσόντες
οἱ Λοκροὶ μικροῦ μὲν κατηκόντισαν ἅπαντας, τινὰς δὲ καὶ
συνήρπασαν τῶν ἱερομνημόνων. ὡς δ' ἅπαξ ἐκ τούτων ἐγκλή- 5
ματα καὶ πόλεμος πρὸς τοὺς Ἀμφισσεῖς ἐταράχθη, τὸ μὲν
πρῶτον ὁ Κόττυφος αὐτῶν τῶν Ἀμφικτυόνων ἤγαγε στρα-
194 τιάν, ὡς δ' οἱ μὲν οὐκ ἦλθον, οἱ δ' ἐλθόντες οὐδὲν ἐποίουν, εἰς
τὴν ἐπιοῦσαν πυλαίαν ἐπὶ τὸν Φίλιππον εὐθὺς ἡγεμόνα ἦγον
οἱ κατεσκευασμένοι καὶ πάλαι πονηροὶ τῶν Θετταλῶν καὶ τῶν 10
ἐν ταῖς ἄλλαις πόλεσι. καὶ προφάσεις εὐλόγους εἰλήφεσαν·
ἢ γὰρ αὐτοὺς εἰσφέρειν καὶ ξένους τρέφειν ἔφασαν δεῖν καὶ
195 ζημιοῦν τοὺς μὴ ταῦτα ποιοῦντας, ἢ 'κεῖνον αἱρεῖσθαι. τί δεῖ
τὰ πολλὰ λέγειν; ᾑρέθη γὰρ ἐκ τούτων ἡγεμών. καὶ μετὰ
ταῦτ' εὐθέως δύναμιν συλλέξας καὶ παρελθὼν ὡς ἐπὶ τὴν Κιρ- 15
ραίαν, ἐρρῶσθαι φράσας πολλὰ Κιρραίοις καὶ Λοκροῖς, τὴν
Ἐλάτειαν καταλαμβάνει. εἰ μὲν οὖν μὴ μετέγνωσαν εὐθέως,
ὡς τοῦτ' εἶδον, οἱ Θηβαῖοι καὶ μεθ' ἡμῶν ἐγένοντο, ὥσπερ
χειμάρρους ἂν ἅπαν τοῦτο τὸ πρᾶγμα εἰς τὴν πόλιν εἰσέπεσε·
196 νῦν δὲ τό γ' ἐξαίφνης ἐπέσχον αὐτὸν ἐκεῖνοι, μάλιστα μὲν, ὦ 20
ἄνδρες Ἀθηναῖοι, θεῶν τινος εὐνοίᾳ πρὸς ὑμᾶς, εἶτα μέντοι
καὶ, ὅσον καθ' ἕνα ἄνδρα, καὶ δι' ἐμέ. δὸς δέ μοι τὰ δόγματα

---

1. κενῇ] καινῇ Σ (sed volgato superscr.) A et socii : vid. annot.   4. κατηκόντισαν
ἅπαντας] Al. ἅπαντας κατηκόντισαν.   15. εὐθέως] Al. εὐθύς.   16. φράσας
πολλά] πολλὰ φράσας A et socii : statim multi inserunt καὶ, et mox iidem plerique om. ὡς
τοῦτ' εἶδον, οἱ.

archonship does the summons date?' Of
course ἐπὶ, the reading of some MSS. and
Edd., is easier. 'In whose archonship was
the summons laid?' ποίας ironically for
what does not exist: so Ar. Nub. 247, 1233,
ποιοὺς θεούς.

1. κενῇ. The reading καινῇ, though perhaps less likely, has rather better MS.
authority. The words are very frequently
confused, as at least in late Greek they were
pronounced almost exactly alike; but though
this accounts for the variation, it does not
prove which variant is right. καινῇ gives a
perfectly good sense, 'a new excuse,' invented
for this occasion only.

§ 193. The Locrians defended themselves
with success against the Amphictyons.

5. ἐγκλήματα καὶ πόλεμος .. ἐταράχθη:
cp. above, § 187, πόλεμον .. καὶ .. ταραχήν.
Tr. 'Stirred up a pother of grievances and
war,' the war to enforce the complaints of
Aesch. in Ctes. §§ 128, 129.

§ 194. So the latter called in Philip.

8. οὐδὲν ἐποίουν. 'Did nothing,' 'got
nothing done,' 'effected nothing.'

εἰς τὴν κ.τ.λ. 'Made a movement
for Philip against the next meeting.'

11. εἰλήφεσαν. 'They had got by this
time' (thanks to Aeschines). He had said
before that Philip's allies could not venture
to move.

§§ 195, 196. Philip was elected champion
of the league: he occupied Elatea. The
Thebans drew back to you by heaven's blessing and by my advice.

14. ἐκ τούτων. 'Hereupon.'

16. ἐρρῶσθαι .. Λοκροῖς. 'Bidding a
hearty farewell to Locrians and Cirrhaeans;'
the legendary examples of the trespass
of which the Locrians were accused. Several
MSS. insert καὶ before Κιρραίοις, which em-
phasises the point : 'Paid as little attention
to the Locrians of his own day, as to the
Cirrhaeans of Solon's.'

20. νῦν δ' .. ἐπέσχον. 'As it was, they
delayed him so far as the surprise went.'

ταῦτα καὶ τοὺς χρόνους ἐν οἷς ἕκαστα πέπρακται, ἵν' εἰδῆτε
ἡλίκα πράγματα ἡ μιαρὰ κεφαλὴ ταράξασα αὕτη δίκην οὐκ
ἔδωκε. λέγε μοι τὰ δόγματα.

ΔΟΓΜΑ ΑΜΦΙΚΤΥΟΝΩΝ.

5   ['Επὶ ἱερέως Κλειναγόρου, ἐαρινῆς πυλαίας, ἔδοξε τοῖς πυλαγόροις 197
καὶ τοῖς συνέδροις τῶν 'Αμφικτυόνων καὶ τῷ κοινῷ τῶν 'Αμφικτυόνων,
ἐπειδὴ 'Αμφισσεῖς ἐπιβαίνουσιν ἐπὶ τὴν ἱερὰν χώραν καὶ σπείρουσι καὶ
βοσκήμασι κατανέμουσιν, ἐπελθεῖν τοὺς πυλαγόρους · αἱ τοὺς συνέδρους,
καὶ στήλαις διαλαβεῖν τοὺς ὅρους, καὶ ἀπειπεῖν τοῖς 'Αμφισσεῦσι τοῦ
10   λοιποῦ μὴ ἐπιβαίνειν.]

ΕΤΕΡΟΝ ΔΟΓΜΑ.

['Επὶ ἱερέως Κλειναγόρου, ἐαρινῆς πυλαίας, ἔδοξε τοῖς πυλαγόροις 198
καὶ τοῖς συνέδροις τῶν 'Αμφικτυόνων καὶ τῷ κοινῷ τῶν 'Αμφικτυόνων,
ἐπειδὴ οἱ ἐξ 'Αμφίσσης τὴν ἱερὰν χώραν κατανειμάμενοι γεωργοῦσι
15   καὶ βοσκήματα νέμουσι, καὶ κωλυόμενοι τοῦτο ποιεῖν, ἐν τοῖς ὅπλοις
παραγενόμενοι, τὸ κοινὸν τῶν 'Ελλήνων συνέδριον κεκωλύκασι μετὰ
βίας, τινὰς δὲ καὶ τετραυματίκασι, τὸν στρατηγὸν τὸν ἡρημένον τῶν 199
'Αμφικτυόνων Κόττυφον τὸν 'Αρκάδα πρεσβεῦσαι πρὸς Φίλιππον τὸν
Μακεδόνα, καὶ ἀξιοῦν ἵνα βοηθήσῃ τῷ τε 'Απόλλωνι καὶ τοῖς 'Αμφικ-
20   τύοσιν, ὅπως μὴ περίδῃ ὑπὸ τῶν ἀσεβῶν 'Αμφισσέων τὸν θεὸν πλημ-
μελούμενον· καὶ διότι αὐτὸν στρατηγὸν αὐτοκράτορα αἱροῦνται οἱ
''Ελληνες οἱ μετέχοντες τοῦ συνεδρίου τῶν 'Αμφικτυόνων.]

Λέγε δὴ καὶ τοὺς χρόνους ἐν οἷς ταῦτ' ἐγίγνετο· εἰσὶ γὰρ 200
καθ' οὓς ἐπυλαγόρησεν οὗτος. λέγε.   •

ΧΡΟΝΟΙ.

25

['Αρχων Μνησιθείδης, μηνὸς ἀνθεστηριῶνος ἕκτῃ ἐπὶ δέκα.]

Δὸς δὴ τὴν ἐπιστολὴν ἣν, ὡς οὐχ ὑπήκουον οἱ Θηβαῖοι, 201
πέμπει πρὸς τοὺς ἐν Πελοποννήσῳ συμμάχους ὁ Φίλιππος,
ἵν' εἰδῆτε καὶ ἐκ ταύτης σαφῶς ὅτι τὴν μὲν ἀληθῆ πρόφασιν
30   τῶν πραγμάτων, τὸ ταῦτ' ἐπὶ τὴν 'Ελλάδα καὶ τοὺς Θηβαίους

---

4. ΔΟΓΜΑ] ΔΟΓΜΑΤΑ Σ.   5, 8. πυλαγόροις .. -ρους] Ita optimi libri passim :
legebatur -παις et -πας.   6. καὶ τῷ κοινῷ τῶν 'Αμφικτυόνων] Om. Σ et alii.
17. τὸν στρατηγὸν] καὶ τὸν στρατηγὸν libri omnes.   26. δέκα] Ita Taylor : libri
δεκάτῃ.   Et in spurio utique decreto fortasse is error non tollendus.   27. δὴ] Sic Σ Α
et socii B. et S. : ceteri et Dind. om.

§§ 197-199.[Decrees of the Amphictyons.]   proves be needed the Amphictyonic pretext.
18. τὸν 'Αρκάδα.   He was a Pharsalian   29. πρόφασιν.   The 'reason' that he
(Aesch. in Ctes. § 125).   put forward sincerely in his own council.
§ 200. [Dates.]   30. τὸ .. πράττειν. ' That he was doing
26. 'Αρχων Μνησιθείδης : cp. Aesch.   this against Greece and Thebes and you,'
in Ctes. § 62, ὁ χρόνος Θεμιστοκλῆς ἄρ-   while he affected to be carrying out a policy
χων.   in which all were interested, and executing
§ 201. Philip's letter to Peloponnese,   Amphictyonic decrees.

καὶ ὑμᾶς πράττειν, ἀπεκρύπτετο, κοινὰ δὲ καὶ τοῖς Ἀμφικτύοσι δόξαντα ποιεῖν προσεποιεῖτο· ὁ δὲ τὰς ἀφορμὰς ταύτας
καὶ τὰς προφάσεις αὐτῷ παρασχὼν οὗτος ἦν. λέγε.

ΕΠΙΣΤΟΛΗ.

202   [Βασιλεὺς Μακεδόνων Φίλιππος Πελοποννησίων τῶν ἐν τῇ συμ- 5
μαχίᾳ τοῖς δημιουργοῖς καὶ τοῖς συνέδροις καὶ τοῖς ἄλλοις συμμάχοις
πᾶσι χαίρειν. ἐπειδὴ Λοκροὶ οἱ καλούμενοι Ὀζόλαι, κατοικοῦντες
ἐν Ἀμφίσσῃ, πλημμελοῦσιν εἰς τὸ ἱερὸν τοῦ Ἀπόλλωνος τοῦ ἐν
Δελφοῖς καὶ τὴν ἱερὰν χώραν ἐρχόμενοι μεθ᾽ ὅπλων λεηλατοῦσι,
βούλομαι τῷ θεῷ μεθ᾽ ὑμῶν βοηθεῖν καὶ ἀμύνασθαι τοὺς παρα- 10
βαίνοντάς τι τῶν ἐν ἀνθρώποις εὐσεβῶν· ὥστε συναντᾶτε μετὰ
τῶν ὅπλων εἰς τὴν Φωκίδα, ἔχοντες ἐπισιτισμὸν ἡμερῶν τετταράκοντα, τοῦ ἐνεστῶτος μηνὸς λῴου, ὡς ἡμεῖς ἄγομεν; ὡς δὲ Ἀθηναῖοι,
βοηδρομιῶνος, ὡς δὲ Κορίνθιοι, πανήμου. τοῖς δὲ μὴ συναντήσασι
πανδημεὶ χρησόμεθα [τοῖς δὲ συμβούλοις ἡμῖν κειμένοις] ἐπιζη- 15
μίοις. εὐτυχεῖτε.]

203   Ὁρᾶθ᾽ ὅτι φεύγει μὲν τὰς ἰδίας προφάσεις, εἰς δὲ τὰς Ἀμφικτυονικὰς καταφεύγει. τίς οὖν ὁ ταῦτα συμπαρασκευάσας
αὐτῷ; τίς ὁ τὰς προφάσεις ταύτας ἐνδούς; τίς ὁ τῶν κακῶν
τῶν γεγενημένων μάλιστα αἴτιος; οὐχ οὗτος; μὴ τοίνυν λέ- 20
γετε, ὦ ἄνδρες Ἀθηναῖοι, περιιόντες ὡς ὑφ᾽ ἑνὸς τοιαῦτα πέ-
204 πονθεν ἡ Ἑλλὰς ἀνθρώπου. οὐχ ὑφ᾽ ἑνός, ἀλλ᾽ ὑπὸ πολλῶν
καὶ πονηρῶν τῶν παρ᾽ ἑκάστοις, ὦ γῆ καὶ θεοί. ὧν εἷς οὑτοσί,
ὅν, εἰ μηδὲν εὐλαβηθέντα τἀληθὲς εἰπεῖν δέοι, οὐκ ἂν ὀκνήσαιμι
ἔγωγε κοινὸν ἀλιτήριον τῶν μετὰ ταῦτα ἀπολωλότων ἁπάντων 25
εἰπεῖν, ἀνθρώπων, τόπων, πόλεων· ὁ γὰρ τὸ σπέρμα παρασχὼν,

3. ἦν] ἦν αὐτῷ A et socii.   12. τετταράκοντα] τεσσαράκοντα Σ et al.
15. κειμένοις] μὴ κειμένοις nonnulli. 'Fort. χρησόμεθα τοῖς διὰ συμβόλων ἡμῖν κειμένοις.'
Sauppius.   17. μὲν] Om. Σ B. et S.   20. λέγετε] Om. pr. Σ.   23. τῶν]
Om. pr. Σ B. et S.   οὑτοσί] Sic Σ: ceteri οὗτός ἐστιν.

§ 202. [Philip's letter.]
13. λῴου. The Boeotian and Corinthian
Panemus coincided with Metageitnion. Lous
came next after Panemus, and of course it is
possible that different states which had the
same names for the months, may have followed different systems of intercalation: cp.
Thuc. 5. 19 init.
14. τοῖς δὲ μὴ.. ἐπιζημίοις. This
seems a confusion of two clauses, τοῖς δὲ
συναντήσασι πανδημεὶ συμβούλοις χρησόμεθα: τοῖς δὲ μὴ [κατὰ τὰς συνθήκας]
ἡμῖν κειμέναις, ἐπιζημίοις. After the
words in brackets fell out, the rest was
sure to follow. There are traces in
some MSS. that μὴ belongs to the second

clause.
§ 203. Aeschines gave him the help he
needed.
18. καταφεύγει. 'Takes refuge in,'
'ensconces himself behind.' φεύγειν is to
fly to a point beyond the reach of danger.
καταφεύγειν, to fly to a point where one is
protected from danger.
21. περιιόντες. We should invert the
verb and participle, 'Don't go about saying.'
Cp. Dem. de F. L. §§ 208, 209, περιιὼν
λέγει, ἐτραγῴδει περιιών.
§ 204. He was one of many, and himself
answerable for all that followed.
26. τόπων, πόλεων. 'Regions and
states.'

οὗτος τῶν φύντων αἴτιος. ὃν ὅπως ποτὲ οὐκ εὐθὺς ἰδόντες
ἀπεστράφητε θαυμάζω. πλὴν πολύ τι σκότος, ὡς ἔοικεν, ἐστὶ
παρ' ὑμῖν πρὸ τῆς ἀληθείας.

Συμβέβηκε τοίνυν μοι τῶν κατὰ τῆς πατρίδος τούτῳ πε- 205
5 πραγμένων ἁψαμένῳ εἰς ἃ τούτοις ἐναντιούμενος αὐτὸς πεπολίτευμαι ἀφῖχθαι· ἃ πολλῶν μὲν ἕνεκ' ἂν εἰκότως ἀκούσαιτέ
μου, μάλιστα δ' ὅτι αἰσχρόν ἐστιν, ὦ ἄνδρες Ἀθηναῖοι, εἰ ἐγὼ
μὲν τὰ ἔργα τῶν ὑπὲρ ὑμῶν πόνων ὑπέμεινα, ὑμεῖς δὲ μηδὲ
τοὺς λόγους αὐτῶν ἀνέξεσθε. ὁρῶν γὰρ ἐγὼ Θηβαίους, σχε- 206
10 δὸν δὲ καὶ ὑμᾶς ὑπὸ τῶν τὰ Φιλίππου φρονούντων καὶ διε-
φθαρμένων παρ' ἑκατέροις, ὃ μὲν ἦν ἀμφοτέροις φοβερὸν καὶ
φυλακῆς πολλῆς δεόμενον, τὸ τὸν Φίλιππον ἐᾶν αὐξάνεσθαι,
παρορῶντας καὶ οὐδὲ καθ' ἓν φυλαττομένους, εἰς ἔχθραν δὲ
καὶ τὸ προσκρούειν ἀλλήλοις ἑτοίμως ἔχοντας, ὅπως τοῦτο μὴ
15 γενήσεται παρατηρῶν διετέλουν, οὐκ ἀπὸ τῆς ἐμαυτοῦ γνώμης 207
μόνον ταῦτα συμφέρειν ὑπολαμβάνων, ἀλλ' εἰδὼς Ἀριστοφῶντα καὶ πάλιν Εὔβουλον πάντα τὸν χρόνον βουλομένους
πρᾶξαι ταύτην τὴν φιλίαν, καὶ περὶ τῶν ἄλλων πολλάκις
ἀντιλέγοντας ἑαυτοῖς τοῦθ' ὁμογνωμονοῦντας ἀεί. οὓς σὺ ζῶν-
20 τας μὲν, ὦ κίναδος, κολακεύων παρηκολούθεις, τεθνεώτων δ' οὐκ
αἰσθάνει κατηγορῶν· ἃ γὰρ περὶ Θηβαίων ἐπιτιμᾷς ἐμοί, ἐκείνων πολὺ μᾶλλον ἢ ἐμοῦ κατηγορεῖς, τῶν πρότερον ἢ ἐγὼ
ταύτην τὴν συμμαχίαν δοκιμασάντων. ἀλλ' ἐκεῖσε ἐπάνειμι, ὅτι 208

1. φύντων] φύντων κακῶν Σ et al. B. et S.   6. ἂν εἰκότως ἀκούσαιτέ] Sic Σ:
A et socii εἰκότως ἀκούσατέ, ceteri εἰκότως ἀκούσετέ.   10. φρονούντων] Sic ΣA et
al.: legebatur πραττόντων.   15. γενήσεται] γένοιτο Σ B. et S. Dind.: est autem
facilior conjectura.   19. ἑαυτοῖς] Om. pr. Σ. Statim εἰς add. A et socii.   21. αἰσθά-
νει] Sic Σ: legebatur αἰσχύνῃ.

1. ὃν .. ἀπεστράφητε. Like the Latin
aversari. ὃν depends on ἀπεστράφητε, not
ἰδόντες.
§ 205. I am brought round from his
treason to my service.
4. συμβέβηκε κ.τ.λ. i. e. 'I now, in the
natural course of my argument, have come
to the time of my chief public services, and
cannot be blamed if I describe them.' Above,
§§ 4, 5, we have a similar but more deferen-
tial apology for self-praise ; here the tone is
so bold, that Dissen doubts if the passage
was actually spoken.
§ 206. I promoted alliance with Thebes,
§ 207. Like Eubulus and Aristophon,
whom you flattered in their life, though you
denounced their policy in my hands,
16. Ἀριστοφῶντα : cp. Aesch. in Ctes.

§ 139. It is possible that Aristophon
desired a close understanding between the
two states as a condition of an active foreign
policy, Eubulus as a guarantee of perpetual
peace. Cp. ad § 26, above : cp. also, for
Demosthenes' respect for Thebes, De F. L.
pp. 384, 385, § 152 sqq.
20. κολακεύων. According to the anonymous life, both these statesmen nominated
him as clerk.
οὐκ αἰσθάνει. So Σ for οὐκ αἰσχύνῃ,
which presupposes the sense of αἰσθάνει.
'You do not give a thought to the effect
your language has on the reputation of your
patrons.'
§ 208. And brought Athens to the brink
of ruin by the antagonism that you and yours
kept up.

τὸν ἐν Ἀμφίσσῃ πόλεμον τούτου μὲν ποιήσαντος, συμπερα-
ναμένων δὲ τῶν ἄλλων τῶν συνεργῶν αὐτῷ τὴν πρὸς Θηβαίους
ἔχθραν, συνέβη τὸν Φίλιππον ἐλθεῖν ἐφ᾽ ἡμᾶς, οὗπερ ἔνεκα τὰς
πόλεις οὗτοι συνέκρουον, καὶ εἰ μὴ προεξανέστημεν μικρὸν, οὐδ᾽
ἀναλαβεῖν ἂν ἐδυνήθημεν· οὕτω μέχρι πόρρω προήγαγον οὗτοι 5
τὴν ἔχθραν. ἐν οἷς δ᾽ ἦτε ἤδη τὰ πρὸς ἀλλήλους, τουτωνὶ
τῶν ψηφισμάτων ἀκούσαντες καὶ τῶν ἀποκρίσεων εἴσεσθε. Καί
μοι λέγε ταῦτα λαβών.

ΨΗΦΙΣΜΑ.

209   [Ἐπὶ ἄρχοντος Ἡροπύθου, μηνὸς ἐλαφηβολιῶνος ἕκτῃ φθίνοντος, 10
φυλῆς πρυτανευούσης Ἐρεχθηίδος, βουλῆς καὶ στρατηγῶν γνώμῃ,
ἐπειδὴ Φίλιππος ἃς μὲν κατείληφε πόλεις τῶν ἀστυγειτόνων, τινὰς
δὲ πορθεῖ, κεφαλαίῳ δὲ ἐπὶ τὴν Ἀττικὴν παρασκευάζεται παραγίγνεσθαι, παρ᾽ οὐδὲν ἡγούμενος τὰς ἡμετέρας συνθήκας, καὶ τοὺς ὅρκους
210   λύειν ἐπιβάλλεται καὶ τὴν εἰρήνην, παραβαίνων τὰς κοινὰς πίστεις, 15
δεδόχθαι τῇ βουλῇ καὶ τῷ δήμῳ πέμπειν πρὸς αὐτὸν πρέσβεις, οἵτινες
αὐτῷ διαλέξονται καὶ παρακαλέσουσιν αὐτὸν μάλιστα μὲν τὴν πρὸς
ἡμᾶς ὁμόνοιαν διατηρεῖν καὶ τὰς συνθήκας, εἰ δὲ μὴ, πρὸς τὸ βουλεύσασθαι δοῦναι χρόνον τῇ πόλει καὶ τὰς ἀνοχὰς ποιήσασθαι μέχρι τοῦ
θαργηλιῶνος μηνός. ᾑρέθησαν ἐκ τῆς βουλῆς Σῖμος Ἀναγυράσιος, 20
Εὐθύδημος Φυλάσιος, Βουλαγόρας Ἀλωπεκῆθεν.]

ΕΤΕΡΟΝ ΨΗΦΙΣΜΑ.

211   [Ἐπὶ ἄρχοντος Ἡροπύθου, μηνὸς μουνυχιῶνος ἕνῃ καὶ νέᾳ, πολεμάρχου γνώμῃ, ἐπειδὴ Φίλιππος εἰς ἀλλοτριότητα Θηβαίους πρὸς ἡμᾶς
ἐπιβάλλεται καταστῆσαι, παρεσκεύασται δὲ καὶ παντὶ τῷ στρατεύματι 25
πρὸς τοὺς ἔγγιστα τῆς Ἀττικῆς παραγίγνεσθαι τόπους, παραβαίνων τὰς
212   πρὸς ἡμᾶς ὑπαρχούσας αὐτῷ συνθήκας, δεδόχθαι τῇ βουλῇ καὶ τῷ δήμῳ
πέμψαι πρὸς αὐτὸν κήρυκα καὶ πρέσβεις, οἵτινες ἀξιώσουσι καὶ παρακαλέσουσιν αὐτὸν ποιήσασθαι τὰς ἀνοχὰς, ὅπως ἐνδεχομένως ὁ δῆμος

6. τὴν ἔχθραν] Sic Σ et al.: usque ad Bekkerum legebatur τὸ πρᾶγμα : om. A et socii
et marg. Σ.   7. εἴσεσθε .. λαβών] οὕτω εἴσεσθε. λέγε δὴ καὶ τὰς ἀποκρίσεις
ΕΠΙΣΤΟΛΗ ΦΙΛΙΠΠΟΥ. ΨΗΦΙΣΜΑ. οὕτω διαθεὶς κ.τ.λ. Α.   9. ΨΗΦΙΣΜΑ]
ΨΗΦΙΣΜΑΤΑ Σ Β. et S.   13. πορθεῖ] † πορθεῖν Σ †.   20. τῆς] Om. ΣF:
mox Ἀναγυρράσιος Σ et al., et Φλιάσιος plerique.   22. ΕΤΕΡΟΝ] Om. Σ, utpote
cujus exemplar supra ΨΗΦΙΣΜΑΤΑ semel tantum pro utriusque decreti titulo scripsisset.

1. τὸν .. ποιήσαντος. The order is
curious, because it implies that Aeschines
made the war and others did something else
to the war. It would make the sentence
more symmetrical to omit τὴν πρὸς Θηβαίους ἔχθραν with some MSS., or even to
substitute τὸ πρᾶγμα for τὴν ἔχθραν
with all the MSS. which insert the phrase
except Σ.

3. συνέβη τὸν Φίλιππον. Reiske wished

to read συνέβη ἄν.

§§ 209, 210. [Decree.]
§§ 211, 212. [Decree.]

3. Ἐπὶ .. Ἡροπύθου. It is possible of
course that the thirty-six days between the
two decrees may have fallen into one prytany: more probably the compiler, instead
of dating the second decree by the right
clerk, meant to date both decrees by the
same archon.

βουλεύσηται· καὶ γὰρ νῦν οὐ κέκρικε βοηθεῖν ἐν οὐδενὶ τῶν μετρίων.
ᾑρέθησαν ἐκ τῆς βουλῆς Νέαρχος Σωσινόμου, Πολυκράτης Ἐπίφρονος,
καὶ κῆρυξ Εὔνομος Ἀναφλύστιος ἐκ τοῦ δήμου.]
Λέγε δὴ καὶ τὰς ἀποκρίσεις.

5   ΑΠΟΚΡΙΣΙΣ ΑΘΗΝΑΙΟΙΣ.

[Βασιλεὺς Μακεδόνων Φίλιππος Ἀθηναίων τῇ βουλῇ καὶ τῷ δήμῳ **213**
χαίρειν. ἣν μὲν ἀπ' ἀρχῆς εἴχετε πρὸς ἡμᾶς αἵρεσιν, οὐκ ἀγνοῶ, καὶ
τίνα σπουδὴν ποιεῖσθε προσκαλέσασθαι βουλόμενοι Θετταλοὺς καὶ
Θηβαίους, ἔτι δὲ καὶ Βοιωτούς· βέλτιον δ' αὐτῶν φρονούντων καὶ μὴ
10   βουλομένων ἐφ' ὑμῖν ποιήσασθαι τὴν ἑαυτῶν αἵρεσιν, ἀλλὰ κατὰ τὸ **214**
συμφέρον ἱσταμένων, νῦν ἐξ ὑποστροφῆς ἀποστείλαντες ὑμεῖς πρός με
πρέσβεις καὶ κήρυκα συνθηκῶν, μνημονεύετε καὶ τὰς ἀνοχὰς αἰτεῖσθε,
κατ' οὐδὲν ὑφ' ἡμῶν πεπλημμελημένοι. ἐγὼ μέντοι ἀκούσας τῶν πρε-
σβευτῶν συγκατατίθεμαι τοῖς παρακαλουμένοις καὶ ἕτοιμός εἰμι ποιεῖ-
15   σθαι τὰς ἀνοχάς, ἄν περ τοὺς οὐκ ὀρθῶς συμβουλεύοντας ὑμῖν παρα-
πέμψαντες τῆς προσηκούσης ἀτιμίας ἀξιώσητε. ἔρρωσθε.]

        ΑΠΟΚΡΙΣΙΣ ΘΗΒΑΙΟΙΣ.

[Βασιλεὺς Μακεδόνων Φίλιππος Θηβαίων τῇ βουλῇ καὶ τῷ δήμῳ **215**
χαίρειν. ἐκομισάμην τὴν παρ' ὑμῶν ἐπιστολήν, δι' ἧς μοι τὴν ὁμό-
20   νοιαν ἀνανεοῦσθε καὶ τὴν εἰρήνην ὄντως ἐμοὶ ποιεῖτε. πυνθάνομαι
μέντοι διότι πᾶσαν ὑμῖν Ἀθηναῖοι προσφέρονται φιλοτιμίαν βουλόμενοι ὑμᾶς συγκαταίνους γενέσθαι τοῖς ὑπ' αὐτῶν παρακαλουμένοις.
πρότερον μὲν οὖν ὑμῶν κατεγίγνωσκον ἐπὶ τῷ μέλλειν πείθεσθαι ταῖς
ἐκείνων ἐλπίσι καὶ ἐπακολουθεῖν αὐτῶν τῇ προαιρέσει. νῦν δ' ἐπι- **216**
25   γνοὺς ὑμᾶς τὰ πρὸς ἡμᾶς ἐζητηκότας ἔχειν εἰρήνην μᾶλλον ἢ ταῖς ἑτέρων
ἐπακολουθεῖν γνώμαις, ἥσθην καὶ μᾶλλον ὑμᾶς ἐπαινῶ κατὰ πολλά,
μάλιστα δ' ἐπὶ τῷ βουλεύσασθαι περὶ τούτων ἀσφαλέστερον καὶ τὰ
πρὸς ἡμᾶς ἔχειν ἐν εὐνοίᾳ· ὅπερ οὐ μικρὰν ὑμῖν οἴσειν ἐλπίζω ῥοπήν,
ἐάν περ ἐπὶ ταύτης μένητε τῆς προθέσεως. ἔρρωσθε.]
30   Οὕτω διαθεὶς ὁ Φίλιππος τὰς πόλεις πρὸς ἀλλήλας διὰ **217**

---

2. τῆς] Om. Σ et al.   5. ΑΠΟΚΡΙΣΙΣ] Libri plerique ΑΠΟΚΡΙΣΕΙΣ, dum
nonnulli ΑΘΗΝΑΙΟΙΣ omittunt.   12. κήρυκα] Sic pr. B: ceteri κήρυκας. Vid. ad
Ae. in Ct. § 62.   17. ΑΠΟΚΡΙΣΙΣ] ΑΠΟΚΡΙΣΕΙΣ iterum habent iidem fere qui
supra.   20. ἀνανεοῦσθε] 'Hoc loco posui cum Φ. Legebatur post εἰρήνην. συμμαχίαν ποιεῖσθαι καὶ τὴν πατρικὴν φιλίαν ἀνανεοῦσθαι dixit Dem. pp. 660, 18. Post εἰρήνην
in Φ est lacuna, cujus quae sit ratio ex scriptura codicis Σ intelligitur, qui post εἰρήνην, omisso
                                                ὀν
verbo ἀνανεοῦσθε, has solus servavit veteris lectionis reliquias : τως εμοι ειτε (literis ον a
manu tertia superscriptis) ex quibus, adscita Dobraei conjectura ποιεῖτε, feci ὄντως ἐμοὶ ποιεῖτε, ut intelligi saltem haec possent' Dind. Ejus lectionem ut ingeniosam recipimus, quan-
quam parum certum videtur, Φ aliquam memoriam habuisse eorum quae in Σ leguntur.
et non solum haesitasse, quonam loco ἀνανεοῦσθε ponendum esset.   25. μᾶλλον]
'Malim abesse' Saupp.   26. κατὰ] καὶ τὰ plerique.

---

§§ 213, 214. [*Reply to Athens.*]
§§ 215, 216. [*Reply to Thebes.*]
§ 217. *Philip counted on the failure of
this policy when he occupied Elatea.*

30. οὕτω διαθείς. 'Philip got the cities
into such dispositions towards each other, as
are set forth in the decrees cited.' Those quoted
by the compiler, if genuine, are irrelevant.

τούτων, καὶ τούτοις ἐπαρθεὶς τοῖς ψηφίσμασι καὶ ταῖς ἀπο-
κρίσεσιν, ἧκεν ἔχων τὴν δύναμιν καὶ τὴν Ἐλάτειαν κατέλαβεν,
ὡς οὐδ᾽ ἂν εἴ τι γένοιτο ἔτι συμπνευσόντων ἡμῶν καὶ τῶν
Θηβαίων. ἀλλὰ μὴν τὸν τότε συμβάντα ἐν τῇ πόλει θόρυβον
ἴστε μὲν ἅπαντες· μικρὰ δ᾽ ἀκούσατε ὅμως, αὐτὰ τἀναγκαιότατα. 5
218 Ἑσπέρα μὲν γὰρ ἦν, ἧκε δ᾽ ἀγγέλλων τις ὡς τοὺς πρυτάνεις
ὡς Ἐλάτεια κατείληπται. καὶ μετὰ ταῦτα οἱ μὲν εὐθὺς ἐξα-
ναστάντες μεταξὺ δειπνοῦντες τούς τ᾽ ἐκ τῶν σκηνῶν τῶν κατὰ
τὴν ἀγορὰν ἐξεῖργον καὶ τὰ γέρρα ἐνεπίμπρασαν, οἱ δὲ τοὺς
στρατηγοὺς μετεπέμποντο καὶ τὸν σαλπικτὴν ἐκάλουν· καὶ θορύ- 10
219 βου πλήρης ἦν ἡ πόλις. τῇ δ᾽ ὑστεραίᾳ ἅμα τῇ ἡμέρᾳ οἱ μὲν πρυτάνεις τὴν βουλὴν ἐκάλουν εἰς τὸ βουλευτήριον, ὑμεῖς δ᾽ εἰς τὴν
ἐκκλησίαν ἐπορεύεσθε, καὶ πρὶν ἐκείνην χρηματίσαι καὶ προβουλεῦ-
σαι πᾶς ὁ δῆμος ἄνω καθῆτο. καὶ μετὰ ταῦτα ὡς ἦλθεν ἡ βουλὴ
καὶ ἀπήγγειλαν οἱ πρυτάνεις τὰ προσηγγελμένα ἑαυτοῖς καὶ τὸν 15
220 ἥκοντα παρήγαγον κἀκεῖνος εἶπεν, ἠρώτα μὲν ὁ κῆρυξ "τίς ἀγορεύειν
βούλεται;" παρῄει δ᾽ οὐδείς. πολλάκις δὲ τοῦ κήρυκος ἐρωτῶντος
οὐδὲν μᾶλλον ἀνίστατ᾽ οὐδείς, ἁπάντων μὲν τῶν στρατηγῶν παρόντων, ἁπάντων δὲ τῶν ῥητόρων, καλούσης δὲ τῆς πατρίδος τῇ κοινῇ

---

3. συμπνευσόντων] συμπνευσόντων ἂν ΣΑ et socii : -σάντων ἂν Dobr. Dind. Statim
ὑμῶν habent nonnulli, ἡμῶν ἂν Dion.   4. ἐν] Om. A et socii.   5. αὐτὰ
τἀναγκαιότατα] ἀναγκαιότατα pr. Σ.   10. σαλπικτὴν] Ita Dind. cum optimis
librorum.   14. ἦλθεν] Ita ΣΦΑ et socii B. et S. : volg. εἰσῆλθεν.   15. ἑαυ-
τοῖς] αὐτοῖς A et socii.   19. τῆς πατρίδος τῇ κοινῇ φωνῇ] Sic Bekk. Dind. cum
γρ. ΣΦ.   τῆς κοινῆς πατρίδος φωνῆς Σ B. et S. : τῇ κοινῇ τῆς πατρίδος φωνῆς A et socii.
τῆς κοινῆς τῆς πατρίδος φωνῆς ceteri.

---

2. τὴν δύναμιν. Almost, 'The whip
hand;' perhaps simply, 'his power,' 'his
forces.'

3. ὡς..Θηβαίων. 'As though Thebes
and Athens could no longer have coalesced
[had lost the power of coalescing], whatever
happened.' The MSS. give συμπνευσόντων,
but Σ and others insert ἂν after the participle, whence Dobree and Dindorf read συμ-
πνευσάντων: we have in fact the choice
between dropping the particle and changing
the tense. If we retain the future, the
earlier ἂν would present no difficulty: the
sense would be, 'They said the Athenians
and Thebans will not, and they would not
whatever might happen.' Cp. the redundant
or elliptical ἂν (whichever we call it) below,
§ 269, etc. : cp. ὥσπερ ἂν εἰ below, § 369.

§§ 218–221. *In your panic I stood forth
alone to answer the call of my country; all
were willing, I alone was ready.*

9. τὰ γέρρα. The γέρρα are the wicker-
work of the booths (σκῆναι): they were

burnt at once to clear the ἀγορά, and give a
signal to citizens without the walls that an
assembly was soon to meet. The assemblies
were held in the morning (Od. 6. 138, 139,
Ar. Eccl. 20, 21, 84, 85), and it appears
from Auctor in Neaeram, p. 376, § 90, that
one object of this was to leave the market-
place free for other business when the assembly rose. Here the ἀγορά was cleared
overnight: as they could not hold the assembly, they relieved their impatience with
these preparations.

14. ἄνω. Up the hill of Pnyx.

16. τίς ἀγορεύειν βούλεται; cp. Ar.
Ach. 45. This simple form had superseded
the more elaborate citation regretted by
Aeschines (in Ctes. § 4), because there was
a class of habitual speakers (τῶν ῥητόρων,
below, § 220) almost as responsible as the
generals. Till this class rose, the theory was
that all the citizens were equally well-
informed, and the eldest entitled to precedence.

φωνῇ τὸν ἐροῦνθ᾽ ὑπὲρ σωτηρίας· ἦν γὰρ ὁ κῆρυξ κατὰ τοὺς
νόμους φωνὴν ἀφίησι, ταύτην κοινὴν τῆς πατρίδος δίκαιόν ἐστιν
ἡγεῖσθαι. καίτοι εἰ μὲν τοὺς σωθῆναι τὴν πόλιν βουλομένους 221
παρελθεῖν ἔδει, πάντες ἂν ὑμεῖς καὶ οἱ ἄλλοι Ἀθηναῖοι ἀνα-
5 στάντες ἐπὶ τὸ βῆμα ἐβαδίζετε· πάντες γὰρ οἶδ᾽ ὅτι σωθῆναι
αὐτὴν ἐβούλεσθε· εἰ δὲ τοὺς πλουσιωτάτους, οἱ τριακόσιοι· εἰ
δὲ τοὺς ἀμφότερα ταῦτα, καὶ εὔνους τῇ πόλει καὶ πλουσίους,
οἱ μετὰ ταῦτα τὰς μεγάλας ἐπιδόσεις ἐπιδόντες· καὶ γὰρ εὐνοίᾳ καὶ πλούτῳ τοῦτ᾽ ἐποίησαν. ἀλλ᾽ ὡς ἔοικεν, ἐκεῖνος ὁ 222
10 καιρὸς καὶ ἡ ἡμέρα ἐκείνη οὐ μόνον εὔνουν καὶ πλούσιον ἄνδρα
ἐκάλει, ἀλλὰ καὶ παρηκολουθηκότα τοῖς πράγμασιν ἐξ ἀρχῆς,
καὶ συλλελογισμένον ὀρθῶς τίνος ἕνεκα ταῦτ᾽ ἔπραττεν ὁ Φίλιππος καὶ τί βουλόμενος· ὁ γὰρ μὴ ταῦτ᾽ εἰδὼς μηδ᾽ ἐξητακὼς
πόρρωθεν ἐπιμελῶς, οὔτ᾽ εἰ εὔνους ἦν οὔτ᾽ εἰ πλούσιος, οὐδὲν
15 μᾶλλον ἔμελλεν ὅ τι χρὴ ποιεῖν εἴσεσθαι οὐδ᾽ ὑμῖν ἕξειν συμβουλεύειν. ἐφάνην τοίνυν οὗτος ἐν ἐκείνῃ τῇ ἡμέρᾳ ἐγώ, καὶ 223
παρελθὼν εἶπον εἰς ὑμᾶς, ἅ μου δυοῖν ἕνεκ᾽ ἀκούσατε προσ-
σχόντες τὸν νοῦν, ἑνὸς μὲν, ἵν᾽ εἰδῆτε ὅτι μόνος τῶν λεγόντων
καὶ πολιτευομένων ἐγὼ τὴν τῆς εὐνοίας τάξιν ἐν τοῖς δεινοῖς
20 οὐκ ἔλιπον, ἀλλὰ καὶ λέγων καὶ γράφων ἐξηταζόμην τὰ δέονθ᾽
ὑπὲρ ὑμῶν ἐν αὐτοῖς τοῖς φοβεροῖς, ἑτέρου δὲ, ὅτι μικρὸν ἀνα-
λώσαντες χρόνον πολλῷ πρὸς τὰ λοιπὰ τῆς πάσης πολιτείας

---

5. οἶδ᾽] Ita Σ: ceteri et volg. εὖ οἶδ᾽. 12. ὀρθῶς] ἐξ ἀρχῆς ὀρθῶς Σ. Vid. annot.
13. μηδ᾽] Ita ΣΑ et socii: volgo μήτ᾽. Mox ἐπιμελῶς om. pr. Σ. 17. προσ-
σχόντες] Ita Φ: προσχόντες Σ: volgo et Bekk. προσέχοντες.

---

1. ἦν .. ἡγεῖσθαι. Aeschines parades
his devotion to constitutional forms : Demosthenes idealises their spirit. There is some
variation in the MSS. as to the order of the
words τῆς πατρίδος τῇ κοινῇ φωνῇ : Dobree
would omit ἦν γὰρ .. ἡγεῖσθαι as weak rhodomontade.

6. οἱ τριακόσιοι. The three hundred
rich men who stood at the head of the
symmoriae.

8. μετὰ ταῦτα κ.τ.λ. 'The men who
gave such large benevolences after this.'

§ 222. A man was required who understood the circumstances, and had followed
Philip's plans.

11. παρηκολουθηκότα: cp. Dem. de F.
L. p. 423, § 291 fin.; in Timocr. p. 703, §
13; Aeschines in Tim. p. 16, § 116 fin.;
Demades, § 1 fin. The repetition of ἐξ
ἀρχῆς after ὀρθῶς in the next line, would
not be unlike the manner of Demosthenes,
though to our taste, and perhaps the taste of

contemporaries to whom he could be denounced as ἐπαχθὴς, the topic seems hardly
suited for emphasis.

14. πόρρωθεν. Starting from a long
way back.

§ 223. That man was I : let me recall
my words.

16. ἐφάνην. 'Such an one was found
that day in me.'

17. εἰς ὑμᾶς go rather with εἶπον than
with παρελθών : the sense here differs
from πρὸς ὑμᾶς, in implying that what
Demosthenes says was spoken εἰς τὸ
μέσον.

19. τὴν τῆς .. ἔλιπον. With more or
less definite reference to Aeschines' reiterated
charge of λιποταξία; perhaps especially to
§ 159 of the speech against Ctesiphon. For
its metaphorical use, cp. Dem. de Synt. p.
176, § 37; Mid. p. 354 init.

22. πρὸς .. πολιτείας. 'For all future
public business.'

224 ἔσεσθ᾽ ἐμπειρότεροι. εἶπον τοίνυν ὅτι "τοὺς μὲν ὡς ὑπαρχόντων Θηβαίων Φιλίππῳ λίαν θορυβουμένους ἀγνοεῖν τὰ παρόντα
πράγμαθ᾽ ἡγοῦμαι· εὖ γὰρ οἶδ᾽ ὅτι, εἰ τοῦθ᾽ οὕτως ἐτύγχανεν
ἔχον, οὐκ ἂν αὐτὸν ἠκούομεν ἐν Ἐλατείᾳ ὄντα, ἀλλ᾽ ἐπὶ τοῖς
ἡμετέροις ὁρίοις. ὅτι μέντοι ἵν᾽ ἕτοιμα ποιήσηται τὰ ἐν Θή- 5
βαις ἥκει, σαφῶς ἐπίσταμαι. ὡς δ᾽ ἔχει" ἔφην "ταῦτα, ἀκού-
225 σατέ μου. ἐκεῖνος ὅσους ἢ πεῖσαι χρήμασι Θηβαίων ἢ ἐξα-
πατῆσαι ἐνῆν, ἅπαντας ηὐτρέπισται· τοὺς δ᾽ ἀπ᾽ ἀρχῆς ἀνθε-
στηκότας αὐτῷ καὶ νῦν ἐναντιουμένους οὐδαμῶς πεῖσαι δύναται.
τί οὖν βούλεται, καὶ τίνος ἕνεκα τὴν Ἐλάτειαν κατείληφεν; 10
πλησίον δύναμιν δείξας καὶ παραστήσας τὰ ὅπλα τοὺς μὲν ἑαυτοῦ φίλους ἐπᾶραι καὶ θρασεῖς ποιῆσαι, τοὺς δ᾽ ἐναντιουμένους
καταπλῆξαι, ἵν᾽ ἢ συγχωρήσωσι φοβηθέντες ἃ νῦν οὐκ ἐθέλου-
226 σιν, ἢ βιασθῶσιν. εἰ μὲν τοίνυν προαιρησόμεθ᾽ ἡμεῖς" ἔφην
"ἐν τῷ παρόντι, εἴ τι δύσκολον πέπρακται Θηβαίοις πρὸς 15
ἡμᾶς, τούτου μεμνῆσθαι καὶ ἀπιστεῖν αὐτοῖς ὡς ἐν τῇ τῶν
ἐχθρῶν οὖσι μερίδι, πρῶτον μὲν ἃ ἂν εὔξαιτο Φίλιππος ποιή-
σομεν, εἶτα φοβοῦμαι μὴ προσδεξαμένων τῶν νῦν ἀνθεστηκό-
των αὐτῷ καὶ μιᾷ γνώμῃ πάντων φιλιππισάντων εἰς τὴν Ἀττικὴν ἔλθωσιν ἀμφότεροι. ἂν μέντοι πεισθῆτ᾽ ἐμοὶ καὶ πρὸς 20
τῷ σκοπεῖν, ἀλλὰ μὴ φιλονεικεῖν περὶ ὧν ἂν λέγω γένησθε,
οἶμαι καὶ τὰ δέοντα λέγειν δόξειν καὶ τὸν ἐφεστηκότα κίνδυνον
227 τῇ πόλει διαλύσειν. τί οὖν φημὶ δεῖν; πρῶτον μὲν τὸν παρόντα ἐπανεῖναι φόβον, εἶτα μεταθέσθαι καὶ φοβεῖσθαι πάντας
ὑπὲρ Θηβαίων· πολὺ γὰρ τῶν δεινῶν εἰσιν ἡμῶν ἐγγυτέρω, 25
καὶ προτέροις αὐτοῖς ἐστιν ὁ κίνδυνος· ἔπειτ᾽ ἐξελθόντας Ἐλευ-

---

2. Φιλίππῳ λίαν] Ita Σ Tiberius: φίλαν post Φιλίππῳ addunt A et socii, ante id ceteri.
4. ὄντα] νῦν ὄντα A et socii.   6. ἔφην, ταῦτα] Sic Σ: ceteri ταῦτα, ἔφην.
8. ηὐτρέπισται] εὐτρέπισται Σ B. et S.   11. πλησίον] ἵνα πλησίον ΣΦ.
12. ἐπᾶραι καὶ θρασεῖς ποιῆσαι] Al. θρασεῖς ποιῆσαι καὶ ἐπᾶραι.   14. τοίνυν]
Sic Σ: ceteri οὖν.   25. ἡμῶν] Al. om.   26. ἐστὶν] Al. om.

---

§ 224. *I told you Philip could not count
upon Thebes yet,*
    1. ὑπαρχόντων .. Φιλίππῳ. 'Are al-
ready secured to Philip.' Cp. Dem. de F.
L. pp. 358, 377, §§ 61, 138.
    § 225. *But came to complete his mastery
by terrorism;*
    8. ηὐτρέπισται. Really a middle per-
fect.
    12. ἐπᾶραι .. ποιῆσαι .. καταπλῆξαι are
all so many answers to the question τί βούλεται; and depend upon it.
    § 226. *That his success depended on the
extent of your generosity;*
    16. ἐν τῇ .. μερίδι. 'In infensorum
loco,' rather than 'in hostium partibus.'

Cp. sup. ad § 78.
    20. ἂν .. γένησθε. 'Should you take
my advice, so far as to weigh my words
rather than wrangle over them.' For γίγνεσθαι πρός, cp. Plat. Phaed. p. 54 C and 65
init.
    § 227. *That you must support your friends
at Thebes, and*
    24. μεταθέσθαι is to be taken absolutely
as a reflexive 'turn round:' one cannot
say either in Greek or English, 'remit
your present fear, and then transfer it,'
etc.
    26. Ἐλευσῖνάδε. And no further, lest
a friendly demonstration should pass for a
menace at Thebes.

σίναδε τοὺς ἐν ἡλικίᾳ καὶ τοὺς ἱππέας δεῖξαι πᾶσιν ὑμᾶς αὐτοὺς
ἐν τοῖς ὅπλοις ὄντας, ἵνα τοῖς ἐν Θήβαις φρονοῦσι τὰ ὑμέτερα
ἐξ ἴσου γένηται τὸ παρρησιάζεσθαι περὶ τῶν δικαίων, εἰδόσιν
ὅτι, ὥσπερ τοῖς πωλοῦσι Φιλίππῳ τὴν πατρίδα πάρεσθ᾽ ἡ
5 βοηθήσουσα δύναμις ἐν Ἐλατείᾳ, οὕτω τοῖς ὑπὲρ τῆς ἐλευθερίας
ἀγωνίζεσθαι βουλομένοις ὑπάρχεθ᾽ ὑμεῖς ἕτοιμοι καὶ βοηθήσετ᾽,
ἐάν τις ἐπ᾽ αὐτοὺς ἴῃ. μετὰ ταῦτα χειροτονῆσαι κελεύω δέκα 228
πρέσβεις, καὶ ποιῆσαι τούτους κυρίους μετὰ τῶν στρατηγῶν
καὶ τοῦ πότε δεῖ βαδίζειν ἐκεῖσε καὶ τῆς ἐξόδου. ἐπειδὰν δ᾽
10 ἔλθωσιν οἱ πρέσβεις εἰς Θήβας, πῶς χρήσασθαι τῷ πράγματι
παραινῶ; τούτῳ πάνυ μοι προσέχετε τὸν νοῦν. μὴ δεῖσθαι 229
Θηβαίων μηδὲν (αἰσχρὸς γὰρ ὁ καιρός), ἀλλ᾽ ἐπαγγέλλεσθαι
βοηθήσειν, ἂν κελεύωσιν, ὡς ἐκείνων μὲν ὄντων ἐν τοῖς ἐσχάτοις,
ἡμῶν δὲ ἄμεινον ἢ 'κεῖνοι τὸ μέλλον προορωμένων· ἵν᾽ ἐὰν μὲν
15 δέξωνται ταῦτα καὶ πεισθῶσιν ἡμῖν, καὶ ἃ βουλόμεθα ὦμεν
διῳκημένοι καὶ μετὰ προσχήματος ἀξίου τῆς πόλεως ταῦτα
πράξωμεν, ἂν δ᾽ ἄρα μὴ συμβῇ κατατυχεῖν, ἐκεῖνοι μὲν αὐτοῖς
ἐγκαλῶσιν, ἄν τι νῦν ἐξαμαρτάνωσιν, ἡμῖν δὲ μηδὲν αἰσχρὸν
μηδὲ ταπεινὸν ᾖ πεπραγμένον." Ταῦτα καὶ παραπλήσια τού- 230
20 τοις εἰπὼν κατέβην. συνεπαινεσάντων δὲ πάντων καὶ οὐδενὸς
εἰπόντος ἐναντίον οὐδὲν οὐκ εἶπον μὲν ταῦτα, οὐκ ἔγραψα δὲ,

2. ὑμέτερα] ἡμέτερα A et socii et corr. Σ. 3. εἰδόσιν] ἰδοῦσιν Σ kr B. et S.,
εἰδοῦσιν AΥΦ. 9. δεῖ βαδίζειν ἐκεῖσε] Sic ΣA et socii : ἐκεῖσε δεῖ βαδίζειν O,
ceteri δεῖ ἐκεῖσε βαδίζειν. 11. δεῖσθαι] Sic Σ et alii plerique, et mox ἐπαγγέλλεσθαι
ΣΦΦ. Utrumque etiam habet Dionysius. Legebatur δεῖσθε .. ἐπαγγέλλεσθε. 13. μὲν]
Om. Σ et plerique. ἐσχάτοις] Sic Σ Dion. : volg. et Bekk. add. κινδύνοις. 14. 'κεῖ-
νοι] κεῖνοι ΣΦ : ἐκεῖνοι A et socii, ceteri κείνων vel ἐκείνων. Vid. annot. 16. προ-
σχήματος] σχήματος et socii et Dion. 18. ἐξαμαρτάνωσιν] Sic Σ Dion.: ceteri
ἐξαμάρτωσιν.

§ 228. *Elect ten ambassadors to share
the control of the army with the generals.*

9. τοῦ πότε δεῖ κ.τ.λ. τῆς ἐξόδου must
mean, ' Of the armed expedition' into Boeotia which was to follow the embassy, and
one can hardly suppose that the ambassadors
were allowed any option as to when they
themselves would start : the whole phrase
therefore will mean, ' Of the time to move
on Thebes, and the force to move with,'
which accounts for the ambassadors being
associated with the generals, who would
have to conduct the ἔξοδος itself.

11. μοί. Not merely = *quaeso*, but a
double dative, ' Give *me* your attention *to*
this point.' So Reiske.

§ 229. *The ambassadors are to offer
everything, ask nothing.*

14. ἡμῶν .. προορωμένων. This clause
would balance ἐκείνων μὲν ὄντων better if

we could translate, ' And we had a better
outlook for the future than they,' than if we
take the common sense of προορᾶν to foresee.
Most MSS. beside Σ give 'κείνων or ἐκείνων
instead of ἐκεῖνοι ; it would be possible to
account for the attraction.

16. μετὰ προσχήματος. 'In accordance with a plan that we could announce as
worthy of the city.'

17. κατατυχεῖν. 'To attain a final
result.'

§ 230. *That was the policy for which
in the fullest sense I made myself responsible.*

21. οὐκ εἶπον κ.τ.λ. 'Did not make
this speech *without* proposing a motion,' etc.,
is perhaps the nearest English equivalent to
the construction. The passage was a
favourite example of climax with the ancient
rhetoricians.

οὐδ᾽ ἔγραψα μὲν, οὐκ ἐπρέσβευσα δὲ, οὐδ᾽ ἐπρέσβευσα μὲν,
οὐκ ἔπεισα δὲ Θηβαίους, ἀλλ᾽ ἀπὸ τῆς ἀρχῆς διὰ πάντων ἄχρι
τῆς τελευτῆς διεξῆλθον, καὶ ἔδωκ᾽ ἐμαυτὸν ὑμῖν ἁπλῶς εἰς τοὺς
περιεστηκότας τῇ πόλει κινδύνους. Καί μοι φέρε τὸ ψήφισμα
τὸ τότε γενόμενον.　　　　　　　　　　　　　　　　　　5

231　Καίτοι τίνα βούλει σὲ, Αἰσχίνη, καὶ τίνα ἐμαυτὸν ἐκείνην
τὴν ἡμέραν εἶναι θῶ; βούλει ἐμαυτὸν μὲν, ὃν ἂν σὺ λοιδορούμενος καὶ διασύρων καλέσαις, Βάτταλον, σὲ δὲ μηδ᾽ ἥρω τὸν
τυχόντα, ἀλλὰ τούτων τινὰ τῶν ἀπὸ τῆς σκηνῆς, Κρεσφόντην
ἢ Κρέοντα ἢ ὃν ἐν Κολλυτῷ ποτὲ Οἰνόμαον κακῶς [ὑποκρι- 10
νόμενος] ἐπέτριψας; τότε τοίνυν κατ᾽ ἐκεῖνον τὸν καιρὸν ὁ
Παιανιεὺς ἐγὼ Βάτταλος Οἰνομάου τοῦ Κοθωκίδου σοῦ πλείονος ἄξιος ὢν ἐφάνην τῇ πατρίδι. σὺ μέν γε οὐδὲν οὐδαμοῦ
χρήσιμος ἦσθα· ἐγὼ δὲ πάντα, ὅσα προσῆκε τὸν ἀγαθὸν πολίτην, ἔπραττον. Λέγε τὸ ψήφισμά μοι.　　　　　　15

ΨΗΦΙΣΜΑ ΔΗΜΟΣΘΕΝΟΥΣ.

232　[Ἐπὶ ἄρχοντος Ναυσικλέους, φυλῆς πρυτανευούσης Αἰαντίδος,
σκιροφοριῶνος ἕκτῃ ἐπὶ δέκα, Δημοσθένης Δημοσθένους Παιανιεὺς
εἶπεν, ἐπειδὴ Φίλιππος ὁ Μακεδόνων βασιλεὺς ἔν τε τῷ παρε-
ληλυθότι χρόνῳ παραβαίνων φαίνεται τὰς γεγενημένας αὐτῷ συν- 20
θήκας πρὸς τὸν Ἀθηναίων δῆμον περὶ τῆς εἰρήνης, ὑπεριδὼν τοὺς

---

2. διὰ πάντων] Om. pr. Σ Β. et S.　　3. ὑμῖν] Om. A et socii.　　8. Βάτταλον]
Sic Σ k : ceteri Βάταλον.　　ἥρω] ἥρωα ΣΓΥ et al. B. et S.　　10. κακῶς] Ita
plerique : legebatur κακὸς κακῶς.　Statim ὑποκρινόμενος om. pr. Σ B. et S. : atque equidem
suspicarer, κακὸς κακῶς ἐπέτριψας veram esse lectionem, κακῶς ὑποκρινόμενος autem glossema esse ad ἐπέτριψας.　　15. μοι] Accessit ex ΣA k.　　19. βασιλεὺς] Om.
ΣΦ; unde suspicari licet, Μακεδὼν pro Μακεδόνων legendum esse, ut est in B.

---

3. ἔδωκ᾽ ἐμαυτόν: cp. below, §§ 250,
278. The latter especially refers to this
passage.

§ 231. *That day you, Aeschines, might
envy me.*

§ 231. Naturally it took the clerk some
time (Lept. p. 482, § 92 fin.) to find the
particular document wanted on the file of
those given him to be read, besides which
the Clepsydra had to be stopped. It was
convenient for the orator to fill up this
interval with a slight digression, humorous,
as here or below, § 331; pathetic, as in
Mid. p. 550 init. § 139, Adv. Lept. pp. 469,
470, §§ 46-50.

8. Βάτταλον: see Life.

9. Κρεσφόντην .. Οἰνόμαον: cp. Dem.
de F. L. p. 418, § 295, where we see that
the τριταγωνίστης had the barren honour of
acting kings; there Creon in the Antigone is
expressly mentioned as a part that Aeschines

had often performed, but with no mention
of a breakdown like the Oenomaus. Cre-
sphontes, so far as we know, only appeared
as a ghost in the Merope of Euripides, which
no longer kept the stage. Cp. Demosthenes
ubi sup., Ar. Ran. 868 : cp. however below,
§ 331. According to Demosthenes (ap.
Vit. Anon. Aesch.), Aeschines lost his place
in the company of the poet Ischander owing
to a breakdown in the Oenomaus, and sank
into a mere strolling player, the tritagonist
of Socrates and Simylus (below, § 326); but
this hardly agrees with ἀρουραῖος Οἰνόμαος
below, § 302.

§§ 232-239. [*Decree of Demosthenes.*]

§ 232. The length of this decree looks as
if it were meant to correspond with that
described by Aeschines (in Ctes. § 100), but
as that was passed before the Amphissian
dispute, and included elaborate statistics, this
is hardly possible.

ὅρκους καὶ τὰ παρὰ πᾶσι τοῖς Ἕλλησι νομιζόμενα εἶναι δίκαια,
καὶ πόλεις παραιρεῖται οὐδὲν αὐτῷ προσηκούσας, τινὰς δὲ καὶ Ἀθηναίων οὔσας δοριαλώτους πεποίηκεν οὐδὲν προαδικηθεὶς ὑπὸ τοῦ
δήμου τοῦ Ἀθηναίων, ἕν τε τῷ παρόντι ἐπὶ πολὺ προάγει τῇ τε
5 βίᾳ καὶ τῇ ὠμότητι· καὶ γὰρ Ἑλληνίδας πόλεις ἃς μὲν ἐμφρούρους 233
ποιεῖ καὶ τὰς πολιτείας καταλύει, τινὰς δὲ καὶ ἐξανδραποδιζόμενος
κατασκάπτει, εἰς ἐνίας δὲ καὶ ἀντὶ Ἑλλήνων βαρβάρους κατοικίζει
ἐπὶ τὰ ἱερὰ καὶ τοὺς τάφους ἐπάγων, οὐδὲν ἀλλότριον ποιῶν οὔτε
τῆς ἑαυτοῦ πατρίδος οὔτε τοῦ τρόπου, καὶ τῇ νῦν αὐτῷ παρούσῃ
10 τύχῃ κατακόρως χρώμενος, ἐπιλελησμένος ἑαυτοῦ ὅτι ἐκ μικροῦ καὶ
τοῦ τυχόντος γέγονεν ἀνελπίστως μέγας. καὶ ἕως μὲν πόλεις ἑώρα 234
παραιρούμενον αὐτὸν βαρβάρους καὶ ἰδίας, ὑπελάμβανεν ἔλαττον
εἶναι ὁ δῆμος ὁ Ἀθηναίων τὸ εἰς αὐτὸν πλημμελεῖσθαι· νῦν δὲ
ὁρῶν Ἑλληνίδας πόλεις τὰς μὲν ὑβριζομένας, τὰς δὲ ἀναστάτους
15 γιγνομένας, δεινὸν ἡγεῖται εἶναι καὶ ἀνάξιον τῆς τῶν προγόνων
δόξης τὸ περιορᾶν τοὺς Ἕλληνας καταδουλουμένους. διὸ δεδόχθαι 235
τῇ βουλῇ καὶ τῷ δήμῳ τῷ Ἀθηναίων, εὐξαμένους καὶ θύσαντας
τοῖς θεοῖς καὶ ἥρωσι τοῖς κατέχουσι τὴν πόλιν καὶ τὴν χώραν τὴν
Ἀθηναίων, καὶ ἐνθυμηθέντας τῆς τῶν προγόνων ἀρετῆς, διότι περὶ
20 πλείονος ἐποιοῦντο τὴν τῶν Ἑλλήνων ἐλευθερίαν διατηρεῖν ἢ τὴν
ἰδίαν πατρίδα, διακοσίας ναῦς καθέλκειν εἰς τὴν θάλατταν καὶ τὸν
ναύαρχον ἀναπλεῖν ἐντὸς Πυλῶν, καὶ τὸν στρατηγὸν καὶ τὸν ἵππαρχον τὰς πεζὰς καὶ τὰς ἱππικὰς δυνάμεις Ἐλευσῖνάδε ἐξάγειν,
πέμψαι δὲ καὶ πρέσβεις πρὸς τοὺς ἄλλους Ἕλληνας, πρῶτον δὲ 236
25 πάντων πρὸς Θηβαίους διὰ τὸ ἐγγυτάτω εἶναι τὸν Φίλιππον τῆς
ἐκείνων χώρας, παρακαλεῖν δὲ αὐτοὺς μηδὲν καταπλαγέντας τὸν
Φίλιππον ἀντέχεσθαι τῆς ἑαυτῶν καὶ τῆς τῶν ἄλλων Ἑλλήνων
ἐλευθερίας, καὶ ὅτι ὁ Ἀθηναίων δῆμος, οὐδὲν μνησικακῶν εἴ τι
πρότερον γέγονεν ἀλλότριον ταῖς πόλεσι πρὸς ἀλλήλας, βοηθήσει
30 καὶ δυνάμεσι καὶ χρήμασι καὶ βέλεσι καὶ ὅπλοις, εἰδὼς ὅτι αὐτοῖς
μὲν πρὸς ἀλλήλους διαμφισβητεῖν περὶ τῆς ἡγεμονίας οὖσιν Ἕλλησι καλόν, ὑπὸ δὲ ἀλλοφύλου ἀνθρώπου ἄρχεσθαι καὶ τῆς ἡγε- 237
μονίας ἀποστερεῖσθαι ἀνάξιον εἶναι καὶ τῆς τῶν Ἑλλήνων δόξης

---

2. παραιρεῖται] παραιτεῖται Σ.   4. τοῦ Ἀθηναίων] Ita ΣΦ: volgo τῶν Ἀθηναίων.
11. μέγας] Om. optimi plerique.   17. τῷ et mox τὴν sic Σ et al.: legebatur τῶν
bis.   24. πρέσβεις] τοὺς πρέσβεις Σ.   33. Ἑλλήνων] προγόνων ΣΓΥΦ et
al. Mox τῆς τῶν προγόνων om. p, et τῶν προγόνων in § proximo om. id.

---

9. τῆς ἑαυτοῦ πατρίδος. Demosthenes
(Olynth. 3. p. 85, § 28, Phil. 3. p. 119, § 40,
etc.) ignores the claim of the Macedonian
royal family to Hellenic descent: the mass
of the nation were confessedly βάρβαροι.
See Shilleto's note on De Fals. Leg. § 248,
and the passages from Thirlwall's Greece
there cited.

12. βαρβάρους καὶ ἰδίας. Probably
both refer to the same places, 'barbarian
cities to which he had a claim;' opposed to
οὐδὲν αὐτῷ προσηκούσας of § 232, or ἰδίας

may mean cities in his territory, the Greek
colonies and old subjects of Athens.

16. διὸ δεδόχθαι. Practically the apodosis to ἐπειδὴ Φίλιππος, § 232.

22. ναύαρχον. An Athenian fleet of any
size was commanded by one or more στρα-
τηγοί: but it appears that ναύαρχος is used
once at least of an Attic officer in temporary
command of a small squadron. Yet τὸν
στρατηγὸν καὶ τὸν ἵππαρχον are curious:
there were ten of the former and two of the
latter.

καὶ τῆς τῶν προγόνων ἀρετῆς. ἔτι δὲ οὐδὲ ἀλλότριον ἡγεῖται
εἶναι ὁ Ἀθηναίων δῆμος τὸν Θηβαίων δῆμον οὔτε τῇ συγγενείᾳ

238 οὔτε τῷ ὁμοφύλῳ. ἀναμιμνήσκεται δὲ καὶ τὰς τῶν προγόνων τῶν
ἑαυτοῦ εἰς τοὺς Θηβαίων προγόνους εὐεργεσίας· καὶ γὰρ τοὺς Ἡρακλέους παῖδας ἀποστερουμένους ὑπὸ Πελοποννησίων τῆς πατρῴας 5
ἀρχῆς κατήγαγον, τοῖς ὅπλοις κρατήσαντες τοὺς ἀντιβαίνειν πειρω-
μένους τοῖς Ἡρακλέους ἐκγόνοις, καὶ τὸν Οἰδίπουν καὶ τοὺς μετ'
ἐκείνου ἐκπεσόντας ὑπεδεξάμεθα, καὶ ἕτερα πολλὰ ἡμῖν ὑπάρχει

239 φιλάνθρωπα καὶ ἔνδοξα πρὸς Θηβαίους· διόπερ οὐδὲ νῦν ἀποστή-
σεται ὁ Ἀθηναίων δῆμος τῶν Θηβαίοις τε καὶ τοῖς ἄλλοις Ἕλλησι 10
συμφερόντων. συνθέσθαι δὲ πρὸς αὐτοὺς καὶ συμμαχίαν καὶ ἐπιγαμίαν
ποιήσασθαι καὶ ὅρκους δοῦναι καὶ λαβεῖν. πρέσβεις Δημοσθένης
Δημοσθένους Παιανιεύς, Ὑπερείδης Κλεάνδρου Σφήττιος, Μνησιθείδης Ἀντιφάνους Φρεάρριος, Δημοκράτης Σωφίλου Φλυεύς, Κάλ-
λαισχρος Διοτίμου Κοθωκίδης.] 15

240 Αὕτη τῶν περὶ Θήβας ἐγίγνετο πραγμάτων ἀρχὴ καὶ κατά-
στασις πρώτη, τὰ πρὸ τούτων εἰς ἔχθραν καὶ μῖσος καὶ ἀπι-
στίαν τῶν πόλεων ὑπηγμένων ὑπὸ τούτων. τοῦτο τὸ ψήφισμα
τὸν τότε τῇ πόλει περιστάντα κίνδυνον παρελθεῖν ἐποίησεν
ὥσπερ νέφος. ἦν μὲν τοίνυν τοῦ δικαίου πολίτου τότε δεῖξαι 20

241 πᾶσιν, εἴ τι τούτων εἶχεν ἄμεινον, μὴ νῦν ἐπιτιμᾶν. ὁ γὰρ
σύμβουλος καὶ ὁ συκοφάντης, οὐδὲ τῶν ἄλλων οὐδὲν ἐοικότες,
ἐν τούτῳ πλεῖστον ἀλλήλων διαφέρουσιν· ὁ μέν γε πρὸ τῶν
πραγμάτων γνώμην ἀποφαίνεται, καὶ δίδωσιν ἑαυτὸν ὑπεύθυνον
τοῖς πεισθεῖσι, τῇ τύχῃ, τοῖς καιροῖς, τῷ βουλομένῳ· ὁ δὲ 25
σιγήσας ἡνίκ' ἔδει λέγειν, ἄν τι δύσκολον συμβῇ, τοῦτο βα-

---

7. ἐκγόνοις] Sic Dind. ex Υ et aliis nonnullis : volg. et Bekk. ἐγγόνοις.   11. καὶ
συμμαχίαν] καὶ om. Dind.   16. ἐγίγνετο] ἐγίνετο ΣΑ, ἐγένετο al. et Dind.
22. οὐδὲ] Sic Σ B. et S. Dind.: οὐδενὶ Α et socii et γρ. Σ: volg. ἐν οὐδενί.   25. τοῖς
καιροῖς] τῷ καιρῷ Σ B. et S.

---

§ 239. The decree, as given here, recites
only six ambassadors instead of ten (above,
§ 228), and Hyperides the orator, who is
probably meant, was Κολλυτεύς, not Σφήττιος.

§ 240. This decree united Thebes and
Athens.

16. ἐγίγνετο. So (or ἐγίνετο) the best
MSS. : volg. ἐγένετο. The imperfect
heightens the sense a little, 'These were the
first steps toward an understanding with
Thebes.'

18. ὑπηγμένων ὑπὸ τούτων. While
the old peace party of Eubulus wished to be
on good terms both with Thebes and Macedon, Aeschines and his friends wished to
crush Thebes by means of Macedon.

20. ἦν μέν. This is resumed after the

parenthesis ὁ γὰρ σύμβουλος .. βασκαίνει,
by ἦν μὲν οὖν, § 242, where οὖν is simply
resumptive, and ἦν μὲν is answered by ἐγὼ
δέ.

§ 241. If unwise, it ought to have been
denounced at the time.

24. ὑπεύθυνον. 'Responsible to those
who take his advice, to fortune, to opportunities (used or abused), to anyone' or anything. As responsibility to fortune and
opportunities seems rather strange (though
not stranger than αὐτὰ τὰ πράγματα κατα-
μαρτυρεῖ Dem. de F. L. p. 377, § 130),
some translate, 'Responsible to whoever will
for his advice, for its success and for circumstances ;' but this would require the genitive
(cp. above, § 142 sqq.), to say nothing of
the awkwardness of one case in two senses.

σκαίνει. ἦν μὲν οὖν, ὅπερ εἶπον, ἐκεῖνος ὁ καιρὸς τοῦ γε 242
φροντίζοντος ἀνδρὸς τῆς πόλεως καὶ τῶν δικαίων λόγων· ἐγὼ
δὲ τοσαύτην ὑπερβολὴν ποιοῦμαι ὥστε, ἂν νῦν ἔχῃ τις δεῖξαί
τι βέλτιον, ἢ ὅλως εἴ τι ἄλλο ἐνῆν πλὴν ὧν ἐγὼ προειλόμην,
5 ἀδικεῖν ὁμολογῶ. εἰ γὰρ ἔσθ' ὅ τι τις νῦν ἑόρακεν, ὃ συνή-
νεγκεν ἂν τότε πραχθέν, τοῦτ' ἐγώ φημι δεῖν ἐμὲ μὴ λαθεῖν.
εἰ δὲ μήτ' ἔστι μήτε ἦν μήτ' ἂν εἰπεῖν ἔχοι μηδεὶς μηδέπω
καὶ τήμερον, τί τὸν σύμβουλον ἐχρῆν ποιεῖν; οὐ τῶν φαινο-
μένων καὶ ἐνόντων τὰ κράτιστα ἑλέσθαι; τοῦτο τοίνυν ἐποίησα 243
10 ἐγώ, τοῦ κήρυκος ἐρωτῶντος, Αἰσχίνη, "τίς ἀγορεύειν βούλεται," οὐ "τίς αἰτιᾶσθαι περὶ τῶν παρεληλυθότων," οὐδὲ "τίς
ἐγγυᾶσθαι τὰ μέλλοντ' ἔσεσθαι." σοῦ δ' ἀφώνου κατ' ἐκείνους τοὺς χρόνους ἐν ταῖς ἐκκλησίαις καθημένου ἐγὼ παριὼν
ἔλεγον. ἐπειδὴ δ' οὐ τότε, ἀλλὰ νῦν δεῖξον. εἰπὲ τίς ἢ λό-
15 γος, ὅντιν' ἐχρῆν εὑρεῖν, ἢ καιρὸς συμφέρων ὑπ' ἐμοῦ παρε-
λείφθη τῇ πόλει; τίς δὲ συμμαχία, τίς πρᾶξις, ἐφ' ἣν μᾶλλον
ἔδει με ἀγαγεῖν τουτουσί;

Ἀλλὰ μὴν τὸ μὲν παρεληλυθὸς ἀεὶ παρὰ πᾶσιν ἀφεῖται, 244
καὶ οὐδεὶς περὶ τούτου προτίθησιν οὐδαμοῦ βουλήν· τὸ δὲ
20 μέλλον ἢ τὸ παρὸν τὴν τοῦ συμβούλου τάξιν ἀπαιτεῖ. τότε
τοίνυν τὰ μὲν ἔμελλεν, ὡς ἐδόκει, τῶν δεινῶν, τὰ δ' ἤδη παρῆν,
ἐν οἷς τὴν προαίρεσίν μου σκόπει τῆς πολιτείας, μὴ τὰ συμβάντα συκοφάντει. τὸ μὲν γὰρ πέρας, ὡς ἂν ὁ δαίμων βου-
βηθῇ, πάντων γίγνεται· ἡ δὲ προαίρεσις αὐτὴ τὴν τοῦ συμ-
25 βούλου διάνοιαν δηλοῖ. μὴ δὴ τοῦτο ὡς ἀδίκημα ἐμὸν θῇς, 245
εἰ κρατῆσαι συνέβη Φιλίππῳ τῇ μάχῃ· ἐν γὰρ τῷ θεῷ τὸ
τούτου τέλος ἦν, οὐκ ἐν ἐμοί. ἀλλ' ὡς οὐχ ἅπαντα ὅσα ἐνῆν

---

1. γε] τε A et socii : al. om.   10. ἐγὼ] Om. Σ et alii multi, B. et S.   11. αἰτιᾶ-
σθαι] αἰτιάσασθαι multi.   13. παριὼν] Sic A et socii : περίων Σ, ceteri παρελθάν.
26. τῇ μάχῃ] Sic ΣFA : ceteri τὴν μάχην.   27. ἐν] Om. ΣA⁴ B. et S.

---

§ 242. But I am willing to be judged
now by the event, and it is clear I did my
duty and chose for the best.

2. ἐγὼ .. ποιοῦμαι. 'I go so far in my
concessions,' surpass so much what could be
required of me. The same phrase occurs in
Dem. de F. L. p. 247, § 381 fin.

§ 243. This was all that could be required,
this I did when you did nothing.

10. τοῦ κήρυκος. Demosthenes will not
leave Aeschines to enjoy undisturbed the
effect of his appeal to constitutional routine
(in Ctes. § 4).

§ 244. A statesman has to deal with con-

tingencies, a sycophant keeps to results.

22. ἐν οἷς κ.τ.λ. 'Consider the general
scope of my policy, do not make captious
objections to events.' προαίρεσις here comes
half way between the popular and psycho-
logical sense : cp. Arist. Eth. Nic. 6. 2. 6,
οὐδεὶς προαιρεῖται Ἴλιον πεπορθηκέναι. From
the next sentence one might illustrate the
difference between πέρας and τέλος, the latter being implied in προαίρεσις.

§ 245. You ought to criticise my policy
now, and not complain of the event.

27. ἅπαντα .. εἱλόμην. 'Made every
choice' I ought, 'secured every advantage.'

κατ᾽ ἀνθρώπινον λογισμὸν εἱλόμην, καὶ δικαίως ταῦτα καὶ ἐπιμελῶς ἔπραξα καὶ φιλοπόνως ὑπὲρ δύναμιν, ἢ ὡς οὐ καλὰ καὶ
τῆς πόλεως ἄξια πράγματα ἐνεστησάμην καὶ ἀναγκαῖα, ταῦτά
246 μοι δεῖξον, καὶ τότ᾽ ἤδη κατηγόρει μου. εἰ δ᾽ ὁ συμβὰς σκηπ-
τὸς μὴ μόνον ἡμῶν, ἀλλὰ καὶ πάντων τῶν ἄλλων Ἑλλήνων 5
μείζων γέγονε, τί χρὴ ποιεῖν; ὥσπερ ἂν εἴ τις ναύκληρον πάντ᾽
ἐπὶ σωτηρίᾳ πράξαντα, καὶ πᾶσι κατασκευάσαντα τὸ πλοῖον
ἀφ᾽ ὧν ὑπελάμβανε σωθήσεσθαι, εἶτα χειμῶνι χρησάμενον καὶ
πονησάντων αὐτῷ τῶν σκευῶν ἢ καὶ συντριβέντων ὅλως, τῆς
ναυαγίας αἰτιῷτο. ἀλλ᾽ οὔτ᾽ ἐκυβέρνων τὴν ναῦν, φήσειεν ἄν, 10
ὥσπερ οὐδ᾽ ἐστρατήγουν ἐγώ, οὔτε τῆς τύχης κύριος ἦν, ἀλλ᾽
247 ἐκείνη τῶν πάντων. ἀλλ᾽ ἐκεῖνο λογίζου καὶ ὅρα, εἰ μετὰ
Θηβαίων ἡμῖν ἀγωνιζομένοις οὕτως εἵμαρτο πρᾶξαι, τί χρῆν
προσδοκᾶν, εἰ μηδὲ τούτους ἔσχομεν συμμάχους, ἀλλὰ Φιλίππῳ
προσέθεντο, ὑπὲρ οὗ τότ᾽ ἐκεῖνος πάσας ἀφῆκε φωνάς; καὶ εἰ 15
νῦν τριῶν ἡμερῶν ἀπὸ τῆς Ἀττικῆς ὁδὸν τῆς μάχης γενομένης
τοσοῦτος κίνδυνος καὶ φόβος περιέστη τὴν πόλιν, τί ἂν, εἴ
που τῆς χώρας ταὐτὸ τοῦτο πάθος συνέβη, προσδοκῆσαι χρῆν;
248 ἆρ᾽ οἶσθ᾽ ὅτι νῦν μὲν στῆναι, συνελθεῖν, ἀναπνεῦσαι, πολλὰ μία
ἡμέρα καὶ δύο καὶ τρεῖς ἔδοσαν τῶν εἰς σωτηρίαν τῇ πόλει, τότε 20
δ᾽—, οὐκ ἄξιον εἰπεῖν, ἅ γε μηδὲ πεῖραν ἔδωκε θεῶν τινος εὐνοίᾳ

---

4. σκηπτὸs] ἢ χειμῶν add. libri : delevit Reisk.   7. πᾶσι] Om. Σ B. et S.
16. ἀπὸ τῆς Ἀττικῆς ὁδὸν] Sic ΣΑ² : ceteri ὁδὸν ἀπὸ τῆς Ἀττικῆς.   18. τῆς
χώρας] πλησίον τῆς χώρας Α et socii.   21. εὐνοίᾳ καὶ τῷ] Ita FΦΩA : ευνοια και
τωι ΣΥ : neque Σ quidem ita constanter : adscriptum dativis adjungit, ut pro testimonio
habendum sit scriptorem non εὐνοίᾳ voluisse.   Alii habent εὔνοια καὶ τό : vid. annot.

---

3. καὶ ἀναγκαῖα. 'And in fact inevitable.' Cp. above, § 242, ὅλως εἴ τι ἄλλο
ἐνῆν.

§ 246. *Though we were beaten I did my
best; the generals and Providence were
answerable for our defeat.*

6. μείζων. 'Too great for,' not κρείττων, 'stronger than.' Cp. sup. ad § 181.

10. οὔτ᾽ ἐκυβέρνων. The ναύκληρος
was the owner, not the captain: he was
legally answerable for his ship being well
formed and seaworthy, not, says Demosthenes,
for her being well managed on the voyage.
Cp. Acts xxvii, 11, for their joint action and
responsibility.

§ 247. *Which would have been far more
fatal if we had fought alone and in our own
territory.*

16. τριῶν ἡμερῶν .. ὁδόν. Defined below,
§ 389, as 700 stadia from Athens.

§ 248. *Three days gave time to do much.*

19. ἆρ᾽ οἶσθ᾽ .. ἔδωκε. 'Do you realise
that as it was [νῦν μὲν] we had one day,

and a second and a third, to recover our
footing, to meet, to take breath, to do many
things to save the state ; but in that case—
God forbid we should speak of things we
never tasted.' Dissen takes μιὰ ἡμέρα κ.τ.λ.
of the days immediately after the occupation
of Elatea, instead of the three days required
for the advance from Chaeronea, which gave
the Athenians time to put on a bold front
and obtain tolerable terms. He translates,
'*factum esse ut stemus, coeamus, respiremus,
alia multa salutis adminicula civitas babeat,*'
i. e. ' liberum vitae quotidianae usum habere.'
Reiske reads ἆρ᾽ οἴεσθε. ἆρ᾽ is 'not equivalent' to ἆρ᾽ οὐ : though Demosthenes
consistently credits Aeschines with knowledge
of Philip's mischievous designs, he asks here,
' Did he really know the full extent of the
danger which Athens in part escaped?'

21. οὐκ ἄξιον, exactly 'indignum.'

εὐνοίᾳ καὶ τῷ. So, apart from accidents, all the best MSS. : others have εὔνοια
καὶ τό. It would be possible, though a little

καὶ τῷ προβάλλεσθαι τὴν πόλιν ταύτην τὴν συμμαχίαν, ἧς
σὺ κατηγορεῖς.
Ἔστι δὲ ταυτὶ πάντα μοι, τὰ πολλὰ, πρὸς ὑμᾶς, ἄνδρες 249
δικασταὶ, καὶ τοὺς περιεστηκότας ἔξωθεν καὶ ἀκροωμένους, ἐπεὶ
πρός γε τοῦτον τὸν κατάπτυστον βραχὺς καὶ σαφὴς ἐξήρκει
λόγος. εἰ μὲν γὰρ ἦν σοὶ πρόδηλα τὰ μέλλοντα, Αἰσχίνη,
μόνῳ τῶν ἄλλων, ὅτ' ἐβουλεύεθ' ἡ πόλις περὶ τούτων, τότ'
ἔδει προλέγειν· εἰ δὲ μὴ προῄδεις, τῆς αὐτῆς ἀγνοίας ὑπεύθυνος
εἶ τοῖς ἄλλοις, ὥστε τί μᾶλλον ἐμοῦ σὺ ταῦτα κατηγορεῖς ἢ
ἐγὼ σοῦ; τοσοῦτον γὰρ ἀμείνων ἐγὼ σοῦ πολίτης γέγονα εἰς 250
αὐτὰ ταῦθ' ἃ λέγω (καὶ οὔπω περὶ τῶν ἄλλων διαλέγομαι),
ὅσον ἐγὼ μὲν ἔδωκα ἐμαυτὸν εἰς τὰ πᾶσι δοκοῦντα συμφέρειν,
οὐδένα κίνδυνον ὀκνήσας ἴδιον οὐδ' ὑπολογισάμενος, σὺ δὲ οὔθ'
ἕτερα εἶπες βελτίω τούτων (οὐ γὰρ ἂν τούτοις ἐχρῶντο), οὔτ'
εἰς ταῦτα χρήσιμον οὐδὲν σαυτὸν παρέσχες, ὅπερ δ' ἂν ὁ φαυ- 251
λότατος καὶ δυσμενέστατος ἄνθρωπος τῇ πόλει, τοῦτο πεποιηκὼς ἐπὶ τοῖς συμβᾶσιν ἐξήτασαι, καὶ ἅμα Ἀρίστρατος ἐν Νάξῳ
καὶ Ἀριστόλεως ἐν Θάσῳ, οἱ καθάπαξ ἐχθροὶ τῆς πόλεως,
τοὺς Ἀθηναίων κρίνουσι φίλους καὶ Ἀθήνησιν Αἰσχίνης Δημοσθένους κατηγορεῖ. καίτοι ὅτῳ τὰ τῶν Ἑλλήνων ἀτυχήματα 252
ἐνευδοκιμεῖν ἀπέκειτο, ἀπολωλέναι μᾶλλον οὗτός ἐστι δίκαιος
ἢ κατηγορεῖν ἑτέρου· καὶ ὅτῳ συνενηνόχασιν οἱ αὐτοὶ καιροὶ

1. **προβάλλεσθαι**] Ita ΣΦΩ B. et S.: volgo *προβαλέσθαι*. 3. **ἄνδρες δικασταὶ**] *ὦ δικασταὶ* A *k*, *ὦ ἄνδρες δικασταὶ* Dind. 5. **τοῦτον**] Ita Σ et *γρ.* Φ: ceteri *τοῦτον αὐτόν*. **ἐξήρκει**] *ἐξήρκει μοι* A et socii. 10. **τοσοῦτον**] *τοσούτῳ* A et socii. 16. **ἄνθρωπος τῇ πόλει**] Ita ΣA et socii: ceteri *ἄνθρωπος ποιήσειε τῇ πόλει*. 18. **Ἀριστόλεως**] Ita A et socii, Ἀριστόλεος Σ: ceteri plerique *-όλαος*.

awkward, to translate the latter reading, 'Which the favour of heaven and the protection of this alliance did not try (i.e. permit to be tried) upon us.' *μηδὲ πεῖραν* is not, 'not even a taste,' but 'we need not talk of them, for we did not feel them either.'

§§ 249, 250. *At any rate I did my duty, as Aeschines did not, by giving the best advice I could.*

3. **τὰ πολλά.** Not 'mostly,' which would be weak after *πάντα*, but 'this long argument.'

5. **πρός γε τοῦτον.** He insinuates that as Aeschines could not honestly prosecute, he could not obtain a conviction: throughout Demosthenes claims that having faced responsibility like a good citizen, he is not to be held accountable to Aeschines, who, like a bad citizen, held aloof.

11. **περὶ τῶν ἄλλων**, i.e. I am speaking of one particular period, that of the war which ended with Chaeronea: during this Aeschines was simply inactive: before it he had done a great deal, though it was mostly harm. Cp. below, § 253, *πολιτεύει καὶ πάλιν οὐ πολιτεύει*.

§ 251. *Now he brings me to trial for what he did not oppose: it is the same all over Greece.*

19. **Αἰσχίνης Δημοσθένους.** The names themselves in juxtaposition, are synonyms of *οἱ καθάπαξ ἐχθροὶ τῆς πόλεως* and *τοὺς Ἀθηναίων φίλους*.

§ 252. *He boasts of our misfortunes, and thrives on them.*

20. **ὅτῳ . . ἀπέκειτο.** 'Whoever kept the misfortunes of Greece laid up as foundations for his own reputation for foresight.'

καὶ τοῖς τῆς πόλεως ἐχθροῖς, οὐκ ἔνι τοῦτον εὔνουν εἶναι τῇ
253 πατρίδι. δηλοῖς δὲ καὶ ἐξ ὧν ζῇς καὶ ποιεῖς καὶ πολιτεύει
καὶ πάλιν οὐ πολιτεύει. πράττεταί τι τῶν ὑμῖν δοκούντων
συμφέρειν, ἄφωνος Αἰσχίνης. ἀντέκρουσέ τι καὶ γέγονεν οἷον
οὐκ ἔδει, πάρεστιν Αἰσχίνης· ὥσπερ τὰ ῥήγματα καὶ τὰ σπά- 5
σματα, ὅταν τι κακὸν τὸ σῶμα λάβῃ, τότε κινεῖται.
254 Ἐπειδὴ δὲ πολὺς τοῖς συμβεβηκόσιν ἔγκειται, βούλομαί τι
καὶ παράδοξον εἰπεῖν. καί μου πρὸς Διὸς καὶ θεῶν μηδεὶς τὴν
ὑπερβολὴν θαυμάσῃ, ἀλλὰ μετ' εὐνοίας ὃ λέγω θεωρησάτω. εἰ
γὰρ ἦν ἅπασι πρόδηλα τὰ μέλλοντα γενήσεσθαι, καὶ προή- 10
δεσαν πάντες, καὶ σὺ προύλεγες, Αἰσχίνη, καὶ διεμαρτύρου
βοῶν καὶ κεκραγώς, ὃς οὐδ' ἐφθέγξω, οὐδ' οὕτως ἀποστατέον
τῇ πόλει τούτων ἦν, εἴπερ δόξης ἢ προγόνων ἢ τοῦ μέλλοντος
255 αἰῶνος εἶχε λόγον. νῦν μέν γε ἀποτυχεῖν δοκεῖ τῶν πραγμάτων, ὃ πᾶσι κοινόν ἐστιν ἀνθρώποις, ὅταν τῷ θεῷ ταῦτα 15
δοκῇ· τότε δ' ἀξιοῦσα προεστάναι τῶν ἄλλων, εἶτ' ἀποστᾶσα
τούτου, Φιλίππῳ προδεδωκέναι πάντας ἂν ἔσχεν αἰτίαν. εἰ
γὰρ ταῦτα προεῖτο ἀκονιτί, περὶ ὧν οὐδένα κίνδυνον ὄντιν' οὐχ
ὑπέμειναν οἱ πρόγονοι, τίς οὐχὶ κατέπτυσεν ἂν σοῦ; μὴ γὰρ
256 τῆς πόλεώς γε, μηδ' ἐμοῦ. τίσι δ' ὀφθαλμοῖς πρὸς Διὸς ἑω- 20
ρῶμεν ἂν τοὺς εἰς τὴν πόλιν ἀνθρώπους ἀφικνουμένους, εἰ τὰ

3. ὑμῖν] ἡμῖν A et socii. 10. γενήσεσθαι] ἔσεσθαι A et socii. 11. Αἰσχίνη]
Om. Dion. et librorum praeter Σ optimi. 14. μέν γε] Sic Σ A et socii: ceteri γάρ.
16. ἄλλων] ἄλλων Ἑλλήνων Dion. et γρ. ΣΦ. 18. ὄντιν' οὐχ] ὀντινοῦν οὐχ ΓΥΦΩ
rw et corr. Σ: ὀντινοῦν t. 19. τίς] τίς ἂν A et socii, et mox μὴ γὰρ δὴ iidem.

§ 253. *When things go well with us he is
dumb: we feel him like an old wound in
sickness.*

5. ὥσπερ .. κινεῖται. 'He is like broken
bones, and sprains : when there is any trouble upon the body, then you feel him stirring.' The same illustration is used in
Olynth. 2. p. 24, § 21, Ad Ep. Phil. pp. 115,
116, § 16, and may perhaps have been suggested by Demosthenes' experience as a
valetudinarian.

§ 254. *Even if I could have foreseen
everything, I was right.*

7. πολὺς τοῖς συμβεβηκόσιν ἔγκειται:
cp. Thuc. 4. 22, Hdt. 7. 158 init. In all
these the sense is vehement *rebuke*.

13. εἴπερ δόξης κ.τ.λ. So Dissen and
Dindorf from the quotation of Dionysius,
on the ground that 'either' is out of
place at the beginning of an enumeration
of similar things. All the MSS. have ἢ
before δόξης except two cursives, which have
καί.

§ 255. *For now Athens is unfortunate,
not base,*

19. μὴ .. ἐμοῦ. 'I hope it would not be
the city or me either.' The hypothetical
case he has put is, 'If Athens had failed of
her duty ;' the natural apodosis would be,
'Then Athens would be disgraced,' but
Demosthenes shrinks from saying this : he
insists that some individual traitor must
have deluded Athens, although he hints that
the city and more honest statesmen might
suffer in reputation from this subservience.
So in the next section he goes on, 'Though
we know that *the city* would not have been
disgraced, still how could the Athenians
have looked foreigners in the face ? They
would have judged us in the light of our
past history.' The sentiment is a democratic parallel to the monarchical fictions
that the king can do no wrong, and the
doctrine of ministerial responsibility.

§ 256. *As she would have been bad she
allowed Philip to conquer unresisted,*

μὲν πράγματ᾽ εἰς ὅπερ νυνὶ περιέστη, ἡγεμὼν δὲ καὶ κύριος
ᾑρέθη Φίλιππος ἁπάντων, τὸν δ᾽ ὑπὲρ τοῦ μὴ γενέσθαι ταῦτ᾽
ἀγῶνα ἕτεροι χωρὶς ἡμῶν ἦσαν πεποιημένοι, καὶ ταῦτα μηδεπώποτε τῆς πόλεως ἐν τοῖς ἔμπροσθε χρόνοις ἀσφάλειαν ἄδοξον
5 μᾶλλον ἢ τὸν ὑπὲρ τῶν καλῶν κίνδυνον ᾑρημένης. τίς γὰρ οὐκ 257
οἶδεν Ἑλλήνων, τίς δὲ βαρβάρων, ὅτι καὶ παρὰ Θηβαίων καὶ
παρὰ τῶν ἔτι τούτων πρότερον ἰσχυρῶν γενομένων Λακεδαιμονίων καὶ παρὰ τοῦ Περσῶν βασιλέως μετὰ πολλῆς χάριτος
τοῦτ᾽ ἂν ἀσμένως ἐδόθη τῇ πόλει, ὅ τι βούλεται λαβούσῃ καὶ
10 τὰ ἑαυτῆς ἐχούσῃ τὸ κελευόμενον ποιεῖν καὶ ἐᾶν ἕτερον τῶν
Ἑλλήνων προεστάναι. ἀλλ᾽ οὐκ ἦν ταῦθ᾽, ὡς ἔοικε, τοῖς τότ᾽ 258
Ἀθηναίοις πάτρια οὐδ᾽ ἀνεκτὰ οὐδ᾽ ἔμφυτα, οὐδ᾽ ἐδυνήθη πώποτε τὴν πόλιν οὐδεὶς ἐκ παντὸς τοῦ χρόνου πεῖσαι τοῖς ἰσχύ-
ουσι μέν, μὴ δίκαια δὲ πράττουσι προσθεμένην ἀσφαλῶς δου-
15 λεύειν, ἀλλ᾽ ἀγωνιζομένη περὶ πρωτείων καὶ τιμῆς καὶ δόξης
κινδυνεύουσα πάντα τὸν αἰῶνα διατετέλεκε. καὶ ταῦθ᾽ οὕτω 259
σεμνὰ καὶ προσήκοντα τοῖς ὑμετέροις ἤθεσιν ὑμεῖς ὑπολαμ-
·βάνετ᾽ εἶναι ὥστε καὶ τῶν προγόνων τοὺς ταῦτα πράξαντας
μάλιστ᾽ ἐπαινεῖτε, εἰκότως. τίς γὰρ οὐκ ἂν ἀγάσαιτο τῶν
20 ἀνδρῶν ἐκείνων τῆς ἀρετῆς, οἳ καὶ τὴν χώραν καὶ τὴν πόλιν
ἐκλιπεῖν ὑπέμειναν εἰς τὰς τριήρεις ἐμβάντες ὑπὲρ τοῦ μὴ τὸ
κελευόμενον ποιῆσαι, τὸν μὲν ταῦτα συμβουλεύσαντα Θεμιστο-
κλέα στρατηγὸν ἑλόμενοι, τὸν δ᾽ ὑπακούειν ἀποφηνάμενον τοῖς

---

1. περιέστη] περιέστησεν A et socii. 3. ἡμῶν] ὑμῶν Σ. 5. ᾑρημένης]
ἀραμένης pr. Σ. 7. γενομένων] γεγενημένων, ut saepe, A et socii. 11. τοῖς
τότε] Ita Σ a m. sec. et A et socii: ceteri τοῖς. 16. κινδυνεύουσα] καὶ κινδυνεύουσα A et socii et Edd. ante Bekk. 17. ὑπολαμβάνετ᾽] ὑπελαμβάνετ᾽ ΓΥΦΩ rsuv.
23. ἀποφηνάμενον τοῖς ἐπιταττομένοις] Ita ΣA et socii et Dion.: ceteri τοῖς ἐπιταττομένοις ἀποφηνάμενον.

3. μηδεπώποτε. Athens never had accepted a dependent position, except in the
short interval between the peace of Lysander
and the battle of Cnidus.

§ 257. *She who never sold herself, as she
might at a high price, to any who sought to
enslave Greece.*

6. παρὰ .. βασιλέως. See the account
of Xerxes' conciliatory embassies, Hdt. 8 fin.,
9 init.

9. τοῦτ᾽ .. ἐδόθη. The gift of course is
ὅ τι βούλεται λαβεῖν and τὰ ἑαυτῆς ἔχειν,
not τὸ κελευόμενον ποιεῖν.

§ 258. *But craven counsels were never
welcome.*

11. ἀλλ᾽ .. διατετέλεκε. 'But it seems
the Athenians that were then had learnt

another lesson and inherited another spirit,
and could not bear that burthen: never
a man was able since time began, to persuade the city to take part with them that
had the power and dealt unrighteously,
and so keep safe in slavery: but in battle,
for pre-eminence and honour and good
fame, she hath continued hitherto in
jeopardy.'

§ 259. *Remember the heroism of Salamis,
and how Cyrsilus was punished.*

§ 259. He suggests, but refrains from
developing the parallel, 'Everyone admires
those who trusted Themistocles and stoned
Cyrsilus: they will equally admire you who
trusted Demosthenes and are going to banish
Aeschines.'

ἐπιταττομένοις Κυρσίλον καταλιθώσαντες, οὐ μόνον αὐτὸν, ἀλλὰ
260 καὶ αἱ γυναῖκες αἱ ὑμέτεραι τὴν γυναῖκ' αὐτοῦ. οὐ γὰρ ἐζήτουν
οἱ τότ' Ἀθηναῖοι οὔτε ῥήτορα οὔτε στρατηγὸν δι' ὅτου δου-
λεύσουσιν εὐτυχῶς, ἀλλ' οὐδὲ ζῆν ἠξίουν, εἰ μὴ μετ' ἐλευθερίας
ἐξέσται τοῦτο ποιεῖν. ἡγεῖτο γὰρ αὐτῶν ἕκαστος οὐχὶ τῷ 5
πατρὶ καὶ τῇ μητρὶ μόνον γεγενῆσθαι, ἀλλὰ καὶ τῇ πατρίδι.
διαφέρει δὲ τί; ὅτι ὁ μὲν τοῖς γονεῦσι μόνον γεγενῆσθαι νομίζων τὸν τῆς εἱμαρμένης καὶ τὸν αὐτόματον θάνατον περιμένει,
ὁ δὲ καὶ τῇ πατρίδι ὑπὲρ τοῦ μὴ ταύτην ἐπιδεῖν δουλεύουσαν
ἀποθνήσκειν ἐθελήσει, καὶ φοβερωτέρας ἡγήσεται τὰς ὕβρεις 10
καὶ τὰς ἀτιμίας, ἃς ἐν δουλευούσῃ τῇ πόλει φέρειν ἀνάγκη,
τοῦ θανάτου.
261 Εἰ μὲν τοίνυν τοῦτ' ἐπεχείρουν λέγειν, ὡς ἐγὼ προήγαγον
ὑμᾶς ἄξια τῶν προγόνων φρονεῖν, οὐκ ἔσθ' ὅστις οὐκ ἂν εἰκότως
ἐπιτιμήσειέ μοι. νῦν δ' ἐγὼ μὲν ὑμετέρας τὰς τοιαύτας προαι- 15
ρέσεις ἀποφαίνω, καὶ δείκνυμι ὅτι καὶ πρὸ ἐμοῦ τοῦτ' εἶχε τὸ
φρόνημα ἡ πόλις, τῆς μέντοι διακονίας τῆς ἐφ' ἑκάστοις τῶν
262 πεπραγμένων καὶ ἐμαυτῷ μετεῖναί φημι, οὗτος δὲ τῶν ὅλων
κατηγορῶν, καὶ κελεύων ὑμᾶς ἐμοὶ πικρῶς ἔχειν ὡς φόβων καὶ
κινδύνων αἰτίῳ τῇ πόλει, τῆς μὲν εἰς τὸ παρὸν τιμῆς ἐμὲ ἀποστε- 20
ρῆσαι γλίχεται, τὰ δ' εἰς ἅπαντα τὸν λοιπὸν χρόνον ἐγκώμια

---

1. Κυρσίλον] Κύρσιλον Σ.　　4. εὐτυχῶς] Om. Σ B. et S.　　5. ἐξέσται] Ita
Σ Dion.: volgo αὐτοῖς ἐξέσται.　　12. τοῦ θανάτου] Om. ΥΠ tiv, in γρ. habent ΦΦ.
13. ὡς ἐγὼ] ὡς ἄρα ἐγὼ Α et socii.　　15. ἐπιτιμήσειε] ἐπετίμησέ Α et socii Υ.
20. πόλει] Addebatur γεγενημένα: om. ΣΑ et socii Dion.

---

1. **Κυρσίλον.** Herodotus 9. 5 names
the traitor Lycidas.

2. **αἱ γυναῖκες.** Here, as usual, the so-
called *nominativus pendens* is a loose kind of
apposition : the citizens' wives are part and
parcel of the citizens. The effect of the
sentence is, ' You stoned not only him, but
his wife, that is, your wives did.'

§ 260. *Our ancestors knew they were the
children, not of their parents only ; but of
freedom and fatherland.*

8. **τὸν .. θάνατον:** cp. Plat. Crit. p. 51,
A, B. The connection of the sentiment is,
' He who recognises none but his natural
birth, will wait for a natural death ; he who
recognises a higher life than that of the
individual, will be ready to sacrifice the
individual life thereto.' It is the Hellenic
counterpart of Romans xiv. 7 sqq.

§ 261. *My own claim is, that I ministered
to their spirit, which survived in you.*

15. **ἐγὼ μὲν** answers to **οὗτος δὲ, προαιρέσεις** to **διακονίας, ὑμετέρας** to **ἐμοί.** Cp.
above, § 110, **ἀλλὰ τίς ἦν .. ὑμεῖς ὦ ἄνδρες.**

Ἀθηναῖοι.

17. **διακονίας** practically comes to the
same as ' execution,' but is a more depreciatory word : cp. Plat. Gorg 517 B, c. 73,
where Socrates complains that statesmen
never rise above ministerial functions.

§ 262. *Therefore Aeschines' envy affects
you more than me.*

18. **τῶν ὅλων κ.τ.λ.** i. e. If he found
fault only with the details of my policy, it
might tell against me alone ; but when he
attacks me on first principles, he attacks the
nation also, whose first principles were the
same. It is noticeable that Demosthenes
does not defend any of the points of detail
attacked by Aeschines (in Ctes. §§ 142-151).
He says generally, that the terms of the
alliance were meant to be liberal towards
Thebes, and his plea, that he was not answerable for military faults, would apply to
the detachment of the 10,000 mercenaries
to Amphissa, though it hardly meets the
specific charges made by Aeschines (in Ctes.
§ 146).

ὑμῶν ἀφαιρεῖται. εἰ γὰρ ὡς οὐ τὰ βέλτιστα ἐμοῦ πο-
λιτευσαμένου τουδὶ καταψηφιεῖσθε, ἡμαρτηκέναι δόξετε, οὐ
τῇ τῆς τύχης ἀγνωμοσύνῃ τὰ συμβάντα παθεῖν. ἀλλ' οὐκ 263
ἔστιν, οὐκ ἔστιν ὅπως ἡμάρτετε, ἄνδρες Ἀθηναῖοι, τὸν ὑπὲρ
5 τῆς ἁπάντων ἐλευθερίας καὶ σωτηρίας κίνδυνον ἀράμενοι, μὰ
τοὺς Μαραθῶνι προκινδυνεύσαντας τῶν προγόνων καὶ τοὺς ἐν
Πλαταιαῖς παραταξαμένους καὶ τοὺς ἐν Σαλαμῖνι ναυμαχήσαντας
καὶ τοὺς ἐπ' Ἀρτεμισίῳ καὶ πολλοὺς ἑτέρους τοὺς ἐν τοῖς
δημοσίοις μνήμασι κειμένους ἀγαθοὺς ἄνδρας, οὓς ἅπαντας ὁμοίως 264
10 ἡ πόλις τῆς αὐτῆς ἀξιώσασα τιμῆς ἔθαψεν, Αἰσχίνη, οὐχὶ τοὺς
κατορθώσαντας αὐτῶν οὐδὲ τοὺς κρατήσαντας μόνους. δικαίως.
ὃ μὲν γὰρ ἦν ἀνδρῶν ἀγαθῶν ἔργον, ἅπασι πέπρακται· τῇ
τύχῃ δ', ἣν ὁ δαίμων ἔνειμεν ἑκάστοις, ταύτῃ κέχρηνται. ἔπειτ', 265
ὦ κατάρατε καὶ γραμματοκύφων, σὺ μὲν τῆς παρὰ τουτωνὶ
15 τιμῆς καὶ φιλανθρωπίας ἔμ' ἀποστερῆσαι βουλόμενος τρόπαια
καὶ μάχας καὶ παλαιὰ ἔργα ἔλεγες, ὧν τίνος προσεδεῖτο ὁ
παρὼν ἀγὼν οὑτοσί; ἐμὲ δὲ, ὦ τριταγωνιστά, τὸν περὶ τῶν
πρωτείων σύμβουλον τῇ πόλει παριόντα τὸ τίνος φρόνημα
λαβόντ' ἀναβαίνειν ἐπὶ τὸ βῆμ' ἔδει; τὸ τοῦ τούτων ἀνάξια
20 ἐροῦντος; δικαίως μεντἂν ἀπέθανον. ἐπεὶ οὐδ' ὑμᾶς, ἄνδρες 266

---

4. ἡμάρτετε] ἡμαρτήκατε A et socii.
θῶνι Σ: volg. ἐν Μαραθῶνι.
πόλις] ἡ πόλις ὁμοίως A et socii.
ΣA et socii Dion.: volg. ἀπένειμεν.
testimonio decepti.   19. λαβόντ'] ἀναλαβόντ' A et socii.
volgo ἔπειτ'.

5. μὰ] Ita Σ: volg. οὐ μά. Mox Μαρα-
7. Πλαταιαῖς] Πλαταιαις Σ.   9. ὁμοίως ἡ
11. αὐτῶν] αὐτοὺς Σ.   13. ἔνειμεν] Sic
17. τὸν] Om. Aℓ et B. et S., falso de codice Σ
20. ἐπεὶ] Sic Σ:

2. τουδί. Ctesiphon: vid. ad Ae. in
Ctes. § 24, p. 57.

§ 263. *You were not wrong, by all the
brave departed.*

6. Μαραθῶνι. 'At Marathon,' distinguished from ἐν Πλαταιαῖς, ἐν Σαλαμῖνι:
Marathon was but a demus, each of the
others included a territory. Strictly the
battle was not fought 'in the streets of
Plataea,' still less the sea-fight 'in Salamis;'
only within their bounds.

προκινδυνεύσαντας. So in Demosthenes' favourite author, Thucydides (1.73),
who also is speaking of Marathon.

7. παραταξαμένους. 'Who stood in
the line:' at Marathon, they met danger
before others were ready, at Plataea they
distinguished themselves among many confederates. Perhaps Demosthenes means to
refer here to discipline, as he referred before
to courage: the Athenians were at their
posts, while most of the army was out of
the way till after the battle was over.

§ 264. *Whom the city honours alike,*

whether they died in victory or defeat.

12. τῇ τυχῇ κ.τ.λ. 'Of fortune, they
had what it pleased Providence to send.'
δαίμων and τὸ δαιμόνιον are used especially
in this sense of 'Providence,' supernatural
power as the disposer of fortune.

§ 265. *And therefore their honour is no
reason why you should refuse to honour me,
who acted in the spirit of your history.*

14. γραμματοκύφων refers to Aeschines'
occupation as usher, not his occupation as
clerk: consequently one cannot translate
'quill-driver.' The sneer is hardly appropriate against a soldier who had distinguished
himself personally in three campaigns.

17. τριταγωνιστά. The point is, that a
man who had never risen above the *tertiae
partes* of the drama, could not criticise the
primae partes, πρωτεῖα, of history.

§ 266. *In that spirit my cause ought to
be tried.*

20. ἐπεὶ οὐδ'. The reading before Reiske
was ἔπειτ' οὐδ'. οὐδ' ὑμᾶς, you, no more
than your advisers.

Ἀθηναῖοι ἀπὸ τῆς αὐτῆς διανοίας δεῖ τάς τε ἰδίας δίκας καὶ
τὰς δημοσίας κρίνειν, ἀλλὰ τὰ μὲν τοῦ καθ᾽ ἡμέραν βίου συμβόλαια ἐπὶ τῶν ἰδίων νόμων καὶ ἔργων σκοποῦντας, τὰς δὲ
κοινὰς προαιρέσεις εἰς τὰ τῶν προγόνων ἀξιώματα ἀποβλέ-
ποντας. καὶ παραλαμβάνειν γε ἅμα τῇ βακτηρίᾳ καὶ τῷ συμ- 5
βόλῳ τὸ φρόνημα τὸ τῆς πόλεως νομίζειν ἕκαστον ὑμῶν δεῖ,
ὅταν τὰ δημόσια εἰσίητε κρινοῦντες, εἴπερ ἄξια ἐκείνων πράττειν οἴεσθε χρῆναι.
267   Ἀλλὰ γὰρ ἐμπεσὼν εἰς τὰ πεπραγμένα τοῖς προγόνοις
ὑμῶν ἔστιν ἃ τῶν ψηφισμάτων παρέβην καὶ τῶν πραχθέντων. 10
ἐπανελθεῖν οὖν, ὁπόθεν εἰς ταῦτ᾽ ἐξέβην, βούλομαι.

Ὡς γὰρ ἀφικόμεθ᾽ εἰς τὰς Θήβας, κατελαμβάνομεν Φιλίππου
καὶ Θετταλῶν καὶ τῶν ἄλλων συμμάχων παρόντας πρέσβεις,
καὶ τοὺς μὲν ἡμετέρους φίλους ἐν φόβῳ, τοὺς δ᾽ ἐκείνου θρασεῖς.
ὅτι δ᾽ οὐ νῦν ταῦτα λέγω τοῦ συμφέροντος ἕνεκα ἐμαυτῷ, 15
λέγε μοι τὴν ἐπιστολὴν ἣν τότ᾽ ἐπέμψαμεν εὐθὺς οἱ πρέσβεις.
268 καίτοι τοσαύτῃ γ᾽ ὑπερβολῇ συκοφαντίας οὗτος κέχρηται ὥστ᾽,
εἰ μέν τι τῶν δεόντων ἐπράχθη, τὸν καιρόν, οὐκ ἐμέ φησιν
αἴτιον γεγενῆσθαι, τῶν δ᾽ ὡς ἑτέρως συμβάντων ἁπάντων ἐμὲ
καὶ τὴν ἐμὴν τύχην αἰτίαν εἶναι. καὶ ὡς ἔοικεν, ὁ σύμβουλος 20
καὶ ῥήτωρ ἐγὼ τῶν μὲν ἐκ λόγου καὶ τοῦ βουλεύσασθαι πραχθέντων οὐδενὸς αὐτῷ συναίτιος εἶναι δοκῶ, τῶν δ᾽ ἐν τοῖς ὅπλοις καὶ κατὰ τὴν στρατηγίαν ἀτυχηθέντων μόνος αἴτιος εἶναι.
πῶς ἂν ὠμότερος συκοφάντης γένοιτ᾽ ἢ καταρατότερος; λέγε
τὴν ἐπιστολήν. 25

11. εἰς ταῦτ᾽] ἐνταῦθ᾽ Σ (volg. est in γρ.) B. et S.   12. κατελαμβάνομεν] καταλαμβάνομεν FΥΦΩ et al.   22. οὐδενὸς] οὐδὲν Σ B. et S.   24. γένοιτ᾽ ἢ
καταρατότερος] Ita ΣA et socii: ceteri plerique γένοιτ᾽ ἂν ἢ καταρατότερος τούτου.

3. τῶν ἰδίων νόμων is taken by Reiske
and Dissen as 'laws affecting private persons,' which would answer very well to ἰδίας
δίκας. If so, the antithesis will be an example of chiasmus, τά .. συμβόλαια will be
opposed to τά .. ἀξιώματα, and ἰδίων νόμων
καὶ ἔργων to κοινὰς προαιρέσεις. It would
be possible also to translate τῶν ἰδίων νόμων
καὶ ἔργων, 'your own laws and experience'
(viz. those of the existing generation), as
opposed to τὰ τῶν προγόνων ἀξιώματα.

§ 267. But I must not forget recent details in this retrospect: our embassy at Thebes
was difficult.

12. κατελαμβάνομεν. Several MSS. give
καταλαμβάνομεν.

15. ὅτι δ᾽ οὐ .. πρέσβεις. The point of
this is an appeal, not from an interested to
a disinterested statement, but from a single
statement made when it could not be checked,

to a joint statement made when it could.
Cp. the argument below, §§ 284, 285.

§ 268. Aeschines has no right to say circumstances made it easy.

17. καίτοι .. ἐπιστολήν. As the course
of the argument is interrupted by the call
for the letter, there is no need to curtail the
virulent apostrophe to Aeschines: cp. sup.,
ad § 231. Here λέγε τὴν ἐπιστολὴν
comes in at the end of the personal attack
as a sort of violent effort of the orator to
calm himself.

18. τὸν καιρόν: cp. Aesch. in Ctes.
§ 141 sqq.

20. ὁ σύμβουλος .. ἐγώ. 'An orator
and statesman when his name is Demosthenes.'

22. συναίτιος. Not to have even 'a
share of the credit:' opposed to μόνος
αἴτιος.

ΕΠΙΣΤΟΛΗ.

Ἐπειδὴ τοίνυν ἐποιήσαντο τὴν ἐκκλησίαν, προσῆγον ἐκείνους 269 προτέρους διὰ τὸ τὴν τῶν συμμάχων τάξιν ἐκείνους ἔχειν. καὶ παρελθόντες ἐδημηγόρουν πολλὰ μὲν Φίλιππον ἐγκωμιάζοντες, 5 πολλὰ δ' ὑμῶν κατηγοροῦντες, πάνθ' ὅσα πώποτ' ἐναντία ἐπράξατε Θηβαίοις ἀναμιμνήσκοντες. τὸ δ' οὖν κεφάλαιον, 270 ἠξίουν ὧν μὲν εὖ πεπόνθεσαν ὑπὸ Φιλίππου χάριν αὐτοὺς ἀποδοῦναι, ὧν δ' ὑφ' ὑμῶν ἠδίκηντο δίκην λαβεῖν, ὁποτέρως βούλονται, ἢ διέντας αὐτοὺς ἐφ' ὑμᾶς ἢ συνεμβαλόντας εἰς τὴν 10 Ἀττικὴν, καὶ ἐδείκνυσαν, ὡς ᾤοντο, ἐκ μὲν ὧν αὐτοὶ συνεβούλευον τὰ ἐκ τῆς Ἀττικῆς βοσκήματα καὶ ἀνδράποδα καὶ τἆλλ' ἀγαθὰ εἰς τὴν Βοιωτίαν ἥξοντα, ἐκ δὲ ὧν ἡμᾶς ἐρεῖν ἔφασαν τὰ ἐν τῇ Βοιωτίᾳ διαρπασθησόμενα ὑπὸ τοῦ πολέμου. καὶ ἄλλα πολλὰ πρὸς τούτοις, εἰς ταὐτὰ δὲ πάντα συντείνοντ' 15 ἔλεγον. ἅ δ' ἡμεῖς πρὸς ταῦτα, τὰ μὲν καθ' ἕκαστα ἐγὼ μὲν 271 ἀντὶ παντὸς ἂν τιμησαίμην εἰπεῖν τοῦ βίου, ὑμᾶς δὲ δέδοικα, μὴ παρεληλυθότων τῶν καιρῶν, ὥσπερ ἂν εἰ κατακλυσμὸν γεγενῆσθαι τῶν πραγμάτων ἡγούμενοι, μάταιον ὄχλον τοὺς περὶ τούτων λόγους νομίσητε· ὅ τι δ' οὖν ἐπείσαμεν ἡμεῖς καὶ ἅ 20 ἡμῖν ἀπεκρίναντο, ἀκούσατε. Λέγε ταυτὶ λαβών.

ΑΠΟΚΡΙΣΙΣ ΘΗΒΑΙΩΝ.

Μετὰ ταῦτα τοίνυν ἐκάλουν ὑμᾶς καὶ μετεπέμποντο. ἐξῆτε, 272

---

5. πάνθ'] Sic ΣΑ et socii: volg. ἄπανθ. 7. πεπόνθεσαν] πεπόνθασιν Α et socii p. αὐτοὺς] αὐτοῖς F et al. Α et socii. 8. ὑμῶν] Al. ἡμῶν. Statim ἠδίκηντο Bekk. et post eum omnes. Ille credebat, hoc a pr. m. in Σ scriptum fuisse, qui sicut ceteri ἠδίκηνται habet. δίκην omiserat prima manus, mox additur 'a m. antiqua, sed erasum, ita tamen ut literas δι et ν agnoscere liceat' Dind. Nobis potius verbum in litura scriptum esse videbatur: et ται syllabam verbi idcirco 'literas paullo quam ceteras nigriores' habere, quia δίκην inter verba ponere conatus erat scriptor. 9. διέντας] Volgo διέντας. Mox pro ὑμᾶς ἡμᾶς habent ΦΑ et socii. 14. ταὐτὰ] ταυτα Σ, ταῦτα ΦΦΩ et al. 15. ἅ δ' ἡμεῖς πρὸς ταῦτα] Ita pr. Σ: ἃ δ' ἡμεῖς εἴπομεν πρὸς ταῦτα sic Σ, ἃ δ' ἡμεῖς πρὸς ταῦτα εἴπομεν Α et socii, ἃ δ' ἡμεῖς πρὸς ταῦτα ἀντείπομεν ΓΥΩ u: volgo ἃ δ' ἡμεῖς πρὸς ταῦτα ἀντείπομεν. 19. ἅ] Om. pr. Σ pr. et tert. Α. Omisso durior videtur locutio. 21. ΑΠΟΚΡΙΣΙΣ] ΑΠΟΚΡΙΣΕΙΣ Σ et al. 22. ἐξῆτε] Ita ΣΓΥΦ: volg. ἐξήειτε.

§ 269. *Philip's ambassadors were heard first,*
2. τὴν ἐκκλησίαν. '*The* assembly' which was to hear the ambassadors.
3. τῶν συμμάχων, i. e. 'They [of the two parties] were the party holding the position of allies.'
§ 270. *And made a plausible appeal to Theban selfishness.*
9. διέντας. If the Thebans adopted this alternative, they would still gain by the plunder of Attica, which would be sold cheap in Boeotia by the conquerors on their re-

turn. This plunder was quite a respectable political motive; in fact Isocrates in the Panegyricus proposes the plunder of Susa as the proper object of Panhellenic patriotism.
§ 271. *I will not repeat my arguments which convinced the Thebans, but they were convinced.*
19. ὅ τι .. ἐπείσαμεν. 'The result of our advice.'
ἅ .. ἀπεκρίναντο. 'The terms of their reply.'
§ 272. *They admitted you into their city, and trusted you with their wives and children.*

ἐβοηθεῖτε, ἵνα τἀν μέσῳ παραλείπω, οὕτως οἰκείως ὑμᾶς ἐδέχοντο ὥστ' ἔξω τῶν ὁπλιτῶν καὶ τῶν ἱππέων ὄντων εἰς τὰς οἰκίας καὶ τὸ ἄστυ δέχεσθαι τὴν στρατιὰν ἐπὶ παῖδας καὶ γυναῖκας καὶ τὰ τιμιώτατα. καίτοι τρία ἐν ἐκείνῃ τῇ ἡμέρᾳ πᾶσιν ἀνθρώποις ἔδειξαν ἐγκώμια Θηβαῖοι καθ' ὑμῶν τὰ κάλ- 5

273 λιστα, ἓν μὲν ἀνδρείας, ἕτερον δὲ δικαιοσύνης, τρίτον δὲ σωφροσύνης. καὶ γὰρ τὸν ἀγῶνα μεθ' ὑμῶν μᾶλλον ἢ πρὸς ὑμᾶς ἑλόμενοι ποιήσασθαι καὶ ἀμείνους εἶναι καὶ δικαιότερ' ἀξιοῦν ὑμᾶς ἔκριναν Φιλίππου· καὶ τὰ παρ' αὑτοῖς καὶ παρὰ πᾶσι δ' ἐν πλείστῃ φυλακῇ, παῖδας καὶ γυναῖκας, ἐφ' ὑμῖν ποιήσαντες 10

274 σωφροσύνης πίστιν περὶ ὑμῶν ἔχοντες ἔδειξαν. ἐν οἷς πᾶσιν, ἄνδρες Ἀθηναῖοι, κατά γ' ὑμᾶς ὀρθῶς ἐφάνησαν ἐγνωκότες. οὔτε γὰρ εἰς τὴν πόλιν εἰσελθόντος τοῦ στρατοπέδου οὐδεὶς οὐδὲν οὐδὲ ἀδίκως ὑμῖν ἐνεκάλεσεν· οὕτω σώφρονας παρέσχετε ὑμᾶς αὐτούς· δίς τε συμπαραταξάμενοι τὰς πρώτας μάχας, 15 τήν τ' ἐπὶ τοῦ ποταμοῦ καὶ τὴν χειμερινήν, οὐκ ἀμέμπτους μόνον ὑμᾶς αὐτούς, ἀλλὰ καὶ θαυμαστοὺς ἐδείξατε τῷ κόσμῳ, ταῖς παρασκευαῖς, τῇ προθυμίᾳ. ἐφ' οἷς παρὰ μὲν τῶν ἄλλων ὑμῖν ἐγίγνοντο ἔπαινοι, παρὰ δ' ὑμῶν θυσίαι καὶ πομπαὶ τοῖς θεοῖς.

275 καὶ ἔγωγε ἡδέως ἂν ἐροίμην Αἰσχίνην, ὅτε ταῦτ' ἐπράττετο 20

---

1. παραλείπω] παραλίπω nonnulli.   5. καθ'] περὶ A et socii.   6. ἀνδρείας] ἀνδρίας Σ, eraso ει ε.   9. αὐτοῖς καὶ παρὰ πᾶσι δ'] αὐτοῖς δὲ καὶ παρὰ πᾶσιν A et socii.   11. πᾶσιν] Ita ΣA et socii : volg. ἅπασιν.   13. τοῦ] Om. Σ. 14. παρέσχετε] Sic ΣA k : legebatur παρέσχεσθε.   15. μάχας] Om. Σ B. et S. 16. τήν τ'] τὴν ΕΥΩ et al.   20. ἐπράττετο] ἐπράττετε nonnulli.

---

2. ἔξω .. ὄντων. 'Although the men-at-arms and cavalry were not in the city, they received the army.' The main Theban force had gone to the front, and yet they admitted the main Athenian force into the city. The sentence is painfully ambiguous in Greek, still more so in English; but τὴν στρατιὰν can hardly be a synonym for ὁπλίτας and ἱππέας.

5. καθ' ὑμῶν. κατά is more frequently used of applying censure than praise : but cp. Ae. in Tim. p. 24, § 169, Phil. 2. p. 68, § 10.

τὰ κάλλιστα. As corresponding to three of the four conventional cardinal virtues. The fact that the Thebans chose to fight with Athens, not against her, is made to do double duty as a proof of her courage and the justice of her cause.

§ 273. *They judged you brave, just, temperate.*

§ 274. *This homage was justified by your discipline and courage, twice successfully displayed.*

12. κατά γ' ὑμᾶς ὀρθῶς. He does not venture to say that the Thebans' decision was not a mistake, only that they were not mistaken in Athens.

16. τὴν ἐπὶ τοῦ ποταμοῦ: cp. above, § 148. 'The battle on the river;' perhaps, though the district of the Cephissus was called Παραποταμία, it is hardly safe to translate after Reiske, 'the battle of Potamus.'

τὴν χειμερινήν. 'The winter battle' for 'the battle in the winter,' seems more possible than 'the stormy battle' for 'the battle in the storm,' which in itself is an odder designation for a battle than the other, though that is far from obvious or precise. But the chronological difficulties in finding room for a winter campaign between the occupation of Elatea and the battle of Chaeronea, are almost, if not quite, insuperable. If the word is corrupt, the corruption must be very old, for the MSS. are unanimous.

§ 275. *Did Aeschines regret its success?*
20. ἐπράττετο. Reiske conj. ἐπράττετε.

καὶ ζήλου καὶ χαρᾶς καὶ ἐπαίνων ἡ πόλις ἦν μεστή,
πότερον συνέθυε καὶ συνευφραίνετο τοῖς πολλοῖς, ἢ λυπούμενος
καὶ στένων καὶ δυσμεναίνων τοῖς κοινοῖς ἀγαθοῖς οἴκοι καθῆτο.
εἰ μὲν γὰρ παρῆν καὶ μετὰ τῶν ἄλλων ἐξητάζετο, πῶς οὐ 276
5 δεινὰ ποιεῖ, μᾶλλον δ' οὐδ' ὅσια, εἰ ὧν ὡς ἀρίστων αὐτὸς τοὺς
θεοὺς ἐποιήσατο μάρτυρας, ταῦθ' ὡς οὐκ ἄριστα νῦν ὑμᾶς ἀξιοῖ
ψηφίσασθαι τοὺς ὀμωμοκότας τοὺς θεούς; εἰ δὲ μὴ παρῆν,
πῶς οὐκ ἀπολωλέναι πολλάκις ἐστὶ δίκαιος, εἰ ἐφ' οἷς ἔχαιρον
οἱ ἄλλοι, ταῦτα ἐλυπεῖτο ὁρῶν; Λέγε δὴ καὶ ταῦτα τὰ ψη-
10 φίσματά μοι.

ΨΗΦΙΣΜΑΤΑ ΘΥΣΙΩΝ.

Οὐκοῦν ἡμεῖς μὲν ἐν θυσίαις ἦμεν τότε, Θηβαῖοι δ' ἐν τῷ 277
δι' ἡμᾶς σεσῶσθαι νομίζειν, καὶ περιειστήκει τοῖς βοηθείας δεή-
σεσθαι δοκοῦσιν ἀφ' ὧν ἔπραττον οὗτοι, αὐτοὺς βοηθεῖν ἑτέροις
15 ἐξ ὧν ἐπείσθητ' ἐμοί. ἀλλὰ μὴν οἵας τότ' ἠφίει φωνὰς ὁ
Φίλιππος καὶ ἐν οἵαις ἦν ταραχαῖς ἐπὶ τούτοις, ἐκ τῶν ἐπι-
στολῶν τῶν ἐκείνου μαθήσεσθε ὧν εἰς Πελοπόννησον ἔπεμπεν.
καί μοι λέγε ταύτας λαβών, ἵν' εἰδῆτε ἡ ἐμὴ συνέχεια καὶ
πλάνοι καὶ ταλαιπωρίαι καὶ τὰ πολλὰ ψηφίσματα, ἃ νῦν
20 οὗτος διέσυρε, τί ἀπειργάσατο.

Καίτοι πολλοὶ παρ' ὑμῖν, ἄνδρες Ἀθηναῖοι, γεγόνασι ῥή- 278
τορες ἔνδοξοι καὶ μεγάλοι πρὸ ἐμοῦ, Καλλίστρατος ἐκεῖνος,

---

1. ἡ πόλις ἦν] Ita ΣΑ et socii: ceteri ἦν ἡ πόλις.   2. τοῖς] Sic ΣΑ s eᵐ: ceteri
ἐπὶ τοῖς.   5. ἀρίστων] δρίστων ὄντων Α et socii: mox ἄξια pro ἄριστα iidem.
11. ΨΗΦΙΣΜΑΤΑ] ΨΗΦΙΣΜΑ Σ.   14. δοκοῦσιν] νομίζουσιν Σ Β. et S.
αὐτοὺς] αὐτοῖς ΓΥΦΩ et socii.   17. ἔπεμπεν] ἔπεμπον pr. Σ, ἔπεμπεν corr. id.:
volg. ἔπεμψεν.   18. Post εἰδῆτε ὅτι add. ΓΥΦΩ et socii et a m. tertia Σ.

---

§ 276. *If he shared your rejoicing, he cannot condemn the policy which produced it: if he did not he is a traitor.*
4. μετὰ τῶν ἄλλων ἐξητάζετο. 'Passed muster with the rest,' 'gave the same signs of patriotic joy.' Of course a man might honestly think an enterprise imprudent, be glad when it seemed succeeding, and denounce the imprudence when it failed.
§ 277. *Philip shewed signs of distress, thanks to my exertions, which Aeschines ridicules,*
12. ἐν .. νομίζειν. Rather a harsh and formal parallelism to ἐν θυσίαις.
18. ἡ ἐμὴ συνέχεια. 'My persistence,' 'my diligence.'
19. πλάνοι. Almost, 'my restlessness;' he is speaking of his journies to negotiate treaties of alliance.
20. διέσυρε. In a passage retrenched

from the speech as we have it: unless the reference of τὰ πολλὰ ψηφίσματα be to Demosthenes' general habit of drawing up long decrees, as described by Ae. in Ctes. § 67, not to 'the many decrees' proposed at this particular period. It is curious that Demosthenes does not speak of Philip's attempts to negotiate, mentioned by Aeschines (in Ctes. §§ 148 sqq.), which were an unmistakable proof of his uneasiness; nor does he justify, as he easily might, his own conduct in rejecting them. They are usually dated rather before this; if so, it was out of place to mention them here, and it might have been embarrassing to mention them in their proper place.
§ 278. *Unprecedented as they were,*
22. Καλλίστρατος. The great anti-Theban orator: his father was Callicrates, his demus Aphidnae.

Ἀριστοφῶν, Κέφαλος, Θρασύβουλος, ἕτεροι μυρίοι· ἀλλ' ὅμως
οὐδεὶς πώποτε τούτων διὰ παντὸς ἔδωκεν ἑαυτὸν εἰς οὐδὲν τῇ
πόλει, ἀλλ' ὁ μὲν γράφων οὐκ ἂν ἐπρέσβευσεν, ὁ δὲ πρεσβεύων
οὐκ ἂν ἔγραψεν. ὑπέλειπε γὰρ αὐτῶν ἕκαστος ἑαυτῷ ἅμα μὲν
279 ῥᾳστώνην, ἅμα δ', εἴ τι γένοιτ', ἀναφοράν. τί οὖν; εἴποι τις 5
ἂν, σὺ τοσοῦτον ὑπερῆρας τοὺς ἄλλους ῥώμῃ καὶ τόλμῃ ὥστε
πάντα ποιεῖν αὐτός; οὐ ταῦτα λέγω, ἀλλ' οὕτως ἐπεπείσμην
μέγαν εἶναι τὸν κατειληφότα κίνδυνον τὴν πόλιν ὥστ' οὐκ
ἐδόκει μοι χώραν οὐδὲ πρόνοιαν οὐδεμίαν τῆς ἰδίας ἀσφαλείας
διδόναι, ἀλλ' ἀγαπητὸν εἶναι, εἰ μηδὲν παραλείπων τις ἃ δεῖ 10
280 πράξειεν. ἐπεπείσμην δ' ὑπὲρ ἐμαυτοῦ, τυχὸν μὲν ἀναισθητῶν,
ὅμως δ' ἐπεπείσμην, μήτε γράφοντ' ἂν ἐμοῦ γράψαι βέλτιον
μηδένα, μήτε πράττοντα πρᾶξαι, μήτε πρεσβεύοντα πρεσβεῦσαι
προθυμότερον μηδὲ δικαιότερον. διὰ ταῦτα ἐν πᾶσιν ἐμαυτὸν
ἔταττον. Λέγε τὰς ἐπιστολὰς τὰς τοῦ Φιλίππου. 15

ΕΠΙΣΤΟΛΑΙ.

281 Εἰς ταῦτα κατέστησε Φίλιππον ἡ ἐμὴ πολιτεία, Αἰ-
σχίνη· ταύτην τὴν φωνὴν ἐκεῖνος ἀφῆκε, πολλοὺς καὶ θρασεῖς
τὰ πρὸ τούτων τῇ πόλει ἐπαιρόμενος λόγους. ἀνθ' ὧν δικαίως

---

2. πώποτε τούτων] τούτων πώποτε ΓΥΦΩ et socii.   4. ὑπέλειπε] Sic Σ: legebatur ὑπελείπετο.   5. γένοιτ'] Sic Σ s, γένοιτο Α, ceteri γίγνοιτο.   6. τοὺς
ἄλλους] Om. Σ, post τολμῇ ponunt ΓΥΦΩ et socii : quod parum abest quin propter sym-
metriam malim, et respondentian ad vocem αὐτούς.   7. ταῦτα λέγω] Sic Σ, ceteri
λέγω ταῦτα.   9. χώραν] ὥραν Α et socii, unde ὥραν Schæfer. Dissen. ὁρᾶν γρ. ΣΦ.
10. παραλείπων] παραλιπὼν ΥΑ et socii.   11. ἀναισθητῶν] Ita solus ω: ceteri
ἀναίσθητον.   14. μηδὲ] Sic Σ p: ceteri μήτε.   πᾶσιν] Sic Σ s: legebatur
ἅπασιν.   15. τὰς τοῦ] Sic ΣΑ et socii : ceteri om.   18. Post ἀφῆκε δι'
ἐμὲ add. omnes praeter Σ.

---

1. Ἀριστοφῶν : cp. ad § 85.
Κέφαλος: cp. ad Aesch. in Ctes. §
195.
Θρασύβουλος : cp. ib. 138.
5. ῥᾳστώνην. 'Some repose at the moment.'
ἀναφοράν. 'Some chance of shifting
the blame.' Cp. Aesch. de F. L. p. 41,
§ 110; also below, § 283, ἀνενεγκεῖν.
§ 279. Not as a display of unprecedented
power, but as called out by unprecedented
danger,
7. οὕτως ἐπεπείσμην. 'I was so
thoroughly persuaded of the greatness of
the danger.' Dissen joins οὕτως with μέγαν.
9. ἐδόκει μοι with διδόναι means, 'I
determined,' with εἶναι, 'I thought;' so
that there is a slight zeugma in the construction, though with both it might be trans-

lated, 'I made up my mind.'
χώραν. The vulgate will mean, 'to
give myself no room to escape, not to waste
a thought on safety.' This is more forcible
than Schæfer and Dissen's reading, 'no care
nor forethought;' though of course ὥραν
goes smoothly with πρόνοιαν, and might
have got altered as an unfamiliar word.
§ 280. Which I felt none could meet
better.
13. πράττοντα. Almost a technical
word for public action, as 'execute' with us:
cp. Xen. Mem. I. 2. 15; 2. 4. 4. It is also
specifically used of negotiations, of a kind to
be discreditable to at least one party, what
were called in Old English 'practices.'
§ 281. I alarmed Philip: I deserved a
crown, which I received without opposition
from Aeschines.

ἐστεφανούμην ὑπὸ τουτωνί, καὶ σὺ παρὼν οὐκ ἀντέλεγες, ὁ δὲ
γραψάμενος Διώνδας τὸ μέρος τῶν ψήφων οὐκ ἔλαβεν. Καί
μοι λέγε ταῦτα τὰ ψηφίσματα τὰ τότε μὲν ἀποπεφευγότα,
ὑπὸ τούτου δ' οὐδὲ γραφέντα.

5 ΨΗΦΙΣΜΑΤΑ.

Ταυτὶ τὰ ψηφίσματ', ἄνδρες Ἀθηναῖοι, τὰς αὐτὰς συλλα- 282
βὰς καὶ ταὐτὰ ῥήματ' ἔχει ἅπερ πρότερον μὲν Ἀριστόνικος,
νῦν δὲ Κτησιφῶν γέγραφεν οὑτοσί. καὶ ταῦτ' Αἰσχίνης οὔτ'
ἐδίωξεν αὐτὸς οὔτε τῷ γραψαμένῳ συγκατηγόρησεν. καίτοι
10 τότε τὸν Δημομέλη τὸν ταῦτα γράφοντα καὶ τὸν Ὑπερείδην,
εἴπερ ἀληθῆ μου νῦν κατηγορεῖ, μᾶλλον ἂν εἰκότως ἢ τόνδ'
ἐδίωκεν. διὰ τί; ὅτι τῷ μὲν ἔστ' ἀνενεγκεῖν ἐπ' ἐκείνους 283
καὶ τὰς τῶν δικαστηρίων γνώσεις καὶ τὸ τοῦτον αὐτὸν ἐκείνων
μὴ κατηγορηκέναι ταὐτὰ γραψάντων ἅπερ οὗτος νῦν, καὶ τὸ
15 τοὺς νόμους μηκέτ' ἐᾶν περὶ τῶν οὕτω πραχθέντων κατηγορεῖν,
καὶ πολλὰ ἕτερα· τότε δ' αὐτὸ τὸ πρᾶγμ' ἂν ἐκρίνετο ἐφ'
αὑτοῦ, πρίν τι τούτων προλαβεῖν. ἀλλ' οὐκ ἦν, οἶμαι, τότε, 284
ὃ νυνὶ ποιεῖ, ἐκ παλαιῶν χρόνων καὶ ψηφισμάτων πολλῶν
ἐκλέξαντα, ἃ μήτε προῄδει μηδεὶς μήτ' ἂν ᾠήθη τήμερον ῥη-
20 θῆναι, διαβάλλειν, καὶ μετενεγκόντα τοὺς χρόνους καὶ προ-

---

2. τὸ μέρος] Ita Σ: volgo τὸ πέμπτον μέρος.   3. λέγε] λάβε Σ B. et S.
τὰ τότε μὲν] Om. pr. Σ.   'Fort. ψηφίσματα τὰ ἀποπεφευγότα' Saupp.   10. Δημο-
μέλη] Ita libri optimi: -λην Dind.   12. διὰ τί; ὅτι τῷ μὲν] τούτῳ μὲν γὰρ A k.
14. νῦν] Ita ΣA et socii B. et S.: ceteri et Dind. νῦν.   18. δ] Ita ΣA et socii:
ceteri ἅ.   Mox ποιεῖν Σ B. et S.

I. οὐκ ἀντέλεγες. These words are introduced to confirm δικαίως, though Demosthenes was probably still ambassador and
already treasurer, so that this decree would
be open to the same technical objection as
Ctesiphon's.
§ 282. Yet the decree then acquitted is
identical with that which he prosecutes now.
9. συγκατηγόρησεν. 'Did not put his
name to the indictment' (Latin subscribere),
'or speak as συνήγορος on the trial.' Cp.
Aesch. in Ctes. § 200.
10. τὸν Δημομέλη .. τὸν Ὑπερείδην.
Each had moved one decree. ταῦτα in the
plural refers to the details of the decree of
Demomeles. Was this Demosthenes' cousin,
with whom Demosthenes had had the questionable quarrel talked of by Aeschines?
§ 283. True, Ctesiphon is protected by
precedent,
12. ἀνενεγκεῖν: cp. sup. ad § 279.
'Throw the responsibility on them, on the
decisions of the courts, on the very silence

of Aeschines, who never prosecuted the
authors of decrees identical with this.' Cp.
Aesch. in Ctes. § 194.
§ 284. But Aeschines can misrepresent
facts now.
18. παλαιῶν χρόνων. The time of the
battle of Chaeronea would be παλαιὸς when
Demosthenes was speaking.
19. προῄδει. From the terms of the
indictment; ἂν ᾠήθη, from its matter. The
reference is partly to the decrees moved to
facilitate the peace of Philocrates (Aesch. in
Ctes. § 60), partly to the decrees connected
with the Theban alliance selected for invidious comment. Ibid. § 142 sqq.
20. μετενεγκόντα τοὺς χρόνους: cp.
Aesch. in Ctes. § 140, πρὶν περὶ συμμαχίας μίαν μόνην συλλαβὴν γράψαι Δημοσθένη.
προφάσεις .. μεταθέντα. As in the
motives he imputes to Demosthenes' conduct
in the matter of the peace of Philocrates, of
Euboea, and of Amphissa.

φάσεις ἀντὶ τῶν ἀληθῶν ψευδεῖς μεταθέντα τοῖς πεπραγμένοις
285 δοκεῖν τι λέγειν. οὐκ ἦν τότε ταῦτα, ἀλλ᾽ ἐπὶ τῆς ἀληθείας,
ἐγγὺς τῶν ἔργων, ἔτι μεμνημένων ὑμῶν καὶ μόνον οὐκ ἐν ταῖς
χερσὶν ἕκαστα ἐχόντων, πάντες ἐγίγνοντ᾽ ἂν οἱ λόγοι. διόπερ
τοὺς παρ᾽ αὐτὰ τὰ πράγματ᾽ ἐλέγχους φυγὼν νῦν ἥκει, ῥητό- 5
ρων ἀγῶνα νομίζων, ὡς γ᾽ ἐμοὶ δοκεῖ, καὶ οὐχὶ τῶν πεπολιτευμένων ἐξέτασιν ποιήσειν ὑμᾶς, καὶ λόγου κρίσιν, οὐχὶ τοῦ τῇ
πόλει συμφέροντος ἔσεσθαι.
286 Εἶτα σοφίζεται, καὶ φησὶ προσήκειν, ἧς μὲν οἴκοθεν ἥκετ᾽
ἔχοντες δόξης περὶ ἡμῶν ἀμελῆσαι, ὥσπερ δ᾽, ὅταν οἰόμενοι 10
περιεῖναι χρήματά τῳ λογίζησθε, ἂν καθαιρῶσιν αἱ ψῆφοι
καὶ μηδὲν περιῇ, συγχωρεῖτε, οὕτω καὶ νῦν τοῖς ἐκ τοῦ λόγου
287 φαινομένοις προσθέσθαι. θεάσασθε τοίνυν ὡς σαθρόν, ὡς ἔοικεν,
ἔστι φύσει πᾶν ὅ τι ἂν μὴ δικαίως ᾖ πεπραγμένον. ἐκ γὰρ
αὐτοῦ τοῦ σοφοῦ τούτου παραδείγματος ὡμολόγηκε νῦν γ᾽ ἡμᾶς 15
ὑπάρχειν ἐγνωσμένους ἐμὲ μὲν λέγειν ὑπὲρ τῆς πατρίδος, αὐτὸν
δ᾽ ὑπὲρ Φιλίππου· οὐ γὰρ ἂν μεταπείθειν ὑμᾶς ἐζήτει μὴ
288 τοιαύτης οὔσης τῆς ὑπαρχούσης ὑπολήψεως περὶ ἑκατέρου. καὶ
μὴν ὅτι γε οὐ δίκαια λέγει μεταθέσθαι ταύτην τὴν δόξαν

---

2. δοκεῖν] δοκεῖ͛ Σ.   ἐπὶ τῆς] Ita ΣA et socii et γρ. Φ, ἐπ᾽ αὐτῆς FΦΩ, volg. ἐπ᾽
αὐτῆς τῆς.   3. Post ἐγγὺς οὔσης add. ΓΥΦΩ et socii.   5. Post νῦν ὕστερον
add. iidem.   6. γ᾽] Om. A et socii.   7. Post ὑμᾶς ὑπολαμβάνων addebatur :
om. ΣA et socii.   οὐχὶ] Sic Σ : volg. οὐ.   11. καθαιρῶσιν] Ita pr. Σ B. et
S.: volgo καθαραὶ ὦσιν. Vid. annot.   15. νῦν γ᾽] Sic Σ, νῦν Ω u, om. A et socii :
legebatur νυνί.   19. τὴν] Om. Σ.

§ 285. *He chooses to bring forward his
accusations when they cannot be tested.*

5. ῥητόρων ἔσεσθαι. 'Thinking, I
must suppose, you will hold a tournament
of oratory, not a review of our policy, and
that the decision will turn upon eloquence,
not the interest of the state.'

§ 286. *Then he pretends you are to judge
by the speeches of a day, not by your lifelong
knowledge of us both :*

9. σοφίζεται. 'Makes a display of
ingenuity ;' as in the next section τοῦ
σοφοῦ παραδείγματος, 'this clever illustration,' the contemptuous or ironical use of
σοφὸς that leads to the ordinary sense of
σοφίζομαι and σοφιστής. See Ae. in Ct.
§ 59.

10. οἰόμενοι .. λογίζησθε. Westermann's
theory, that these words refer to Lycurgus,
who was expected to have a balance after
his five years' administration, is quite unsupported by the parallel passage in Aeschines : but his construction, taking τῳ
with περιεῖναι χρήματα, is certainly better
than Dissen's, who joins it with λογίζησθε,

for fear of making the other words too emphatic.

11. καθαιρῶσιν. It might be taken,
'If they prove this point,' the sense of
καθαιρεῖν being 'to convict,' like the
simple αἱρεῖν, as in Soph. Ant. 384.
Perhaps it is more like Demosthenes to
make καθαιρῶσιν correlative to καὶ μηδὲν
περιῇ, 'If the figures (the several items)
exhaust (the sum-total), and there is no
remainder.' The common reading, καθαραὶ
ὦσιν, would mean simply 'come out even.'

§ 287. *Confessing thereby, that this test
condemns him.*

15. ἡμᾶς .. ἐγνωσμένους. This reading
is now received from Σ by Dindorf, as well
as B. and S. Baiter refers to his own note
on Lyc. in Leocr. p. 125, § 82, for evidence
that ἐγνωσμένος is always strictly passive.
If we retained the old reading ὑμᾶς, we
should have to give ἐγνωσμένους a semi-
active meaning, like 'decided,' 'that your
minds were already made up.'

§§ 288, 289. *Naturally : I gained Thebes,
and Euboea and the Hellespont,*

ἀξιῶν, ἐγὼ διδάξω ῥᾳδίως, οὐ τιθεὶς ψήφους (οὐ γάρ ἐστιν ὁ
τῶν πραγμάτων οὗτος λογισμός), ἀλλ' ἀναμιμνήσκων ἕκαστα
ἐν βραχέσι, λογισταῖς ἅμα καὶ μάρτυσι τοῖς ἀκούουσιν ὑμῖν
χρώμενος. ἡ γὰρ ἐμὴ πολιτεία, ἧς οὗτος κατηγορεῖ, ἀντὶ μὲν
5 τοῦ Θηβαίους μετὰ Φιλίππου συνεμβαλεῖν εἰς τὴν χώραν, ὃ 289
πάντες ᾤοντο, μεθ' ἡμῶν παραταξαμένους ἐκεῖνον κωλύειν ἐποίησεν, ἀντὶ δὲ τοῦ ἐν τῇ Ἀττικῇ τὸν πόλεμον εἶναι ἑπτακόσια
στάδια ἀπὸ τῆς πόλεως ἐπὶ τοῖς Βοιωτῶν ὁρίοις γενέσθαι,
ἀντὶ δὲ τοῦ τοὺς λῃστὰς ἡμᾶς φέρειν καὶ ἄγειν ἐκ τῆς Εὐβοίας
10 ἐν εἰρήνῃ τὴν Ἀττικὴν ἐκ θαλάττης εἶναι πάντα τὸν πόλεμον,
ἀντὶ δὲ τοῦ τὸν Ἑλλήσποντον ἔχειν Φίλιππον, λαβόντα Βυζάντιον, συμπολεμεῖν τοὺς Βυζαντίους μεθ' ἡμῶν πρὸς ἐκεῖνον.
ἆρά σοι ψήφοις ὅμοιος ὁ τῶν ἔργων λογισμὸς φαίνεται ; ἢ 290
δεῖν ἀντανελεῖν ταῦτα, ἀλλ' οὐχ ὅπως τὸν ἅπαντα χρόνον μνη-
15 μονευθήσεται σκέψασθαι ; καὶ οὐκέτι προστίθημι ὅτι τῆς μὲν
ὠμότητος, ἣν ἐν οἷς καθάπαξ τινῶν κύριος κατέστη Φίλιππος
ἔστιν ἰδεῖν, ἑτέροις πειραθῆναι συνέβη, τῆς δὲ φιλανθρωπίας,
ἣν τὰ λοιπὰ τῶν πραγμάτων ἐκεῖνος περιβαλλόμενος ἐπλάττετο, ὑμεῖς καλῶς ποιοῦντες τοὺς καρποὺς κεκόμισθε. ἀλλ'
20 ἐῶ ταῦτα.

Καὶ μὴν οὐδὲ τοῦτ' εἰπεῖν ὀκνήσω, ὅτι ὁ τὸν ῥήτορα βου- 291
λόμενος δικαίως ἐξετάζειν καὶ μὴ συκοφαντεῖν, οὐκ ἂν οἷα σὺ νῦν

---

1. Post ἀξιῶν volg. et Bekk. add. ὑμᾶς.　Om. ΣΑ et socii.　6. Post ᾤοντο
ἔσεσθαι add. ΓΥΦΩ et socii omnes et Bekk.　παραταξαμένους] συμπαραταξαμένους
Α et socii.　12. Post ἐκεῖνον ἐποίησεν add. Α et socii.　16. κύριος κατέστη]
κατέστη κύριος k Dion.　18. Post περιβαλλόμενος volgo et Bekk. add. πρὸς ὑμᾶς:
om. Σ.　21. τοῦτ'] ταῦτ' ΣΦ.

1. οὐ γάρ ἐστιν κ.τ.λ.　'For the calculation of state affairs is not simply arith-
metical,' anticipating the point afterwards
worked out in § 290 init.
3. λογισταῖς ἅμα καὶ μάρτυσι.　'With
you who hear me, for me vouchers and
auditors both,' to testify to the facts and
decide the result.　Perhaps there is the
same point as in § 142, 'I am not afraid of
submitting to the strictest legitimate εὔθυναι.'
§ 290. To say nothing of making Philip
respect us in defeat. Are these mere items
in an overdrawn account?
13. ἆρά σοι .. φαίνεται.　'Are deeds to
be reckoned like counters, and cancelled as
lightly? are they not to be remembered for
ever?'　'You are not,' says Demosthenes,
'to ignore services done to the state, even
when counterbalanced by misfortune or treason.　Statesmanship is not merely a matter
of profit and loss, where, if the loss be

greater than the profit, the profit counts for
nothing.'　Vid. ad Ae. in Ct. § 59, for the
question of the relevancy of this reply.
15. οὐκέτι.　'After this, I have no need
to add ...'
16. ἣν .. ἐπλάττετο.　'Which he feigned,
as a means of compassing what remained of
supremacy,' viz. the being acknowledged as
chief of Greece by a nominally free election.
It might be just possible to translate ἣν ..
περιβαλλόμενος ἐπλάττετο, 'which he
fashioned as a cloak for the rest he had to
do.'
19. καλῶς ποιοῦντες.　Often, as in Ae.
in Ct. § 233, a mere expletive of good
omen, 'and good luck to you with it !' here
more gravely, 'and very rightly ;' almost,
'and it does you honour.'
§§ 291, 292. Nay, these are the tests of
statesmanship ; not your paltry etiquette.
But I must apply them, as you did not.

ἔλεγες, τοιαῦτα κατηγόρει, παραδείγματα πλάττων καὶ ῥήματα καὶ
σχήματα μιμούμενος (πάνυ γὰρ παρὰ τοῦτο, οὐχ ὁρᾷς; γέγονε
τὰ τῶν Ἑλλήνων, εἰ τουτὶ τὸ ῥῆμα, ἀλλὰ μὴ τουτὶ διελέχθην
292 ἐγώ, ἢ δευρὶ τὴν χεῖρα, ἀλλὰ μὴ δευρὶ παρήνεγκα), ἀλλ᾽ ἐπ᾽
αὐτῶν τῶν ἔργων ἂν ἐσκόπει τίνας εἶχεν ἀφορμὰς ἡ πόλις καὶ 5
τίνας δυνάμεις, ὅτ᾽ εἰς τὰ πράγματ᾽ εἰσήειν, καὶ τίνας συνήγαγον αὐτῇ μετὰ ταῦτ᾽ ἐπιστὰς ἐγώ, καὶ πῶς εἶχε τὰ τῶν
ἐναντίων. εἶτ᾽ εἰ μὲν ἐλάττους ἐποίησα τὰς δυνάμεις, παρ᾽
ἐμοὶ τἀδίκημ᾽ ἂν ἐδείκνυεν ὄν, εἰ δὲ πολλῷ μείζους, οὐκ ἂν
ἐσυκοφάντει. ἐπειδὴ δὲ σὺ τοῦτο πέφευγας, ἐγὼ ποιήσω· καὶ 10
σκοπεῖτε εἰ δικαίως χρήσομαι τῷ λόγῳ.
293 Δύναμιν μὲν τοίνυν εἶχεν ἡ πόλις τοὺς νησιώτας, οὐχ ἅπαντας,
ἀλλὰ τοὺς ἀσθενεστάτους· οὔτε γὰρ Χίος οὔτε Ῥόδος οὔτε
Κέρκυρα μεθ᾽ ἡμῶν ἦν· χρημάτων δὲ σύνταξιν εἰς πέντε καὶ
τετταράκοντα τάλαντα, καὶ ταῦτ᾽ ἦν προεξειλεγμένα· ὁπλίτην 15
δ᾽ ἢ ἱππέα πλὴν τῶν οἰκείων οὐδένα. ὃ δὲ πάντων καὶ φοβερώ-
τατον καὶ μάλισθ᾽ ὑπὲρ τῶν ἐχθρῶν, οὗτοι παρεσκευάκεισαν
τοὺς περιχώρους πάντας ἔχθρας ἢ φιλίας ἐγγυτέρω, Μεγαρέας,
294 Θηβαίους, Εὐβοέας. τὰ μὲν τῆς πόλεως οὕτως ὑπῆρχεν ἔχοντα,
καὶ οὐδεὶς ἂν ἔχοι παρὰ ταῦτ᾽ εἰπεῖν ἄλλο οὐδέν· τὰ δὲ τοῦ 20

---

3. Post Ἑλλήνων addebatur πράγματα : om. ΣΑ et socii. 6. εἰσήειν] εἰσήει ΓΥ
et al. 11. δικαίως] δικαίῳ Dobr. 16. ἢ] Om. ΣΦΩ et al. B. et S., laudato
Bernhardy, Synt. Gr. p. 448, nimis tamen id durum videtur. 19. τὰ μὲν] καὶ τὰ μὲν
A et socii.

---

1. παραδείγματα πλάττων κ.τ.λ.
'Making up models (of what I had done, or
ought to do), and imitating phrases and
gestures.' Perhaps παραδείγματα refers to
his putting words into Demosthenes' mouth,
as in §§ 210, 212: ῥήματα .. μιμούμενος,
to verbal criticisms like §§ 72, 166. Of
course the imitation of gestures does not
appear in the written speech, but § 167
would suggest it, and in § 212 we have
clearly an imitation of voice. For Aeschines'
proneness to lay stress on such matters, cp.
D. de F. L. p. 420, § 281 sqq.
2. οὐχ ὁρᾷς. Pointing an irony just like
videlicet in Latin, or 'you see' in English:
so below, § 330.
4. ἐπ᾽ αὐτῶν τῶν ἔργων. The preposition has the same force as in § 266.
5. ἀφορμὰς .. δυνάμεις. Supplementary
rather than synonymous, 'opportunities and
resources.'
8. εἶτ᾽. 'If he had done so,' had adopted
this test, then he would either have accused
me justly, or found no materials for accusing
me at all.

§ 293. Our resources as I found them
were the minor islands : the more powerful
were alienated, our nearer neighbours hostile.
13. οὔτε γὰρ Χίος κ.τ.λ. Having revolted from the confederacy in B.C. 358.
Cp. ad Ae. in Ct. § 42.
15. προεξειλεγμένα. 'Raised in advance,'
the reverse of 'in arrear:' the confederacy
was in debt to its members. ἐκλέγειν is
the technical word for raising a tax, e.g.
Thuc. 8. 44 fin. : also παρεκλέγειν, of
'embezzling' (raising for by-ends), D. de
F. L. p. 435, § 336.
17. παρεσκευάκεισαν. By their appeals
to Athenian selfishness.
§ 294. Philip had full control over his
resources, was rich enough to carry out his
designs, absolute enough to keep his se-
crets,
20. παρὰ ταῦτ᾽. One can hardly say
whether 'besides these' or 'against this' is
the more accurate translation : such passages
shew how the first meaning leads to the
second.

Φιλίππου, πρὸς ὃν ἦν ἡμῖν ὁ ἀγών, σκέψασθε πῶς. πρῶτον
μὲν ἦρχε τῶν ἀκολουθούντων αὐτὸς αὐτοκράτωρ, ὃ τῶν εἰς τὸν
πόλεμον μέγιστόν ἐστιν ἁπάντων· εἶθ' οὗτοι τὰ ὅπλα εἶχον
ἐν ταῖς χερσὶν ἀεί· ἔπειτα χρημάτων ηὐπόρει, καὶ ἔπραττεν
5 ἃ δόξειεν αὐτῷ, οὐ προλέγων ἐν τοῖς ψηφίσμασιν, οὐδ' ἐν τῷ
φανερῷ βουλευόμενος [οὐδ' ὑπὸ τῶν συκοφαντούντων κρινόμενος],
οὐδὲ γραφὰς φεύγων παρανόμων, οὐδ' ὑπεύθυνος ὢν οὐδενί, ἀλλ'
ἁπλῶς αὐτὸς δεσπότης, ἡγεμών, κύριος πάντων. ἐγὼ δ' ὁ πρὸς 295
τοῦτον ἀντιτεταγμένος (καὶ γὰρ τοῦτ' ἐξετάσαι δίκαιον) τίνος
10 κύριος ἦν; οὐδενός· αὐτὸ γὰρ τὸ δημηγορεῖν πρῶτον, οὗ μόνου
μετεῖχον ἐγώ, ἐξ ἴσου προὐτίθεθ' ὑμεῖς τοῖς παρ' ἐκείνου μισθαρνοῦσι καὶ ἐμοί, καὶ ὅσα οὗτοι περιγένοιντο ἐμοῦ (πολλὰ δ'
ἐγίγνετο ταῦτα, δι' ἣν ἕκαστον τύχοι πρόφασιν), ταῦθ' ὑπὲρ
τῶν ἐχθρῶν ἀπῆτε βεβουλευμένοι. ἀλλ' ὅμως ἐκ τοιούτων ἐλατ- 296
15 τωμάτων ἐγὼ συμμάχους μὲν ὑμῖν ἐποίησα Εὐβοέας, Ἀχαιούς,
Κορινθίους, Θηβαίους, Μεγαρέας, Λευκαδίους, Κερκυραίους, ἀφ'
ὧν μύριοι μὲν καὶ πεντακισχίλιοι ξένοι, δισχίλιοι δ' ἱππεῖς
ἄνευ τῶν πολιτικῶν δυνάμεων συνήχθησαν· χρημάτων δὲ ὅσων
ἐδυνήθην ἐγὼ πλείστην συντέλειαν ἐποίησα. εἰ δὲ λέγεις ἢ 297
20 τὰ πρὸς Θηβαίους δίκαια, Αἰσχίνη, ἢ τὰ πρὸς Βυζαντίους
ἢ τὰ πρὸς Εὐβοέας, ἢ περὶ τῶν ἴσων νυνὶ διαλέγει, πρῶτον

---

2. Post αὐτοκράτωρ ὢν add. A et socii: atque ita Bekk. Dind.   6. οὐδ' ὑπὸ
συκοφαντούντων κρινόμενος] In margine habet Σ, om. B. et S., uncis inclusit Dind.
11. προὐτίθεθ'] προὐτίθεσθ' ΣΦ.   14. ἀπῆτε] ἀπῄειτε AB et volg. ante Bekk.
18. ὅσων] ὅσην Dobr.

2. αὐτοκράτωρ. ὢν was added after
this word, an easy but not needful gloss,
with no sufficient MS. authority.

3. εἶθ' οὗτοι κ.τ.λ. Whereas the Athenians were too civilised to serve in person,
except at an emergency like Chaeronea
itself; and then of course shewed the want
of habitual training.

5. οὐ προλέγων κ.τ.λ. It was a real
weakness in the Athenian constitution, that
it had no vigorous executive, untrammeled
in action even though responsible afterwards. The complaint that a statesman at
Athens was responsible is a less fair one;
but as it is obviously made, it seems likely
that the clause οὐδ' ὑπὸ τῶν συκοφαντούντων κρινόμενος is genuine, as it puts Demosthenes' point in the most invidious light.

§ 295. And as well off for Athenian
speakers as Athens.

12. ὅσα οὗτοι .. βεβουλευμένοι. As
τίνος κύριος ἦν balances αὐτὸς δεσπότης,
ἡγεμὼν, κύριος πάντων, so this clause may

be said to balance ἔπραττεν ἃ δόξειεν αὐτῷ.
'Philip had absolute power over affairs, and
conducted them in his own interest; I had
only a hearing, equally with other men
(μετεῖχον), in a debate that often ended in
our opponent's interest.'

§ 296. Yet, though Philip had these
advantages over me, I gained you many
profitable allies, and enriched the military
chest:

§§ 297, 298. Without committing Athens
to greater sacrifices than she had already
made to Greece, from Salamis onward.

20. τὰ πρὸς Θηβαίους δίκαια. 'If you
are going into our just grievances against
these individual states' (the force of the repeated ἢ πρὸς), 'or insisting on general
principles of equity ...' The first clause
speaks of the argument, that Athens ought
not to have helped these particular states at
all; the second, that Athens ought to have
received more benefit from any state she
helped.

μὲν ἀγνοεῖς ὅτι καὶ πρότερον τῶν ὑπὲρ τῶν Ἑλλήνων ἐκείνων
ἀγωνισαμένων τριήρων, τριακοσίων οὐσῶν τῶν πασῶν, τὰς δια-
298 κοσίας ἡ πόλις παρέσχετο, καὶ οὐκ ἐλαττοῦσθαι νομίζουσα
οὐδὲ κρίνουσα τοὺς ταῦτα συμβουλεύσαντας οὐδὲ ἀγανακτοῦσα
ἐπὶ τούτοις ἑωρᾶτο (αἰσχρὸν γάρ), ἀλλὰ τοῖς θεοῖς ἔχουσα 5
χάριν, εἰ κοινοῦ κινδύνου τοῖς Ἕλλησι περιστάντος αὐτὴ διπλά-
σια τῶν ἄλλων εἰς τὴν ἁπάντων σωτηρίαν παρέσχετο. εἶτα
299 κενὰς χαρίζει χάριτας τουτοισὶ συκοφαντῶν ἐμέ. τί γὰρ νῦν
λέγεις οἷα ἐχρῆν πράττειν, ἀλλ᾽ οὐ τότ᾽ ὢν ἐν τῇ πόλει καὶ
παρὼν ταῦτ᾽ ἔγραφες, εἴπερ ἐνεδέχετο παρὰ τοὺς παρόντας 10
καιροὺς, ἐν οἷς οὐχ ὅσα ἐβουλόμεθα, ἀλλ᾽ ὅσα δοίη τὰ πράγ-
ματ᾽ ἔδει δέχεσθαι· ὁ γὰρ ἀντωνούμενος καὶ ταχὺ τοὺς παρ᾽
ἡμῶν ἀπελαυνομένους προσδεξόμενος καὶ χρήματα προσθήσων
ὑπῆρχεν ἕτοιμος. ✓
300 Ἀλλ᾽ εἰ νῦν ἐπὶ τοῖς πεπραγμένοις κατηγορίας ἔχω, τί ἂν 15

---

2. τριήρων] τριηρῶν ΣΓΥΦ t.   8. κενὰς] κενάς γε A et socii Bekk. Statim
χαρίζῃ Σ.   11. ἐβουλόμεθα] ἠβουλόμεθα Σ p Dind. in edit. Oxon., ἂν βουλώμεθα
ΓΥ et socii.

---

2. τριακοσίων κ.τ.λ. The statements of
the numbers of the fleet at Salamis present
a well-known difficulty. Of the two principal authorities, Aeschylus (Persae, 341,
342) states the Greek fleet at 310 (or 300
as some understand him), Herodotus (8. 42)
at 366 or 378, according as we accept his
calculation of the aggregate force, or his
enumeration of the several contingents: and,
according to him, the Athenian ships num-
bered 180. He is describing the muster,
not the actual battle, so it is possible that
the force engaged was 310, while the larger
number were present, but some of them not
fit for action But we are told (Hdt. 8. 18)
that the Athenians had suffered especially at
Artemisium, so that if the efficient strength
of the fleet be reckoned instead of the
nominal, the number of their contingent
ought to be reduced in at least as great
a proportion as that of the total. Yet it
was a constant boast of the Athenians, that
they had furnished two-thirds of the fleet
that fought at Salamis (see, especially, Thuc.
1. 74, where the total force is said, by most
MSS., to have reached ἐς τὰς τετρακοσίας).
This could be justified, if Herodotus be right
as to the number of Athenian ships, and
Aeschylus as to the total: but it is arbitrary
to suppose this. Probably (as Arnold in
Thuc. l. c.) we have the truth coloured by
national vanity. If we count all the ships
that were on the coast of Salamis before the
battle, there were 180 Athenian triremes

there: if we count only those that actually
fought, there were 310 Greek triremes in
all, and 180 out of 310 might, without
much exaggeration, be called two-thirds, or
200 out of 300. But if we reckon fairly,
and make either no deductions, or make the
same from the parts as the whole, the
Athenian contingent was less than half the
fleet—180 out of 366, or 150 (perhaps) out
of 310.

τὰς διακοσίας. 'Two hundred out of
three,' the two hundred which make two-
thirds. The article is thus constantly used
in Greek for defining one portion out of a
larger number, even when the remainder is
not specified.

§ 299. And your criticism on me comes
too late to save our resources.

9. ὢν ἐν τῇ πόλει καὶ παρών. παρὼν is
not simply synonymous with ὢν ἐν τῇ πόλει,
but means that he actually attended the
assembly: below, § 337 init.

12. ἀντωνούμενος. Not exactly 'one
to bid against us,' but 'one to buy in the
same market with us,' to pay money
down to get what we rejected. The
bargain is in terms of military help, of
which Philip was always ready to pay
any sum to secure a bargain declined by
Athens.

§§ 300, 301. If I am accused now, what
would have been said if these states had
joined Philip?

15. ἐπὶ τοῖς πεπραγμένοις. The pre-

οἴεσθε, εἰ τότ' ἐμοῦ περὶ τούτων ἀκριβολογουμένου, ἀπῆλθον
αἱ πόλεις καὶ προσέθεντο Φιλίππῳ, καὶ ἅμα Εὐβοίας καὶ Θηβῶν καὶ Βυζαντίου κύριος κατέστη, τί ποιεῖν ἂν ἢ τί λέγειν
τοὺς ἀσεβεῖς ἀνθρώπους τουτουσί; οὐχ ὡς ἐξεδόθησαν; οὐχ 301
5 ὡς ἀπηλάθησαν βουλόμενοι μεθ' ἡμῶν εἶναι; εἶτα τοῦ μὲν Ἑλ-
λησπόντου διὰ Βυζαντίων ἐγκρατὴς καθέστηκε, καὶ τῆς σιτοπομπίας τῆς τῶν Ἑλλήνων κύριος, πόλεμος δ' ὅμορος καὶ
βαρὺς εἰς τὴν Ἀττικὴν διὰ Θηβαίων κεκόμισται, ἄπλους δ' ἡ
θάλαττα ὑπὸ τῶν ἐκ τῆς Εὐβοίας ὁρμωμένων λῃστῶν γέγονεν;
10 οὐκ ἂν ταῦτ' ἔλεγον, καὶ πολλά γε πρὸς τούτοις ἕτερα; πονηρὸν, 302
ἄνδρες Ἀθηναῖοι, πονηρὸν ὁ συκοφάντης ἀεὶ καὶ πανταχόθεν
βάσκανον καὶ φιλαίτιον· τοῦτο δὲ καὶ φύσει κίναδος τἀνθρώ-
πιόν ἐστιν, οὐδὲν ἐξ ἀρχῆς ὑγιὲς πεποιηκὸς οὐδ' ἐλεύθερον,
αὐτοτραγικὸς πίθηκος, ἀρουραῖος Οἰνόμαος, παράσημος ῥήτωρ.
15 τί γὰρ ἡ σὴ δεινότης εἰς ὄνησιν ἥκει τῇ πατρίδι; νῦν ἡμῖν 303
λέγεις περὶ τῶν παρεληλυθότων; ὥσπερ ἂν εἴ τις ἰατρὸς ἀσθε-
νοῦσι μὲν τοῖς κάμνουσιν εἰσιὼν μὴ λέγοι μηδὲ δεικνύοι δι' ὧν
ἀποφεύξονται τὴν νόσον, ἐπειδὴ δὲ τελευτήσειέ τις αὐτῶν καὶ
τὰ νομιζόμεν' αὐτῷ φέροιτο, ἀκολουθῶν ἐπὶ τὸ μνῆμα διεξίοι

---

1. εἰ τότ'] εἴ ποτ' FΥ et socii.   τούτων] τούτου Σ τούτου FB.   3. Post λέγειν
al. add. οἴεσθε: alii post τί vel post τυντουσί.   4. Alterum οὐχ ὡς om. pr. Σ B.
et S.   Mox pro ἡμῶν, ὑμῶν Σ.   6. καθέστηκε] κατέστη ΥΑ et socii: statim Φίλιππος add. Σ a m. sec.   7. Post κύριος addebatur γέγονεν.   Om. ΣΑ et socii.
9. ἐκ] Om. Σ.   15. τῇ] Om. pr. Σ B. et S.   • 17. δεικνύοι] δεικνύη Σ.
19. φέροιτο] φαίνοιτο ΣΦ.

---

position has the same force as ἐπ' ἐξειργα-
σμένοις, Aesch. Ag. 1379.
    τί ἂν οἴεσθε . . τί ποιεῖν ἄν. Cp. Phil.
3. p. 120, § 45, for the repetition of the
interrogative, when the thread of the main
question is resumed. This view seems
better than to put a note of interrogation
after κατέστη, and take τί ἂν οἴεσθε, 'What
do you think would have happened?' No
good MSS. repeat οἴεσθε after λέγειν.
    1. τούτων. It seems hard to find a sin-
gular substantive designating the benefit
Athens ought to have insisted on, that will
justify the reading τούτου. Yet Σ is not
unsupported in it.
    4. ἐξεδόθησαν, sc. οἱ Θηβαῖοι καὶ Εὐ-
βοεῖς καὶ Βυζάντιοι. That οὐχ ὡς should
be repeated, seems more like Demosthenes,
though one might accept its omission, if we
were sure it was not accidental on the part
of the transcriber of Σ.
    5. εἶτα τοῦ μὲν Ἑλλησπόντου κ.τ.λ.
He passes into oratio recta by simply dropping the ὡς.

§§ 302, 303. But no inconsistency is too
bad for a sycophant, who speaks after the
event, like a doctor prescribing at the funeral.
    11. ἀεὶ καὶ πανταχόθεν. Whatever
has happened, and wherever he has to get
his accusations: else, to say merely that a
συκοφάντης was always φιλαίτιος, would be
a truism. The neuter predicates give a very
intelligible sarcasm: you regard the man
simply as an embodied nuisance, and despise
him too much to recognise his personality.
    12. καὶ φύσει. As well as by pro-
fession.
    14. αὐτοτραγικὸς κ.τ.λ.   'He is an ape
of an actor in grain, the very Oenomaus for
a fair, but a counterfeit as a statesman.' It
appears from Arist. Poet. c. 27, that πίθηκος
was a cant name for a ranting actor.
    παράσημος carries a reference to the
model statesman described by Aeschines, and
already criticised: above, § 157.
    § 303. Aeschines attempts to reply, in Ct.
§ 226.
    19. τὰ νομιζόμενα. He does not pre-

"εἰ τὸ καὶ τὸ ἐποίησεν ἄνθρωπος οὑτοσὶ, οὐκ ἂν ἀπέθανεν."
ἐμβρόντητε, εἶτα νῦν λέγεις;
304 Οὐ τοίνυν οὐδὲ τὴν ἧτταν, εἰ ταύτῃ γαυριᾷς ἐφ᾽ ᾗ στένειν
σε, ὦ κατάρατε, προσῆκεν, ἐν οὐδενὶ τῶν παρ᾽ ἐμοὶ γεγονυῖαν
εὑρήσετε τῇ πόλει. οὑτωσὶ δὲ λογίζεσθε. οὐδαμοῦ πώποθ᾽ 5
ὅποι πρεσβευτὴς ἐπέμφθην ὑφ᾽ ὑμῶν ἐγώ, ἡττηθεὶς ἀπῆλθον
τῶν παρὰ Φιλίππου πρέσβεων, οὐκ ἐκ Θετταλίας, οὐκ ἐξ Ἀμβρακίας, οὐκ ἐξ Ἰλλυριῶν, οὐ παρὰ τῶν Θρᾳκῶν βασιλέων,
οὐκ ἐκ Βυζαντίου, οὐκ ἄλλοθεν οὐδαμόθεν, οὐ τὰ τελευταῖα
ἐκ Θηβῶν, ἀλλ᾽ ἐν οἷς κρατηθεῖεν οἱ πρέσβεις αὐτοῦ τῷ λόγῳ, 10
305 ταῦτα τοῖς ὅπλοις ἐπιὼν κατεστρέφετο. ταῦτ᾽ οὖν ἀπαιτεῖς
παρ᾽ ἐμοῦ, καὶ οὐκ αἰσχύνει τὸν αὐτὸν εἴς τε μαλακίαν σκώπ-
των καὶ τῆς Φιλίππου δυνάμεως ἀξιῶν ἕνα ὄντα κρείττω γενέσθαι; καὶ ταῦτα τοῖς λόγοις; τίνος γὰρ ἄλλου κύριος ἦν
ἐγώ; οὐ γὰρ τῆς γε ἑκάστου ψυχῆς, οὐδὲ τῆς τύχης τῶν 15
παραταξαμένων, οὐδὲ τῆς στρατηγίας, ἧς ἔμ᾽ ἀπαιτεῖς εὐθύνας·
306 οὕτω σκαιὸς εἶ. ἀλλὰ μὴν ὧν γ᾽ ἂν ὁ ῥήτωρ ὑπεύθυνος εἴη,
πᾶσαν ἐξέτασιν λάμβανε· οὐ παραιτοῦμαι. τίνα οὖν ἐστι

---

1. ἄνθρωπος] Ita Bekk.: † Σ ἄνθρωπος †, ceteri ἄνθρωπος.   3. Post ἧτταν αὑτὴν add.
A et socii.   4. ἐμοί] Ita ΣΦΩ et al. B. et S. et nunc Dind.: volgo ἐμοῦ.   6. ὅποι]
ὅπου ΦΦΩ et socii.   ἐπέμφθην] ἐξεπέμφθην A et socii.   7. οὐκ ἐξ Ἀμβρακίας]
Ita A et socii p: ceteri οὐδ᾽ ἐξ Ἀμβρακίας. Εt Σ οὐδ᾽ ἐξ Ἰλλυρίων οὐδὲ παρὰ τῶν Θρᾳκῶν
βασιλέων, οὐκ ἐκ Βυζαντίου κ.τ.λ. habet.   9. Post τελευταῖα volg. usque ad Bekk.
add. πρώην, νῦν A et socii, Σ om.   12. αἰσχύνει] Sic Σ, volg. -νη.   13. γενέσθαι]
γεγενῆσθαι A et socii.   18. λάμβανε] λαμβάνετε Σ B. et S.

---

scribe immediately after death, but waits for
the public funeral (τὰ ἔνατα, as Aeschines
l. c. understands it) to make a shew of his
sham sorrow.

§§ 304, 305. *My defeats were military,
where I was not responsible: my diplomatic
successes were uninterrupted,*

4. παρ᾽ ἐμοί. Reiske reads παρ᾽ ἐμοῦ, and
so Dind. in his Oxford Edition, against the best
MSS., and with perhaps a harsher sense. It
would have to mean, 'in any result of my
action,' the text, 'in anything that lay at my
door,' much like κατ᾽ ἐμὲ below, § 307.

7. οὐκ ἐξ Ἀμβρακίας. Nearly all MSS.
have οὐδὲ for οὐκ here, and Σ has it so
three times; but then reads οὐκ ἐκ Βυζαντίου, οὐκ ἄλλοθεν οὐδαμόθεν, οὐ τὰ τελευταῖα, and it is harder to give a reason for
this change than to suppose an error, recti-
fied in the middle of the passage. It would
be far-fetched to regard οὐδὲ παρὰ τῶν Θρᾳκῶν βασιλέων as ending one enumeration,
and οὐκ ἐκ Βυζαντίου.. Θηβῶν as making
a fresh one, on the ground that Byzantium,
Thebes, and the places gained in between,

were those on account of which Aeschines
specially censured him.

9. τὰ τελευταῖα. νῦν and πρήην, one of
which follows these words in all MSS. but
Σ, are clearly rival glosses on them.

14. καὶ ταῦτα τοῖς λόγοις. 'You call
me a coward, yet you ask me to defeat
Philip by my single prowess, and that as a
speaker.'

15. τῶν παραταξαμένων. 'Of the men
who stood in line with me,' hinting that he
deserved credit for having brought them
into line at all, and perhaps that he had
done all the military duty that could be .
expected of one man—fought like any other
soldier.

16. στρατηγίας.. εὐθύνας. Referring,
probably, to the charge of having separated
and sacrificed two-thirds of his 15,000 mercenaries, Ae. in Ct. §§ 146, 147.

§ 306. *My political foresight unclouded,
my political courage unwavering:*

18. λάμβανε. Σ has λαμβάνετε, but it
would weaken the passage to turn from Aeschines to the court.

ταῦτα; ἰδεῖν τὰ πράγματα ἀρχόμενα καὶ προαισθέσθαι καὶ
προειπεῖν τοῖς ἄλλοις. ταῦτα πέπρακταί μοι. καὶ ἔτι τὰς
ἑκασταχοῦ βραδυτῆτας, ὄκνους, ἀγνοίας, φιλονεικίας, ἃ πολιτικὰ ταῖς πόλεσι πρόσεστιν ἁπάσαις καὶ ἀναγκαῖα ἁμαρτή-
5 ματα, ταῦθ᾽ ὡς εἰς ἐλάχιστα συστεῖλαι, καὶ τοὐναντίον εἰς
ὁμόνοιαν καὶ φιλίαν καὶ τοῦ τὰ δέοντα ποιεῖν ὁρμὴν προ-
τρέψαι. καὶ ταῦτά μοι πάντα πεποίηται, καὶ οὐδεὶς μήποθ᾽
εὕρη κατ᾽ ἐμὲ οὐδὲν ἐλλειφθέν. εἰ τοίνυν τις ἔροιτο ὁντινοῦν 307
τίσι τὰ πλεῖστα Φίλιππος ὧν κατέπραξε διῳκήσατο, πάντες
10 ἂν εἴποιεν τῷ στρατοπέδῳ καὶ τῷ διδόναι καὶ διαφθείρειν τοὺς
ἐπὶ τῶν πραγμάτων. οὐκοῦν τῶν μὲν δυνάμεων οὔτε κύριος
οὔθ᾽ ἡγεμὼν ἦν ἐγώ, ὥστε οὐδ᾽ ὁ λόγος τῶν κατὰ ταῦτα πραχθέντων πρὸς ἐμέ. καὶ μὴν τῷ διαφθαρῆναι χρήμασιν ἢ μὴ
κεκράτηκα Φιλίππου· ὥσπερ γὰρ ὁ ὠνούμενος νενίκηκε τὸν
15 λαβόντα, ἐὰν πρίηται, οὕτως ὁ μὴ λαβὼν μηδὲ διαφθαρεὶς
νενίκηκε τὸν ὠνούμενον. ὥστε ἀήττητος ἡ πόλις τὸ κατ᾽ ἐμέ.

Ἃ μὲν τοίνυν ἐγὼ παρεσχόμην εἰς τὸ δικαίως τοιαῦτα γρά- 308
φειν τουτονὶ περὶ ἐμοῦ, πρὸς πολλοῖς ἑτέροις ταῦτα καὶ παραπλήσια τούτοις ἐστίν· ἃ δ᾽ οἱ πάντες ὑμεῖς, ταῦτ᾽ ἤδη λέξω.
20 μετὰ γὰρ τὴν μάχην εὐθὺς ὁ δῆμος, εἰδὼς καὶ ἑορακὼς πάντα

---

3. πολιτικὰ] πηλίκα Α et socii.   5. ἐλάχιστα] Sic Σ: volg. usque ad Bekk.
ἐλάχιστον.   8. κατ᾽ ἐμὲ] Ita Σ Β. et S.: ceteri τὸ κατ᾽ ἐμέ.   ἔροιτο ὀντι-
νοῦν] ὀντινοῦν ἔροιτο ΓΥΦΩ et socii.   13. τῷ διαφθαρῆναι χρήμασιν ἢ μὴ] Ita Σ:
legebatur τῷ γε μὴ διαφθαρῆναι χρήμασιν, τῷ γε διαφθαρῆναι χρήμασιν ἢ μὴ habent Υ p Α
et socii.   15. μηδὲ διαφθαρεὶς] καὶ διαφθαρεὶς pr. Σ Β. et S.   18. τουτονὶ]
Sic Α et socii ΓΩ p Bekk. Dind.: ceteri et Β. et S. τούτου.   19. οἱ πάντες] πάντες
Α et al.   20. ἑορακὼς] Ita Dind.: libri ἑωρακώς.

---

3. πολιτικὰ ταῖς πόλεσι. 'Inherent
weaknesses in cities as such,' the name πόλις
almost implying a free government (πόλις
γὰρ οὐκ ἔσθ᾽, ᾗ τις ἀνδρὸς ἔσθ᾽ ἑνός): these
weaknesses, inseparable from freedom, were
explained in § 294. 'Constitutional infirmities in constitutional states,' would be too
mere a pun, but would exactly express the
meaning.

8. κατ᾽ ἐμέ. Almost 'at my post,' in
the matters where I was on duty: exactly
like καθ᾽ ἡμᾶς in Soph. Aj. 775. So, again,
τὸ κατ᾽ ἐμὲ at the end of the next section.
All MSS. but Σ have τὸ κατ᾽ ἐμὲ here also;
but the article seems to break the flow of
the sense, and the following passage is weaker
if verbally the same as this.

§ 307. And I conquered Philip on the
one point that rested with me—incorruptibility.

12. οὐδ᾽ ὁ λόγος. 'So that neither was
the responsibility mine,' any more than the

power.

13. τῷ διαφθαρῆναι χρήμασιν ἢ μή.
'On the point whether I should take or not
take bribes.' Dindorf compares D. de Rhod.
Lib. p. 197, § 29, De F. L. p. 429, § 312,
for the construction, which the second group
of MSS. changed into τῷ γε μὴ διαφθαρῆναι
χρήμασιν, with great detriment to the force
of the passage. γε is read by the other
MSS. except Σ, and may be right: if so, its
force is, 'incorruptibility at any rate might
be required of me,' though generalship
could not.

14. ὠνούμενος .. πρίηται. 'The bid-
der' .. 'if he effect the bargain.'

16. τὸ κατ᾽ ἐμέ. See on the last section.

§ 308. I have said what ground I gave
Ctesiphon for his decree: I will now say
what ground you gave.

§ 308. I gave him a right to propose a
vote of thanks by serving you, you by
acceptance and appreciation of the service.

ὅσα ἔπραττον ἐγώ, ἐν αὐτοῖς τοῖς δεινοῖς καὶ φοβεροῖς ἐμβε-
309 βηκώς, ἡνίκ' οὐδ' ἀγνωμονῆσαί τι θαυμαστὸν ἦν τοὺς πολλοὺς
πρὸς ἐμέ, πρῶτον μὲν περὶ σωτηρίας τῆς πόλεως τὰς ἐμὰς
γνώμας ἐχειροτόνει, καὶ πάνθ' ὅσα τῆς φυλακῆς ἕνεκα ἐπράττετο, ἡ διάταξις τῶν φυλάκων, αἱ τάφροι, τὰ εἰς τὰ τείχη 5
χρήματα, διὰ τῶν ἐμῶν ψηφισμάτων ἐγίγνετο· ἔπειθ' αἱρού-
310 μενος σιτώνην ἐκ πάντων ἐμὲ ἐχειροτόνησεν ὁ δῆμος. καὶ μετὰ
ταῦτα συστάντων οἷς ἦν ἐπιμελὲς κακῶς ἐμὲ ποιεῖν, καὶ γραφὰς, εὐθύνας, εἰσαγγελίας, πάντα ταῦτ' ἐπαγόντων μοι, οὐ δι'
ἑαυτῶν τό γε πρῶτον, ἀλλὰ δι' ὧν μάλισθ' ὑπελάμβανον ἀγνο- 10
ήσεσθαι (ἴστε γὰρ δήπου καὶ μέμνησθε ὅτι τοὺς πρώτους
χρόνους κατὰ τὴν ἡμέραν ἑκάστην ἐκρινόμην ἐγώ, καὶ οὔτ'
ἀπόνοια Σωσικλέους οὔτε συκοφαντία Φιλοκράτους οὔτε Διών-
δου καὶ Μελάντου μανία οὔτ' ἄλλ' οὐδὲν ἀπείρατον ἦν τούτοις
κατ' ἐμοῦ), ἐν τοίνυν τούτοις πᾶσι μάλιστα μὲν διὰ τοὺς θεούς, 15
δεύτερον δὲ δι' ὑμᾶς καὶ τοὺς ἄλλους Ἀθηναίους ἐσῳζόμην. ᵥ
311 δικαίως· τοῦτο γὰρ καὶ ἀληθές ἐστι καὶ ὑπὲρ τῶν ὀμωμοκότων
καὶ γνόντων τὰ εὔορκα δικαστῶν. οὐκοῦν ἐν μὲν οἷς εἰσηγ-
γελλόμην, ὅτ' ἀπεψηφίζεσθέ μου καὶ τὸ μέρος τῶν ψήφων
τοῖς διώκουσιν οὐ μετεδίδοτε, τότ' ἐψηφίζεσθε τὰ ἄριστά με 20
πράττειν· ἐν οἷς δὲ τὰς γραφὰς ἀπέφευγον, ἔννομα καὶ γράφειν καὶ λέγειν ἀπεδεικνύμην· ἐν οἷς δὲ τὰς εὐθύνας ἐπεση-
μαίνεσθε, δικαίως καὶ ἀδωροδοκήτως πάντα πεπρᾶχθαί μοι

---

3. Post πόλεως βουλευόμενος Σ a m. sec. 5. φυλάκων] φυλακῶν Σ. 9. πάντα
ταῦτ'] ταῦτα πάντ' Σ et pr. A. 12. κατὰ τὴν ἡμέραν ἑκάστην] Sic Σ k et (prae-
fixo σχεδὸν) A s : volgo καθ' ἑκάστην ἡμέραν. 16. Post ἄλλους ἅπαντας add. F
et socii. 18. γνόντων τὰ εὔορκα] ὑπὲρ παντὰ εὔορκα γνόντων F et socii. 19. τὸ
μέρος] Ita Σ : ceteri τὸ πέμπτον μέρος.

§§ 309-312. *You maintained my policy
against all assailants : your acquittal was
my praise.*

5. **φυλάκων.** φυλακῶν, the reading of
Σ, would be harsh after τῆς φυλακῆς.

αἱ τάφροι . . χρήματα. 'The stockades, the money for the fortifications, were
provided by decrees of mine.' He hints that
in the matter of the stockades, he did more
than assign public money to them, providing private : while yet their plan and construction was a public act.

12. **ἐκρινόμην.** 'I was always being
brought to trial ;' **ἐσῳζόμην,** 'I was preserved as often.'

13. **ἀπόνοια . . . συκοφαντία . . . μανία.**
The first is the deliberate desperation of a
man with nothing to lose, the last the desperation of blind passion ; the second merely
a combination of craft and malice. Philo-

crates cannot be the ambassador : even
if the general amnesty after Chaeronea
had allowed him to return to Athens, it
is clear that he was thrown over even by
the Macedonian party, so he can have
had no hope of a hearing against Demosthenes.

17. **δικαίως κ.τ.λ.** 'Rightly, too : I say
this, for it is true, and a testimony due to
the judges, who had taken the same oath
as you have, and kept it,' as I know you
will. It seems as if Demosthenes blended
the two thoughts of the former judges who
voted honestly, and the present ones who
have still to vote. But the tense of γνόντων
shews that the primary reference is to the
former.

20. **τὰ ἄριστά με πράττειν.** With special reference to the terms of Ctesiphon's
decree.

Q 2

προσωμολογεῖτε. τούτων οὖν οὕτως ἐχόντων τί προσῆκον ἢ τί 312
δίκαιον ἦν τοῖς ὑπ' ἐμοῦ πεπραγμένοις θέσθαι τὸν Κτησιφῶντα ὄνομα, οὐχ ὃ τὸν δῆμον ἑώρα τιθέμενον, οὐχ ὃ τοὺς
ὀμωμοκότας δικαστὰς, οὐχ ὃ, τὴν ἀλήθειαν παρὰ πᾶσι βεβαι-
5 οῦσαν;
Ναὶ, φησὶν, ἀλλὰ τὸ τοῦ Κεφάλου καλὸν, τὸ μηδεμίαν 313
γραφὴν φεύγειν. καὶ νὴ Δί' εὔδαιμόν γε. ἀλλὰ τί μᾶλλον
ὁ πολλάκις μὲν φυγὼν, μηδεπώποτε δ' ἐξελεγχθεὶς ἀδικῶν ἐν
ἐγκλήματι γίγνοιτ' ἂν διὰ τοῦτο δικαίως; καίτοι πρός γε
10 τοῦτον, ἄνδρες Ἀθηναῖοι, καὶ τὸ τοῦ Κεφάλου καλὸν εἰπεῖν
ἔστι μοι. οὐδεμίαν γὰρ πώποτ' ἐγράψατό με οὐδ' ἐδίωξε
γραφὴν, ὥστε ὑπὸ σοῦ γε ὡμολόγημαι μηδὲν εἶναι τοῦ Κεφάλου χείρων πολίτης.
Πανταχόθεν μὲν τοίνυν ἄν τις ἴδοι τὴν ἀγνωμοσύνην αὐτοῦ 314
15 καὶ τὴν βασκανίαν, οὐχ ἥκιστα δ' ἀφ' ὧν περὶ τῆς τύχης
διελέχθη. ἐγὼ δ' ὅλως μὲν, ὅστις ἄνθρωπος ὢν ἀνθρώπῳ τύχην

---

1. προσῆκον] Ita ΣΦΩ et socii et B. et S.: volgo προσῆκεν. 7. φεύγειν] Ita
ΣΦΑ et socii B. et S.: Σ a m. sec. et ce:teri φυγεῖν. 14. πανταχόθεν] Ita Σ: legebatur πολλαχόθεν. 16. διελέχθη] † διελέγχθη Σ †.

---

1. προσῆκον .. δίκαιον. Aeschines has
said (In Ct. § 212) that a crown tc Demosthenes was in bad taste, even if it had been
justified by facts.
3. τὸν δῆμον .. τοὺς ὀμωμοκότας δικαστάς .. τὴν ἀλήθειαν. Corresponding to
the three forms of trial, by εἰσαγγελία,
γραφὴ παρανόμων, and εὔθυναι, in all of
which, he has just said, he was acquitted.
The climax of τὴν ἀλήθειαν is rather rhetorical than logical: but it may be said that
in questions of accounts the figures would
speak for themselves, and that acquittal
would prove more about facts and less about
opinions, than in the other cases.
§ 313. And if never to bave been prosecuted for public measures is a distinction, it
is no thanks to Aeschines if I cannot claim
that.
6. τὸ τοῦ Κεφάλου καλόν. 'Nay, but
the glorious boast of Cephalus,' is more
accurately the force than 'the boast of
Cephalus is a noble one,' as appears from τὸ
τοῦ Κεφάλου καλὸν being repeated substan-
tivally in the next sentence. Vid. Ae. in Ct.
§ 195.
7. φεύγειν. For the merits of the reading φυγεῖν, vid. ad Ae. in Ct. § 221.
καὶ νὴ Δί' εὔδαιμόν γε. 'Glorious it
is, indeed, and not less fortunate ;' he was
more fortunate than me or Ctesiphon, not
necessarily more upright.

11. ἐδίωξε γραφήν. As συνήγορος: cp.
above, § 282, οὐδὲ τῷ γραψαμένῳ συγκατηγόρησεν. 'He cannot say that he would
have prosecuted me, had not others taken
the duty off his hands: for he let them
lose their cases without a word to help
them.'
12. μηδὲν εἶναι. Not οὐδὲν, lest he
should appear to make the claim to equality
with Cephalus in his own person, which he
disclaims as invidious : below, § 387 sqq.
§§ 314, 315. He reviles me as unlucky—
no legitimate ground for reviling : but to
meet him.
15. τῆς τύχης. The topic perhaps is
suggested at this particular point, by the
mention of Cephalus' distinction as depending rather on fortune than merit. The
point of Demosthenes' ill-fortune, as having
ruined all whom he professed to help, even
apart from his treachery, is urged by Aeschines repeatedly, §§ 114, 157, etc. One
may illustrate the superstitious notion which
Demosthenes thinks worth refuting, by the
popular Italian belief that the national movement of 1848 failed, because the Pope with
the evil eye blessed it.
16. ὅλως μέν. 'As a general principle :'
in the particular case of Aeschines, I feel
justified by his violence in making an exception, and twitting him with bis personal ill-
fortune.

προφέρει, ἀνόητον ἡγοῦμαι· ἢν γὰρ ὁ βέλτιστα πράττειν
νομίζων καὶ ἀρίστην ἔχειν οἰόμενος οὐκ οἶδεν εἰ μενεῖ τοιαύτη
315 μέχρι τῆς ἑσπέρας, πῶς χρὴ περὶ ταύτης λέγειν ἢ πῶς ὀνειδίζειν ἑτέρῳ; ἐπειδὴ δ' οὗτος πρὸς πολλοῖς ἄλλοις καὶ περὶ
τούτων ὑπερηφάνως χρῆται τῷ λόγῳ σκέψασθ', ὦ ἄνδρες 5
Ἀθηναῖοι, καὶ θεωρήσατε ὅσῳ καὶ ἀληθέστερον καὶ ἀνθρω-
316 πινώτερον ἐγὼ περὶ τῆς τύχης τούτου διαλεχθήσομαι. ἐγὼ
τὴν μὲν τῆς πόλεως τύχην ἀγαθὴν ἡγοῦμαι, καὶ ταῦθ' ὁρῶ καὶ
τὸν Δία τὸν Δωδωναῖον ἡμῖν μαντευόμενον, τὴν μέντοι τῶν
πάντων ἀνθρώπων, ἣ νῦν ἐπέχει, χαλεπὴν καὶ δεινήν· τίς γὰρ 10
Ἑλλήνων ἢ τίς βαρβάρων οὐ πολλῶν κακῶν ἐν τῷ παρόντι
317 πεπείραται; τὸ μὲν τοίνυν προελέσθαι τὰ κάλλιστα καὶ τὸ
τῶν οἰηθέντων Ἑλλήνων, εἰ πρόοιντο ἡμᾶς, ἐν εὐδαιμονίᾳ διά-
ξειν, αὐτῶν ἄμεινον πράττειν τῆς ἀγαθῆς τύχης τῆς πόλεως
εἶναι τίθημι· τὸ δὲ προσκροῦσαι καὶ μὴ πάνθ' ὡς ἐβουλόμεθ' 15
ἡμῖν συμβῆναι τῆς τῶν ἄλλων ἀνθρώπων τύχης τὸ ἐπιβάλλον
ἐφ' ἡμᾶς μέρος μετειληφέναι νομίζω τὴν πόλιν. τὴν δ' ἰδίαν
τύχην τὴν ἐμὴν καὶ τὴν ἑνὸς ἡμῶν ἑκάστου ἐν τοῖς ἰδίοις ἐξετά-
318 ζειν δίκαιον εἶναι νομίζω. ἐγὼ μὲν οὑτωσὶ περὶ τῆς τύχης

---

1. ἀνόητον] Ita ΣFA: ceteri plerique παντελῶς ἀνόητον.   βέλτιστα] τὰ βέλτιστα
Σ a m. sec.   2. μενεῖ] μένει Σ.   5. χρῆται] Sic Σ et γρ. Φ; ceteri et Bekk.
κέχρηται.   9. Post ἡμῖν addebatur καὶ τὸν Ἀπόλλω τὸν Πύθιον: quae om. ΣΦ, in
margine habent AB k.   † In Σ additur a m. recentissima καὶ τὰ πολλὰ τῶν Πυθίων †.

14. αὐτῶν] Ita ΣΦ B. et S.: αὐτοὺς γρ. Σ: αὐτῶν ἐκείνων ΥΩ et al. et γρ. Φ, αὐτῶν F,
volg. τούτων αὐτῶν.   15. ὡς] ὅσα ΥΑ et socii et γρ. FΩ.   19. μὲν] μὲν
οὖν FΦΥ et socii et volgo.   Mox post τύχης ante Bekk. addebatur ἐξετάζειν.   Post
τύχης συνδοκεῖν add. FΦΥ et socii: quod primus uncis inclusit Bekk., om. B. et S. Dind.

---

6. θεωρήσατε ὅσῳ κ.τ.λ. Aeschines'
point was that Demosthenes' enterprises
turned out badly. Demosthenes distinguishes
his personal fortune from that of his enterprises, accounts for the failure of the latter
by the evil times, and contrasts his personal
fortune with that of Aeschines.

§ 316. I say that the luck of Athens is
always relatively good, but that of mankind
at large is in our generation bad. The last
is obvious.

9. τὸν Δία τὸν Δωδωναῖον. The reference is to the oracle said to have been given
to an early king of Attica, in which Athens
is compared to a bladder, sure always to rise
to the surface after being submerged: at the
same time, the oracle seems to have been
often consulted by Athens in historical times,
when Delphi was under Spartan influence.
The words that are added after these in the
text or margin of most MSS., καὶ τὸν Ἀπόλλω τὸν Πύθιον, are no doubt an interpola-

tion for the sake of symmetry: but the
interpolation is old, as it appears to be
known to the imitator of this passage who
wrote the fourth Epistle of Demosthenes.

11. ἢ τίς βαρβάρων. He is doubtless
thinking especially of the Persian king, as
Ae. in Ct. § 132. Philip's violent death,
and, as it proved, Alexander's untimely
one, would prevent the kings of Macedon
being exempted from the supposed universal
curse.

§§ 317-319. The first is proved by our
having saved our honour, and faring better
than those who sacrificed us and their own
honour. As for my luck, that is not a public
question: but it is better than Aeschines'.

16. τῆς τῶν ἄλλων ἀνθρώπων τύχης.
The sentence would have been complete
here, but Demosthenes continues it so as to
vary the construction, τὸ δὲ προσκρούειν ..
συμβῆναι being put in apposition with τὸ
ἐπιβάλλον ἐφ' ἡμᾶς μέρος.

230   ΔΗΜΟΣΘΕΝΟΥΣ   §§ 319-321.

ἀξιῶ, ὀρθῶς καὶ δικαίως, ὡς ἐμαυτῷ δοκῶ, νομίζω δὲ καὶ ὑμῖν·
ὁ δὲ τὴν ἰδίαν τύχην τὴν ἐμὴν τῆς κοινῆς τῆς πόλεως κυριωτέ-
ραν εἶναί φησι, τὴν μικρὰν καὶ φαύλην τῆς ἀγαθῆς καὶ μεγάλης. καὶ πῶς ἔνι τοῦτο γενέσθαι;

5 Καὶ μὴν εἴ γε τὴν ἐμὴν τύχην πάντως ἐξετάζειν, Αἰσχίνη, 319
προαιρεῖ, πρὸς τὴν σεαυτοῦ σκόπει, κἂν εὕρῃς τὴν ἐμὴν βελτίω
τῆς σῆς, παῦσαι λοιδορούμενος αὐτῇ. σκόπει τοίνυν εὐθὺς ἐξ
ἀρχῆς. καί μου πρὸς Διὸς μηδεμίαν ψυχρότητα καταγνῷ
μηδείς. ἐγὼ γὰρ οὔτ' εἴ τις πενίαν προπηλακίζει, νοῦν ἔχειν
10 ἡγοῦμαι, οὔτ' εἴ τις ἐν ἀφθόνοις τραφεὶς ἐπὶ τούτῳ σεμνύνεται·
ἀλλ' ὑπὸ τῆς τουτουὶ τοῦ χαλεποῦ βλασφημίας καὶ συκοφαντίας εἰς τοιούτους λόγους ἐμπίπτειν ἀναγκάζομαι, οἷς ἐκ
τῶν ἐνόντων ὡς ἂν δύνωμαι μετριώτατα χρήσομαι.

Ἐμοὶ μὲν τοίνυν ὑπῆρξεν, Αἰσχίνη, παιδὶ μὲν ὄντι φοιτᾶν 320
15 εἰς τὰ προσήκοντα διδασκαλεῖα, καὶ ἔχειν ὅσα χρὴ τὸν μηδὲν
αἰσχρὸν ποιήσοντα δι' ἔνδειαν, ἐξελθόντι δὲ ἐκ παίδων ἀκόλουθα τούτοις πράττειν, χορηγεῖν, τριηραρχεῖν, εἰσφέρειν, μηδεμιᾶς φιλοτιμίας μήτε ἰδίας μήτε δημοσίας ἀπολείπεσθαι, ἀλλὰ
καὶ τῇ πόλει καὶ τοῖς φίλοις χρήσιμον εἶναι, ἐπειδὴ δὲ πρὸς 321
20 τὰ κοινὰ προσελθεῖν ἔδοξέ μοι, τοιαῦτα πολιτεύματα ἑλέσθαι
ὥστε καὶ ὑπὸ τῆς πατρίδος καὶ ὑπ' ἄλλων Ἑλλήνων πολλῶν
πολλάκις ἐστεφανῶσθαι, καὶ μηδὲ τοὺς ἐχθροὺς ὑμᾶς, ὡς οὐ
καλά γ' ἦν ἃ προειλόμην, ἐπιχειρεῖν λέγειν. ἐγὼ μὲν δὴ
τοιαύτῃ συμβεβίωκα τύχῃ, καὶ πόλλ' ἂν ἔχων ἕτερ' εἰπεῖν περὶ

14. μὲν ὄντι φοιτᾶν εἰς] Oni. pr. Σ B. et S.
Ita Σ: ante Bekk. legebatur τῶν ἄλλων Ἑλλήνων.
γῆν αι Σ, † spatiis verborum, si verba vocanda sunt, distinctis †: ita ut paene crediderim
haec ὡς οὐκ ἄλλα γ' ἦν εἰ μὴ ἃ προειλόμην indicare. Peccavit librarius dum dictata parum
accurate auscultat.

21. ἄλλων Ἑλλήνων πολλῶν]
22. οὐ καλά γ' ἦν ἃ] οὐκ αλλα

3. τὴν μικρὰν καὶ φαύλην. Demosthenes concedes the first epithet, and imputes the second.
8. ψυχρότητα. 'Dulness,' at once moral
and rhetorical, unfeeling introduction of a
topic the audience will not feel. Cp. Xen.
Symp. 6. 7.
12. ἐκ τῶν ἐνόντων. 'As moderately as
the case allows,' hinting what he expresses
in § 328, that it is hard to describe Aeschines' private life without scurrility.
§§ 310, 321. I was well educated, and
served with honour as a private citizen and
as a statesman:
15. τὰ προσήκοντα διδασκαλεῖα. He
omits to state that his school fees were not
paid, in Aph. 1. p. 828, § 53.
16. ἐξελθόντι δὲ ἐκ παίδων. It is re-

marked, that Demosthenes had been called
on for an εἰσφορά in his childhood; but
these services generally are characteristic of
mature life, and the λειτούργιαι peculiar to
it. Demosthenes had served his first trierarchy immediately on attaining manhood :
D. in Mid. p. 539 sq., § 100 sqq.
17. μηδεμιᾶς φιλοτιμίας κ.τ.λ. Demosthenes says he spent his money in a high-
minded way, no doubt speaking of the same
habits that Aeschines calls ridiculous extravagance.
20. ἔδοξέ μοι. He did so of free choice,
not, like Aeschines, as a last resource, when
all trades failed. Aeschines makes the same
imputation, In Ct. § 173.
23. καλά γ'. If not either prudent or
profitable.

αὐτῆς παραλείπω, φυλαττόμενος τὸ λυπῆσαί τινα ἐν οἷς σεμ-
322 νύνομαι. σὺ δ' ὁ σεμνὸς ἀνὴρ καὶ διαπτύων τοὺς ἄλλους σκόπει πρὸς ταύτην ποίᾳ τινὶ κέχρησαι τύχῃ, δι' ἣν παῖς μὲν
ὢν μετὰ πολλῆς ἐνδείας ἐτράφης, ἅμα τῷ πατρὶ πρὸς τῷ διδα-
σκαλείῳ προσεδρεύων, τὸ μέλαν τρίβων καὶ τὰ βάθρα σπογ- 5
323 γίζων καὶ τὸ παιδαγωγεῖον κορῶν, οἰκέτου τάξιν, οὐκ ἐλευθέρου
παιδὸς ἔχων, ἀνὴρ δὲ γενόμενος τῇ μητρὶ τελούσῃ τὰς βίβλους
ἀνεγίγνωσκες καὶ τἆλλα συνεσκευωροῦ, τὴν μὲν νύκτα νεβρίζων
καὶ κρατηρίζων καὶ καθαίρων τοὺς τελουμένους καὶ ἀπομάττων
τῷ πηλῷ καὶ τοῖς πιτύροις καὶ ἀνιστὰς ἀπὸ τοῦ καθαρμοῦ 10
κελεύων λέγειν "ἔφυγον κακόν, εὗρον ἄμεινον," ἐπὶ τῷ μηδένα
πώποτε τηλικοῦτ' ὀλολύξαι σεμνυνόμενος (καὶ ἔγωγε νομίζω·
μὴ 'γὰρ οἴεσθ' αὐτὸν φθέγγεσθαι μὲν οὕτω μέγα, ὀλολύζειν
324 δ' οὐχ ὑπέρλαμπρον), ἐν δὲ ταῖς ἡμέραις τοὺς καλοὺς θιάσους
ἄγων διὰ τῶν ὁδῶν, τοὺς ἐστεφανωμένους τῷ μαράθῳ καὶ τῇ 15
λεύκῃ, τοὺς ὄφεις τοὺς παρείας θλίβων καὶ ὑπὲρ τῆς κεφαλῆς
αἰωρῶν, καὶ βοῶν εὐοῖ σαβοῖ, καὶ ἐπορχούμενος ὑῆς ἄττης ἄττης
ὑῆς, ἔξαρχος καὶ προηγεμὼν καὶ κιστοφόρος καὶ λικνοφόρος

---

1. τινα] Sic ΣΦΩ A et socii: volg. et Bekk. τινας.   2. σεμνὸς] σεμνὸς ὢν Herodian., σεμνυνόμενος Σ B. et S. Cum σεμνύνομαι praecesserit, illud fortasse nonnullis place-
bit, tanquam diceret, 'Equidem invidiam fugio τὴν ἀπὸ τοῦ σεμνύνεσθαι: tu autem es re vera
σεμνὸς, neque alius cujusquam infirmitates curas.'   11. κελεύων] Volg. usque ad
Bekk. καὶ κελεύων: καὶ om. ΣΑ et socii.   15. μαράθῳ] μαράθρῳ nonnulli.

18. κιστοφόρος] Ita s † et fortasse superscr. Σ. Habet enim κιττοφόρος, et lineola super
prius τ a m. pr., ut nobis videbatur, erat posita †. Ceteri κιττοφόρος.

---

1. τινα. Those of the audience who
are less fortunate.

§ 322. *You were first a school fag,*

5. προσεδρεύων. Almost 'tied to the
spot.'

τὰ βάθρα : cp. Plat. Protag. p. 325.

6. τὸ παιδαγωγεῖον. The waiting-room
of the παιδαγωγαί, not merely the school-
room : you had to wait upon slaves as well
as freemen.

§ 323. *Then a deputy sorcerer*

8. νεβρίζων καὶ κρατηρίζων must both
be transitive, though against the Scholiast :
'Clothing with fawn-skins, and drenching
with holy wine.' κρατηρίζω is, indeed,
quoted as intransitive in a fragment of
Sophron, but there is a passive of it in
Hesychius ; and the construction flows much
more naturally, if τοὺς τελουμένους is the
object to all the verbs.

10. πιτύροις. Cp. the *meal* in the initia-
tion of Strepsiades, Ar. Nub. 263.

§ 324. [*By night, a deputy greengrocer
by day*],

16. λεύκῃ. The Homeric ἀχερωΐς, considered as an infernal plant, perhaps on account of the name : though in Homer (Od.
10. 510) the infernal tree is the kindred
αἴγειρος. Sabazius was identified with Bac-
chus, but was no doubt more or less of a
chthonian deity. The Eleusinian Dionysus,
also, was a brother of Persephone ; and
probably the difference of these mysteries
and the more reputable ones was rather
social, and perhaps ritual, than theological.

τοὺς ὄφεις τοὺς παρείας. Cp. the
fourth fragment of Hyperides' speech against
Demades. They are perhaps 'hooded snakes.'
The bacchanals certainly claimed power over
serpents : as the ritual is outlandish, it may
perhaps be relevant to compare the position
of the Cobra in Hindoo idolatry.

17. ἄττης. In St. Clement Alex., Pro-
trepticon, p. 6, we find a theory of the iden-
tification of Dionysus and Attis, as having
undergone the same mutilation.

18. κιστοφόρος. So one MS. for κιττοφόρος ; the variation is as old as Harpocra-

καὶ τοιαῦτα ὑπὸ τῶν γραδίων προσαγορευόμενος, μισθὸν λαμβάνων τούτων ἔνθρυπτα καὶ στρεπτοὺς καὶ νεήλατα, ἐφ' οἷς
τίς οὐκ ἂν ὡς ἀληθῶς αὐτὸν εὐδαιμονίσειε καὶ τὴν αὑτοῦ τύχην;
ἐπειδὴ δ' εἰς τοὺς δημότας ἐνεγράφης ὁπωσδήποτε, ἐῶ γὰρ 325
5 τοῦτό γε, ἐπειδὴ δ' οὖν ἐνεγράφης, εὐθέως τὸ κάλλιστον ἐξε-
λέξω τῶν ἔργων, γραμματεύειν καὶ ὑπηρετεῖν τοῖς ἀρχιδίοις.
ὡς δ' ἀπηλλάγης ποτὲ καὶ τούτου, πάνθ' ἃ τῶν ἄλλων κατηγορεῖς αὐτὸς ποιήσας, οὐ κατῄσχυνας μὰ Δί' οὐδὲν τῶν προϋ-
πηργμένων τῷ μετὰ ταῦτα βίῳ, ἀλλὰ μισθώσας σαυτὸν τοῖς 326
10 βαρυστόνοις ἐπικαλουμένοις ἐκείνοις ὑποκριταῖς, Σιμύλῳ καὶ
Σωκράτει, ἐτριταγωνίστεις, σῦκα καὶ βότρυς καὶ ἐλάας συλ-

1. τοιαῦτα] Sic Σ: ceteri τὰ τοιαῦτα.   5. τοῦτό γε] τοῦτο ΣΦΩ ν.   δ' οὖν]
γ' ΣΓΥΦ ι B. et S.   ἐπειδὴ .. ἐνεγράφης om. A et socii.   6. ἀρχιδίοις] ἀρχείοις A et
socii, et Υ in litura, et ρ, et γρ. ΣΦ.   7. κατηγορεῖς] κατηγόρεις A et socii.
9. σαυτὸν] αὑτὸν Σ B. et S., ἑαυτὸν Harpocr.   10. ἐπικαλουμένοις ἐκείνοις]
ἐκείνοις ἐπικαλουμένοις A et socii.   Σιμύλῳ] Σιμύδῳ Υ, Σιμύκκᾳ Φ et al., Σιμύλλῳ
ς ἢ Σιμύδῳ γρ. F, † σιμύκ και και σωκρατει Σ, ita ut videatur potius prius και et mera διττογραφία esse, quam librarius Σιμύκκᾳ in animo habuisse †.

tion. In Σ there is an obscure mark over
the τ, probably meant for a σ, though more
like a modern cursive α: it seemed to us to
be by the original hand. If we are right in
thus reading it, we should have a fresh
testimony to the antiquity of the variant;
and modern editors are entitled to choose,
as most have done, on grounds of internal
evidence rather than mediaeval authority.
From Hermogenes' manner of quotation, it
would seem to be here that some editions in
his time added the passage quoted at § 167,
which critics objected to, as below the dignity of a *public* speech. It is likely to be
genuine, but we cannot tell how or where
to work it into the present text.

§ 325. *Then, being enrolled as a citizen,
first a clerk and a swindler,*

4. ἐῶ γὰρ τοῦτό γε. 'I do not say that
you *are* no citizen,' only that you *were* not
by birth; for τὸ τοὺς δημότας ἐγγρά-
φεσθαι ought to have coincided with, not
followed, τὸ ἀνὴρ γενέσθαι of § 323.

6. ἀρχιδίοις. 'The petty offices of routine;' yet, according to one biographer, he
attended in this capacity on men of as much
note as Aristophon and Eubulus, which receives some support from Demosthenes' own
language: below, § 333.

7. ὡς δ' ἀπηλλάγης ποτὲ καὶ τούτου.
It seems hard to suppose that the point is
(as Shilleto ad D. de F. L. § 100), that he
'actually rose in caste when he emerged
from this menial office and became a third-
rate actor,' though it seems as if Libanius
had understood it so (Vit. Dem. p. 3, v. 21).
But, comparing the parallel taunt (Ae in Ct.

§ 173), it seems likelier to mean, 'You were
discharged even from this mean place, for
malversations such as you now impute to
others.' Cp. D. de F. L. p. 403, § 222 init.
This would prevent ἃ τῶν ἄλλων κατηγορεῖς
referring to Timarchus: and, in spite of D.
de F. L. ibid. ad fin., it is hardly likely
that so vague an insinuation would have
told on a man of Aeschines' age and character.

§ 326. *Then a player and a thief, often
thrashed in both capacities,*

10. Σιμύλῳ καὶ Σωκράτει. See Consp.
Lect. for the evidence as to the name of
the former of these worthies. According to
Demochares (quoted in the anonymous Life
of Aeschines). he had at first been tritagonist
to Ischander the tragic poet (his senior colleagues being perhaps Theodorus and Aristodemus, D. de F. L. p. 418, § 274), but
was dismissed by him as incompetent, and
then joined a mere strolling company.

11. σῦκα .. ὥσπερ ὀπωρώνης. 'You
collected figs, etc., from other people's land,
like the farmer of a crop from his neighbour's farms.' One or two MSS., and more
editors, add ἐκεῖνος after ὀπωρώνης, as though
there was some well-known or proverbial
story of such dishonesty: and Dissen asks
if we are to suppose that all ὀπωρῶναι did
so. Surely it is likely that they should have
borne a name for doing so as a class: if you
contracted for one season's crop from an
orchard, the temptation to encroach on an
adjoining one would be greater, and the
risk of detection less, than if you had a
more permanent tenure.

λέγων ὥσπερ ὀπωρώνης ἐκ τῶν ἀλλοτρίων χωρίων, πλείω λαμβάνων ἀπὸ τούτων [τραύματα] ἢ τῶν ἀγώνων, οὓς ὑμεῖς περὶ
τῆς ψυχῆς ἠγωνίζεσθε· ἦν γὰρ ἄσπονδος καὶ ἀκήρυκτος ὑμῖν
πρὸς τοὺς θεατὰς πόλεμος, ὑφ' ὧν πολλὰ τραύματ' εἰληφὼς
εἰκότως τοὺς ἀπείρους τῶν τοιούτων κινδύνων ὡς δειλοὺς σκώπ- 5
327 τεις. ἀλλὰ γὰρ παρεὶς ὧν τὴν πενίαν αἰτιάσαιτ' ἄν τις, πρὸς
αὐτὰ τὰ τοῦ τρόπου σου βαδιοῦμαι κατηγορήματα. τοιαύτην
γὰρ εἵλου πολιτείαν, ἐπειδή ποτε καὶ τοῦτ' ἐπῆλθέ σοι ποιῆσαι, δι' ἢν εὐτυχούσης μὲν τῆς πατρίδος λαγὼ βίον ἔζης δεδιὼς
καὶ τρέμων καὶ ἀεὶ πληγήσεσθαι προσδοκῶν ἐφ' οἷς σαυτῷ 10
συνήδεις ἀδικοῦντι, ἐν οἷς δ' ἠτύχησαν οἱ ἄλλοι, θρασὺς ὢν ὑφ'
328 ἁπάντων ὦψαι. καίτοι ὅστις χιλίων πολιτῶν ἀποθανόντων
ἐθάρρησε, τί οὗτος παθεῖν ὑπὸ τῶν ζώντων δίκαιός ἐστιν;
πολλὰ τοίνυν ἕτερ' εἰπεῖν ἔχων περὶ αὐτοῦ παραλείψω· οὐ
γὰρ ὅσ' ἂν δείξαιμι προσόντ' αἰσχρὰ τούτῳ καὶ ὄνειδη, πάντ' 15
οἶμαι δεῖν εὐχερῶς λέγειν, ἀλλ' ὅσα μηδὲν αἰσχρόν ἐστιν εἰπεῖν
ἐμοί.
329 Ἐξέτασον τοίνυν παρ' ἄλληλα τὰ σοὶ κἀμοὶ βεβιωμένα,
πράως, μὴ πικρῶς, Αἰσχίνη· εἶτ' ἐρώτησον τουτουσὶ τὴν ποτέρου τύχην ἂν ἔλοιθ' ἕκαστος αὐτῶν. ἐδίδασκες γράμματα, ἐγὼ 20
δ' ἐφοίτων. ἐτέλεις, ἐγὼ δ' ἐτελούμην. [ἐχόρευες, ἐγὼ δ' ἐχορήγουν.] ἐγραμμάτευες, ἐγὼ δ' ἠκκλησίαζον. ἐτριταγωνίστεις,

---

1. Post ὀπωρώνης ἐκεῖνος add. k.   2. τραύματα] Om. pr. Σ, nec nisi a m. recenti
ibi est additum.   4. πρὸς] Ita Σ: legebatur ὁ πρὸς.   18. κἀμοὶ] † καὶ μοὶ
Σ †.   19. μὴ] καὶ μὴ omnes praeter Σ, quod hoc tantum a m. rec. habet.
ποτέρου] Ita ΣΑ: ceteri ὁ ποτέρου.   21. ἐχόρευες .. ἐχορήγουν] Om. Σ et grammatici.   22. ἠκκλησίαζον] Ita BF : ἠκκλησίαζον Σ (ε superscr. a m. ant.): ceteri
ἐκκλησίαζον. k annotatum habet 'ὅρα τὸ ἐκκλησίαζον. οἶμαι ἐξεκλησίαζον ἔδει.' Vid.
annot.

1. πλείω λαμβάνων ἀπὸ κ.τ.λ. So Σ:
the other MSS., Bekker (in brackets), and
Dissen, add τραύματα after λαμβάνων, 'Your
thefts brought you into more trouble than
even your bad acting.' And it would be
just possible to understand the text the same
way, illustrating the ellipse with πλείω by
πολλὰς in D. de F. L. p. 403, § 219, etc.
But probably it means simply, 'You made
more income by your thefts than by your
profession.'

§§ 327, 328. At last a politician, keeping
in a corner till Athens was in distress.

8. ἐπειδή ποτε .. ποιῆσαι. Correlative
to the ἐδοξέ μοι of § 320.

10. πληγήσεσθαι. Perhaps continuing
the illustration of the hare, perhaps expect-
ing a thrashing, as not being worth a prosecution.

12. χιλίων πολιτῶν ἀποθανόντων ἐθάρρησε. Cp. § 350, describing Aeschines'
avowed attitude after Chaeronea.

§ 329. Now compare your life and mine
quietly, and ask the judges which they prefer.

19. μὴ πικρῶς. For you cannot afford.
καὶ, omitted by Σ, seems rather to weaken
the irony of the quasi-friendly appeal.

21. ἐχόρευες, ἐγὼ δ' ἐχορήγουν. Not
only Σ, but most rhetorical and grammatical
writers who quote the passage, omit this
clause. Internal evidence, or taste, can
hardly be said to decide either way. Whether
genuine or no, ἐχόρευες must refer to the
mystical chorus described in § 324: for there
is no evidence of Aeschines ever having
served in a dramatic chorus.

22. ἠκκλησίαζον. So one would natur-
ally write, and it has quite sufficient authority,

234 ΔΗΜΟΣΘΕΝΟΥΣ §§ 330, 331.

ἐγὼ δ' ἐθεώρουν. ἐξέπιπτες, ἐγὼ δ' ἐσύριττον. ὑπὲρ τῶν
ἐχθρῶν πεπολίτευσαι πάντα, ἐγὼ δ' ὑπὲρ τῆς πατρίδος.
ἐῶ τἆλλα, ἀλλὰ νυνὶ τήμερον ἐγὼ μὲν ὑπὲρ τοῦ στεφανω- 330
θῆναι δοκιμάζομαι, τὸ δὲ μηδ' ὁτιοῦν ἀδικεῖν ἀνωμολόγημαι,
5 σοὶ δὲ συκοφάντῃ μὲν εἶναι δοκεῖν ὑπάρχει, κινδυνεύεις δὲ εἴτε
δεῖ σ' ἔτι τοῦτο ποιεῖν, εἴτ' ἤδη πεπαῦσθαι μὴ μεταλαβόντα
τὸ πέμπτον μέρος τῶν ψήφων. ἀγαθῇ γ', οὐχ ὁρᾷς; τύχῃ
συμβεβιωκὼς τῆς ἐμῆς ὡς φαύλης κατηγορεῖς.

Φέρε δὴ καὶ τὰς τῶν λειτουργιῶν μαρτυρίας, ὧν λελειτούρ- 331
10 γηκα, ὑμῖν ἀναγνῶ. παρ' ἃς παραναγνωθι καὶ σύ μοι τὰς
ῥήσεις ἃς ἐλυμαίνου,

ἥκω λιπὼν κευθμῶνα καὶ σκότου πύλας

καὶ

κακαγγελεῖν μὲν ἴσθι μὴ θέλοντά με,

15 καὶ κακὸν κακῶς σε μάλιστα μὲν οἱ θεοί, ἔπειτα οὗτοι πάντες
ἀπολέσειαν, πονηρὸν ὄντα καὶ πολίτην καὶ τριταγωνιστήν.
Λέγε τὰς μαρτυρίας.

7. πέμπτον] Om. Dind, quia alibi meliores libri omittunt: hic autem omnes habent;
neque est cur eadem passim formula sit Demosthenes usus.　　γ'] δὲ FΥΦΩ et socii.
8. συμβεβιωκὼς] συμβεβηκὼς pr. Σ.　　ὡς φαύλης] Om. Σ B. et S.　　9. λει-
τουργιῶν] λειτουργιῶν Σ.　　10. ἀναγνῶ.　παρ' ἃς] Sic ΣΦ: ceteri ἀναγνῶ πάσας.
καὶ σύ μοι] Sic ΣΦ: δὴ καὶ σύ μοι A et socii: ceteri δ' ἡμῖν καὶ σύ.　　12. λιπὼν]
νεκρῶν pr. Σ, nec nisi a m. recentissimæ est mutatum.　Idque recepit Dind.　14. κακαγ-
γελεῖν] κακ' ἀγγέλλειν vel κακαγγέλλειν ΣΦΑ et socii.　　16. καὶ πολίτην] Sic
ΣΦ: καὶ est deletum in Σ a m. sec.: legebatur πολίτην καὶ προδότην, cum paucis neque
optimis librorum.

even in this place alone. The custom of
writing, on a false analogy, ἐξεκλησίαζον,
seems to have arisen early, but to be decidedly post-Attic: and ἐκκλησίαζον is likely
to be nothing but a confusion between the
two.

1. ἐξέπιπτες, ἐγὼ δ' ἐσύριττον. We
should view the two actions as coming in the
opposite order, as cause and effect: 'You
were in the stage, I in the stalls: I hissed
you, you went off.' Demosthenes reaps the
advantage of being able to use a neuter verb
in a sense where most languages would require a passive.

§ 330. *Even to-day, the question for me
is of a reward for my services; for you,
whether to expel you from your profession,
such as it is.*

4. τὸ δὲ μηδ' ὁτιοῦν κ.τ.λ. As you only
prosecute Ctesiphon.

7. τὸ πέμπτον μέρος τῶν ψήφων. In
the other passages where this phrase occurs,
the best MSS. omit πέμπτον, and accordingly Dindorf does so here. But the fact that
they do not introduce it where it is only a
gloss, is rather a reason that they should be
trusted where they have it.

§§ 331-333. *As to my private generosity,
I will let facts speak for themselves, rather
than talk of my own good deeds:*

9. τῶν λειτουργιῶν. A proof at once of
prosperity and patriotism: 'I served the
state well, therefore I did not hurt it wilfully:
I was in a position to serve it handsomely,
so I cannot have entangled it in ill-fortune.'

12. λιπών. So all MSS. but Σ, which
has νεκρῶν, as in Eur. Hec. 1. It is more
likely that a thoughtful copyist restored the
text of the Hecuba, than that Demosthenes
should have delivered the sentence incomplete. He probably took λιπὼν from the
next line, not from a slip of memory, but to
complete the construction without too long
a quotation. See on §§ 166, 231, for part
of the possible point: Aeschines was a ghost
from the womb!

14. κακαγγελεῖν. Clearly the right reading, though a ἅπαξ λεγόμενον, and though
the MSS. are in a little confusion, from not
being familiar with it. It is not known
from what play the quotation is taken; but
the allusion no doubt is to Aeschines' 'reluctance to give bad news' on the embassy,
about Philip's Phocian expedition.

ΜΑΡΤΥΡΙΑΙ.

332 Ἐν μὲν τοίνυν τοῖς πρὸς τὴν πόλιν τοιοῦτος· ἐν δὲ τοῖς
ἰδίοις εἰ μὴ πάντες ἴστε ὅτι κοινὸς καὶ φιλάνθρωπος καὶ τοῖς
δεομένοις ἐπαρκῶν, σιωπῶ καὶ οὐδὲν ἂν εἴποιμι οὐδὲ παρασχοί-
μην περὶ τούτων οὐδεμίαν μαρτυρίαν, οὔτ᾽ εἴ τινας ἐκ τῶν 5
πολεμίων ἐλυσάμην, οὔτ᾽ εἴ τισι θυγατέρας συνεξέδωκα, οὔτε
333 τῶν τοιούτων οὐδέν. καὶ γὰρ οὕτω πως ὑπείληφα. ἐγὼ
νομίζω τὸν μὲν εὖ παθόντα δεῖν μεμνῆσθαι πάντα τὸν χρόνον,
τὸν δὲ ποιήσαντα εὐθὺς ἐπιλελῆσθαι, εἰ δεῖ τὸν μὲν χρηστοῦ,
τὸν δὲ μὴ μικροψύχου ποιεῖν ἔργον ἀνθρώπου. τὸ δὲ τὰς 10
ἰδίας εὐεργεσίας ὑπομιμνήσκειν καὶ λέγειν μικροῦ δεῖν ὅμοιόν
ἐστι τῷ ὀνειδίζειν. οὐ δὴ ποιήσω τοιοῦτον οὐδέν, οὐδὲ προαχθήσομαι, ἀλλ᾽ ὅπως ποθ᾽ ὑπείλημμαι περὶ τούτων, ἀρκεῖ μοι.
334 Βούλομαι δὲ τῶν ἰδίων ἀπαλλαγεὶς ἔτι μικρὰ πρὸς ὑμᾶς
εἰπεῖν περὶ τῶν κοινῶν. εἰ μὲν γὰρ ἔχεις, Αἰσχίνη, τῶν ὑπὸ 15
τοῦτον τὸν ἥλιον εἰπεῖν ἀνθρώπων ὅστις ἀθῷος τῆς Φιλίππου
πρότερον καὶ νῦν τῆς Ἀλεξάνδρου δυναστείας γέγονεν, ἢ τῶν
Ἑλλήνων ἢ τῶν βαρβάρων, ἔστω, συγχωρῶ σοι τὴν ἐμὴν εἴτε
τύχην εἴτε δυστυχίαν ὀνομάζειν βούλει πάντων αἰτίαν γεγενῆ-
335 σθαι. εἰ δὲ καὶ τῶν μηδεπώποτ᾽ ἰδόντων ἐμὲ μηδὲ φωνὴν 20
ἀκηκοότων ἐμοῦ πολλοὶ πολλὰ καὶ δεινὰ πεπόνθασι, μὴ μόνον
κατ᾽ ἄνδρα, ἀλλὰ καὶ πόλεις ὅλαι καὶ ἔθνη, πόσῳ δικαιότερον
καὶ ἀληθέστερον τὴν ἁπάντων, ὡς ἔοικεν, ἀνθρώπων τύχην κοινὴν καὶ φοράν τινα πραγμάτων χαλεπὴν καὶ οὐχ οἵαν ἔδει

---

8. πάντα τὸν] Sic ΣΦΑ et socii : ceteri τὸν πάντα. 9. ποιήσαντα] εὖ ποιήσαντα
A et alii. 16. τοῦτον] Ita Σ : ceteri et Bekk. τουτονί. 18. σοι] Om. Σ.
19. αἰτίαν] Om. pr. Σ.

5. εἴ τινας .. ἐλυσάμην. As on his second
embassy in Macedonia, D. de F. L. p. 396,
§ 186 sqq., A. de F. L. pp. 29, 41, §§ 12, 106.
7. ἐγὼ νομίζω κ.τ.λ. . It is perhaps
worth noticing that the Iambic rhythm arises
less from accident than from the sententious
fulness of expression : there is a very similar
verse in the Midias, p. 547, § 129.
8. δεῖν .. εἰ δεῖ. 'We are to expect .. ,
if we are to expect the one to act like an
honest man, and the other not to act like a
mean-spirited one.'
12. οὐδὲ προαχθήσομαι. Not even
under provocation, such as your slanders.
§§ 334, 335. About public affairs I have
a little more to say. If there be a single
man under the sun that is free from Macedon,
let it be held my fault that Athens is not free.

15. τῶν ὑπὸ τοῦτον τὸν ἥλιον. All
west of the Adriatic had fallen out of the
political horizon.
17. δυναστείας. The most accurate
word afforded by Greek political nomenclature for the informal but absolute and, in
Demosthenes' view, unjust and oppressive
supremacy of the Macedonian kings. The
transference of the word from domestic
power to international, may be illustrated
from what is said of the τυραννὶς of Athens,
Thuc. I. 122, 124 ; 3. 37 ; and so Demosthenes has applied the same word to Philip,
in the era of his conquests, above, § 80.
18. τὴν ἐμὴν .. δυστυχίαν. He only
gives this verbal alternative ; even in a hypothetical case, he will not admit a suspicion
of his loyalty.

τούτων αἰτίαν ἡγεῖσθαι. σὺ τοίνυν ταῦτ' ἀφεὶς ἐμὲ τὸν παρὰ 336
τουτοισὶ πεπολιτευμένον αἰτιᾷ, καὶ ταῦτ' εἰδὼς ὅτι, καὶ εἰ μὴ
τὸ ὅλον, μέρος γ' ἐπιβάλλει τῆς βλασφημίας ἅπασι, καὶ μάλιστα σοί. εἰ μὲν γὰρ ἐγὼ κατ' ἐμαυτὸν αὐτοκράτωρ περὶ
5 τῶν πραγμάτων ἐβουλευόμην, ἦν ἂν τοῖς ἄλλοις ῥήτορσιν ὑμῖν
ἐμὲ αἰτιᾶσθαι· εἰ δὲ παρῆτε μέν ἐν ταῖς ἐκκλησίαις ἁπάσαις, 337
ἀεὶ δ' ἐν κοινῷ τὸ συμφέρον ἡ πόλις προὐτίθει σκοπεῖν, πᾶσι
δὲ ταῦτ' ἐδόκει τότ' ἄριστ' εἶναι, καὶ μάλιστα σοὶ (οὐ γὰρ
ἐπ' εὐνοίᾳ γ' ἐμοὶ παρεχώρεις ἐλπίδων καὶ ζήλου καὶ τιμῶν,
10 ἃ πάντα προσῆν τοῖς τότε πραττομένοις ὑπ' ἐμοῦ, ἀλλὰ τῆς
ἀληθείας ἡττώμενος δηλονότι καὶ τῷ μηδὲν ἔχειν εἰπεῖν βέλτιον), πῶς οὐκ ἀδικεῖς καὶ δεινὰ ποιεῖς τούτοις νῦν ἐγκαλῶν
ὧν τότ' οὐκ εἶχες λέγειν βελτίω; παρὰ μὲν τοίνυν τοῖς ἄλλοις 338
ἔγωγ' ὁρῶ πᾶσιν ἀνθρώποις διωρισμένα καὶ τεταγμένα πως τὰ
15 τοιαῦτα. ἀδικεῖ τις ἑκών, ὀργὴν καὶ τιμωρίαν κατὰ τούτου.
ἐξήμαρτέ τις ἄκων, συγγνώμην ἀντὶ τῆς τιμωρίας τούτῳ. οὔτ'
ἀδικῶν τις οὔτ' ἐξαμαρτάνων, εἰς τὰ πᾶσι δοκοῦντα συμφέρειν
ἑαυτὸν δοὺς οὐ κατώρθωσε μεθ' ἁπάντων; οὐκ ὀνειδίζειν οὐδὲ
λοιδορεῖσθαι τῷ τοιούτῳ δίκαιον, ἀλλὰ συνάχθεσθαι. φανή- 339
20 σεται ταῦτα πάντα οὕτως οὐ μόνον ἐν τοῖς νομίμοις, ἀλλὰ
καὶ ἡ φύσις αὐτὴ τοῖς ἀγράφοις νόμοις καὶ τοῖς ἀνθρωπίνοις
ἤθεσι διώρικεν. Αἰσχίνης τοίνυν τοσοῦτον ὑπερβέβληκεν ἅπαν-

---

4. αὐτοκράτωρ] Ita ΣΑ et socii B. et S. Volgo et Dind. αὐτοκράτωρ ὤν. 15. ὀργὴν
καὶ τιμωρίαν] Ita ΣΑ et socii: legebatur ὀργὴ καὶ τιμωρία, et mox συγγνώμη.
17. ἐξαμαρτάνων] ἐξαμαρτὼν Α et socii. δοκοῦντα συμφέρειν] τὰ φέρειν pr. Σ,
spatio praecedente, in quo δοκοῦντα a m. rec. est insertum. 20. ταῦτα] Legebatur
τοίνυν ταῦτα : τοίνυν om, Σ. ἐν] Om. ΣΑ et socii. Mox νόμοις pro νομίμοις habent
iidem. 21. νόμοις] νομίμοις libri : νόμοις et νομίμοις inter se permutavit Reisk.
22. ἤθεσι] Om. Σ : vid. annot.

---

§ 336. There is none, yet you throw blame
on me that you know must fall upon Athens.
1. τὸν παρὰ τουτοισὶ πεπολιτευμένον.
My sphere of action has been limited to
Athens, yet you attribute to it world-wide
effects: it has been visible to all Athens, yet
you expect to deceive Athenians as to its
character.
3. καὶ μάλιστα σοί. Who hated me
most.
4. αὐτοκράτωρ. Addebatur ὤν ut ad
§ 294.
§ 337. And on you, who might have
opposed me.
9. ἐλπίδων. Hopes of future influence,
to be founded on success.
ζήλου. Present rivalry in the contest.
τιμῶν. Present respect.

§§ 338, 339. Other men punish crime,
forgive error, and pity misfortune: Aeschines
holds me criminally responsible for ill-success.
13. παρὰ μὲν τοίνυν κ.τ.λ. Answered
by Αἰσχίνης τοίνυν in the next section.
'All other men make a difference between
the three cases of crime, blunder, and misfortune: Aeschines confuses even the first
and last.' Cp. Ar. Rhet. I. 13.
20. νομίμοις .. νόμοις. All MSS. have
νομίμοις in the second place, and Σ and
others have νόμοις in the first. Reiske's
transposition is generally accepted : νόμιμα
is the more formal word, and being originally
an adjective, τὰ ἄγραφα νόμιμα is rare, and
would be harsh.
22. ἤθεσι. So the MSS. (Σ omits it,
doubtless by accident), Bekker, B. and S.

τας ἀνθρώπους ὠμότητι καὶ συκοφαντίᾳ ὥστε καὶ ὧν αὐτὸς
ὡς ἀτυχημάτων ἐμέμνητο, καὶ ταῦτ' ἐμοῦ κατηγορεῖ.

340 Καὶ πρὸς τοῖς ἄλλοις, ὥσπερ αὐτὸς ἁπλῶς καὶ μετ' εὐνοίας
πάντας εἰρηκὼς τοὺς λόγους, φυλάττειν ἐμὲ καὶ τηρεῖν ἐκέλευεν,
ὅπως μὴ παρακρούσομαι μηδ' ἐξαπατήσω, δεινὸν καὶ γόητα 5
καὶ σοφιστὴν καὶ τὰ τοιαῦτ' ὀνομάζων, ὡς ἐὰν πρότερός τις
εἴπῃ τὰ προσόνθ' ἑαυτῷ περὶ ἄλλου, καὶ δὴ ταῦθ' οὕτως ἔχοντα,
καὶ οὐκέτι τοὺς ἀκούοντας σκεψομένους τίς ποτ' αὐτός ἐστιν ὁ
ταῦτα λέγων. ἐγὼ δ' οἶδ' ὅτι γιγνώσκετε τοῦτον ἅπαντες,
καὶ πολὺ τούτῳ μᾶλλον ἢ ἐμοὶ νομίζετε ταῦτα προσεῖναι. 10
341 κἀκεῖνο εὖ οἶδ' ὅτι τὴν ἐμὴν δεινότητα—ἔστω γάρ. καίτοι
ἔγωγ' ὁρῶ τῆς τῶν λεγόντων δυνάμεως τοὺς ἀκούοντας τὸ
πλεῖστον κυρίους· ὡς γὰρ ἂν ὑμεῖς ἀποδέξησθε καὶ πρὸς ἕκαστον ἔχητ' εὐνοίας, οὕτως ὁ λέγων ἔδοξε φρονεῖν. εἰ δ' οὖν
ἐστι καὶ παρ' ἐμοί τις ἐμπειρία τοιαύτη, ταύτην μὲν εὑρήσετε 15
πάντες ἐν τοῖς κοινοῖς ἐξεταζομένην ὑπὲρ ὑμῶν ἀεὶ καὶ οὐδαμοῦ καθ' ὑμῶν οὐδ' ἰδίᾳ, τὴν δὲ τούτου τοὐναντίον οὐ μόνον
τῷ λέγειν ὑπὲρ τῶν ἐχθρῶν, ἀλλὰ καὶ εἴ τις ἐλύπησέ τι τοῦ-
342 τον ἢ προσέκρουσέ που, κατὰ τούτων. οὐ γὰρ αὐτῇ δικαίως,
οὐδ' ἐφ' ἃ συμφέρει τῇ πόλει, χρῆται. οὔτε γὰρ τὴν ὀργὴν 20

---

5. παρακρούσομαι] Sic Σ: legebatur παρακρούσωμαι.   11. κἀκεῖνο] Ita A et
socii, καὶ ἐκεῖνο Σ, κἀκεῖνο δὲ ceteri.   13. πλεῖστον κυρίους] Ita Σ: legebatur
ante Bekk. πλεῖστον μέρος κυρίους ὄντας.

Dindorf has ἔθεσι, as at § 115. So far as
the words were really distinct in popular
language, ἤθεσι seems more appropriate
here: the sense is not 'habits,' so much as
'universal moral traditions or feelings.'

Αἰσχίνης τοίνυν. As ἔπειτα without
δὲ is sufficient to mark the antithesis to
πρῶτον μὲν, so is the proper name without
δὲ sufficient to answer to παρὰ μὲν τοῖς
ἄλλοις.

§§ 340-343. Then, as if he had spoken
fairly and moderately, he charges me not to
mislead you:—you, who know him for a
trickster—as if an intelligent audience was
so easy to mislead. If I have been able to
lead you, it was always for your good, like a
good citizen, who places the common weal
before all things. He exerts himself for the
public good,

5. δεινὸν καὶ γόητα κ.τ.λ.: cp. Ae. in
Ct. §§ 16, 207.

6. ὡς ἐὰν .. οὕτως ἔχοντα. καὶ δὴ introduces the apodosis: 'As if, should a man
come first to charge his neighbour with his
own faults, presently the charge is forsooth
to be true, and the hearers are too late to

examine the accuser.' For the construction
of the accusatives, vid. ad Ae. in Ct. § 112.

11. δεινότητα—ἔστω γάρ. δεινότης
being not exactly a word of blame, but a
suspicious quality that it is doubtful praise
to impute. That he was γόης καὶ σοφιστὴς
of course he could not admit at all.

καίτοι ἔγωγ' ὁρῶ. I am a successful
speaker, Aeschines is not: he thinks everything depends on the speaker, I on the
audience.

18. ὑπὲρ τῶν ἐχθρῶν answers to ὑπὲρ
ὑμῶν ἀεὶ καὶ οὐδαμοῦ καθ' ὑμῶν.

εἴ τις ἐλύπησέ τι κατὰ τούτων an-
swers to οὐδ' ἰδίᾳ. Dissen thinks that the last
words are meant to describe Aeschines' developing his personal quarrel with himself on the
embassy into a political antagonism: but surely
Demosthenes, by his prosecution, was himself chiefly responsible for that. The same
might be said of Timarchus. Possibly a
private quarrel with Ctesiphon is referred to.

20. τὴν ὀργὴν ·· βεβαιοῦν. Almost
'endorse his passion or his spite,' secure him
the luxury of feeling it, by deciding in accordance with it.

οὔτε τὴν ἔχθραν οὔτ᾽ ἄλλο οὐδὲν τῶν τοιούτων τὸν καλὸν
κἀγαθὸν πολίτην δεῖ τοὺς ὑπὲρ τῶν κοινῶν εἰσεληλυθότας δικαστὰς ἀξιοῦν αὐτῷ βεβαιοῦν, οὐδ᾽ ὑπὲρ τούτων εἰς ὑμᾶς εἰσιέναι,
ἀλλὰ μάλιστα μὲν μὴ ἔχειν ταῦτ᾽ ἐν τῇ φύσει, εἰ δ᾽ ἄρ᾽
5 ἀνάγκη, πράως καὶ μετρίως διακείμεν᾽ ἔχειν. ἐν τίσιν οὖν 343
σφοδρὸν εἶναι τὸν πολιτευόμενον καὶ τὸν ῥήτορα δεῖ; ἐν οἷς
τῶν ὅλων τι κινδυνεύεται τῇ πόλει, καὶ ἐν οἷς πρὸς τοὺς ἐναν-
τίους ἐστὶ τῷ δήμῳ ἐν τούτοις· ταῦτα γὰρ γενναίου καὶ ἀγαθοῦ
πολίτου. μηδενὸς δὲ ἀδικήματος πώποτε δημοσίου, προσθήσω 344
10 δὲ μηδ᾽ ἰδίου, δίκην ἀξιώσαντα λαβεῖν παρ᾽ ἐμοῦ μήθ᾽ ὑπὲρ
τῆς πόλεως μήθ᾽ ὑπὲρ αὐτοῦ, στεφάνου καὶ ἐπαίνου κατηγορίαν ἥκειν συνεσκευασμένον, καὶ τοσουτουσὶ λόγους ἀνηλωκέναι
ἰδίας ἔχθρας καὶ φθόνου καὶ μικροψυχίας ἐστὶ σημεῖον, οὐδενὸς χρηστοῦ. τὸ δὲ δὴ καὶ τοὺς πρὸς ἐμὲ αὐτὸν ἀγῶνας ἐά-
15 σαντα νῦν ἐπὶ τόνδ᾽ ἥκειν καὶ πᾶσαν ἔχει κακίαν. καί μοι 345
δοκεῖς ἐκ τούτων, Αἰσχίνη, λόγων ἐπίδειξίν τινα καὶ φωνασκίας βουλόμενος ποιήσασθαι τοῦτον προελέσθαι τὸν ἀγῶνα,
οὐκ ἀδικήματος οὐδενὸς λαβεῖν τιμωρίαν. ἔστι δ᾽ οὐχ ὁ λόγος
τοῦ ῥήτορος, Αἰσχίνη, τίμιον, οὐδ᾽ ὁ τόνος τῆς φωνῆς, ἀλλὰ
20 τὸ ταὐτὰ προαιρεῖσθαι τοῖς πολλοῖς καὶ τὸ τοὺς αὐτοὺς μισεῖν
καὶ φιλεῖν οὕσπερ ἂν ἡ πατρίς. ὁ γὰρ οὕτως ἔχων τὴν ψυχήν, 346
οὗτος ἐπ᾽ εὐνοίᾳ πάντ᾽ ἐρεῖ· ὁ δ᾽ ἀφ᾽ ὧν ἡ πόλις προορᾶταί
τινα κίνδυνον ἑαυτῇ, τούτους θεραπεύων οὐκ ἐπὶ τῆς αὐτῆς ὁρμεῖ
τοῖς πολλοῖς, οὔκουν οὐδὲ τῆς ἀσφαλείας τὴν αὐτὴν ἔχει προσ-
25 δοκίαν. . ἀλλ᾽, ὁρᾷς; ἐγώ· ταὐτὰ γὰρ συμφέρονθ᾽ εἱλόμην
τουτοισί, καὶ οὐδὲν ἐξαίρετον οὐδ᾽ ἴδιον πεποίημαι. ἆρ᾽ οὖν 347

---

5. ἀνάγκη] † ἂν ἀνάγκη Σ †.   διακείμεν᾽] διακείμενον ΓΥΦΩ et socii.   8. γεν-
ναίου] ἐστι γενναίου Α et socii.   11. κατηγορίαν] Ita Σ: ceteri νῦν κατηγορίαν
vel κατηγορίαν νῦν.   14. ἐμὲ αὐτὸν] Sic ΣΩ et al.: volg. ἐμαυτὸν.   15. καὶ
πᾶσαν] Ita Α kst: ceteri πᾶσαν.   16. λόγων] Sic ΣΦ: legebatur ante Bekk. τῶν
λόγων, mox omisso καὶ, quod omittunt iidem qui articulum habent.   19. τίμιον]
Sic Σ: ceteri τίμιος.

6. σφοδρόν. Conceding that Aeschines
might have a case for charging him with
violence of language or manner, e. g. §
150.
§§ 344, 345. *You in a private quarrel,
or a mere rhetorical display:*
16. λόγων ἐπίδειξιν καὶ φωνασκίας.
' To shew how well you can talk, and that
your voice is still in good training.' For
φωνασκία, cp. ad Ae. in Ct. § 210, though
the occurrence of ὁ τόνος τῆς φωνῆς here
prevents one's pressing the contrast.
20. τὸ ταὐτὰ προαιρεῖσθαι τοῖς πολλοῖς is the loyalty that serves Athens her

own way,
τὸ τοὺς αὐτοὺς μισεῖν καὶ φιλεῖν οὕσπερ ἂν ἡ πατρίς, the patriotism that takes
sides with Athens, in any conflict, for or
against whomsoever.
§§ 346, 347. *Which has no value from a
bad citizen, who rejoices in the success of the
public enemy.*
24. οὐδὲ τῆς ἀσφαλείας κ.τ.λ. As his
hope of security rests upon different grounds,
so he does not look to its realisation either
to come in the same way. If he looks to
Philip for safety, he is safest when Philip
succeeds.

οὐδὲ σύ; καὶ πῶς; ὃς εὐθέως μετὰ τὴν μάχην πρεσβευτὴς
ἐπορεύου πρὸς Φίλιππον, ὃς ἦν τῶν ἐν ἐκείνοις τοῖς χρόνοις
συμφορῶν αἴτιος τῇ πατρίδι, καὶ ταῦτ᾿ ἀρνούμενος πάντα τὸν
348 ἔμπροσθε χρόνον ταύτην τὴν χρείαν, ὡς πάντες ἴσασιν. καίτοι
τίς ὁ τὴν πόλιν ἐξαπατῶν; οὐχ ὁ μὴ λέγων ἃ φρονεῖ; τῷ δ᾿ 5
ὁ κῆρυξ καταρᾶται δικαίως; οὐ τῷ τοιούτῳ; τί δὲ μεῖζον ἔχοι
τις ἂν εἰπεῖν ἀδίκημα κατ᾿ ἀνδρὸς ῥήτορος ἢ εἰ μὴ ταὐτὰ φρο-
349 νεῖ καὶ λέγει; σὺ τοίνυν οὗτος εὑρέθης. εἶτα σὺ φθέγγει καὶ
βλέπειν εἰς τὰ τουτωνὶ πρόσωπα τολμᾷς; πότερ᾿ οὐχ ἡγεῖ
γιγνώσκειν αὐτοὺς ὅστις εἶ; ἢ τοσοῦτον ὕπνον καὶ λήθην ἅπαν- 10
τας ἔχειν ὥστ᾿ οὐ μεμνῆσθαι τοὺς λόγους οὓς ἐδημηγόρεις ἐν
τῷ πολέμῳ, καταρώμενος καὶ διομνύμενος μηδὲν εἶναι σοὶ καὶ
Φιλίππῳ πρᾶγμα, ἀλλ᾿ ἐμὲ τὴν αἰτίαν σοι ταύτην ἐπάγειν
350 τῆς ἰδίας ἕνεκ᾿ ἔχθρας, οὐκ οὖσαν ἀληθῆ. ὡς δ᾿ ἀπηγγέλθη
τάχισθ᾿ ἡ μάχη, οὐδὲν τούτων φροντίσας εὐθέως ὡμολόγεις καὶ 15
προσεποιοῦ φιλίαν, καὶ ξενίαν εἶναί σοι πρὸς αὐτόν, τῇ μισθαρ-
νίᾳ ταῦτα μετατιθέμενος τὰ ὀνόματα· ἐκ ποίας γὰρ ἴσης ἢ
δικαίας προφάσεως Αἰσχίνῃ τῷ Γλαυκοθέας τῆς τυμπανιστρίας
351 ξένος ἢ φίλος ἢ γνώριμος ἦν Φίλιππος; ἐγὼ μὲν οὐχ ὁρῶ,
ἀλλ᾿ ἐμισθώθης ἐπὶ τῷ τὰ τουτωνὶ συμφέροντα διαφθείρειν. 20
ἀλλ᾿ ὅμως οὕτω φανερῶς αὐτὸς εἰλημμένος προδότης καὶ
κατὰ σαυτοῦ μηνυτὴς ἐπὶ τοῖς συμβᾶσι γεγονὼς ἐμοὶ

---

2. ἐν] Om. Σ.   6. καταρᾶται δικαίως] καταρᾶται καθ᾿ ἑκάστην ἐκκλησίαν
δικαίως γρ. ΣΦΦ: legebatur ante Bekk. καταρᾶται δικαίως καθ᾿ ἑκάστην ἐκκλησίαν.
7. ἦ] Om. F p A et socii.   9. τουτωνὶ] τούτων ΣΤ r B. et S.   12. πολέμῳ]
Sic ΣA k: volg. et Bekk. δήμῳ.   15. εὐθέως] Sic pr. Σ: volg. et Bekk. εὐθύς.

---

1. πρεσβευτής: Ae. in Ct. § 228.
3. ἀρνούμενος: vide ad § 349.
§§ 348–351. *You are convicted of insincerity, having denied connection with Philip
till the battle, and proclaimed it afterwards,
in a form absurd from its arrogance.*
6. ὁ κῆρυξ καταρᾶται: cp. above, § 165
fin. The reading given as a γρ. in three
MSS., καθ᾿ ἑκάστην ἐκκλησίαν, is no doubt
a gloss, and right as a gloss. We may suppose that it was a part of the ceremonial of
opening the Assembly, to proclaim a curse
on every one who should not utter his sincere views.
8. οὗτος. Not merely τοιοῦτος, but *the*
typical specimen of the class described, ὁ τὴν
πόλιν ἐξαπατῶν, ὁ μὴ λέγων ἃ φρονεῖ, ὁ
τοιοῦτος ὃν ὁ κῆρυξ καταρᾶται δικαίως.
11. ὥστ᾿ οὐ μεμνῆσθαι. οὐ, not μή,
because the infinitive is only due to the

oratio obliqua : the sentiment attributed to
Aeschines is, τοσοῦτος ὕπνος καὶ λήθη ἅπαντας ἔχει, ὥστ᾿ οὐ μέμνηνται. Cp. Shilleto's
D. de F. L. Exc.
12. μηδὲν εἶναι σοὶ καὶ Φιλίππῳ πρᾶγμα.
Aeschines did not directly contradict himself, if we may press Demosthenes' words.
What he denied was that he had any practical connection or communication with
Philip; what he affirmed was, that he had
with him the relation of personal hospitality,
the φιλία of § 350.
17. ἐκ ποίας γὰρ .. προφάσεως. The
πρόφασις was, that he and his colleagues
had received Philip's hospitality on the embassy.
18. Γλαυκοθέας. He admits it was her
real name: admits also, perhaps, that Atro-
metus was not altogether a parent to be
ashamed of.

λοιδορεῖ καὶ ὀνειδίζεις ταῦτα, ὧν πάντας μᾶλλον αἰτίους
εὑρήσεις. Πολλὰ καὶ καλὰ καὶ μεγάλα ἡ πόλις, Αἰσχίνη, καὶ προεί- 352
λετο καὶ κατώρθωσε δι' ἐμοῦ, ὧν οὐκ ἠμνημόνησεν. σημεῖον
5 δέ· χειροτονῶν γὰρ ὁ δῆμος τὸν ἐροῦντ' ἐπὶ τοῖς τετελευτηκόσι
παρ' αὐτὰ τὰ συμβάντα οὐ σὲ ἐχειροτόνησε προβληθέντα, καίπερ εὔφωνον ὄντα, οὐδὲ Δημάδην, ἄρτι πεποιηκότα τὴν εἰρήνην,
οὐδ' Ἡγήμονα, οὐδ' ἄλλον ὑμῶν οὐδένα, ἀλλ' ἐμέ. καὶ παρελ-
θόντος σοῦ καὶ Πυθοκλέους ὠμῶς καὶ ἀναιδῶς, ω Ζεῦ καὶ θεοὶ,
10 καὶ κατηγορούντων ἐμοῦ ταῦτὰ ἃ καὶ σὺ νυνί, καὶ λοιδορου-
μένων, ἔτ' ἄμεινον ἐχειροτόνησεν ἐμέ. τὸ δ' αἴτιον οὐκ ἀγνοεῖς 353
μὲν, ὅμως δὲ φράσω σοι κἀγώ. ἀμφότερ' ᾔδεσαν αὐτοί, τὴν
τ' ἐμὴν εὔνοιαν καὶ προθυμίαν, μεθ' ἧς τὰ πράγματ' ἔπραττον,
καὶ τὴν ὑμετέραν ἀδικίαν· ἃ γὰρ εὐθενούντων τῶν πραγμάτων
15 ἠρνεῖσθε διομνύμενοι, ταῦτ' ἐν οἷς ἔπταισεν ἡ πόλις ὡμολογή-
σατε. τοὺς οὖν ἐπὶ τοῖς κοινοῖς ἀτυχήμασιν ὧν ἐφρόνουν λαβόντας ἄδειαν ἐχθροὺς μὲν πάλαι, φανεροὺς δὲ τόθ' ἡγήσαντο
αὐτοῖς γεγενῆσθαι. εἶτα καὶ προσήκειν ὑπολαμβάνοντες τὸν 354
ἐροῦντ' ἐπὶ τοῖς τετελευτηκόσι καὶ τὴν ἐκείνων ἀρετὴν κοσμή-
20 σοντα μήθ' ὁμωρόφιον μήθ' ὁμόσπονδον γεγενημένον εἶναι τοῖς

---

1. μᾶλλον αἰτίους] αἰτίους μᾶλλον Υ p A et socii.　　2. Post εὑρήσεις ante Bekk.
addebatur ἢ ἐμέ.　Om. Σ.　　6. οὐ σὲ] οὐ σ' Σ, et mox ἐχειροτόνησέ με.
8. Ἡγήμονα] Sic A, Ἡγημόνα k, Ἡγεμόνα s, ceteri, ut videtur, Ἡγέμονα. Literam ter-
tiam in rasura habet Σ.　　10. ταῦτὰ] ταῦτα praeter Σ plerique.　　12. κἀγώ]
καὶ ἐγώ Σ.　　αὐτοί] Om. Υ p, οὗτοι A et socii Bekk. Dind.　　18. ὑπολαμ-
βάνοντες] Sic ΣΦ : ceteri et Bekk. ὑπελάμβανον.

---

1. **πάντας μᾶλλον αἰτίους.** Possibly as
in § 92, etc.: 'I did not really do as much
as others to precipitate the *war*,' but it is
more in harmony with the sense of the passage to take it, 'I did more than any man
to prevent the *defeat*.'

§§ 352-354. *The City chose me for the
funeral oration, in spite of you: it knew us
both, and that my grief was sincere.*

4. **σημεῖον δέ** refers quite as much to δι'
ἐμοῦ as to οὐκ ἠμνημόνησεν.

5. **ὁ δῆμος.** According to Plato's Me-
nexenus (p. 234 B), the senate appointed.
The practice *may* have been changed, but it
is far likelier that Plato speaks inaccurately.
It is scarcely possible that Demosthenes
should.

6. **παρ' αὐτὰ τὰ συμβάντα.** Here clearly
of time.

7. **Δημάδην.** He not only had negotiated the peace, so as to have some claim
to the people's gratitude, but had fought in
the battle and been made prisoner, so as to

have the claim of a comrade to speak for
the dead.

11. **ἔτ' ἄμεινον.** 'Yet more heartily,' in
a second assembly after the charge broke
down.

12. **αὐτοί.** So Σ and most other MSS.
for the vulgate οὗτοι: 'They knew of their
personal experience.' Even apart from authority, the transition, from speaking to
Aeschines of the people, to speaking consciously in the presence of the people, would
be harsh and inartistic.

16. **ὧν ἐφρόνουν .. ἄδειαν.** Exactly
equivalent to the common Gallicism, 'the
courage of their opinions.'

20. **μήθ' ὁμωρόφιον κ.τ.λ.** Demosthenes
must mean τοῖς πρὸς ἐκείνους παραταξαμένοις not merely as a designation of persons,
but as implying the time after the battle :
else he himself had partaken of Philip's hospitality, on the first embassy at least. Perhaps the use of γεγενημένον εἶναι expresses
this distinction : Demosthenes might be

πρὸς ἐκείνους παραταξαμένοις, μηδ' ἐκεῖ μὲν κωμάζειν καὶ παιανί-
ζειν ἐπὶ ταῖς τῶν Ἑλλήνων συμφοραῖς μετὰ τῶν αὐτοχείρων
τοῦ φόνου, δεῦρο δ' ἐλθόντα τιμᾶσθαι, μηδὲ τῇ φωνῇ δακρύειν
ὑποκρινόμενον τὴν ἐκείνων τύχην, ἀλλὰ τῇ ψυχῇ συναλγεῖν.
355 τοῦτο δ' ἑώρων παρ' ἑαυτοῖς καὶ παρ' ἐμοί, παρὰ δ' ὑμῖν οὔ. 5
διὰ ταῦτ' ἔμ' ἐχειροτόνησαν καὶ οὐχ ὑμᾶς. καὶ οὐχ ὁ μὲν
δῆμος οὕτως, οἱ δὲ τῶν τετελευτηκότων πατέρες καὶ ἀδελφοὶ
οἱ ὑπὸ τοῦ δήμου τόθ' αἱρεθέντες ἐπὶ τὰς ταφὰς ἄλλως πως,
ἀλλὰ δέον ποιεῖν αὐτοὺς τὸ περίδειπνον ὡς παρ' οἰκειοτάτῳ
τῶν τετελευτηκότων, ὥσπερ τἄλλ' εἴωθε γίγνεσθαι, τοῦτ' ἐποί- 10
356 ησαν παρ' ἐμοί. εἰκότως· γένει μὲν γὰρ ἕκαστος ἑκάστῳ μᾶλλον οἰκεῖος ἦν ἐμοῦ, κοινῇ δὲ πᾶσιν οὐδεὶς ἐγγυτέρω· ᾧ γὰρ
ἐκείνους σωθῆναι καὶ κατορθῶσαι μάλιστα διέφερεν, οὗτος καὶ
παθόντων ἃ μήποτ' ὤφελον τῆς ὑπὲρ ἁπάντων λύπης πλεῖστον μετεῖχεν. 15
357 Λέγε δ' αὐτῷ τουτὶ τὸ ἐπίγραμμα, ὃ δημοσίᾳ προείλετο
ἡ πόλις αὐτοῖς ἐπιγράψαι, ἵν' εἰδῇς, Αἰσχίνη, καὶ ἐν αὐτῷ
τούτῳ σαυτὸν ἀγνώμονα καὶ συκοφάντην ὄντα καὶ μιαρόν.
Λέγε.

ΕΠΙΓΡΑΜΜΑ.   20

358   Οἵδε πάτρας ἕνεκα σφετέρας εἰς δῆριν ἔθεντο
        ὅπλα, καὶ ἀντιπάλων ὕβριν ἀπεσκέδασαν.

οδ'
3. δεῦρο δ' ἐλθόντα] δεῦρ ελθόντα Σ, δ' om. etiam s.   4. ὑποκρινόμενον] Ita A
et socii : ceteri, B. et S., ὑποκρινομένους.   8. οἱ ὑπὸ] Ita Σ B. et S. Dind. : ceteri
et Bekk. ὑπό.   9. οἰκειοτάτῳ τῶν] οἰκιοτάτῳ pr. Σ, οἰκειοτάτῳ Ω, οἰκειοτάτων Υ
et pr. r.   13. ἐκείνους] Ita ΣΦ : ceteri τὸ ἐκείνους.   20. Totum epigramma
om. ΣΑ et socii.

said, as a separate past fact, ὁμωρόφιον καὶ
ὁμόσπονδον γεγενῆσθαι. Cp. ad Ae. in Ct.
§ 64.

4. ὑποκρινόμενον. The emphatic word,
opposed to τῇ ψυχῇ συναλγεῖν. But as
Aeschines was apparently the only other
candidate proposed, it conveys the usual
sneer at the actor.

§§ 355, 356. *The kindred of the dead
chose my house for the funeral feast :*
8. αἱρεθέντες. A committee of the relatives of the dead, appointed by the state.

9. ὡς παρ' οἰκειοτάτῳ τῶν τετελευτηκότων. They 'had to hold the supper *as
it were* in the nearest kinsman's house,' in
accordance with the custom in common
funerals, where of course it would be the
actual next kinsman who gave it.

§§ 357–359. *And the public monument re-
pudiates your principle of judging by the event.*

16. λέγε δ' αὐτῷ. The quotation of
the inscription serves to balance those quoted
by Aeschines in honour of ancient worthies
(in Ct. §§ 184–186, 191).

21. ἔθεντο ὅπλα apparently has come to
be merely equivalent to παρετάξαντο, as in
Thuc. 2. 2, θέμενοι εἰς τὴν ἀγορὰν τὰ ὅπλα :
and again, θέσθαι παρ' αὑτοὺς τὰ ὅπλα. But
perhaps εἰς δῆριν is meant to recal the words
from the technical sense to the literal, ' advanced their arms into battle.'

22. ἀντιπάλων ὕβριν ἀπεσκέδασαν.
'Put away the reproach of their enemies,'
made it impossible for even their enemies
to despise or insult them. It would have
been absurd to speak of 'scattering the
enemies' pride,' in reference to the two
earlier successes, when the object of the
whole piece is to confess that all is lost but
honour.

R

μαρνάμενοι δ' ἀρετῆς καὶ δείματος οὐκ ἐσάωσαν
ψυχὰς, ἀλλ' Ἀΐδην κοινὸν ἔθεντο βραβῆ,
οὕνεκεν Ἑλλήνων, ὡς μὴ ζυγὸν αὐχένι θέντες
δουλοσύνης στυγερὰν ἀμφὶς ἔχωσιν ὕβριν.
5 γαῖα δὲ πατρὶς ἔχει κόλποις τῶν πλεῖστα καμόντων
σώματ', ἐπεὶ θνητοῖς ἐκ Διὸς ἥδε κρίσις·
μηδὲν ἁμαρτεῖν ἐστι θεῶν καὶ πάντα κατορθοῦν,
ἐν βιοτῇ μοῖραν δ' οὔ τι φυγεῖν ἔπορεν.

Ἀκούεις, Αἰσχίνη, καὶ ἐν αὐτῷ τούτῳ μηδὲν ἁμαρτεῖν ἐστι 359
10 θεοῦ καὶ πάντα κατορθοῦν; οὐ τῷ συμβούλῳ τὴν τοῦ κατορ-

1. δείματος] Al. λήματος: vid. annot. 7. θεῶν] θεοῦ nunc legit Dind., ut in proximo §, quamvis hic libri omnes pluralem habent. θεοῦ sane citant Liban. et anon. ap. Suidam. Probabile est, θεοῦ fuisse in illo epigrammatis apographo, quo Demosthenes vel potius scriba dicasterii usus est, θεῶν ex anthologia nescio qua in archytypum venisse familiae eorum codd. qui soli id habent. 8. ἔπορεν] ἔπορον Ω et corr. r, μερόπων Dissen. Vid. annot. 9. Post τούτῳ Volg. et Bekk. add. ὡς τό: om. ΣΑ et socii. τό in Σ 'a m. tertia est insertum, sed rursus deletum ' Dind. 10. θεοῦ] Ita ΣΥΑ et socii: nempe omnes praeter Υ, qui supra θεῶν habent, id quod Demosthenis dixit suo textui accommodaverunt. οὐ τῷ .. κατορθοῦν] Ob homoeoteleuton om. pr. Σ.

1. μαρνάμενοι .. ὕβριν. 'And in the battle, they did not save their lives, but chose Death to judge in behalf of Greece, whether the soldiers of freedom or slavery (κοινὸν) were brave or cowards; trusting that his judgment would deliver Greece.' Valckenaer's emendation ἀρετῆς καὶ λήματος is meant to be translated, 'fighting the fight of courage and spirit;' no really parallel example is adduced of that construction. It seems therefore necessary to make ἀρετῆς καὶ δείματος depend on βραβῆ, by a hyperbaton, or in other words, taking οὐκ ἐσάωσον ψυχὰς ἀλλ' as parenthetical. On either view, the quatrain is a crabbed cramped conceit.

3. ζυγὸν αὐχένι θέντες. One would have expected θέμενοι, but the active makes the idea of voluntary submission more prominent.

4. ἀμφίς. As in Od. 3. 186, ζυγὸν ἀμφὶς ἔχοντες, of the yoke pressing evenly all round and over the neck.

6. ἐπεὶ .. ἥδε κρίσις. The connection is, 'We bury them honourably, though unsuccessful, because Zeus' decree permits uniform success only to the gods,' so that it is not their fault that they had it not. Some put a full stop after κρίσις, which would imply that ἥδε referred to the preceding words, 'this (viz. that their souls should go to Hades, and their bodies to the tomb) is the decree of Zeus for mortals,' but there is no need to depart from its usual sense.

7. θεῶν. In the next section the best MSS. have θεοῦ, and so Dindorf now reads here. But Zeus could hardly be said to assign the lot of God as he might of the gods: where the line is quoted out of the context. θεοῦ makes sense.

8. ἐν βιοτῇ must mean, 'in mortal life,' unless we adopt the conjecture μερόπων for ἔπορεν or -pον. It would have no point connected with the former line, as in Bekker's punctuation, πάντα κατορθοῦν ἐν βιοτῇ: the unfitness of the word to be used of the gods, illustrates the way in which it comes to imply mortality.

μοῖραν δ' οὔ τι φυγεῖν. The obvious translation is, 'But in human life he has given no means of escaping fate;' but it seems to suit the sense better, if one could give to φυγεῖν the sense 'to flee from,' so that the line should mean, 'But to meet fate fearlessly is the best he allows to man.' Demosthenes' paraphrase alone determines against this.

ἔπορεν. 'He [Zeus] granted:' if we read ἔπορον with some MSS., the subject must be θεοί. From the latter reading some have conjectured μερόπων, which makes clearer what must in any case be the sense. Conjecture has a freer scope in this piece than in the body of the speech, as Σ and most of the third family of MSS. omit it. Those which have it, no doubt took it from an anthology.

10. οἳ τῷ συμβούλῳ .. τοῖς θεοῖς. Probably not so much a paraphrase of the line which he has quoted (which clearly must mean, 'God succeeds in bis own designs'), as of the one following it, of which it fixes the sense. The plural τοῖς θεοῖς would support the reading ἔπορον, but that we have the change from θεῶν to θεοῦ in the former line.

θοῦν τοὺς ἀγωνιζομένους ἀνέθηκε δύναμιν, ἀλλὰ τοῖς θεοῖς. τί
οὖν, ὦ κατάρατ', ἐμοὶ περὶ τούτων λοιδορεῖ, καὶ λέγεις ἃ σοὶ
καὶ τοῖς σοῖς οἱ θεοὶ τρέψειαν εἰς κεφαλήν;

360 Πολλὰ τοίνυν, ὦ ἄνδρες Ἀθηναῖοι, καὶ ἄλλα κατηγορηκότος
αὐτοῦ καὶ κατεψευσμένου, μάλιστ' ἐθαύμασα πάντων, ὅτε τῶν 5
συμβεβηκότων τότε τῇ πόλει μνησθεὶς οὐχ ὡς ἂν εὔνους καὶ
δίκαιος πολίτης ἔσχε τὴν γνώμην, οὐδ' ἐδάκρυσεν, οὐδ' ἔπαθε
τοιοῦτον οὐδὲν τῇ ψυχῇ, ἀλλ' ἐπάρας τὴν φωνὴν καὶ γεγηθὼς
καὶ λαρυγγίζων ᾤετο μὲν ἐμοῦ κατηγορεῖν δηλονότι, δεῖγμα
δ' ἐξέφερε καθ' ἑαυτοῦ ὅτι τοῖς γεγενημένοις ἀνιαροῖς οὐδὲν 10
361 ὁμοίως ἔσχε τοῖς ἄλλοις. καίτοι τὸν τῶν νόμων καὶ τῆς πολιτείας φάσκοντα φροντίζειν, ὥσπερ οὗτος νυνί, καὶ εἰ μηδὲν
ἄλλο, τοῦτό γ' ἔχειν δεῖ, ταὐτὰ λυπεῖσθαι καὶ ταὐτὰ χαίρειν
τοῖς πολλοῖς, καὶ μὴ τῇ προαιρέσει τῶν κοινῶν ἐν τῷ τῶν
ἐναντίων μέρει τετάχθαι· ὃ σὺ νυνὶ πεποιηκὼς εἶ φανερός, ἐμὲ 15
πάντων αἴτιον καὶ δι' ἐμὲ εἰς πράγματα φάσκων ἐμπεσεῖν τὴν
πόλιν, οὐκ ἀπὸ τῆς ἐμῆς πολιτείας οὐδὲ προαιρέσεως ἀρξαμέ-
362 νων ὑμῶν τοῖς Ἕλλησι βοηθεῖν, ἐπεὶ ἔμοιγ' εἰ τοῦτο δοθείη
παρ' ὑμῶν, δι' ἐμὲ ὑμᾶς ἠναντιῶσθαι τῇ κατὰ τῶν Ἑλλήνων
ἀρχῇ πραττομένῃ, μείζων ἂν δοθείη δωρεὰ συμπασῶν ὧν τοῖς 20
ἄλλοις δεδώκατε. ἀλλ' οὔτ' ἂν ἐγὼ ταῦτα φήσαιμι (ἀδικοίην
γὰρ ἂν ὑμᾶς), οὔτ' ἂν ὑμεῖς εὖ οἶδ' ὅτι συγχωρήσαιτε· οὗτός
τ' εἰ δίκαια ἐποίει, οὐκ ἂν ἕνεκα τῆς πρὸς ἐμὲ ἔχθρας τὰ μέγιστα τῶν ὑμετέρων καλῶν ἔβλαπτε καὶ διέβαλλεν.

363 Ἀλλὰ τί ταῦτ' ἐπιτιμῶ, πολλῷ σχετλιώτερα ἄλλα κατη- 25

---

5. μάλιστ'] Volg. et Bekk. ἐν μάλιστ': ἐν om. ΣΑ et socii.   ὅτε] Sic ΣΑ k B.
et S.: ceteri, Bekk., Dind., ὅτι.   6. καὶ] οὐδὲ ΓΥΦΩ et socii.   10. ὅτι] ὅτι
ἐπὶ s ᶜᵐ Bekk.   13. ταὐτὰ] τὸ ταὐτὰ ΓΥΦΩ et socii et r.   19. δι' ἐμέ] Ita
ΣΥ p A et socii : ceteri τοσαῦτα δι' ἐμέ.

---

§§ 360-362. *He rejoiced, as his whole
manner shewed, at your calamities, because
he could impute them to me. But that was
not his only reason: he rejoiced at the success
of his master. Even otherwise, did you need
me to make you defend Greece?*

5. ὅτε. So B. and S. from ΣΑ: it seems
more appropriate and vivid than the vulgate
ὅτι, as the reference is obviously to Aeschines' manner at a particular part of his
speech, probably §§ 133, 134.

7. ἔπαθε .. τῇ ψυχῇ. You would have
expected him to be moved to tears: in fact
he was not moved at all.

9. δεῖγμα δ' ἐξέφερε. So Mid. p. 573
extr., § 232, Plat. Laws, 788 C.

ᴵ 14. τῇ προαιρέσει τῶν κοινῶν. Not so
much 'in his scheme of public life,' as 'in
his sympathies and desires for the course of
public events.' The charge is not merely
that Aeschines advocated the *policy* of friendship with Macedon, but that he gave Macedon his *sympathy*, even when the
avowed enemy of Athens; and he argues,
'when you blame me for opposing Philip's
schemes of domination, you prove you
shared them.'

§§ 363-365. *But he has uttered slanders
yet more bitter, charging me with Philippising: whereas it was the partners of Aeschines who throughout Greece did Philip's business.*

R 2

γορηκότος αὐτοῦ καὶ κατεψευσμένου· ὃς γὰρ ἐμοῦ φιλιππισ-
μὸν, ὦ γῆ καὶ θεοὶ, κατηγορεῖ, τί οὗτος οὐκ ἂν εἴποι; καίτοι
νὴ τὸν Ἡρακλέα καὶ πάντας θεούς, εἴ γ' ἐπ' ἀληθείας δέοι
σκοπεῖσθαι, τὸ καταψεύδεσθαι καὶ δι' ἔχθραν τι λέγειν ἀνε-
5 λόντας ἐκ μέσου, τίνες ὡς ἀληθῶς εἰσὶν οἷς ἂν εἰκότως καὶ
δικαίως τὴν τῶν γεγενημένων αἰτίαν ἐπὶ τὴν κεφαλὴν ἀναθεῖεν
ἅπαντες, τοὺς ὁμοίους τούτῳ παρ' ἑκάστῃ τῶν πόλεων εὕροιτ'
ἂν, οὐ τοὺς ἐμοί· οἳ, ὅτ' ἦν ἀσθενῆ τὰ Φιλίππου πράγματα 364
καὶ κομιδῇ μικρὰ, πολλάκις προλεγόντων ἡμῶν καὶ παρα-
10 καλούντων καὶ διδασκόντων τὰ βέλτιστα, τῆς ἰδίας ἕνεκ' αἰ-
σχροκερδείας τὰ κοινῇ συμφέροντα προΐεντο, τοὺς ὑπάρχοντας
ἕκαστοι πολίτας ἐξαπατῶντες καὶ διαφθείροντες, ἕως δούλους
ἐποίησαν, Θετταλοὺς Δάοχος, Κινέας, Θρασυδαῖος, Ἀρκάδας 365
Κερκιδᾶς, Ἱερώνυμος, Εὐκαμπίδας, Ἀργείους Μύρτις, Τελέδαμος,
15 Μνασέας, Ἠλείους Εὐξίθεος, Κλεότιμος, Ἀρίσταιχμος, Μεσ-
σηνίους οἱ Φιλιάδου τοῦ θεοῖς ἐχθροῦ παῖδες Νέων καὶ Θρασύ-
λοχος, Σικυωνίους Ἀρίστρατος, Ἐπιχάρης, Κορινθίους Δεί-
ναρχος, Δημάρατος, Μεγαρέας Πτοιόδωρος, Ἕλιξος, Περίλαος,
Θηβαίους Τιμόλας, Θεογείτων, Ἀνεμοίτας, Εὐβοέας Ἵππαρχος,
20 Κλείταρχος, Σωσίστρατος. ἐπιλείψει με λέγοντα ἡ ἡμέρα
τὰ τῶν προδοτῶν ὀνόματα. οὗτοι πάντες εἰσὶν, ἄνδρες Ἀθη- 366
ναῖοι τῶν αὐτῶν βουλευμάτων ἐν ταῖς αὐτῶν πατρίσιν ὧνπερ
οὗτοι παρ' ὑμῖν, ἄνθρωποι μιαροὶ καὶ κόλακες καὶ ἀλάστορες,
ἠκρωτηριασμένοι τὰς ἑαυτῶν ἕκαστοι πατρίδας, τὴν ἐλευθερίαν

---

3. θεούς] Ita ΣΑ et socii, ceteri τοὺς θεούς.   7. εὕροιτ' ἄν, οὐ] Ita ΣΥΑ et socii,
ceteri et Bekk. εὕροι τις ἄν, οὐχί.   εὕροιτ' etiam γρ. F.   10. αἰσχροκερδείας]
αἰσχροκερδίας Σ.   13. Θρασυδαῖος] Ita nunc Dind., cum Σ Θρασύδαος habeat, et
multi Θρασύδαιος Υ p pr. A et socii Bekk. B. et S. et Dind. in ed. Oxon.
18. Δημάρατος] Δημάρετος ΣΑ k.   Περίλαος] Περίαλος Σ, Πέριλλος Υ et γρ. F.
19. Τιμόλας] Ita Σ: ceteri Τιμόλαος.   Ἀνεμοίτας] Ἀνεμύτας r, codex Harpocrationis Palatinus, Suidas et alii grammatici.

---

1. φιλιππισμόν. Recurring to the part
of Aeschines' speech introduced by the illustration of the λογισμοὶ already commented
on (Ae. in Ct. §§ 60 sqq.)
3. εἴ γ' ἐπ' ἀληθείας .. ἐκ μέσου. If I
could say all the truth, and not be slandered
for saying it.
11. τοὺς ὑπάρχοντας ἕκαστοι πολίτας.
'The countrymen they had at home,' not
'who were on their side.' Demosthenes
does not admit, whether it was the fact or
no, that there was an honest Macedonian
party in each state, as distinct from traitors
in the pay of Macedon.
§ 365. Naturally, the spelling of several

of these proper names varies much in MSS.
The only variation of much interest is Ἀνεμοίτας, for which one MS. of Harpocration
has Ἀνεμύτας, which would be a Boeotian
form, and is supported by Suidas and several
grammarians. If it be accepted, says Dindorf, one ought to read Θεογίτων : it is as
easy to say, if it be not genuine one ought
to read Τιμόλαος. For Clitarchus, cp. Ae.
in Ct. § 103; for Aristratus and Perilaus, §
60. It is hardly likely that the Aristratus
of § 251 can be the Sicyonian.
§ 366. Men whose standard of happiness
is too carnal to include honour.
24. ἠκρωτηριασμένοι. Probably the

προπεπωκότες πρότερον μὲν Φιλίππῳ, νῦν δὲ Ἀλεξάνδρῳ, τῇ
γαστρὶ μετροῦντες καὶ τοῖς αἰσχίστοις τὴν εὐδαιμονίαν, τὴν δ᾽
ἐλευθερίαν καὶ τὸ μηδένα ἔχειν δεσπότην αὐτῶν, ἃ τοῖς προτέροις Ἕλλησιν ὅροι τῶν ἀγαθῶν ἦσαν καὶ κανόνες, ἀνατετρα-
φότες.   5

367   Ταύτης τοίνυν τῆς οὕτως αἰσχρᾶς καὶ περιβοήτου συστά-
σεως καὶ κακίας, μᾶλλον δ᾽, ὦ ἄνδρες Ἀθηναῖοι, προδοσίας,
εἰ δεῖ μὴ ληρεῖν, τῆς τῶν Ἑλλήνων ἐλευθερίας, ἥ τε πόλις
παρὰ πᾶσιν ἀνθρώποις ἀναίτιος γέγονεν ἐκ τῶν ἐμῶν πολιτευμάτων καὶ ἐγὼ παρ᾽ ὑμῖν. εἶτά μ᾽ ἐρωτᾷς ἀντὶ ποίας 10

368   ἀρετῆς ἀξιῶ τιμᾶσθαι; ἐγὼ δή σοι λέγω ὅτι τῶν πολιτευομένων παρὰ τοῖς Ἕλλησι διαφθαρέντων ἁπάντων, ἀρξαμένων
ἀπὸ σοῦ, πρότερον μὲν ὑπὸ Φιλίππου, νῦν δ᾽ ὑπ᾽ Ἀλεξάνδρου,
ἐμὲ οὔτε καιρὸς οὔτε φιλανθρωπία λόγων οὔτ᾽ ἐπαγγελιῶν
μέγεθος οὔτ᾽ ἐλπὶς οὔτε φόβος οὔτ᾽ ἄλλο οὐδὲν ἐπῆρεν οὐδὲ 15
προηγάγετο ὧν ἔκρινα δικαίων καὶ συμφερόντων τῇ πατρίδι
οὐδὲν προδοῦναι, οὐδ᾽, ὅσα συμβεβούλευκα πώποτε τουτοισὶ

369   ὁμοίως ὑμῖν ὡσπερανεὶ τρυτάνη ῥέπων ἐπὶ τὸ λῆμμα συμβε-

---

4. ἀνατετραφότες] Sic Σ p : ceteri ἀνατετροφότες.   7. ὦ] Om. A.   11. δή
σοι] δέ σοι Σ B. et S.   15. Post φόβος οὔτε χάρις add. Σ a m. sec. et A et socii.

---

word is used with full consciousness of the
metaphor, 'having mutilated her after the
murder, lest her ghost should avenge the
parricide,' since the correlative word ἀλάστορες, those exposed to be haunted by her,
has just been used, and is explained by it.
For this quaint superstition, cp. Ae. in Ct.
§ 245, and the note there : also the practice
in the Norse Sagas of laying a slain man's
head under his thigh, with the same object,
to prevent his ghost walking.

1. προπεπωκότες. Here no doubt simply
'sacrificed recklessly,' as e. g. Demosth.
Olynth. 3. p. 34 extr., § 26, though it would
be just possible to take it, 'handed to Philip
across the wine-table,' in exchange for his
gold and silver cups (D. de F. L. p. 384, §
152). Yet Shilleto l. c. seems to deny this
generally recognised sense of the word.

τῇ γαστρὶ .. καὶ τοῖς αἰσχίστοις. Cp.
D. de F. L. p. 412, § 254, πορνὰς ἠγόραζε
καὶ ἰχθύας περιιών (of Philocrates).

4. ὅροι .. καὶ κανόνες. Not that they
thought these the only goods, but recognised
nothing as good without them.

§ 367. Athens is pure of this treachery in
Greece, and I in Athens :
6. αἰσχρᾶς καὶ περιβοήτου. So that
the shame was great and public.
7. μᾶλλον δ᾽ .. ἐλευθερίας. 'It was a

conspiracy, and a foul one; nay, in plain
language, high treason against the liberties
of Greece.' For εἰ δεῖ μὴ ληρεῖν, cp. ad Ae.
in Ct. § 143.

10. εἶτά μ᾽ ἐρωτᾷς κ.τ.λ. refers especially
perhaps to Ae. in Ct. § 237.

§§ 368, 369. And for this unshaken incorruptibility, contrasting so with you, I claim
honour,

11. ἐγὼ δή σοι seems more forcible than
ἐγὼ δέ σοι, the reading of Σ and, of course,
of B. and S. The force is not merely, 'Well,
I will tell you,' but 'Why, that is just what
I am telling you.'

15. οὔτε φόβος. There is fair authority
for adding here οὔτε χάρις. It is not unlike
Demosthenes, but perhaps makes the enumeration too long, and may be a gloss on
ἄλλο οὐδὲν, explaining what other induce-
ments there might be.

ἐπῆρεν, of vanity or excitement; προηγάγετο, of interest.

18. ὁμοίως ὑμῖν may be joined either
with συμβεβούλευκα or with what follows :
'the advice I gave, as you did yours' (cp.
above, § 295); or better, 'the advice I gave
I never gave, as you did, from self-interest.'

ὡσπερανεὶ .. λῆμμα. Cp. Dem. de
Pace, p. 60, § 12, where the metaphor is
more clearly worked out. The statesman

βούλευκα, ἀλλ' ἀπ' ὀρθῆς καὶ δικαίας καὶ ἀδιαφθόρου τῆς ψυχῆς, καὶ μεγίστων δὴ πραγμάτων τῶν κατ' ἐμαυτὸν ἀνθρώπων
προστὰς πάντα ταῦτα ὑγιῶς καὶ δικαίως πεπολίτευμαι. διὰ 370
ταῦτ' ἀξιῶ τιμᾶσθαι. τὸν δὲ τειχισμὸν τοῦτον, ὃν σύ μου
5 διέσυρες, καὶ τὴν ταφρείαν ἄξια μὲν χάριτος καὶ ἐπαίνου κρίνω,
πῶς γὰρ οὔ; πόρρω μέντοι που τῶν ἐμαυτῷ πεπολιτευμένων
τίθεμαι. οὐ λίθοις ἐτείχισα τὴν πόλιν οὐδὲ πλίνθοις ἐγώ,
οὐδ' ἐπὶ τούτοις μέγιστον τῶν ἐμαυτοῦ φρονῶ· ἀλλ' ἐὰν τὸν
ἐμὸν τειχισμὸν βούλῃ δικαίως σκοπεῖν, εὑρήσεις ὅπλα καὶ πόλεις
10 καὶ τόπους καὶ λιμένας καὶ ναῦς καὶ ἵππους καὶ πολλοὺς τοὺς
ὑπὲρ τούτων ἀμυνο[υ]μένους. ταῦτα προὐβαλόμην ἐγὼ πρὸ 371
τῆς Ἀττικῆς, ὅσον ἦν ἀνθρωπίνῳ λογισμῷ δυνατόν, καὶ τούτοις
ἐτείχισα τὴν χώραν, οὐχὶ τὸν κύκλον τοῦ Πειραιῶς οὐδὲ τοῦ
ἄστεως. οὐδέ γ' ἡττήθην ἐγὼ τοῖς λογισμοῖς Φιλίππου, πολ-
15 λοῦ γε καὶ δεῖ, οὐδὲ ταῖς παρασκευαῖς, ἀλλ' οἱ τῶν συμμάχων
στρατηγοὶ καὶ αἱ δυνάμεις τῇ τύχῃ. τίνες αἱ τούτων ἀποδείξεις; ἐναργεῖς καὶ φανεραί. σκοπεῖτε δέ.

1. Post ψυχῆς addebatur usque ad Bekk. τὰ πάντα μοι πέπρακται quae om. ΣΑ ks: τὰ r, ut videtur, solus habet, ut μοι om. Φ.   2. τῶν] Om. pr. Σ : inter versus est positum sed erasum.   3. προστὰς] πρὸς pr. Σ.   7. Post οὐ Volg. ante Bekk. add. γάρ: om. ΣΦΑ et socii.   10. ἵππους καὶ πολλοὺς] Elegantem Dindorfi conjecturam recepimus; libri πολλοὺς ἵππους καὶ habent.   πολλοὺς uncis incl. Reisk. Bekk., om. Dind. in edit. Oxon.   11. ἀμυνομένους] ἀμυνομένους Bekk. et Dind. ἀμυνουμένους elegantius, et Graeco idiomati accommodatius. Sed ἀμυνομένους habent ΣΦ p A et socii, quos omnes incuriae arguere vix ausim: idque receperunt B. et Ꞩ. ἀγωνιζομένους Ω u, quod praesenti favere videtur.   13. Post κύκλον addebatur ante Bekk. μόνον: om. ΣΑ et socii.

is conceived as standing in one scale: if personal profit is in the opposite scale to the country's interest, it carries him away into the air. 'I,' says Demosthenes, 'have always kept my equilibrium.'

§§ 370, 371. *As well as for my minor though real services in repair of the walls. Our true fortification was the alliance I gained: I did what prudence could do, though accident overpowered me.*

5. διέσυρες: Ae. in Ct. § 237 fin.

7. οὐ λίθοις κ.τ.λ. Apparently alluded to by Ae. in Ct. § 84.

10. τόπους. Especially the Chersonese.

11. ἀμυνομένους. So the preponderance of the MSS., and Dissen refers to Isocr. de Pace, § 139, for a parallel use of the present (πολλοὺς ἕξομεν τοὺς .. συναγωνιζομένους), where there is no various reading, and where the text would not be as easy to alter. But here the difference is so slight, that as the future is decidedly the commoner in this sense ('men *to* fight for them'), it seems

that it might be introduced without much rashness.

13. τὴν χώραν. The whole extent of Attica, not the capital only.

14. τοῖς λογισμοῖς. Plans for getting allies, and still more calculations (such as those ridiculed by Aeschines, In Ct. §§ 97 sqq.) as to the various contingents to be brought into the field: the part of a war minister, as distinct from that of a general.

15. ταῖς παρασκευαῖς. The actual raising and equipping of the estimated forces.

τῶν συμμάχων. Apparently, 'of the confederates,' including Athens herself.

16. τῇ τύχῃ. Perhaps Dissen is right in thinking that he hints his disapproval of the condemnation of Lysicles: 'Our defeat was not my fault, and only the *misfortune* of the generals,' whose fault it might have been. Below, § 375, he speaks of στρατηγῶν φαυλότης as a possible cause of the defeat; but by omitting the article with either word, he avoids asserting that it was the real one.

372 Τί χρῆν τὸν εὔνουν πολίτην ποιεῖν, τί τὸν μετὰ πάσης
προνοίας καὶ προθυμίας καὶ δικαιοσύνης ὑπὲρ τῆς πατρίδος πολιτευόμενον; οὐκ ἐκ μὲν θαλάττης τὴν Εὔβοιαν προβαλέσθαι
πρὸ τῆς Ἀττικῆς, ἐκ δὲ τῆς μεσογείας τὴν Βοιωτίαν, ἐκ δὲ
τῶν πρὸς Πελοπόννησον τόπων τοὺς ὁμόρους ταύτῃ; οὐ τὴν 5
σιτοπομπίαν, ὅπως παρὰ πᾶσαν φιλίαν ἄχρι τοῦ Πειραιῶς
373 κομισθήσεται, προΐδεσθαι; καὶ τὰ μὲν σῶσαι τῶν ὑπαρχόντων
ἐκπέμποντα βοηθείας καὶ λέγοντα καὶ γράφοντα τοιαῦτα, τὴν
Προκόννησον, τὴν Χερρόνησον, τὴν Τένεδον, τά δ' ὅπως οἰκεῖα
καὶ σύμμαχ' ὑπάρξει πρᾶξαι, τὸ Βυζάντιον, τὴν Ἄβυδον, τὴν 10
Εὔβοιαν; καὶ τῶν μὲν τοῖς ἐχθροῖς ὑπαρχουσῶν δυνάμεων τὰς
μεγίστας ἀφελεῖν, ὧν δ' ἐνέλειπε τῇ πόλει, ταῦτα προσθεῖναι;
374 ταῦτα τοίνυν ἅπαντα πέπρακται τοῖς ἐμοῖς ψηφίσμασι καὶ
τοῖς ἐμοῖς πολιτεύμασιν, ἃ καὶ βεβουλευμένα, ὦ ἄνδρες Ἀθηναῖοι, ἐὰν ἄνευ φθόνου τις βούληται σκοπεῖν, ὀρθῶς εὑρήσει 15
καὶ πεπραγμένα πάσῃ δικαιοσύνῃ, καὶ τὸν ἑκάστου καιρὸν οὐ
παρεθέντα οὐδ' ἀγνοηθέντα οὐδὲ προεθέντα ὑπ' ἐμοῦ, καὶ ὅσα
εἰς ἑνὸς ἀνδρὸς δύναμιν καὶ λογισμὸν ἧκεν, οὐδὲν ἐλλειφθέν.
375 εἰ δὲ ἢ δαίμονός τινος ἢ τύχης ἰσχὺς ἢ στρατηγῶν φαυλότης
ἢ τῶν προδιδόντων τὰς πόλεις ὑμῶν κακία ἢ πάντα ταῦτα ἅμα 20
ἐλυμαίνετο τοῖς ὅλοις, ἕως ἀνέτρεψαν, τί Δημοσθένης ἀδικεῖ;
εἰ δ' οἷος ἐγὼ παρ' ὑμῖν κατὰ τὴν ἐμαυτοῦ τάξιν, εἷς ἐν ἑκάστῃ
376 τῶν Ἑλληνίδων πόλεων ἀνὴρ ἐγένετο, μᾶλλον δ' εἰ ἕνα ἄνδρα

6. σιτοπομπίαν] Sic optimi plerique : scribebatur σιτοπομπείαν. Πειραιῶς]
Πειρέως pr. Σ, fortasse pro Πειραιέως. 10. ὑπάρξει] Sic ΣΦ p Α s: ceteri ὑπάρξῃ.
12. ἐνέλειπε] Sic ΣΥ p Α: ceteri ἐνέλιπε. 13. Post τοίνυν addebatur ὑμῖν: om.
ΣΑ et socii. 17. προεθέντα] Sic ΣΥΑ et socii, παρεθέντα F p Bekk., ceteri προδο-
θέντα. 20. ἅμα] Non nisi in γρ. habet Σ, om. k B. et S. 22. εἰ δ' οἷος]
δ'οἷ
εἷος Σ, ubi lectio superscr. est a m. sec.: et εἰ ος teste Bekk. habet etiam Τ. Statim usque
ad Bekk. addebatur ἦν, quod om. ΣΤΑ et socii.

In the absence of any definite mention of Lysicles' condemnation in any of the contemporary orators, especially in the extant speech of Lycurgus, the alleged prosecutor, one is tempted to doubt the fact.

§§ 372-375. *I made Attica secure on every side, from invasion and from famine, leaving no weak point:*

5. τοὺς ὁμόρους ταύτῃ. Megara and Corinth, and perhaps Achaia. The enumeration of these neighbour states describes what he calls the fortification of Attica: the account of the arrangement for supplies, perhaps, pursues the metaphor of provisioning the fortress.

6. παρὰ πᾶσαν φιλίαν. 'Along a continuous line of friendly coast.' Byzantium,

the Chersonese, Abydus, and Tenedus, would command the exit from the Euxine more completely than any part of Philip's dominions; and the other islands southward and westward to Euboea would complete the chain of communication.

11. τῶν μὲν τοῖς ἐχθροῖς .. ἀφελεῖν. The Theban alliance, on which Philip had reckoned.

17. παρεθέντα. Negligently.
προεθέντα. Corruptly.

21. Δημοσθένης. A man, a civilian, and a patriot, opposed to δαίμονος ἢ τύχης, στρατηγῶν, τῶν προδιδόντων .. ὑμῶν, especially the last.

§ 376. *One man like me in Thessaly, one in Arcadia, would have saved Greece.*

μόνον Θετταλία καὶ ἕνα ἄνδρα Ἀρκαδία ταὐτὰ φρονοῦντα
ἔσχεν ἐμοί, οὐδεὶς οὔτε τῶν ἔξω Πυλῶν Ἑλλήνων οὔτε τῶν
εἴσω τοῖς παροῦσι κακοῖς ἐκέχρητ᾿ ἄν, ἀλλὰ πάντες ἂν ὄντες
ἐλεύθεροι καὶ αὐτόνομοι μετὰ πάσης ἀδείας ἀσφαλῶς ἐν εὐδαι-
5 μονίᾳ τὰς ἑαυτῶν ᾤκουν πατρίδας, τῶν τοσούτων καὶ τοιούτων
ἀγαθῶν ὑμῖν καὶ τοῖς ἄλλοις Ἀθηναίοις ἔχοντες χάριν δι᾿ ἐμέ.
ἵνα δ᾿ εἰδῆτε ὅτι πολλῷ τοῖς λόγοις ἐλάττοσι χρῶμαι τῶν 377
ἔργων, εὐλαβούμενος τὸν φθόνον, λέγε μοι ταυτὶ καὶ ἀνάγνωθι
λαβὼν [τὸν ἀριθμὸν τῶν βοηθειῶν κατὰ τὰ ἐμὰ ψηφίσματα].

10   ΑΡΙΘΜΟΣ ΒΟΗΘΕΙΩΝ.

Ταῦτα καὶ τοιαῦτα πράττειν, Αἰσχίνη, τὸν καλὸν κἀγαθὸν 378
πολίτην δεῖ, ὧν κατορθουμένων μὲν μεγίστοις ἀναμφισβητήτως
ὑπῆρχεν εἶναι, καὶ τὸ δικαίως προσῆν, ὡς ἑτέρως δὲ συμβάντων
τὸ γοῦν εὐδοκιμεῖν περίεστι καὶ τὸ μηδένα μέμφεσθαι τὴν
15 πόλιν μηδὲ τὴν προαίρεσιν αὐτῆς, ἀλλὰ τὴν τύχην κακίζειν
τὴν οὕτω τὰ πράγματα κρίνασαν, οὐ μὰ Δί᾿ οὐκ ἀποστάντα 379
τῶν συμφερόντων τῇ πόλει, μισθώσαντα δ᾿ αὑτὸν τοῖς ἐναντίοις, τοὺς ὑπὲρ τῶν ἐχθρῶν καιροὺς ἀντὶ τῶν τῆς πατρίδος
θεραπεύειν, οὐδὲ τὸν μὲν πράγματ᾿ ἄξια τῆς πόλεως ὑποστάντα
20 λέγειν καὶ γράφειν καὶ μένειν ἐπὶ τούτων βασκαίνειν, ἂν δέ

---

2. ἔσχεν] Sic ΣΑ et socii: ceteri ἔσχον.   3. ἐκέχρητ᾿] ἐκέχρηντ᾿ Σ.   5. τῶν]
τούτων Σ: 'fort. τούτων τῶν' B. et S.   9. τὸν ἀριθμὸν .. ψηφίσματα] Om. Σ
B. et S., uncis inclusit Bekk.   Potest esse διττογραφία quaedam: nam in titulo
10. ΑΡΙΘΜΟΣ ΒΟΗΘΕΙΩΝ] ΚΑΤΑ ΤΑ ΕΜΑ ΨΗΦΙΣΜΑΤΑ add. ΣΥΦΑ et al.   Pro-
babilius autem credimus esse volgatum.   12. Post μὲν ὦ γῆ καὶ θεοὶ addebatur usque
ad Bekk.: om. ΣΥ.   20. Post ἐπὶ τούτων Volg. Bekk. Dind. add. προελόμενον:
om. ΣΓΥΦΩ et socii, B. et S.

---

1. Θετταλία .. Ἀρκαδία. Philip's party
in the one opened Northern Greece to him,
and in the other neutralised Peloponnesus.
    5. τὰς ἑαυτῶν ᾤκουν πατρίδας. As it
was, individuals were exiled as well as cities
reduced to subjection.
    § 377. *I understate what facts will prove.*
    9. τὸν ἀριθμὸν .. ψηφίσματα. It is
of course possible (vid. Consp. Lectt.)
that these words got into the text from
the title; but it is not like Demosthenes'
general manner, nor indeed that of other
orators, to leave the court to find out from
the clerk what is the subject of the document.
    § 378. *The success of my policy would
have secured you a just supremacy: even in
failure, it saved your honour:*
    12. μεγίστοις ἀναμφισβητήτως .. δι-
καίως. Your supremacy would have been

uncontested, your greatness undisputed.
    14. περίεστι. 'Is saved,' rather than
'is won.'
    15. κακίζειν might etymologically mean
simply 'think it bad,' like ὀλβίζω or εὐδαι-
μονίζω; but by its usage it would be a
stronger word than μέμφεσθαι: to deprive
glorious deeds of their effect is worse than
not to do them.
    § 379. *Unlike that of Aeschines, who sold
himself to the enemy to libel patriots, and
keep his eloquence for private quarrels,*
    19. ὑποστάντα. The notion is of mov-
ing to support a burden, and so exactly
equivalent to 'undertaken.'
    20. μένειν ἐπὶ τούτων. Volg. and Dind.
add προελόμενον. But that the MSS. are
against it, it would somewhat relieve the
weight of infinitives that are dependent on
ὑποστάντα; and as προελόμενον implies

τις ἰδίᾳ τι λυπήσῃ, τοῦτο μεμνῆσθαι καὶ τηρεῖν, οὐδέ γ᾽ ἡσυ-
380 χίαν ἄγειν ἄδικον καὶ ὕπουλον, ὃ σὺ ποιεῖς πολλάκις. ἔστι
γάρ, ἔστιν ἡσυχία δικαία καὶ συμφέρουσα τῇ πόλει, ἣν οἱ
πολλοὶ τῶν πολιτῶν ὑμεῖς ἁπλῶς ἄγετε. ἀλλ᾽ οὐ ταύτην
οὗτος ἄγει τὴν ἡσυχίαν, πολλοῦ γε καὶ δεῖ, ἀλλ᾽ ἀποστὰς 5
ὅταν αὐτῷ δόξῃ τῆς πολιτείας (πολλάκις δὲ δοκεῖ) φυλάττει
πηνίκ᾽ ἔσεσθε μεστοὶ τοῦ συνεχῶς λέγοντος ἢ παρὰ τῆς τύχης
τι συμβέβηκεν ἐναντίωμα ἢ ἄλλο τι δύσκολον γέγονε (πολλὰ
381 δὲ τἀνθρώπινα)· εἶτ᾽ ἐπὶ τούτῳ τῷ καιρῷ ῥήτωρ ἐξαίφνης ἐκ
τῆς ἡσυχίας ὥσπερ πνεῦμ᾽ ἐφάνη, καὶ πεφωνασκηκὼς καὶ συνει- 10
λοχὼς ῥήματα καὶ λόγους συνείρει τούτους σαφῶς καὶ ἀπνευστὶ,
ὄνησιν μὲν οὐδεμίαν φέροντας οὐδ᾽ ἀγαθοῦ κτῆσιν οὐδενός, συμ-
382 φορὰν δὲ τῷ τυχόντι τῶν πολιτῶν καὶ κοινὴν αἰσχύνην. καίτοι
ταύτης τῆς μελέτης καὶ τῆς ἐπιμελείας, Αἰσχίνη, εἴπερ ἐκ ψυχῆς δικαίας ἐγίγνετο καὶ τὰ τῆς πατρίδος συμφέροντα προη- 15
ρημένης, τοὺς καρποὺς ἔδει γενναίους καὶ καλοὺς καὶ πᾶσιν
ὠφελίμους εἶναι, συμμαχίας πόλεων, πόρους χρημάτων, ἐμπο-
ρίου κατασκευήν, νόμων συμφερόντων θέσεις, τοῖς ἀποδειχθεῖσιν
383 ἐχθροῖς ἐναντιώματα. τούτων γὰρ ἁπάντων ἦν ἐν τοῖς ἄνω
χρόνοις ἐξέτασις, καὶ ἔδωκεν ὁ παρελθὼν χρόνος πολλὰς ἀπο- 20
δείξεις ἀνδρὶ καλῷ τε κἀγαθῷ, ἐν οἷς οὐδαμοῦ σὺ φανήσει

---

1. οὐδέ γ᾽] Sic ΣΥ et praeter ipsum A tertia codd. familia legebatur οὐδ᾽.　2. ὃ]
Sic ΣΑ k : ceteri ὡs.　7. πηνίκ᾽] Sic Σ : volg. et Bekk. ὁπηνίκ᾽.　ἔσεσθε]
ἔσεσθαι Σ; legebatur ἐστέ.　ἢ om. pr. Σ.　10. ἐφάνη] ἀνεφάνη Α et
socii.　συνειλοχὼς] συνειλεχὼς Σ et al., συνειληχὼς nonnulli.　11. συνείρει]
συνῆρει Σ.　ἀπνευστὶ] ἀπνευστεὶ Σ.　20. ἔδωκεν] † Bis habet Σ, fortasse
non fortuito †.

---

more of resolute persistency, one can hardly
say that it would be a mere synonym.

ἂν δέ τις ἰδίᾳ τι λυπήσῃ: cp. above,
§§ 341, 344. Here, again, Timarchus might
be alluded to ; but the offence he gave Aeschines could scarcely be called private, and
it would be harsh to translate λυπήσῃ, 'give
offence' absolutely.

§ 380. Avoiding politics from treachery,
not simplicity.

3. ἡσυχία. Nearly equivalent to ἀπραγ-
μοσύνη. In Demosthenes' time it was not
as unpopular a temper as in Pericles' (Thuc.
2. 40).

§ 381. And only declaiming when he
knows it will be useless to Athens.

9. ῥήτωρ .. ἐφάνη. Having all this while
affected to be an ἰδιώτηs. ἀνεφάνη, the
reading of one group of MSS., is an obvious
alteration for ἐφάνη, but would alter the
sense. Demosthenes says, ' You find all of

a sudden that he is a rhetorician,' not merely
' All of a sudden he starts up as one.'

10. πεφωνασκηκὼς κ.τ.λ. 'With his
voice in fine training, and phrases and topics
ready culled ; and strings them together so
that you never miss a word, though he does
not stop for breath.'

12. συμφορὰν δὲ κ.τ.λ. ' A trouble to
his butt of the moment, and a disgrace to all.'

§ 382. Diligence like yours must have
served Athens much if it had been honest.

§§ 383, 384. But she has gained no
material assistance from you.

19. τούτων γὰρ .. ἐξέτασις. ' If he had
done any such service, our memory of the
past would testify to it,' even if the material
benefit itself were lost now, like those of my
own policy.

21. ἐν οἷς. The antecedent is to be supplied from the abstract or typical singular,
ἀνδρὶ καλῷ τε κἀγαθῷ.

γεγονὼς, οὐ πρῶτος, οὐ δεύτερος, οὐ τρίτος, οὐ τέταρτος, οὐ
πέμπτος, οὐχ ἕκτος, οὐχ ὁποστοσοῦν, οὔκουν ἐπί γ᾽ οἷς ἡ
πατρὶς ηὐξάνετο. τίς γὰρ συμμαχία σοῦ πράξαντος γέγονε
τῇ πόλει; τίς δὲ βοήθεια ἢ κτῆσις εὐνοίας ἢ δόξης; τίς δὲ 384
5 πρεσβεία, τίς διακονία δι᾽ ἣν ἡ πόλις ἐντιμοτέρα; τί τῶν
οἰκείων ἢ τῶν Ἑλληνικῶν καὶ ξενικῶν, οἷς ἐπέστης, ἐπηνώρθωται; ποῖαι τριήρεις; ποῖα βέλη; ποῖοι νεώσοικοι; τίς ἐπι-
σκευὴ τειχῶν; ποῖον ἱππικόν; τί τῶν ἁπάντων σὺ χρήσιμος
εἶ; τίς ἢ τοῖς εὐπόροις ἢ τοῖς ἀπόροις πολιτικὴ καὶ κοινὴ
10 βοήθεια χρημάτων; οὐδεμία. ἀλλ᾽, ὦ τᾶν, εἰ μηδὲν τούτων, 385
εὔνοιά γε καὶ προθυμία· ποῦ; πότε; ὅστις, ὦ πάντων ἀδικώ-
τατε, οὐδ᾽ ὅτε ἅπαντες, ὅσοι πώποτ᾽ ἐφθέγξαντ᾽ ἐπὶ τοῦ βήματος, εἰς σωτηρίαν ἐπεδίδοσαν, καὶ τὸ τελευταῖον Ἀριστόνικος τὸ συνειλεγμένον εἰς τὴν ἐπιτιμίαν ἀργύριον, οὐδὲ τότε
15 οὔτε παρῆλθες οὔτ᾽ ἐπέδωκας οὐδέν, οὐκ ἀπορῶν, πῶς· γὰρ; ὅς

2. ἐπί γ᾽ οἷς] Sic ΣΑ, ἐπεί γε καὶ plerique utriusque familiae.   5. ἐντιμοτέρα]
† ἐντιμωτέρα Σ †.   Statim γέγονε add. volg. et Bekk. om. Σ et Alexander.   6. οἷς]
ἃς Σ, et variant aliquid ceteri.   Post ἐπηνώρθωται Volg. et B. et S. add. διά σε:
om. Σ.   10. χρημάτων; οὐδεμία] Sic Σ: χρημάτων; οὐδεμία παρὰ σοῦ k et (nisi
quod περὶ pro παρὰ habet) s, χρημάτων παρὰ σοῦ; r: ceteri et Bekk. χρημάτων παρὰ σοῦ;
οὐδεμία.   παρὰ σοῦ οὐδεμία ponat A an in margine tantum habeat, ex Dindorfi nota
parum liquet.   ὦ τᾶν] † ὅ ταν Σ †.   11. ποῦ] ὅτου correctus Σ teste Dind.:
nobis videbatur prima esse lectio.   14. ἀργύριον] Om. Σ B. et S.: post συνειλεγμένον ponunt ΓΥΦΩ et socii et r.   15. οὔτε] Om. ΦΦ stv, et mox οὐδ᾽ Φ.

1. οὐ πρῶτος, οὐ δεύτερος κ.τ.λ. Proverbial: cp. Or. ap. Schol. ad Theocr. 14.
48.
2. οὔκουν ἐπί γ᾽ οἷς κ.τ.λ. If you did
not discharge routine duties of patriotism,
still less could you be expected to perform
the extraordinary services which exalt a
state.
3. τίς γὰρ συμμαχία κ.τ.λ. There is a
curiously close imitation of it in Dinarchus'
speech against Demosthenes himself, p. 102,
§ 99.
4. ἢ κτῆσις. Reiske quotes from Alexander a reading ἐκ τῆς σῆς, and regrets not
having adopted it.
9. ἢ τοῖς εὐπόροις. According to Reiske,
a mere διττογραφία. The allusion is clearly
to Demosthenes' own trierarchic law, which
he regards as a benefit chiefly τοῖς ἀπόροις
(above, § 135); but a sound financial measure might well benefit the rich also, by a
fairer adjustment of burdens within the tax-
paying class, or by more efficient and eco-
nomical expenditure.
§§ 385, 386. *Not even your bare good
will: you only come forward to insult our
calamities.*
10. ὦ τᾶν. Being clearly not friendly,

and hardly ironical, this use of the word
seems almost fatal to the ὦ 'τὰν etymology.
12. ὅτε ἅπαντες κ.τ.λ. It is disputed
whether this refers to the panic after Chaeronea, or to the time of the revolt of Thebes,
after Philip's death. What Aeschines says
about the scanty supply of money at Athens
(In Ct. § 241, etc.) makes the latter unlikely.
13. Ἀριστόνικος. Perhaps the same as
the mover of the crown to Demosthenes,
mentioned in §§ 103 sqq., 282. One may
suppose that he had tried a motion of doubtful legality once too often.
14. εἰς τὴν ἐπιτιμίαν. To pay off a
fine and recover his civic rights. Probably
the fine could not be paid by instalments:
he had hoped to get the whole sum together
by degrees, but in the public need gave up
at once all he had, and so had to begin
again at the beginning. It seems hardly
possible to omit ἀργύριον, though not only
Σ does so, but its place varies in other MSS.
15. ὅς γε κεκληρονόμηκας κ.τ.λ. He
says nothing of what he had, according to
him, received from Macedon: his Boeotian
estate (above, § 54) of course did not come
in till afterwards.

γε κεκληρονόμηκας μὲν τῶν Φίλωνος τοῦ κηδεστοῦ χρημάτων.
πλειόνων ἢ πεντεταλάντων, διτάλαντον δ' εἶχες ἔρανον δωρεὰν
παρὰ τῶν ἡγεμόνων τῶν συμμοριῶν ἐφ' οἷς ἐλυμήνω τὸν τριη-
386 ραρχικὸν νόμον. ἀλλ' ἵνα μὴ λόγον ἐκ λόγου λέγων τοῦ
παρόντος ἐμαυτὸν ἐκκρούσω, παραλείψω ταῦτα. ἀλλ' ὅτι γ' 5
οὐχὶ δι' ἔνδειαν οὐκ ἐπέδωκας, ἐκ τούτων δῆλον, ἀλλὰ φυλάττων τὸ μηδὲν ἐναντίον γενέσθαι παρὰ σοῦ τούτοις οἷς ἅπαντα
πολιτεύει. ἐν τίσιν οὖν σὺ νεανίας καὶ πηνίκα λαμπρός; ἡνίκ'
ἂν κατὰ τουτωνὶ δέῃ, ἐν τούτοις λαμπροφωνότατος, μνημονικώτατος, ὑποκριτὴς ἄριστος, τραγικὸς Θεοκρίνης.   10
387 Εἶτα τῶν πρότερον γεγενημένων ἀγαθῶν ἀνδρῶν μέμνησαι.
καὶ καλῶς ποιεῖς. οὐ μέντοι δίκαιόν ἐστιν, ἄνδρες Ἀθηναῖοι,
τὴν πρὸς τοὺς τετελευτηκότας εὔνοιαν ὑπάρχουσαν προλαβόντα
παρ' ὑμῶν πρὸς ἐκείνους ἐξετάζειν καὶ παραβάλλειν ἐμὲ τὸν
388 νῦν ζῶντα μεθ' ὑμῶν. τίς γὰρ οὐκ οἶδε τῶν πάντων ὅτι τοῖς 15
μὲν ζῶσι πᾶσιν ὕπεστί τις ἢ πλείων ἢ ἐλάττων φθόνος, τοὺς
τεθνεῶτας δὲ οὐδὲ τῶν ἐχθρῶν οὐδεὶς ἔτι μισεῖ; οὕτως οὖν
ἐχόντων τούτων τῇ φύσει, πρὸς τοὺς πρὸ ἐμαυτοῦ νῦν ἐγὼ
κρίνωμαι καὶ θεωρῶμαι; μηδαμῶς· οὔτε γὰρ δίκαιον οὔτ' ἴσον,
Αἰσχίνη, ἀλλὰ πρὸς σὲ καὶ ἄλλον εἴ τινα βούλει τῶν ταῦτά 20
389 σοι προῃρημένων καὶ ζώντων. κἀκεῖνο σκόπει. πότερον κάλλιον

---

2. πεντεταλάντων] In libris πέντε ταλάντων divisim scribitur.   7. παρὰ σοῦ
τούτοις] † παρὰ τούτοις pr. Σ †.   9. κατὰ τουτωνὶ δέῃ] κατὰ τούτων τι δέῃ pr.
Σ B. et S. : κατὰ τούτων εἰπεῖν τι δέῃ rec. Σ et A et socii : legebatur εἰπεῖν κατὰ τούτων τι
δέῃ. Statim δέοι ΓΥΦΩ rt.   11. ἀγαθῶν ἀνδρῶν] Ita ΣΤΦ p et praeter A cognati :
ceteri et Bekk. ἀνδρῶν ἀγαθῶν.   13. προλαβόντα] προσλαβόντα ΓΦ piv krs.
15. νῦν ζῶντα] Ita ΣΤΩ u et corr. v : volg. ante Bekk. συζῶντα.   17. τεθνεῶτας
δὲ] δὲ τεθνεῶτας Υ v Α² k Bekk.   19. κρίνωμαι καὶ θεωρῶμαι] κρίνομαι καὶ θεω-
ροῦμαι Ω et al. A et socii : κρίνομαι etiam ΥΦ.

---

2. πλειόνων ἢ πεντεταλάντων. The
MSS. write πέντε ταλάντων as two words,
which would mean, 'more than five talents
of your brother-in-law's property.' As the
sense 'your brother-in-law's property of
more than five talents,' is more natural
and appropriate, the vulgate is no doubt
right.

δωρεὰν includes the sense, 'at no cost
to yourself,' but is hardly a mere adverb.

3. ἐφ' οἷς ἐλυμήνω. 'Your wages for
mangling:' cp. above, § 129. Apparently
Demosthenes was really induced or compelled
to accept modifications in the measure: Aeschines was able to take credit for having
opposed him. (In Ct. § 223).

7. παρὰ σοῦ τούτοις. παρὰ τούτοις, the
reading of Σ, might be defended, and is probably not accidental, 'that there may be no
offence given in the eyes of those ...' But the

text gives a completer and more elegant sense.

9. μνημονικώτατος. A necessary quali-
fication to an actor or to a stagy orator.

10. Θεοκρίνης. According to Erasmus
ap. H. Wolf, an actor and dramatic critic.
Though the Theocrines attacked in the
speech among the works of Demosthenes is
represented as a συκοφάντης, there seems no
likelihood that his name was already proverbial in that character.

§§ 387-389. *Then you recall the memory
of ancient worthies, whom of course the
court ranks above me:*

11. εἶτα .. μέμνησαι : Ae. in Ct. § 181 ;
perhaps also §§ 258, 259.

12. καλῶς ποιεῖς. For they ought to be
imitated, though they cannot be equalled.

15. τοῖς μὲν ζῶσι. There is the same
sentiment in Thuc. 2. 42, φθόνος γὰρ τοῖς
ζῶσι πρὸς τἀντίπαλον.

καὶ ἄμεινον τῇ πόλει διὰ τὰς τῶν πρότερον εὐεργεσίας,
οὔσας ὑπερμεγέθεις, οὐ μὲν οὖν εἴποι τις ἂν ἡλίκας, τὰς ἐπὶ
τὸν παρόντα βίον γιγνομένας εἰς ἀχαριστίαν καὶ προπηλακισμὸν ἄγειν, ἢ πᾶσιν, ὅσοι τι μετ' εὐνοίας πράττουσι, τῆς παρὰ
5 τούτων τιμῆς καὶ φιλανθρωπίας μετεῖναι; καὶ μὴν εἰ καὶ τοῦτ' 390
ἄρα δεῖ με εἰπεῖν, ἡ μὲν ἐμὴ πολιτεία καὶ προαίρεσις, ἄν τις
ὀρθῶς σκοπῇ, ταῖς τῶν τότ' ἐπαινουμένων ἀνδρῶν ὁμοία καὶ
ταὐτὰ βουλομένη φανήσεται, ἡ δὲ σὴ ταῖς τῶν τοὺς τοιούτους
τότε συκοφαντούντων· δῆλον γὰρ ὅτι καὶ κατ' ἐκείνους ἦσάν
10 τινες, οἱ διασύροντες τοὺς ὄντας τότε, τοὺς δὲ πρότερον γεγενημένους ἐπῄνουν, βάσκανον πρᾶγμα καὶ ταὐτὸ ποιοῦντες σοί.
εἶτα λέγεις ὡς οὐδὲν ὅμοιός εἰμι ἐκείνοις ἐγώ; σὺ δ' ὅμοιος, 391
Αἰσχίνη; ὁ δ' ἀδελφὸς ὁ σός; ἄλλος δέ τις τῶν νῦν ῥητόρων;
ἐγὼ μὲν γὰρ οὐδένα φημί. ἀλλὰ πρὸς τοὺς ζῶντας, ὦ χρη-
15 στέ, ἵνα μηδὲν ἄλλ' εἴπω, τὸν ζῶντα ἐξέταζε καὶ τοὺς καθ'
αὑτόν, ὥσπερ τἆλλα πάντα, τοὺς ποιητάς, τοὺς χοροὺς, τοὺς
ἀγωνιστάς. ὁ Φιλάμμων οὐχ ὅτι Γλαύκου τοῦ Καρυστίου καὶ 392
τινων ἑτέρων πρότερον γεγενημένων ἀθλητῶν ἀσθενέστερος ἦν,
ἀστεφάνωτος ἐκ τῆς Ὀλυμπίας ἀπῄει, ἀλλ' ὅτι τῶν εἰσελ-
20 θόντων πρὸς αὐτὸν ἄριστα ἐμάχετο, ἐστεφανοῦτο καὶ νικῶν
ἀνηγορεύετο. καὶ σὺ πρὸς τοὺς νῦν ὅρα με ῥήτορας, πρὸς
σαυτόν, πρὸς ὅντινα βούλει τῶν ἁπάντων· οὐδένα ἐξίσταμαι.

---

4. τῆς παρὰ τούτων τιμῆς] 'τῆς om. γρ. Σ, παρὰ om. ΣϮ' Bekk. Dind., τῆς τούτων
τιμῆς legunt B. et S. † Nisi nos fallehamur, pr. Σ habet τῆς τιμῆς, quod si verum est, παρὰ
τούτων potest esse scholium quoddam, articuli explicandi caussa †.   7. ταῖς τῶν]
τίς; τῶν γρ. ΣΦ.   9. ἐκείνους] Ita ΣΥ: volg. usque ad Bekk. ἐκείνους τοὺς χρόνους.   10. οἱ διασύροντες] Sic ΣΓΥΦΩ et socii B. et S. Volgo, Bekk., Dind., οἱ
διέσυρον.   13. ὁ δ'] ὁ Σ.   22. οὐδένα] Ita ΣΥ: ceteri et Bekk. οὐδενί.

---

2. ἐπὶ τὸν παρόντα βίον. Possibly, 'In
order to enable the present generation to
live and thrive.' But vid. Dissen, p. 450.

§ 390. *But I deserve thanks when I do
my little all, like them, who did more, and
yet had their detractors.*

9. κατ' ἐκείνους. 'In their times,' by
far the most forcible sense. Most MSS. add
τοὺς χρόνους here or after τινες.

ἦσάν τινες οἱ διασύροντες. So most
MSS. for the vulgate οἱ διέσυρον μέν. The
construction, though less obvious, is more
forcible: 'There were in their time men
who reviled the living, and they no doubt
also praised the men of former times, with
the same spiteful temper as your own.' It
is scarcely possible to retain μὲν after διασύροντες, though two MSS. have it of those
that read the participle.

§ 391. *I challenge comparison with you*

and yours—yes, or any contemporaries.

13. ὁ δ' ἀδελφὸς ὁ σός. He had two
brothers (D. de F. L. p. 415, § 262, Ae. de
F. L. fin.) Probably this is Philochares, as
he only seems to have been a public man.

14 πρὸς τοὺς ζῶντας .. εἴπω. I claim
the advantage of being compared with my
contemporaries: I will not say what *they*
are, though the contrast is in my favour.

§ 392. *That is enough: that is the standard in other things: that I can meet boldly.*

17. Φιλάμμων: vid. ad Ae. in Ct. § 190.
He is selected as an Athenian, well-known,
and doubtless popular; not, as some conjecture in ignorance of his reputation, as having won in a bad year. Vid. Ar. Rhet. 3.
11. 5.

Γλαύκου. He was victor in Ol. 25,
and was celebrated by Simonides.

22. οὐδένα ἐξίσταμαι. As in Soph.

393 ὧν, ὅτε μὲν τῇ πόλει τὰ βέλτιστα ἑλέσθαι παρῆν, ἐφαμίλλου
τῆς εἰς τὴν πατρίδα εὐνοίας ἐν κοινῷ πᾶσι κειμένης, ἐγὼ κράτιστα λέγων ἐφαινόμην, καὶ τοῖς ἐμοῖς καὶ ψηφίσμασι καὶ
νόμοις καὶ πρεσβείαις ἅπαντα διῳκεῖτο, ὑμῶν δὲ οὐδεὶς ἦν οὐδα-
394 μοῦ, πλὴν εἰ τούτοις ἐπηρεάσαι τι δέοι· ἐπειδὴ δὲ α μήποτ' 5
ὤφελε συνέβη, καὶ οὐκέτι συμβούλων, ἀλλὰ τῶν τοῖς ἐπιταττομένοις ὑπηρετούντων καὶ τῶν κατὰ τῆς πατρίδος μισθαρνεῖν
ἑτοίμων καὶ τῶν κολακεύειν ἕτερον βουλομένων ἐξέτασις ἦν, τηνικαῦτα σὺ καὶ τούτων ἕκαστος ἐν τάξει καὶ μέγας καὶ λαμπρὸς
ἱπποτρόφος, ἐγὼ δ' ἀσθενής, ὁμολογῶ, ἀλλ' εὔνους μᾶλλον 10
395 ὑμῶν τουτοισί. δύο δ', ἄνδρες Ἀθηναῖοι, τὸν φύσει μέτριον
πολίτην ἔχειν δεῖ (οὕτω γάρ μοι περὶ ἐμαυτοῦ λέγοντι ἀν-
επιφθονώτατον εἰπεῖν), ἐν μὲν ταῖς ἐξουσίαις τὴν τοῦ γενναίου
καὶ τοῦ πρωτείου τῇ πόλει προαίρεσιν διαφυλάττειν, ἐν παντὶ
δὲ καιρῷ καὶ πράξει τὴν εὔνοιαν· τούτου γὰρ ἡ φύσις κυρία, 15
τοῦ δύνασθαι δὲ καὶ ἰσχύειν ἕτερα. ταύτην τοίνυν παρ' ἐμοὶ
396 μεμενηκυῖαν εὑρήσετε ἁπλῶς. ὁρᾶτε δέ. οὐκ ἐξαιτούμενος, οὐκ
Ἀμφικτυονικὰς δίκας ἐπαγόντων, οὐκ ἀπειλούντων, οὐκ ἐπαγ-
γελλομένων, οὐχὶ τοὺς καταράτους τούτους ὥσπερ θηρία μοι
προσβαλλόντων, οὐδαμῶς ἐγὼ προδέδωκα τὴν εἰς ὑμᾶς εὔνοιαν. 20
τὸ γὰρ ἐξ ἀρχῆς εὐθὺς ὀρθὴν καὶ δικαίαν τὴν ὁδὸν τῆς πολιτείας

3. Ante ψηφίσμασι καὶ om. Bekk., cum codd. praeter ΣΥΩ *tiv.* 8. ἕτερον] Sic
ΣΥ: ceteri et (quia Bekkerum fefellerat, illud in Σ legi) B. et S., ἑτέρους· Mox ἦν om. Σ
B. et S. 11. Post Ἀθηναῖοι ταῦτα add. Bekk. cum omnibus praeter Σ. 14. τοῦ
πρωτείου] Ita ΣΑ: τὴν πρωτείον Ω *w* ks: volg. ante Bekk. τὴν τοῦ πρωτείου. 16. δύνασθαι δὲ] δὲ δύνασθαι Ω *w* Α et socii, et volg. usque ad Bekk. 18. Ἀμφικτυονικὰς]
εἰς Ἀμφικτυονικὰς † Σ † ΥΑ. Mox post ἐπαγόντων, ante Bekk. addebatur μοι, quod om.
ΣΩ *w* Α et socii. οὐκ ἀπειλούντων] Om. pr. Σ, B. et S.

Aj. 92. Most MSS., surprised at the
quasi-transitive construction, substitute οὐδενί.

§ 393. *I surpassed you when Athens was
free to judge between us:*
1. ὧν. 'Among whom.' Note the contrast, or at least distinction, between βέλτιστα, 'what *was* best,' and κράτιστα, 'what
was carried.' He states nothing of himself
but what is undeniable.

§ 394. *And share Athens' fall, which is
your rise.*
5. ἐπειδὴ κ.τ.λ. supports the view that
Aeschines was not paid in advance; that he
was not put in a thriving condition until
Athens was subdued, and Philip and Alexander had to pay for having her managed.
Cp. ad § 385.
8. ἐξέτασις. When they were mustered
for service.

§ 395. *I laboured for Athens when I
could, and loved her always.*
12. οὕτω γὰρ κ.τ.λ. I will not boast of
my devotion to you after you cast me off:
I will call it only what a good citizen ought
to shew.
13. ἐν μὲν ταῖς ἐξουσίαις = ὁσάκις ἐξῆν,
' In all times of opportunity.'

§ 396. *In spite of the persecution, from
which the nation could hardly protect me,*
18. ἐπαγόντων clearly refers to Macedonia, τοὺς καταράτους .. προβαλλόντων
excluding his enemies at Athens. δίκας
ἐπαγόντων is a common phrase; εἰς δίκας
ἐπαγόντων, the reading of Σ, is hardly
Greek for 'bringing me into suits.'
20. προσβαλλόντων. 'Setting them on,'
hardly used elsewhere in exactly this sense;
but one may compare προσβαλλόντων δεῖμα
in Eur. Ion 584.

εἱλόμην, τὰς τιμὰς, τὰς δυναστείας, τὰς εὐδοξίας τὰς τῆς
πατρίδος θεραπεύειν, ταύτας αὔξειν, μετὰ τούτων εἶναι.   οὐκ
ἐπὶ μὲν τοῖς ἑτέρων εὐτυχήμασι φαιδρὸς ἐγὼ καὶ γεγηθὼς 397
κατὰ τὴν ἀγορὰν περιέρχομαι, τὴν δεξιὰν προτείνων καὶ εὐαγ-
5 γελιζόμενος τούτοις οὓς ἂν ἐκεῖσε ἀπαγγέλλειν οἴωμαι, τῶν
δὲ τῆς πόλεως ἀγαθῶν πεφρικὼς ἀκούω καὶ στένων καὶ κύπτων
εἰς τὴν γῆν, ὥσπερ οἱ δυσσεβεῖς οὗτοι, οἳ τὴν μὲν πόλιν διασύ-
ρουσιν, ὥσπερ οὐχ αὑτοὺς διασύροντες, ὅταν τοῦτο ποιῶσιν,
ἔξω δὲ βλέπουσι, καὶ ἐν οἷς ἀτυχησάντων τῶν Ἑλλήνων εὐτύ-
10 χησεν ἕτερος, ταῦτ' ἐπαινοῦσι καὶ ὅπως τὸν ἅπαντα χρόνον
μενεῖ φασὶ δεῖν τηρεῖν.

Μὴ δῆτ', ὦ πάντες θεοὶ, μηδεὶς ταῦθ' ὑμῶν ἐπινεύσειεν, ἀλλὰ 398
μάλιστα μὲν καὶ τούτοις βελτίω τινὰ νοῦν καὶ φρένας ἐνθείητε,
εἰ δ' ἄρ' ἔχουσιν ἀνιάτως, τούτους μὲν αὐτοὺς καθ' ἑαυτοὺς
15 ἐξώλεις ἐν γῇ καὶ θαλάττῃ ποιήσατε, ἡμῖν δὲ τοῖς λοιποῖς τὴν
ταχίστην ἀπαλλαγὴν τῶν ἐπηρτημένων φόβων δότε καὶ σωτηρίαν ἀσφαλῆ.

9. εὐτύχησεν ἕτερος] ἕτερος εὐτύχησεν Ω κ Α et socii.   11. μενεῖ] Sic Σ, μένει
Α et socii, ceteri et Bekk. διαμενεῖ.   12. ταῦθ' ὑμῶν] ὑμῶν ταῦτ' Ω κ Α et socii.
14. ἀνιάτως] Ita ΣΥΩ κ Α et socii: volg. ante Bekk. οὕτως ἀνιάτως.   15. Post
ἐξώλεις καὶ προώλεις om. Α et socii.   ποιήσατε] Ita Σ k: ceteri ποιήσαιτε.

16. δότε] δοῖτε Σ.

- § 397. *I have never made the nation's humiliation my pride and hope.*

4. εὐαγγελιζόμενος. Telling it as good news, to those whom I expect to repeat to their master that I have told them.   This ulterior design accounts for the middle.

7. τὴν μὲν πόλιν .. δεῖν τηρεῖν. The view censured is, 'Athens is a paltry town: the fortunes of Greece are bound up with those of the conqueror of Persia.   It is a good thing that he should put down Thebes and Sparta; and we have only to hope that Greece may continue to rule the world under him.'

§ 398. *May they who have find their due reward.*

15. ἐξώλεις .. ποιήσατε. 'Give them up to destruction,' rather than 'destroy them.'

16. τῶν ἐπηρτημένων φόβων. The victorious return of Alexander.

INDICES.

I. OF WORDS AND PHRASES.

II. OF PROPER NAMES.

The Numbers in Index I refer to the Section of the speech (according to the division of the *Oxford* Edition of Bekker's Attic Orators, which is here followed, and of which the Numerals are given in the inner margin of the present volume): those in Index II refer to the Page of this Edition. In both Indices, the letter D. after a figure indicates that the passage referred to is in one of the Documents inserted in Demosthenes' speech.

INDEX I.

s

INDEX II.